CABBAGES AND KINGS
THE FOUR MILLION
THE TRIMMED LAMP

O. HENRY
(WILLIAM SIDNEY PORTER)
1862-1910

69 SHORT STORIES

comprising
CABBAGES AND KINGS
THE FOUR MILLION
THE TRIMMED LAMP

O. HENRY

With an Introduction by
WOODROW WYATT

COLLINS
LONDON AND GLASGOW

GENERAL EDITOR: G. F. MAINE

CABBAGES AND KINGS *first published*, 1904
THE FOUR MILLION *first published*, 1906
THE TRIMMED LAMP *first published*, 1907
This Edition, 1967

PRINTED IN GREAT BRITAIN BY
COLLINS CLEAR-TYPE PRESS

O. HENRY
(WILLIAM SIDNEY PORTER)

O. Henry's real name was William Sidney Porter. He was born on September 11th, 1862 at Greensboro, North Carolina, U.S.A. His father was Dr. Algernon Sidney Porter, a man of genial disposition and an able physician who in later life devoted most of his time to unsuccessful inventions; among them a steam driven automobile, a washing machine, a flying machine, a mechanical contrivance for picking cotton and a water-driven *perpetuum mobile*. His mother was a gifted and scholarly woman who, at the Greensboro Female College (one of the first institutions of its kind), had studied rhetoric, algebra, geometry, logic, astronomy and French. She also had a talent for painting and drawing which her son inherited from her. She died of tuberculosis aged thirty, when O. Henry was three years old.

His only teacher was his aunt Evelina Maria Porter—affectionately known as ' aunt Lina ' to all in Greensboro—who kept a small private school. She had a passionate devotion for literature which she succeeded in instilling into her pupils. O. Henry's life-long love of good books was mainly due to her inspired way of teaching.

When he was fifteen he entered as a clerk into his uncle's drug store, and soon acquired local fame, both for his kindly, humorous manner and for his consummate art as a cartoonist. However, the work in the confined space of the store, together with his incessant reading and lack of exercise, affected his health, and when some years later (1882) a local doctor, whose sons had gone to Texas where they had made their fame and fortune, invited him to join them, he seized the opportunity and went to live at their ranch in La Salle County, later immortalized in many of his Texas stories. After two years he moved to Austin, Texas, becoming first a book-keeper with a real estate firm and subsequently an assistant draftsman in the General Land Office, a position he held until 1891. In 1887, after a romantic elopement, he married Athol Estes, then seventeen years old, by whom he had a daughter.

After leaving the Land Office, he entered the First National Bank of Austin as paying and receiving teller. On the side he tried his hand at publishing a small weekly magazine *The Rolling Stone* which had but a brief existence. In 1895 he accepted a

5

position on the Houston *Daily Post* where his contributions and drawings quickly gained him a reputation as a clever journalist. In July 1896 he was summoned by the Federal Authorities to return to Austin to stand trial for alleged embezzlement of funds while working at the First National Bank. The total amount involved was $1153, 68c. made up of three separate items, of which the last, amounting to $299, 60c. was taken when he had been out of the bank for several months, a fact which seems to have been overlooked by jurors, lawyers, the judge and O. Henry himself. He was most certainly completely innocent, and a victim of someone **else's** errors or misdeeds in a bank which had been notorious for the unbusinesslike and lax conduct of its affairs. He would have been acquitted but for an act of folly, born of his too vivid imagination. Alone on the train taking him to Austin, the visualisation of the impending trial, his possible conviction and attending humiliation so took possession of him that it overshadowed his reasoning power. Instead of proceeding to Austin, he changed trains and went to New Orleans, from where he eventually sailed for Honduras, hoping to make a new existence for himself and his family. In the company of Al Jennings and brother fugitives from justice, like himself, he travelled several months in Latin America, but early in 1897, on learning that his wife (who had been ill for some time) was dying, he returned to the United States and gave himself up. He was allowed bail and not tried until a year later. During the whole of his trial he remained completely aloof and silent, and was convicted and sentenced to five years' imprisonment at the Ohio Penitentiary, Columbus. He entered prison on April 25th, 1898.

The five years he had worked in his uncle's pharmacy store now stood him in good stead. He was given the job of night drug clerk at the prison dispensary, a post which he filled with great conscientiousness and efficiency.

It gave him almost complete freedom from prison routine, good living quarters, plentiful food and many other privileges, among them the opportunity to employ his free time for writing. His stories began to appear in various magazines, mostly under the pseudonym O. Henry which he had adopted shortly before going to prison. One of the most famous stories of this period was *A Retrieved Reformation*, the plot of which was given to him by a fellow convict. It was later dramatised and presented on Broadway under the title *Alias Jimmy Valentine*. When he left the penitentiary on 24th July, 1901, having served only 3 years and 3 months of his sentence, he was an accomplished writer and a man ennobled by suffering, with boundless charity for his fellow men and free of bitterness. He went first to Pittsburg where his parents-in-law owned a hotel and from there to New York, which was to be his residence for the eight remaining years of his life. New York, which he liked to call " Little Old Bagdad-on-the Subway," was to him an inexhaustible source of inspiration. When not at work he spent most of his time, in cafes, restaurants and cabarets, mixing with cabmen, shop-girls, actors, clerks; in short with the ordinary people, in whose lives he took a profound and compassionate interest. Most of his stories were about these people, " The Four Million " as he called them. His literary output was prodigious. In the year 1904 he wrote 65 stories of which 52, i.e. one every week, appeared in the New York journal *World,* which also printed fifty of his stories in 1905.

His earnings were considerable, but he was always short of money mainly because of his extravagant generosity. In 1905 his first book, stories on South American themes strung together as a novel, appeared under the title *Cabbages and Kings.* In 1906 came his second book *The Four Million* and each succeeding year until after his death was to be marked by the publication of two collections of his stories. In the beginning of 1908 he was at the height of his fame, but his health was broken through overwork and the onset of tuberculosis. His heavy drinking was probably a contributory cause. In 1907 he had married again. His second wife was Sallie Coleman of Asheville N.C. In the Autumn 1909 he went to Asheville to recuperate, returned to New York in the Spring of 1910, and died on June 5th the same year.

H. d. R.

CONTENTS

INTRODUCTION

O. Henry (William Sidney Porter) was born on the 11th of September, 1862 at Greensboro, North Carolina, remote from the bustling life and opportunities of the big cities. His childhood was as unsheltered as the rest of his life. His mother died when he was three. His father, nominally a doctor, was more interested in trying to perfect a perpetual motion water-wheel than in providing effectively for his son's welfare. O. Henry may have inherited from his father much of his ingenuity, but he acquired nothing else either material or spiritual.

For a while O. Henry went to a Dame's school run by his aunt, but he left it, and all formal learning, at the age of fifteen. From then on his education came from his observation and from the tragic pattern of his own life. He began his acquaintance with the adult world in his uncle's drug store where he worked for five years. Afterwards the inhabitants of Greensboro remembered him as a boy who was quick and cheerful, bright and willing, and with artistic inclinations expressed in drawing. From the start he approached life eagerly and hopefully. The world was not his oyster—it was he who was the oyster, lying wide open to receive the impressions which flowed over his sensitive soul and which in their movements often bruised it.

When he was twenty O. Henry left Greensboro for Texas, where he worked on a ranch for two years and began to write short stories. They were of indifferent merit but he was not discouraged. After he had moved to Austin, the capital of Texas, to take work as a clerk, he persevered with his writing and began at the age of twenty-five to contribute humorous sketches to the *Detroit Free Press*. His writing developed steadily during the next eight years, in course of which he married. For the first five he worked as a draftsman, and for the next three as a cashier in the First National Bank. In 1894 he left the bank to edit a paper, called *Rolling Stone,* which soon failed. In the following year he left Austin for Houston where the reputation he had made as a writer enabled him to secure a daily column in the *Houston Daily Post*. From working in his uncle's drug store he had painfully progressed through a process of self-education until at last he had fulfilled his ambition of becoming a whole-time writer. Then tragedy hit him.

In 1896 he was summoned to Austin to answer a charge of

misappropriating a little over a thousand dollars while he was a cashier at the First National Bank. O. Henry was terrified. Instead of facing it out, he fled to New Orleans and from there to Honduras, where he absorbed the South American atmosphere which permeates *Cabbages and Kings*. Towards the end of 1897 he heard of his wife's serious illness. Fearful and miserable he returned to Austin in time to be with her during her last days. Immediately after her death his trial began.

Nobody will ever know for certain whether he had actually been dishonest. The affairs of the bank were in a tangle and the deficiency in O. Henry's accounts was only one of many irregularities. It is probable that if he had not run away the errors in his books would have been held to be merely a part of the general muddle which prevailed in the bank, and that he would have been acquitted. His flight ensured his conviction. I feel, without evidence, that he was probably not so much dishonest as inefficient; that when the summons came from Austin, his strong sense of the tragedy in life, and the timidity in his nature, made him despair of proving his innocence, and his nerve gave. That would have been more in keeping with the character which comes through his writings than a dishonourable act. We know that O. Henry suffered for the remainder of his life from the deep sense of shame and humiliation which resulted from the five year prison sentence awarded him in March, 1898. He was released in June, 1901, before the five years were up, having obtained the usual remission for good conduct. Nine years later he was dead.

In those nine years he wrote the stories, apart from a few written in prison, for which he is famous, including all in this volume. After he was released he went for a brief period to Pittsburgh and then to New York, where he remained. For a time he spent his days in the streets, parks and restaurants, observing and noting. He watched the life of the city absorbedly and minutely, with a sympathy and compassion born of his own harrowing experience. He loved the poor, the hardworked, and the wretched, and he understood them. When he began to write he wrote prodigiously at the rate of fifty or sixty stories a year, and this with a technical skill that amazed by its virtuosity and even now blinds many to his true merits.

Too often he is dismissed as nothing more than a master of trick endings. The sheer knockout brilliance of most of his endings is startling, but the trick is rarely forced. It fits into the theme and texture of the story and reveals some irony or aspect of humanity which gives a rounded completion to the picture. That his endings were so often ingenious should be accounted to skill and not to shallowness. Nor are his endings, although neat and quick, like the final knot tied in the string round a parcel by the fingers of a practised shop assistant, always unexpected. The reader who is familiar with O. Henry's work is not invariably deceived or surprised. He has suffered from shoddy imitations of his endings made by writers who seek to make up for their lack of perception by applying a terminal shock barely related to their theme. It is a vice common among inexperienced writers who strive for effect and who cling to the notion that short stories must have a beginning, a middle and an end. That may be true, but the three should be blended naturally.

So much attention has been focussed on O. Henry's endings that his superb beginnings have been almost ignored. Look (and this is a chance selection) at the beginnings of some of the stories in this volume.

One dollar and eighty-seven cents. That was all. And sixty cents of it was in pennies. Pennies saved one and two at a time by bulldozing the grocer and the vegetable man and the butcher until one's cheeks burned with the silent imputation of parsimony that such close dealing implied. Three times Della counted it. One dollar and eighty-seven cents. And the next day would be Christmas.

The Gift of the Magi.

On his bench in Madison Square, Soapy moved uneasily. When wild geese honk high of nights, and when women without sealskin coats grow kind to their husbands, and when Soapy moves uneasily on his bench in the park, you may know that winter is near at hand.

The Cop and the Anthem.

This document is intended to strike somewhere between a temperance lecture and the Bartender's guide. Relative to the latter, drink shall swell the theme and be set forth in abundance. Agreeably to the former, not an elbow shall be crooked.

The Rubaiyat of a Scotch Highball.

In an art exhibition the other day I saw a painting that had been sold for 5,000 dollars. The painter was a young scrub out of the West named Kraft, who had a favourite food and a pet theory. His pabulum was an unquenchable belief in the Unerring Artistic Adjustment of Nature. His theory was fixed around corned-beef hash with poached egg. There was a story behind the picture, so I went home and let it drip out of a fountain-pen.

An Adjustment of Nature.

At once the reader is caught and put right into the atmosphere and situation. He is beckoned, and is listening, before he has time to consider whether he wants to be one of the audience or not. There are no preliminary perambulations in which the author demands the admiration of the reader for the delicacy and elegance of his descriptive manner—frequently to succeed in doing nothing more than induce boredom. O. Henry revolutionized the art of beginning the short story, and few writers today can start one without bowing, even if subconsciously, to his influence. His opening sentences and paragraphs were acquired from his journalism, but they were soundly conceived : there is no time to waste time in a short story.

O. Henry's method was to cram the small space he allotted himself with incident and matter, to reveal much in brief. Sometimes, but not often, he tried to push too much into the tiny container, as in *The Buyer from Cactus City* where the girl's feelings and the events develop too rapidly for credibility. This technique of exposing a wide area quickly has provoked the charge that he was like a superficial camera man who darts into a street or a nightclub and snaps only the momentary picture. It is indisputable that O. Henry had an eye for compostion and for the unusual, that to focus his episode he would put up his hand to life and call 'Halt !' while with accurate observation and sharp clarity he detailed the characters and the scene, but the deduction that he saw nothing but the externals cannot be upheld. His splendid sense of drama, his amazing gift for plots, and his objective, comprehensive reporting never prevented him from driving deep into the human mind and exposing its charm, its tragedy, its kindliness, its humour, its weakness and its lovability. His short excursions tell more, and leave a stronger impression, than many full-length novels.

The humour of *A Harlem Tragedy*, the sweet delicacy of *The Gift of the Magi*, the pathos of the girl and General Kitchener's picture in *An Unfinished Story*, live in the memory. O. Henry's work is infused with his understanding of human nature, his acceptance of vice and crime without moralising, his sensitive knowledge of motives and simple hopes. At the time, he was thought to be a sensationalist who, like a tabloid journalist, deliberately tried to shock, and the unfair criticism still lingers. It arose because O. Henry was one of the first to write with feeling and without condescension about the sort of people he met in the Ohio State Penitentiary and in the slums of New York. He had suffered as they had. He did not seek to sit in judgment over them or to represent them as quaint, or to put a haze around them to placate the genteel reader. He made no concessions to convention.

He was given to sentiment, but not often to sentimentality : there was the world as he saw it and he would not distort it.

From his childhood he saw life as a series of pictures but his pictures open up far more than a faithful recording. The difference between him and the man with the box camera is the difference between a great portrait painter and a press photographer. He could see the beauty of the spirit through the ugliness of the face, but he shows us both. It was because his mind worked from and on pictures that the short story was his natural medium. Even his one novel, *Cabbages and Kings,* which has a connected thread running through it, breaks up into short stories before it has gone halfway. The concentration of his great talents on the short story gave it a new status and popularity which has persisted. He exploited its possibilities to the limit.

But he could not have become so famous and have maintained his fame on the technical excellence of his work alone. He administered shocks to complacency and he cast away false prudery. Above all, he elevated the common man and forced us to take him seriously as a human being in his own dignity. The Ohio State Penitentiary was his tragedy but it gave him immortality. O. Henry, writing in the first decade after 1900, was the prophet of the century of the common man.

WOODROW WYATT

CABBAGES AND KINGS

CONTENTS

THE PROEM

BY THE CARPENTER

THEY will tell you in Anchuria, that President Miraflores, of that volatile republic, died by his own hand in the coast town of Coralio; that he had reached thus far in flight from the inconveniences of an imminent revolution; and that one hundred thousand dollars, government funds, which he carried with him in an American leather valise as a souvenir of his tempestuous administration, was never afterward recovered.

For a *real,* a boy will show you his grave. It is back of the town near a little bridge that spans a mangrove swamp. A plain slab of wood stands at its head. Some one has burned upon the headstone with a hot iron this inscription :

RAMON ANGEL DE LAS CRUZES
Y MIRAFLORES
PRESIDENTE DE LA REPUBLICA
DE ANCHURIA
QUE SEA SU JUEZ DIOS

It is characteristic of this buoyant people that they pursue no man beyond the grave. " Let God be his judge ! "—Even with the hundred thousand unfound, though they greatly coveted, the hue and cry went no further than that.

To the stranger or the guest the people of Coralio will relate the story of the tragic end of their former president; how he strove to escape from the country with the public funds and also with Doña Isabel Guilbert, the young American opera singer; and how, being apprehended by members of the opposing political party in Coralio, he shot himself through the head rather than give up the funds, and, in consequence, the Señorita Guilbert. They will relate further that Doña Isabel, her adventurous bark of fortune shoaled by the simultaneous loss of her distinguished admirer and the souvenir hundred thousand, dropped anchor on this stagnant coast, awaiting a rising tide.

They say, in Coralio, that she found a prompt and prosperous tide in the form of Frank Goodwin, an American resident of the town, an investor who had grown wealthy by dealing in the products of the country—a banana king, a rubber prince, a sarsaparilla, indigo, and mahogany baron. The Señorita Guilbert,

21

you will be told, married Señor Goodwin one month after the
president's death, thus, in the very moment when Fortune had
ceased to smile, wresting from her a gift greater than the prize
withdrawn.

Of the American, Don Frank Goodwin, and of his wife the
natives have nothing but good to say. Don Frank has lived among
them for years, and has compelled their respect. His lady is easily
queen of what social life the sober coast affords. The wife of the
governor of the district, herself, who was of the proud Castilian
family of Monteleon y Dolorosa de los Santos y Mendez, feels
honoured to unfold her napkin with olive-hued, ringed hands at
the table of Señora Goodwin. Were you to refer (with your
northern prejudices) to the vivacious past of Mrs. Goodwin when
her audacious and gleeful abandon in light opera captured the
mature president's fancy, or to her share in that statesman's down-
fall and malfeasance, the Latin shrug of the shoulder would be
your only answer and rebuttal. What prejudices there were in
Coralio concerning Señora Goodwin seemed now to be in her
favour, whatever they had been in the past.

It would seem that the story is ended, instead of begun; that
the close of tragedy and the climax of a romance have covered the
ground of interest; but, to the more curious reader it shall be some
slight instruction to trace the close threads that underlie the
ingenuous web of circumstances.

The headpiece bearing the name of President Miraflores is daily
scrubbed with soap-bark and sand. An old half-breed Indian tends
the grave with fidelity and the dawdling minuteness of inherited
sloth. He chops down the weeds and ever-springing grass with his
machete, he plucks ants and scorpions and beetles from it with his
horny fingers, and sprinkles its turf with water from the plaza
fountain. There is no grave anywhere so well kept and ordered.

Only by following out the underlying threads will it be made
clear why the old Indian, Galvez, is secretly paid to keep green the
grave of President Miraflores by one who never saw that unfortunate statesman in life, or in death, and why that one was wont
to walk in the twilight, casting from a distance looks of gentle
sadness upon that unhonored mound.

Elsewhere than at Coralio one learns of the impetuous career of
Isabel Guilbert. New Orleans gave her birth and the mingled
French and Spanish creole nature that tinctured her life with such
turbulence and warmth. She had little education, but a knowledge
of men and motives that seemed to have come by instinct. Far
beyond the common woman was she endowed with intrepid rash-
ness, with a love for the pursuit of adventure to the brink of danger,
and with desire for the pleasures of life. Her spirit was one to chafe

under any curb; she was Eve after the fall, but before the bitterness of it was felt. She wore life as a rose in her bosom.

Of the legion of men who had been at her feet it was said that but one was so fortunate as to engage her fancy. To President Miraflores, the brilliant but unstable ruler of Anchuria, she yielded the key to her resolute heart. How, then, do we find her (as the Coralians would have told you) the wife of Frank Goodwin, and happily living a life of dull and dreamy inaction?

The underlying threads reach far, stretching across the sea. Following them out it will be made plain why "Shorty" O'Day, of the Columbia Detective Agency, resigned his position. And, for a lighter pastime, it shall be a duty and a pleasing sport to wander with Momus beneath the tropic stars where Melpomene once stalked austere. Now to cause laughter to echo from those lavish junglos and frowning crags where formerly rang the cries of pirates' victims; to lay aside pike and cutlass and attack with quip and jollity; to draw one saving titter of mirth from the rusty casque of Romance—this were pleasant to do in the shade of the lemon-trees on that coast that is curved like lips set for smiling.

For there are yet tales of the Spanish Main. That segment of continent washed by the tempestuous Caribbean, and presenting to the sea a formidable border of tropical jungle topped by the overweening Cordilleras, is still begirt by mystery and romance. In past times buccaneers and revolutionists roused the echoes of its cliffs, and the condor wheeled perpetually above where, in the green groves, they made food for him with their matchlocks and toledos. Taken and retaken by sea rovers, by adverse powers and by sudden uprising of rebellious factions, the historic 300 miles of adventurous coast has scarcely known for hundreds of years whom rightly to call its master. Pizarro, Balboa, Sir Francis Drake, and Bolivar did what they could to make it a part of Christendom. Sir John Morgan, Lafitte, and other eminent swashbucklers bombarded and pounded it in the name of Abaddon.

The game still goes on. The guns of the rovers are silenced; but the tintype man, the enlarged photograph brigand, the kodaking tourist and the scouts of the gentle brigade of fakirs have found it out, and carry on the work. The hucksters of Germany, France, and Sicily now bag its small change across their counters. Gentleman adventurers throng the waiting-rooms of its rulers with proposals for railways and concessions. The little *opéra-bouffe* nations play at government and intrigue until some day a big, silent gun-boat glides into the offing and warns them not to break their toys. And with these changes comes also the small adventurer, with empty pockets to fill, light of heart, busy-brained—the modern fairy prince, bearing an alarm clock with which, more surely than by the sentimental kiss, to awaken the beautiful tropics from their centuries' sleep. Generally he wears a shamrock, which he matches pridefully against the extravagant palms; and it is he who has driven Melpomene to the wings, and set Comedy to dancing before the footlights of the Southern Cross.

So, there is a little tale to tell of many things. Perhaps to the promiscuous ear of the Walrus it shall come with most avail; for in it there are indeed shoes and ships and sealing-wax and cabbage-palms and presidents instead of kings.

Add to these a little love and counterplotting, and scatter everywhere throughout the maze a trail of tropical dollars—dollars warmed no more by the torrid sun than by the hot palms of the scouts of Fortune—and, after all, here seems to be Life, itself, with talk enough to weary the most garrulous of Walruses.

"FOX-IN-THE-MORNING"

CORALIO reclined, in the mid-day heat, like some vacuous beauty lounging in a guarded harem. The town lay at the sea's edge on a strip of alluvial coast. It was set like a little pearl in an emerald band. Behind it, and seeming almost to topple, imminent, above it, rose the sea-following range of the Cordilleras. In front the sea was spread, a smiling jailer, but even more incorruptible than the frowning mountains. The waves swished along the smooth beach; the parrots screamed in the orange and ceiba-trees; the palms waved their limber fronds foolishly like an awkward chorus at the prima donna's cue to enter.

Suddenly the town was full of excitement. A native boy dashed down a grass-grown street, shrieking : " *Busca el Señor* Goodwin. *Ha venido un telegrama por él !* "

The word passed quickly. Telegrams do not often come to any-one in Coralio. The cry for Señor Goodwin was taken up by a dozen officious voices. The main street running parallel to the beach became populated with those who desired to expedite the delivery of the despatch. Knots of women with complexions varying from palest olive to deepest brown gathered at street corners and plaintively carolled : " *Un telegrama por Señor* Goodwin ! " The *comandante,* Don Señor el Coronel Encarnación Rios, who was loyal to the Ins and suspected Goodwin's devotion to the Outs, hissed : "Aha ! " and wrote in his secret memorandum book the accusive fact that Señor Goodwin had on that momentous date received a telegram.

In the midst of the hullabaloo a man stepped to the door of a small wooden building and looked out. Above the door was a sign that read " Keogh and Clancy "—a nomenclature that seemed not to be indigenous to that tropical soil. The man in the door was Billy Keogh, scout of fortune and progress and latterly rover of the Spanish Main. Tintypes and photographs were the weapons with which Keogh and Clancy were at that time assailing the hopeless shores. Outside the shop were set two large frames filled with specimens of their art and skill.

Keogh leaned in the doorway, his bold and humorous countenance wearing a look of interest at the unusual influx of life and sound into the street. When the meaning of the disturbance became clear to him he placed a hand beside his mouth and shouted : " Hey ! Frank ! " in such a robustious voice that the feeble clamor of the natives was drowned and silenced.

Fifty yards away, on the seaward side of the street, stood the abode of the consul for the United States. Out from the door of this building tumbled Goodwin at the call. He had been smoking with Willard Geddie, the consul, on the back porch of the consulate, which was conceded to be the coolest spot in Coralio.

" Hurry up," shouted Keogh. " There's a riot in town on account of a telegram that's come for you. You want to be careful about these things, my boy. It won't do to trifle with the feelings of the public this way. You'll be getting a pink note some day with violet scent on it; and then the country'll be steeped in the throes of a revolution."

Goodwin had strolled up the street and met the boy with the message. The ox-eyed women gazed at him with shy admiration, for his type drew them. He was big, blond, and jauntily dressed in white linen, with buckskin *zapatos*. His manner was courtly, with a sort of kindly truculence in it tempered by a merciful eye. When the telegram had been delivered, and the bearer of it dismissed with a gratuity, the relieved populace returned to the contiguities of shade from which curiosity had drawn it—the women to their baking in the mud ovens under the orange-trees, or to the interminable combing of their long, straight hair; the men to their cigarettes and gossip in the cantinas.

Goodwin sat on Keogh's doorstep and read his telegram. It was from Bob Englehart, an American, who lived in San Mateo, the capital city of Anchuria, eighty miles in the interior. Englehart was a gold miner, an ardent revolutionist and " good people." That he was a man of resource and imagination was proven by the telegram he had sent. It had been his task to send a confidential message to his friend in Coralio. This could not have been accomplished in either Spanish or English, for the eye politic in Anchuria was an active one. The Ins and the Outs were perpetually on their guard. But Englehart was a diplomatist. There existed but one code upon which he might make requisition with promise of safety—the great and potent code of Slang. So, here is the message that slipped, unconstrued, through the fingers of curious officials, and came to the eye of Goodwin :

His Nibs skedalled yesterday per jack-rabbit line with all the coin in the kitty and the bundle of muslin he's spoony about. The boodle is six figures short. Our crowd in good shape, but we need the spondulicks. You collar it. The main guy and the dry goods are headed for the briny. You know what to do.

BOB.

This screed, remarkable as it was, had no mystery for Goodwin. He was the most successful of the small advance-guard of speculative Americans that had invaded Anchuria, and he had not reached that enviable pinnacle without having well exercised the arts of foresight and deduction. He had taken up political intrigue as a matter of business. He was acute enough to wield a certain influence among the leading schemers, and he was prosperous enough to be able to purchase the respect of the petty office-holders. There was always a revolutionary party; and to it he had always allied himself; for the adherents of a new administration received the rewards of their labors. There was now a Liberal party seeking to overturn President Miraflores. If the wheel successfully revolved, Goodwin stood to win a concession to 30,000 manzanas of the finest coffee lands in the interior. Certain incidents in the recent career of President Miraflores had excited a shrewd suspicion in Goodwin's mind that the government was near a dissolution from another cause than that of a revolution, and now Englehart's telegram had come as a corroboration of his wisdom.

The telegram, which had remained unintelligible to the Anchurian linguists who had applied to it in vain their knowledge of Spanish and elemental English, conveyed a stimulating piece of news to Goodwin's understanding. It informed him that the president of the republic had decamped from the capital city with the contents of the treasury. Furthermore, that he was accompanied in his flight by that winning adventuress Isabel Guilbert, the opera singer, whose troupe of performers had been entertained by the president at San Mateo during the past month on a scale less modest than that with which royal visitors are often content. The reference to the " jack-rabbit line " could mean nothing else than the mule-back system of transport that prevailed between Coralio and the capital. The hint that the " boodle " was " six figures short " made the condition of the national treasury lament-

ably clear. Also it was convincingly true that the ingoing party—
its way now made a pacific one—would need the " spondulicks."
Unless its pledges should be fulfilled, and the spoils held for the
delectation of the victors, precarious indeed would be the position
of the new government. Therefore it was exceedingly necessary to
" collar the main guy," and recapture the sinews of war and
government.

Goodwin handed the message to Keogh.

" Read that, Billy," he said. " It's from Bob Englehart. Can
you manage the cipher ? "

Keogh sat in the other half of the doorway, and carefully perused
the telegram.

" 'Tis not a cipher," he said, finally. " 'Tis what they call
literature, and that's a system of language put in the mouths of
people that they've never been introduced to by writers of imagination. The magazines invented it, but I never knew before that
President Norvin Green had stamped it with the seal of his
approval. 'Tis now no longer literature, but language. The
dictionaries tried, but they couldn't make it go for anything but
dialect. Sure, now that the Western Union indorses it, it won't
be long till a race of people will spring up that speaks it."

" You're running too much to philology, Billy," said Goodwin.
" Do you make out the meaning of it ? "

" Sure," replied the philosopher of Fortune. "All languages
come easy to the man who must know 'em. I've even failed to
misunderstand an order to evacuate in classical Chinese when it
was backed up by the muzzle of a breech-loader. This little
literary essay, I hold in my hands means a game of Fox-in-the-
Morning. Ever play that, Frank, when you was a kid ? "

" I think so," said Goodwin, laughing. " You join hands all
'round, and——"

" You do not," interrupted Keogh. " You've got a fine sporting
game mixed up in your head with 'All Around the Rosebush.'
The spirit of ' Fox-in-the-Morning ' is opposed to the holding of
hands. I'll tell you how it's played. This president man and his
companion in play, they stand up over in San Mateo, ready for
the run, and shout : ' Fox-in-the-Morning ! ' Me and you,
standing here, we say : ' Goose and the Gander ! ' They say :
' How many miles is it to London town ? ' ' We say : ' Only a
few, if your legs are long enough. How many comes out ? ' They
say : ' More than you're able to catch.' And then the game
commences."

" I catch the idea," said Goodwin. " It won't do to let the goose
and gander slip through our fingers, Billy; their feathers are too
valuable. Our crowd is prepared and able to step into the shoes

of the government at once; but with the treasury empty we'd stay in power about as long as a tenderfoot would stick on an untamed bronco. We must play the fox on every foot of the coast to prevent their getting out of the country."

" By the mule-back schedule," said Keogh, " it's five days down from San Mateo. We've got plenty of time to set our outposts. There's only three places on the coast where they can hope to sail from—here and Solitas and Alazan. They're the only points we'll have to guard. It's as easy as a chess problem—fox to play, and mate in three moves. Oh, goosey, goosey, gander, whither do you wander ? By the blessing of the literary telegraph the boodle of this benighted fatherland shall be preserved to the honest political party that is seeking to overthrow it."

The situation had been justly outlined by Keogh. The down trail from the capital was at all times a weary road to travel. A jiggety-joggety journey it was; ice-cold and hot, wet and dry. The trail climbed appalling mountains, wound like a rotten string about the brows of breathless precipices, plunged through chilling snow-fed streams, and wriggled like a snake through sunless forests teeming with menacing insect and animal life. After descending to the foothills it turned to a trident, the central prong ending at Alazan. Another branched off to Coralio; the third penetrated to Solitas. Between the sea and the foothills stretched the five miles breadth of alluvial coast. Here was the flora of the tropics in its rankest and most prodigal growth. Spaces here and there had been wrested from the jungle and planted with bananas and cane and orange groves. The rest was a riot of wild vegetation, the home of monkeys, tapirs, jaguars, alligators and prodigious reptiles and insects. Where no road was cut a serpent could scarcely make its way through the tangle of vines and creepers. Across the treacherous mangrove swamps few things without wings could safely pass. Therefore the fugitives could hope to reach the coast only by one of the routes named.

" Keep the matter quiet, Billy," advised Goodwin. " We don't want the Ins to know that the president is in flight. I suppose Bob's information is something of a scoop in the capital as yet. Otherwise he would not have tried to make his message a confidential one; and besides, everybody would have heard the news. I'm going around now to see Dr. Zavalla, and start a man up the trail to cut the telegraph wire."

As Goodwin rose, Keogh threw his hat upon the grass by the door and expelled a tremendous sigh.

" What's the trouble, Billy ? " asked Goodwin, pausing. " That's the first time I ever heard you sigh."

" 'Tis the last," said Keogh. " With that sorrowful puff of wind

I resign myself to a life of praiseworthy but harassing honesty. What are tintypes, if you please, to the opportunities of the great hilarious class of ganders and geese ? Not that I would be a president, Frank—and the boodle he's got is too big for me to handle— but in some ways I feel my conscience hurting me for addicting myself to photographing a nation instead of running away with it. Frank, did you ever see the ' bundle of muslin ' that His Excellency has wrapped up and carried off ? "

" Isabel Guilbert ? " said Goodwin, laughing. " No, I never did. From what I've heard of her, though, I imagine that she wouldn't stick at anything to carry her point. Don't get romantic, Billy. Sometimes I begin to fear that there's Irish blood in your ancestry."

" I never saw her either," went on Keogh ; " but they say she's got all the ladies of mythology, sculpture, and fiction reduced to chromos. They say she can look at a man once, and he'll turn monkey and climb trees to pick cocoanuts for her. Think of that president man with Lord knows how many hundreds of thousands of dollars in one hand, and this muslin siren in the other, galloping down hill on a sympathetic mule amid songbirds and flowers ! And here is Billy Keogh, because he is virtuous, condemned to the unprofitable swindle of slandering the faces of missing links on tin for an honest living ! 'Tis an injustice of nature."

" Cheer up," said Goodwin. " You are a pretty fox to be envying a gander. Maybe the enchanting Guilbert will take a fancy to you and your tintypes after we impoverish her royal escort."

" She could do worse," reflected Keogh; " but she won't. 'Tis not a tintype gallery, but the gallery of the gods that she's fitted to adorn. She's a very wicked lady, and the president man is in luck. But I hear Clancy swearing in the back room for having to do all the work." And Keogh plunged for the rear of the " gallery," whistling gaily in a spontaneous way that belied his recent sigh over the questionable good luck of the flying president.

Goodwin turned from the main street into a much narrower one that intersected it at a right angle.

These side streets were covered by a growth of thick, rank grass, which was kept to a navigable shortness by the machetes of the police. Stone sidewalks, little more than a ledge in width, ran along the base of the mean and monotonous adobe houses. At the outskirts of the village these streets dwindled to nothing; and here were set the palm-thatched huts of the Caribs and the poorer natives, and the shabby cabins of negroes from Jamaica and the West India islands. A few structures raised their heads above the red-tiled roofs of the one-story houses—the bell tower of the *Calaboza,* the Hotel de los Estranjeros, the residence of the Vesuvius

Fruit Company's agent, the store and residence of Bernard Brannigan, a ruined cathedral in which Columbus had once set foot,
and, most imposing of all, the Casa Morena—the summer " White
House " of the President of Anchuria. On the principal street
running along the beach—the Broadway of Coralio—were the
larger stores, the government *bodega* and post-office, the *cuartel*,
the rum-shops and the market place.

On his way Goodwin passed the house of Bernard Brannigan.
It was a modern wooden building, two stories in height. The
ground floor was occupied by Brannigan's store, the upper one
contained the living apartments. A wide cool porch ran around
the house half way up its outer walls. A handsome, vivacious girl
neatly dressed in flowing white leaned over the railing and smiled
down upon Goodwin. She was no darker than many an Anda-
lusian of high descent, and she sparkled and glowed like a tropical
moonlight.

" Good evening, Miss Paula," said Goodwin, taking off his hat,
with his ready smile. There was little difference in his manner
whether he addressed women or men. Everybody in Coralio liked
to receive the salutation of the big American.

" Is there any news, Mr. Goodwin ? Please don't say no. Isn't
it warm ? I feel just like Mariana in her moated grange—or was
it a range ?—it's hot enough."

" No, there's no news to tell, I believe," said Goodwin, with a
mischievous look in his eye, " except that old Geddie is getting
grumpier and crosser every day. If something doesn't happen to
relieve his mind I'll have to quit smoking on his back porch—and
there's no other place available that is cool enough."

" He isn't grumpy," said Paula Brannigan, impulsively, " when
he——"

But she ceased suddenly, and drew back with a deepening
colour; for her mother had been a *mestizo* lady, and the Spanish
blood had brought Paula a certain shyness that was an adornment
to the other half of her demonstrative nature.

THE LOTUS AND THE BOTTLE

WILLARD GEDDIE, consul for the United States in Coralio, was working leisurely on his yearly report. Goodwin, who had strolled in as he did daily for a smoke on the much coveted porch, had found him so absorbed in his work that he departed after roundly abusing the consul for his lack of hospitality.

" I shall complain to the civil service department," said Goodwin;—" or is it a department?—perhaps it's only a theory. One gets neither civility nor service from you. You won't talk; and you won't set out anything to drink. What kind of a way is that of representing your government? "

Goodwin strolled out and across the hotel to see if he could bully the quarantine doctor into a game on Coralio's solitary billiard table. His plans were completed for the interception of the fugitives from the capital; and now it was but a waiting game that he had to play.

The consul was interested in his report. He was only twenty-four; and he had not been in Coralio long enough for his enthusiasm to cool in the heat of the tropics—a paradox that may be allowed between Cancer and Capricorn.

So many thousand bunches of bananas, so many thousand oranges and cocoanuts, so many ounces of gold dust, pounds of rubber, coffee, indigo and sarsaparilla—actually, exports were twenty per cent. greater than for the previous year!

A little thrill of satisfaction ran through the consul. Perhaps, he thought, the State Department, upon reading his introduction, would notice—and then he leaned back in his chair and laughed. He was getting as bad as the others. For the moment he had forgotten that Coralio was an insignificant town in an insignificant republic lying along the by-ways of a second-rate sea. He thought of Gregg, the quarantine doctor, who subscribed for the London *Lancet*, expecting to find it quoting his reports to the home Board of Health concerning the yellow fever germ. The consul knew that not one in fifty of his acquaintances in the States had ever heard of Coralio. He knew that two men, at any rate, would have to read his report—some underling in the State Department and a compositor in the Public Printing Office. Perhaps the typesticker would note the increase of commerce in Coralio, and speak of it, over the cheese and beer, to a friend.

He had just written: " Most unaccountable is the supineness

31

of the large exporters in the United States in permitting the French
and German houses to practically control the trade interests of
this rich and productive country "—when he heard the hoarse
notes of a steamer's siren.

Geddie laid down his pen and gathered his Panama hat and
umbrella. By the sound he knew it to be the *Valhalla,* one of the
line of fruit vessels plying for the Vesuvius Company. Down to
niños of five years, everyone in Coralio could name you each incoming steamer by the note of her siren.

The consul sauntered by a roundabout, shaded way to the beach.
By reason of long practice he gauged his stroll so accurately that
by the time he arrived on the sandy shore the boat of the customs
officials was rowing back from the steamer, which had been
boarded and inspected according to the laws of Anchuria.

There is no harbour at Coralio. Vessels of the draught of the
Valhalla must ride at anchor a mile from shore. When they take
on fruit it is conveyed on lighters and freighter sloops. At Solitas,
where there was a fine harbour, ships of many kinds were to be
seen, but in the roadstead off Coralio scarcely any save the fruiters
paused. Now and then a tramp coaster, or a mysterious brig from
Spain, or a saucy French barque would hang innocently for a few
days in the offing. Then the custom-house crew would become
doubly vigilant and wary. At night a sloop or two would be making
strange trips in and out along the shore; and in the morning the
stock of Three-Star Hennessey, wines and drygoods in Coralio
would be found vastly increased. It has also been said that the
customs officials jingled more silver in the pockets of their red-
striped trousers, and the record books showed no increase in import
duties received.

The customs boat and the *Valhalla* gig reached the shore at the
same time. When they grounded in the shallow water there was
still five yards of rolling surf between them and dry sand. Then
half-clothed Caribs dashed into the water, and brought in on their
backs the *Valhalla's* purser and the little native officials in their
cotton undershirts, blue trousers with red stripes, and flapping
straw hats.

At college Geddie had been a treasure as a first-baseman. He
now closed his umbrella, stuck it upright in the sand, and stooped,
with his hands resting upon his knees. The purser, burlesquing the
pitcher's contortions, hurled at the consul the heavy roll of newspapers, tied with a string, that the steamer always brought for him.
Geddie leaped high and caught the roll with a sounding " thwack."
The loungers on the beach—about a third of the population of the
town—laughed and applauded delightedly. Every week they
expected to see that roll of papers delivered and received in that

same manner, and they were never disappointed. Innovations did not flourish in Coralio.

The Consul re-hoisted his umbrella and walked back to the consulate.

This home of a great nation's representative was a wooden structure of two rooms, with a native-built gallery of poles, bamboo and nipa palm running on three sides of it. One room was the official apartment, furnished chastely with a flat-top desk, a hammock, and three uncomfortable cane-seated chairs. Engravings of the first and latest president of the country represented hung against the wall. The other room was the consul's living apartment.

It was eleven o'clock when he returned from the beach, and therefore breakfast time. Chanca, the Carib woman who cooked for him, was just serving the meal on the side of the gallery facing the sea—a spot famous as the coolest in Coralio. The breakfast consisted of shark's fin soup, stew of land crabs, breadfruit, a boiled iguana steak, aguacates, a freshly cut pineapple, claret and coffee.

Geddie took his seat, and unrolled with luxurious laziness his bundle of newspapers. Here in Coralio for two days or longer he would read of goings-on in the world very much as we of the world read those whimsical contributions to inexact science that assume to portray the doings of the Martians. After he had finished with the papers they would be sent on the rounds of the other English-speaking residents of the town.

The paper that came first to his hand was one of those bulky mattresses of printed stuff upon which the readers of certain New York journals are supposed to take their Sabbath literary nap. Opening this the consul rested it upon the table, supporting its weight with the aid of the back of a chair. Then he partook of his meal deliberately, turning the leaves from time to time and glancing half idly at the contents.

Presently he was struck by something familiar to him in a picture—a half-page, badly printed reproduction of a photograph of a vessel. Languidly interested, he leaned for a nearer scrutiny and a view of the florid headlines of the column next to the picture.

Yes; he was not mistaken. The engraving was of the eight-hundred-ton yacht *Idalia*, belonging to " that prince of good fellows, Midas of the money market, and society's pink of perfection, J. Ward Tolliver."

Slowly sipping his black coffee, Geddie read the column of print. Following a listed statement of Mr. Tolliver's real estate and bonds, came a description of the yacht's furnishings, and then the grain of news no bigger than a mustard seed. Mr. Tolliver, with a party of favoured guests, would sail the next day on a six weeks' cruise along the Central American and South American coasts and among the

Bahama Islands. Among the guests were Mrs. Cumberland Payne and Miss Ida Payne, of Norfolk.

The writer, with the fatuous presumption that was demanded of him by his readers, had concocted a romance suited to their palates. He bracketed the names of Miss Payne and Mr. Tolliver until he had well-nigh read the marriage ceremony over them. He played coyly and insinuatingly upon the strings of " *on dit* " and " Madame Rumour " and " a little bird " and " no one would be surprised," and ended with congratulations.

Geddie, having finished his breakfast, took his papers to the edge of the gallery, and sat there in his favourite steamer chair with his feet on the bamboo railing. He lighted a cigar, and looked out upon the sea. He felt a glow of satisfaction at finding he was so little disturbed by what he had read. He told himself that he had conquered the distress that had sent him, a voluntary exile, to this far land of the lotus. He could never forget Ida, of course; but there was no longer any pain in thinking about her. When they had had that misunderstanding and quarrel he had impulsively sought his consulship with the desire to retaliate upon her by detaching himself from her world and presence. He had succeeded thoroughly in that. During the twelve months of his life in Coralio no word had passed between them, though he had sometimes heard of her through the dilatory correspondence with the few friends to whom he still wrote. Still he could not repress a little thrill of satisfaction at knowing that she had not yet married Tolliver or any one else. But evidently Tolliver had not yet abandoned hope.

Well, it made no difference to him now. He had eaten of the lotus. He was happy and content in this land of perpetual afternoon. Those old days of life in the States seemed like an irritating dream. He hoped Ida would be as happy as he was. The climate as balmy as that of distant Avalon; the fetterless, idyllic round of enchanted days; the life among this indolent, romantic people— a life full of music, flowers, and low laughter; the influence of the imminent sea and mountains, and the many shapes of love and magic and beauty that bloomed in the white tropic nights—with all he was more than content. Also, there was Paula Brannigan.

Geddie intended to marry Paula—if, of course, she would consent; but he felt rather sure that she would do that. Somehow, he kept postponing his proposal. Several times he had been quite near to it; but a mysterious something always held him back. Perhaps it was only the unconscious, instinctive conviction that the act would sever the last tie that bound him to his old world.

He could be very happy with Paula. Few of the native girls could be compared with her. She had attended a convent school in New Orleans for two years; and when she chose to display her accomplishments no one could detect any difference between her and the girls of Norfolk and Manhattan. But it was delicious to see her at home dressed, as she sometimes was, in the native costume, with bare shoulders and flowing sleeves.

Bernard Brannigan was the great merchant of Coralio. Besides his store, he maintained a train of pack mules, and carried on a lively trade with the interior towns and villages. He had married a native lady of high Castilian descent, but with a tinge of Indian brown showing through her olive cheek. The union of the Irish and the Spanish had produced, as it so often has, an offshoot of rare beauty and variety. They were very excellent people indeed, and the upper story of their house was ready to be placed at the service of Geddie and Paula as soon as he should make up his mind to speak about it.

By the time two hours were whiled away the consul tired of reading. The papers lay scattered about him on the gallery. Reclining there, he gazed dreamily out upon an Eden. A clump of banana plants interposed their broad shields between him and the sun. The gentle slope from the consulate to the sea was covered with the dark-green foliage of lemon-trees and orange-trees just bursting into bloom. A lagoon pierced the land like a dark, jagged crystal, and above it a pale ceiba-tree rose almost to the clouds. The waving cocoanut palms on the beach flared their decorative green leaves against the slate of an almost quiescent sea. His senses were cognizant of brilliant scarlet and ochres amid the vert of the coppice, of odours of fruit and bloom and the smoke from Chanca's clay oven under the calabash-tree; of the treble laughter of the native women in their huts, the song of the robin, the salt taste of the breeze, the diminuendo of the faint surf running along the shore—and, gradually, of a white speck, growing to a blur, that intruded itself upon the drab prospect of the sea.

Lazily interested, he watched this blur increase until it became the *Idalia* steaming at full speed, coming down the coast. Without changing his position he kept his eyes upon the beautiful white yacht as she drew swiftly near and came opposite to Coralio. Then, sitting upright, he saw her float steadily past and on. Scarcely a mile of sea had separated her from the shore. He had seen the frequent flash of her polished brass work and the stripes of her deck-awnings—so much, and no more. Like a ship on a magic lantern slide the *Idalia* had crossed the illuminated circle of the consul's little world, and was gone. Save for the tiny cloud of smoke that was left hanging over the brim of the sea, she might have been an immaterial thing, a chimera of his idle brain.

Geddie went into his office and sat down to dawdle over his

report. If the reading of the article in the paper had left him unshaken, this silent passing of the *Idalia* had done for him still more. It had brought the calm and peace of a situation from which all uncertainty had been erased. He knew that men sometimes hope without being aware of it. Now, since she had come two thousand miles and had passed without a sign, not even his unconscious self need cling to the past any longer.

After dinner, when the sun was low behind the mountains, Geddie walked on the little strip of beach under the cocoanuts. The wind was blowing mildly landward, and the surface of the sea was rippled by tiny wavelets.

A miniature breaker, spreading with a soft " swish " upon the sand, brought with it something round and shiny that rolled back again as the wave receded. The next influx beached it clear, and Geddie picked it up. The thing was a long-necked wine bottle of colourless glass. The cork had been driven in tightly to the level of the mouth, and the end covered with dark-red sealing-wax. The bottle contained only what seemed to be a sheet of paper, much curled from the manipulation it had undergone while being inserted. In the sealing-wax was the impression of a seal—probably of a signet-ring, bearing the initials of a monogram; but the impression had been hastily made, and the letters were past anything more certain than a shrewd conjecture. Ida Payne had always worn a signet-ring in preference to any other finger decoration. Geddie thought he could make out the familiar " I P "; and a queer sensation of disquietude went over him. More personal and intimate was this reminder of her than had been the sight of the vessel she was doubtless on. He walked back to his house, and set the bottle on his desk.

Throwing off his hat and coat, and lighting a lamp—for the night had crowded precipitately upon the brief twilight—he began to examine his piece of sea salvage.

By holding the bottle near the light and turning it judiciously, he made out that it contained a double sheet of note-paper filled with close writing; further, that the paper was of the same size and shade as that always used by Ida; and that, to the best of his belief, the handwriting was hers. The imperfect glass of the bottle so distorted the rays of light that he could read no word of the writing; but certain capital letters, of which he caught comprehensive glimpses, were Ida's, he felt sure.

There was a little smile of perplexity and amusement in Geddie's eyes as he set the bottle down, and laid three cigars side by side on his desk. He fetched his steamer chair from the gallery, and stretched himself comfortably. He would smoke those three cigars while considering the problem.

For it amounted to a problem. He almost wished that he had not found the bottle; but the bottle was there. Why should it have drifted in from the sea, whence come so many disquieting things, to disturb his peace?

In this dreamy land, where time seemed so redundant, he had fallen into the habit of bestowing much thought upon even trifling matters.

He began to speculate upon many fanciful theories concerning the story of the bottle, rejecting each in turn.

Ships in danger of wreck or disablement sometimes cast forth such precarious messengers calling for aid. But he had seen the *Idalia* not three hours before, safe and speeding. Suppose the crew had mutinied and imprisoned the passengers below, and the message was one begging for succour! But, premising such an improbable outrage, would the agitated captives have taken the pains to fill four pages of note-paper which carefully penned arguments to their rescue?

Thus by elimination he soon rid the matter of the more unlikely theories, and was reduced—though aversely—to the less assailable one that the bottle contained a message to himself. Ida knew he was in Coralio; she must have launched the bottle while the yacht was passing and the wind blowing fairly toward the shore.

As soon as Geddie reached this conclusion a wrinkle came between his brows and a stubborn look settled around his mouth. He sat looking out through the doorway at the gigantic fire-flies traversing the quiet streets.

If this was a message to him from Ida, what could it mean save an overture toward a reconciliation? And if that, why had she not used the safe methods of the post instead of this uncertain and even flippant means of communication? A note in an empty bottle, cast into the sea! There was something light and frivolous about it, if not actually contemptuous.

The thought stirred his pride and subdued whatever emotions had been resurrected by the finding of the bottle.

Geddie put on his coat and hat and walked out. He followed a street that led him along the border of the little plaza where a band was playing and people were rambling, care-free and indolent. Some timorous *señoritas* scurrying past with fire-flies tangled in the jetty braids of their hair glanced at him with shy, flattering eyes. The air was languorous with the scent of jasmin and orange-blossoms.

The consul stayed his steps at the house of Bernard Brannigan. Paula was swinging in a hammock on the gallery. She rose from it like a bird from its nest. The colour came to her cheek at the sound of Geddie's voice.

He was charmed at the sight of her costume—a flounced muslin dress, with a little jacket of white flannel, all made with neatness and style. He suggested a stroll, and they walked out to the old Indian well on the hill road. They sat on the curb, and there Geddie made the expected but long-deferred speech. Certain though he had been that she would not say him nay, he was thrilled with joy at the completeness and sweetness of her surrender. Here was surely a heart made for love and steadfastness. Here was no caprice or questionings or captious standards of convention.

When Geddie kissed Paula at her door that night he was happier than he had ever been before. " Here in this hollow lotus land, ever to live and lie reclined " seemed to him, as it seemed to many mariners, the best as well as the easiest. His future would be an ideal one. He had attained a Paradise without a serpent. His Eve would be indeed a part of him, unbeguiled, and therefore more beguiling. He had made his decision to-night, and his heart was full of serene, assured content.

Geddie went back to his house whistling that finest and saddest love song, " La Golondrina." At the door his tame monkey leaped down from his shelf, chattering briskly. The consul turned to his desk to get him some nuts he usually kept there. Reaching in the half-darkness, his hand struck against the bottle. He started as if he had touched the cold rotundity of a serpent.

He had forgotten that the bottle was there.

He lighted the lamp and fed the monkey. Then, very deliberately, he lighted a cigar, and took the bottle in his hand, and walked down the path to the beach.

There was a moon, and the sea was glorious. The breeze had shifted, as it did each evening, and was now rushing steadily seaward.

Stepping to the water's edge, Geddie hurled the unopened bottle far out into the sea. It disappeared for a moment, and then shot upward twice its length. Geddie stood still, watching it. The moonlight was so bright that he could see it bobbing up and down with the little waves. Slowly it receded from the shore, flashing and turning as it went. The wind was carrying it out to sea. Soon it became a mere speck, doubtfully discerned at irregular intervals; and then the mystery of it was swallowed up by the greater mystery of the ocean. Geddie stood still upon the beach, smoking and looking out upon the water.

" Simon !—Oh, Simon !—wake up there, Simon ! " bawled a sonorous voice at the edge of the water.

Old Simon Cruz was a half-breed fisherman and smuggler who lived in a hut on the beach. Out of his earliest nap Simon was thus awakened.

He slipped on his shoes and went outside. Just landing from one of the *Valhalla's* boats was the third mate of that vessel, who was an acquaintance of Simon's, and three sailors from the fruiter.

" Go up, Simon," called the mate, " and find Dr. Gregg or Mr. Goodwin or anybody that's a friend to Mr. Geddie, and bring 'em here at once."

" Saints of the skies ! " said Simon, sleepily, " nothing has happened to Mr. Geddie ? "

" He's under that tarpauling," said the mate, pointing to the boat, " and he's rather more than half drowned. We seen him from the steamer nearly a mile out from shore, swimmin' like mad after a bottle that was floatin' in the water, outward bound. We lowered the gig and started for him. He nearly had his hand on the bottle, when he gave out and went under. We pulled him out in time to save him, maybe ; but the doctor is the one to decide that."

"A bottle ? ' said the old man, rubbing his eyes. He was not yet fully awake. " Where is the bottle ? "

" Driftin' along out there some'eres," said the mate, jerking his thumb toward the sea. " Get on with you, Simon."

SMITH

GOODWIN and the ardent patriot, Zavalla, took all the precautions that their foresight could contrive to prevent the escape of President Miraflores and his companion. They sent trusted messengers up the coast to Solitas and Alazan to warn the local leaders of the flight, and to instruct them to patrol the water line and arrest the fugitives at all hazards should they reveal themselves in that territory. After this was done there remained only to cover the district about Coralio and await the coming of the quarry. The nets were well spread. The roads were so few, the opportunities for embarkation so limited, and the two or three probable points of exit so well guarded that it would be strange indeed if there should slip through the meshes so much of the country's dignity, romance, and collateral. The president would, without doubt, move as secretly as possible, and endeavour to board a vessel by stealth from some secluded point along the shore.

On the fourth day after the receipt of Englehart's telegram the *Karlsefin*, a Norwegian steamer chartered by the New Orleans fruit trade, anchored off Coralio with three hoarse toots of her siren. The *Karlsefin* was not one of the line operated by the Vesuvius Fruit Company. She was something of a dilettante, doing odd jobs for a company that was scarcely important enough to figure as a rival to the Vesuvius. The movements of the *Karlsefin* were dependent upon the state of the market. Sometimes she would ply steadily between the Spanish Main and New Orleans in the regular transport of fruit; next she would be making erratic trips to Mobile or Charleston, or even as far north as New York, according to the distribution of the fruit supply.

Goodwin lounged upon the beach with the usual crowd of idlers that had gathered to view the steamer. Now that President Miraflores might be expected to reach the borders of his adjured country at any time, the orders were to keep a strict and unrelenting watch. Every vessel that approached the shores might now be considered a possible means of escape for the fugitives; and an eye was kept even on the sloops and dories that belonged to the seagoing contingent of Coralio. Goodwin and Zavalla moved everywhere, but without ostentation, watching the loopholes of escape.

The customs officials crowded importantly into their boat and rowed out to the *Karlsefin*. A boat from the steamer landed her purser with his papers, and took out the quarantine doctor with his green umbrella and clinical thermometer. Next a swarm of Caribs began to load upon lighters the thousands of bunches of bananas heaped upon the shore and row them out to the steamer. The *Karlsefin* had no passenger list, and was soon done with the attention of the authorities. The purser declared that the steamer would remain at anchor until morning, taking on her fruit during the night. The *Karlsefin* had come, he said, from New York, to which port her latest load of oranges and cocoanuts had been conveyed. Two or three of the freighter sloops were engaged to assist in the work, for the captain was anxious to make a quick return in order to reap the advantage offered by a certain dearth of fruit in the States.

About four o'clock in the afternoon another of those marine monsters, not very familiar in those waters, hove in sight, following the fateful *Idalia*—a graceful steam yacht, painted a light buff, clean-cut as a steel engraving. The beautiful vessel hovered off shore, see-sawing the waves as lightly as a duck in a rain barrel. A swift boat manned by a crew in uniform came ashore, and a stocky-built man leaped to the sands.

The new-comer seemed to turn a disapproving eye upon the rather motley congregation of native Anchurians, and made his way at once toward Goodwin, who was the most conspicuously Anglo-Saxon figure present. Goodwin greeted him with courtesy.

Conversation developed that the newly landed one was named Smith, and that he had come in a yacht. A meagre biography, truly; for the yacht was most apparent; and the " Smith " not beyond a reasonable guess before the revelation. Yet to the eye of Goodwin, who had seen several things, there was a discrepancy between Smith and his yacht. A bullet-headed man Smith was, with an oblique, dead eye and the moustache of a cocktail-mixer. And unless he had shifted costumes before putting off for shore he had affronted the deck of his correct vessel clad in a pearl-gray derby, a gay plaid suit and vaudeville neckwear. Men owning pleasure yachts generally harmonize better with them.

Smith looked business, but he was no advertiser. He commented upon the scenery, remarking upon its fidelity to the pictures in the geography; and then inquired for the United States consul. Goodwin pointed out the starred-and-striped bunting hanging above the little consulate, which was concealed behind the orange-trees.

" Mr. Geddie, the consul, will be sure to be there," said Goodwin. " He was very nearly drowned a few days ago while taking a swim in the sea, and the doctor has ordered him to remain indoors for some time."

Smith plowed his way through the sand to the consulate, his haberdashery creating violent discord against the smooth tropical blues and greens.

Geddie was lounging in his hammock, somewhat pale of face and languid in pose. On that night when the *Valhalla's* boat had brought him ashore apparently drenched to death by the sea, Dr. Gregg and his other friends had toiled for hours to preserve the little spark of life that remained to him. The bottle, with its impotent message, was gone out to sea, and the problem that it had provoked was reduced to a simple sum in addition—one and one make two, by the rule of arithmetic; one by the rule of romance.

There is a quaint old theory that man may have two souls—a peripheral one which serves ordinarily, and a central one which is stirred only at certain times, but then with activity and vigor. While under the domination of the former a man will shave, vote, pay taxes, give money to his family, buy subscription books and comport himself on the average plan. But let the central soul suddenly become dominant, and he may, in the twinkling of an eye, turn upon the partner of his joys with furious execration; he may change his politics while you could snap your fingers; he may deal out deadly insult to his dearest friend ; he may get him, instanter, to a monastery or a dance hall; he may elope, or hang himself—or he may write a song or poem, or kiss his wife unasked, or give his funds to the search of a microbe. Then the peripheral soul will return; and we have our safe, sane citizen again. It is but the revolt of the Ego against Order; and its effect is to shake up the atoms only that they may settle where they belong.

Geddie's revulsion had been a mild one—no more than a swim in a summer sea after so inglorious an object as a drifting bottle. And now he was himself again. Upon his desk, ready for the post, was a letter to his government tendering his resignation as consul, to be effective as soon as another could be appointed in his place. For Bernard Brannigan, who never did things in a half-way manner, was to take Geddie at once for a partner in his very profitable and various enterprises; and Paula was happily engaged in plans for refurnishing and decorating the upper story of the Brannigan house.

The consul rose from his hammock when he saw the conspicuous stranger in his door.

" Keep your seat, old man," said the visitor, with an airy wave of his large hand. " My name's Smith; and I've come in a yacht. You are the consul—is that right ? A big, cool guy on the beach directed me here. Thought I'd pay my respects to the flag."

" Sit down," said Geddie. " I've been admiring your craft ever since it came in sight. Looks like a fast sailer. What's her tonnage?"

" Search me ! " said Smith. " I don't know what she weighs in at. But she's got a tidy gait. The *Rambler*—that's her name— don't take the dust of anything afloat. This is my first trip on her. I'm taking a squint along this coast just to get an idea of the countries where the rubber and red pepper and revolutions come from. I had no idea there was so much scenery down here. Why, Central Park ain't in it with this neck of the woods. I'm from New York. They get monkeys, and cocoanuts, and parrots down here—is that right ? "

" We have them all," said Geddie. " I'm quite sure that our fauna and flora would take a prize over Central Park."

" Maybe they would," admitted Smith, cheerfully. " I haven't seen them yet. But I guess you've got us skinned on the animal and vegetation question. You don't have much travel here, do you ? "

" Travel ? " queried the consul. " I suppose you mean passengers on the steamers. No; very few people land in Coralio. An investor now and then—tourists and sightseers generally go further down the coast to one of the larger towns where there is a harbor."

" I see a ship out there loading up with bananas," said Smith. "Any passengers come on her ? "

" That's the *Karlsefin*," said the consul. " She's a tramp fruiter —made her last trip to New York, I believe. No; she brought no passengers. I saw her boat come ashore, and there was no one. About the only exciting recreation we have here is watching steamers when they arrive; and a passenger on one of them generally causes the whole town to turn out. If you are going to remain in Coralio a while, Mr. Smith, I'll be glad to take you around to meet some people. There are four or five American chaps that are good to know, besides the native high-fliers."

"Thanks," said the yachtsman, "but I wouldn't put you to the trouble. I'd like to meet the guys you speak of, but I won't be here long enough to do much knocking around. That cool gent on the beach spoke of a doctor; can you tell me where I could find him? The *Rambler* ain't quite as steady on her feet as a Broadway hotel; and a fellow gets a touch of seasickness now and then. Thought I'd strike the croaker for a handful of the little sugar pills, in case I need 'em."

"You will be apt to find Dr. Gregg at the hotel," said the consul. "You can see it from the door—it's that two-story building with the balcony, where the orange-trees are."

The Hotel de los Estranjeros was a dreary hostelry, in great disuse both by strangers and friends. It stood at a corner of the Street of the Holy Sepulchre. A grove of small orange-trees crowded against one side of it, enclosed by a low, rock wall over which a tall man might easily step. The house was of plastered adobe, stained a hundred shades of colour by the salt breeze and the sun. Upon its upper balcony opened a central door and two windows containing broad jalousies instead of sashes.

The lower floor communicated by two doorways with the narrow, rock-paved sidewalk. The *pulpería*—or drinking shop—of the proprietress, Madama Timotea Ortiz, occupied the ground floor. On the bottles of brandy, *anisada*, Scotch "smoke" and inexpensive wines behind the little counter the dust lay thick save where the fingers of infrequent customers had left irregular prints. The upper story contained four or five guest-rooms which where rarely put to their destined use. Sometimes a fruit-grower, riding in from his plantation to confer with his agent, would pass a melancholy night in the dismal upper story; sometimes a minor native official on some trifling government quest would have his pomp and majesty awed by Madama's sepulchral hospitality. But Madama sat behind her bar content, nor desiring to quarrel with Fate. If any one required meat, drink, or lodging at the Hotel de los Estranjeros they had but to come, and be served. *Está bueno.* If they came not, why, then, they came not. *Está bueno.*

As the exceptional yachtsman was making his way down the precarious sidewalk of the Street of the Holy Sepulchre, the solitary permanent guest of that decaying hotel sat at its door, enjoying the breeze from the sea.

Dr. Gregg, the quarantine physician, was a man of fifty or sixty, with a florid face and the longest beard between Topeka and Terra del Fuego. He held his position by virtue of an appointment by the Board of Health of a seaport city in one of the Southern states. That city feared the ancient enemy of every Southern seaport—the yellow fever—and it was the duty of Dr. Gregg to examine crew and passengers of every vessel leaving Coralio for preliminary symptons. The duties were light, and the salary, for one who lived in Coralio, ample. Surplus time there was in plenty; and the good doctor added to his gains by a large private practice among the residents of the coast. The fact that he did not know ten words of Spanish was no obstacle; a pulse could be felt and a fee collected without one being a linguist. Add to the description the facts that the doctor had a story to tell concerning the operation of trepanning which no listener had ever allowed him to conclude, and that he believed in brandy as a prophylactic; and the special points of interest possessed by Dr. Gregg will have become exhausted.

The doctor had dragged a chair to the sidewalk. He was coatless, and he leaned back against the wall and smoked, while he stroked his beard. Surprise came into his pale blue eyes when he caught sight of Smith in his unusual and prismatic clothes.

" You're Dr. Gregg—is that right ? " said Smith, feeling the dog's head pin in his tie. " The constable—I mean the consul, told me you hung out at this caravansary. My name's Smith; and I came in a yacht. Taking a cruise around, looking at the monkeys and pineapple-trees. Come inside and have a drink, Doc. This café looks on the blink, but I guess it can set out something wet."

" I will join you, sir, in just a taste of brandy," said Dr. Gregg, rising quickly. " I find that as a prophylactic a little brandy is almost a necessity in this climate."

As they turned to enter the *pulperia* a native man, barefoot, glided noiselessly up and addressed the doctor in Spanish. He was yellowish-brown, like an over-ripe lemon; he wore a cotton shirt and ragged linen trousers girded by a leather belt. His face was like an animal's, live and wary, but without promise of much intelligence. This man jabbered with animation and so much seriousness that it seemed a pity that his words were to be wasted.

Dr. Gregg felt his pulse.

" You sick ? " he inquired.

" *Mi mujer está enferma en la casa,*" said the man, thus endeavoring to convey the news, in the only language open to him, that his wife lay ill in her palm-thatched hut.

The doctor drew a handful of capsules filled with a white powder from his trousers pocket. He counted ten of them into the native's hand, and held up his forefinger impressively.

" Take one," said the doctor, " every two hours." He then held up two fingers, shaking them emphatically before the native's face. Next he pulled out his watch and ran his finger round its dial twice. Again the two fingers confronted the patient's nose. " Two—two—two hours," repeated the doctor.

" *Si señor*," said the native, sadly.

He pulled a cheap silver watch from his own pocket and laid it in the doctor's hand. " Me bring," said he, struggling painfully with his scant English, " other watchy to-morrow." Then he departed down-heartedly with his capsules.

"A very ignorant race of people, sir," said the doctor, as he slipped the watch into his pocket. " He seems to have mistaken my directions for taking the physic for the fee. However, it is all right. He owes me an account, anyway. The chances are that he won't bring the other watch. You can't depend on anything they promise you. About that drink, now ? How did you come to Coralio, Mr. Smith ? I was not aware that any boats except the *Karlsefin* had arrived for some days."

The two leaned against the deserted bar; and Madama set out a bottle without waiting for the doctor's order. There was no dust on it.

After they had drank twice Smith said :

" You say there were no passengers on the *Karlsefin*, Doc ? Are you sure about that ? It seems to me I heard somebody down on the beach say that there was one or two aboard."

" They were mistaken, sir. I myself went out and put all hands through a medical examination, as usual. The *Karlsefin* sails as soon as she gets her bananas loaded, which will be about daylight in the morning, and she got everything ready this afternoon. No, sir, there was no passenger list. Like that Three-Star ? A French schooner landed two slooploads of it a month ago. If any customs duties on it went to the distinguished republic of Anchuria you may have my hat. If you won't have another, come out and let's sit in the cool a while. It isn't often we exiles get a chance to talk with somebody from the outside world."

The doctor brought out another chair to the sidewalk for his new acquaintance. The two seated themselves.

" You are a man of the world," said Dr. Gregg; " a man of travel and experience. Your decision in a matter of ethics and, no doubt, on the points of equity, ability, and professional probity should be of value. I would be glad if you will listen to the history of a case that I think stands unique in medical annals.

"About nine years ago, while I was engaged in the practice of medicine in my native city, I was called to treat a case of contusion of the skull. I made the diagnosis that a splinter of bone was pressing upon the brain, and that the surgical operation known as trepanning was required. However, as the patient was a gentleman of wealth and position, I called in for consultation, Dr.——"

Smith rose from his chair, and laid a hand, soft with apology, upon the doctor's shirt sleeve.

" Say, Doc," he said, solemnly, " I want to hear that story. You've got me interested; and I don't want to miss the rest of it. I know it's a loola by the way it begins; and I want to tell it at the next meeting of the Barney O'Flynn Association, if you don't mind. But I've got one or two matters to attend to first. If I get 'em attended to in time I'll come right back and hear you spiel the rest before bedtime—is that right ? "

" By all means," said the doctor, " get your business attended to, and then return. I shall wait up for you. You see, one of the most prominent physicians at the consultation diagnosed the trouble as a blood clot; another said it was an abscess, but I——"

" Don't tell me now, Doc. Don't spoil the story. Wait till I come back. I want to hear it as it runs off the reel—is that right ? "

The mountains reached up their bulky shoulders to receive the level gallop of Apollo's homing steeds, the day died in the lagoons and in the shadowed banana groves and in the mangrove swamps, where the great blue crabs were beginning to crawl to land for their nightly ramble. And it died, at last, upon the highest peaks. Then the brief twilight, ephemeral as the flight of a moth, came and went; the Southern Cross peeped with its topmost eye above a row of palms, and the fire-flies heralded with their torches the approach of soft-footed night.

In the offing the *Karlsefin* swayed at anchor, her lights seeming to penetrate the water to countless fathoms with their shimmering, lanceolate reflections. The Caribs were busy loading her by means of the great lighters heaped full from the piles of fruit ranged upon the shore.

On the sandy beach, with his back against a cocoanut-tree and the stubs of many cigars lying around him, Smith sat waiting, never relaxing his sharp gaze in the direction of the steamer.

The incongruous yachtsman had concentrated his interest upon the innocent fruiter. Twice had he been assured that no passengers had come to Coralio on board of her. And yet, with a persistence not to be attributed to an idling voyager, he had appealed the case to the higher court of his own eye-sight. Surprisingly like some gay-coated lizard, he crouched at the foot of the cocoanut palm, and with the beady, shifting eyes of the selfsame reptile, sustained his espionage on the *Karlsefin*.

On the white sands a whiter gig belonging to the yacht was drawn up, guarded by one of the white-ducked crew. Not far away in a *pulperia* on the shore-following Calle Grande three other sailors swaggered with their cues around Coralio's solitary billiard-table. The boat lay there as if under orders to be ready for use at any moment. There was in the atmosphere a hint of expectation, of waiting for something to occur, which was foreign to the air of Coralio.

Like some passing bird of brilliant plumage, Smith alights on this palmy shore but to preen his wings for an instant and then to fly away upon silent pinions. When morning dawned there was no Smith, no waiting gig, no yacht in the offing. Smith left no intimation of his mission there, no footprints to show where he had followed the trail of his mystery on the sands of Coralio that night. He came; he spake his strange jargon of the asphalt and the cafés; he sat under the cocoanut-tree, and vanished. The next morning Coralio, Smithless, ate its fried plantain and said : " The man of pictured clothing went himself away." With the *siesta* the incident passed, yawning, into history.

So, for a time, must Smith pass behind the scenes of the play. He comes no more to Coralio nor to Dr. Gregg, who sits in vain, wagging his redundant beard, waiting to enrich his derelict audience with his moving tale of trepanning and jealousy.

But prosperity to the lucidity of these loose pages, Smith shall flutter among them again. In the nick of time he shall come to tell us why he strewed so many anxious cigar stumps around the cocoanut palm that night. This he must do; for, when he sailed away before the dawn in his yacht *Rambler*, he carried with him the answer to a riddle so big and preposterous that few in Anchuria had ventured even to propound it.

CAUGHT

THE plans for the detention of the flying President Miraflores and his companion at the coast line seemed hardly likely to fail. Dr. Zavalla himself had gone to the port of Alazan to establish a guard at that point. At Coralio the Liberal patriot Varras could be depended upon to keep close watch. Goodwin held himself responsible for the district about Coralio.

The news of the president's flight had been disclosed to no one in the coast towns save trusted members of the ambitious political party that was desirous of succeeding to power. The telegraph wire running from San Mateo to the coast had been cut far up on the mountain trail by an emissary of Zavalla's. Long before this could be repaired and word received along it from the capital the fugitives would have reached the coast and the question of escape or capture been solved.

Goodwin had stationed armed sentinels at frequent intervals along the shore for a mile in each direction from Coralio. They were instructed to keep a vigilant lookout during the night to prevent Miraflores from attempting to embark stealthily by means of some boat or sloop found by chance at the water's edge. A dozen patrols walked the streets of Coralio, ready to intercept the truant official should he show himself there.

Goodwin was very well convinced that no precautions had been overlooked. He strolled about the streets that bore such high-sounding names and were but narrow, grass-covered lanes, lending his own aid to the vigil that had been intrusted to him by Bob Englehart.

The town had begun the tepid round of its nightly diversions. A few leisurely dandies, clad in white duck, with flowing neckties, and swinging slim bamboo canes, threaded the grassy by-ways toward the houses of their favored señoritas. Those who wooed the art of music dragged tirelessly at whining concertinas, or fingered lugubrious guitars at doors and windows. An occasional soldier from the *cuartel*, with flapping straw hat, without coat or shoes, hurried by, balancing his long gun like a lance in one hand. From every density of the foliage the giant tree frogs sounded their loud and irritating clatter. Further out, where the by-ways perished at the brink of the jungle, the guttural cries of marauding baboons and the coughing of the alligators in the black estuaries fractured the vain silence of the wood.

By ten o'clock the streets were deserted. The oil lamps that had burned, a sickly yellow, at random corners, had been extinguished by some economical civic agent. Coralio lay sleeping calmly between toppling mountains and encroaching sea like a stolen babe in the arms of its abductors. Somewhere over in that tropical darkness—perhaps already threading the profundities of the alluvial lowlands—the high adventurer and his mate were moving toward land's end. The game of Fox-in-the-Morning should be coming soon to its close.

Goodwin, at his deliberate gait, passed the long, low *cuartel* where Coralio's contingent of Anchuria's military force slumbered, with its bare toes pointed heavenward. There was a law that no civilian might come so near the headquarters of the citadel of war after nine o'clock, but Goodwin was always forgetting the minor statutes.

" *Quién vive ?* " shrieked the sentinel, wrestling prodigiously with his lengthy musket.

" *Americano*," growled Goodwin, without turning his head, and passed on, unhalted.

To the right he turned, and to the left up the street that ultimately reached the Plaza Nacional. When within the toss of a cigar stump from the intersecting Street of the Holy Sepulchre, he stopped suddenly in the pathway.

He saw the form of a tall man, clothed in black and carrying a large valise, hurry down the cross-street in the direction of the beach. And Goodwin's second glance made him aware of a woman at the man's elbow on the farther side, who seemed to urge forward, if not even to assist, her companion in their swift but silent progress. They were no Coralians, those two.

Goodwin followed at increased speed, but without any of the artful tactics that are so dear to the heart of the sleuth. The American was too broad to feel the instinct of the detective. He stood as an agent for the people of Anchuria, and but for political reasons he would have demanded then and there the money. It was the design of his party to secure the imperilled fund, to restore it to the treasury of the country, and to declare itself in power without bloodshed or resistance.

The couple halted at the door of the Hotel de los Estranjeros, and the man struck upon the wood with the impatience of one unused to his entry being stayed. Madama was long in response; but after a time her light showed, the door was opened, and the guests housed.

Goodwin stood in the quiet street, lighting another cigar. In two minutes a faint gleam began to show between the slats of the jalousies in the upper story of the hotel. " They have engaged rooms," said Goodwin to himself. " So, then, their arrangements for sailing have yet to be made."

At that moment there came along one Estebán Delgado, a barber, an enemy to existing government, a jovial plotter against stagnation in any form. This barber was one of Coralio's saddest dogs, often remaining out of doors as late as eleven, post meridian. He was a partisan Liberal; and he greeted Goodwin with flatulent importance as a brother in the cause. But he had something important to tell.

" What think you, Don Frank ! " he cried, in the universal tone of the conspirator. " I have to-night shaved *la barba*—what you call the 'weeskers' of the *Presidente* himself, of this countree ! Consider ! He sent for me to come. In the poor *casita* of an old woman he awaited me—in a verree leetle house in a dark place. *Carramba !* —el Señor Presidente to make himself thus secret and obscured ! I think he desired not to be known—but, *carajo !* can you shave a man and not see his face ? This gold piece he gave me, and said it was to be all quite still. I think, Don Frank, there is what you call a chip over the bug."

" Have you ever seen President Miraflores before ? " asked Goodwin.

" But once," answered Estebán. " He is tall, and he had weeskers, verree black and sufficient."

" Was any one else present when you shaved him ? "

"An old Indian woman, Señor, that belonged with the *casa*, and one señorita—a ladee of so much beautee !—*ah, Dios !* "

"All right, Estebán," said Goodwin. " It's very lucky that you happened along with your tonsorial information. The new administration will be likely to remember you for this."

Then in a few words he made the barber acquainted with the crisis into which the affairs of the nation had culminated, and instructed him to remain outside, keeping watch upon the two sides of the hotel that looked upon the street, and observing whether any one should attempt to leave the house by any door or window. Goodwin himself went to the door through which the guests had entered, opened it and stepped inside.

Madama had returned downstairs from her journey above to see after the comfort of her lodgers. Her candle stood upon the bar. She was about to take a thimbleful of rum as a solace for having her rest disturbed. She looked up without surprise or alarm as her third caller entered.

"Ah ! it is the Señor Goodwin. Not often does he honor my poor house by his presence."

" I must come oftener," said Goodwin, with the Goodwin smile. " I hear that your cognac is the best between Belize to the north and Rio to the south. Set out the bottle, Madama, and let us have the proof in *un vasito* for each of us."

" My *aguardiente*," said Madama, with pride, " is the best. It grows, in beautiful bottles, in the dark places among the banana-trees. *Si, Señor.* Only at midnight can they be picked by sailor-men who bring them, before daylight comes, to your back door. Good *aguardiente* is a verree difficult fruit to handle, Señor Goodwin."

Smuggling, in Coralio, was much nearer than competition to being the life of trade. One spoke of it slyly, yet with a certain conceit, when it had been well accomplished.

" You have guests in the house to-night," said Goodwin, laying a silver dollar upon the counter.

" Why not ? " said Madama, counting the change. " Two; but the smallest while finished to arrive. One señor, not quite old, and one señorita of sufficient handsomeness. To their rooms they have ascended, not desiring the to-eat nor the to-drink. Two rooms—*Número* 9 and *Número* 10."

"I was expecting that gentleman and that lady," said Goodwin. "I have important *negocios* that must be transacted. Will you allow me to see them?"

"Why not?" sighed Madama, placidly. "Why should not Señor Goodwin ascend and speak to his friends? *Está bueno.* Room *Número* 9 and room *Número* 10."

Goodwin loosened in his coat pocket the American revolver that he carried, and ascended the steep, dark stairway.

In the hallway above, the saffron light from a hanging lamp allowed him to select the gaudy numbers on the doors. He turned the knob of Number 9, entered and closed the door behind him.

If that was Isabel Guilbert seated by the table in that poorly furnished room, report had failed to do her charms justice. She rested her head upon one hand. Extreme fatigue was signified in every line of her figure; and upon her countenance a deep perplexity was written. Her eyes were gray-irised, and of that mould that seems to have belonged to the orbs of all the famous queens of hearts. Their whites were singularly clear and brilliant, concealed above the irises by heavy horizontal lids, and showing a snowy line below them. Such eyes denote great nobility, vigor, and, if you can conceive of it, a most generous selfishness. She looked up when the American entered with an expression of surprised inquiry, but without alarm.

Goodwin took off his hat and seated himself, with his characteristic deliberate ease, upon a corner of the table. He held a lighted cigar between his fingers. He took this familiar course because he was sure that preliminaries would be wasted upon Miss Guilbert. He knew her history, and the small part that the conventions had played in it.

"Good evening," he said. "Now, madame, let us come to business at once. You will observe that I mention no names, but I know who is in the next room, and what he carries in that valise. That is the point which brings me here. I have come to dictate terms of surrender."

The lady neither moved nor replied, but steadily regarded the cigar in Goodwin's hand.

"We," continued the dictator, thoughtfully regarding the neat buckskin shoe on his gently swinging foot—"I speak for a considerable majority of the people—demand the return of the stolen funds belonging to them. Our terms go very little further than that. They are very simple. As an accredited spokesman, I promise that our interference will cease if they are accepted. Give up the money, and you and your companion will be permitted to proceed wherever you will. In fact, assistance will be given you in the matter of securing a passage by any outgoing vessel you may choose. It is on my personal responsibility that I add congratulations to the gentleman in Number 10 upon his taste in feminine charms."

Returning his cigar to his mouth, Goodwin observed her, and saw that her eyes followed it and rested upon it with icy and significant concentration. Apparently she had not heard a word he had said. He understood, tossed the cigar out of the window, and, with an amused laugh, slid from the table to his feet.

"That is better," said the lady. "It makes it possible for me to listen to you. For a second lesson in good manners, you might now tell me by whom I am being insulted."

"I am sorry," said Goodwin, leaning one hand on the table, "that my time is too brief for devoting much of it to a course of etiquette. Come, now; I appeal to your good sense. You have shown yourself, in more than one instance, to be well aware of what is to your advantage. This is an occasion that demands the exercise of your undoubted intelligence. There is no mystery here. I am Frank Goodwin; and I have come for the money. I entered this room at a venture. Had I entered the other I would have had it before now. Do you want it in words? The gentleman in Number 10 has betrayed a great trust. He has robbed his people of a large sum, and it is I who will prevent their losing it. I do not say who that gentleman is; but if I should be forced to see him and he should prove to be a certain high official of the republic, it will be my duty to arrest him. The house is guarded. I am offering you liberal terms. It is not absolutely necessary that I confer personally with the gentleman in the next room. Bring me the valise containing the money, and we will call the affair ended."

The lady arose from her chair and stood for a moment, thinking deeply.

"Do you live here, Mr. Goodwin?" she asked, presently.

"Yes."

"What is your authority for this intrusion?"

"I am an instrument of the republic. I was advised by wire of the movements of the—gentleman in Number 10."

"May I ask you two or three questions? I believe you to be a man more apt to be truthful than—timid. What sort of a town is this—Coralio, I think they call it?"

"Not much of a town," said Goodwin, smiling. "A banana town, as they run. Grass huts, 'dobes, five or six two-story houses, accommodations limited, population half-breed Spanish and Indian, Caribs and blackamoors. No sidewalks to speak of, no amusements. Rather unmoral. That's an offhand sketch, of course."

"Are there any inducements, say in a social or in a business way, for people to reside here?"

" Oh, yes," answered Goodwin, smiling broadly. " There are no afternoon teas, no hand-organs, no department stores—and there is no extradition treaty."

" He told me," went on the lady, speaking as if to herself, and with a slight frown, " that there were towns on this coast of beauty and importance; that there was a pleasing social order—especially an American colony of cultured residents."

" There is an American colony," said Goodwin, gazing at her in some wonder. " Some of the members are all right. Some are fugitives from justice from the States. I recall two exiled bank presidents, one army paymaster under a cloud, a couple of man-slayers, and a widow—arsenic, I believe, was the suspicion in her case. I myself complete the colony, but, as yet, I have not distinguished myself by any particular crime."

" Do not lose hope," said the lady, dryly; " I see nothing in your actions tonight to guarantee your further obscurity. Some mistake has been made; I do not know just where. But *him* you shall not disturb to-night. The journey has fatigued him so that he has fallen asleep, I think, in his clothes. You talk of stolen money ! I do not understand you. Some mistake has been made. I will convince you. Remain where you are and I will bring you the valise that you seem to covet so, and show it to you."

She moved toward the closed door that connected the two rooms, but stopped, and half turned and bestowed upon Goodwin a grave, searching look that ended in a quizzical smile.

" You force my door," she said, " and you follow your ruffianly behavior with the basest accusations; and yet "—she hesitated, as if to reconsider what she was about to say—" and yet—it is a puzzling thing—I am sure there has been some mistake."

She took a step toward the door, but Goodwin stayed her by a light touch upon her arm. I have said before that women turned to look at him in the streets. He was the viking sort of man, big, good-looking, and with an air of kindly truculence. She was dark and proud, glowing or pale as her mood moved her. I do not know if Eve were light or dark, but if such a woman had stood in the garden I know that the apple would have been eaten. This woman was to be Goodwin's fate, and he did not know it; but he must have felt the first throes of destiny, for, as he faced her, the knowledge of what report named her turned bitter in his throat.

" If there has been any mistake," he said, hotly, " it was yours. I do not blame the man who has lost his country, his honor, and is about to lose the poor consolation of his stolen riches as much as I blame you, for, by Heaven ! I can very well see how he was brought to it. I can understand, and pity him. It is such women as you that strew this degraded coast with wretched exiles, that make men forget their trusts, that drag——"

The lady interrupted him with a weary gesture.

" There is no need to continue your insults," she said, coldly. " I do not understand what you are saying, nor do I know what mad blunder you are making; but if the inspection of the contents of a gentleman's portmanteau will rid me of you, let us delay it no longer."

She passed quickly and noiselessly into the other room, and returned with the heavy leather valise, which she handed to the American with an air of patient contempt.

Goodwin set the valise quickly upon the table and began to unfasten the straps. The lady stood by, with an expression of infinite scorn and weariness upon her face.

The valise opened wide to a powerful, sidelong wrench. Goodwin dragged out two or three articles of clothing, exposing the bulk of its contents—package after package of tightly packed United States bank and treasury notes of large denomination. Reckoning from the high figures written upon the paper bands that bound them, the total must have come closely upon the hundred thousand mark.

Goodwin glanced swiftly at the woman, and saw, with surprise and a thrill of pleasure that he wondered at, that she had experienced an unmistakable shock. Her eyes grew wide, she gasped, and leaned heavily against the table. She had been ignorant, then, he inferred, that her companion had looted the government treasury. But why, he angrily asked himself, should he be so well pleased to think this wandering and unscrupulous singer not so black as report had painted her?

A noise in the other room startled them both. The door swung open, and a tall, elderly, dark complexioned man, recently shaven, hurried into the room.

All the pictures of President Miraflores represent him as the possessor of a luxuriant supply of dark and carefully tended whiskers; but the story of the barber, Estebán, had prepared Goodwin for the change.

The man stumbled in from the dark room, his eyes blinking at the lamplight, and heavy from sleep.

" What does this mean ? " he demanded in excellent English, with a keen and perturbed look at the American—" robbery ? "

" Very near it," answered Goodwin. " But I rather think I'm in time to prevent it. I represent the people to whom this money belongs, and I have come to convey it back to them." He thrust his hand into a pocket of his loose linen coat.

The other man's hand went quickly behind him.

"Don't draw," called Goodwin, sharply; "I've got you covered from my pocket."

The lady stepped forward, and laid one hand upon the shoulder of her hesitating companion. She pointed to the table. "Tell me the truth—the truth," she said, in a low voice. "Whose money is that?"

The man did not answer. He gave a deep, long-drawn sigh, leaned and kissed her on the forehead, stepped back into the other room and closed the door.

Goodwin foresaw his purpose, and jumped for the door, but the report of the pistol echoed as his hand touched the knob. A heavy fall followed, and some one swept him aside and struggled into the room of the fallen man.

A desolation, thought Goodwin, greater than that derived from the loss of cavalier and gold must have been in the heart of the enchantress to have wrung from her, in that moment, the cry of one turning to the all-forgiving, all-comforting earthly consoler—to have made her call out from that bloody and dishonored room —"Oh, mother, mother, mother!"

But there was an alarm outside. The barber, Estebán, at the sound of the shot, had raised his voice; and the shot itself had aroused half the town. A pattering of feet came up the street, and official orders rang out on the still air. Goodwin had a duty to perform. Circumstances had made him the custodian of his adopted country's treasure. Swiftly cramming the money into the valise, he closed it, leaned far out of the window and dropped it into a thick orange-tree in the little inclosure below.

They will tell you in Coralio, as they delight in telling the stranger, of the conclusion of that tragic flight. They will tell you how the upholders of the law came apace when the alarm was sounded—the *Comandante* in red slippers and a jacket like a head waiter's and girded sword, the soldiers with their interminable guns, followed by outnumbering officers struggling into their gold lace and epaulettes; the bare-footed policemen (the only capables in the lot), and ruffled citizens of every hue and description.

They say that the countenance of the dead man was marred sadly by the effects of the shot; but he was identified as the fallen president by both Goodwin and the barber Estebán. On the next morning messages began to come over the mended telegraph wire; and the story of the flight from the capital was given out to the public. In San Mateo the revolutionary party had seized the sceptre of government, without opposition, and the *vivas* of the mercurial populace quickly effaced the interest belonging to the unfortunate Miraflores.

They will relate to you how the new government sifted the towns and raked the roads to find the valise containing Anchuria's surplus capital, which the president was known to have carried with him, but all in vain. In Coralio Señor Goodwin himself led the searching party which combed that town as carefully as a woman combs her hair; but the money was not found.

So they buried the dead man, without honors, back of the town near the little bridge that spans the mangrove swamp; and for a *real* a boy will show you his grave. They say that the old woman in whose hut the barber shaved the president placed the wooden slab at his head, and burned the inscription upon it with a hot iron.

You will hear also that Señor Goodwin, like a tower of strength, shielded Doña Isabel Guilbert through those subsequent distressful days; and that his scruples as to her past career (if he had any) vanished; and her adventuresome waywardness (if she had any) left her, and they were wedded and were happy.

The American built a home on a little foothill near the town. It is a conglomerate structure of native woods that, exported, would be worth a fortune, and of brick, palm, glass, bamboo and adobe. There is a paradise of nature about it; and something of the same sort within. The natives speak of its interior with hands uplifted in admiration. There are floors polished like mirrors and covered with hand-woven Indian rugs of silk fibre, tall ornaments and pictures, musical instruments and papered walls—" figure-it-to-yourself ! " they exclaim.

But they cannot tell you in Coralio (as you shall learn) what became of the money that Frank Goodwin dropped into the orange-tree. But that shall come later; for the palms are fluttering in the breeze, bidding us to sport and gaiety.

CUPID'S EXILE NUMBER TWO

THE United States of America, after looking over its stock-of consular timber, selected Mr. John De Graffanreid Atwood, of Dalesburg, Alabama, for a successor to Willard Geddie, resigned.

Without prejudice to Mr. Atwood, it will have to be acknowledged that, in this instance, it was the man who sought the office. As with the self-banished Geddie, it was nothing less than the artful smiles of lovely women that had driven Johnny Atwood to the desperate expedient of accepting office under a despised Federal Government so that he might go far, far away and never see again the false, fair face that had wrecked his young life. The consulship at Coralio seemed to offer a retreat sufficiently removed and romantic enough to inject the necessary drama into the pastoral scenes of Dalesburg life.

It was while playing the part of Cupid's exile that Johnny added his handiwork to the long list of casualties along the Spanish Main by his famous manipulation of the shoe market, and his unparalleled feat of elevating the most despised and useless weed in his own country from obscurity to be a valuable product in international commerce.

The trouble began, as trouble often begins instead of ending with a romance. In Dalesburg there was a man named Elijah Hemstetter, who kept a general store. His family consisted of one daughter called Rosine, a name that atoned much for " Hemstetter." This young woman was possessed of plentiful attractions, so that the young men of the community were agitated in their bosoms. Among the more agitated was Johnny, the son of Judge Atwood, who lived in the big colonial mansion on the edge of Dalesburg.

It would seem that the desirable Rosine should have been pleased to return the affection of an Atwood, a name honored all over the state long before and since the war. It does seem that she should have gladly consented to have been led into that stately but rather empty colonial mansion. But not so. There was a cloud on the horizon, a threatening cumulus, cloud, in the shape of a lively and shrewd young farmer in the neighborhood who dared to enter the lists as a rival to the high-born Atwood.

One night Johnny propounded to Rosine a question that is considered of much importance by the young of the human species. The accessories were all there—moonlight, oleanders, magnolias, the mock-bird's song. Whether or no the shadow of Pinkney Dawson, the prosperous young farmer, came between them on that occasion is not known; but Rosine's answer was unfavorable. Mr. John De Graffenreid Atwood bowed till his hat touched the lawn grass, and went away with his head high, but with a sore wound in his pedigree and heart. A Hemstetter refuse an Atwood! Zounds !

Among other accidents of that year was a Democratic president. Judge Atwood was a warhorse of Democracy. Johnny persuaded him to set the wheels moving for some foreign appointment. He would go away—away. Perhaps in years to come Rosine would think how true, how faithful his love had been, and would drop a tear—maybe in the cream she would be skimming for Pink Dawson's breakfast.

The wheels of politics revolved; and Johnny was appointed consul to Coralio. Just before leaving he dropped in at Hem-

stetter's to say good-bye. There was a queer, pinkish look about
Rosine's eyes; and had the two been alone, the United States
might have had to cast about for another consul. But Pink Dawson
was there, of course, talking about his 400-acre orchard, and the
three-mile alfalfa tract, and the 200-acre pasture. So Johnny
shook hands with Rosine as coolly as if he were only going to run
up to Montgomery for a couple of days. They had the royal
manner when they chose, those Atwoods.

" If you happen to strike anything in the way of a good invest-
ment down there, Johnny," said Pink Dawson, "just let me know,
will you ? I reckon I could lay my hands on a few extra thousands
'most any time for a profitable deal."

" Certainly, Pink," said Johnny, pleasantly. " If I strike anything of the sort I'll let you in with pleasure."

So Johnny went down to Mobile and took a fruit steamer for
the coast of Anchuria.

When the new consul arrived in Coralio the strangeness of the
scenes diverted him much. He was only twenty-two; and the
grief of youth is not worn like a garment as it is by older men.
It has its seasons when it reigns; and then it is unseated for a
time by the assertion of the keen senses.

Billy Keogh and Johnny seemed to conceive a mutual friendship at once. Keogh took the new consul about town and presented
him to the handful of Americans and the smaller number of French
and Germans who made up the " foreign " contingent. And then,
of course, he had to be more formally introduced to the native
officials, and have his credentials transmitted through an
interpreter.

There was something about the young Southerner that the
sophisticated Keogh liked. His manner was simple almost to
boyishness; but he possessed the cool carelessness of a man of far
greater age and experience. Neither uniforms nor titles, red tape
nor foreign languages, mountains nor sea weighed upon his spirits.
He was heir to all the ages, an Atwood, of Dalesburg; and you
might know every thought conceived in his bosom.

Geddie came down to the consulate to explain the duties and
workings of the office. He and Keogh tried to interest the new
consul in their description of the work that his government
expected him to perform.

" It's all right," said Johnny from the hammock that he had
set up as the official reclining place. " If anything turns up that
has to be done I'll let you fellows do it. You can't expect a Demo-
crat to work during his first term of holding office."

" You might look over these headings," suggested Geddie, " of
the different lines of exports you will have to keep account of.

The fruit is classified; and there are the valuable woods, coffee, rubber——"

" That last account sounds all right," interrupted Mr. Atwood. " Sounds as if it could be stretched. I want to buy a new flag, a monkey, a guitar and a barrel of pineapples. Will that rubber account stretch over 'em ? "

" That's merely statistics," said Geddie, smiling. " The expense account is what you want. It is supposed to have a slight elasticity. The ' stationery ' items are sometimes carelessly audited by the State Department."

" We're wasting our time," said Keogh. " This man was born to hold office. He penetrates to the root of the art at one step of his eagle eye. The true genius of government shows its hand in every word of his speech."

" I didn't take this job with any intention of working," explained Johnny, lazily. " I wanted to go somewhere in the world where they didn't talk about farms. There are none here, are there ? "

" Not the kind you are acquainted with," answered the ex-consul. " There is no such art here as agriculture. There never was a plow or a reaper within the boundaries of Anchuria."

" This is the country for me," murmured the consul and immediately he fell asleep.

The cheerful tintypist pursued his intimacy with Johnny in spite of open charges that he did so to obtain a preëmption on a seat in the coveted spot, the rear gallery of the consulate. But whether his designs were selfish or purely friendly, Keogh achieved that desirable privilege. Few were the nights on which the two could not be found reposing there in the sea breeze, with their heels on the railing, and the cigars and brandy conveniently near.

One evening they had sat thus, mainly silent, for their talk had dwindled before the stilling influence of an unusual night.

There was a great, full moon; and the sea was mother-of-pearl. Almost every sound was hushed, for the air was but faintly stirring; and the town lay panting, waiting for the night to cool. Off-shore lay the fruit steamer *Andador*, of the Vesuvius line, full-laden and scheduled to sail at six in the morning. There were no loiterers on the beach. So bright was the moonlight that the two men could see the small pebbles shining on the beach where the gentle surf wetted them.

Then down the coast, tacking close to shore, slowly swam a little sloop, white-winged like some snowy sea fowl. Its course lay within twenty points of the wind's eye; so it veered in and out again in long slow strokes like the movements of a graceful skater.

Again the tactics of its crew brought it close in shore, this time nearly opposite the consulate; and then there blew from the sloop clear and surprising notes as if from a horn of elfland. A fairy bugle it might have been, sweet and silvery and unexpected, playing with spirit the familiar air of " Home, Sweet Home."

It was a scene set for the land of the lotus. The authority of the sea and the tropics, the mystery that attends unknown sails, and the prestige of drifting music on moonlit waters gave it an anodynous charm. Johnny Atwood felt it, and thought of Dalesburg; but as soon as Keogh's mind had arrived at a theory concerning the peripatetic solo he sprang to the railing, and his ear-rending yawp fractured the silence of Coralio like a cannon shot.

" Mel-lin-ger a-hoy ! "

The sloop was now on its outward tack; but from it came a clear, answering hail :

" Good-bye, Billy . . . go-ing home—bye! "

The *Andador* was the sloop's destination. No doubt some passenger with a sailing permit from some up-the-coast point had come down in this sloop to catch the regular fruit steamer on its return trip. Like a coquettish pigeon the little boat tacked on its eccentric way until at last its white sail was lost to sight against the larger bulk of the fruiter's side.

" That's old H. P. Mellinger," explained Keogh, dropping back into his chair. " He's going back to New York. He was private secretary of the late hot-foot president of this grocery and fruit stand that they call a country. His job's over now; and I guess old Mellinger is glad."

" Why does he disappear to music, like Zo-zo, the magic queen ? " asked Johnny. " Just to show 'em that he doesn't care ? "

" That noise you heard is a phonograph," said Keogh. " I sold him that. Mellinger had a graft in this country that was the only thing of its kind in the world. The tooting machine saved it for him once, and he always carried it around with him afterward."

" Tell me about it," demanded Johnny, betraying interest.

" I'm no disseminator of narratives," said Keogh. " I can use language for purposes of speech; but when I attempt a discourse the words come out as they will, and they make sense when they strike the atmosphere, or they may not."

" I want to hear about that graft," persisted Johnny. " You've got no right to refuse. I've told you all about every man, woman and hitching post in Dalesburg."

" You shall hear it," said Keogh. " I said my instincts of narrative were perplexed. Don't you believe it. It's an art I've acquired along with many other of the graces and sciences."

THE PHONOGRAPH AND THE GRAFT

WHAT was this graft?" asked Johnny, with the impatience of the great public to whom tales are told.

" 'Tis contrary to art and philosophy to give you the information," said Keogh, calmly. " The art of narrative consists in concealing from your audience everything it wants to know until after you expose your favorite opinions on topics foreign to the subject. A good story is like a bitter pill with the sugar coating inside of it. I will begin, if you please, with a horoscope located in the Cherokee Nation ; and end with a moral tune on the phonograph.

" Me and Henry Horsecollar brought the first phonograph to this country. Henry was a quarter-breed, quarter-back Cherokee, educated East in the idioms of football, and West in contraband whisky, and a gentleman, the same as you and me. He was easy and romping in his ways; a man about six foot, with a kind of rubber-tire movement. Yes, he was a little man about five foot five, or five foot eleven. He was what you would call a medium tall man of average smallness. Henry had quit college once, and the Muscogee jail three times—the last-named institution on account of introducing and selling whisky in the territories. Henry Horsecollar never let any cigar stores come up and stand behind him. He didn't belong to that tribe of Indians.

" Henry and me met at Texarkana, and figured out this phonograph scheme . He had $360 which came to him out of a land allotment in the reservation. I had run down from Little Rock on account of a distressful scene I had witnessed on the street there. A man stood on a box and passed around some gold watches, screw case, stem-winders, Elgin movement, very elegant. Twenty bucks they cost you over the counter. At three dollars the crowd fought for the tickets. The man happened to find a valise full of them handy, and he passed them out like putting hot biscuits on a plate. The backs were hard to unscrew, but the crowd put its ear to the case, and they ticked mollifying and agreeable. Three of these watches were genuine tickers; the rest were only kickers. Hey ? Why, empty cases with one of them horny black bugs that fly around electric lights in 'em. Them bugs kick off minutes and seconds industrious and beautiful. So, this man I was speaking of cleaned up $288; and then he went away, because he knew that when it came time to wind watches in Little Rock an entomologist would be needed, and he wasn't one.

" So, as I say, Henry had $360, and I had $288. The idea of introducing the phonograph to South America was Henry's; but I took to it freely, being fond of machinery of all kinds.

" 'The Latin races,' says Henry, explaining easily in the idioms he learned at college, 'are peculiarly adapted to be victims of the phonograph. They have the artistic temperament. They yearn for music and color and gaiety. They give wampum to the hand-organ man and the four-legged chicken in the tent when they're months behind with the grocery and the bread-fruit tree.'

" 'Then,' says I, 'we'll export canned music to the Latins; but I'm mindful of Mr. Julius Cæsar's account of 'em where he says : " *Omnia Gallia in tres partes divisa est* "; which is the same as to say, " We will need all of our gall in devising means to tree them parties." '

" I hated to make a show of education; but I was disinclined to be overdone in syntax by a mere Indian, a member of a race to which we owe nothing except the land on which the United States is situated.

" We bought a fine phonograph in Texarkana—one of the best make—and half a trunkful of records. We packed up, and took the T. and P. for New Orleans. From that celebrated centre of molasses and disfranchised coon songs we took a steamer for South America.

" We landed at Solitas, forty miles up the coast from here. 'Twas a palatable enough place to look at. The houses were clean and white; and to look at 'em stuck around among the scenery they reminded you of hard-boiled eggs served with lettuce. There was a block of skyscraper mountains in the suburbs; and they kept pretty quiet, like they had crept up there and were watching the town. And the sea was remarking ' Sh-sh-sh' on the beach; and now and then a ripe cocoanut would drop kerblip in the sand; and that was all there was doing. Yes, I judge that town was considerably on the quiet. I judge that after Gabriel quits blowing his horn, and the car starts, with Philadelphia swinging to the last strap, and Pine Gully, Arkansas, hanging onto the rear step, this town of Solitas will wake up and ask if anybody spoke.

" The captain went ashore with us, and offered to conduct what he seemed to like to call the obsequies. He introduced Henry and me to the United States Consul, and a roan man, the head of the Department of Mercenary and Licentious Dispositions, the way it reads upon his sign.

" 'I touch here a week again from to-day,' says the captain.

" 'By that time,' we told him, 'we'll be amassing wealth in the interior towns with our galvanized prima donna and correct imitations of Sousa's band excavating a march from a tin mine.'

" 'Ye'll not,' says the captain. 'Ye'll be hypnotized. Any gentle-man in the audience who kindly steps upon the stage and looks this country in the eye will be converted to the hypothesis that he's but a fly in the Elgin creamery. Ye'll be standing knee deep in the surf waiting for me, and your machine for making Hamburger steak out of the hitherto respected art of music will be playing " There's no place like home." '

" Henry skinned a twenty off his roll, and received from the Bureau of Mercenary Dispositions a paper bearing a red seal and a dialect story, and no change.

" Then we got the consul full of red wine, and struck him for a horoscope. He was a thin, youngish kind of a man, I should say past fifty, sort of French-Irish in his affections, and puffed up with disconsolation. Yes, he was a flattened kind of a man, in whom drink lay stagnant, inclined to corpulence and misery. Yes, I think he was a kind of Dutchman, being very sad and genial in his ways.

" 'The marvellous invention,' he says, ' entitled the phono-graph, has never invaded these shores. The people have never heard it. They would not believe it if they should. Simple-hearted children of nature, progress has never condemned them to accept the work of a can-opener as an overture, and rag-time might incite them to a bloody revolution. But you can try the experiment. The best chance you have is that the populace may not wake up when you play. There's two ways,' says the consul, 'they may take it. They may become inebriated with attention, like an Atlanta colonel listening to " Marching Through Georgia," or they will get excited and transpose the key of the music with an axe and yourselves into a dungeon. In the latter case,' says the consul, ' I'll do my duty by cabling to the State Department, and I'll wrap the Stars and Stripes around you when you come to be shot, and threaten them with the vengeance of the greatest gold export and financial reserve nation on earth. The flag is full of bullet holes now,' says the consul, 'made in that way. Twice before,' says the consul, ' I have cabled our government for a couple of gunboats to protect American citizens. The first time the Depart-ment sent me a pair of gum boots. The other time was when a man named Pease was going to be executed here. They referred that appeal to the Secretary of Agriculture. Let us now disturb the señor behind the bar for a subsequence of the red wine.'

" Thus soliloquized the consul of Solitas to me and Henry Horsecollar.

" But, notwithstanding, we hired a room that afternoon in the Calle de los Angeles, the main street that runs along the shore, and puts our trunks there. 'Twas a good-sized room, dark and cheerful, but small. 'Twas on a various street, diversified by houses and conservatory plants. The peasantry of the city passed to and fro on the fine pasturage between the sidewalks. 'Twas, for the world, like an opera chorus when the Royal Kafoozlum is about to enter.

" We were rubbing the dust off the machine and getting fixed to start business the next day, when a big, fine-looking white man in white clothes stopped at the door and looked in. We extended the invitations, and he walked inside and sized us up. He was chewing a long cigar, and wrinkling his eyes, meditative, like a girl trying to decide which dress to wear to the party.

" 'New York ? ' he says to me finally.

" 'Originally, and from time to time,' I says. 'Hasn't it rubbed off yet ? '

" 'It's simple,' says he, 'when you know how. It's the fit of the vest. They don't cut vests right anywhere else. Coats, maybe, but not vests.'

" The white man looks at Henry Horsecollar and hesitates.

" 'Injun,' says Henry ! ' tame Injun.'

" 'Mellinger,' says the man—' Homer P. Mellinger. Boys, you're confiscated. You're babies in the wood without a chaperon or referee, and it's my duty to start you going. I'll knock out the props and launch you proper in the pellucid waters of this tropical mud puddle. You'll have to be christened, and if you'll come with me I'll break a bottle of wine across your bows, according to Hoyle.'

" Well, for two days Homer P. Mellinger did the honors. That man cut ice in Anchuria. He was It. He was the Royal Kafoozlum. If me and Henry was babes in the wood, he was a Robin Redbreast from the topmost bough. Him and me and Henry Horsecollar locked arms, and toted that phonograph around, and had wassail and diversions. Everywhere we found doors open we went inside and set the machine going, and Mellinger called upon the people to observe the artful music and his two lifelong friends, the Señores Américanos. The opera chorus was agitated with esteem, and followed us from house to house. There was a different kind of drink to be had with every tune. The natives had acquirements of a pleasant thing in the way of a drink that gums itself to the recollection. They chop off the end of a green cocoanut, and pour in on the juice of it French brandy and other adjuvants. We had them and other things.

" Mine and Henry's money was counterfeit. Everything was on Homer P. Mellinger. That man could find rolls of bills concealed in places on his person where Hermann the Wizard couldn't have conjured out a rabbit or an omelette. He could have founded universities, and made orchid collections, and then had enough left to purchase the colored vote of his country. Henry and me wondered what his graft was. One evening he told us.

" 'Boys,' said he, ' I've deceived you. You think I'm a painted butterfly; but in fact I'm the hardest worked man in this country. Ten years ago I landed on its shores; and two years ago on the point of its jaw. Yes, I guess I can get the decision over this ginger cake commonwealth at the end of any round I choose. I'll confide in you because you are my countrymen and guests, even if you have assaulted my adopted shores with the worst system of noises ever set to music.

" 'My job is private secretary to the president of this republic; and my duties are running it. I'm not headlined in the bills, but I'm the mustard in the salad dressing just the same. There isn't a law goes before Congress, there isn't a concession granted, there isn't an import duty levied but what H. P. Mellinger he cooks and seasons it. In the front office I fill the president's inkstand and search visiting statesmen for dirks and dynamite; but in the back room I dictate the policy of the government. You'd never guess in the world how I got my pull. It's the only graft of its kind on earth. I'll put you wise. You remember the old top-liner in the copy book—" Honesty is the Best Policy " ? That's it. I'm working honesty for a graft. I'm the only honest man in the republic. The government knows it; the people know it; the boodlers know it; the foreign investors know it. I make the government keep its faith. If a man is promised a job he gets it. If outside capital buys a concession it gets the goods. I run a monopoly of square dealing here. There's no competition. If Colonel Diogenes were to flash his lantern in this precinct he'd have my address inside of two minutes. There isn't big money in it, but it's a sure thing, and let's a man sleep of nights.'

" Thus Homer P. Mellinger made oration to me and Henry Horsecollar. And, later, he divested himself of this remark.

" 'Boys, I'm to hold a *soirée* this evening with a gang of leading citizens, and I want your assistance. You bring the musical corn sheller and give the affair the outside appearance of a function. There's important business on hand, but it mustn't show. I can talk to you people. I've been pained for years on account of not having anybody to blow off and brag to. I get homesick sometimes, and I'd swap the entire perquisites of office for just one hour to have a stein and a caviare sandwich somewhere on Thirty-fourth Street, and stand and watch the street cars go by, and smell the peanut roaster at old Giuseppe's fruit stand.'

" 'Yes,' said I, ' there's fine caviare at Billy Renfrow's café, corner of Thirty-fourth and——'

" 'God knows it,' interrupts Mellinger, 'and if you'd told me you knew Billy Renfrow I'd have invented tons of ways of making you happy. Billy was my side-kicker in New York. There is a man who never knew what crooked was. Here I am working Honesty for a graft, but that man loses money on it. Carrambos! I get sick at times of this country. Everything's rotten. From the executive down to the coffee pickers, they're plotting to down each other and skin their friends. If a mule driver takes off his hat to an official, that man figures it out that he's a popular idol, and sets his pegs to stir up a revolution and upset the administration. It's one of my little chores as private secretary to smell out these revolutions and affix the kibosh before they break out and scratch the paint off the government property. That's why I'm down here now in this mildewed coast town. The governor of the district and his crew are plotting to uprise. I've got every one of their names, and they're invited to listen to the phonograph to-night, compliment of H. P. M. That's the way I'll get them in a bunch, and things are on the programme to happen to them."

" We three were sitting at table in the cantina of the Purified Saints. Mellinger poured out wine, and was looking some worried; I was thinking.

" 'They're a sharp crowd,' he says, kind of fretful. 'They're capitalized by a foreign syndicate after rubber, and they're loaded to the muzzle for bribing. I'm sick,' goes on Mellinger, ' of comic opera. I want to smell East River and wear suspenders again. At times I feel like throwing up my job, but I'm d—n fool enough to be sort of proud of it. " There's Mellinger," they say here. " *Por Dios !* you can't touch him with a million." I'd like to take that record back and show it to Billy Renfrow some day; and that tightens my grip whenever I see a fat thing that I could corral just by winking one eye—and losing my graft. By —, they can't monkey with me. They know it. What money I get I make honest and spend it. Some day I'll make a pile and go back and eat caviare with Billy. To-night I'll show you how to handle a bunch of corruptionists. I'll show them what Mellinger, private secretary, means when you spell it with cotton and tissue paper off.'

" Mellinger appears shaky, and breaks his glass against the neck of the bottle.

" I says to myself, ' White man, if I'm not mistaken there's been a bait laid out where the tail of your eye could see it.'

" That night, according to arrangements, me and Henry took the phonograph to a room in a 'dobe house in a dirty side street, where the grass was knee high. 'Twas a long room, lit with smoky oil lamps. There was plenty of chairs, and a table at the back end. We set the phonograph on the table. Mellinger was there, walking up and down, disturbed in his predicaments. He chewed cigars and spat 'em out, and he bit the thumb nail of his left hand.

" By and by the invitations to the musicale came sliding in by pairs and threes and spade flushes. Their color was of a diversity, running from a three-days' smoked meerschaum to a patent-leather polish. They were as polite as wax, being devastated with enjoyments to give Señor Mellinger the good evenings. I understood their Spanish talk—I ran a pumping engine two years in a Mexican silver mine, and had it pat—but I never let on.

" Maybe fifty of 'em had come, and was seated, when in slid the king bee, the governor of the district. Mellinger met him at the door, and escorted him to the grand stand. When I saw that Latin man I knew that Mellinger, private secretary, had all the dances on his card taken. That was a big, squashy man, the color of a rubber overshoe, and he had an eye like a head waiter's.

Mellinger explained, fluent, in the Castilian idioms, that his soul was disconcerted with joy at introducing to his respected friends America's greatest invention, the wonder of the age. Henry got the cue and run on an elegant brass-band record and the festivities became initiated. The governor man had a bit of English under his hat, and when the music was choked off he says :

" 'Ver-r-ree fine. *Gr-r-r-r-racias*, the American gentleemen, the so esplendeed moosic as to playee.'

" The table was a long one, and Henry and me sat at the end of it next the wall. The governor sat at the other end. Homer P. Mellinger stood at the side of it. I was just wondering how Mellinger was going to handle his crowd, when the home talent suddenly opened the services.

" That governor man was suitable for uprisings and policies. I judge he was a ready kind of man, who took his own time. Yes, he was full of attention and immediateness. He leaned his hands on the table and imposed his face toward the secretary man.

" 'Do the American señores understand Spanish ? ' he asks in his native accents.

" 'They do not,' says Mellinger.

" 'Then listen,' goes on the Latin man, prompt. ' The musics are of sufficient prettiness, but not of necessity. Let us speak of business. I well know why we are here, since I observe my compatriots. You had a whisper yesterday Señor Mellinger, of our proposals. To-night we will speak out. We know that you stand in the president's favor, and we know your influence. The government will be changed. We know the worth of your services. We esteem your friendship and aid so much that'—Mellinger raises his hand, but the governor man bottles him up. ' Do not speak until I have done.'

" The governor man then draws a package wrapped in paper from his pocket, and lays it on the table by Mellinger's hand.

" 'In that you will find fifty thousand dollars in money of your country. You can do nothing against us, but you can be worth that for us. Go back to the capital and obey our instructions. Take that money now. We trust you. You will find with it a paper giving in detail the work you will be expected to do for us. Do not have the unwiseness of refuse."

" The governor man paused, with his eyes fixed on Mellinger, full of expressions and observances. I looked at Mellinger, and was glad Billy Renfrow couldn't see him then. The sweat was popping out on his forehead, and he stood dumb, tapping the little package with the ends of his fingers. The colorado-maduro gang was after his graft. He had only to change his politics, and stuff five fingers in his inside pocket.

" Henry whispers to me and wants the pause in the programme interpreted. I whisper back : ' H. P. is up against a bribe, senator's size, and the coons have got him going.' I saw Mellinger's hand moving closer to the package. ' He's weakening,' I whispered to Henry. ' We'll remind him,' says Henry, ' of the peanut-roaster on Thirty-fourth Street, New York.'

" Henry stooped down and got a record from the basketful we'd brought, slid it in the phonograph, and started her off. It was a cornet solo, very neat and beautiful, and the name of it was ' Home, Sweet Home.' Not one of them fifty-odd men in the room moved while it was playing, and the governor man kept his eyes steady on Mellinger. I saw Mellinger's head go up little by little, and his hand came creeping away from the package. Not until the last note sounded did anybody stir. And then Homer P. Mellinger takes up the bundle of boodle and slams it in the governor man's face.

" 'That's my answer,' says Mellinger, private secretary, 'and there'll be another in the morning. I have proofs of conspiracy against every man of you. The show is over, gentlemen.'

" 'There's one more act,' puts in the governor man. ' You are a servant, I believe, employed by the president to copy letters and answer raps at the door. I am governor here. *Señores*, I call upon you in the name of the cause to seize this man.'

" That brindled gang of conspirators shoved back their chairs and advanced in force. I could see where Mellinger had made a mistake in massing his enemy so as to make a grand-stand play. I think he made another one, too; but we can pass that, Mellinger's idea of a graft and mine being different, according to estimations and points of view.

" There was only one window and door in that room, and they were in the front end. Here was fifty odd Latin men coming in a bunch to obstruct the legislation of Mellinger. You may say there were three of us, for me and Henry, simultaneous, declared New

York City and the Cherokee Nation in sympathy with the weaker party.

" Then it was that Henry Horsecollar rose to a point of disorder and intervened, showing, admirable, the advantages of education as applied to the American Indian's natural intellect and native refinement. He stood up and smoothed back his hair on each side with his hands as you have seen little girls do when they play.

" 'Get behind me, both of you,' says Henry.

" 'What's it to be chief? ' I asked.

" 'I'm going to buck centre,' says Henry, in his football idioms. ' There isn't a tackle in the lot of them. Follow me close, and rush the game.'

" Then that cultured Red Man exhaled an arrangement of sounds with his mouth that made the Latin aggregation pause, with thoughtfulness and hesitations. The matter of his proclamation seemed to be a co-operation of the Carlisle war-whoop with the Cherokee college yell. He went at the chocolate team like a bean out of a little boy's nigger shooter. His right elbow laid out the governor man on the gridiron, and he made a lane the length of the crowd so wide that a woman could have carried a step-ladder through it without striking against anything. All Mellinger and me had to do was to follow.

" It took us just three minutes to get out of that street around to military headquarters, where Mellinger had things his own way. A colonel and a battalion of bare-toed infantry turned out and went back to the scene of the musicale with us, but the conspirator gang was gone. But we recaptured the phonograph with honors of war, and marched back to the *cuartel* with it playing 'All Coons Look Alike to Me.'

" The next day Mellinger takes me and Henry to one side, and begins to shed tens and twenties.

" 'I want to buy that phonograph,' says he. 'I liked that last tune it played at the *soirée*.'

" 'This is more money than the machine is worth,' says I.

" ' 'Tis government expense money,' says Mellinger. ' The government pays for it, and it's getting the tune-grinder cheap.'

" Me and Henry knew that pretty well. We knew that it had saved Homer P. Mellinger's graft when he was on the point of losing it; but we never let him know we knew it.

" 'Now you boys better slide off further down the coast for a while,' says Mellinger, 'till I get the screws put on these fellows here. If you don't they'll give you trouble. And if you ever happen to see Billy Renfrow again before I do, tell him I'm coming back to New York as soon as I can make a stake—honest.'

" Me and Henry laid low until the day the steamer came back.

When we saw the captain's boat on the beach we went down and stood in the edge of the water. The captain grinned when he saw us.

" 'I told you you'd be waiting,' he says. ' Where's the Hamburger machine ? '

" 'It stays behind,' I says, 'to play " Home, Sweet Home." '

" 'I told you so,' says the captain again. 'Climb in the boat.'

"And that," said Keogh, " is the way me and Henry Horsecollar introduced the phonograph into this country. Henry went back to the States, but I've been rummaging around in the tropics ever since. They say Mellinger never travelled a mile after that without his phonograph. I guess it kept him reminded about his graft whenever he saw the siren voice of the boodler tip him the wink with a bribe in its hand."

" I suppose he's taking it home with him as a souvenir," remarked the consul.

" Not as a souvenir," said Keogh. " He'll need two of 'em in New York, running day and night."

MONEY MAZE

THE new administration of Anchuria entered upon its duties and privileges with enthusiasm. Its first act was to send an agent to Coralio with imperative orders to recover, if possible, the sum of money ravished from the treasury by the ill-fated Miraflores.

Colonel Emilio Falcon, the private secretary of Losada, the new president, was despatched from the capital upon this important mission.

The position of private secretary to a tropical president is a responsible one. He must be a diplomat, a spy, a ruler of men, a body-guard to his chief, and a smeller-out of plots and nascent revolutions. Often he is the power behind the throne, the dictator of policy; and a president chooses him with a dozen times the care with which he selects a matrimonial mate.

Colonel Falcon, a handsome and urbane gentleman of Castilian courtesy and débonnaire manners, came to Coralio with the task before him of striking upon the cold trail of the lost money. There he conferred with the military authorities, who had received instructions to co-operate with him in the search.

Colonel Falcon established his headquarters in one of the rooms of the Casa Morena. Here for a week he held informal sittings—must as if he were a kind of unified grand jury—and summoned before him all those whose testimony might illumine the financial tragedy that had accompanied the less momentous one of the late president's death.

Two or three who were thus examined, among whom was the barber Estebán, declared that they had identified the body of the president before its burial.

" Of a truth," testified Estebán before the mighty secretary, " it was he, the president. Consider !—how could I shave a man and not see his face ? He sent for me to shave him in a small house. He had a beard very black and thick. Had I ever seen the president before ? Why not ? I saw him once ride forth in a carriage from the *vapor* in Solitas. When I shaved him he gave me a gold piece, and said there was to be no talk. But I am a Liberal—I am devoted to my country—and I spake of these things to Señor Goodwin."

" It is known," said Colonel Falcon, smoothly, " that the late President took with him an American leather valise, containing a large amount of money. Did you see that ? "

" *De veras*—no," Estebán answered. " The light in the little house was but a small lamp by which I could scarcely see to shave the President. Such a thing there may have been, but I did not see it. No. Also in the room was a young lady—a señorita of much beauty—that I could see even in so small a light. But the money, señor, or the thing in which it was carried—that I did not see."

The *comandante* and other officers gave testimony that they had been awakened and alarmed by the noise of a pistol-shot in the Hotel de los Estranjeros. Hurrying thither to protect the peace and dignity of the republic, they found a man lying dead, with a pistol clutched in his hand. Beside him was a young woman, weeping sorely. Señor Goodwin was also in the room when they entered it. But of the valise of money they saw nothing.

Madame Timotea Ortiz, the proprietress of the hotel in which the game of Fox-in-the-Morning had been played out, told of the coming of the two guests to her house.

" To my house they came," said she—" one *señor*, not quite old, and one *señorita* of sufficient handsomeness. They desired not to eat or to drink—not even of my *aguardiente*, which is the best. To their rooms they ascended—*Número Nueve* and *Número Diez*. Later came Señor Goodwin, who ascended to speak with them. Then I heard a great noise like that of a *canon*, and they said that the *pobre Presidente* had shot himself. *Está bueno*. I saw nothing of money or of the thing you call *veliz* that you say he carried it in."

Colonel Falcon soon came to the reasonable conclusion that if any one in Coralio could furnish a clue to the vanished money, Frank Goodwin must be the man. But the wise secretary pursued a different course in seeking information from the American. Goodwin was a powerful friend to the new administration, and one who was not to be carelessly dealt with in respect to either his honesty or his courage. Even the private secretary of His Excellency hesitated to have this rubber prince and mahogany baron haled before him as a common citizen of Anchuria. So he sent Goodwin a flowery epistle, each word-petal dripping with honey, requesting the favor of an interview. Goodwin replied with an invitation to dinner at his own house.

Before the hour named the American walked over to the Casa Morena, and greeted his guest frankly and friendly. Then the two strolled, in the cool of the afternoon, to Goodwin's home in the environs.

The American left Colonel Falcon in a big, cool, shadowed room with a floor of inlaid and polished woods that any millionaire in the States would have envied, excusing himself for a few minutes. He crossed a *patio*, shaded with deftly arranged awnings and plants, and entered a long room looking upon the sea in the opposite wing of the house. The broad jalousies were opened wide, and the ocean breeze flowed in through the room, an invisible current of coolness and health. Goodwin's wife sat near one of the windows, making a water-color sketch of the afternoon seascape.

Here was a woman who looked to be happy. And more—she looked to be content. Had a poet been inspired to pen just similes concerning her favor, he would have likened her full, clear eyes, with their white-encircled, gray irises, to moonflowers. With none of the goddesses whose traditional charms have become coldly classic would the discerning rhymester have compared her. She was purely Paradisaic, not Olympian. If you can imagine Eve, after the eviction, beguiling the flaming warriors and serenely re-entering the Garden, you will have her. Just so human, and still so harmonious with Eden seemed Mrs. Goodwin.

When her husband entered she looked up, and her lips curved and parted; her eyelids fluttered twice or thrice—a movement remindful (Poesy forgive us !) of the tail-wagging of a faithful dog —and a little ripple went through her like the commotion set up in a weeping willow by a puff of wind. Thus she ever acknowledged his coming, were it twenty times a day. If they who sometimes sat over their wine in Coralio, reshaping old, diverting stories of the madcap career of Isabel Guilbert, could have seen the wife of Frank Goodwin that afternoon in the estimable aura of her happy wifehood, they might have disbelieved, or have agreed to forget, those graphic annals of the life of the one for whom their president gave up his country and his honor.

" I have brought a guest to dinner," said Goodwin. " One

Colonel Falcon, from San Mateo. He is come on government business. I do not think you will care to see him, so I prescribe for you one of those convenient and indisputable feminine headaches."

" He has come to inquire about the lost money, has he not ? " asked Mrs. Goodwin, going on with her sketch.

"A good guess ! " acknowledged Goodwin. " He has been holding an inquisition among the natives for three days. I am next on his list of witnesses, but as he feels shy about dragging one of Uncle Sam's subjects before him, he consents to give it the outward appearance of a social function. He will apply the torture over my own wine and provender."

" Has he found any one who saw the valise of money ? "

" Not a soul. Even Madame Ortiz, whose eyes are so sharp for the sight of a revenue official, does not remember that there was any baggage."

Mrs. Goodwin laid down her brush and sighed.

" I am so sorry, Frank," she said, " that they are giving you so much trouble about the money. But we can't let them know about it, can we ? "

" Not without doing our intelligence a great injustice," said Goodwin, with a smile and a shrug that he had picked up from the natives. " *Americano*, though I am, they would have me in the *calaboza* in half an hour if they knew we had appropriated that valise. No; we must appear as ignorant about the money as the other ignoramuses in Coralio."

" Do you think that this man they have sent suspects you ? " she asked, with a little pucker of her brows.

" He'd better not," said the American, carelessly. " It's lucky that no one caught a sight of the valise except myself. As I was in the rooms when the shot was fired, it is not surprising that they should want to investigate my part in the affair rather closely. But there's no cause for alarm. This colonel is down on the list of events for a good dinner, with a dessert of American ' bluff ' that will end the matter, I think."

Mrs. Goodwin rose and walked to the window. Goodwin followed and stood by her side. She leaned to him, and rested in the protection of his strength, as she had always rested since that dark night on which he had first made himself her tower of refuge. Thus they stood for a little while.

Straight through the lavish growth of tropical branch and leaf and vine that confronted them had been cunningly trimmed a vista, that ended at the cleared environs of Coralio, on the banks of the mangrove swamp. At the other end of the aërial tunnel they could see the grave and wooden headpiece that bore the name of the unhappy President Miraflores. From this window when the rains forbade the open, and from the green and shady slopes of Goodwin's fruitful lands when the skies were smiling, his wife was wont to look upon that grave with a gentle sadness that was now scarcely a mar to her happiness.

" I loved him so, Frank ! " she said, " even after that terrible flight and its awful ending. And you have been so good to me, and have made me so happy. It has all grown into such a strange puzzle. If they were to find out that we got the money do you think they would force you to make the amount good to the government ? "

" They would undoubtedly try," answered Goodwin. " You are right about its being a puzzle. And it must remain a puzzle to Falcon and all his countrymen until it solves itself. You and I, who know more than any one else, only know half of the solution. We must not let even a hint about this money get abroad. Let them come to the theory that the president concealed it in the mountains during his journey, or that he found means to ship it out of the country before he reached Coralio. I don't think that Falcon suspects me. He is making a close investigation, according to his orders, but he will find out nothing."

Thus they spake together. Had any one overheard or overseen them as they discussed the lost funds of Anchuria there would have been a second puzzle presented. For upon the faces and in the bearing of each of them was visible (if countenances are to be believed) Saxon honesty and pride and honorable thoughts. In Goodwin's steady eyes and firm lineaments, moulded into material shape by the inward spirit of kindness and generosity and courage, there was nothing reconcilable with his words.

As for his wife, physiognomy championed her even in the face of their accusive talk. Nobility was in her guise; purity was in her glance. The devotion that she manifested had not even the appearance of that feeling that now and then inspires a woman to share the guilt of her partner out of the pathetic greatness of her love. No, there was a discrepancy here between what the eye would have seen and the ear have heard.

Dinner was served to Goodwin and his guest in the *patio*, under cool foliage and flowers. The American begged the illustrious secretary to excuse the absence of Mrs. Goodwin, who was suffering, he said, from a headache brought on by a slight *calentura*.

After the meal they lingered, according to the custom, over their coffee and cigars. Colonel Falcon, with true Castilian delicacy, waited for his host to open the question that they had met to discuss. He had not long to wait. As soon as the cigars were lighted, the American cleared the way by inquiring whether the secretary's investigations in the town had furnished him with any clue to the lost funds.

" I have found no one yet," admitted Colonel Falcon, " who even had sight of the valise or the money. Yet I have persisted. It has been proven in the capital that President Miraflores set out from San Mateo with one hundred thousand dollars belonging to the government, accompanied by *Señorita* Isabel Guilbert, the opera singer. The Government, officially and personally, is loath to believe," concluded Colonel Falcon, with a smile, " that our last president's tastes would have permitted him to abandon on the route, as excess baggage, either of the desirable articles with which his flight was burdened."

" I suppose you would like to hear what I have to say about the affair," said Goodwin, coming directly to the point. " It will not require many words.

" On that night, with others of our friends here, I was keeping a lookout for the President, having been notified of his flight by a telegram in our national cipher from Englehart, one of our leaders in the capital. About ten o'clock that night I saw a man and a woman hurrying along the streets. They went to the Hotel de los Estranjeros, and engaged rooms. I followed them upstairs, leaving Estebán, who had come up, to watch outside. The barber had told me that he had shaved the beard from the President's face that night; therefore I was prepared, when I entered the rooms, to find him with a smooth face. When I apprehended him in the name of the people he drew a pistol and shot himself instantly. In a few minutes many officers and citizens were on the spot. I suppose you have been informed of the subsequent facts."

Goodwin paused. Losada's agent maintained an attitude of waiting, as if he expected a continuance.

"And now," went on the American, looking steadily into the eyes of the other man, and giving each word a deliberate emphasis, " you will oblige me by attending carefully to what I have to add. I saw no valise or receptacle of any kind, or any money belonging to the Republic of Anchuria. If President Miraflores decamped with any funds belonging to the treasury of this country. or to himself, or to any one else, I saw no trace of it in the house or elsewhere, at that time or at any other. Does that statement cover the ground of the inquiry you wished to make of me ? "

Colonel Falcon bowed, and described a fluent curve with his cigar. His duty was performed. Goodwin was not to be disputed. He was a loyal supporter of the government, and enjoyed the full confidence of the new president. His rectitude had been the capital that had brought him fortune in Anchuria, just as it had formed the lucrative " graft " of Mellinger, the secretary of Miraflores.

" I thank you, *Señor* Goodwin," said Falcon, " for speaking plainly. Your word will be sufficient for the President. But, *Señor* Goodwin, I am instructed to pursue every clue that presents itself in this matter. There is one that I have not yet touched upon. Our friends in France, *señor*, have a saying, ' *Cherchez la femme,*' when there is a mystery without a clue. But here we do not have to search. The woman who accompanied the late president in his flight must surely——"

" I must interrupt you there," interposed Goodwin. " It is true that when I entered the hotel for the purpose of intercepting President Miraflores I found a lady there. I must beg of you to remember that that lady is now my wife. I speak for her as I do for myself. She knows nothing of the fate of the valise or of the money that you are seeking. You will say to his excellency that I guarantee her innocence. I do not need to add to you, Colonel Falcon, that I do not care to have her questioned or disturbed."

Colonel Falcon bowed again.

" *Por supuesto,* no ! " he cried. And to indicate that the inquiry was ended he added : "And now, *señor,* let me beg of you to show me that sea view from your *galeria* of which you spoke. I am a lover of the sea."

In the early evening Goodwin walked back to the town with his guest, leaving him at the corner of the Calle Grande. As he was returning homeward one " Beelzebub " Blythe, with the air of a courtier and the outward aspect of a scarecrow, pounced upon him hopefully from the door of a *pulperia.*

Blythe had been re-christened "Beelzebub" as an acknowledgment of the greatness of his fall. Once in some distant Paradise Lost, he had foregathered with the angels of the earth. But Fate had hurled him headlong down to the tropics, where flamed in his bosom a fire that was seldom quenched. In Coralio they called him a beachcomber; but he was, in reality, a categorical idealist who strove to anamorphosize the dull verities of life by the means of brandy and rum. As Beelzebub, himself, might have held in his clutch with unwitting tenacity his harp or crown during his tremendous fall, so his namesake had clung to his gold-rimmed eyeglasses as the only souvenir of his lost estate. These he wore with impressiveness and distinction while he combed beaches and extracted toll from his friends. By some mysterious means he kept his drink-reddened face always smoothly shaven. For the rest he sponged gracefully upon whomsoever he could for enough to keep him pretty drunk, and sheltered from the rains and night dews.

" Hallo, Goodwin ! " called the derelict, airily. " I was hoping I'd strike you. I wanted to see you particularly. Suppose we go where we can talk. Of course you know there's a chap down here looking up the money old Miraflores lost."

" Yes," said Goodwin, " I've been talking with him. Let's go into Espada's place. I can spare you ten minutes."

They went into the *pulpería* and sat at a little table upon stools with rawhide tops.

" Have a drink ? " said Goodwin.

" They can't bring it too quickly," said Blythe. " I've been in a drought ever since morning. Hi—*muchacho !—el aguardiente por acá.*"

" Now, what do you want to see me about?" asked Goodwin, when the drinks were before them.

" Confound it, old man," drawled Blythe, " why do you spoil a golden moment like this with business ? I wanted to see you—well, this has the preference." He gulped down his brandy, and gazed longingly into the empty glass.

" Have another ? " suggested Goodwin.

" Between gentlemen," said the fallen angel, " I don't quite like your use of that word ' another.' It isn't quite delicate. But the concrete idea that the word represents is not displeasing."

The glasses were refilled. Blythe sipped blissfully from his, as he began to enter the state of a true idealist.

" I must trot along in a minute or two," hinted Goodwin. " Was there anything in particular ? "

Blythe did not reply at once.

" Old Losada would make it a hot country," he remarked at length, " for the man who swiped that gripsack of treasury boodle, don't you think ? "

" Undoubtedly, he would," agreed Goodwin calmly, as he rose leisurely to his feet. " I'll be running over to the house now, old man. Mrs. Goodwin is alone. There was nothing important you had to say, was there ? "

" That's all," said Blythe. " Unless you wouldn't mind sending in another drink from the bar as you go out. Old Espada has closed my account to profit and loss. And pay for the lot, will you, like a good fellow ? "

" All right," said Goodwin. " *Buenas noches.*"

" Beelzebub " Blythe lingered over his cups, polishing his eye-glasses with a disreputable handkerchief.

" I thought I could do it, but I couldn't," he muttered to himself after a time. " A gentleman can't blackmail the man that he drinks with."

THE ADMIRAL

SPILLED milk draws few tears from an Anchurian administration. Many are its lacteal sources; and the clocks' hands point forever to milking time. Even the rich cream skimmed from the treasury by the bewitched Miraflores did not cause the newly-installed patriots to waste time in unprofitable regrets. The government philosophically set about supplying the deficiency by increasing the import duties and by "suggesting" to wealthy private citizens that contributions according to their means would be considered patriotic and in order. Prosperity was expected to attend the reign of Losada, the new president. The ousted office-holders and military favorites organized a new "Liberal" party, and began to lay their plans for a resuccession. Thus the game of Anchurian politics began, like a Chinese comedy, to unwind slowly its serial length. Here and there Mirth peeps for an instant from the wings and illumines the florid lines.

A dozen quarts of champagne in conjunction with an informal sitting of the president and his cabinet led to the establishment of the navy and the appointment of Felipe Carrera as its admiral.

Next to the champagne the credit of the appointment belongs to Don Sabas Placido, the newly confirmed Minister of War.

The President had requested a convention of his cabinet for the discussion of questions politic and for the transaction of certain routine matters of state. The session had been signally tedious; the business and the wine prodigiously dry. A sudden, prankish humor of Don Sabas, impelling him to the deed, spiced the grave affairs of state with a whiff of agreeable playfulness.

In the dilatory order of business had come a bulletin from the coast department of Orilla del Mar reporting the seizure by the custom-house officers at the town of Coralio of the sloop *Estrella del Noche* and her cargo of drygoods, patent medicines, granulated sugar and three-star brandy. Also six Martini rifles and a barrel of American whisky. Caught in the act of smuggling, the sloop with its cargo was now, according to law, the property of the republic.

The Collector of Customs, in making his report, departed from the conventional forms so far as to suggest that the confiscated vessel be converted to the use of the government. The prize was the first capture to the credit of the department in ten years. The collector took opportunity to pat his department on the back.

It often happened that government officers required transportation from point to point along the coast, and means were usually lacking. Furthermore, the sloop could be manned by a loyal crew and employed as a coast guard to discourage the pernicious art of smuggling. The collector also ventured to nominate one to whom the charge of the boat could be safely intrusted—a young man of Coralio, Felipe Carrera—not, be it understood, one of extreme wisdom, but loyal and the best sailor along the coast.

It was upon this hint that the Minister of War acted, executing a rare piece of drollery that so enlivened the tedium of executive session.

In the constitution of this small, maritime banana republic was a forgotten section that provided for the maintenance of a navy. This provision—with many other wiser ones—had lain inert since the establishment of the republic. Anchuria had no navy and had no use for one. It was characteristic of Don Sabas—a man at once merry, learned, whimsical and audacious—that he should have disturbed the dust of this musty and sleeping statute to increase the humor of the world by so much as a smile from his indulgent colleagues.

With delightful mock seriousness the Minister of War proposed the creation of a navy. He argued its need and the glories it might achieve with such gay and witty zeal that the traversty overcame with its humor even the swart dignity of President Losada himself.

The champagne was bubbling trickily in the veins of the mercurial statesmen. It was not the custom of the grave governors of Anchuria to enliven their sessions with a beverage so apt to cast a veil of disparagement over sober affairs. The wine had been a thoughtful compliment tendered by the agent of the Vesuvius Fruit Company as a token of amicable relations—and certain consummated deals—between that company and the republic of Anchuria.

The jest was carried to its end. A formidable, official document was prepared, encrusted with chromatic seals and jaunty with fluttering ribbons, bearing the florid signatures of state. This commission conferred upon el Señor Don Felipe Carrera the title of Flag Admiral of the Republic of Anchuria. Thus within the space of a few minutes and the dominion of a dozen " extra dry," the country took its place among the naval powers of the world, and Felipe Carrera became entitled to a salute of nineteen guns whenever he might enter port.

The southern races are lacking in that particular kind of humor that finds entertainment in the defects and misfortunes bestowed by Nature. Owing to this defect in their constitution they are not moved to laughter (as are their northern brothers) by the spectacle of the deformed, the feeble-minded or the insane.

Felipe Carrera was sent upon earth with but half his wits. Therefore, the people of Coralio called him " *El pobrecito loco* "— " the poor little crazed one "—saying that God had sent but half of him to earth, retaining the other half.

A sombre youth, glowering, and speaking only at the rarest times, Felipe was but negatively " loco." On shore he generally refused all conversation. He seemed to know that he was badly handicapped on land, where so many kinds of understanding are needed; but on the water his only talent set him equal with most men. Few sailors whom God had carefully and completely made could handle a sailboat as well. Five points nearer the wind than even the best of them he could sail his sloop. When the elements raged and set other men to cowering, the deficiencies of Felipe seemed of little importance. He was a perfect sailor, if an imperfect man. He owned no boat, but worked among the crews of the schooners and sloops that skimmed the coast, trading and freighting fruit out to the steamers where there was no harbor. It was through his famous skill and boldness on the sea, as well as for the pity felt for his mental imperfections, that he was recommended by the collector as a suitable custodian of the captured sloop.

When the outcome of Don Sabas' little pleasantry arrived in the form of the imposing and preposterous commission, the collector smiled. He had not expected such prompt and overwhelming response to his recommendation. He despatched a *muchacho* at once to fetch the future admiral.

The collector waited in his official quarters. His office was in the Calle Grande, and the sea breezes hummed through its windows all day. The collector, in white linen and canvas shoes, philandered with papers on an antique desk. A parrot, perched on a pen rack, seasoned the official tedium with a fire of choice Castilian imprecations. Two rooms opened into the collector's. In one the clerical force of young men of variegated complexions transacted with glitter and parade their several duties. Through the open door of the other room could be seen a bronze babe, guiltless of clothing, that rollicked upon the floor. In a grass hammock a thin woman, tinted a pale lemon, played a guitar and swung contentedly in the breeze. Thus surrounded by the routine of his high duties and the visible tokens of agreeable domesticity, the collector's heart was further made happy by the power placed in his hands to brighten the fortunes of the " innocent " Felipe.

Felipe came and stood before the collector. He was a lad of twenty, not ill-favored in looks, but with an expression of distant and pondering vacuity. He wore white cotton trousers, down the seams of which he had sewed red stripes with some vague aim at military decoration. A flimsy blue shirt fell open at his throat; his feet were bare; he held in his hand the cheapest of straw hats from the States.

"Señor Carrera," said the collector, gravely, producing the showy commission, "I have sent for you at the President's bidding. This document that I present to you confers upon you the title of Admiral of this great republic, and gives you absolute command of the naval forces and fleet of our country. You may think, friend Felipe, that we have no navy—but yes! The sloop the *Estrella del Noche*, that my brave men captured from the coast smugglers, is to be placed under your command. The boat is to be devoted to the services of your country. You will be ready at all times to convey officials of the government to points along the coast where they may be obliged to visit. You will also act as a coast-guard to prevent, as far as you may be able, the crime of smuggling. You will uphold the honor and prestige of your country at sea, and endeavor to place Anchuria among the proudest naval powers of the world. These are your instructions as the Minister of War desires me to convey them to you. *Por Dios!* I do not know how all this is to be accomplished, for not one word did his letter contain in respect to a crew or to the expenses of this navy. Perhaps you are to provide a crew yourself, Señor Admiral—I do not know—but it is a very high honor that has descended upon you. I now hand you your commission. When you are ready for the boat I will give orders that she shall be made over into your charge. That is as far as my instructions go."

Felipe took the commission that the collector handed to him. He gazed through the open window at the sea for a moment, with his customary expression of deep but vain pondering. Then he turned without having spoken a word, and walked swiftly away through the hot sand of the street.

"*Pobrecito loco!*" sighed the collector; and the parrot on the pen racks screeched "Loco!—loco!—loco!"

The next morning a strange procession filed through the streets to the collector's office. At its head was the admiral of the navy. Somewhere Felipe had raked together a pitiful semblance of a military uniform—a pair of red trousers, a dingy blue short jacket heavily ornamented with gold braid, and an old fatigue cap that must have been cast away by one of the British soldiers in Belize and brought away by Felipe on one of his coasting voyages. Buckled around his waist was an ancient ship's cutlass contributed to his equipment by Pedro Lafitte, the baker, who proudly asserted its inheritance from his ancestor, the illustrious buccaneer.

At the admiral's heels tagged his newly shipped crew—three grinning, glossy, black Caribs, bare to the waist, the sand spurting in showers from the spring of their naked feet.

Briefly and with dignity Felipe demanded his vessel of the collector. And now a fresh honor awaited him. The collector's wife, who played the guitar and read novels in the hammock all day, had more than a little romance in her placid yellow bosom. She had found in an old book an engraving of a flag that purported to be the naval flag of Anchuria. Perhaps it had so been designed by the founders of the nation; but, as no navy had ever been established, oblivion had claimed the flag. Laboriously with her own hands she had made a flag after the pattern—a red cross upon a blue-and-white ground. She presented it to Felipe with these words : " Brave sailor, this flag is of your country. Be true, and defend it with your life. Go you with God."

For the first time since his appointment the admiral showed a flicker of emotion. He took the silken emblem, and passed his hand reverently over its surface. " I am the admiral," he said to the collector's lady. Being on land he could bring himself to no more exuberant expression of sentiment. At sea with the flag at the masthead of his navy, some more eloquent exposition of feelings might be forthcoming.

Abruptly the admiral departed with his crew. For the next three days they were busy giving the *Estrella del Noche* a new coat of white paint trimmed with blue. And then Felipe further adorned himself by fastening a handful of brilliant parrot's plumes in his cap. Again he tramped with his faithful crew to the collector's office and formerly notified him that the sloop's name had been changed to *El Nacional*.

During the next few months the navy had its troubles. Even an admiral is perplexed to know what to do without any orders. But none came. Neither did any salaries. *El Nacional* swung idly at anchor.

When Felipe's little store of money was exhausted he went to the collector and raised the question of finances.

" Salaries ! " exclaimed the collector, with hands raised; " *Valgame Dios !* not one *centavo* of my own pay have I received for the last seven months. The pay of an admiral, do you ask ? *Quién sabe ?* Should it be less than three thousand *pesos ? Mira !* you will see a revolution in this country very soon. A good sign of it is when the government calls all the time for *pesos, pesos, pesos,* and pays none out."

Felipe left the collector's office with a look of almost content on his sombre face. A revolution would mean fighting, and then the government would need his services. It was rather humiliating to be an admiral without anything to do, and have a hungry crew at your heels begging for *reales* to buy plantains and tobacco with.

When he returned to where his happy-go-lucky Caribs were waiting they sprang up and saluted, as he had drilled them to do.

" Come, *muchachos*," said the admiral; " it seems that the government is poor. It had no money to give us. We will earn what we need to live upon. Thus will we serve our country. Soon "—his heavy eyes almost lighted up—" it may gladly call upon us for help."

Thereafter *El Nacional* turned out with the other coast craft and became a wage-earner. She worked with the lighters freighting bananas and oranges out to the fruit steamers that could not approach nearer than a mile from the shore. Surely a self-supporting navy deserves red letters in the budget of any nation.

After earning enough at freighting to keep himself and his crew in provisions for a week Felipe would anchor the navy and hang about the little telegraph office, looking like one of the chorus of an insolvent comic opera troupe besieging the manager's den. A hope for orders from the capital was always in his heart. That his services as admiral had never been called into requirement hurt his pride and patriotism. At every call he would inquire, gravely and expectantly, for despatches. The operator would pretend to make a search, and then reply :

" Not yet, it seems, *Señor el Almirante—poco tiempo !* "

Outside in the shade of the lime-trees the crew chewed sugar cane or slumbered, well content to serve a country that was contented with so little service.

One day in the early summer the revolution predicted by the collector flamed out suddenly. It had long been smoldering. At the first note of alarm the admiral of the navy force and fleet made all sail for a larger port on the coast of a neighboring republic, where he traded a hastily collected cargo of fruit for its value in cartridges for the five Martini rifles, the only guns that the navy could boast. Then to the telegraph office sped the admiral. Sprawling in his favorite corner, in his fast-decaying uniform, with his prodigious sabre distributed between his red legs, he waited for the long-delayed, but now soon expected, orders.

" Not yet, *Señor el Almirante*," the telegraph clerk would call to him—" *poco tiempo !* "

At the answer the admiral would plump himself down with a great rattling of scabbard to await the infrequent tick of the little instrument on the table.

" They will come," would be his unshaken reply; " I am the admiral."

THE FLAG PARAMOUNT

A T the head of the insurgent party appeared that Hector and learned Theban of the southern republic, Don Sabás Placido. A traveller, a soldier, a poet, a scientist, a statesman, and a connoisseur—the wonder was that he could content himself with the petty, remote life of his native country.

"It is a whim of Placido's," said a friend who knew him well, "to take up political intrigue. It is not otherwise than as if he had come upon a new *tempo* in music, a new bacillus in the air, a new scent, or rhyme, or explosive. He will squeeze this revolution dry of sensations, and a week afterward will forget it, skimming the seas of the world in his brigantine to add to his already world-famous collections. Collections of what? *Por Dios!* of everything from postage stamps to prehistoric stone idols."

But, for a mere dilettante, the æsthetic Placido seemed to be creating a lively row. The people admired him; they were fascinated by his brilliancy and flattered by his taking an interest in so small a thing as his native country. They rallied to the call of his lieutenants in the capital, where (somewhat contrary to arrangements) the army remained faithful to the government. There was also lively skirmishing in the coast towns. It was rumored that the revolution was aided by the Vesuvius Fruit Company, the power that forever stood with chiding smile and uplifted finger to keep Anchuria in the class of good children. Two of its steamers, the *Traveler* and the *Salvador*, were known to have conveyed insurgent troops from point to point along the coast.

As yet there had been no actual uprising in Coralio. Military law prevailed, and the ferment was bottled for the time. And then came the word that everywhere the revolutionists were encountering defeat. In the capital the president's forces triumphed; and there was a rumor that the leaders of the revolt had been forced to fly, hotly pursued.

In the little telegraph office at Coralio there was always a gathering of officials and loyal citizens, awaiting news from the seat of government. One morning the telegraph key began clicking, and presently the operator called, loudly : " One telegram for *el Almirante,* Don Señor Felipe Carrera ! "

There was a shuffling sound, a great rattling of tin scabbard, and the admiral, prompt at his spot of waiting, leaped across the room to receive it.

The message was handed to him. Slowly spelling it out, he found it to be his first official order—thus running :

Proceed immediately with your vessel to mouth of Rio Ruiz; transport beef and provisions to barracks at Alforan.

                                        Martinez, General.

Small glory, to be sure, in this, his country's first call. But it had called, and joy surged in the admiral's breast. He drew his cutlass belt to another buckle hole, roused his dozing crew, and in a quarter of an hour *El Nacional* was tacking swiftly down coast in a stiff landward breeze.

The Rio Ruiz is a small river, emptying into the sea ten miles below Coralio. That portion of the coast is wild and solitary. Through a gorge in the Cordilleras rushes the Rio Ruiz, cold and bubbling, to glide, at last, with breadth and leisure, through an alluvial morass into the sea.

In two hours *El Nacional* entered the river's mouth. The banks were crowded with a disposition of formidable trees. The sumptuous undergrowth of the tropics overflowed the land, and drowned itself in the fallow waters. Silently the sloop entered there, and met a deeper silence. Brilliant with greens and ochres and floral scarlets, the umbrageous mouth of the Rio Ruiz furnished no sound or movement save of the sea-going water as it purled against the prow of the vessel. Small chance there seemed of wresting beef or provisions from that empty solitude.

The admiral decided to cast anchor, and, at the chain's rattle, the forest was stimulated to instant and resounding uproar. The mouth of the Rio Ruiz had only been taking a morning nap. Parrots and baboons screeched and barked in the trees; a whirring and a hissing and a booming marked the awakening of animal life; a dark bulk was visible for an instant, as a startled tapir fought his way through the vines.

The navy, under orders, hung in the mouth of the little river for hours. The crew served the dinner of shark's fin soup, plantains, crab gumbo and sour wine. The admiral, with a three-foot telescope, closely scanned the impervious foliage fifty yards away.

It was nearly sunset when a reverberating " hallo-o-o ! " came from the forest to their left. It was answered; and three men, mounted upon mules, crashed through the tropic tangle to within a dozen yards of the river's bank. There they dismounted; and one, unbuckling his belt, struck each mule a violent blow with his sword scabbard, so that they, with a fling of heels, dashed back again into the forest.

Those were strange-looking men to be conveying beef and

provisions. One was a large and exceedingly active man, of
striking presence. He was of the purest Spanish type, with curling,
gray-besprinkled, dark hair, blue, sparkling eyes, and the pro-
nounced air of a *caballero grande*. The other two were small, brown-
faced men, wearing white military uniforms, high riding boots and
swords. The clothes of all were drenched, bespattered and rent by
the thicket. Some stress of circumstance must have driven them,
diable à quatre, through flood, mire and jungle.

" *O-hé! Señor Almirante*," called the large man. " Send to us
your boat."

The dory was lowered, and Felipe, with one of the Caribs,
rowed toward the left bank.

The large man stood near the water's brink, waist deep in the
curling vines. As he gazed upon the scarecrow figure in the stern
of the dory a sprightly interest beamed upon his mobile face.

Months of wageless and thankless service had dimmed the
admiral's splendor. His red trousers were patched and ragged.
Most of the bright buttons and yellow braid were gone from his
jacket. The visor of his cap was torn, and depended almost to his
eyes. The admiral's feet were bare.

" Dear admiral," cried the large man, and his voice was like
a blast from a horn, " I kiss your hands. I knew we could build
upon your fidelity. You had our despatch—from General Martinez.
A little nearer with your boat, dear Admiral. Upon these devils
of shifting vines we stand with the smallest security."

Felipe regarded him with a stolid face.

" Provisions and beef for the barracks at Alforan," he quoted.

" No fault of the butchers, *Almirante mio*, that the beef awaits
you not. But you are come in time to save the cattle. Get us
aboard your vessel, señor, at once. You first, *caballeros—á priesa !*
Come back for me. The boat is too small."

The dory conveyed the two officers to the sloop, and returned
for the large man.

" Have you so gross a thing as food, good admiral ? " he cried,
when aboard. "And, perhaps, coffee ? Beef and provisions !
Nombre de Dios ! a little longer and we could have eaten one of
those mules that you, Colonel Rafael, saluted so feelingly with
your sword scabbard at parting. Let us have food; and then we
will sail—for the barracks at Alforan—no ? "

The Caribs prepared a meal, to which the three passengers of
El Nacional set themselves with famished delight. About sunset, as
was its custom, the breeze veered and swept back from the mountains, cool and steady, bringing a taste of the stagnant lagoons and
mangrove swamps that guttered the lowlands. The mainsail of the
sloop was hoisted and swelled to it, and at that moment they heard

shouts and a waxing clamor from the bosky profoundities of the shore.

"The butchers, my dear admiral," said the large man, smiling, "too late for the slaughter."

Further than his orders to his crew, the admiral was saying nothing. The topsail and jib were spread, and the sloop glided out of the estuary. The large man and his companions had bestowed themselves with what comfort they could about the bare deck. Belike, the thing big in their minds had been their departure from that critical shore; and now that the hazard was so far reduced their thoughts were loosed to the consideration of further deliverance. But when they saw the sloop turn and fly up coast again they relaxed, satisfied with the course the admiral had taken.

The large man sat at ease, his spirited blue eye engaged in the contemplation of the navy's commander. He was trying to estimate this sombre and fantastic lad, whose impenetrable stolidity puzzled him. Himself a fugitive, his life sought, and chafing under the smart of defeat and failure, it was characteristic of him to transfer instantly his interest to the study of a thing new to him. It was like him, too, to have conceived and risked all upon this last desperate and madcap scheme—this message to a poor, crazed *fanático* cruising about with his grotesque uniform and his farcical title. But his companions had been at their wits' end; escape had seemed incredible; and now he was pleased with the success of the plan they had called crack-brained and precarious.

The brief tropic twilight seemed to slide swiftly into the pearly splendor of a moonlight night. And now the lights of Coralio appeared, distributed against the darkening shore to their right. The admiral stood, silent, at the tiller; the Caribs, like black panthers, held the sheets, leaping noiselessly at his short commands. The three passengers were watching intently the sea before them, and when at length they came in sight of the bulk of a steamer lying a mile out from the town, with her lights radiating deep into the water, they held a sudden voluble and close-headed converse. The sloop was speeding as if to strike midway between ship and shore.

The large man suddenly separated from his companions and approached the scarecrow at the helm.

"My dear admiral," he said, "the government has been exceedingly remiss. I feel all the shame for it that only its ignorance of your devoted service has prevented it from sustaining. An inexcusable oversight has been made. A vessel, a uniform and a crew worthy of your fidelity shall be furnished you. But just now, dear admiral, there is business of moment afoot. The steamer lying there is the *Salvador*. I and my friends desire to be conveyed to her, where we are sent on the government's business. Do us the favor to shape your course accordingly."

Without replying, the admiral gave a sharp command, and put the tiller hard to port. *El Nacional* swerved, and headed straight as an arrow's course for the shore.

" Do me the favor," said the large man, a trifle restively, " to acknowledge, at least, that you catch the sound of my words." It was possible that the fellow might be lacking in senses as well as intellect.

The admiral emitted a croaking, harsh laugh, and spake.

" They stand you," he said, " with your face to a wall and shoot you dead. That is the way they kill traitors. I knew you when you stepped into my boat. I have seen your picture in a book. You are Sabas Placido, traitor to your country. With your face to a wall. So, you will die. I am the admiral, and I will take you to them. With your face to a wall. Yes."

Don Sabas half turned and waved his hand, with a ringing laugh, toward his fellow fugitives. " To you, *caballeros*, I have related the history of that session when we issued that O ! so ridiculous commission. Of a truth our jest has been turned against us. Behold the Frankenstein's monster we have created ! "

Don Sabas glanced toward the shore. The lights of Coralio were drawing near. He could see the beach, the warehouse of the *Bodega Nacional*, the long, low *cuartel* occupied by the soldiers, and, behind that, gleaming in the moonlight, a stretch of high adobe wall. He had seen men stood with their faces to that wall and shot dead.

Again he addressed the extravagant figure at the helm.

" It is true," he said, " that I am fleeing the country. But, receive the assurance that I care very little for that. Courts and camps everywhere are open to Sabas Placido. *Vaya !* what is this molehill of a republic—this pig's head of a country—to a man like me ? I am a *paisano* of everywhere. In Rome, in London, in Paris, in Vienna, you will hear them say : ' Welcome back, Don Sabas.' Come !—*tonto*—baboon of a boy—admiral, whatever you call yourself, turn your boat. Put us on board the *Salvador*, and here is your pay—five hundred *pesos* in money of the *Estados Unidos*— more than your lying government will pay you in twenty years."

Don Sabas pressed a plump purse against the youth's hand. The admiral gave no heed to the words or the movement. Braced against the helm, he was holding the sloop dead on her shoreward course. His dull face was lit almost to intelligence by some inward conceit that seemed to afford him joy, and found utterance in another parrot-like cackle.

" That is why they do it," he said—" so that you will not see the guns. They fire—boom !—and you fall dead. With your face to the wall. Yes."

The admiral called a sudden order to his crew. The lithe, silent Caribs made fast the sheets they held, and slipped down the hatchway into the hold of the sloop. When the last one had disappeared, Don Sabas, like a big, brown leopard, leaped forward, closed and fastened the hatch and stood, smiling.

" No rifles, if you please, dear admiral," he said. " It was a whimsey of mine once to compile a dictionary of the Carib *lengua.* So, I understood your order. Perhaps now you will——"

He cut short his words, for he heard the dull " swish " of iron scraping along tin. The admiral had drawn the cutlass of Pedro Lafitte, and was darting upon him. The blade descended, and it was only by a display of surprising agility that the large man escaped, with only a bruised shoulder, the glancing weapon. He was drawing his pistol as he sprang, and the next instant he shot the admiral down.

Don Sabas stooped over him, and rose again.

" In the heart," he said briefly. " *Señores,* the navy is abolished."

Colonel Rafael sprang to the helm, and the other officer hastened to loose the mainsail sheets. The boom swung round; *El Nacional* veered and began to tack industriously for the *Salvador.*

" Strike that flag, señor," called Colonel Rafael. " Our friends on the steamer will wonder why we are sailing under it."

" Well said," cried Don Sabas. Advancing to the mast he lowered the flag to the deck, where lay its too loyal supporter. Thus ended the Minister of War's little piece of after-dinner drollery, and by the same hand that began it.

Suddenly Don Sabas gave a great cry of joy, and ran down the slanting deck to the side of Colonel Rafael. Across his arm he carried the flag of the extinguished navy.

" *Mire ! mire ! señor.* Ah, *Dios !* Already can I hear the great bear of an *Oestreicher* shout, ' *Du hast mein herz gebrochen !* ' *Mire !* Of my friend, Herr Grunitz, of Vienna, you have heard me relate. That man has travelled to Ceylon for an orchid—to Patagonia for a headdress—to Benares for a slipper—to Mozambique for a spearhead to add to his famous collections. Thou knowest, also, *amigo* Rafael, that I have been a gatherer of curios. My collection of battle flags of the world's navies was the most complete in existence until last year. Then Herr Grunitz secured two, O ! such rare specimens. One of a Barbary state, and one of the Makarooroos, a tribe on the west coast of Africa. I have not those, but they can be procured. But this flag, señor—do you know what it is ? Name of God ! do you know ? See that red cross upon the blue-and-white ground ! You never saw it before ? *Seguarmente no.*

It is the naval flag of your country. *Mire.!* This rotten tub we stand
upon is its navy—that dead cockatoo lying there was its commander—that stroke of cutlass and single pistol shot a sea battle.
All a piece of absurd foolery, I grant you—but authentic. There
has never been another flag like this, and there never will be
another. No. It is unique in the whole world. Yes. Think of what
that means to a collector of flags ! Do you know, *Coronel mio,* how
many golden crowns Herr Grunitz would give for this flag ? Ten
thousand, likely. Well, a hundred thousand would not buy it.
Beautiful flag ! Only flag ! Little devil of a most heaven-born
flag ! *O-hé !* old grumbler beyond the ocean. Wait till Don Sabas
comes again to the Königin Strasse. He will let you kneel and
touch the folds of it with one finger. *O-hé !* old spectacled ran-
sacker of the world ! "

Forgotten was the impotent revolution, the danger, the loss, the
gall of defeat. Possessed solely by the inordinate and unparalleled
passion of the collector, he strode up and down the little deck,
clasping to his breast with one hand the paragon of a flag. He
snapped his fingers triumphantly toward the east. He shouted
the paean to his prize in trumpet tones, as though he would make
old Grunitz hear in his musty den beyond the sea.

They were waiting, on the *Salvador,* to welcome them. The sloop
came close alongside the steamer where her sides were sliced almost
to the lower deck for the loading of fruit. The sailors of the *Salvador*
grappled and held her there.

Captain McLeod leaned over the side.

" Well, *señor,* the jig is up, I'm told."

" The jig is up ? " Don Sabas looked perplexed for a moment.
" That revolution—ah, yes ! " With a shrug of his shoulders he
dismissed the matter.

The captain learned of the escape and the imprisoned crew.

" Caribs ? " he said; " no harm in them." He slipped down
into the sloop and kicked loose the hasp of the hatch. The black
fellows came tumbling up, sweating but grinning.

" Hey ! black boys ! " said the captain, in a dialect of his own;
" you sabe, catchy boat and vamos back same place quick."

They saw him point to themselves, the sloop and Coralio. " Yas,
yas ! " they cried, with broader grins and many nods.

The four—Don Sabas, the two officers and the captain—moved
to quit the sloop. Don Sabas lagged a little behind, looking at the
still form of the late admiral, sprawled in his paltry trappings.

" *Pobrecito loco,* " he said softly.

He was a brilliant cosmopolite and a *cognoscente* of high rank;
but, after all, he was of the same race and blood and instinct as
this people. Even as the simple *paisanos* of Coralio had said it, so

said Don Sabas. Without a smile, he looked, and said, "The poor little crazed one!"

Stooping he raised the limp shoulders, drew the priceless and induplicable flag under them and over the breast, pinning it there with the diamond star of the Order of San Carlos that he took from the collar of his own coat.

He followed after the others, and stood with them upon the deck of the *Salvador*. The sailors that steadied *El Nacional* shoved her off. The jabbering Caribs hauled away at the rigging; the sloop headed for the shore.

And Herr Grunitz's collection of naval flags was still the finest in the world.

THE SHAMROCK AND THE PALM

ONE night when there was no breeze, and Coralio seemed closer than ever to the gratings of Avernus, five men were grouped about the door of the photograph establishment of Keogh and Clancy. Thus, in all the scorched and exotic places of the earth, Caucasians meet when the day's work is done to preserve the fulness of their heritage by the aspersion of alien things.

Johnny Atwood lay stretched upon the grass in the undress uniform of a Carib, and prated feebly of the cool water to be had in the cucumber-wood pumps of Dalesburg. Dr. Gregg, through the prestige of his whiskers and as a bribe against the relation of his imminent professional tales, was conceded the hammock that was swung between the door jamb and a calabash-tree. Keogh had moved out upon the grass a little table that held the instrument for burnishing completed photographs. He was the only busy one of the group. Industriously from between the cylinders of the burnisher rolled the finished depictments of Coralio's citizens. Blanchard, the French mining engineer, in his cool linen viewed the smoke of his cigarette through his calm glasses, impervious to the heat. Clancy sat on the steps, smoking his short pipe. His mood was the gossip's; the others were reduced, by the humidity, to the state of disability desirable in an audience.

Clancy was an American with an Irish diathesis and cosmopolitan proclivities. Many businesses had claimed him, but not for long. The roadster's blood was in his veins. The voice of the tintype was but one of the many callings that had wooed him upon so many roads. Sometimes he could be persuaded to oral construction of his voyages into the informal and egregious. To-night there were symptons of divulgement in him.

" 'Tis elegant weather for filibusterin'," he volunteered. " It reminds me of the time I struggled to liberate a nation from the poisonous breath of a tyrant's clutch. 'Twas hard work. 'Tis strainin' to the back and makes corns on the hands."

" I didn't know you had ever lent your sword to an oppressed people," murmured Atwood, from the grass.

" I did," said Clancy; " and they turned it into a plowshare."

" What country was so fortunate as to secure your aid ? " airily inquired Blanchard.

" Where's Kamchatka ? " asked Clancy, with seeming irrelevance.

" Why, off Siberia somewhere in the Arctic regions," somebody answered, doubtfully.

" I thought that was the cold one," said Clancy, with a satisfied nod. " I'm always gettin' the two names mixed. 'Twas Guatemala, then—the hot one—I've been filibusterin' with. Ye'll find that country on the map. 'Tis in the district known as the tropics. By the foresight of Providence, it lies on the coast so the geography man could run the names of the towns off into the water. They're an inch long, small type, composed of Spanish dialects, and, 'tis my opinion, of the same system of syntax that blew up the *Maine*. Yes, 'twas that country I sailed against, single-handed, and endeavored to liberate it from a tyrannical government with a single-barreled pickaxe, unloaded at that. Ye don't understand, of course. 'Tis a statement demandin' elucidation and apologies.

" 'Twas in New Orleans one morning about the first of June ; I was standin' down on the wharf, lookin' about at the ships in the river. There was a little steamer moored right opposite me that seemed about ready to sail. The funnels of it were throwin' out smoke, and a gang of roustabouts were carryin' aboard a pile of boxes that was stacked up on the wharf. The boxes were about two feet square, and somethin' like four feet long, and they seemed to be pretty heavy.

" I walked over, careless, to the stack of boxes. I saw one of them had been broken in handlin'. 'Twas curiosity made me pull up the loose top and look inside. The box was packed full of Winchester rifles. ' So, so,' says I to myself; ' somebody's gettin' a twist on the neutrality laws. Somebody's aidin' with munitions of war. I wonder where the popguns are goin ' ? '

" I heard somebody cough, and I turned around. There stood a little, round, fat man with a brown face and white clothes, a first-class-looking little man, with a four-karat diamond on his finger and his eye full of interrogations and respects. I judged he was a kind of foreigner—may be from Russia or Japan or the archipelagoes.

" 'Hist ! ' says the round man, full of concealments and confidences. ' Will the señor respect the discoveryments he has made, that the mans on the ship shall not be acquaint ? The señor will be a gentleman that shall not expose one thing that by accident occur.'

" 'Monseer,' says I—for I judged him to be a kind of Frenchman—' receive my most exasperated assurances that your secret is safe with James Clancy. Furthermore, I will go so far as to remark, Veev la Liberty—veev it good and strong. Whenever you hear of a Clancy obstructin' the abolishment of existin' governments you may notify me by return mail.'

" 'The señor is good,' says the dark, fat man, smilin' under his black mustache. ' Wish you to come aboard my ship and drink of wine a glass.'

" Bein' a Clancy, in two minutes me and the foreigner man were seated at a table in the cabin of the steamer, with a bottle between us. I could hear the heavy boxes bein' dumped into the hold. I judged that cargo must consist of at least 2,000 Winchesters. Me and the brown man drank the bottle of stuff, and he called the steward to bring another. When you amalgamate a Clancy with the contents of a bottle you practically instigate secession. I had heard a good deal about these revolutions in them tropical localities, and I begun to want a hand in it.

" 'You goin' to stir things up in your country ain't you, monseer ? ' says I, with a wink to let him know I was on.

" 'Yes, yes,' said the little man, pounding his fist on the table. 'A change of the greatest will occur. Too long have the people been oppressed with the promises and the never-to-happen things to become. The great work it shall be carry on. Yes. Our forces shall in the capital city strike of the soonest. *Carrambos !* '

" '*Carrambos* is the word,' says I, beginning to invest myself with enthusiasm and more wine, ' likewise veeva, as I said before. May the shamrock of old—I mean the banana-vine or the pie-plant, or whatever the imperial emblem may be of your downtrodden country, wave forever.'

" 'A thousand thank-yous,' says the round man, ' for your emission of amicable utterances. What our cause needs of the very most is mans who will work do, to lift it along. Oh, for one thousands strong, good mans to aid the General De Vega that he shall to his country bring those success and glory ! It is hard—oh, so hard to find good mans to help in the work.'

" 'Monseer,' says I, leanin' over the table and graspin' his hand, ' I don't know where your country is, but me heart bleeds for it. The heart of a Clancy was never deaf to the sight of an oppressed people. The family is filibusterers by birth, and foreigners by trade.

If you can use James Clancy's arms and his blood in denudin'
your shores of the tyrant's yoke they're yours to command.'

" General De Vega was overcome with joy to confiscate my
condolence of his conspiracies and predicaments. He tried to
embrace me across the table, but his fatness, and the wine that had
been in the bottles, prevented. Thus was I welcomed into the ranks
of filibustery. Then the general man told me his country had the
name of Guatemala, and was the greatest nation laved by any
ocean whatever anywhere. He looked at me with tears in his eyes,
and from time to time he would emit the remark, 'Ah ! big, strong,
brave mans ! That is what my country need.'

" General De Vega, as was the name by which he denounced
himself, brought out a document for me to sign, which I did,
makin' a fine flourish and curlycue with the tail of the ' y.'

" 'Your passage-money,' says the general, business-like, ' shall
from your pay be deduct.'

" 'Twill not,' says I, haughty. ' I'll pay my own passage.' A
hundred and eighty dollars I had in my inside pocket, and 'twas
no common filibuster I was goin' to be, filibusterin' for me board
and clothes.

" The steamer was to sail in two hours, and I went ashore to
get some things together I'd need. When I came aboard I showed
the general with pride the outfit. 'Twas a fine Chinchilla overcoat,
Arctic overshoes, fur cap and earmuffs, with elegant fleece-lined
gloves and woolen muffler.

" *'Carrambos !'* says the little general. ' What clothes are these
that shall go to the tropic ? ' And then the little spalpeen laughs,
and he calls the captain, and the captain calls the purser, and they
pipe up the chief engineer, and the whole gang leans against the
cabin and laughs at Clancy's wardrobe for Guatemala.

" I reflects a bit, serious, and asks the general again to denomi-
nate the terms by which his country is called. He tells me, and
I see then that 'twas the t'other one, Kamchatka, I had in mind.
Since then I've had difficulty in separatin' the two nations in name,
climate and geographic disposition.

" I paid my passage—twenty-four dollars, first cabin—and ate
at table with the officer crowd. Down on the lower deck was a gang
of second-class passengers, about forty of them, seemin' to be
Dagoes and the like. I wondered what so many of them were
goin' along for.

" Well, then, in three days we sailed alongside that Guatemala.
'Twas a blue country, and not yellow as 'tis miscolored on the
map. We landed at a town on the coast, where a train of cars was
waitin' for us on a dinky little railroad. The boxes on the steamer
were brought ashore and loaded on the cars. The gang of Dagoes

got aboard, too, the general and me in the front car. Yes, me and General De Vega headed the revolution, as it pulled out of the seaport town. That train travelled about as fast as a policeman goin' to a riot. It penetrated the most conspicuous lot of fuzzy scenery ever seen outside a geography. We run some forty miles in seven hours, and the train stopped. There was no more railroad. 'Twas a sort of camp in a damp gorge full of wildness and melancholies. They was gradin' and choppin' out the forests ahead to continue the road. ' Here,' says I to myself, ' is the romantic haunt of the revolutionists. Here will Clancy, by the virtue that is in a superior race and the inculcation of Fenian tactics, strike a tremendous blow for liberty.'

" They unloaded the boxes from the train and begun to knock the tops off. From the first one that was open I saw General De Vega take the Winchester rifles and pass them around to a squad of morbid soldiery. The other boxes was opened next, and, believe me or not, divil another gun was to be seen. Every other box in the load was full of pickaxes and spades.

"And then—sorrow be upon them tropics—the proud Clancy and the dishonored Dagoes, each one of them, had to shoulder a pick or a spade, and march away to work on that dirty little railroad. Yes; 'twas that the Dagoes shipped for, and 'twas that the filibusterin' Clancy signed for, though unbeknownst to himself at the time. In after days I found out about it. It seems 'twas hard to get hands to work on the road. The intelligent natives of the country was too lazy to work. Indeed the saints know, 'twas unnecessary. By stretchin' out one hand, they could seize the most delicate and costly fruits of the earth, and, by stretchin' out the other, they could sleep for days at a time without hearin' a seven-o'clock whistle or the footsteps of the rent man upon the stairs. So, regular, the steamers travelled to the United States to seduce labor. Usually the imported spade-slingers died in two or three months from eatin' the over-ripe water and breathin' the violent tropical scenery. Wherefore they made them sign contracts for a year, when they hired them, and put an armed guard over the poor divils to keep them from runnin' away.

" 'Twas thus I was double-crossed by the tropics through a family failin' of goin' out of the way to hunt disturbances.

" They gave me a pick, and I took it, meditatin' an insurrection on the spot; but there was the guards handlin' the Winchesters careless, and I come to the conclusion that discretion was the best part of filibusterin'. There was about a hundred of us in the gang startin' out to work, and the word was given to move. I steps out of the ranks and goes up to that General De Vega man, who was smokin' a cigar and gazin' upon the scene with satisfactions and glory. He smiles at me polite and devilish. ' Plenty work,' says he, ' for big, strong mans in Guatemala. Yes. T'irty dollars in the month. Good pay. Ah, yes. You strong, brave man. Bimeby we push those railroad in the capital very quick. They want you go work now. *Adios,* strong mans.'

" 'Monseer,' says I, lingerin', 'will you tell a poor little Irishman this : When I set foot on your cockroachy steamer, and breathed liberal and revolutionary sentiments into your sour wine, did you think I was conspirin' to sling a pick on your contemptuous little railroad ? And when you answered me with patriotic recitations, humping up the star-spangled cause of liberty, did you have meditations of reducin' me to the ranks of the stump-grubbin' Dagoes in the chain-gangs of your vile and grovelin' country ? '

" The general man expanded his rotundity and laughed considerable. Yes, he laughed very long and loud, and I, Clancy, stood and waited.

" 'Comical mans ! ' he shouts, at last. ' So you will kill me from the laughing. Yes; it is hard to find the brave, strong mans to aid my country. Revolutions ? Did I speak of r-r-revolutions ? Not one word. I say, big, strong mans is need in Guatemala. So. The mistake is of you. You have looked in those one box containing those gun for the guard. You think all boxes is contain gun ? No.

" 'There is not war in Guatemala. But work ? Yes. Good. T'irty dollar in the month. You shall shoulder one pickaxe, señor, and dig for the liberty and prosperity of Guatemala. Off to your work. The guard waits for you.'

" 'Little, fat poodle dog of a brown man,' says I, quiet, but full of indignations and discomforts, ' things shall happen to you. Maybe not right away, but as soon as J. Clancy can formulate somethin' in the way of repartee.'

" The boss of the gang orders us to work. I tramps off with the Dagoes, and I hears the distinguished patriot and kidnapper laughin' hearty as we go.

" 'Tis a sorrowful fact, for eight weeks I built railroads for that misbehavin' country. I filibustered twelve hours a day with a heavy pick and a spade, choppin' away the luxurious landscape that grew upon the right of way. We worked in swamps that smelled like there was a leak in the gas mains, trampin' down a fine assortment of the most expensive hot-house plants and vegetables. The scene was tropical beyond the wildest imagination of the geography man. The trees was all sky-scrapers; the under-brush was full of needles and pins; there was monkeys jumpin' around and crocodiles and pink-tailed mockin'-birds, and ye stood knee-deep in the rotten water and grabbed roots for the liberation of Guatemala. Of nights we would build smudges in camp to discourage the mosquitoes, and sit in the smoke, with the guards pacin' all around us. There was two hundred men workin' on the road—mostly Dagoes, nigger-men, Spanish-men and Swedes. Three or four were Irish. ..

" One old man named Halloran—a man of Hibernian entitlements and discretions, explained it to me. He had been workin' on the road a year. Most of them died in less than six months. He was dried up to gristle and bone and shook with chills every third night.

"'When you first come,' says he, ' ye think ye'll leave right away. But they hold out your first month's pay for your passage over, and by that time the tropics has its grip on ye. Ye're surrounded by a ragin' forest full of disreputable beasts—lions and baboons and anacondas—waitin' to devour ye. The sun strikes ye hard, and melts the marrow in your bones. Ye get similar to the lettuce-eaters the poetry-book speaks about. Ye forget the elevated sintiments of life, such as patriotism, revenge, disturbances of the peace and the dacint love of a clane shirt. Ye do your work, and ye swallow the kerosene ile and rubber pipestems dished up to ye by the Dago cook for food. Ye light your pipeful, and say to yoursilf, " Next week I'll break away," and ye go to sleep and call yersilf a liar, for ye know ye'll never do it.'

"'Who is this general man,' asks I, ' that calls himself De Vega ?'

"' 'Tis the man,' says Halloran, ' who is tryin' to complete the finishin' of the railroad. 'Twas the project of a private corporation, but it was busted, and then the government took it up. De Vegy is a big politician, and wants to be president. The people want the railroad completed, as they're taxed mighty on account of it. The De Vegy man is pushin' it along as a campaign move.'

"' 'Tis not my way,' says I, ' to make threats against any man, but there's an account to be settled between the railroad man and James O'Dowd Clancy.'

"' 'Twas that way I thought, mesilf, at first,' Halloran says, with a big sigh, ' until I got to be a lettuce-eater. The fault's wid these tropics. They rejuices a man's system. 'Tis a land, as the poet says, " Where it always seems to be after dinner." I does me work and smokes me pipe and sleeps. There's little else in life, anyway. Ye'll get that way yersilf, mighty soon. Don't be harborin' any sintiments at all, Clancy.'

"' I can't help it,' says I; ' I'm full of 'em. I enlisted in the revolutionary army of this dark country in good faith to fight for its liberty, honors and silver candlesticks; instead of which I am set to amputatin' its scenery and grubbin' its roots. 'Tis the general man will have to pay for it.'

" Two months I worked on that railroad before I found a chance to get away. One day a gang of us was sent back to the end of the completed line to fetch some picks that had been sent down to Port Barrios to be sharpened. They were brought on a hand-car, and I noticed, when I started away, that the car was left there on the track.

"That night, about twelve, I woke up Halloran and told him my scheme.

"'Run away?' says Halloran. 'Good Lord, Clancy, do ye mean it? Why, I ain't got the nerve. It's too chilly, and I ain't slept enough. Run away? I told you, Clancy, I've eat the lettuce. I've lost my grip. 'Tis the tropics that's done it. 'Tis like the poet says: "Forgotten are our friends that we have left behind; in the hollow lettuce-land we will live and lay reclined." You better go on, Clancy, I'll stay, I guess. It's too early and cold, and I'm sleepy.'

"So I had to leave Halloran. I dressed quiet, and slipped out of the tent we were in. When the guard came along I knocked him over, like a ninepin, with a green cocoanut I had, and made for the railroad. I got on that hand-car and made it fly. 'Twas yet a while before daybreak when I saw the lights of Port Barrios about a mile away. I stopped the hand-car there and walked to the town. I stepped inside the corporations of that town with care and hesitations. I was not afraid of the army of Guatemala, but me soul quaked at the prospect of a hand-to-hand struggle with its employment bureau. 'Tis a country that hires its help easy and keeps 'em long. Sure I can fancy Missis America and Missis Guatemala passin' a bit of gossip some fine, still night across the mountains. 'Oh, dear,' says Missis America, 'and it's a lot of trouble I'm havin' ag'in with the help, señora, ma'am.' 'Laws, now!' says Missis Guatemala, 'you don't say so, ma'am! Now, mine never think of leavin' me—te-he! ma'am,' snickers Missis Guatemala.

"I was wonderin' how I was goin' to move away from them tropics without bein' hired again. Dark as it was, I could see a steamer ridin' in the harbor, with smoke emergin' from her stacks. I turned down a little grass street that run down to the water. On the beach I found a little brown nigger-man just about to shove off in a skiff.

"'Hold on, Sambo,' says I, 'savve English?'

"'Heap plenty, yes,' says he, with a pleasant grin.

"'What steamer is that?' I asks him, 'and where is it going? And what's the news, and the good word and the time of day?'

"'That steamer the Conchita,' said the little brown man, affable and easy, rollin' a cigarette. 'Him come from New Orleans for load banana. Him got load last night. I think him sail in one, two hour. Verree nice day we shall be goin' to have. You hear some talkee 'bout big battle, maybe so ? You think catchee General De Vega, señor ? Yes ? No ? '

" 'How's that, Sambo ? ' says I. ' Big battle ? What battle ? Who wants catchee General De Vega ? I've been up at my old gold mines in the interior for a couple of months, and haven't heard any news.'

" 'Oh,' says the nigger-man, proud to speak the English, ' verree great revolution in Guatemala one week ago. General De Vega, him try be president. Him raise armee—one—five—ten thousand mans for fight at the government. Those one government send five—forty—hundred thousand soldiers to suppress revolution. They fight big battle yesterday at Lomagrande—that about nineteen or fifty mile in the mountain. That government soldier wheep General De Vega—oh, most bad. Five hundred—nine hundred—two thousand of his mans is kill, That revolution is smash suppress —bust—very quick. General De Viga, him r-r-run away fast on one big mule. Yes, *carrambos !* The general, him r-r-run away, and his armee is kill. That government soldier, they try to find General De Vega verree much. They want catchee him for shoot. You think they catchee that general, señor ? '

" 'Saints grant it ! ' says I. ' 'Twould be the judgment of Providence for settin' the warlike talent of a Clancy to gradin' the tropics with a pick and shovel. But 'tis so much a question of insurrections now, me little man, as 'tis of the hired-man problem. 'Tis anxious I am to resign a situation of responsibility and trust with the white wings department of your great and degraded country. Row me in your little boat out to that steamer, and I'll give ye five dollars—sinker pacers—sinker pacers,' says I, reducin' the offer to the language and denomination of the tropic dialects.

" '*Cinco pesos,* repeats the little man. ' Five dollee, you give ? '

" 'Twas not such a bad little man. He had hesitations at first, sayin' that passengers leavin' the country had to have papers and passports, but at last he took me out alongside the steamer.

" Day was just breakin' as we struck her, and there wasn't a soul to be seen on board. The water was very still, and the nigger-man gave me a lift from the boat, and I climbed onto the steamer where her side was sliced to the deck for loadin' fruit. The hatches was open, and I looked down and saw the cargo of bananas that filled the hold to within six feet of the top. I thinks to myself, ' Clancy, you better go as a stowaway. It's safer. The steamer men might hand you back to the employment bureau. The tropic'll get you, Clancy, if you don't watch out.'

" So I jumps down easy among the bananas and digs out a hole to hide in among the bunches. In an hour or so I could hear the engines goin', and feel the steamer rockin', and I knew we were off to sea. They left the hatches open for ventilation, and pretty soon it was light enough in the hold to see fairly well. I got feelin' a bit hungry, and thought I'd have a light fruit lunch, by way of refreshment. I creeped out of the hole I'd made and stood up straight. Just then I saw another man crawl up about ten feet away and reach out and skin a banana and stuff it into his mouth. 'Twas a dirty man, black-faced and ragged and disgraceful of aspect. Yes, the man was a ringer for the pictures of the fat Weary Willie in the funny papers. I looked again, and saw it was my general man—De Vega, the great revolutionist, mule-rider and pick-axe importer. When he saw me the general hesitated with his mouth filled with banana and his eyes the size of cocoanuts.

" 'Hist !' I says. ' Not a word, or they'll put us off and make us walk. " Veev la Liberty !" ' I adds, copperin' the sentiment by shovin' a banana into the source of it. I was certain the general wouldn't recognize me. The nefarious work of the tropics had left me lookin' different. There was half an inch of roan whiskers coverin' me face, and me costume was a pair of blue overalls and a red shirt.

" 'How you come in the ship, señor ? ' asked the general as soon as he could speak.

" 'By the back door—whist ! ' says I. ' 'Twas a glorious blow for liberty we struck,' I continues; ' but we was overpowered by numbers. Let us accept our defeat like brave men and eat another banana.'

" 'Were you in the cause of liberty fightin', señor ? ' says the general, sheddin' tears on the cargo.

" 'To the last,' says I. ' 'Twas I led the last desperate charge against the minions of the tyrant. But it made them mad, and we was forced to retreat. 'Twas I, general, procured the mule upon which you escaped. Could you give that ripe bunch a little boost this way, general ? It's a bit out of my reach. Thanks.'

" 'Say you so, brave patriot ? ' said the general, again weepin'. 'Ah, *Dios !* And I have not the means to reward your devotion. Barely did I my life bring away. *Carrambos !* what a devil's animal was that mule, señor ! Like ships in one storm was I dashed about. The skin on myself was ripped away with the thorns and vines. Upon the bark of a hundred trees did that beast of the infernal bump, and cause outrage to the legs of mine. In the night to Port Barrios I came. I dispossess myself of that mountains of mule and hasten along the water shore. I find a little boat to be tied. I launch myself and row to the steamer. I cannot see any mans on board, so I climbed one rope which hang at the side. I then myself hide in the bananas. Surely, I say, if the ship captains view me, they shall throw me again to those Guatemala. Those things are not good. Guatemala will shoot General De Vega. Therefore, I am hide and remain silent. Life itself is glorious. Liberty, it is pretty good; but so good as life I do not think.'

"Three days, as I said, was the trip to New Orleans. The general man and me got to be cronies of the deepest dye. Bananas we ate until they were distasteful to the sight and an eyesore to the palate, but to bananas alone was the bill of fare reduced. At night I crawls out, careful, on the lower deck, and gets a bucket of fresh water.

"That General De Vega was a man inhabited by an engorgement of words and sentences. He added to the monotony of the voyage by divestin' himself of conversation. He believed I was a revolutionist of his own party, there bein', as he told me, a good many Americans and other foreigners in its ranks. 'Twas a braggart and a conceited little gabbler it was, though he considered himself a hero. 'Twas on himself he wasted all his regrets at the failin' of his plot. Not a word did the little balloon have to say about the other misbehavin' idiots that had been shot, or run themselves to death in his revolution.

"The second day out he was feelin' pretty braggy and uppish for a stowed-away conspirator that owed his existence to a mule and stolen bananas. He was tellin' me about the great railroad he had been buildin', and he relates what he calls a comic incident about a fool Irishman he inveigled from New Orleans to sling a pick on his little morgue of a narrow-guage line. 'Twas sorrowful to hear the little, dirty general tell the opprobrious story of how he put salt upon the tail of that reckless and silly bird, Clancy. Laugh, he did, hearty and long. He shook with laughin', the black-faced rebel and outcast, standin' neck-deep in bananas, without friends or country.

"'Ah, señor,' he snickers, ' to the death you would have laughed at that drollest Irish. I say to him : " Strong, big mans is need very much in Guatemala." " I will blows strike for your down-pressed country," he say. " That shall you do," I tell him. Ah ! it was an Irish so comic. He sees one box break upon the wharf that contain for the guard a few gun. He think there is gun in all the box. But that is all pick-axe. Yes. Ah ! señor, could you the face of that Irish have seen when they set him to the work ! '

"'Twas thus the ex-boss of the employment bureau contributed to the tedium of the trip with merry jests and anecdote. But now and then he would weep upon the bananas and make oration about the lost cause of liberty and the mule.

"'Twas a pleasant sound when the steamer bumped againt the pier in New Orleans. Pretty soon we heard the pat-a-pat of hundreds of bare feet, and the Dago gang that unloads the fruit jumped on the deck and down into the hold. Me and the general worked a while at passin' up the bunches, and they thought we were part of the gang. After about an hour we managed to slip off the steamer onto the wharf.

" 'Twas a great honor on the hands of an obscure Clancy, havin' the entertainment of the representative of a great foreign filibusterin' power. I first bought for the general and myself many long drinks and things to eat that were not bananas. The general man trotted along at my side, leavin' all the arrangements to me. I led him up to Lafayette Square and set him on a bench in the little park. Cigarettes I had bought for him, and he humped himself down on the seat like a little fat, contented hobo. I look him over as he sets there, and what I see pleases me. Brown by nature and instinct, he is now brindled with dirt and dust. Praise to the mule, his clothes is mostly strings and flaps. Yes, the looks of the general man is agreeable to Clancy.

" I ask him, delicate, if, by any chance, he brought away anybody's money with him from Guatemala. He sighs and bumps his shoulders against the bench. Not a cent. All right. Maybe, he tells me, some of his friends in the tropic outfit will send him funds later. The general was as clear a case of no visible means as I ever saw.

" I told him not to move from the bench, and then I went up to the corner of Poydras and Carondelet. Along there is O'Hara's beat. In five minutes along comes O'Hara, a big, fine man, red-faced, with shinin' buttons, swingin' his club. 'Twould be a fine thing for Guatemala to move into O'Hara's precinct. 'Twould be a fine bit of recreation for Danny to suppress revolutions and uprisin's once or twice a week with his club.

" 'Is 5046 workin' yet Danny ? ' says I, walkin' up to him.

" 'Overtime,' says O'Hara, lookin' over me suspicious. ' Want some of it ? '

" Fifty-forty-six is the celebrated city ordinance authorizin' arrest, conviction, and imprisonment of persons that succeed in concealin' their crimes from the police.

" 'Don't ye know Jimmy Clancy ? ' says I. ' Ye pink-gilled monster.' So, when O'Hara recognized me beneath the scandalous exterior bestowed upon me by the tropics, I backed him into a doorway and told him what I wanted, and why I wanted it. 'All right, Jimmy,' says O'Hara. ' Go back and hold the bench. I'll be along in ten minutes.'

" In that time O'Hara strolled through Lafayette Square and spied two Weary Willies disgracin' one of the benches. In ten minutes more J. Clancy and General De Vega, late candidate for the presidency of Guatemala, was in the station house. The general is badly frightened, and calls upon me to proclaim his distinguish-ments and rank.

" 'The man,' says I to the police, 'used to be a railroad man. He's on the bum now. 'Tis a little bughouse he is, on account of losin' his job.'

" '*Carrambos!* ' says the general, fizzin' like a little soda-water fountain, ' you fought, señor, with my forces in my native country. Why do you say the lies? You shall say I am the General De Vega, one soldier, one *caballero*——'

" 'Railroader,' says I again. ' On the hog. No good. Been livin' for three days on stolen bananas. Look at him. Ain't that enough ?'

" Twenty-five dollars or sixty days, was what the recorder gave the general. He didn't have a cent, so he took the time. They let me go, as I knew they would, for I had money to show, and O'Hara spoke for me. Yes; sixty days he got. 'Twas just so long that I slung a pick for the great country of Kam—Guatemala."

Clancy paused. The bright starlight showed a reminiscent look of happy content on his seasoned features. Keogh leaned in his chair and gave his partner a slap on his thinly-clad back that sounded like the crack of the surf on the sands.

" Tell 'em, you divil," he chuckled, " how you got even with the tropical general in the way of agricultural maneuvrings."

" Havin' no money," concluded Clancy, with unction, "they set him to work his fine out with a gang from the parish prison clearing Ursulines Street. Around the corner was a saloon deco-rated genially with electric fans and cool merchandise. I made that me headquarters, and every fifteen minutes I'd walk around and take a look at the little man filibusterin' with a rake and shovel. 'Twas just such a hot broth of a day as this has been. And I'd call at him ' Hey, monseer ! ' and he'd look at me black, with the damp showin' through his shirt in places.

" 'Fat, strong mans,' says I to General De Vega, ' is needed in New Orleans. Yes. To carry on the good work. Carrambos ! Erin go bragh ! ' "

Breakfast in Coralio was at eleven. Therefore the people did not go to market early. The little wooden market-house stood on a patch of short-trimmed grass, under the vivid green foliage of a bread-fruit tree.

Thither one morning the venders leisurely convened, bringing their wares with them. A porch or platform six feet wide encircled the building, shaded from the mid-morning sun by the projecting, grass-thatched roof. Upon this platform the venders were wont to display their goods—newly-killed beef, fish, crabs, fruit of the country, cassava, eggs, *dulces* and high, tottering stacks of native tortillas as large around as the sombrero of a Spanish grandee.

But on this morning they whose stations lay on the seaward side of the market-house, instead of spreading their merchandise formed themselves into a softly jabbering and gesticulating group. For there upon their space of the platform was sprawled, asleep, the unbeautiful figure of " Beelzebub " Blythe. He lay upon a ragged strip of cocoa matting, more than ever a fallen angel in appearance. His suit of coarse flax, soiled, bursting at the seams, crumpled into a thousand diversified wrinkles and creases, inclosed him absurdly, like the garb of some effigy that had been stuffed in sport and thrown there after indignity had been wrought upon it. But firmly upon the high bridge of his nose reposed his gold-rimmed glasses, the surviving badge of his ancient glory.

The sun's rays, reflecting quiveringly from the rippling sea upon his face, and the voices of the marketmen woke " Beelzebub " Blythe. He sat up, blinking, and leaned his back against the wall of the market. Drawing a blighted silk handkerchief from his pocket, he assiduously rubbed and burnished his glasses. And while doing this he became aware that his bedroom had been invaded, and that polite brown and yellow men were beseeching him to vacate in favor of their market stuff.

If the señor would have the goodness—a thousand pardons for bringing to him molestation—but soon would come the *compradores* for the day's provisions—surely they had ten thousand regrets at disturbing him !

In this manner they expanded to him the intimation that he must clear out and cease to clog the wheels of trade.

Blythe stepped from the platform with the air of a prince leaving his canopied couch. He never quite lost that air, even at the lowest point of his fall. It is clear that the college of good breeding does not necessarily maintain a chair of morals within its walls.

Blythe shook out his wry clothing, and moved slowly up the Calle Grande through the hot sand. He moved without a destination in his mind. The little town was languidly stirring to its daily life. Golden-skinned babies tumbled over one another in the grass. The sea breeze brought him appetite, but nothing to satisfy it. Throughout Coralio were its morning odors—those from the heavily fragrant tropical flowers and from the bread baking in the outdoor ovens of clay and the pervading smoke of their fires. Where the smoke cleared, the crystal air, with some of the efficacy of faith, seemed to remove the mountains almost to the sea, bringing them so near that one might count the scarred glades on their wooded sides. The light-footed Caribs were swiftly gliding to their tasks at the waterside. Already along the bosky trails from the banana groves files of horses were slowly moving, concealed, except for their nodding heads and plodding legs, by the bunches of green-golden fruit heaped upon their backs. On doorsills sat women combing their long, black hair and calling, one to another, across the narrow thoroughfares. Peace reigned in Coralio—arid and bald peace; but still peace.

On that bright morning when Nature seemed to be offering the lotus on the Dawn's golden platter " Beelzebub " Blythe had reached rock bottom. Further descent seemed impossible. That last night's slumber in a public place had done for him. As long as he had had a roof to cover him there had remained, unbridged, the space that separates a gentleman from the beasts of the jungle and the fowls of the air. But now he was little more than a whimpering oyster led to be devoured on the sands of a Southern sea by the artful walrus, Circumstance, and the implacable carpenter, Fate.

To Blythe money was now but a memory. He had drained his friends of all that their good-fellowship had to offer; then he had squeezed them to the last drop of their generosity; and at the last, Aaron-like, he had smitten the rock of their hardening bosoms for their scattering, ignoble drops of Charity itself.

He had exhausted his credit to the last *real*. With the minute keenness of the shameless sponger he was aware of every source in Coralio from which a glass of rum, a meal, or a piece of silver could be wheedled. Marshalling each such source in his mind, he considered it with all the thoroughness and penetration that hunger and thirst lent him for the task. All his optimism failed to thresh a grain of hope from the chaff of his postulations. He had played out the game. That one night in the open had shaken his nerves. Until then there had been left to him at least a few grounds upon which he could base his unblushing demands upon his neighbors' stores. Now he must beg instead of borrowing. The most brazen sophistry could not dignify by the name of " loan " the coin contemptuously flung to a beach-comber who slept on the bare boards of the public market.

But on this morning no beggar would have more thankfully received a charitable coin, for the demon thirst had him by the throat—the drunkard's matutinal thirst that requires to be slaked at each morning station on the road to Tophet.

Blythe walked slowly up the street, keeping a watchful eye for any miracle that might drop manna upon him in his wilderness. As he passed the popular eating house of Madama Vasquez, Madama's boarders were just sitting down to freshly-baked bread, *aguacates,* pines and delicious coffee that sent forth odorous guarantee of its quality upon the breeze. Madama was serving; she turned her shy, stolid, melancholy gaze for a moment out the window; she saw Blythe, and her expression turned more shy and embarrassed. " Beelzebub " owed her twenty *pesos.* He bowed as he had once bowed to less embarrassed dames to whom he owed nothing, and passed on.

Merchants and their clerks were throwing open the solid wooden doors of their shops. Polite but cool were the glances they cast upon Blythe as he lounged tentatively by with the remains of his old jaunty air; for they were his creditors almost without exception.

At the little fountain in the *plaza* he made an apology for a toilet with his wetted handkerchief. Across the open square filed the dolorous line of friends of the prisoners in the *calaboza,* bearing the morning meal of the immured. The food in their hands aroused small longing in Blythe. It was drink that his soul craved, or money to buy it.

In the streets he met many with whom he had been friends and equals, and whose patience and liberality he had gradually exhausted. Willard Geddie and Paula cantered past him with the coolest of nods, returning from their daily horseback ride along the old Indian road. Keogh passed him at another corner, whistling cheerfully and bearing a prize of newly-laid eggs for the breakfast of himself and Clancy. The jovial scout of Fortune was one of Blythe's victims who had plunged his hand oftenest into his pocket to aid him. But now it seemed that Keogh, too, had fortified himself against further invasions. His curt greeting and the ominous light in his full gray eye quickened the steps of " Beelzebub," whom desperation had almost incited to attempt an additional " loan."

Three drinking shops the forlorn one next visited in succession. In all of these his money, his credit, and his welcome had long since been spent; but Blythe felt that he would have fawned in the dust at the feet of an enemy that morning for one draught of *aguardiente*. In two of the *pulperías* his courageous petition for drink was met with a refusal so polite that it stung worse than abuse. The third establishment had acquired something of American methods ; and here he was seized bodily and cast out upon his hands and knees.

This physical indignity caused a singular change in the man. As he picked himself up and walked away, an expression of absolute relief came upon his features. The specious and conciliatory smile that had been graven there was succeeded by a look of calm and sinister resolve. " Beelzebub " had been floundering in the sea of improbity, holding by a slender life-line to the respectable world that had cast him overboard. He must have felt that with this ultimate shock the line had snapped, and have experienced the welcome ease of the drowning swimmer who has ceased to struggle.

Blythe walked to the next corner and stood there while he brushed the sand from his garments and repolished his glasses.

" I've got to do it—oh, I've got to do it," he told himself, aloud. " If I had a quart of rum I believe I could stave it off yet—for a little while. But there's no more rum for—' Beelzebub,' as they call me. By the flames of Tartarus ! if I'm to sit at the right hand of Satan somebody has got to pay the court expenses. You'll have to pony up, Mr. Frank Goodwin. You're a good fellow; but a gentleman must draw the line at being kicked into the gutter. Blackmail isn't a pretty word, but it's the next station on the road I'm travelling."

With purpose in his steps Blythe now moved rapidly through the town by way of its landward environs. He passed through the squalid quarters of the improvident negroes and on beyond the picturesque shacks of the poorer *mestizos*. From many points along his course he could see, through the umbrageous glades, the house of Frank Goodwin on its wooded hill. And as he crossed the little bridge over the lagoon he saw the old Indian, Galvez, scrubbing at the wooden slab that bore the name of Miraflores. Beyond the lagoon the lands of Goodwin began to slope gently upward. A grassy road, shaded by a munificent and diverse array of tropical flora, wound from the edge of an outlying banana grove to the dwelling. Blythe took this road with long and purposeful strides.

Goodwin was seated on his coolest gallery, dictating letters to his secretary, a sallow and capable native youth. The household adhered to the American plan of breakfast; and that meal had been a thing of the past for the better part of an hour.

The castaway walked to the steps, and flourished a hand.

" Good morning, Blythe," said Goodwin, looking up. " Come in and have a chair. Anything I can do for you ? "

" I want to speak to you in private."

Goodwin nodded at his secretary, who strolled out under a mango tree and lit a cigarette. Blythe took the chair that he had left vacant.

" I want some money," he began, doggedly.

" I'm sorry," said Goodwin, with equal directness, " but you can't have any. You're drinking yourself to death, Blythe. Your friends have done all they could to help you to brace up. You won't help yourself. There's no use furnishing you with money to ruin yourself with any longer."

" Dear man," said Blythe, tilting back his chair, " it isn't a question of social economy now. It's past that. I like you, Goodwin; and I've come to stick a knife between your ribs. I was kicked out of Espada's saloon this morning; and Society owes me reparation for my wounded feelings."

" I didn't kick you out."

" No; but in a general way you represent Society; and in a particular way you represent my last chance. I've had to come down to it, old man—I tried to do it a month ago when Losada's man was here turning things over; but I couldn't do it then. Now it's different. I want a thousand dollars, Goodwin; and you have to give it to me."

" Only last week," said Goodwin, with a smile, " a silver dollar was all you were asking for."

"An evidence," said Blythe, flippantly, " that I was still virtuous —though under heavy pressure. The wages of sin should be something higher than a *peso* worth forty-eight cents. Let's talk business. I am the villain in the third act; and I must have my merited, if only temporary, triumph. I saw you collar the late president's valiseful of boodle. Oh, I know it's blackmail; but I'm liberal about the price. I know I'm a cheap villain—one of the regular sawmill-drama kind—but you're one of my particular friends, and I don't want to stick you hard."

" Suppose you go into details," suggested Goodwin, calmly arranging his letters on the table.

"All right," said " Beelzebub." " I like the way you take it. I despise histrionics; so you will please prepare yourself for the facts without any red fire, calcium or grace notes on the saxophone.

" On the night that His Fly-by-night Excellency arrived in town I was very drunk. You will excuse the pride with which I state that fact; but it was quite a feat for me to attain that desirable state. Somebody had left a cot out under the orange trees in the yard of Madama Ortiz's hotel. I stepped over the wall, laid down upon it, and fell asleep. I was awakened by an orange that dropped from the tree upon my nose; and I laid there for awhile cursing

Sir Isaac Newton, or whoever it was that invented gravitation, for not confining his theory to apples.

"And then along came Mr. Miraflores and his true-love with the treasury in a valise, and went into the hotel. Next you hove in sight, and held a pow-wow with the tonsorial artist who insisted upon talking shop after hours. I tried to slumber again; but once more my rest was disturbed—this time by the noise of the popgun that went off upstairs. Then that valise came crashing down into an orange tree just above my head; and I arose from my couch, not knowing when it might begin to rain Saratoga trunks. When the army and the constabulary began to arrive, with their medals and decorations hastily pinned to their pajamas, and their snicker-snees drawn, I crawled into the welcome shadow of a banana plant. I remained there for an hour, by which time the excitement and the people had cleared away. And then, my dear Goodwin—excuse me—I saw you sneak back and pluck that ripe and juicy valise from the orange tree. I followed you, and saw you take it to your own house. A hundred-thousand-dollar crop from one orange tree in a season about breaks the record of the fruit-growing industry.

" Being a gentleman at that time, of course, I never mentioned the incident to any one. But this morning I was kicked out of a saloon, my code of honor is all out at the elbows, and I'd sell my mother's prayer-book for three fingers of *aguardiente.* I'm not putting on the screws hard. It ought to be worth a thousand to you for me to have slept on that cot through the whole business without waking up and seeing anything."

Goodwin opened two more letters, and made memoranda in pencil on them. Then he called " Manuel ! " to his secretary, who came, spryly.

" The *Ariel*—when does she sail ? " asked Goodwin.

" Señor," answered the youth, " at three this afternoon. She drops down-coast to Punta Soledad to complete her cargo of fruit. From there she sails for New Orleans without delay."

" *Bueno !* " said Goodwin. " These letters may wait yet awhile."

The secretary returned to his cigarette under the mango tree.

" In round numbers," said Goodwin, facing Blythe squarely, " how much money do you owe in this town, not including the sums you have ' borrowed ' from me ? "

" Five hundred—at a rough guess," answered Blythe, lightly.

" Go somewhere in the town and draw up a schedule of your debts," said Goodwin. " Come back here in two hours, and I will send Manuel with the money to pay them. I will also have a decent outfit of clothing ready for you. You will sail on the *Ariel* at three. Manuel will accompany you as far as the deck of the steamer. There he will hand you one thousand dollars in cash. I suppose that we needn't discuss what you will be expected to do in return."

"Oh, I understand," piped Blythe, cheerily. "I was asleep all the time on the cot under Madama Ortiz's orange trees; and I shake off the dust of Coralio forever. I'll play fair. No more of the lotus for me. Your proposition is O.K. You're a good fellow, Goodwin; and I let you off light. I'll agree to everything. But in the meantime—I've a devil of a thirst on, old man——"

"Not a *centavo*," said Goodwin, firmly, "until you are on board the *Ariel*. You would be drunk in thirty minutes if you had money now."

But he noticed the blood-streaked eyeballs, the relaxed form, and the shaking hands of "Beelzebub"; and he stepped into the dining room through the low window, and brought out a glass and a decanter of brandy.

"Take a bracer, anyway, before you go," he proposed, even as a man to the friend whom he entertains.

"Beelzebub" Blythe's eyes glistened at the sight of the solace for which his soul burned. To-day for the first time his poisoned nerves had been denied their steadying dose; and their retort was a mounting torment. He grasped the decanter and rattled its crystal mouth against the glass in his trembling hand. He flushed the glass, and then stood erect, holding it aloft for an instant. For one fleeting moment he held his head above the drowning waves of his abyss. He nodded easily at Goodwin, raised his brimming glass and murmered a "health" that men had used in his ancient Paradise Lost. And then so suddenly that he spilled the brandy over his hand, he set down his glass, untasted.

"In two hours," his dry lips muttered to Goodwin, as he marched down the steps and turned his face toward the town.

In the edge of the cool banana grove "Beelzebub" halted, and snapped the tongue of his belt buckle into another hole.

"I couldn't do it," he explained, feverishly, to the waving banana fronds. "I wanted to, but I couldn't. A gentleman can't drink with the man that he blackmails."

SHOES

JOHN DE GRAFFENREID ATWOOD ate of the lotus, root, stem, and flower. The tropics gobbled him up. He plunged enthusiastically into his work, which was to try to forget Rosine.

Now, they who dine on the lotus rarely consume it plain. There is a sauce *au diable* that goes with it; and the distillers are the chefs who prepare it. And on Johnny's menu card it read " brandy." With a bottle between them, he and Billy Keogh would sit on the porch of the little consulate at night and roar out great, indecorous songs, until the natives, slipping hastily past, would shrug a shoulder and mutter things to themselves about the "*Americanos diablos*."

One day Johnny's *mozo* brought the mail and dumped it on the table. Johnny leaned from his hammock, and fingered the four or five letters dejectedly. Keogh was sitting on the edge of the table chopping lazily with a paper knife at the legs of a centipede that was crawling among the stationery. Johnny was in that phase of lotus-eating when all the world tastes bitter in one's mouth.

" Same old thing ! " he complained. " Fool people writing for information about the country. They want to know all about raising fruit, and how to make a fortune without work. Half of 'em don't even send stamps for a reply. They think a consul hasn't anything to do but write letters. Slit those envelopes for me, old man, and see what they want. I'm feeling too rocky to move."

Keogh, acclimated beyond all possibility of ill-humor, drew his chair to the table with smiling compliance on his rose-pink countenance, and began to slit open the letters. Four of them were from citizens in various parts of the United States who seemed to regard the consul at Coralio as a cyclopædia of information. They asked long lists of questions, numerically arranged, about the climate, products, possibilities, laws, business chances, and statistics of the country in which the consul had the honor of representing his own government.

" Write 'em, please, Billy," said that inert official, " just a line, referring them to the latest consular report. Tell 'em the State Department will be delighted to furnish the literary gems. Sign my name. Don't let your pen scratch, Billy ; it'll keep me awake."

" Don't snore," said Keogh, amiably, " and I'll do your work for you. You need a corps of assistants, anyhow. Don't see how you ever get out a report. Wake up a minute !—here's one more letter—it's from your own town, too—Dalesburg."

" That so ? " murmured Johnny, showing a mild obligatory interest. " What's it about ? "

" Postmaster writes," explained Keogh. " Says a citizen of the town wants some facts and advice from you. Says the citizen has an idea in his head of coming down where you are and opening a shoe store. Wants to know if you think the business would pay. Says he's heard of the boom along this coast, and wants to get in on the ground floor."

In spite of the heat and his bad temper, Johnny's hammock swayed with his laughter. Keogh laughed too; and the pet monkey on the top shelf of the bookcase chattered in shrill sympathy with the ironical reception of the letter from Dalesburg.

" Great bunions ! " exclaimed the consul. " Shoe store ! What'll they ask about next, I wonder ? Overcoat factory, I reckon. Say, Billy—of our 3,000 citizens, how many do you suppose ever had on a pair of shoes ? "

Keogh reflected judicially.

" Let's see—there's you and me and——"

" Not me," said Johnny, promptly and incorrectly, holding up a foot encased in a disreputable deerskin *zapato*. " I haven't been a victim to shoes in months."

" But you've got 'em, though," went on Keogh. "And there's Goodwin and Blanchard and Geddie and old Lutz and Doc Gregg and that Italian that's agent for the banana company, and there's old Delgado—no; he wears sandals. And, oh, yes; there's Madama Ortiz, ' what kapes the hotel' —she had on a pair of red slippers at the *baile* the other night. And Miss Pasa, her daughter, that went to school in the States—she brought back some civilized notions in the way of footgear. And there's the *comandante's* sister that dresses up her feet on feastdays—and Mrs. Geddie, who wears a two with a Castilian instep—and that's about all the ladies. Let's see—don't some of the soldiers at the *cuartel*—no : that's so; they're allowed shoes only when on the march. In barracks they turn their little toeses out to grass."

" 'Bout right," agreed the consul. " Not over twenty out of the three thousand ever felt leather on their walking arrangements. Oh, yes; Coralio is just the town for an enterprising shoe store— that doesn't want to part with its goods. Wonder if old Patterson is trying to jolly me ! He always was full of things he called jokes. Write him a letter, Billy. I'll dictate it. We'll jolly him back a few."

Keogh dipped his pen, and wrote at Johnny's dictation. With many pauses, filled in with smoke and sundry travellings of the bottle and glasses, the following reply to the Dalesburg communication was perpetrated :

Mr. Obadiah Patterson,
> Dalesburg, Ala.

Dear Sir: In reply to your favor of July 2d, I have the honor to inform you that, according to my opinion, there is no place on the habitable globe that presents to the eye stronger evidence of the need of a first-class shoe store than does the town of Coralio. There are 3,000 inhabitants in the place, and not a single shoe store ! The situation speaks for itself. This coast is rapidly becoming the goal of enterprising business men, but the shoe business is one that has been sadly overlooked or neglected. In fact, there are a considerable number of our citizens actually without shoes at present.

Besides the want above mentioned, there is also a crying need for a brewery, a college of higher mathematics, a coal yard, and a clean and intellectual Punch and Judy show. I have the honor to be, sir,

Your Obt. Servant,

John de Graffenreid Atwood,

U.S. Consul at Coralio.

P. S.—Hello ! Uncle Obadiah. How's the old burg racking along ? What would the government do without you and me ? Look out for a green-headed parrot and a bunch of bananas soon, from your old friend

Johnny.

" I throw in that postscript," explained the consul, " so Uncle Obadiah won't take offence at the official tone of the letter ! Now, Billy, you get that correspondence fixed up, and send Pancho to the post-office with it. The *Ariadne* takes the mail out to-morrow if they make up that load of fruit to-day."

The night programme in Coralio never varied. The recreations of the people were soporific and flat. They wandered about, barefoot and aimless, speaking lowly and smoking cigar or cigarette. Looking down on the dimly lighted ways one seemed to see a threading maze of brunette ghosts tangled with a procession of insane fire-flies.

In some houses the thrumming of lugubrious guitars added to the depression of the *triste* night. Giant tree-frogs rattled in the foliage as loudly as the end man's " bones " in a minstrel troupe. By nine o'clock the streets were almost deserted.

Not at the consulate was there often a change of bill. Keogh would come there nightly, for Coralio's one cool place with the little seaward porch of that official residence.

The brandy would be kept moving; and before midnight sentiment would begin to stir in the heart of the self-exiled consul.

Then he would relate to Keogh the story of his ended romance. Each night Keogh would listen patiently to the tale, and be ready with untiring sympathy.

"But don't you think for a minute "—thus Johnny would always conclude his woeful narrative—" that I'm grieving about that girl, Billy. I've forgotten her. She never enters my mind. If she were to enter that door right now, my pulse wouldn't gain a beat. That's all over long ago."

"Don't I know it?" Keogh would answer. "Of course you've forgotten her. Proper thing to do. Wasn't quite O. K. of her to listen to the knocks that—er—Dink Pawson kept giving you."

"Pink Dawson!"—a world of contempt would be in Johnny's tones—"Poor white trash! That's what he was. Had five hundred acres of farming land, though; and that counted. Maybe I'll have a chance to get back at him some day. The Dawsons weren't anybody. Everybody in Alabama knows the Atwoods. Say, Billy—did you know my mother was a De Graffenreid?"

"Why, no," Keogh would say; "is that so?" He had heard it some three hundred times.

"Fact. The De Graffenreids of Hancock County. But I never think of that girl any more, do I, Billy?"

"Not for a minute, my boy," would be the last sounds heard by the conqueror of Cupid.

At this point Johnny would fall into a gentle slumber, and Keogh would saunter out to his own shack under the calabash tree at the edge of the plaza.

In a day or two the letter from the Dalesburg postmaster and its answer had been forgotten by the Coralio exiles. But on the 26th day of July the fruit of the reply appeared upon the tree of events.

The *Andador*, a fruit steamer that visited Coralio regularly, drew into the offing and anchored. The beach was lined with spectators while the quarantine doctor and the custom-house crew rowed out to attend to their duties.

An hour later Billy Keogh lounged into the consulate, clean and cool in his linen clothes, and grinning like a pleased shark.

"Guess what?" he said to Johnny, lounging in his hammock.

"Too hot to guess," said Johnny, lazily.

"Your shoe-store man's come," said Keogh, rolling the sweet morsel on his tongue, "with a stock of goods big enough to supply the continent as far down as Terra del Fuego. They're carting his cases over to the custom-house now. Six barges full they brought ashore and have paddled back for the rest. Oh, ye saints in glory! won't there be regalements in the air when he gets onto the joke

and has an interview with Mr. Consul ? It'll be worth nine years
in the tropics just to witness that one joyful moment."

Keogh loved to take his mirth easily. He selected a clean place
on the matting and lay upon the floor. The walls shook with his
enjoyment. Johnny turned half over and blinked.

"Don't tell me," he said, "that anybody was fool enough to
take that letter seriously."

"Four-thousand-dollar stock of goods ! " gasped Keogh, in
ecstasy. "Talk about coals to Newcastle ! Why didn't he take a
ship-load of palm-leaf fans to Spitzbergen while he was about it ?
Saw the old codger on the beach. You ought to have been there
when he put on his specs and squinted at the five hundred or so
barefooted citizens standing around."

"Are you telling the truth, Billy ? " asked the consul, weakly.

"Am I ? You ought to see the buncoed gentleman's daughter
he brought along. Looks ! She makes the brick-dust señoritas
here look like tar-babies."

"Go on," said Johnny, "if you can stop that asinine giggling.
I hate to see a grown man make a laughing hyena of himself."

"Name is Hemstetter," went on Keogh. "He's a—— Hello !
what's the matter now ? "

Johnny's moccasined feet struck the floor with a thud as he
wriggled out of his hammock.

"Get up, you idiot," he said, sternly, "or I'll brain you with
this inkstand. That's Rosine and her father. Gad ! what a drivelling idiot old Patterson is ! Get up, here, Billy Keogh, and help
me. What the devil are we going to do ? Has all the world gone
crazy ? "

Keogh rose and dusted himself. He manged to regain a decorous
demeanor.

"Situation has got to be met, Johnny," he said, with some
success at seriousness. "I didn't think about its being your girl
until you spoke. First thing to do is to get them comfortable
quarters. You go down and face the music, and I'll trot out to
Goodwin's and see if Mrs. Goodwin won't take them in. They've
got the decentest house in town."

"Bless you, Billy ! " said the consul. "I knew you wouldn't
desert me. The world's bound to come to an end, but maybe we
can stave it off for a day or two."

Keogh hoisted his umbrella and set out for Goodwin's house.
Johnny put on his coat and hat. He picked up the brandy bottle,
but set it down again without drinking, and marched bravely
down to the beach.

In the shade of the custom-house walls he found Mr. Hemstetter
and Rosine surrounded by a mass of gaping citizens. The customs

officers were ducking and scraping, while the captain of the *Andador* interpreted the business of the new arrivals. Rosine looked healthy and very much alive. She was gazing at the strange scenes around her with amused interest. There was a faint blush upon her round cheek as she greeted her old admirer. Mr. Hemstetter shook hands with Johnny in a very friendly way. He was an oldish, impractical man—one of that numerous class of erratic business men who are forever dissatisfied, and seeking a change.

" I am very glad to see you, John—may I call you John ? " he said. " Let me thank you for your prompt answer to our post-master's letter of inquiry. He volunteered to write to you on my behalf. I was looking about for something different in the way of a business in which the profits would be greater. I had noticed in the papers that this coast was receiving much attention from investors. I am extremely grateful for your advice to come. I sold out everything that I possess, and invested the proceeds in as fine a stock of shoes as could be bought in the North. You have a picturesque town here, John. I hope business will be as good as your letter justifies me in expecting."

Johnny's agony was abbreviated by the arrival of Keogh, who hurried up with the news that Mrs. Goodwin would be much pleased to place rooms at the disposal of Mr. Hemstetter and his daughter. So there Mr. Hemstetter and Rosine were at once conducted and left to recuperate from the fatigue of the voyage, while Johnny went down to see that the cases of shoes were safely in the customs warehouse pending their examination by the officials. Keogh, grinning like a shark, skirmished about to find Goodwin, to instruct him not to expose to Mr. Hemstetter the true state of Coralio as a shoe market until Johnny had been given a chance to redeem the situation, if such a thing were possible.

That night the consul and Keogh held a desperate consultation on the breezy porch of the consulate.

" Send 'em back home," began Keogh, reading Johnny's thoughts.

" I would," said Johnny, after a little silence; " but I've been lying to you, Billy."

"All right about that," said Keogh, affably.

" I've told you hundreds of times." said Johnny, slowly, " that I had forgotten that girl, haven't I ? "

"About three hundred and seventy-five," admitted the monument of patience.

" I lied," repeated the consul, " every time. I never forgot her for one minute. I was an obstinate ass for running away just because she said ' No ' once. And I was too proud a fool to go back. I talked with Rosine a few minutes this evening up at Goodwin's.

I found out one thing. You remember that farmer fellow who was always after her ? "

" Dink Pawson ? " asked Keogh.

" Pink Dawson. Well, he wasn't a hill of beans to her. She says she didn't believe a word of the things he told her about me. But I'm sewed up now, Billy. That tomfool letter we sent ruined whatever chance I had left. She'll despise me when she finds out that her old father has been made the victim of a joke that a decent school boy wouldn't have been guilty of. Shoes ! Why he couldn't sell twenty pairs of shoes in Coralio if he kept store here for twenty years. You put a pair of shoes on one of these Caribs or Spanish brown boys and what'd he do ? Stand on his head and squeal until he'd kicked 'em off. None of 'em ever wore shoes and they never will. If I send 'em back home I'll have to tell the whole story, and what'll she think of me ? I want that girl worse than ever, Billy, and now when she's in reach I've lost her forever because I tried to be funny when the thermometer was at 102."

" Keep cheerful," said the optimistic Keogh. "And let 'em open the store. I've been busy myself this afternoon. We can stir up a temporary boom in foot-gear anyhow. I'll buy six pairs when the doors open. I've been around and seen all the fellows and explained the catastrophe. They'll all buy shoes like they was centipedes. Frank Goodwin will take cases of 'em. The Geddes want about eleven pairs between 'em. Clancy is going to invest the savings of weeks, and even old Doc Gregg wants three pairs of alligator-hide slippers if they've got any tens. Blanchard got a look at Miss Hemstetter; and as he's a Frenchman, no less than a dozen pairs will do for him."

"A dozen customers," said Johnny, " for a $4,000 stock of shoes ! It won't work. There's a big problem here to figure out. You go home, Billy, and leave me alone. I've got to work at it all by myself. Take that bottle of Three-star along with you—no, sir; not another ounce of booze for the United States consul. I'll sit here to-night and pull out the think stop. If there's a soft place on this proposition anywhere I'll land on it. If there isn't there'll be another wreck to the credit of the gorgeous tropics."

Keogh left, feeling that he could be of no use. Johnny laid a handful of cigars on a table and stretched himself in a steamer chair. When the sudden daylight broke, silvering the harbor ripples, he was still sitting there. Then he got up, whistling a little tune, and took his bath.

At nine o'clock he walked down to the dingy little cable office and hung for half an hour over a blank. The result of his application was the following message, which he signed and had transmitted at a cost of $33 :

To PINKEY DAWSON,
    Dalesburg, Ala.

Draft for $100 comes to you next mail. Ship me immediately 500 pounds stiff, dry cockleburrs. New use here in arts. Market price twenty cents pound. Further orders likely. Rush.

SHIPS

WITHIN a week a suitable building had been secured in the Calle Grande, and Mr. Hemstetter's stock of shoes arranged upon their shelves. The rent of the store was moderate; and the stock made a fine showing of neat white boxes, attractively displayed.

Johnny's friends stood by him loyally. On the first day Keogh strolled into the store in a casual kind of way about once every hour, and bought shoes. After he had purchased a pair each of extension soles, congress gaiters, button kids, low-quartered calfs, dancing pumps, rubber boots, tans of various hues, tennis shoes and flowered slippers, he sought out Johnny to be prompted as to names of other kinds that he might inquire for. The other English-speaking residents also played their parts nobly by buying often and liberally. Keogh was grand marshal, and made them distribute their patronage, thus keeping up a fair run of customers for several days.

Mr. Hemstetter was gratified by the amount of business done thus far; but expressed surprise that the natives were so backward with their custom.

" Oh, they're awfully shy," explained Johnny, as he wiped his forehead nervously. " They'll get the habit pretty soon. They'll come with a rush when they do come."

One afternoon Keogh dropped into the consul's office, chewing an unlighted cigar thoughtfully.

" Got anything up your sleeve ? " he inquired of Johnny. " If you have it's about time to show it. If you can borrow some gent's hat in the audience, and make a lot of customers for an idle stock of shoes come out of it, you'd better spiel. The boys have all laid in enough foot-wear to last 'em ten years; and there's nothing doing in the shoe store but dolcy far nienty. I just came by there. Your venerable victim was standing in the door, gazing through his specs at the bare toes passing by his emporium. The natives here have got the true artistic temperament. Me and Clancy took eighteen tin-types this morning in two hours. There's been but one pair of shoes sold all day. Blanchard went in and bought a pair of fur-lined house-slippers because he thought he saw Miss Hemstetter go into the store. I saw him throw the slippers into the lagoon afterwards."

" There's a Mobile fruit steamer coming in to-morrow or next day," said Johnny. " We can't do anything until then."

" What are you going to do—try to create a demand ? "

" Political economy isn't your strong point," said the consul, impudently. " You can't create a demand. But you can create a necessity for a demand. That's what I am going to do."

Two weeks after the consul sent his cable, a fruit steamer brought him a huge, mysterious brown bale of some unknown commodity. Johnny's influence with the custom-house people was sufficiently strong for him to get the goods turned over to him without the usual inspection. He had the bale taken to the consulate and snugly stowed in the back room.

That night he ripped open a corner of it and took out a handful of the cockle-burrs. He examined them with the care with which a warrior examines his arms before he goes forth to battle for his lady-love and life. The burrs were the ripe August product, as hard as filberts, and bristling with spines as tough and sharp as needles. Johnny whistled softly a little tune, and went out to find Billy Keogh.

Later in the night, when Coralio was steeped in slumber, he and Billy went forth into the deserted streets with their coats bulging like balloons. All up and down the Calle Grande they went, sowing the sharp burrs carefully in the sand, along the narrow sidewalks, in every foot of grass between the silent houses. And then they took the side streets and byways, missing none. No place where the foot of man, woman or child might fall was slighted. Many trips they made to and from the prickly hoard. And then, nearly at the dawn, they laid themselves down to rest calmly, as great generals do after planning a victory according to the revised tactics, and slept, knowing that they had sowed with the accuracy of Satan sowing tares and the perseverance of Paul planting.

With the rising sun came the purveyors of fruits and meats, and arranged their wares in and around the little market-house. At one end of the town near the seashore the market-house stood; and the sowing of the burrs had not been carried that far. The dealers waited long past the hour when their sales usually began. None came to buy. " *Qué hay ?* " they began to exclaim, one to another.

At their accustomed time, from every 'dobe and palm hut and grass-thatched shack and dim *patio* glided women—black women, brown women, lemon-colored women, women dun and yellow and tawny. They were the marketers starting to purchase the family supply of cassava, plantains, meat, fowls, and tortillas. Décolleté they were and bare-armed and bare-footed, with a single skirt reaching below the knee. Stolid and ox-eyed, they stepped from their doorways into the narrow paths or upon the soft grass of the streets.

The first to emerge uttered ambiguous squeals, and raised one foot quickly. Another step and they sat down, with shrill cries of alarm, to pick at the new and painful insects that had stung them upon the feet. " *Qué picadores diablos !* " they screeched to one another across the narrow ways. Some tried the grass instead of the paths, but there they were also stung and bitten by the strange little prickly balls. They plumped down in the grass, and added their lamentations to those of their sisters in the sandy paths. All through the town was heard the plaint of the feminine jabber. The venders in the market still wondered why no customers came.

Then men, lords of the earth, came forth. They, too, began to hop, to dance, to limp, and to curse. They stood stranded and foolish, or stooped to pluck at the scourge that attacked their feet and ankles. Some loudly proclaimed the pest to be poisonous spiders of an unknown species.

And then the children ran out for their morning romp. And now to the uproar was added the howls of limping infants and cockle-burred childhood. Every minute the advancing day brought forth fresh victims.

Doña Maria Castillas y Buenventura de las Casas stepped from her honored doorway, as was her daily custom, to procure fresh bread from the *panadería* across the street. She was clad in a skirt of flowered yellow satin, a chemise of ruffled linen, and wore a purple mantilla from the looms of Spain. Her lemon-tinted feet, alas ! were bare. Her progress was majestic, for were not her ancestors hidalgos of Aragon ? Three steps she made across the velvety grass, and set her aristocratic sole upon a bunch of Johnny's burrs. Doña Maria Castillas y Buenventura de las Casas emitted a yowl even as a wild-cat. Turning about, she fell upon hands and knees, and crawled—ay, like a beast of the field she crawled back to her honorable door-sill.

Don Señor Ildefonso Federico Valdazar, *Juez de la Paz*, weighing twenty stone, attempted to convey his bulk to the *pulpería* at the corner of the plaza in order to assuage his matutinal thirst. The first plunge of his unshod foot into the cool grass struck a concealed mine. Don Ildefonso fell like a crumpled cathedral, crying out that he had been fatally bitten by a deadly scorpion. Everywhere were the shoeless citizens hopping, stumbling, limping, and picking from their feet the venomous insects that had come in a single night to harass them.

The first to perceive the remedy was Estebán Delgado, the barber, a man of travel and education. Sitting upon a stone, he plucked burrs from his toes, and made oration :

" Behold, my friend, these bugs of the devil ! I know them well. They soar through the skies in swarms like pigeons. These are the dead ones that fell during the night. In Yucatan I have seen them as large as oranges. Yes ! There they hiss like serpents, and have wings like bats. It is the shoes—the shoes that one needs ! *Zapatos —zapatos para mí !* "

Estebán hobbled to Mr. Hemstetter's store, and bought shoes. Coming out, he swaggered down the street with impunity, reviling loudly the bugs of the devil. The suffering ones sat up or stood upon one foot and beheld the immune barber. Men, women, and children took up the cry : " *Zapatos ! zapatos !* "

The necessity for the demand had been created. The demand followed. That day Mr. Hemstetter sold three hundred pairs of shoes.

" It is really surprising," he said to Johnny, who came up in the evening to help him straighten out the stock, " how trade is picking up. Yesterday I made but three sales."

" I told you they'd whoop things up when they got started," said the consul.

" I think I shall order a dozen more cases of goods, to keep the stock up," said Mr. Hemstetter, beaming through his spectacles.

" I wouldn't send in any orders yet," advised Johnny. " Wait till you see how the trade holds up."

Each night Johnny and Keogh sowed the crop that grew dollars by day. At the end of ten days two-thirds of the stock of shoes had been sold; and the stock of cockleburrs was exhausted. Johnny cabled to Pink Dawson for another 500 pounds, paying twenty cents per pound as before. Mr. Hemstetter carefully made up an order for $1,500 worth of shoes from Northern firms. Johnny hung about the store until this order was ready for the mail, and succeeded in destroying it before it reached the post office.

That night he took Rosine under the mango tree by Goodwin's porch, and confessed everything. She looked him in the eye, and said : " You are a very wicked man. Father and I will go back home. You say it was a joke ? I think it is a very serious matter."

But at the end of half an hour's argument the conversation had been turned upon a different subject. The two were considering the respective merits of pale blue and pink wall paper with which the old colonial mansion at the Atwoods in Dalesburg was to be decorated after the wedding.

On the next morning Johnny confessed to Mr. Hemstetter. The

shoe merchant put on his spectacles, and said through them :
" You strike me as being a most extraordinary young scamp. If
I had not managed this enterprise with good business judgment
my entire stock of goods might have been a complete loss. Now,
how do you propose to dispose of the rest of it ? "

When the second invoice of cockleburrs arrived Johnny loaded
them and the remainder of the shoes into a schooner, and sailed
down the coast to Alazan.

There, in the same dark and diabolical manner, he repeated
his success; and came back with a bag of money and not so much
as a shoestring.

And then he besought his great Uncle of the waving goatee and
starred vest to accept his resignation, for the lotus no longer lured
him. He hankered for the spinach and cress of Dalesburg.

The services of Mr. William Terence Keogh as acting consul,
pro tem., were suggested and accepted, and Johnny sailed with the
Hemstetters back to his native shores.

Keogh slipped into the sinecure of the American consulship with
the ease that never left him even in such high places. The tintype
establishment was soon to become a thing of the past, although
its deadly work along the peaceful and helpless Spanish Main was
never effaced. The restless partners were about to be off again,
scouting ahead of the slow ranks of Fortune. But now they would
take different ways. There were rumors of a promising uprising
in Peru; and thither the martial Clancy would turn his adventurous steps. As for Keogh, he was figuring in his mind and on
quires of Government letter-heads a scheme that dwarfed the art
of misrepresenting the human countenance upon tin.

" What suits me," Keogh used to say, " in the way of a business
proposition is something diversified that looks like a longer shot
than it is—something in the way of a genteel graft that isn't worked
enough for the correspondence schools to be teaching it by mail.
I take the long end; but I like to have at least as good a chance to
win as a man learning to play poker on an ocean steamer, or
running for governor of Texas on the Republican ticket. And when
I cash in my winnings, I don't want to find any widows' and
orphans' chips in my stack."

The grass-grown globe was the green table on which Keogh
gambled. The games he played were of his own invention. He was
no grubber after the diffident dollar. Nor did he care to follow
it with horn and hounds. Rather he loved to coax it with egregious
and brilliant flies from its habitat in the waters of strange streams.
Yet Keogh was a business man; and his schemes, in spite of their
singularity, were as solidly set as the plans of a building contractor.
In Arthur's time Sir William Keogh would have been a Knight

of the Round Table. In these modern days he rides abroad, seeking the Graft instead of the Grail.

Three days after Johnny's departure, two small schooners appeared off Coralio. After some delay a boat put off from one of them, and brought a sunburned young man ashore. This young man had a shrewd and calculating eye; and he gazed with amazement at the strange things that he saw. He found on the beach some one who directed him to the consul's office; and thither he made his way at a nervous gait.

Keogh was sprawled in the official chair, drawing caricatures of his uncle's head on an official pad of paper. He looked up at his visitor.

"Where's Johnny Atwood?" inquired the sunburned young man, in a business tone.

"Gone," said Keogh, working carefully at Uncle Sam's necktie.

"That's just like him," remarked the nut-brown one, leaning against the table. "He always was a fellow to gallivant around instead of 'tending to business. Will he be in soon?"

"Don't think so," said Keogh, after a fair amount of deliberation.

"I s'pose he's out at some of his tomfoolery," conjectured the visitor, in a tone of virtuous conviction. "Johnny never would stick to anything long enough to succeed. I wonder how he manages to run his business here, and never be 'round to look after it."

"I'm looking after the business just now," admitted the *pro tem.* consul.

"Are you--then, say!--where's the factory?"

"What factory?" asked Keogh, with a mildly polite interest.

"Why, the factory where they use them cockleburrs. Lord knows what they use 'em for, anyway! I've got the basements of both them ships out there loaded with 'em. I'll give you a bargain in this lot. I've had every man, woman, and child around Dalesburg that wasn't busy pickin' 'em for a month. I hired these ships to bring 'em over. Everybody thought I was crazy. Now, you can have this lot for fifteen cents a pound, delivered on land. And if you want more I guess old Alabam' can come up to the demand. Johnny told me when he left home that if he struck anything down here that there was any money in he'd let me in on it. Shall I drive the ships in and hitch?"

A look of supreme, almost incredulous, delight dawned in Keogh's ruddy countenance. He dropped his pencil. His eyes turned upon the sunburned young man with joy in them mingled with fear lest his ecstasy should prove a dream.

"For God's sake, tell me," said Keogh, earnestly, "are you Dink Pawson?"

" My name is Pinkney Dawson," said the cornerer of the cockle-
burr market.

Billy Keogh slid rapturously and gently from his chair to his
favorite strip of matting on the floor.

There were not many sounds in Coralio on that sultry afternoon.
Among those that were may be mentioned a noise of enraptured
and unrighteous laughter from a prostrate Irish-American, while
a sunburned young man, with a shrewd eye, looked on him with
wonder and amazement. Also the " tramp, tramp, tramp " of
many well-shod feet in the streets outside. Also the lonesome wash
of the waves that beat along the historic shores of the Spanish Main.

MASTERS OF ARTS

A TWO-INCH stub of a blue pencil was the wand with which
Keogh performed the preliminary acts of his magic. So,
with this he covered paper with diagrams and figures while he
waited for the United States of America to send down to Coralio
a successor to Atwood, resigned.

The new scheme that his mind had conceived, his stout heart
indorsed, and his blue pencil corroborated, was laid around the
characteristics and human frailties of the new president of Anchuria.
These characteristics, and the situation out of which Keogh hoped
to wrest a golden tribute, deserve chronicling contributive to the
clear order of events.

President Losada—many called him Dictator—was a man whose
genius would have made him conspicuous even among Anglo-
Saxons, had not that genius been intermixed with other traits that
were petty and subversive. He had some of the lofty patriotism of
Washington (the man he most admired), the force of Napoleon,
and much of the wisdom of the sages. These characteristics might
have justified him in the assumption of the title of "The Illustrious
Liberator," had they not been accompanied by a stupendous and
amazing vanity that kept him in the less worthy ranks of the
dictators.

Yet he did his country great service. With a mighty grasp he
shook it nearly free fom the shackles of ignorance and sloth and
the vermin that fed upon it, and all but made it a power in the
council of nations. He established schools and hospitals, built
roads, bridges, railroads and palaces, and bestowed generous
subsidies upon the arts and sciences. He was the absolute despot
and the idol of his people. The wealth of the country poured into
his hands. Other presidents had been rapacious without reason.

Losada amassed enormous wealth, but his people had their share of the benefits.

The joint in his armor was his insatiate passion for monuments and tokens commemorating his glory. In every town he caused to be erected statues of himself bearing legends in praise of his greatness. In the walls of every public edifice, tablets were fixed reciting his splendor and the gratitude of his subjects. His statuettes and portraits were scattered throughout the land in every house and hut. One of the sycophants in his court painted him as St. John, with a halo and a train of attendants in full uniform. Losada saw nothing incongruous in this picture, and had it hung in a church in the capital. He ordered from a French sculptor a marble group including himself with Napoleon, Alexander the Great, and one or two others whom he deemed worthy of the honor.

He ransacked Europe for decorations, employing policy, money and intrigue to cajole the orders he coveted from kings and rulers. On state occasions his breast was covered from shoulder to shoulder with crosses, stars, golden roses, medals and ribbons. It was said that the man who could contrive for him a new decoration, or invent some new method of extolling his greatness, might plunge a hand deep into the treasury.

This was the man upon whom Billy Keogh had his eye. The gentle buccaneer had observed the rain of favors that fell upon those who ministered to the president's vanities, and he did not deem it his duty to hoist his umbrella against the scattering drops of liquid fortune.

In a few weeks the new consul arrived, releasing Keogh from his temporary duties. He was a young man fresh from college, who lived for botany alone. The consulate at Coralio gave him the opportunity to study tropical flora. He wore smoked glasses, and carried a green umbrella. He filled the cool, back porch of the consulate with plants and specimens so that space for a bottle and chair was not to be found. Keogh gazed on him sadly, but without rancour, and began to pack his gripsack. For his new plot against stagnation along the Spanish Main required of him a voyage overseas.

Soon came the *Karlsefin* again—she was of the trampish habits —gleaning a cargo of cocoanuts for a speculative descent upon the New York market. Keogh was booked for a passage on the return trip.

" Yes, I'm going to New York," he explained to the group of his countrymen that had gathered on the beach to see him off. " But I'll be back before you miss me. I've undertaken the art education of this piebald country, and I'm not the man to desert it while it's in the early throes of tintypes."

With this mysterious declaration of his intentions Keogh boarded the *Karlesfin*.

Ten days later, shivering, with the collar of his thin coat turned high, he burst into the studio of Carolus White at the top of a tall building in Tenth Street, New York City.

Carolus White was smoking a cigarette and frying sausages over an oil stove. He was only twenty-three, and had noble theories about art.

" Billy Keogh ! " exclaimed White, extending the hand that was not busy with the frying pan. " From what part of the uncivilized world, I wonder ! "

" Hello, Carry," said Keogh, dragging forward a stool, and holding his fingers close to the stove. " I'm glad I found you so soon. I've been looking for you all day in the directories and art galleries. The free-lunch man on the corner told me where you were, quick. I was sure you'd be painting pictures yet."

Keogh glanced about the studio with the shrewd eye of a connoisseur in business.

" Yes, you can do it," he declared, with many gentle nods of his head. " That big one in the corner with the angels and green clouds and band-wagon is just the sort of thing we want. What would you call that, Carry—scene from Coney Island, ain't it ? "

" That," said White, " I had intended to call ' The Translation of Elijah,' but you may be nearer right than I am."

" Name doesn't matter," said Keogh, largely; " it's the frame and the varieties of paint that does the trick. Now, I can tell you in a minute what I want. I've come on a little voyage of two thousand miles to take you in with me on a scheme. I thought of you as soon as the scheme showed itself to me. How would you like to go back with me and paint a picture ? Ninety days for the trip, and five thousand dollars for the job."

" Cereal food or hair-tonic posters ? " asked White.

" It isn't an ad."

" What kind of a picture is it to be ? "

" It's a long story," said Keogh.

" Go ahead with it. If you don't mind, while you talk I'll just keep my eye on these sausages. Let 'em get one shade deeper than a Vandyke brown and you spoil 'em."

Keogh explained his project. They were to return to Coralio, where White was to pose as a distinguished American portrait painter who was touring in the tropics as a relaxation from his arduous and remunerative professional labors. It was not an unreasonable hope, even to those who had trod in the beaten paths of business, that an artist with so much prestige might secure a commission to perpetuate upon canvas the lineaments of the president, and secure a share of the *pesos* that were raining upon the caterers to his weaknesses.

Keogh had set his price at ten thousand dollars. Artists had been paid more for portraits. He and White were to share the expenses of the trip, and divide the possible profits. Thus he laid the scheme before White, whom he had known in the West before one declared for Art and the other became a Bedouin.

Before long the two machinators abandoned the rigor of the bare studio for a snug corner of a café. There they sat far into the night, with old envelopes and Keogh's stub of blue pencil between them.

At twelve o'clock White doubled up in his chair, with his chin on his fist, and shut his eyes at the unbeautiful wall-paper.

" I'll go you, Billy," he said, in the quiet tones of decision. " I've got two or three hundred saved up for sausages and rent; and I'll take the chance with you. Five thousand ! It will give me two years in Paris and one in Italy. I'll begin to pack to-morrow."

" You'll begin in ten minutes," said Keogh. " It's to-morrow now. The *Karlsefin* starts back at four P.M. Come on to your painting shop, and I'll help you."

For five months in the year Coralio is the Newport of Anchuria. Then only does the town possess life. From November to March it is practically the seat of government. The president with his official family sojourns there; and society follows him. The pleasure-loving people make the season one long holiday of amusement and rejoicing. *Fiestas,* balls, games, sea bathing, processions and small theatres contribute to their enjoyment. The famous Swiss band from the capital plays in the little plaza every evening, while the fourteen carriages and vehicles in the town circle in funereal but complacent procession. Indians from the interior mountains, looking like prehistoric stone idols, come down to peddle their handiwork in the streets. The people throng the narrow ways, a chattering, happy, careless stream of buoyant humanity. Preposterous children rigged out with the shortest of ballet skirts and gilt wings, howl, underfoot, among the effervescent crowds. Especially is the arrival of the presidential party, at the opening of the season, attended with pomp, show and patriotic demonstrations of enthusiasm and delight.

When Keogh and White reached their destination, on the return trip of the *Karlsefin,* the gay winter season was well begun. As they stepped upon the beach they could hear the band playing in the plaza. The village maidens, with fireflies already fixed in their dark locks, were gliding, barefoot and coy-eyed, along the paths. Dandies in white linen, swinging their canes, were beginning their seductive strolls. The air was full of human essence, of artificial enticement, of coquetry, indolence, pleasure—the man-made sense of existence.

The first two or three days after their arrival were spent in preliminaries. Keogh escorted the artist about town, introducing him to the little circle of English-speaking residents and pulling whatever wires he could to effect the spreading of White's fame as a painter. And then Keogh planned a more spectacular demonstration of the idea he wished to keep before the public.

He and White engaged rooms in the Hotel de los Estranjeros. The two were clad in new suits of immaculate duck, with American straw hats, and carried canes of remarkable uniqueness and inutility. Few caballeros in Coralio—even the gorgeously uniformed officers of the Anchurian army—were as conspicuous for ease and elegance of demeanor as Keogh and his friend, the great American painter, Señor White.

White set up his easel on the beach and made striking sketches of the mountain and sea views. The native population formed at his rear in a vast, chattering semicircle to watch his work. Keogh, with his care for details, had arranged for himself a pose which he carried out with fidelity. His rôle was that of friend to the great artist, a man of affairs and leisure. The visible emblem of his position was a pocket camera.

"For branding the man who owns it," said he, "a genteel dilettante with a bank account and an easy conscience, a steam-yacht ain't in it with a camera. You see a man doing nothing but loafing around making snap-shots, and you know right away he reads up well in 'Bradstreet.' You notice these old millionaire boys—soon as they get through taking everything else in sight they go to taking photographs. People are more impressed by a kodak than they are by a title or a four-carat scarf-pin." So Keogh strolled blandly about Coralio, snapping the scenery and the shrinking señoritas, while White posed conspicuously in the higher regions of art.

Two weeks after their arrival, the scheme began to bear fruit. An aide-de-camp of the president drove to the hotel in a dashing victoria. The president desired that Señor White come to the Casa Morena for an informal interview.

Keogh gripped his pipe tightly between his teeth. "Not a cent less than ten thousand," he said to the artist—"remember the price. And in gold or its equivalent—don't let him stick you with this bargain-counter stuff they call money here."

"Perhaps it isn't that he wants," said White.

"Get out!" said Keogh, with splendid confidence. "I know what he wants. He wants his picture painted by the celebrated young American painter and filibuster now sojourning in this down-trodden country. Off you go."

The victoria sped away with the artist. Keogh walked up and down, puffing great clouds of smoke from his pipe, and waited. In an hour the victoria swept again to the door of the hotel, deposited White, and vanished. The artist dashed up the stairs, three at a step. Keogh stopped smoking, and became a silent interrogation point.

"Landed," exclaimed White, with his boyish face flushed with elation. "Billy, you are a wonder. He wants a picture. I'll tell you all about it. By Heavens! that dictator chap is a corker! He's a dictator clear down to his finger-ends. He's a kind of combination of Julius Cæsar, Lucifer and Chauncey Depew done in sepia. Polite and grim—that's his way. The room I saw him in was about ten acres big, and looked like a Mississippi steamboat with its gilding and mirrors and white paint. He talks English better than I can ever hope to. The matter of the price came up. I mentioned ten thousand. I expected him to call the guard and have me taken out and shot. He didn't move an eyelash. He just waved one of his chestnut hands in a careless way, and said, 'Whatever you say.' I am to go back to-morrow and discuss with him the details of the picture,"

Keogh hung his head. Self-abasement was easy to read in his downcast countenance.

"I'm failing, Carry," he said, sorrowfully. "I'm not fit to handle these man's-size schemes any longer. Peddling oranges in a push-cart is about the suitable graft for me. When I said ten thousand, I swear I thought I had sized up that brown man's limit to within two cents. He'd have melted down for fifteen thousand just as easy. Say—Carry—you'll see the old man Keogh safe in some nice, quiet idiot asylum, won't you, if he makes a break like that again?"

The Casa Morena, although only one story in height, was a building of brown stone, luxurious as a palace in its interior. It stood on a low hill in a walled garden of splendid tropical flora at the upper edge of Coralio. The next day the president's carriage came again for the artist. Keogh went out for a walk along the beach, where he and his " picture box " were now familiar sights. When he returned to the hotel White was sitting in a steamer-chair on the balcony.

"Well," said Keogh, " did you and His Nibs decide on the kind of chromo he wants?"

White got up and walked back and forth on the balcony a few times. Then he stopped and laughed strangely. His face was flushed, and his eyes were bright with a kind of angry amusement.

"Look here, Billy," he said, somewhat roughly, "when you first came to me in my studio and mentioned a picture, I thought you wanted a Smashed Oats or a Hair Tonic poster painted on a range of mountains or the side of a continent. Well, either of those jobs would have been Art in its highest form compared to the one you've steered me against. I can't paint that picture, Billy. You've got to let me out. Let me try to tell you what that barbarian wants. He had it all planned out and even a sketch made of his idea. The old boy doesn't draw badly at all. But, ye goddesses of Art! listen to the monstrosity he expects me to paint. He wants himself in the centre of the canvas, of course. He is to be painted as Jupiter sitting on Olympus, with the clouds at his feet. At one side of him stands George Washington, in full regimentals, with his hand on the president's shoulder. An angel with outstretched wings hovers overhead, and is placing a laurel wreath on the president's head, crowning him—Queen of the May, I suppose. In the background is to be cannon, more angels and soldiers. The man who would paint that picture would have to have the soul of a dog, and would deserve to go down into oblivion without even a tin can tied to his tail to sound his memory."

Little beads of moisture crept out all over Billy Keogh's brow. The stub of his blue pencil had not figured out a contingency like this. The machinery of his plan had run with flattering smoothness until now. He dragged another chair upon the balcony, and got White back to his seat. He lit his pipe with apparent calm.

"Now, sonny," he said, with gentle grimness, "you and me will have an Art to Art talk. You've got your art and I've got mine. Yours is the real Pierian stuff that turns up its nose at bock-beer signs and oleographs of the Old Mill. Mine's the art of Business. This was my scheme, and it worked out like two-and-two. Paint that president man as Old King Cole, or Venus, or a landscape, or a fresco, or a bunch of lilies, or anything he thinks he looks like. But get the paint on the canvas and collect the spoils. You wouldn't throw me down, Carry, at this stage of the game. Think of that ten thousand."

"I can't help thinking of it," said White, "and that's what hurts. I'm tempted to throw every ideal I ever had down in the mire, and steep my soul in infamy by painting that picture. That five thousand meant three years of foreign study to me, and I'd almost sell my soul for that."

"Now it ain't as bad as that," said Keogh, soothingly. "It's a business proposition. It's so much paint and time against money. I don't fall in with your idea that that picture would so everlastingly jolt the art side of the question. George Washington was all right, you know, and nobody could say a word against the angel.

I don't think so bad of that group. If you was to give Jupiter a pair of epaulets and a sword, and kind of work the clouds around to look like a blackberry patch, it wouldn't make such a bad battle scene. Why, if we hadn't already settled on the price, he ought to pay an extra thousand for Washington, and the angel ought to raise it five hundred."

"You don't understand, Billy," said White, with an uneasy laugh. "Some of us fellows who try to paint have big notions about Art. I wanted to paint a picture some day that people would stand before and forget that it was made of paint. I wanted it to creep into them like a bar of music and mushroom there like a soft bullet. And I wanted 'em to go away and ask, 'What else has he done?' And I didn't want 'em to find a thing; not a portrait nor a magazine cover nor an illustration nor a drawing of a girl—nothing but *the* picture. That's why I've lived on fried sausages, and tried to keep true to myself. I persuaded myself to do this portrait for the chance it might give me to study abroad. But this howling, screaming caricature! Good Lord! can't you see how it is?"

"Sure," said Keogh, as tenderly as he would have spoken to a child, and he laid a long fore-finger on White's knee. "I see. It's bad to have your art all slugged up like that. I know. You wanted to paint a big thing like the panorama of the battle of Gettysburg. But let me kalsomine you a little mental sketch to consider. Up to date we're out $385.50 on this scheme. Our capital took every cent both of us could raise. We've got about enough left to get back to New York on. I need my share of that ten thousand. I want to work a copper deal in Idaho, and make a hundred thousand. That's the business end of the thing. Come down off your art perch, Carry, and let's land that hatful of dollars."

"Billy," said White, with an effort, "I'll try. I won't say I'll do it, but I'll try. I'll go at it, and put it through if I can."

"That's business," said Keogh heartily. "Good boy! Now, here's another thing—rush that picture—crowd it through as quick as you can. Get a couple of boys to help you mix the paint if necessary. I've picked up some pointers around town. The people here are beginning to get sick of Mr. President. They say he's been too free with concessions; and they accuse him of trying to make a dicker with England to sell out the country. We want that picture done and paid for before there's any row."

In the great *patio* of Casa Morena, the president caused to be stretched a huge canvas. Under this White set up his temporary studio. For two hours each day the great man sat to him.

White worked faithfully. But, as the work progressed, he had seasons of bitter scorn, of infinite self-contempt, of sullen gloom and sardonic gaiety. Keogh, with the patience of a great general, soothed, coaxed, argued—kept him at the picture.

At the end of a month, White announced that the picture was completed—Jupiter, Washington, angels, clouds, cannon and all. His face was pale and his mouth drawn straight when he told Keogh. He said the president was much pleased with it. It was to be hung in the National Gallery of Statesmen and Heroes. The artist had been requested to return to Casa Morena on the following day to receive payment. At the appointed time he left the hotel, silent under his friend's joyful talk of their success.

An hour later he walked into the room where Keogh was waiting, threw his hat on the floor, and sat upon the table.

" Billy," he said, in strained and laboring tones, " I've a little money out West in a small business that my brother is running. It's what I've been living on while I've been studying art. I'll draw out my share and pay you back what you've lost on this scheme."

" Lost ! " exclaimed Keogh, jumping up. " Didn't you get paid for the picture ? "

" Yes, I got paid," said White. " But just now there isn't any picture, and there isn't any pay. If you care to hear about it, here are the edifying details. The president and I were looking at the painting. His secretary brought a bank draft on New York for ten thousand dollars and handed it to me. The moment I touched it I went wild. I tore it into little pieces and threw them on the floor. A workman was repainting the pillars inside the *patio*. A bucket of his paint happened to be convenient. I picked up his brush and slapped a quart of blue paint all over that ten-thousand-dollar nightmare. I bowed, and walked out. The president didn't move or speak. That was one time he was taken by surprise. It's tough on you, Billy, but I couldn't help it."

There seemed to be excitement in Coralio. Outside there was a confused, rising murmer pierced by high-pitched cries. "*Abajo el traidor—Muerte al traidor !* were the words they seemed to form.

" Listen to that ! " exclaimed White, bitterly : " I know that much Spanish. They're shouting, ' Down with the traitor ! ' I heard them before. I felt that they meant me. I was a traitor to Art. The picture had to go."

" 'Down with the blank fool' would have suited your case better," said Keogh, with fiery emphasis. " You tear up ten thousand dollars like an old rag because the way you've spread on five dollars' worth of paint hurts your conscience. Next time I pick a side-partner in a scheme the man has got to go before a notary and swear he never even heard the word ' ideal ' mentioned."

Keogh strode from the room, white-hot. White paid little attention to his resentment. The scorn of Billy Keogh seemed a trifling thing beside the greater self-scorn he had escaped.

In Coralio the excitement waxed. An outburst was imminent. The cause of this demonstration of displeasure was the presence in the town of a big, pink-cheeked Englishman, who, it was said, was an agent of his government come to clinch the bargain by which the president placed his people in the hands of a foreign power. It was charged that not only had he given away priceless concessions, but that the public debt was to be transferred into the hands of the English, and the custom-houses turned over to them as a guarantee. The long-enduring people had determined to make their protest felt.

On that night, in Coralio and in other towns, their ire found vent. Yelling mobs, mercurial but dangerous, roamed the streets. They overthrew the great bronze statue of the president that stood in the centre of the plaza, and hacked it to shapeless pieces. They tore from public buildings the tablets set there proclaiming the glory of the " Illustrious Liberator." His pictures in the government office were demolished. The mobs even attacked the Casa Morena, but were driven away by the military, which remained faithful to the executive. All the night terror reigned.

The greatness of Losada was shown by the fact that by noon the next day order was restored, and he was still absolute. He issued proclamations denying positively that any negotiations of any kind had been entered into with England. Sir Stafford Vaughn, the pink-cheeked Englishman, also declared in placards and in public print that his presence there had no international significance. He was a traveller without guile. In fact (so he stated), he had not even spoken with the president or been in his presence since his arrival.

During this disturbance, White was preparing for his homeward voyage in the steamship that was to sail within two or three days. About noon, Keogh, the restless, took his camera out with the hope of speeding the lagging hours. The town was now as quiet as if peace had never departed from her perch on the red-tiled roofs.

About the middle of the afternoon, Keogh hurried back to the hotel with something decidedly special in his air. He retired to the little room where he developed his pictures.

Later on he came out to White on the balcony, with a luminous, grim, predatory smile on his face.

" Do you know what that is ? " he asked, holding up a 4 x 5 photograph mounted on cardboard.

" Snap-shot of a señorita sitting in the sand—alliteration unintentional," guessed White, lazily.

"Wrong," said Keogh with shining eyes. "It's a slung-shot. It's a can of dynamite. It's a gold mine. It's a sight-draft on your president man for twenty thousand dollars—yes, sir—twenty thousand this time, and no spoiling the picture. No ethics of art in the way. Art! You with your smelly little tubes! I've got you skinned to death with a kodak. Take a look at that."

White took the picture in his hand, and gave a long whistle.

"Jove," he exclaimed, "but wouldn't that stir up a row in town if you let it be seen. How in the world did you get it, Billy?"

"You know that high wall around the president man's back garden? I was up there trying to get a bird's-eye of the town. I happened to notice a chink in the wall where a stone and a lot of plaster had slid out. Thinks I, I'll take a peep through to see how Mr. President's cabbages are growing. The first thing I saw was him and this Sir Englishman sitting at a little table about twenty feet away. They had the table all spread over with documents, and they were hobnobbing over them as thick as two pirates. 'Twas a nice corner of the garden, all private and shady with palms and orange trees, and they had a pail of champagne set by handy in the grass. I knew then was the time for me to make my big hit in Art. So I raised the machine up to the crack, and pressed the button. Just as I did so them old boys shook hands on the deal—you see they took that way in the picture."

Keogh put on his coat and hat.

"What are you going to do with it?" asked White.

"Me," said Keogh in a hurt tone, "why, I'm going to tie a pink ribbon to it and hang it on the what-not, of course. I'm surprised at you. But while I'm out you just try to figure out what gingercake potentate would be most likely to want to buy this work of art for his private collection—just to keep it out of circulation."

The sunset was reddening the tops of the cocoanut palms when Billy Keogh came back from Casa Morena. He nodded to the artist's questioning gaze; and lay down on a cot with his hands under the back of his head.

"I saw him. He paid the money like a little man. They didn't want to let me in at first. I told 'em it was important. Yes, that president man is on the plenty-able list. He's got a beautiful business system about the way he uses his brains. All I had to do was to hold up the photograph so he could see it, and name the price. He just smiled, and walked over to a safe and got the cash. Twenty one-thousand-dollar brand-new United States Treasury notes he laid on the table, like I'd pay out a dollar and a quarter. Fine notes, too—they crackled with a sound like burning the brush off a ten-acre lot."

"Let's try the feel of one," said White, curiously. "I never saw a thousand-dollar bill." Keogh did not immediately respond.

"Carry," he said, in an absent-minded way, "you think a heap of your art, don't you?"

"More," said White, frankly, "than has been for the financial good of myself and my friends."

"I thought you were a fool the other day," went on Keogh, quietly, "and I'm not sure now that you wasn't. But if you was, so am I. I've been in some funny deals, Carry, but I've always managed to scramble fair, and match my brains and capital against the other fellow's. But when it comes to—well, when you've got the other fellow cinched, and the screws on him, and he's got to put up—why, it don't strike me as being a man's game. They've got a name for it, you know; it's—confound you, don't you understand? A fellow feels—it's something like that blamed art of yours—he—well, I tore that photograph up and laid the pieces on that stack of money and shoved the whole business back across the table. 'Excuse me, Mr. Losada,' I said, 'but I guess I've made a mistake in the price. You get the photo for nothing.' Now, Carry, you get out the pencil, and we'll do some more figuring. I'd like to save enough out of our capital for you to have some fried sausages in your joint when you get back to New York."

DICKY

THERE is little consecutiveness along the Spanish Main. Things happen there intermittently. Even Time seems to hang his scythe daily on the branch of an orange tree while he takes a siesta and a cigarette.

After the ineffectual revolt against the administration of President Losada, the country settled again into quiet toleration of the abuses with which he had been charged. In Coralio old political enemies went arm-in-arm, lightly eschewing for the time all differences of opinion.

The failure of the art expedition did not stretch the cat-footed Keogh upon his back. The ups and downs of Fortune made smooth travelling for his nimble steps. His blue pencil stub was at work again before the smoke of the steamer on which White sailed had cleared away from the horizon. He had but to speak a word to Geddie to find his credit negotiable for whatever goods he wanted from the store of Brannigan & Company. On the same day on which White arrived in New York, Keogh, at the rear of a train of five pack mules loaded with hardware and cutlery, set his face toward the grim, interior mountains. There the Indian tribes wash gold dust from the auriferous streams; and when a market is brought trading to them is brisk and *muy bueno* in the Cordilleras.

In Coralio Time folded his wings and paced wearily along his drowsy path. They who had most cheered the torpid hours were gone. Clancy had sailed on a Spanish barque for Colon, contemplating a cut across the isthmus and then a further voyage to end at Calao, where the fighting was said to be on. Geddie, whose quiet and genial nature had once served to mitigate the frequent dull reaction of lotus eating, was now a home-man, happy with even his bright orchid, Paula, and never dreaming of or regretting the unsolved, sealed and monogramed Bottle whose contents, now inconsiderable, were held safely in the keeping of the sea.

Well may the Walrus, most discerning and eclectic of beasts, place sealing-wax midway on his programme of topics that fall pertinent and diverting upon the ear.

Atwood was gone—he was of the hospitable back porch and ingenuous cunning. Dr. Gregg, with his trepanning story smouldering within him, was a whiskered volcano, always showing signs of imminent eruption, and was not to be considered in the ranks of those who might contribute to the amelioration of ennui. The new consul's note chimed with the sad sea waves and the violent tropical greens—he had not a bar of Scheherezade or of the Round Table in his lute. Goodwin was employed with large projects : what time he was loosed from them found him at his home, where he loved to be. Therefore it will be seen that there was a dearth of fellowship and entertainment among the foreign contingent of Coralio.

And then Dicky Maloney dropped down from the clouds upon the town, and amused it.

Nobody knew where Dicky Maloney hailed from or how he reached Coralio. He appeared there one day; and that was all. He afterward said that he came on the fruit steamer *Thor;* but an inspection of the *Thor's* passenger list of that date was found to be Maloneyless. Curiosity, however, soon perished; and Dicky took his place among the odd fish cast up by the Caribbean.

He was an active, devil-may-care, rollicking fellow with an engaging gray eye, the most irresistible grin, a rather dark or much sunburned complexion, and a head of the fieriest red hair ever seen in that country. Speaking the Spanish language as well as he spoke English, and seeming always to have plenty of silver in his pockets, it was not long before he was a welcome companion withersoever he went. He had an extreme fondness for *vino blanco,* and gained the reputation of being able to drink more of it than any three men in town. Everybody called him " Dicky "; everybody cheered up at the sight of him—especially the natives, to whom his marvellous red hair and his free-and-easy style were a constant delight and envy. Wherever you went in the town you would soon see Dicky or hear his genial laugh, and find around him a group of admirers who appreciated him both for his good nature and the white wine he was always so ready to buy.

A considerable amount of speculation was had concerning the object of his sojourn there, until one day he silenced this by opening a small shop for the sale of tobacco, *dulces* and the handiwork of the interior Indians—fibre-and-silk-woven goods, deerskin *zapatos* and basket work of *tule* reeds. Even then he did not change his habits; for he was drinking and playing cards half the day and night with the *comandante*, the collector of customs, the *Jefe Politico* and other gay dogs among the native officials.

One day Dicky saw Pasa, the daughter of Madama Ortiz, sitting in the side-door of the Hotel des los Estranjeros. He stopped in his tracks, still, for the first time in Coralio; and then he sped, swift as a deer, to find Vasquez, a gilded native youth, to present him.

The young men had named Pasa " *La Santita Naranjadita*." *Naranjadita* is a Spanish word for a certain color that you must go to more trouble to describe in English. By saying " The little saint, tinted the most beautiful delicate-slightly-orange-golden," you will approximate, the description of Madama Ortiz's daughter.

La Madama Ortiz sold rum in addition to other liquors. Now, you must know that the rum expiates whatever opprobrium attends upon the other commodities. For rum-making, mind you, is a government monopoly; and to keep a government dispensary assures respectability if not preëminence. Moreover, the saddest of precisions could find no fault with the conduct of the shop. Customers drank there in the lowest of spirits and fearsomely, as in the shadow of the dead; for Madama's ancient and vaunted lineage counteracted even the rum's behest to be merry. For, was she not of the Iglesias, who landed with Pizarro? And had not her deceased husband been *comisionado de caminos y puentes* for the district ?

In the evenings Pasa sat by the window in the room next to the one where they drank, and strummed dreamily upon her guitar. And then, by twos and threes, would come visiting young caballeros and occupy the prim line of chairs set against the wall of this room. They were there to beseige the heart of " *La Santita*." Their method (which is not proof against intelligent competition) consisted of expanding the chest, looking valorous, and consuming a gross or two of cigarettes. Even saints delicately oranged prefer to be wooed differently.

Doña Pasa would tide over the vast chasms of nicotinized silence with music from her guitar, while she wondered if the romances she had read about gallant and more—more contiguous cavaliers were all lies. At somewhat regular intervals Madama would glide in from the dispensary with a sort of drought-suggesting gleam in her eye, and there would be a rustling of stiffly-starched white trousers as one of the caballeros would propose an adjournment to the bar.

That Dick Maloney would, sooner or later, explore this field was a thing to be foreseen. There were few doors in Coralio into which his red head had not been poked.

In an incredibly short space of time after his first sight of her he was there, seated close beside her rocking chair. There were no back-against-the-wall poses in Dicky's theory of wooing. His plan of subjection was an attack at close range. To carry the fortress with one concentrated, ardent, eloquent, irresistible *escalade*—that was Dicky's way.

Pasa was descended from the proudest Spanish families in the country. Moreover, she had had unusual advantages. Two years in a New Orleans school had elevated her ambitions and fitted her for a fate above the ordinary maidens of her native land. And yet here she succumbed to the first red-haired scamp with a glib tongue and a charming smile that came along and courted her properly.

Very soon Dicky took her to the little church in the corner of the plaza, and " Mrs. Maloney " was added to her string of distinguished names.

And it was her fate to sit, with her patient, saintly eyes and figure like a bisque Psyche, behind the sequestered counter of the little shop, while Dicky drank and philandered with his frivolous acquaintances.

The women, with their naturally fine instinct, saw a chance for vivisection, and delicately taunted her with his habits. She turned upon them in a beautiful, steady blaze of sorrowful contempt.

" You meat-cows," she said, in her level, crystal-clear tones; " you know nothing of a man. Your men are *maromeros*. They are fit only to roll cigarettes in the shade until the sun strikes and shrivels them up. They drone in your hammocks and you comb their hair and feed them with fresh fruit. My man is no such blood. Let him drink of the wine. When he has taken sufficient of it to drown one of your *flaccitos* he will come home to me more of a man than one thousand of your *pobrecitos*. *My* hair he smooths and braids; to me he sings; he himself removes my *zapatos*, and there, there, upon each instep leaves a kiss. He holds—Oh, you will never understand ! Blind ones who have never known a *man*."

Sometimes mysterious things happened at night about Dicky's shop. While the front of it was dark, in the little room back of it Dicky and a few of his friends would sit about a table carrying on some kind of very quiet *negocios* until quite late. Finally he would let them out the front door very carefully, and go upstairs to his little saint. These visitors were generally conspirator-like men with dark clothes and hats. Of course, these dark doings were noticed after a while, and talked about.

Dicky seemed to care nothing at all for the society of the alien residents of the town. He avoided Goodwin, and his skilful escape from the trepanning story of Dr. Gregg is still referred to, in Coralio, as a masterpiece of lightning diplomacy.

Many letters arrived, addressed to " Mr. Dicky Maloney," or " Señor Dickee Maloney," to the considerable pride of Pasa. That so many people should desire to write to him only confirmed her own suspicion that the light from his red head shone around the world. As to their contents she never felt curiosity. There was a wife for you !

The one mistake Dicky made in Coralio was to run out of money at the wrong time. Where his money came from was a puzzle, for the sales of his shop were next to nothing, but that source failed, and at a peculiarly unfortunate time. It was when the *comandante,* Don Señor el Coronel Encarnation Rios, looked upon the little saint seated in the shop and felt his heart go pitapat.

The *comandante,* who was versed in all the intricate arts of gallantry, first delicately hinted at his sentiments by donning his dress uniform and strutting up and down fiercely before her window. Pasa, glancing demurely with her saintly eyes, instantly perceived his resemblance to her parrot, Chichi, and was diverted to the extent of a smile. The *comandante* saw the smile, which was not intended for him. Convinced of an impression made, he entered the shop, confidently, and advanced to open compliment. Pasa froze; he pranced; she flamed royally; he was charmed to injudicious persistence; she commanded him to leave the shop; he tried to capture her hand,—and Dicky entered, smiling broadly, full of white wine and the devil.

He spent five minutes in punishing the *comandante* scientifically and carefully, so that the pain might be prolonged as far as possible. At the end of that time he pitched the rash wooer out of the door upon the stones of the street, senseless.

A barefooted policeman who had been watching the affair from across the street blew a whistle. A squad of four soldiers came running from the *cuartel* around the corner. When they saw that the offender was Dicky, they stopped, and blew more whistles, which brought out reënforcements of eight. Deeming the odds against them sufficiently reduced, the military advanced upon the disturber.

Dicky, being thoroughly imbued with the martial spirit, stooped and drew the *comandante's* sword, which was girded about him, and charged his foe. He chased the standing army four squares, playfully prodding its squealing rear and hacking at its ginger-colored heels.

But he was not so successful with the civic authorities. Six muscular, nimble policeman overpowered him and conveyed him, triumphantly but warily, to jail. " *El Diablo Colorado* " they dubbed him, and derided the military for its defeat.

Dicky, with the rest of the prisoners, could look out through the barred door at the grass of the little plaza, at a row of orange trees and the red tile roofs and 'dobe walls of a line of insignificant stores.

At sunset along a path across this plaza came a melancholy procession of sad-faced women bearing plantains, cassaba, bread and fruit—each coming with food to some wretch behind those bars to whom she still clung and furnished the means of life. Twice a day—morning and evening—they were permitted to come. Water was furnished to her compulsory guests by the republic but no food.

That evening Dicky's name was called by the sentry, and he stepped before the bars of the door. There stood his little saint, a black mantilla draped about her head and shoulders, her face like glorified melancholy, her clear eyes gazing longingly at him as if they might draw him between the bars to her. She brought a chicken, some oranges, *dulces* and a loaf of white bread. A soldier inspected the food, and passed it in to Dicky. Pasa spoke calmly as she always did, briefly, in her thrilling, flute-like tones. "Angel of my life," she said, " let it not be long that thou art away from me. Thou knowest that life is not a thing to be endured with thou not at my side. Tell me if I can do aught in this matter. If not, I will wait—a little while. I come again in the morning."

Dicky, with his shoes removed so as not to disturb his fellow prisoners, tramped the floor of the jail half the night condemning his lack of money and the cause of it—whatever that might have been. He knew very well that money would have brought his release at once.

For two days succeeding Pasa came at the appointed times and brought him food. He eagerly inquired each time if a letter or package had come for him, and she mournfully shook her head.

On the morning of the third day she brought only a small loaf of bread. There were dark circles under her eyes. She seemed as calm as ever.

" By jingo," said Dicky, who seemed to speak in English or

Spanish as the whim seized him, " this is dry provender, *muchachita.* Is this the best you can dig up for a fellow ? "

Pasa looked at him as a mother looks at a beloved but capricious babe.

" Think better of it," she said, in a low voice; " since for the next meal there will be nothing. The last *centavo* is spent." She pressed close against the grating.

" Sell the goods in the shop—take anything for them."

" Have I not tried ? Did I not offer them for one-tenth their cost ? Not even one *peso* would any one give. There is not one *real* in this town to assist Dickee Malonee."

Dick clenched his teeth grimly. " That's the *comandante,*" he growled. " He's responsible for that sentiment. Wait, oh, wait till the cards are all out."

Pasa lowered her voice to almost a whisper. "And, listen, heart of my heart," she said, " I have endeavored to be brave, but I cannot live without thee. Three days now——"

Dicky caught a faint gleam of steel from the folds of her mantilla. For once she looked in his face and saw it without a smile, stern, menacing and purposeful. Then he suddenly raised his hand and his smile came back like a gleam of sunshine. The hoarse signal of an incoming steamer's siren sounded in the harbor. Dicky called to the sentry who was pacing before the door : " What steamer comes ? "

" The *Catarina.*"

" Of the Vesuvius line ? "

" Without doubt, of that line."

" Go you, *picarilla,*" said Dicky joyously to Pasa, " to the American consul. Tell him I wish to speak with him. See that he comes at once. And look you ! let me see a different look in those eyes, for I promise your head shall rest upon this arm to-night."

It was an hour before the consul came. He held his green umbrella under his arm, and mopped his forehead impatiently.

" Now, see here, Maloney," he began, captiously, " you fellows seem to think you can cut up any kind of row, and expect me to pull you out of it. I'm neither the War Department nor a gold mine. This country has its laws, you know, and there's one against pounding the senses out of the regular army. You Irish are forever getting into trouble. I don't see what I can do. Anything like tobacco, ow, to make you comfortable—or newspapers——"

" Son of Eli," interrupted Dicky, gravely, " you haven't changed an iota. That is almost a duplicate of the speech you made when old Koen's donkeys and geese got into the chapel loft, and the culprits wanted to hide in your room."

" Oh, heavens ! " exclaimed the consul, hurriedly adjusting his spectacles. "Are you a Yale man, too ? Were you in that crowd ? I don't seem to remember any one with red—any one named Maloney. Such a lot of collegemen seem to have misused their advantages. One of the best mathematicians of the class of '91 is selling lottery tickets in Belize. A Cornell man dropped off here last month. He was second steward on a guano boat. I'll write to the department if you like, Maloney. Or if there's any tobacco, or newspa——"

" There's nothing," interrupted Dicky, shortly, " but this. You go tell the captain of the *Catarina* that Dicky Maloney wants to see him as soon as he can conveniently come. Tell him where I am. Hurry. That's all."

The consul, glad to be let off so easily, hurried away. The captain of the *Catarina,* a stout man, Sicilian born, soon appeared, shoving, with little ceremony, through the guards to the jail door. The Vesuvius Fruit Company had a habit of doing things that way in Anchuria.

" I am exceedingly sorry—exceedingly sorry," said the captain, " to see this occur. I place myself at your service, Mr. Maloney. What you need shall be furnished. Whatever you say shall be done."

Dickey looked at him unsmilingly. His red hair could not detract from his attitude of severe dignity as he stood, tall and calm, with his now grim mouth forming a horizontal line.

" Captain De Lucco, I believe I still have funds in the hands of your company—ample and personal funds. I ordered a remittance last week. The money has not arrived. You know what is needed in this game. Money and money and more money. Why has it not been sent.?"

" By the *Cristóbal,*" replied De Lucco, gesticulating, " it was despatched. Where is the *Cristóbal ?* Off Cape Antonio I spoke her with a broken shaft. A tramp coaster was towing her back to New Orleans. I brought money ashore thinking your need for it might not withstand delay. In this envelope is one thousand dollars. There is more if you need it, Mr. Maloney."

" For the present it will suffice," said Dicky, softening as he crinkled the envelope and looked down at the half-inch thickness of smooth, dingy bills.

" The long green ! " he said, gently, with a new reverence in his gaze. " Is there anything it will not buy, Captain ? "

" I had three friends," replied De Lucco, who was a bit of a philosopher, " who had money. One of them speculated in stocks and made ten million; another is in heaven, and the third married a poor girl whom he loved."

"The answer, then," said Dicky, "is held by the Almighty, Wall Street and Cupid. So, the question remains."

"This," queried the captain, including Dicky's surroundings in a significant gesture of his hand, "is it—it is not—it is not connected with the business of your little shop? There is no failure in your plans?"

"No, no," said Dicky. "This is merely the result of a little private affair of mine, a digression from the regular line of business. They say for a complete life a man must know poverty, love, and war. But they don't go well together, *capitán mío*. No; there is no failure in my business. The little shop is doing very well."

When the captain had departed Dicky called the sergeant of the jail and asked:

"Am I *preso* by the military or the civil authority?"

"Surely there is no martial law in effect now, señor."

"*Bueno.* Now go or send to the alcalde, the *Juez de la Paz* and the *Jefe de los Policios*. Tell them I am prepared at once to satisfy the demands of justice." A folded bill of the "long green" slid into the sergeant's hands.

Then Dicky's smile came back again, for he knew that the hours of his captivity were numbered; and he hummed, in time with the sentry's tread:

> "*They're hanging men and women now,*
> *For lacking of the green.*"

So, that night Dicky sat by the window of the room over his shop and his little saint sat close by, working at something silken and dainty. Dicky was thoughtful and grave. His red hair was in an unusual state of disorder. Pasa's fingers often ached to smooth and arrange it, but Dicky would never allow it. He was poring, to-night, over a great litter of maps and books and papers on his table until that perpendicular line came between his brows that always distressed Pasa. Presently she went and brought his hat, and stood with it until he looked up, inquiringly.

"It is sad for you here," she explained. "Go out and drink *vino blanco*. Come back when you get that smile you used to wear. That is what I wish to see."

Dicky laughed and threw down his papers. "The *vino blanco* stage is past. It has served its turn. Perhaps, after all, there was less entered my mouth and more my ears than people thought. But, there will be no more maps or frowns to-night. I promise you that. Come."

They sat upon a red *silleta* at the window and watched the quivering gleams from the lights of the *Catarina* reflected in the harbor.

Presently Pasa rippled out one of her infrequent chirrups of audible laughter.

" I was thinking," she began, anticipating Dicky's question, " of the foolish things girls have in their minds. Because I went to school in the States I used to have ambitions. Nothing less than to be the president's wife would satisfy me. And, look, thou red picaroon, to what obscure fate thou hast stolen me ! "

" Don't give up hope," said Dicky, smiling. " More than one Irishman has been the ruler of a South American country. There was a dictator of Chili named O'Higgins. Why not a President Maloney, of Anchuria ? Say the word, *santita mia*, and we'll make the race."

" No, no, no, thou red-haired, reckless one ! " sighed Pasa; " I am content "—she laid her head against his arm—" here."

ROUGE ET NOIR

IT has been indicated that disaffection followed the elevation of Losada to the presidency. This feeling continued to grow. Throughout the entire republic there seemed to be a spirit of silent, sullen discontent. Even the old Liberal party to which Goodwin, Zavalla and other patriots had lent their aid was disappointed. Losada had failed to become a popular idol. Fresh taxes, fresh import duties and, more than all, his tolerance of the outrageous oppression of citizens by the military had rendered him the most obnoxious president since the despicable Alforan. The majority of his own cabinet were out of sympathy with him. The army, which he had courted by giving it license to tyrannize, had been his main, and thus far adequate support.

But the most impolitic of the administration's moves had been when it antagonized the Vesuvius Fruit Company, an organization plying twelve steamers and with cash and capital somewhat larger than Anchuria's surplus and debt combined.

Reasonably an established concern like the Vesuvius would become irritated at having a small, retail republic with no rating at all attempt to squeeze it. So when the government proxies applied for a subsidy they encountered a polite refusal. The president at once retaliated by clapping an export duty of one *real* per bunch on bananas—a thing unprecedented in fruit-growing countries. The Vesuvius Company had invested large sums in wharves and plantations along the Anchuria coast, their agents had erected fine homes in the towns where they had their headquarters, and heretofore had worked with the republic in good-will and with advantage to both. It would lose an immense sum if compelled to move out. The selling price of bananas from Vera Cruz to Trinidad was three *reals* per bunch. This new duty of one *real* would have ruined the fruit growers in Anchuria and have seriously discommoded the Vesuvius Company had it declined to pay it. But for some reason, the Vesuvius continued to buy Anchuria fruit, paying four *reals* for it; and not suffering the growers to bear the loss.

This apparent victory deceived His Excellency; and he began to hunger for more of it. He sent an emissary to request a conference with a representative of the fruit company. The Vesuvius sent Mr. Franzoni, a little, stout, cheerful man, always cool, and whistling airs from Verdi's operas. Señor Espirition, of the office of the Minister of Finance, attempted the sandbagging in behalf of Anchuria. The meeting took place in the cabin of the *Salvador*, of the Vesuvius line.

Señor Espirition opened negotiations by announcing that the government contemplated the building of a railroad to skirt the alluvial coast lands. After touching upon the benefits such a road would confer upon the interests of the Vesuvius, he reached the definite suggestion that a contribution to the road's expenses of, say, fifty thousand *pesos* would not be more than an equivalent to benefits received.

Mr. Franzoni denied that his company would receive any benefits from a contemplated road. As its representative he must decline to contribute fifty thousand *pesos*. But he would assume the responsibility of offering twenty-five.

Did Señor Espirition understand Señor Franzoni to mean twenty-five thousand *pesos* ?

By no means. Twenty-five *pesos*. And in silver; not in gold.

"Your offer insults my government," cried Señor Espirition, rising with indignation.

"Then," said Mr. Franzoni, in warning tone, "*we will change it*."

The offer was never changed. Could Mr. Franzoni have meant the government ?

This was the state of affairs in Anchuria when the winter season opened at Coralio at the end of the second year of Losada's administration. So, when the government and society made its annual exodus to the seashore it was evident that the presidential advent would not be celebrated by unlimited rejoicing. The tenth of November was the day set for the entrance into Coralio of the gay company from the capital. A narrow-gauge railroad runs twenty miles into the interior from Solitas. The government party travels by carriage from San Mateo to this road's terminal point, and proceeds by train to Solitas. From here they march in grand procession to Coralio where, on the day of their coming, festivities and ceremonies abound. But this season saw an ominous dawning of the tenth of November.

Although the rainy season was over, the day seemed to hark back to reeking June. A fine drizzle of rain fell all during the forenoon. The procession entered Coralio amid a strange silence.

President Losada was an elderly man, grizzly bearded, with a considerable ratio of Indian blood revealed in his cinnamon complexion. His carriage headed the procession, surrounded and guarded by Captain Cruz and his famous troop of one hundred light horse " *El Ciento Huilando*." Colonel Rocas followed, with a regiment of the regular army.

The president's sharp, beady eyes glanced about him for the expected demonstration of welcome; but he faced a stolid, indifferent array of citizens. Sightseers the Anchurians are by birth and habit, and they turned out to their last able-bodied unit to witness the scene; but they maintained an accusive silence. They crowded the streets to the very wheel ruts; they covered the red tile roofs to the eaves, but there was never a " *viva* " from them. No wreaths of palm and lemon branches or gorgeous strings of paper roses hung from the windows and balconies as was the custom. There was an apathy, a dull, dissenting disapprobation, that was more ominous because it puzzled. No one feared an outburst, a revolt of the discontents, for they had no leader. The president and those loyal to him had never even heard whispered a name among them capable of crystallizing the dissatisfaction into opposition. No, there could be no danger. The people always procured a new idol before they destroyed an old one.

At length, after a prodigious galloping and curvetting of red-sashed majors, gold-laced colonels and epauletted generals, the procession formed for its annual progress down the Calle Grande to the Casa Morena, where the ceremony of welcome to the visiting president always took place.

The Swiss band led the line of march. After it pranced the local *comandante*, mounted, and a detachment of his troops. Next came a carriage with four members of the cabinet, conspicuous among them the Minister of War, old General Pilar, with his white moustache and his soldierly bearing. Then the president's vehicle, containing also the Ministers of Finance and State; and surrounded by Captain Cruz's light horse formed in a close double file of fours. Following them, the rest of the officials of state, the judges and distinguished military and social ornaments of public and private life.

As the band struck up, and the movement began, like a bird of ill-omen the *Valhalla*, the swiftest steamship of the Vesuvius line,

glided into the harbor in plain view of the president and his train.
Of course, there was nothing menacing about its arrival—a
business firm does not go to war with a nation—but it reminded
Señor Espirición and others in those carriages that the Vesuvius
Fruit Company was undoubtedly carrying something up its sleeve
for them.

By the time the van of the procession had reached the government building, Captain Cronin, of the *Valhalla*, and Mr. Vincenti,
member of the Vesuvius Company, had landed and were pushing
their way, bluff, hearty, and nonchalant, through the crowd on
the narrow sidewalk. Clad in white linen, big, debonair, with an
air of good-humored authority, they made conspicuous figures
among the dark mass of unimposing Anchurians, as they penetrated to within a few yards of the steps of the Casa Morena.
Looking easily above the heads of the crowd, they perceived another that towered above the undersized natives. It was the fiery
poll of Dicky Maloney against the wall close by the lower step;
and his broad, seductive grin showed that he recognized their
presence.

Dicky had attired himself becomingly for the festive occasion
in a well-fitting black suit. Pasa was close by his side, her head
covered with the ubiquitous black mantilla.

Mr. Vincenti looked at her attentively.

" Botticelli's Madonna," he remarked, gravely. " I wonder
when she got into the game. I don't like his getting tangled with
the women. I hoped he would keep away from them."

Captain Cronin's laugh almost drew attention from the parade.

" With that head of hair ! Keep away from the women ! And
a Maloney ! Hasn't he got a license ? But, nonsense aside, what
do you think of the prospects ? It's a species of filibustering out
of my line."

Vincenti glanced again at Dicky's head and smiled.

" *Rouge et noir*," he said. " There you have it. Make your play,
gentlemen. Our money is on the red."

" The lad's game," said Cronin, with a commending look at
the tall, easy figure by the steps. " But 'tis all like fly-by-night
theatricals to me. The talk's bigger than the stage; there's a smell
of gasoline in the air, and they're their own audience and scene-
shifters."

They ceased talking, for General Pilar had descended from the
first carriage and had taken his stand upon the top step of Casa
Morena. As the oldest member of the cabinet, custom had decreed
that he should make the address of welcome, presenting the keys
of the official residence to the president at its close.

General Pilar was one of the most distinguished citizens of the republic. Hero of three wars and innumerable revolutions, he was an honored guest at European courts and camps. An eloquent speaker and a friend to the people, he represented the highest type of the Anchurians.

Holding in his hand the gilt keys of Casa Morena, he began his address in a historical form, touching upon each administration and the advance of civilization and prosperity from the first striving after liberty down to present times. Arriving at the rêgime of President Losada, at which point, according to precedent, he should have delivered a eulogy upon its wise conduct and the happiness of the people, General Pilar paused. Then he silently held up the bunch of keys high above his head, with his eyes closely regarding it. The ribbon with which they were bound fluttered in the breeze.

" It still blows," cried the speaker, exultantly. " Citizens of Anchuria, give thanks to the saints this night that our air is still free."

Thus disposing of Losada's administration, he abruptly reverted to that of Olivarra, Anchuria's most popular ruler. Olivarra had been assassinated nine years before while in the prime of life and usefulness. A faction of the Liberal party led by Losada himself had been accused of the deed. Whether guilty or not, it was eight years before the ambitious and scheming Losada had gained his goal.

Upon this theme General Pilar's eloquence loosed. He drew the picture of the beneficent Olivarra with a loving hand. He reminded the people of the peace, the security, and the happiness they had enjoyed during that period. He recalled in vivid detail and with significant contrast the last winter sojourn of President Olivarra in Coralio, when his appearance at their fiestas was the signal for thundering *vivas* of love and approbation.

The first public expression of sentiment from the people that day followed. A low, sustained murmer went among them like the surf rolling along the shore.

" Ten dollars to a dinner at the Saint Charles," remarked Mr. Vincenti, " that *rouge* wins."

" I never bet against my own interests," said Captain Cronin, lighting a cigar. " Long-winded old boy, for his age. What's he talking about ? "

" My Spanish," replied Vincenti, " runs about ten words to the minute; his is something around two hundred. Whatever he's saying, he's getting them warmed up."

" Friends and brothers," General Pilar was saying, " could I reach out my hand this day across the lamentable silence of the grave to Olivarra ' the Good,' to the ruler who was one of you, whose tears fell when you sorrowed, and whose smile followed your joy—I would bring him back to you, but—Olivarra is dead—dead at the hands of a craven assassin!"

The speaker turned and gazed boldly into the carriage of the president. His arm remained extended aloft as if to sustain his peroration. The president was listening, aghast, at this remarkable address of welcome. He was sunk back upon his seat, trembling with rage and dumb surprise, his dark hands tightly gripping the carriage cushions.

Half rising, he extended one arm toward the speaker, and shouted a harsh command at Captain Cruz. The leader of the "Flying Hundred" sat his horse, immovable, with folded arms, giving no sign of having heard. Losada sank back again, his dark features distinctly paling.

"Who says that Olivarra is dead?" suddenly cried the speaker, his voice, old as he was, sounding like a battle trumpet. "His body lies in the grave, but to the people he loved he has bequeathed his spirit—yes, more—his learning, his courage, his kindness—yes, more—his youth, his image—people of Anchuria, have you forgotten Ramon, the son of Olivarra?"

Cronin and Vincenti, watching closely, saw Dicky Maloney suddenly raise his hat, tear off his shock of red hair, leap up the steps and stand at the side of General Pilar. The Minister of War laid his arm across the young man's shoulders. All who had known President Olivarra saw again his same lion-like pose, the same frank, undaunted expression, the same high forehead with the peculiar line of the clustering, crisp black hair.

General Pilar was an experienced orator. He seized the moment of breathless silence that preceded the storm.

"Citizens of Anchuria," he trumpeted, holding aloft the keys to Casa Morena, "I am here to deliver these keys—the keys to your homes and liberty—to your chosen president. Shall I deliver them to Enrico Olivarra's assassin, or to his son?"

"Olivarra! Olivarra!" the crowd shrieked and howled. All vociferated the magic name—men, women, children and the parrots.

And the enthusiasm was not confined to the blood of the plebs. Colonel Rocas ascended the steps and laid his sword theatrically at young Ramon Olivarra's feet. Four members of the cabinet embraced him. Captain Cruz gave a command, and twenty of *El Ciento Huilando* dismounted and arranged themselves in a cordon about the steps of Casa Morena.

But Ramon Olivarra seized that moment to prove himself a born genius and politician. He waved those soldiers aside, and descended the steps to the street. There, without losing his dignity or the distinguished elegance that the loss of his red hair brought him, he took the proletariat to his bosom—the barefooted, the dirty, Indians, Caribs, babies, beggars old, young, saints, soldiers and sinners—he missed none of them.

While this act of the drama was being presented, the scene shifters had been busy at the duties that had been assigned to them. Two of Cruz's dragoons had seized the bridle reigns of Losada's horses; others formed a close guard around the carriage; and they galloped off with the tyrant and his two unpopular Ministers. No doubt a place had been prepared for them. There are a number of well-barred stone apartments in Coralio.

" *Rouge* wins," said Mr. Vincenti, calmly lighting another cigar.

Captain Cronin had been intently watching the vicinity of the stone steps for some time.

" Good boy ! " he exclaimed suddenly, as if relieved. " I wondered if he was going to forget his Kathleen Mavourneen."

Young Olivarra had reascended the steps and spoken a few words to General Pilar. Then that distinguished veteran descended to the ground and approached Pasa, who still stood, wonder-eyed, where Dicky had left her. With his plumed hat in his hand, and his medals and decorations shining on his breast, the general spoke to her and gave her his arm, and they went up the stone steps of the Casa Morena together. And then Ramon Olivarra stepped forward and took both her hands before all the people.

And while the cheering was breaking out afresh everywhere, Captain Cronin and Mr. Vincenti turned and walked back toward the shore where the gig was waiting for them.

" There'll be another ' *presidente proclamada* ' in the morning," said Mr. Vincenti, musingly. "As a rule they are not as reliable as the elected ones, but this youngster seems to have some good stuff in him. He planned and manœuvred the entire campaign. Olivarra's widow, you know, was wealthy. After her husband was assassinated she went to the States, and educated her son at Yale The Vesuvius Company hunted him up, and backed him in the little game."

" It's a glorious thing," said Cronin, half jestingly, " to be able to discharge a government, and insert one of your own choosing, in these days."

" Oh, it is only a matter of business," said Vincenti, stopping and offering the stump of his cigar to a monkey that swung down from a lime tree ; " and that is what moves the world of today. That extra *real* on the price of bananas had to go. We took the shortest way of removing it."

TWO RECALLS

THERE remain three duties to be performed before the curtain falls upon the patched comedy. Two have been promised : the third is no less obligatory.

It was set forth in the programme of this tropic vaudeville that it would be made known why Shorty O'Day, of the Columbia Detective Agency, lost his position. Also that Smith should come again to tell us what mystery he followed that night on the shores of Anchuria when he strewed so many cigar stumps around the cocoanut palm during his lonely night vigil on the beach. These things were promised; but a bigger thing yet remains to be accomplished—the clearing up of a seeming wrong that has been done according to the array of chronicled facts (truthfully set forth) that have been presented. And one voice, speaking, shall do these three things.

Two men sat on a stringer of a North River pier in the City of New York. A steamer from the tropics had begun to unload bananas and oranges on the pier. Now and then a banana or two would fall from an overripe bunch, and one of the two men would shamble forward, seize the fruit and return to share it with his companion.

One of the men was in the ultimate stage of deterioration. As far as rain and wind and sun could wreck the garments he wore, it had been done. In his person the ravages of drink were as plainly visible. And yet, upon his high-bridged, rubicund nose was jauntily perched a pair of shining and flawless gold-rimmed glasses.

The other man was not so far gone upon the descending Highway of the Incompetents. Truly, the flower of his manhood had gone to seed—seed, that, perhaps, no soil might sprout. But there were still cross-cuts along where he travelled through which he might yet regain the pathway of usefulness without disturbing the slumbering Miracles. This man was short and compactly built. He had an oblique, dead eye, like that of a string-ray, and the moustache of a cocktail mixer. We know the eye and the moustache; we know that Smith of the luxurious yacht, the gorgeous raiment, the mysterious mission, the magic disappearance, has come again, though shorn of the accessories of his former state.

At his third banana, the man with the nose glasses spat it from him with a shudder.

" Deuce take the fruit ! " he remarked, in a patrician tone of disgust. " I lived for two years where these things grow. The memory of their taste lingers with you. The oranges are not so bad. Just see if you can gather a couple of them, O'Day, when the next broken crate comes up."

"Did you live down with the monkeys?" asked the other, made tepidly garrulous by the sunshine and the alleviating meal of juicy fruit. "I was down there, once myself. But only for a few hours. That was when I was with the Columbia Detective Agency. The monkey people did me up. I'd have my job yet if it hadn't been for them. I'll tell you about it.

"One day the chief sent a note around to the office that read : 'Send O'Day here at once for a big piece of business.' I was the crack detective of the agency at that time. They always handed me the big jobs. The address the chief wrote from was down in the Wall Street district.

"When I got there I found him in a private office with a lot of directors who were looking pretty fuzzy. They stated the case. The president of the Republic Insurance Company had skipped with about a tenth of a million dollars in cash. The directors wanted him back pretty bad, but they wanted the money worse. They said they needed it. They had traced the old gent's movements to where he boarded a tramp fruit steamer bound for South America that same morning with his daughter and the big grip-sack—all the family he had.

"One of the directors had his steam yacht coaled and with steam up, ready for the trip; and he turned her over to me, cart blongsh. In four hours I was on board of her, and hot on the trail of the fruit tub. I had a pretty good idea where old Wahrfield—that was his name, J. Churchill Wahrfield—would head for. At that time we had a treaty with about every foreign country except Belgium and that banana republic Anchuria. There wasn't a photo of old Wahrfield to be had in New York—he had been foxy there—but I had his description. And besides, the lady with him would be a dead-give-away anywhere. She was one of the high-flyers in Society—not the kind that have their pictures in the Sunday papers—but the real sort that open chrysanthemum shows and christen battleships.

"Well, sir, we never got a sight of that fruit tub on the road. The ocean is a pretty big place; and I guess we took different paths across it. But we kept going toward this Anchuria, where the fruiterer was bound for.

"We struck the monkey coast one afternoon about four. There was a ratty-looking steamer off shore taking on bananas. The monkeys were loading her up with big barges. It might be the one the old man had taken, and it might not. I went ashore to look around. The scenery was pretty good. I never saw any finer on the New York stage. I struck an American on shore, a big, cool chap, standing around with the monkeys. He showed me the consul's office. The consul was a nice young fellow. He said the fruiter was the *Karlsefin*, running generally to New Orleans, but took her last cargo to New York. Then I was sure my people were on board, although everybody told me that no passengers had landed. I didn't think they would land until after dark, for they might have been shy about it on account of seeing that yacht of mine hanging around. So, all I had to do was to wait and nab 'em when they came ashore. I couldn't arrest old Wahrfield without extradition papers, but my play was to get the cash. They generally give up if you strike 'em when they're tired and rattled and short on nerve.

"After dark I sat under a cocoanut tree on the beach for a while, and then I walked around and investigated that town some, and it was enough to give you the lions. If a man could stay in New York and be honest, he'd better do it than to hit that monkey town with a million.

" Dinky little mud houses; grass over your shoe tops in the streets; ladies in low-neck-an-short-sleeves walking around smoking cigars; tree frogs rattling like a hose cart going to a ten blow; big mountains dropping gravel in the back yards; and the sea licking the paint off in front—no, sir—a man had better be in God's country living on free lunch than there.

" The main street ran along the beach, and I walked down it, and then turned up a kind of lane where the houses were made of poles and straw. I wanted to see what the monkeys did when they weren't climbing cocoanut trees. The very first shack I looked in I saw my people. They must have come ashore while I was promenading. A man about fifty, smooth face, heavy eyebrows, dressed in black broadcloth, looking like he was just about to say, ' Can any little boy in the Sunday School answer that ? ' He was freezing on to a grip that weighed like a dozen gold bricks, and a swell girl —a regular peach, with a Fifth Avenue cut—was sitting on a wooden chair. An old black woman was fixing some coffee and beans on a table. The light they had came from a lantern hung on a nail. I went and stood in the door, and they looked at me, and I said :

" 'Mr. Wahrfield, you are my prisoner. I hope, for the lady's sake, you will take the matter sensibly. You know why I want you.'

" 'Who are you ? ' says the old gent.

" 'O'Day,' says I, ' of the Columbia Detective Agency. And now, sir, let me give you a piece of good advice. You go back and take your medicine like a man. Hand 'em back the boodle; and maybe they'll let you off light. Go back easy, and I'll put in a word for you. I'll give you five minutes to decide.' I pulled out my watch and waited.

" Then the young lady chipped in. She was one of the genuine high-steppers. You could tell by the way her clothes fit and the style she had that Fifth Avenue was made for her.

" 'Come inside,' she says. Don't stand in the door and disturb the whole street with that suit of clothes. Now, what is it you want?'

" 'Three minutes gone,' I said. ' I'll tell you again while the other two tick off.

" 'You'll admit being the president of the Republic, won't you?'

" 'I am,' says he.

" 'Well, then,' says I, ' it ought to be plain to you. Wanted, in New York, J. Churchill Wahrfield, president of the Republic Insurance Company.

" 'Also the funds belonging to said company, now in that grip, in the unlawful possession of said J. Churchill Wahrfield.'

" 'Oh-h-h-h ! ' says the young lady, as if she was thinking, ' you want to take us back to New York ? '

" 'To take Mr. Wahrfield. There's no charge against you, miss. There'll be no objection, of course, to your returning with your father.'

" Of a sudden the girl gave a tiny scream and grabbed the old boy around the neck. ' Oh, father, father ! ' she says, kind of contralto, ' can this be true ? Have you taken money that is not yours ? Speak, father ! ' It made you shiver to hear the tremolo stop she put on her voice.

" The old boy looked pretty bughouse when she first grappled him, but she went on, whispering in his ear and patting his off shoulder till he stood still, but sweating a little.

" She got him to one side and they talked together a minute, and then he put on some gold eyeglasses and walked up and handed me the grip.

" 'Mr. Detective,' he says, talking a little broken. ' I conclude to return with you. I have finished to discover that life on this desolate and displeased coast would be worse than to die, itself. I will go back and hurl myself upon the mercy of the Republic Company. Have you brought a sheep ? '

" 'Sheep ! ' says I; ' I haven't a single——'

" 'Ship,' cut in the young lady. ' Don't get funny. Father is of German birth, and doesn't speak perfect English. How did you come ? '

" The girl was all broke up. She had a handkerchief to her face, and kept saying every little bit, " Oh, father ! father ! ' She walked up to me and laid her lily-white hand on the clothes that had pained her at first. I told her I came in a private yacht.

" 'Mr. O'Day,' she says. ' Oh, take us away from this horrid country at once. Can you ! Will you ! Say you will.'

" 'I'll try,' I said, concealing the fact that I was dying to get them on salt water before they could change their mind.

" One thing they both kicked against was going through the town to the boat landing. Said they dreaded publicity, and now that they were going to return, they had a hope that the thing might yet be kept out of the papers. They swore they wouldn't go unless I got them out to the yacht without any one knowing it, so I agreed to humor them.

" The sailors who rowed me ashore were playing billiards in a bar-room near the water, waiting for orders, and I proposed to have them take the boat down the beach half a mile or so, and take us up there. How to get them word was the question, for I couldn't leave the grip with the prisoner, and I couldn't take it with me, not knowing but what the monkeys might stick me up.

" The young lady says the old colored woman would take them a note. I sat down and wrote it, and gave it to the dame with plain directions what to do, and she grins like a baboon and shakes her head.

" Then Mr. Wahrfield handed her a string of foreign dialect, and she nods her head and says, ' See, señor,' maybe fifty times, and lights out with the note.

" 'Old Augusta only understands German,' said Miss Wahrfield, smiling at me. ' We stopped in her house to ask where we could find lodging, and she insisted upon our having coffee. She tells us she was raised in a German family in San Domingo.'

" 'Very likely,' I said. ' But you can search me for German words, except *nix verstay* and *noch einst*. I would have called that " See, señor " French, though, on a gamble.'

" Well, we three make a sneak around the edge of town so as not to be seen. We got tangled in vines and ferns and the banana bushes and tropical scenery a good deal. The monkey suburbs was as wild as places in Central Park. We came out of the beach a good half mile below. A brown chap was lying asleep under a cocoanut tree, with a ten-foot musket beside him. Mr. Wahrfield takes up the gun and pitches it into the sea. ' The coast is guarded,' he says. ' Rebellion and plots ripen like fruit.' He pointed to the sleeping man, who never stirred. ' Thus,' he says, ' they perform trusts. Children ! '

" I saw our boat coming, and I struck a match and lit a piece of newspaper to show them where we were. In thirty minutes we were on board the yacht.

" The first thing, Mr. Wahrfield and his daughter and I took the grip into the owner's cabin, opened it up and took an inventory.

There was one hundred and five thousand dollars, United States treasury notes, in it, beside a lot of diamond jewelry and a couple of hundred Havana cigars. I gave the old man the cigars and a receipt for the rest of the lot, as agent for the company, and locked the stuff up in my private quarters.

" I never had a pleasanter trip than that one. After we got to sea the young lady turned out to be the jolliest ever. The very first time we sat down to dinner, and the steward filled her glass with champagne—that director's yacht was a regular floating Waldorf-Astoria—she winks at me and says, ' What's the use to borrow trouble, Mr. Fly Cop ? Here's hoping you may live to eat the hen that scratches on your grave.' There was a piano on board, and she sat down to it and sung better than you give up two cases to hear plenty times. She knew about nine operas clear through. She was sure enough *bon ton* and swell. She wasn't one of the ' among others present' kind; she belonged on the special mention list !

" The old man, too, perked up amazingly on the way. He passed the cigars, and says to me once, quite chipper, out of a cloud of smoke, ' Mr. O'Day, somehow I think the Republic Company will not give me the much trouble. Guard well the gripvalise of the money, Mr. O'Day, for that it must be returned to them that it belongs when we finish to arrive.'

" When we landed in New York I 'phoned to the chief to meet us in that director's office. We got in a cab and went there. I carried the grip, and we walked in, and I was pleased to see that the chief had got together that same old crowd of moneybugs with pink faces and white vests to see us march in. I set the grip on the table. ' There's the money,' I said.

" 'And your prisoner ? ' said the chief.

" I pointed to Mr. Wahrfield, and he stepped forward and say :

" 'The honor of a word with you, sir, to explain.'

" He and the chief went into another room and stayed ten minutes. When they came back the chief looked as black as a ton of coal.

" 'Did this gentleman,' he says to me, ' have this valise in his possession when you first saw him ? '

" 'He did,' said I.

" The chief took up the grip and handed it to the prisoner with a bow, and says to the director crowd : ' Do any of you recognize this gentleman ? '

" They all shook their pink faces.

" 'Allow me to present,' he goes on, 'Señor Miraflores, president of the Republic of Anchuria. The señor has generously consented to overlook this outrageous blunder, on condition that we undertake to secure him against the annoyance of public comment.

It is a concession on his part to overlook an insult for which he might claim international redress. I think we can gratefully promise him secrecy in the matter.'

"They gave him a pink nod all round.

" 'O'Day,' he says to me. 'As a private detective you're wasted. In a war, where kidnapping governments is in the rules, you'd be invaluable. Come down to the office at eleven.'

" I knew what that meant.

" 'So that's the president of the monkeys,' says I. ' Well, why couldn't he have said so ? '

" Wouldn't it jar you ? "

THE VITAGRAPHOSCOPE

VAUDEVILLE is intrinsically episodic and discontinuous. Its audiences do not demand dénouements. Sufficient unto each " turn " is the evil thereof. No one cares how many romances the singing comédienne may have had if she can capably sustain the limelight and a high note or two. The audiences reck not if the performing dogs get to the pound the moment they have jumped through their last hoop. They do not desire bulletins about the possible injuries received by the comic bicyclist who retires head-first from the stage in a crash of (property) china-ware. Neither do they consider that their seat coupons entitle them to be in-structed whether or no there is a sentiment between the lady solo banjoist and the Irish monologist.

Therefore let us have no lifting of the curtain upon a tableau of the united lovers, backgrounded by defeated villainy and dero-gated by the comic, osculating maid and butler, thrown in as a sop to the Cerberi of the fifty-cent seats.

But our programme ends with a brief " turn " or two; and then to the exits. Whoever sits the show out may find, if he will, the slender thread that binds together, though ever so slightly, the story that, perhaps, only the Walrus will understand.

Extracts from a letter from the first vice-president of the Republic Insurance Company, of New York City, to Frank Goodwin, of Coralio, Republic of Anchuria.

My Dear Mr. Goodwin :—Your communication per Messrs. Howland and Fourchet, of New Orleans, has reached us. Also their draft on N.Y. for $100,000, the amount abstracted from the funds of this company by the late J. Churchill Wahrfield, its former president. . . . The officers and directors unite in requesting me to express to you their sincere esteem and thanks for your prompt and much appreciated return of the entire missing sum within two weeks from the time of its diasppearance. . . . Can assure you that the matter will not be allowed to receive the least publicity. . . . Regret exceedingly the distressing death of Mr. Wahrfield by his own hand, but. . . . Congratulations on your marriage to Miss Wahrfield . . . many charms, winning manners, noble and womanly nature and envied position in the best metropolitan society. . . .

Cordially yours,

Lucius E. Applegate.

First Vice-President of the Republic Insurance Company.

The Vitagraphoscope

(Moving Pictures)

The Last Sausage

SCENE—*An Artist's Studio.* The artist, a young man of prepossessing appearance, sits in a dejected attitude, amid a litter of sketches, with his head resting upon his hand. An oil stove stands on a pine box in the centre of the studio. The artist rises, tightens his waist belt to another hole, and lights the stove. He goes to a tin bread box, half-hidden by a screen, takes out a solitary link of sausage, turns the box up-side-down to show that there is no more, and chucks the sausage into a frying-pan, which he sets upon the stove. The flame of the stove goes out, showing that there is no more oil. The artist, in evident despair, seizes the sausage, in a sudden access of rage, and hurls it violently from him. At the same time a door opens, and a man who enters receives the sausage forcibly against his nose. He seems to cry out; and is observed to make a dance step or two, vigorously. The newcomer is a ruddy-faced, active, keen-looking man, apparently of Irish ancestry. Next he is observed to laugh immoderately; he kicks over the stove; he claps the artist (who is vainly striving to grasp his hand) vehemently upon the back. Then he goes through a pantomime which to the sufficiently intelligent spectator reveals that he has acquired large sums of money by trading pot-metal hatchets and razors to the Indians of the Cordillera Mountains for gold dust. He draws a roll of money as large as a small loaf of bread from his pocket, and waves it above his head, while at the same time he makes pantomime of drinking from a glass. The artist hurriedly secures his hat, and the two leave the studio together.

The Writing on the Sands

SCENE—*The Beach at Nice.* A woman, beautiful, still young, exquisitely clothed, complacent, poised, reclines near the water, idly scrawling letters in the sand with the staff of her silken parasol. The beauty of her face is audacious; her languid pose is one that you feel to be impermanent—you wait, expectant, for her to spring or glide or crawl, like a panther that has unaccountably become stock-still, She idly scrawls in the sand; and the word that she always writes is " Isabel." A man sits a few yards away. You can see that they are companions, even if no longer comrades. His face dark and smooth, and almost inscrutable—but not quite. The two speak little together. The man also scratches on the sand with his cane. And the word that he writes is "Anchuria." And then he looks out where the Mediterranean and the sky intermingle, with death in his gaze.

The Wilderness and Thou

SCENE—*The Borders of a Gentleman's Estate in a Tropical Land.* An old Indian, with a mahogany-colored face, is trimming the grass on a grave by a mangrove swamp. Presently he rises to his feet and walks slowly toward a grove that is shaded by the gathering, brief twilight. In the edge of the grove stands a man who is stalwart, with a kind and courteous air, and a woman of a serene and clear-cut loveliness. When the old Indian comes up to them the man drops money in his hand. The grave-tender, with the stolid pride of his race, takes it as his due, and goes his way. The two in the edge of the grove turn back along the dim pathway, and walk close, close—for, after all, what is the world at its best but a little round field of the moving pictures with two walking together in it ?

CURTAIN

THE FOUR MILLION

CONTENTS

TOBIN'S PALM

Tobin and me, the two of us, went down to Coney one day, for there was four dollars between us, and Tobin had need of distractions. For there was Katie Mahorner, his sweetheart, of County Sligo, lost since she started for America three months before with two hundred dollars, her own savings, and one hundred dollars from the sale of Tobin's inherited estate, a fine cottage and pig on the Bog Shannaugh. And since the letter that Tobin got saying that she had started to come to him not a bit of news had he heard or seen of Katie Mahorner. Tobin advertised in the papers, but nothing could be found of the colleen.

So, to Coney me and Tobin went, thinking that a turn at the chutes and the smell of the popcorn might raise the heart in his bosom. But Tobin was a hard-headed man, and the sadness stuck in his skin. He ground his teeth at the crying balloons; he cursed the moving pictures; and, though he would drink whenever asked, he scorned Punch and Judy, and was for licking the tintype men as they came.

So I gets him down on a side way on a board walk where the attractions were some less violent. At a little six by eight stall Tobin halts, with a more human look in his eye.

" 'Tis here," says he, " I will be diverted. I'll have the palm of me hand investigated by the wonderful palmist of the Nile, and see if what is to be will be."

Tobin was a believer in signs and the unnatural in nature. He possessed illegal convictions in his mind along the subjects of black cats, lucky numbers, and the weather predictions in the papers.

We went into the enchanted chicken coop, which was fixed mysterious with red cloth and pictures of hands with lines crossing 'em like a railroad centre. The sign over the door says it is Madame Zozo the Egyptian Palmist. There was a fat woman inside in a red jumper with pothooks and beasties embroidered upon it. Tobin gives her ten cents and extends one of his hands. She lifts Tobin's hand, which is own brother to the hoof of a drayhorse, and examines it to see whether 'tis a stone in the frog or a cast shoe he has come for.

" Man," says this Madame Zozo, " the line of your fate shows——"

" 'Tis not me foot at all," says Tobin, interrupting. " Sure, 'tis no beauty, but ye hold the palm of me hand."

"The line shows," says the Madame, "that ye've not arrived at your time of life without bad luck. And there's more to come. The mount of Venus—or is that a stone bruise?—shows that ye've been in love. There's been trouble in your life on account of your sweetheart."

"'Tis Katie Mahorner she has references with," whispers Tobin to me in a loud voice to one side.

"I see," says the palmist, "a great deal of sorrow and tribulation with one whom ye cannot forget. I see the lines of designation point to the letter K and the letter M in her name."

"Whist!" says Tobin to me; "do ye hear that?"

"Look out," goes on the palmist, "for a dark man and a light woman; for they'll both bring ye trouble. Ye'll make a voyage upon the water very soon, and have a financial loss. I see one line that brings good luck. There's a man coming into your life who will fetch ye good fortune. Ye'll know him when ye see him by his crooked nose."

"Is his name set down?" asks Tobin. "'Twill be convenient in the way of greeting when he backs up to dump off the good luck."

"His name," says the palmist, thoughtful looking, "is not spelled out by the lines, but they indicate 'tis a long one, and the letter ' o ' should be in it. There's no more to tell. Good-evening. Don't block up the door."

"'Tis wonderful how she knows," says Tobin as we walk to the pier.

As we squeezed through the gates a nigger man sticks his lighted segar against Tobin's ear, and there is trouble. Tobin hammers his neck, and the women squeal, and by presence of mind I drag the little man out of the way before the police comes. Tobin is always in an ugly mood when enjoying himself.

On the boat going back, when the man calls "Who wants the good-looking waiter?" Tobin tried to plead guilty, feeling the desire to blow the foam off a crock of suds, but when he felt in his pocket he found himself discharged for lack of evidence. Somebody had disturbed his change during the commotion. So we sat, dry, upon the stools, listening to the Dagoes fiddling on deck. If anything, Tobin was lower in spirits and less congenial with his misfortunes than when we started.

On a seat against the railing was a young woman dressed suitable for red automobiles, with hair the color of an unsmoked meerschaum. In passing by Tobin kicks her foot without intentions, and, being polite to ladies when in drink, he tries to give his hat a twist while apologizing. But he knocks it off, and the wind carries it overboard.

Tobin came back and sat down, and I began to look out for him, for the man's adversities were becoming frequent. He was apt, when pushed so close by hard luck, to kick the best dressed man he could see, and try to take command of the boat.

Presently Tobin grabs my arm and says, excited : " Jawn," says he, " do ye know what we're doing ? We're taking a voyage upon the water."

" There now," says I; " subdue yeself. The boat'll land in ten minutes more."

" Look," says he, " at the light lady upon the bench. And have ye forgotten the nigger man that burned me ear ? And isn't the money I had gone—a dollar sixty-five it was ? "

I thought he was no more than summing up his catastrophes so as to get violent with good excuse, as men will do, and I tried to make him understand such things was trifles.

" Listen," says Tobin. " Ye've no ear for the gift of prophecy or the miracles of the inspired. What did the palmist lady tell ye out of me hand ? 'Tis coming true before your eyes. ' Look out,' says she, ' for a dark man and a light woman; they'll bring ye trouble.' Have ye forgot the nigger man, though he got some of it back from me fist ? Can ye show me a lighter woman than the blonde lady that was the cause of me hat falling in the water ? And where's the dollar sixty-five I had in me vest when we left the shooting gallery ? "

The way Tobin put it, it did seem to corroborate the art of prediction, though it looked to me that these accidents could happen to any one at Coney without the implication of palmistry.

Tobin got up and walked around on deck, looking close at the passengers out of his little red eyes. I asked him the interpretation of his movements. Ye never know what Tobin has in his mind until he begins to carry it out.

" Ye should know," says he, " I'm working out the salvation promised by the lines in me palm. I'm looking for the crooked-nose man that's to bring the good luck. 'Tis all that will save us. Jawn, did ye ever see a straighter-nosed gang of hellions in the days of your life ? "

'Twas the nine-thirty boat, and we landed and walked up-town through Twenty-second Street, Tobin being without his hat.

On a street corner, standing under a gas-light and looking over the elevated road at the moon, was a man. A long man he was, dressed decent, with a segar between his teeth, and I saw that his nose made two twists from bridge to end, like the wriggle of a snake. Tobin saw it at the same time, and I heard him breathe hard like a horse when you take the saddle off. He went straight up to the man, and I went with him.

" Good-night to ye," Tobin says to the man. The man takes out a segar and passes the compliments, sociable.

" Would ye hand us your name," asks Tobin, " and let us look at the size of it ? It may be our duty to become acquainted with ye."

" My name," says the man, polite, " is Friedenhausman— Maximus G. Friedenhausman."

" 'Tis the right length," says Tobin. " Do you spell it with an ' o ' anywhere down the stretch of it ? "

" I do not," says the man.

" *Can* ye spell it with an ' o ' ? " inquires Tobin, turning anxious.

" If your conscience," says the man with the nose, " is indisposed toward foreign idioms ye might, to please yourself, smuggle the letter into the penultimate syllable."

" 'Tis well," says Tobin. " Ye're in the presence of Jawn Malone and Daniel Tobin."

" 'Tis highly appreciated," says the man, with a bow. "And now since I cannot conceive that ye would hold a spelling bee upon the street corner, will ye name some reasonable excuse for being at large ? "

" By the two signs," answers Tobin, trying to explain, " which ye display according to the reading of the Egyptian palmist from the sole of me hand, ye've been nominated to offset with good luck the lines of trouble leading to the nigger man and the blonde lady with her feet crossed in the boat, besides the financial loss of a dollar sixty-five, all so far fulfilled according to Hoyle."

The man stopped smoking and looked at me.

" Have ye any amendments," he asks, " to offer to that statement, or are ye one too ? I thought by the looks of ye ye might have him in charge."

" None," says I to him, " except that as one horseshoe resembles another so are ye the picture of good luck as predicted by the hand of me friend. If not, then the lines of Danny's hand may have been crossed, I don't know."

" There's two of ye," says the man with the nose, looking up and down for the sight of a policeman. " I've enjoyed your company immense. Good-night."

With that he shoves his segar in his mouth and moves across the street, stepping fast. But Tobin sticks close to one side of him and me at the other.

" What ! " says he, stopping on the opposite sidewalk and pushing back his hat; " do ye follow me ? I tell ye," he says, very loud, " I'm proud to have met ye. But it is my desire to be rid of ye. I am off to me home."

" Do," says Tobin, leaning against his sleeve. " Do be off to your home. And I will sit at the door of it till ye come out in the morning. For the dependence is upon ye to obviate the curse of the nigger man and the blonde lady and the financial loss of the one-sixty-five."

" 'Tis a strange hallucination," says the man, turning to me as a more reasonable lunatic. " Hadn't ye better get him home ? "

" Listen, man," says I to him. " Daniel Tobin is as sensible as he ever was. Maybe he is a bit deranged on account of having drink enough to disturb but not enough to settle his wits, but he is no more than following out the legitimate path of his superstitions and predicaments, which I will explain to you." With that I relates the facts about the palmist lady and how the finger of suspicion points to him as an instrument of good fortune. " Now, understand I concludes, " my position in this riot. I am the friend of me friend Tobin, according to me interpretations. 'Tis easy to be a friend to the prosperous, for it pays; 'tis not hard to be a friend to the poor, for ye get puffed up by gratitude and have your picture printed standing in front of a tenement with a scuttle of coal and an orphan in each hand. But it strains the art of friendship to be true friend to a born fool. And that's what I'm doing," says I, " for, in my opinion, there's no fortune to be read from the palm of me hand that wasn't printed there with the handle of a pick. And, though ye've got the crookedest nose in New York City, I misdoubt that all the fortune-tellers doing business could milk good luck from ye. But the lines of Danny's hand pointed to ye fair, and I'll assist him to experiment with ye until he's convinced ye're dry."

After that the man turns, sudden, to laughing. He leans against a corner and laughs considerable. Then he claps me and Tobin on the backs of us and takes us by an arm apiece.

" 'Tis my mistake," says he. " How could I expecting anything so fine and wonderful to be turning the corner upon me ? I came near being found unworthy. Hard by," says he, ' 'is a cafe, snug and suitable for the entertainment of idiosyncrasies. Let us go there and have a drink while we discuss the unavailability of the categorical."

So saying, he marched me and Tobin to the back room of a saloon, and ordered the drinks, and laid the money on the table. He looks at me and Tobin like brothers of his, and we have the segars.

" Ye must know," says the man of destiny, " that me walk in life is one that is called the literary. I wander abroad be night seeking idiosyncrasies in the masses and truth in the heavens above. When ye came upon me I was in contemplation of the elevated road in conjunction with the chief luminary of night. The rapid transit is poetry and art : the moon but a tedious, dry body, moving by rote. But these are private opinions, for, in the business of literature, the conditions are reversed. 'Tis me hope to be writing a book to explain the strange things I have discovered in life."

" Ye will put me in a book," says Tobin, disgusted; " will ye put me in a book ? "

" I will not," says the man, " for the covers will not hold ye. Not yet. The best I can do is to enjoy ye meself, for the time is not ripe for destroying the limitations of print. Ye would look fantastic in type. All alone by meself must I drink this cup of joy. But, I thank ye, boys; I am truly grateful."

" The talk of ye," says Tobin, blowing through his moustache and pounding the table with his fist, " is an eyesore to me patience. There was good luck promised out of the crook of your nose, but ye bear fruit like the bang of a drum. Ye resemble, with your noise of books, the wind blowing through a crack. Sure, now, I would be thinking the palm of me hand lied but for the coming true of the nigger man and the blonde lady and——"

" Whist ! " says the long man; " would ye be led astray by physiognomy ? Me nose will do what it can within bounds. Let us have these glasses filled again, for 'tis good to keep idiosyncrasies well moistened, they being subject to deterioration in a dry moral atmosphere."

So, the man of literature makes good, to my notion, for he pays, cheerful, for everything, the capital of me and Tobin being exhausted by prediction. But Tobin is sore, and drinks quiet, with the red showing in his eye.

By and by we moved out, for 'twas eleven o'clock, and stands a bit upon the sidewalk. And then the man says he must be going home, and invites me and Tobin to walk that way. We arrives on a side street two blocks away where there is a stretch of brick houses with high stoops and iron fences. The man stops at one of them and looks at the top windows which he finds dark.

" 'Tis me humble dwelling," says he, " and I begin to perceive the signs that me wife has retired to slumber. Therefore I will venture a bit in the way of hospitality. 'Tis me wish that ye enter the basement room, where we dine, and partake of a reasonable refreshment. There will be some fine fowl cold and cheese and a bottle or two of ale. Ye will be welcome to enter and eat, for I am indebted to ye for diversions.

The appetite and conscience of me and Tobin was congenial to the proposition, though 'twas sticking hard in Danny's superstitions to think that a few drinks and a cold lunch should represent the good fortune promised by the palm of his hand.

"Step down the steps," says the man with the crooked nose, "and I will enter by the door above and let ye in. I will ask the new girl we have in the kitchen," says he, "to make ye a pot of coffee to drink before ye go. 'Tis fine coffee Katie Mahorner makes for a green girl just landed three months. Step in," says the man, "and I'll send her down to ye."

THE GIFT OF THE MAGI

ONE dollar and eighty-seven cents. That was all. And sixty cents of it was in pennies. Pennies saved one and two at a time by bulldozing the grocer and the vegetable man and the butcher until one's cheeks burned with the silent imputation of parsimony that such close dealing implied. Three times Della counted it. One dollar and eighty-seven cents. And the next day would be Christmas.

There was clearly nothing to do but flop down on the shabby little couch and howl. So Della did it. Which instigates the moral reflection that life is made up of sobs, with sniffles predominating.

While the mistress of the home is gradually subsiding from the first stage to the second, take a look at the home. A furnished flat at $8 per week. It did not exactly beggar description, but it certainly had that word on the lookout for the mendicancy squad.

In the vestibule below was a letter-box into which no letter would go, and an electric button from which no mortal finger could coax a ring. Also appertaining thereunto was a card bearing the name "Mr. James Dillingham Young."

The "Dillingham" had been flung to the breeze during a former period of prosperity when its possessor was being paid $30 per week. Now, when the income was shrunk to $20, the letters of "Dillingham" looked blurred, as though they were thinking seriously of contracting to a modest and unassuming D. But whenever Mr. James Dillingham Young came home and reached his flat above he was called "Jim" and greatly hugged by Mrs. James Dillingham Young, already introduced to you as Della. Which is all very good.

Della finished her cry and attended to her cheeks with the powder rag. She stood by the window and looked out dully at a gray cat walking a gray fence in a gray backyard. Tomorrow would be Christmas Day, and she had only $1.87 with which to buy Jim a present. She had been saving every penny she could for months, with this result. Twenty dollars a week doesn't go far. Expenses had been greater than she had calculated. They always are. Only $1.87 to buy a present for Jim. Her Jim. Many a happy hour she had spent planning for something nice for him. Something fine and rare and sterling—something just a little bit near to being worthy of the honor of being owned by Jim.

There was a pier-glass between the windows of the room. Perhaps you have seen a pier-glass in an $8 flat. A very thin and very agile person may, by observing his reflection in a rapid sequence of longitudinal strips, obtain a fairly accurate conception of his looks. Della, being slender, had mastered the art.

Suddenly she whirled from the window and stood before the glass. Her eyes were shining brilliantly, but her face had lost its color within twenty seconds. Rapidly she pulled down her hair and let it fall to its length.

Now, there were two possessions of the James Dillingham Youngs in which they both took a mighty pride. One was Jim's gold watch that had been his father's and his grandfather's. The other was Della's hair. Had the Queen of Sheba lived in the flat across the airshaft, Della would have let her hair hang out the window some day to dry just to depreciate Her Majesty's jewels and gifts. Had King Solomon been the janitor, with all his treasures piled up in the basement, Jim would have pulled out his watch every time he passed, just to see him pluck at his beard from envy.

So now Della's beautiful hair fell about her rippling and shining like a cascade of brown waters. It reached below her knee and made itself almost a garment for her. And then she did it up again nervously and quickly. Once she faltered for a minute and stood still while a tear or two splashed on the worn red carpet.

On went her old brown jacket; on went her old brown hat. With a whirl of skirts and with the brilliant sparkle still in her eyes, she fluttered out the door and down the stairs to the street.

Where she stopped the sign read : " Mme. Sofronie. Hair Goods of All Kinds." One flight up Della ran, and collected herself, panting. Madame, large, too white, chilly, hardly looked the " Sofronie."

" Will you buy my hair ? " asked Della.

" I buy hair," said Madame. " Take yer hat off and let's have a sight at the looks of it."

Down rippled the brown cascade.

" Twenty dollars," said Madame, lifting the mass with a practised hand.

" Give it to me quick," said Della.

Oh, and the next two hours tripped by on rosy wings. Forget the hashed metaphor. She was ransacking the stores for Jim's present.

She found it at last. It surely had been made for Jim and no

one else. There was no other like it in any of the stores, and she had
turned all of them inside out. It was a platinum fob chain simple
and chaste in design, properly proclaiming its value by substance
alone and not by meretricious ornamentation—as all good things
should do. It was even worthy of The Watch. As soon as she saw
it she knew that it must be Jim's. It was like him. Quietness and
value—the description applied to both. Twenty-one dollars they
took from her for it, and she hurried home with the 87 cents. With
that chain on his watch Jim might be properly anxious about the
time in any company. Grand as the watch was, he sometimes
looked at it on the sly on account of the old leather strap that he
used in place of a chain.

When Della reached home her intoxication gave way a little
to prudence and reason. She got out her curling irons and lighted
the gas and went to work repairing the ravages made by generosity
added to love. Which is always a tremendous task, dear friends
—a mammoth task.

Within forty minutes her head was covered with tiny, close-lying
curls that made her look wonderfully like a truant schoolboy. She
looked at her reflection in the mirror long, carefully, and critically.

" If Jim doesn't kill me," she said to herself, " before he takes
a second look at me, he'll say I look like a Coney Island chorus
girl. But what could I do—oh ! what could I do with a dollar and
eighty-seven cents ? "

At 7 o'clock the coffee was made and the frying-pan was on the
back of the stove hot and ready to cook the chops.

Jim was never late. Della doubled the fob chain in her hand
and sat on the corner of the table near the door that he always
entered. Then she heard his step on the stair away down on the
first flight, and she turned white for just a moment. She had a
habit of saying little silent prayers about the simplest everyday
things, and now she whispered : " Please God, make him think
I am still pretty."

The door opened and Jim stepped in and closed it. He looked
thin and very serious. Poor fellow, he was only twenty-two—and
to be burdened with a family ! He needed a new overcoat and
he was without gloves.

Jim stopped inside the door, as immovable as a setter at the
scent of quail. His eyes were fixed upon Della, and there was an
expression in them that she could not read, and it terrified her.
It was not anger, nor surprise, nor disapproval, nor horror, nor
any of the sentiments that she had been prepared for. He simply
stared at her fixedly with that peculiar expression on his face.

Della wriggled off the table and went for him.

" Jim, darling," she cried, " don't look at me that way. I had my hair cut off and sold it because I couldn't haved lived through Christmas without giving you a present. It'll grow out again—you won't mind, will you ? I just had to do it. My hair grows awfully fast. Say 'Merry Christmas ! ' Jim, and let's be happy. You don't know what a nice—what a beautiful, nice gift I've got for you."

"You've cut off your hair ? " asked Jim, laboriously, as if he had not arrived at that patent fact yet even after the hardest mental labor.

"Cut it off and sold it," said Della. "Don't you like me just as well, anyhow ? I'm me without my hair, ain't I ? "

Jim looked about the room curiously.

"You say your hair is gone ? " he said, with an air almost of idiocy.

"You needn't look for it," said Della. "It's sold, I tell you—sold and gone, too, It's Christmas Eve, boy. Be good to me, for it went for you. Maybe the hairs of my head were numbered," she went on with a sudden serious sweetness, "but nobody could ever count my love for you. Shall I put the chops on, Jim ? "

Out of his trance Jim seemed quickly to wake. He enfolded his Della. For ten seconds let us regard with discreet scrutiny some inconsequential object in the other direction. Eight dollars a week or a million a year—what is the difference ? A mathematician or a wit would give you the wrong answer. The magi brought valuable gifts, but that was not among them. This dark assertion will be illuminated later on.

Jim drew a package from his overcoat pocket and threw it upon the table.

"Don't make any mistake, Dell," he said, "about me. I don't think there's anything in the way of a haircut or a shave or a shampoo that could make me like my girl any less. But if you'll unwrap that package you may see why you had me going a while at first."

White fingers and nimble tore at the string and paper. And then an ecstatic scream of joy; and then, alas ! a quick feminine change to hysterical tears and wails, necessitating the immediate employment of all the comforting powers of the lord of the flat.

For there lay The Combs—the set of combs, side and back, that Della had worshipped for long in a Broadway window. Beautiful combs, pure tortoise shell, with jewelled rims—just the shade to wear in the beautiful vanished hair. They were expensive combs, she knew, and her heart had simply craved and yearned over them without the least hope of possession. And now, they were hers, but the tresses that should have adorned the coveted adornments were gone.

But she hugged them to her bosom, and at length she was able to look up with dim eyes and a smile and say : " My hair grows so fast, Jim ! "

And then Della leaped up like a little singed cat and cried, " Oh, oh ! "

Jim had not yet seen his beautiful present. She held it out to him eagerly upon her open palm. The dull precious metal seemed to flash with a reflection of her bright and ardent spirit.

" Isn't it a dandy, Jim ? I hunted all over town to find it. You'll have to look at the time a hundred times a day now. Give me your watch. I want to see how it looks on it."

Instead of obeying, Jim tumbled down on the couch and put his hands under the back of his head and smiled.

" Dell," said he, " let's put our Christmas presents away and keep 'em a while. They're too nice to use just at present. I sold the watch to get the money to buy your combs. And now suppose you put the chops on."

The magi, as you know, were wise men—wonderfully wise men —who brought gifts to the Babe in the manger. They invented the art of giving Christmas presents. Being wise, their gifts were no doubt wise ones, possibly bearing the privilege of exchange in case of duplication. And here I have lamely related to you the un-eventful chronicle of two foolish children in a flat who most un-wisely sacrificed for each other the greatest treasures of their house. But in a last word to the wise of these days let it be said that of all who give gifts these two were the wisest. Of all who give and receive gifts, such as they are wisest. Everywhere they are the wisest. They are the magi.

A COSMOPOLITE IN A CAFÉ

At midnight the café was crowded. By some chance the little table at which I sat had escaped the eye of incomers, and two vacant chairs at it extended their arms with venal hospitality to the influx of patrons.

And then a cosmopolite sat in one of them, and I was glad, for I held a theory that since Adam no true citizen of the world has existed. We hear of them, and we see foreign labels on much luggage, but we find travellers instead of cosmopolites.

I invoke your consideration of the scene—the marble-topped tables, the range of leather-upholstered wall seats, the gay com-pany, the ladies dressed in demi-state toilets, speaking in an exquisite visible chorus of taste, economy, opulence or art; the sedulous and largess-loving *garçons*, the music wisely catering to all with its raids upon the composers; the *mélange* of talk and laughter—and, if you will, the Würzburger in the tall glass cones that bend to your lips as a ripe cherry sways on its branch to the beak of a robber jay. I was told by a sculptor from Mauch Chunk that the scene was truly Parisian.

My cosmopolite was named E. Rushmore Coglan, and he will be heard from next summer at Coney Island. He is to establish a new " attraction " there, he informed me, offering kingly diversion. And then his conversation rang along parallels of latitude and longitude. He took the great, round world in his hand, so to speak, familiarly, contemptuously, and it seemed no larger than the seed of a Maraschino cherry in a *table d'hôte* grape fruit. He spoke disrespectfully of the equator, he skipped from continent to continent, he derided the zones, he mopped up the high seas with his napkin. With a wave of his hand he would speak of a certain bazaar in Hyderabad. Whiff ! He would have you on skis in Lapland. Zip ! Now you rode the breakers with the Kanakas at Kealaikahiki. Presto ! He dragged you through an Arkansas post-oak swamp, let you dry for a moment on the alkali plains of his Idaho ranch, then whirled you into the society of Viennese archdukes. Anon he would be telling you of a cold he acquired in a Chicago lake breeze and how old Escamila cured it in Buenos Ayres with a hot infusion of the *chuchula* weed. You would have addressed a letter to " E. Rushmore Coglan, Esq., the Earth, Solar System, the Universe," and mailed it, feeling confident that it would be delivered to him.

I was sure that I had found at last the one true cosmopolite since Adam, and I listened to his world-wide discourse fearful lest I should discover in it the local note of the mere globe-trotter. But his opinions never fluttered or drooped; he was as impartial to cities, countries, and continents as the winds or gravitation.

And as E. Rushmore Coglan prattled of this little planet I thought with glee of a great almost-cosmopolite who wrote for the whole world and dedicated himself to Bombay. In a poem he has to say that there is pride and rivalry between the cities of the earth, and that " the men that breed from them, they traffic up and down, but cling to their cities' hem as a child to the mother's gown." And whenever they walk " by roaring streets unknown " they remember their native city " most faithful, foolish, fond ; making her mere-breathed name their bond upon their bond." And my glee was roused because I had caught Mr. Kipling napping. Here I had found a man not made from dust; one who had no narrow boasts of birthplace or country, one who, if he bragged at all, would brag of his whole round globe against the Martians and the inhabitants of the Moon.

Expression on these subjects were precipitated from E. Rushmore Coglan by the third corner to our table. While Coglan was describing to me the topography along the Siberian Railway the orchestra glided into a medley. The concluding air was " Dixie," and as the exhilarating notes tumbled forth they were almost overpowered by a great clapping of hands from almost every table.

It is worth a paragraph to say that this remarkable scene can be witnessed every evening in numerous cafés in the City of New York. Tons of brew have been consumed over theories to account for it. Some have conjectured hastily that all Southerners in town hie themselves to cafés at nightfall. This applause of the " rebel " air in a Northern city does puzzle a little; but it is not insolvable. The war with Spain, many years' generous mint and watermelon crops, a few long-shot winners at the New Orleans race track, and the brilliant banquets given by the Indiana and Kansas citizens who compose the North Carolina Society have made the South rather a " fad " in Manhattan. Your manicure will lisp softly that your left forefinger reminds her so much of a gentleman's in Richmond, Va. Oh, certainly; but many a lady has to work now— the war, you know.

When " Dixie " was being played a dark-haired young man sprang up from somewhere with a Mosby guerrilla yell and waved frantically his soft-brimmed hat. Then he strayed through the smoke, dropped into the vacant chair at our table and pulled out cigarettes.

The evening was at the period when reserve is thawed. One of us mentioned three Würzburgers to the waiter; the dark-haired young man acknowledged his inclusion in the order by a smile and a nod. I hastened to ask him a question because I wanted to try out a theory I had.

" Would you mind telling me," I began, " whether you are from——"

The fist of E. Rushmore Coglan banged the table and I was jarred into silence.

" Excuse me," said he, " but that's a question I never like to hear asked. What does it matter where a man is from ? Is it fair to judge a man by his post-office address ? Why, I've seen Kentuckians who hated whiskey, Virginians who weren't descended from Pocahontas, Indianians who hadn't written a novel, Mexicans who didn't wear velvet trousers with silver dollars sewed along the seams, funny Englishmen, spendthrift Yankees, cold-blooded Southerners, narrow-minded Westerners, and New Yorkers who were too busy to stop for an hour on the street to watch a one-armed grocer's clerk do up cranberries in paper bags. Let a man be a man and don't handicap him with the label of any section."

"Pardon me," I said, "but my curiosity was not altogether an idle one. I know the South, and when the band plays ' Dixie ' I like to observe. I have formed the belief that the man who applauds that air with special violence and ostensible sectional loyalty is invariably a native of either Secausus, N. J., or the district between Murray Hill Lyceum and the Harlem River, this city. I was about to put my opinion to the test by inquiring of this gentleman when you interrupted with your own—larger theory, I must confess."

And now the dark-haired young man spoke to me, and it became evident that his mind also moved along its own set of grooves.

"I should like to be a periwinkle," said he, mysteriously, " on the top of a valley, and sing too-ralloo-ralloo."

This was clearly too obscure, so I turned again to Coglan.

"I've been around the world twelve times," said he. " I know an Esquimau in Upernavik who sends to Cincinnati for his neck-ties, and I saw a goat-herder in Uruguay who won a prize in a Battle Creek breakfast food puzzle competition. I pay rent on a room in Cairo, Egypt, and another in Yokohama all the year around. I've got slippers waiting for me in a tea-house in Shanghai, and I don't have to tell 'em how to cook my eggs in Rio Janeiro or Seattle. It's a mighty little old world. What's the use of brag-ging about being from the North, or the South, or the old manor house in the dale, or Euclid Avenue, Cleveland, of Pike's Peak, or Fairfax County, Va., or Hooligan's Flats or any place ? It'll be a better world when we quit being fools about some mildewed town or ten acres of swampland just because we happened to be born there."

"You seem to be a genuine cosmopolite," I said, admiringly. " But it also seems that you would decry patriotism."

"A relic of the stone age," declared Coglan, warmly. " We are all brothers—Chinamen, Englishmen, Zulus, Patagonians and the people in the bend of the Kaw River. Some day all this petty pride in one's city or state or section or country will be wiped out, and we'll all be citizens of the world, as we ought to be."

"But while you are wandering in foreign lands," I persisted, " do not your thoughts revert to some spot—some dear and——"

"Nary a spot," interrupted E. R. Coglan, flippantly. " The terrestial, globular, planetary hunk of matter, slightly flattened at the poles, and known as the Earth, is my abode. I've met a good many object-bound citizens of this country abroad. I've seen men from Chicago sit in a gondola in Venice on a moonlight night and brag about their drainage canal. I've seen a Southerner on being introduced to the King of England hand that monarch, without batting his eyes, the information that his grand-aunt on his mother's side was related by marriage to the Perkinses, of Charleston. I knew a New Yorker who was kidnapped for ransom by some Afghanistan bandits. His people sent over the money and he came back to Kabul with the agent. 'Afghanistan?' the natives said to him through an interpreter. 'Well, not so slow, do you think?' 'Oh, I don't know,' says he, and he begins to tell them about a cab driver at Sixth Avenue and Broadway. Those ideas don't suit me. I'm not tied down to anything that isn't 8,000 miles in diameter. Just put me down as E. Rushmore Coglan, citizen of the terrestial sphere."

My cosmopolite made a large adieu and left me, for he thought he saw some one through the chatter and smoke whom he knew. So I was left with the would-be periwinkle, who was reduced to Würzburger without further ability to voice his aspirations to perch, melodious, upon the summit of a valley.

I sat reflecting upon my evident cosmopolite and wondering how the poet had managed to miss him. He was my discovery and I believed in him. How was it? " The men that breed from them they traffic up and down, but cling to their cities' hem as a child to the mother's gown."

Not so E. Rushmore Coglan. With the whole world for his——

My meditations were interrupted by a tremendous noise and conflict in another part of the café. I saw above the heads of the seated patrons E. Rushmore Coglan and a stranger to me engaged in terrific battle. They fought between the tables like Titans, and glasses crashed, and men caught their hats up and were knocked down, and a brunette screamed, and a blonde began to sing " Teasing."

My cosmopolite was sustaining the pride and reputation of the Earth when the waiters closed in on both combatants with their famous flying wedge formation and bore them outside, still resisting.

I called McCarthy, one of the French garçons, and asked him the cause of the conflict.

" The man with the red tie " (that was my cosmopolite), said he, " got hot on account of things said about the bum sidewalks and water supply of the place he come from by the other guy."

" Why," said I, bewildered, " that man is a citizen of the world —a cosmopolite. He——"

" Originally from Mattawamkeag, Maine, he said," continued McCarthy, " and he wouldn't stand for no knockin' the place."

THE May moon shone bright upon the private boarding-house of Mrs. Murphy. By reference to the almanac a large amount of territory will be discovered upon which its rays also fell. Spring was in its heydey, with hay fever soon to follow. The parks were green with new leaves and buyers for the Western and Southern trade. Flowers and summer-resort agents were blowing; the air and answers to Lawson were growing milder; hand-organs, fountains and pinochle were playing everywhere.

The windows of Mrs. Murphy's boarding-house were open. A group of boarders were seated on the high stoop upon round, flat mats like German pancakes.

In one of the second-floor front windows Mrs. McCaskey awaited her husband. Supper was cooling on the table. Its heat went into Mrs. McCaskey.

At nine McCaskey came. He carried his coat on his arm and his pipe in his teeth; and he apologized for disturbing the boarders on the steps as he selected spots of stone between them on which to set his size 9, width Ds.

As he opened the door of his room he received a surprise. Instead of the usual stove-lid or potato-masher for him to dodge, came only words.

Mr. McCaskey reckoned that the benign May moon had softened the breast of his spouse.

" I heard ye," came the oral substitutes for kitchenware. " Ye can apollygize to riff-raff of the streets for settin' yer unhandy feet on the tails of their frocks, but ye'd walk on the neck of yer wife the length of a clothes-line without so much as a ' Kiss me fut,' and I'm sure it's that long from rubberin' out the windy for ye and the victuals cold such as there's money to buy after drinkin' up yer wages at Gallegher's every Saturday evenin', and the gas man here twice to-day for his."

" Woman ! " said Mr. McCaskey, dashing his coat and hat upon a chair, " the noise of ye is an insult to me appetite. When ye run down politeness ye take the mortar from between the bricks of the foundations of society. 'Tis no more than exercisin' the acrimony of a gentleman when ye ask the dissent of ladies blockin' the way for steppin' between them. Will ye bring the pig's face of ye out of the windy and see to the food ? "

Mrs. McCaskey arose heavily and went to the stove. There was something in her manner that warned Mr. McCaskey. When the corners of her mouth went down suddenly like a barometer it usually foretold a fall of crockery and tinware.

" Pig's face, is it ? " said Mrs. McCaskey, and hurled a stewpan full of bacon and turnips at her lord.

Mr. McCaskey was no novice at repartee. He knew what should follow the entrée. On the table was a roast sirloin of pork, garnished with shamrocks. He retorted with this, and drew the appropriate return of a bread pudding in an earthen dish. A hunk of Swiss cheese accurately thrown by her husband struck Mrs. McCaskey below one eye. When she replied with a well-aimed coffee-pot full of a hot, black, semi-fragrant liquid the battle, according to courses, should have ended.

But Mr. McCaskey was no 50-cent *table d'hôter*. Let cheap Bohemians consider coffee the end, if they would. Let them make that *faux pas*. He was foxier still. Finger-bowls were not beyond the compass of his experience. They were not to be had in the Pension Murphy; but their equivalent was at hand. Triumphantly he sent the granite-ware wash-basin at the head of his matrimonial adversary. Mrs. McCaskey dodged in time. She reached for a flatiron, with which, as a sort of cordial, she hoped to bring the gastronomical duel to a close. But a loud, wailing scream downstairs caused both her and Mr. McCaskey to pause in a sort of involuntary armistice.

On the sidewalk at the corner of the house Policeman Cleary was standing with one ear upturned, listening to the crash of household utensils.

" 'Tis Jawn McCaskey and his missis at it again," meditated the policeman. " I wonder shall I go up and stop the row. I will not. Married folks they are : and few pleasures they have. 'Twill not last long. Sure, they'll have to borrow more dishes to keep it up with."

And just then came the load scream belowstairs, betokening fear or dire extremity. " 'Tis probably the cat," said Policeman Cleary, and walked hastily in the other direction.

The boarders on the steps were fluttered. Mr. Toomey, an insurance solicitor by birth and an investigator by profession, went inside to analyze the scream. He returned with the news that Mrs. Murphy's little boy, Mike, was lost. Following the messenger, out bounced Mrs. Murphy—two hundred pounds in tears and hysterics, clutching the air and howling to the sky for the loss of thirty pounds of freckles and mischief. Bathos, truly; but Mr. Toomey sat down at the side of Miss Purdy, millinery, and their hands came together in sympathy. The two old maids, Misses Walsh, who complained every day about the noise in the halls, inquired immediately if anybody had looked behind the clock.

Major Grigg, who sat by his fat wife on the top step, arose and buttoned his coat. " The little one lost ? " he exclaimed. " I will scour the city." His wife never allowed him out after dark. But now she said : " Go, Ludovic ! " in a baritone voice. " Whoever can look upon that mother's grief without springing to her relief has a heart of stone." " Give me some thirty or—sixty cents, my love," said the Major. " Lost children sometimes stray far. I may need car-fares."

Old man Denny, hall room, fourth floor back, who sat on the lowest step, trying to read a paper by the street lamp, turned over a page to follow up the article about the carpenter's strike. Mrs. Murphy shrieked to the moon : " Oh, ar-r-Mike, f'r Gawd's sake, where is me little bit av a boy ? "

" When'd ye see him last ? " asked old man Denny, with one eye on the report of the Building Trades League.

" Oh," wailed Mrs. Murphy, " 'twas yisterday, or maybe four hours ago ! I dunno. But it's lost he is, me little boy Mike. He was playin' on the sidewalk only this mornin'—or was it Wednesday ? I'm that busy with work, 'tis hard to keep up with dates. But I've looked the house over from top to cellar, and it's gone he is. Oh, for the love av Hiven——"

Silent, grim, colossal, the big city has ever stood against its revilers. They call it hard as iron; they say that no pulse of pity beats in its bosom; they compare its streets with lonely forests and deserts of lava.

But beneath the hard crust of the lobster is found a delectable and luscious food. Perhaps a different simile would have been wiser. Still, nobody should take offence. We would call no one a lobster without good and sufficient claws.

No calamity so touches the common heart of humanity as does the straying of a little child. Their feet are so uncertain and feeble; the ways are so steep and strange.

Major Grigg hurried down to the corner, and up the avenue into Billy's place. " Gimme a rye-high," he said to the servitor. " Haven't seen a bow-legged, dirty-faced little devil of a six-year old lost kid around here anywhere, have you ? "

Mr. Toomey retained Miss Purdy's hand on the steps. " Think of that dear dear little babe," said Miss Purdy, " lost from his mother's side—perhaps already fallen beneath the iron hoofs of galloping steeds—oh, isn't it dreadful ? "

"Ain't that right ? " agreed Mr. Toomey, squeezing her hand. " Say I start out and help look for um ! "

" Perhaps," said Miss Purdy, " you should. But, oh, Mr. Toomey, you are so dashing—so reckless—suppose in your enthusiasm some accident should befall you, then what——"

Old man Denny read on about the arbitration agreement, with one finger on the lines.

In the second floor front Mr. and Mrs. McCaskey came to the window to recover their second wind. Mr. McCaskey was scooping turnips out of his vest with a crooked forefinger, and his lady was wiping an eye that the salt of the roast pork had not benefited. They heard the outcry below, and thrust their heads out of the window.

" 'Tis little Mike is lost," said Mr. McCaskey, in a hushed voice, " the beautiful, little, trouble-making angel of a gossoon ! "

" The bit of a boy mislaid ? " said Mrs. McCaskey, leaning out of the window. " Why, now, that's bad enough, entirely. The childer, they be different. If 'twas a woman I'd be willin', for they leave peace behind 'em when they go."

Disregarding the thrust, Mrs. McCaskey caught her husband's arm.

" Jawn," she said, sentimentally, " Missis Murphy's little bye is lost. 'Tis a great city for losing little boys. Six years old he was. Jawn, 'tis the same age our little bye would have been if we had had one six years ago."

" We never did," said Mr. McCaskey, lingering with the fact.

" But if we had, Jawn, think what sorrow would be in our hearts this night, with our little Phelan run away and stolen in the city nowheres at all."

" Ye talk foolishness," said Mr. McCaskey. " 'Tis Pat he would be named, after me old father in Cantrim."

" Ye lie ! " said Mrs. McCaskey, without anger. " Me brother was worth tin dozen bog-trotting McCaskeys. After him would the bye be named." She leaned over the window-sill and looked down at the hurrying and bustle below.

" Jawn," said Mrs. McCaskey, softly, " I'm sorry I was hasty wid ye."

" 'Twas hasty puddin', as ye say," said her husband, " and hurry-up turnips and get-a-move-on-ye coffee. 'Twas what ye could call a quick lunch, all right, and tell no lie."

Mrs. McCaskey slipped her arm inside her husband's and took his rough hand in hers.

" Listen at the cryin' of poor Mrs. Murphy," she said. " 'Tis an awful thing for a bit of a bye to be lost in this great big city. If 'twas our little Phelan, Jawn, I'd be breakin' me heart."

Awkwardly Mr. McCaskey withdrew his hand. But he laid it around the nearing shoulder of his wife.

" 'Tis foolishness, of course," said he, roughly, " but I'd be cut up some meself if our little—Pat was kidnapped or anything. But there never was any childer for us. Sometimes I've been ugly and hard with ye, Judy. Forget it."

They leaned together, and looked down at the heart-drama being acted below.

Long they sat thus. People surged along the sidewalk, crowding, questioning, filling the air with rumors, and inconsequent surmises. Mrs. Murphy plowed back and forth in their midst, like a soft mountain down which plunged an audible cataract of tears. Couriers came and went.

Loud voices and a renewed uproar were raised in front of the boarding-house.

'What's up now, Judy ? " asked Mr. McCaskey.

" 'Tis Missis Murphy's voice," said Mrs. McCaskey, harking. " She says she's after finding little Mike asleep behind the roll of linoleum under the bed in her room."

Mr. McCaskey laughed loudly.

" That's yer Phelan," he shouted, sardonically. " Divil a bit would a Pat have done that trick. If the bye we never had is strayed and stole, by the powers, call him Phelan, and see him hide out under the bed like a mangy pup."

Mrs. McCaskey arose heavily, and went toward the dish closet, with the corners of her mouth drawn down.

Policeman Cleary came back around the corner as the crowd dispersed. Surprised, he upturned an ear toward the McCaskey apartment, where the crash of irons and chinaware and the ring of hurled kitchen utensils seemed as loud as before. Policeman Cleary took out his timepiece.

" By the deported snakes ! " he exclaimed. " Jawn McCaskey and his lady have been fightin' for an hour and a quarter by the watch. The missis could give him forty pounds weight. Strength to his arm."

Policeman Cleary strolled back around the corner.

Old man Denny folded his paper and hurried up the steps just as Mrs. Murphy was about to lock the door for the night.

THE SKYLIGHT ROOM

FIRST Mrs. Parker would show you the double parlors. You would dare to interrupt her description of their advantages and of the merits of the gentleman who had occupied them for eight years. Then you would manage to stammer forth the confession that you were neither a doctor nor a dentist. Mrs. Parker's manner of receiving the admisssion was such that you could never afterward entertain the same feeling toward your parents, who had neglected to train you up in one of the professions that fitted Mrs. Parker's parlors.

Next you ascended one flight of stairs and looked at the second-floor-back at $8. Convinced by her second-floor manner that it was worth the $12 that Mr. Toosenberry always paid for it until he left to take charge of his brother's orange plantation in Florida near Palm Beach, where Mrs. McIntyre always spent the winters that had the double front room with private bath, you managed to babble that you wanted something still cheaper.

If you survived Mrs. Parker's scorn, you were taken to look at Mr. Skidder's large hall room on the third floor. Mr. Skidder's room was not vacant. He wrote plays and smoked cigarettes in it all day long. But every room-hunter was made to visit his room to admire the lambrequins. After each visit, Mr. Skidder, from the fright caused by possible eviction, would pay something on his rent.

Then—oh, then—if you still stood on one foot, with your hot hand clutching the three moist dollars in your pocket, and hoarsely proclaimed your hideous and culpable poverty, nevermore would Mrs. Parker be cicerone of yours. She would honk loudly the word "Clara," she would show you her back, and march downstairs. Then Clara, the colored maid, would escort you up the carpeted ladder that served for the fourth flight, and show you the Skylight Room, It occupied 7 x 8 feet of floor space in the middle of the hall. On each side of it was a dark lumber closet or storeroom.

In it was an iron cot, a washstand and a chair. A shelf was the dresser. Its four bare walls seemed to close in upon you like the sides of a coffin. Your hand crept to your throat, you gasped, you looked up as from a well—and breathed once more. Through the glass of the little skylight you saw a square of blue infinity.

"Two dollars, suh," Clara would say in her half-contemptuous, half-Tuskegeenial tones.

One day Miss Leeson came hunting for a room. She carried a typewriter made to be lugged around by a much larger lady. She was a very little girl, with eyes and hair that had kept on growing after she had stopped and that always looked as if they were saying : " Goodness me ! Why didn't you keep up with us ? "

Mrs. Parker showed her the double parlors. " In this closet," she said, " one could keep a skeleton or anæsthetic or coal——"

" But I am neither a doctor nor a dentist," said Miss Leeson, with a shiver.

Mrs. Parker gave her the incredulous, pitying, sneering, icy stare that she kept for those who failed to qualify as doctors or dentists, and led the way to the second-floor-back.-

" Eight dollars ? " said Miss Leeson. " Dear me ! I'm not Hetty

if I do look green. I'm just a poor little working girl. Show me
something higher and lower."

Mr. Skidder jumped and strewed the floor with cigarette stubs
at the rap on his door.

" Excuse me, Mr. Skidder," said Mrs. Parker, with her demon's
smile at his pale looks. " I didn't know you were in. I asked the
lady to have a look at your lambrequins."

" They're too lovely for anything," said Miss Leeson, smiling
in exactly the way the angels do.

After they had gone Mr. Skidder got very busy erasing the tall,
black-haired heroine from his latest (unproduced) play and inserted a small, roguish one with heavy, bright hair and vivacious
features.

"Anna Held'll jump at it," said Mr. Skidder to himself, putting
his feet up against the lambrequins and disappearing in a cloud
of smoke like an aërial cuttlefish.

Presently the tocsin call of " Clara ! " sounded to the world the
state of Miss Leeson's purse. A dark goblin seized her, mounted a
Stygian stairway, thrust her into a vault with a glimmer of light
in its top and muttered the menacing and cabalistic words " Two
dollars ! "

" I'll take it ! " sighed Miss Leeson, sinking down upon the
squeaky iron bed.

Every day Miss Leeson went out to work. At night she brought
home papers with handwriting on them and made copies with her
typewriter. Sometimes she had no work at night, and then she
would sit on the steps of the high stoop with the other roomers.
Miss Leeson was not intended for a skylight room when the plans
were drawn for her creation. She was gay-hearted and full of
tender, whimsical fancies. Once she let Mr. Skidder read to her
three acts of his great (unpublished) comedy, " It's No Kid; or,
The Heir of the Subway."

There was rejoicing among the gentlemen roomers whenever
Miss Leeson had time to sit on the steps for an hour or two. But
Miss Longnecker, the tall blonde who taught in a public school
and said, " Well, really ! " to everything you said, sat on the top
step and sniffed. And Miss Dorn, who shot at the moving ducks
at Coney every Sunday and worked in a department store, sat
on the bottom step and sniffed. Miss Leeson sat on the middle
step and the men would quickly group around her.

Especially Mr. Skidder, who had cast her in his mind for the
star part in a private, romantic (unspoken) drama in real life. And
especially Mr. Hoover, who was forty-five, fat, flush and foolish.
And especially very young Mr. Evans, who set up a hollow cough
to induce her to ask him to leave off cigarettes. The men voted

her " the funniest and jolliest ever," but the sniffs on the top step and the lower step were implacable.

I pray you let the drama halt while Chorus stalks to the footlights and drops an epicedian tear upon the fatness of Mr. Hoover. Tune the pipes to the tragedy of tallow, the bane of bulk, the calamity of corpulence. Tried out, Falstaff might have rendered more romance to the ton than would have Romeo's rickety ribs to the ounce. A lover may sigh, but he must not puff. To the train of Momus are the fat men remanded. In vain beats the faithfullest heart above a 52-inch belt. Avaunt, Hoover ! Hoover, forty-five, flush and foolish, might carry off Helen herself; Hoover, forty-five, flush, foolish and fat is meat for perdition. There was never a chance for you, Hoover.

As Mrs. Parker's roomers sat thus one summer's evening, Miss Leeson looked up into the firmament and cried with her little gay laugh :

" Why, there's Billy Jackson ! I can see him from down here, too."

All looked up—some at the windows of skyscrapers, some casting about for an airship, Jackson-guided..

" It's that star," explained Miss Leeson, pointing with a tiny finger. " Not the big one that twinkles—the steady blue one near it. I can see it every night through my skylight. I named it Billy Jackson."

" Well, really ! " said Miss Longnecker. " I didn't know you were an astronomer, Miss Leeson."

" Oh, yes," said the small star gazer, " I know as much as any of them about the style of sleeves they're going to wear next fall in Mars."

" Well, really ! " said Miss Longnecker. " The star you refer to is Gamma, of the constellation Cassiopeia. It is nearly of the second magnitude, and its meridian passage is——"

" Oh," said the very young Mr. Evans, " I think Billy Jackson is a much better name for it."

" Same here," said Mr. Hoover, loudly breathing defiance to Miss Longnecker. " I think Miss Leeson has just as much right to name stars as any of these old astrologers had."

" Well, really ! " said Miss Longnecker.

" I wonder whether it's a shooting star," remarked Miss Dorn. " I hit nine ducks and a rabbit out of ten in the gallery at Coney Sunday."

" He doesn't show up very well from down here," said Miss Leeson. " You ought to see him from my room. You know you can see stars even in the daytime from the bottom of a well. At night my room is like the shaft of a coal mine, and it makes Billy Jackson look like the big diamond pin that Night fastens her kimono with."

There came a time after that when Miss Leeson brought no formidable papers home to copy. And when she went out in the morning, instead of working, she went from office to office and let her heart melt away in the drip of cold refusals transmitted through insolent office boys. This went on.

There came an evening when she wearily climbed Mrs. Parker's stoop at the hour when she always returned from her dinner at the restaurant. But she had had no dinner.

As she stepped into the hall Mr. Hoover met her and seized his chance. He asked her to marry him, and his fatness hovered above her like an avalanche. She dodged, and caught the balustrade. He tried for her hand, and she raised it and smote him weakly in the face. Step by step she went up, dragging herself by the railing. She passed Mr. Skidder's door as he was red-inking a stage direction for Myrtle Delorme (Miss Leeson) in his (unaccepted) comedy, to " pirouette across stage from L to the side of the Count." Up the carpeted ladder she crawled at last and opened the door of the skylight room.

She was too weak to light the lamp or to undress. She fell upon the iron cot, her fragile body scarcely hollowing the worn springs. And in that Erebus of a room she slowly raised her heavy eyelids, and smiled.

For Billy Jackson was shining down on her, calm and bright and constant through the skylight. There was no world about her. She was sunk in a pit of blackness, with but that small square of pallid light framing the star that she had so whimsically and oh, so ineffectually, named. Miss Longnecker must be right : it was Gamma, of the constellation Cassiopeia, and not Billy Jackson. And yet she could not let it be Gamma.

As she lay on her back, she tried twice to raise her arm. The third time she got two thin fingers to her lips and blew a kiss out of the black pit to Billy Jackson. Her arm fell back limply.

" Good-bye, Billy, she murmured, faintly. " You're millions of miles away and you won't even twinkle once. But you kept where I could see you most of the time up there when there wasn't anything else but darkness to look at, didn't you ? . . . Millions of miles. . . .Good-bye, Billy Jackson."

Clara, the colored maid, found the door locked at 10 the next day, and they forced it open. Vinegar, and the slapping of wrists and burnt feathers proving of no avail, some one ran to 'phone for an ambulance.

In due time it backed up to the door with much gong-clanging and the capable young medico, in his white linen coat, ready, active, confident, with his smooth face half debonair, half grin, danced up the steps.

" Ambulance call to 49," he said, briefly. " What's the trouble?"

" Oh, yes, doctor," sniffed Mrs. Parker, as though her trouble that there should be trouble in the house was the greater. " I can't think what can be the matter with her. Nothing we could do would bring her to. It's a young woman, a Miss Elsie—yes, a Miss Elsie Leeson. Never before in my house——"

" What room ? " cried the doctor in a terrible voice, to which Mrs. Parker was a stranger.

" The skylight room. It——"

Evidently the ambulance doctor was familiar with the location of skylight rooms. He was gone up the stairs, four at a time. Mrs. Parker followed slowly, as her dignity demanded.

On the first landing she met him coming back bearing the astronomer in his arms. He stopped and let loose the practised scalpel of his tongue, not loudly. Gradually Mrs. Parker crumpled as a stiff garment that slips down from a nail. Ever afterward there remained crumples in her mind and body. Sometimes her curious roomers would ask her what the doctor said to her.

" Let that be," she would answer. " If I can get forgiveness for having heard it I will be satisfied."

The ambulance physician strode with his burden through the pack of hounds that follow the curiosity chase, and even they fell back along the sidewalk abashed, for his face was that of one who bears his own dead.

They noticed that he did not lay down upon the bed prepared for it in the ambulance the form that he carried, and all that he said was : " Drive like h—l, Wilson," to the driver.

That is all. Is it a story ? In the next morning's paper I saw a little news item, and the last sentence of it may help you (as it helped me) to weld the incidents together.

It recounted the reception into Bellevue Hospital of a young woman who had been removed from No. 49 East —— Street, suffering from debility induced by starvation. It concluded with these words :

" Dr. William Jackson, the ambulance physician who attended the case, says the patient will recover."

A SERVICE OF LOVE

WHEN one loves one's Art no service seems too hard.

That is our premise. This story shall draw a conclusion from it, and show at the same time that the premise is incorrect. That will be a new thing in logic, and a feat in story-telling somewhat older than the great wall of China.

Joe Larrabee came out of the post-oak flats of the Middle West pulsing with a genius for pictorial art. At six he drew a picture of the town pump with a prominent citizen passing it hastily. This effort was framed and hung in the drug-store window by the side of the ear of corn with an uneven number of rows. At twenty he left for New York with a flowing necktie and a capital tied up somewhat closer.

Delia Caruthers did things in six octaves so promisingly in a pine-tree village in the South that her relatives chipped in enough in her chip hat for her to go " North " and " finish." They could not see her f——, but that is our story.

Joe and Delia met in an atelier where a number of art and music students had gathered to discuss chiaroscuro, Wagner, music, Rembrandt's works, pictures, Waldteufel, wall paper, Chopin and Oolong.

Joe and Delia became enamored one of the other, or each of the other, as you please, and in a short time were married—for (see above), when one loves one's Art no service seems too hard.

Mr. and Mrs. Larrabee began housekeeping in a flat. It was a lonesome flat—something like the A sharp way down at the left-hand end of the keyboard. And they were happy; for they had their Art, and they had each other. And my advice to the rich young man would be—sell all thou hast, and give it to the poor —janitor for the privilege of living in a flat with your Art and your Delia.

Flat-dwellers shall indorse my dictum that theirs is the only true happiness. If a home is happy it cannot fit too close—let the dresser collapse and become a billiard table; let the mantel turn to a rowing machine, the escritoire to a spare bedchamber, the washstand to an upright piano; let the four walls come together, if they will, so you and your Delia are between. But if home be the other kind, let it be wide and long—enter you at the Golden Gate, hang your hat on Hatteras, your cape on Cape Horn and go out by the Labrador.

Joe was painting in the class of the great Magister—you know his fame. His fees are high; his lessons are light—his high-lights have brought him renown. Delia was studying under Rosenstock you know his repute as a disturber of the piano keys.

They were mighty happy as long as their money lasted. So is every—but I will not be cynical. Their aims were very clear and defined. Joe was to become capable very soon of turning out pictures that old gentlemen with thin side-whiskers and thick pocketbooks would sandbag one another in his studio for the privilege of buying. Delia was to become familiar and then contemptuous with Music, so that when she saw the orchestra seats and boxes unsold she could have sore throat and lobster in a private dining-room and refuse to go on the stage.

But the best, in my opinion, was the home life in the little flat —the ardent, voluble chats after the day's study; the cozy dinners and fresh, light breakfasts; the interchange of ambitions—ambitions interwoven each with the other's or else inconsiderable—the mutual help and inspiration; and—overlook my artlessness— stuffed olives and cheese sandwiches at 11 P.M.

But after a while Art flagged. It sometimes does, even if some switchman doesn't flag it. Everything going out and nothing coming in, as the vulgarians say. Money was lacking to pay Mr. Magister and Herr Rosenstock their prices. When one loves one's Art no service seems too hard. So, Delia said she must give music lessons to keep the chafing dish bubbling.

For two or three days she went out canvassing for pupils. One evening she came home elated.

" Joe, dear," she said, gleefully, " I've a pupil. And, oh, the loveliest people. General—General A. B. Pinkney's daughter— on Seventy-first street. Such a splendid house, Joe—you ought to see the front door ! Byzantine I think you would call it. And inside ! Oh, Joe, I never saw anything like it before.

" My pupil is his daughter Clementina. I dearly love her already. She's a delicate thing—dresses always in white; and the sweetest, simplest manners ! Only eighteen years old. I'm to give three lessons a week; and, just think, Joe ! $5 a lesson. I don't mind it a bit; for when I get two or three more pupils I can resume my lessons with Herr Rosenstock. Now, smooth out that wrinkle between your brows, dear, and let's have a nice supper."

" That's all right for you, Dele," said Joe, attacking a can of peas with a carving knife and a hatchet, " but how about me ? Do you think I'm going to let you hustle for wages while I philander in the regions of high art ? Not by the bones of Benvenuto Cellini ! I guess I can sell papers or lay cobblestones, and bring in a dollar or two."

Delia came and hung about his neck.

" Joe, dear, you are silly. You must keep on at your studies. It is not as if I had quit my music and gone to work at something else. While I teach I learn. I am always with my music. And we can live as happily as millionaires on $15 a week. You mustn't think of leaving Mr. Magister."

"All right," said Joe, reaching for the blue scalloped vegetable dish. " But I hate for you to be giving lessons. It isn't Art. But you're a trump and a dear to do it."

" When one loves one's Art no service seems to hard," said Delia.

" Magister praised the sky in that sketch I made in the park," said Joe. "And Tinkle gave me permission to hang two of them in his window. I may sell one if the right kind of a moneyed idiot sees them."

" I'm sure you will," said Delia, sweetly. "And now let's be thankful for Gen. Pinkney and this veal roast."

During all of the next week the Larrabees had an early breakfast. Joe was enthusiastic about some morning-effect sketches he was doing in Central Park, and Delia packed him off breakfasted, coddled, praised and kissed at 7 o'clock. Art is an engaging mistress. It was most times 7 o'clock when he returned in the evening.

At the end of the week Delia, sweetly proud but languid, triumphantly tossed three five -dollar bills on the 8 x 10 (inches) centre table of the 8 x 10 (feet) flat parlor.

" Sometimes," she said, a little wearily, " Clementina tries me. I'm afraid she doesn't practise enough, and I have to tell her the same things so often. And then she always dresses entirely in white, and that does get monotonous. But Gen. Pinkney is the dearest old man ! I wish you could know him, Joe. He comes in sometimes when I am with Clementina at the piano—he is a widower, you know—and stands there pulling his white goatee. 'And how are the semiquavers and the demisemiquavers progressing?' he always asks.

" I wish you could see the wainscoting in that drawing room, Joe ! And those Astrakhan rug portières. And Clementina has such a funny little cough. I hope she is stronger than she looks. Oh, I really am getting attached to her, she is so gentle and high bred. Gen. Pinkney's brother was once Minister to Bolivia."

And then Joe, with the air of a Monte Cristo, drew forth a ten, a five, a two and a one—all legal tender notes—and laid them beside Delia's earnings.

" Sold that watercolor of the obelisk to a man from Peoria," he announced, overwhelmingly.

" Don't joke with me," said Delia—" not from Peoria ! "

" All the way. I wish you could see him, Dele. Fat man with

a woolen muffler and a quill toothpick. He saw the sketch in Tinkle's window and thought it was a windmill at first. He was game, though, and bought it anyhow. He ordered another—an oil sketch of the Lackawanna freight depot—to take back with him. Music lessons ! Oh, I guess Art is still in it."

" I'm so glad you're kept on," said Delia, heartily. " You're bound to win, dear. Thirty-three dollars ! We never had so much to spend before. We'll have oysters to-night."

" And filet mignon with champignons," said Joe. " Where is the olive fork ? "

On the next Saturday evening Joe reached home first. He spread his $18 on the parlor table and washed what seemed to be a great deal of dark paint from his hands.

Half an hour later Delia arrived, her right hand tied up in a shapeless bundle of wraps and bandages.

" How is this ? " asked Joe after the usual greetings. Delia laughed, but not very joyously.

" Clementina," she explained, " insisted upon a Welsh rabbit after her lesson. She is such a queer girl. Welsh rabbits at 5 in the afternoon. The General was there. You should have seen him run for the chafing dish, Joe, just as if there wasn't a servant in the house. I know Clementina isn't in good health; she is so nervous. In serving the rabbit she spilled a great lot of it, boiling hot, over my hand and wrist. It hurt awfully, Joe. And the dear girl was so sorry ! But Gen. Pinkney !—Joe, that old man nearly went distracted. He rushed downstairs and sent somebody—they said the furnace man or somebody in the basement—out to a drug store for some oil and things to bind it up with. It doesn't hurt so much now."

" What's this ? " asked Joe, taking the hand tenderly and pulling at some white strands beneath the bandages.

" It's something soft," said Delia, " that had oil on it. Oh, Joe, did you sell another sketch ? " she had seen the money on the table.

" Did I ? " said Joe; " just ask the man from Peoria. He got his depot to-day, and he isn't sure but he thinks he wants another parkscape and a view on the Hudson. What time this afternoon did you burn your hand, Dele ? "

" Five o'clock, I think," said Dele, plaintively. " The iron—I mean the rabbit came off the fire about that time. You ought to have seen Gen. Pinkney, Joe, when——"

" Sit down here a moment, Dele," said Joe. He drew her to the couch, sat beside her and put his arm across her shoulders.

" What have you been doing for the last two weeks, Dele ? " he asked.

She braved it for a moment or two with an eye full of love and stubbornness, and murmured a phrase or two vaguely of Gen. Pinkney; but at length down went her head and out came the truth and tears.

" I couldn't get any pupils," she confessed. "And I couldn't bear to have you give up your lessons; and I got a place ironing shirts in that big Twenty-fourth Street laundry. And I think I did very well to make up both General Pinkney and Clementina, don't you, Joe ? And when a girl in the laundry set down a hot iron on my hand this afternoon I was all the way home making up that story about the Welsh rabbit. You're not angry, are you, Joe ? And if I hadn't got the work you mightn't have sold your sketches to that man from Peoria."

" He wasn't from Peoria," said Joe, slowly.

" Well, it doesn't matter where he was from. How clever you are, Joe—and—kiss me, Joe—and what made you ever suspect that I wasn't giving music lessons to Clementina ? "

" I didn't," said Joe, " until to-night. And I wouldn't have then, only I sent up this cotton waste and oil from the engine-room this afternoon for a girl upstairs who had her hand burned with a smoothing-iron. I've been firing the engine in that laundry for the last two weeks."

" And then you didn't——"

" My purchaser from Peoria," said Joe, " and Gen. Pinkney are both creations of the same art—but you wouldn't call it either painting or music."

And then they both laughed, and Joe began :

" When one loves one's Art no service seems——"

But Delia stopped him with her hand on his lips. " No," she said—" just ' When one loves.' "

THE COMING-OUT OF MAGGIE

Every Saturday night the Clover Leaf Social Club gave a hop in the hall of the Give and Take Athletic Association on the East Side. In order to attend one of these dances you must be a member of the Give and Take—or, if you belong to the division that starts off with the right foot in waltzing, you must work in Rhinegold's paper-box factory. Still, any Clover Leaf was privileged to escort or be escorted by an outsider to a single dance. But mostly each Give and Take brought the paper-box girl that he affected; and few strangers could boast of having shaken a foot at the regular hops.

Maggie Toole, on account of her dull eyes, broad mouth and left-handed style of footwork in the two-step, went to the dances with Anna McCarty and her " fellow." Anna and Maggie worked side by side in the factory, and were the greatest chums ever. So Anna always made Jimmy Burns take her by Maggie's house every Saturday night so that her friend could go to the dance with them.

The Give and Take Athletic Association lived up to its name. The hall of the association in Orchard Street was fitted out with muscle-making inventions. With the fibres thus builded up the members were wont to engage the police and rival social and athletic organizations in joyous combat. Between these more serious occupations the Saturday night hops with the paper-box factory girls came as a refining influence and as an efficient screen. For sometimes the tip went 'round, and if you were among the elect that tiptoed up the dark back stairway you might see as neat and satisfying a little welter-weight affair to a finish as ever happened inside the ropes.

On Saturdays Rhinegold's paper-box factory closed at 3 P.M. On one such afternoon Anna and Maggie walked homeward together. At Maggie's door Anna said, as usual : " Be ready at seven sharp, Mag, and Jimmy and me'll come by for you."

But what was this ? Instead of the customary humble and grateful thanks from the non-escorted one there was to be perceived a high poised head, a prideful dimpling at the corners of a broad mouth, and almost a sparkle in a dull brown eye.

" Thanks, Anna," said Maggie; " but you and Jimmy needn't bother to-night. I've a gentleman friend that's coming round to escort me to the hop."

The comely Anna pounced upon her friend, shook her, chided and beseeched her. Maggie Toole catch a fellow ! Plain, dear, loyal, unattractive Maggie, so sweet as a chum, so unsought for a two-step or a moonlit bench in the little park. How was it ? When did it happen ? Who was it ?

" You'll see to-night," said Maggie, flushed with the wine of the first grapes she had gathered in Cupid's vineyard. " He's swell all right. He's two inches taller than Jimmy, and an up-to-date dresser. I'll introduce him, Anna, just as soon as we get to the hall."

Anna and Jimmy were among the first Clover Leafs to arrive that evening. Anna's eyes were brightly fixed upon the door of the hall to catch the first glimpse of her friend's " catch."

At 8 : 30 Miss Toole swept into the hall with her escort. Quickly her triumphant eye discovered her chum under the wing of her faithful Jimmy.

" Oh, gee ! " cried Anna, " Mag ain't made a hit—oh, no ! Swell fellow ? well, I guess ! Style ? Look at 'um."

" Go as far as you like," said Jimmy, with sandpaper in his voice. " Cop him out if you want him. These new guys always win out with the push. Don't mind me. He don't squeeze all the lines, I guess. Huh ! "

" Shut up, Jimmy. You know what I mean. I'm glad for Mag. First fellow she ever had. Oh, here they come."

Across the floor Maggie sailed like a coquettish yacht convoyed by a stately cruiser. And truly, her companion justified the encomiums of the faithful chum. He stood two inches taller than the average Give and Take athlete; his dark hair curled; his eyes and his teeth flashed whenever he bestowed his frequent smiles. The young men of the Clover Leaf Club pinned not their faith to the graces of person as much as they did to its prowess, its achievements in hand-to-hand conflicts, and its preservation from the legal duress that constantly menaced it. The member of the association who would bind a paper-box maiden to his conquering chariot scorned to employ Beau Brummel airs. They were not considered honorable methods of warfare. The swelling biceps, the coat straining at its buttons over the chest, the air of conscious conviction of the super-eminence of the male in the cosmogony of creation, even a calm display of bow legs as subduing and enchanting agents in the gentle tourneys of Cupid—these were the approved arms and ammunition of the Clover Leaf gallants. They viewed, then, the genuflexions and alluring poses of this visitor with their chins at a new angle.

"A friend of mine, Mr. Terry O'Sullivan," was Maggie's formula of introduction. She led him around the room, presenting him to each new-arriving Clover Leaf. Almost was she pretty now, with the unique luminosity in her eyes that comes to a girl with her first suitor and a kitten with its first mouse.

" Maggie Toole's got a fellow at last," was the word that went round among the paper-box girls. " Pipe Mag's floor-walker " —thus the Give and Takes expressed their indifferent contempt.

Usually at the weekly hops Maggie kept a spot on the wall warm with her back. She felt and showed so much gratitude whenever a self-sacrificing partner invited her to dance that his pleasure was cheapened and diminished. She had even grown used to noticing Anna joggle the reluctant Jimmy with her elbow as a signal for him to invite her chum to walk over his feet through a two-step.

But to-night the pumpkin had turned to a coach and six. Terry O'Sullivan was a victorious Prince Charming, and Maggie Toole winged her first butterfly flight. And though our tropes of fairy-

land be mixed with those of entomology they shall not spill one
drop of ambrosia from the rose-crowned melody of Maggie's one
perfect night.

The girls besieged her for introduction to her " fellow." The
Clover Leaf young men, after two years of blindness, suddenly
perceived charms in Miss Toole. They flexed their compelling
muscles before her and bespoke her for the dance.

Thus she scored; but to Terry O'Sullivan the honors of the
evening fell thick and fast. He shook his curls; he smiled and
went easily through the seven motions for acquiring grace in your
own room before an open window ten minutes each day. He
danced like a faun; he introduced manner and style and atmosphere; his words came trippingly upon his tongue, and—he
waltzed twice in succession with the paper-box girl that Dempsey
Donovan brought.

Dempsey was the leader of the association. He wore a dress
suit, and could chin the bar twice with one hand. He was one of
" Big Mike " O'Sullivan's lieutenants, and was never troubled
by trouble. No cop dared to arrest him. Whenever he broke a
pushcart man's head or shot a member of the Heinrick B. Sweeney
Outing and Literary Association in the kneecap, an officer would
drop around and say :

" The Cap'n'd like to see ye a few minutes round to the office
whin ye have time, Dempsey, me boy."

But there would be sundry gentlemen there with large gold fob
chains and black cigars; and somebody would tell a funny story,
and then Dempsey would go back and work half an hour with the
six-pound dumbells. So, doing a tight-rope act on a wire stretched
across Niagara was a safe terpsichorean performance compared
with waltzing twice with Dempsey Donovan's paper-box girl. At
10 o'clock the jolly round face of " Big Mike " O'Sullivan shone
at the door for five minutes upon the scene. He always looked in
for five minutes, smiled at the girls and handed out real perfectos
to the delighted boys.

Dempsey Donovan was at his elbow instantly, talking rapidly.
" Big Mike " looked carefully at the dancers, smiled, shook his
head and departed.

The music stopped. The dancers scattered to the chairs along
the walls. Terry O'Sullivan, with his entrancing bow, relinquished
a pretty girl in blue, to her partner and started back to find Maggie.
Dempsey intercepted him in the middle of the floor.

Some fine instinct that Rome must have bequeathed to us
caused nearly every one to turn and look at them—there was a
subtle feeling that two gladiators had met in the arena. Two or
three Give and Takes with tight coat sleeves drew nearer.

" One moment, Mr. O'Sullivan," said Dempsey. " I hope you're enjoying yourself. Where did you say you lived ? "

The two gladiators were well matched. Dempsey had, perhaps, ten pounds of weight to give away. The O'Sullivan had breadth with quickness. Dempsey had a glacial eye, a dominating slit of a mouth, an indestructible jaw, a complexion like a belle's and the coolness of a champion. The visitor showed more fire in his contempt and less control over his conspicuous sneer. They were enemies by the law written when the rocks were molten. They were each too splendid, too mighty, too incomparable to divide pre-eminence. One only must survive.

" I live on Grand," said O'Sullivan, insolently; " and no trouble to find me at home. Where do you live ? "

Dempsey ignored the question.

" You say your name's O'Sullivan," he went on. " Well, ' Big Mike ' says he never saw you before."

" Lots of things he never saw," said the favorite of the hop.

"As a rule," went on Dempsey, huskily sweet, " O'Sullivans in this district know one another. You escorted one of our lady members here, and we want a chance to make good. If you've got a family tree let's see a few historical O'Sullivan buds come out on it. Or do you want us to dig it out of you by the roots ? "

" Suppose you mind your own business," suggested O'Sullivan, blandly.

Dempsey's eye brightened. He held up an inspired forefinger as though a brilliant idea had struck him.

" I've got it now," he said, cordially. " It was just a little mistake. You ain't no O'Sullivan. You are a ring-tailed monkey. Excuse us for not recognizing you at first."

O'Sullivan's eye flashed. He made a quick movement, but Andy Geoghan was ready and caught his arm.

Dempsey nodded at Andy and William McMahan, the secretary of the club, and walked rapidly toward a door at the rear of the hall. Two other members of the Give and Take Association swiftly joined the little group. Terry O'Sullivan was now in the hands of the Board of Rules and Social Referees. They spoke to him briefly and softly, and conducted him out through the same door at the rear.

This movement on the part of the Clover Leaf members requires a word of elucidation. Back of the association hall was a smaller room rented by the club. In this room personal difficulties that arose on the ballroom floor were settled, man to man, with the weapons of nature, under the supervision of the Board. No lady could say that she had witnessed a fight at a Clover Leaf hop in several years. It's gentlemen members guaranteed that.

So easily and smoothly had Dempsey and the Board done their preliminary work that many in the hall had not noticed the checking of the fascinating O'Sullivan's social triumph. Among these was Maggie. She looked about for her escort.

"Smoke up!" said Rose Cassidy. "Wasn't you on? Demps Donovan picked a scrap with your Lizzie-boy, and they've waltzed out to the slaughter room with him. How's my hair look done up this way, Mag?"

Maggie laid a hand on the bosom of her cheese-cloth waist.

"Gone to the fight with Dempsey!" she said, breathlessly. "They've got to be stopped. Dempsey Donovan can't fight him. Why, he'll—he'll kill him!"

"Ah, what do you care?" said Rosa. "Don't some of 'em fight every hop?"

But Maggie was off, darting her zig-zag way through the maze of dancers. She burst through the rear door into the dark hall and then threw her solid shoulder against the door of the room of single combat. It gave way, and in the instant that she entered her eye caught the scene—the Board standing about with open watches; Dempsey Donovan in his shirt sleeves dancing lightfooted, with the wary grace of the modern pugilist, within easy reach of his adversary; Terry O'Sullivan standing with arms folded and a murderous look in his dark eyes. And without slacking the speed of her entrance she leaped forward with a scream—leaped in time to catch and hang upon the arm of O'Sullivan that was suddenly uplifted, and to whisk from it the long, bright stiletto that he had drawn from his bosom.

The knife fell and rang upon the floor. Cold steel drawn in the rooms of the Give and Take Association! Such a thing had never happened before. Everyone stood motionless for a minute. Andy Geoghan kicked the stiletto with the toe of his shoe curiously, like an antiquarian who has come upon some ancient weapon unknown to his learning.

And then O'Sullivan hissed something unintelligible between his teeth. Dempsey and the Board exchanged looks. And then Dempsey looked at O'Sullivan without anger, as one looks at a stray dog, and nodded his head in the direction of the door. "The back stairs, Giuseppi," he said, briefly. "Somebody'll pitch your hat down after you."

Maggie walked up to Dempsey Donovan. There was a brilliant spot of red in her cheeks, down which slow tears were running. But she looked him bravely in the eye.

"I knew it, Dempsey," she said, as her eyes grew dull even in their tears. "I knew he was a Guinea. His name's Tony Spinelli. I hurried in when they told me you and him was scrappin'. Them Guineas always carries knives. But you don't understand, Dempsey. I never had a fellow in my life. I got tired of comin' with Anna and Jimmy every night, so I fixed it with him to call himself O'Sullivan, and brought him along. I knew there'd be nothin' doin' for him if he came as a Dago. I guess I'll resign from the club now."

Dempsey turned to Andy Geoghan.

" Chuck that cheese slicer out of the window," he said, " and tell 'em inside that Mr. O'Sullivan has had a telephone message to go down to Tammany Hall."

And then he turned back to Maggie.

" Say, Mag," he said, " I'll see you home. And how about next Saturday night ? Will you come to the hop with me if I call around for you ? "

It was remarkable how quickly Maggie's eyes could change from dull to a shining brown.

" With you, Dempsey ? " she stammered. " Say—will a duck swim ? "

MAN ABOUT TOWN

THERE were two or three things that I wanted to know. I do not care about a mystery. So I began to inquire.

It took me two weeks to find out what women carry in dress suit cases. And then I began to ask why a mattress is made in two pieces. This serious query was at first received with suspicion because it sounded like a conundrum. I was at last assured that its double form of construction was designed to make lighter the burden of woman, who makes up beds. I was so foolish as to persist, begging to know why, then, they were not made in two equal pieces; whereupon I was shunned.

The third draught that I craved from the fount of knowledge was enlightenment concerning the character known as A Man About Town. He was more vague in my mind than a type should be. We must have a concrete idea of anything, even if it be an imaginary idea, before we can comprehend it. Now, I have a mental picture of John Doe that is as clear as a steel engraving. His eyes are weak blue; he wears a brown vest and a shiny black serge coat. He stands always in the sunshine chewing something; and he keeps half-shutting his pocket knife and opening it again with his thumb. And, if the Man Higher Up is ever found, take my assurance for it, he will be a large, pale man with blue wristlets showing under his cuffs, and he will be sitting to have his shoes

polished within sound of a bowling alley, and there will be somewhere about him turquoises.

But the canvas of my imagination, when it came to limning
the Man About Town, was blank. I fancied that he had a detach-
able sneer (like the smile of the Cheshire Cat) and attached cuffs;
and that was all. Whereupon I asked a newspaper reporter about
him.

" Why," said he, " a ' Man About Town ' is something between
a ' rounder ' and a ' clubman.' He isn't exactly—well, he fits in
between Mrs. Fish's receptions and private boxing bouts. He
doesn't—well, he doesn't belong either to the Lotos Club or to the
Jerry McGeoghegan Galvanized Iron Workers' Apprentices' Left
Hook Chowder Association. I don't exactly know how to describe
him to you. You'll see him everywhere there's anything doing.
Yes, I suppose he's a type. Dress clothes every evening; knows
the ropes; calls every policeman and waiter in town by their first
names. No; he never travels with the hydrogen derivatives. You
generally see him alone or with another man."

My friend the reporter left me, and I wandered further afield.
By this time the 3126 electric lights on the Rialto were alight.
People passed, but they held me not. Paphian eyes rayed upon
me, and left me unscathed. Diners, heim-gangers, shop-girls,
confidence men, panhandlers, actors, highwaymen, millionaires,
and outlanders hurried, skipped, strolled, sneaked, swaggered,
and scurried by me; but I took no note of them. I knew them all;
I had read their hearts; they had served. I wanted my Man About
Town. He was a type, and to drop him would be an error—a
typograph—but no ! let us continue.

Let us continue with a moral digression. To see a family reading
the Sunday paper gratifies. The sections have been separated.
Papa is earnestly scanning the page that pictures the young lady
exercising before an open window, and bending—but there, there !
Mamma is interested in trying to guess the missing letters in the
word N—w Yo—k. The oldest girls are eagerly perusing the financial reports, for a certain young man remarked last Sunday night
that he had taken a flyer in Q., X. & Z. Willie, the eighteen-year-
old son, who attends the New York public school, is absorbed in
the weekly article describing how to make over an old shirt, for
he hopes to take a prize in sewing on graduation day.

Grandma is holding to the comic supplement with a two-hours'
grip; and little Tottie, the baby, is rocking along the best she can
with the real estate transfers. This view is intended to be reassuring,
for it is desirable that a few lines of this story be skipped. For it
introduces strong drink.

I went into a café to—and while it was being mixed I asked the

man who grabs up your hot Scotch spoon as soon as you lay it down
what he understood by the term, epithet, description, designation,
characterization or appellation, viz. : a " Man About Town."

" Why," said he, carefully, " it means a fly guy that's wise to
the all-night push—see ? It's a hot sport that you can't bump to
the rail anywhere between the Flatirons—see ? I guess that's
about what it means."

I thanked him and departed.

On the sidewalk a Salvation lassie shook her contribution
receptacle gently against my waistcoat pocket.

" Would you mind telling me," I asked her, " if you ever meet
with the character commonly denominated as 'A Man About
Town' during your daily wanderings ? "

" I think I know whom you mean," she answered, with a gentle
smile. " We see them in the same places night after night. They
are the devil's body guard, and if the soldiers of any army are as
faithful as they are, their commanders are well served. We go
among them, diverting a few pennies from their wickedness to the
Lord's service."

She shook the box again and I dropped a dime into it.

In front of a glittering hotel a friend of mine, a critic, was
climbing from a cab. He seemed at leisure; and I put my question
to him. He answered me conscientiously, as I was sure he would.

" There is a type of ' Man About Town ' in New York," he
answered. " The term is quite familiar to me, but I don't think
I was ever called upon to define the character before. It would
be difficult to point you out an exact specimen. I would say, offhand, that it is a man who had a hopeless case of the peculiar New
York disease of wanting to see and know. At 6 o'clock each day
life begins with him. He follows rigidly the conventions of dress
and manners; but in the business of poking his nose into places
where he does not belong he could give pointers to a civet cat or
a jackdaw. He is the man who has chased Bohemia about the
town from rathskeller to roof garden and from Hester Street to
Harlem until you can't find a place in the city where they don't
cut their spaghetti with a knife. Your ' Man About Town ' has
done that. He is always on the scent of something new. He is
curiosity, impudence, and omnipresence. Hansoms were made
for him, and gold-banded cigars ; and the curse of music at dinner.
There are not so many of him; but his minority report is adopted
everywhere.

" I'm glad you brought up the subject; I've felt the influence
of this nocturnal blight upon our city, but I never thought to
analyze it before. I can see now that your ' Man About Town '
should have been classified long ago. In his wake spring up wine

agents and cloak models; and the orchestra plays ' Let's All Go
Up to Maud's' for him, by request, instead of Handel. He makes
his rounds every evening; while you and I see the elephant once
a week. When the cigar store is raided, he winks at the officer,
familiar with his ground, and walks away immune, while you and
I search among the Presidents for names, and among the stars for
addresses to give the desk sergeant."

My friend, the critic, paused to acquire breath for fresh eloquence. I seized my advantage.

" You have classified him," I cried with joy. " You have painted
his portrait in the gallery of city types. But I must meet one face
to face. I must study the Man About Town at first hand. Where
shall I find him? How shall I know him? "

Without seeming to hear me, the critic went on. And his cab-
driver was waiting for his fare, too.

" He is the sublimated essence of Butt-in; the refined, intrinsic
extract of Rubber; the concentrated, purified, irrefutable, un-
avoidable spirit of Curiosity and Inquisitiveness. A new sensation
is the breath in his nostrils; when his experience is exhausted he
explores new fields with the indefatigability of a——"

" Excuse me," I interrupted, " but can you produce one of this
type? It is a new thing to me. I must study it. I will search
the town over until I find one. Its habitat must be here on
Broadway."

" I am about to dine here," said my friend. " Come inside, and
if there is a Man About Town present I will point him out to you.
I know most of the regular patrons here."

" I am not dining yet," I said to him. " You will excuse me.
I am going to find my Man About Town this night if I have to rake
New York from the Battery to Little Coney Isalnd."

I left the hotel and walked down Broadway. The pursuit of my
type gave a pleasant savor of life and interest to the air I breathed.
I was glad to be in a city so great, so complex and diversified.
Leisurely and with something of an air I strolled along with my
heart expanding at the thought that I was a citizen of great
Gotham, a sharer in its magnificence and pleasures, a partaker
in its glory and prestige.

I turned to cross the street. I heard something buzz like a bee,
and then I took a long, pleasant ride with Santos-Dumont.

When I opened my eyes I remembered a smell of gasoline, and
I said aloud: " Hasn't it passed yet? "

A hospital nurse laid a hand that was not particularly soft upon
my brow that was not at all fevered. A young doctor came along,
grinned, and handed me a morning newspaper.

" Want to see how it happened? " he asked, cheerily. I read

the article. Its headlines began where I heard the buzzing leave off the night before. It closed with these lines :

"——Bellevue Hospital, where it was said that his injuries were not serious. He appeared to be a typical Man About Town."

THE COP AND THE ANTHEM

ON his bench in Madison Square Soapy moved uneasily. When wild geese honk high of nights, and when women without sealskin coats grow kind to their husbands, and when Soapy moves uneasily on his bench in the park, you may know that winter is near at hand.

A dead leaf fell in Soapy's lap. That was Jack Frost's card. Jack is kind to the regular denizens of Madison Square, and gives fair warning of his annual call. At the corners of four streets he hands his pasteboard to the North Wind, footman of the mansion of All Outdoors, so that the inhabitants thereof may make ready.

Soapy's mind became cognizant of the fact that the time had come for him to resolve himself into a singular Committee of Ways and Means to provide against the coming rigor. And therefore he moved uneasily on his bench.

The hibernatorial ambitions of Soapy were not of the highest. In them were no considerations of Mediterranean cruises, of soporific Southern skies or drifting in the Vesuvian Bay. Three months on the Island was what his soul craved. Three months of assured board and bed and congenial company, safe from Boreas and bluecoats, seemed to Soapy the essence of things desirable.

For years the hospitable Blackwell's had been his winter quarters. Just as his more fortunate fellow New Yorkers had bought their tickets to Palm Beach and the Riviera each winter, so Soapy had made his humble arrangements for his annual hegira to the Island. And now the time was come. On the previous night three Sabbath newspapers, distributed beneath his coat, about his ankles and over his lap, had failed to repulse the cold as he slept on his bench near the spurting fountain in the ancient square. So the Island loomed big and timely in Soapy's mind. He scorned the provisions made in the name of charity for the city's dependents. In Soapy's opinion the Law was more benign than Philanthropy. There was an endless round of institutions, municipal and eleemosynary, on which he might set out and receive lodging and food accordant with the simple life. But to one of Soapy's proud spirit the gifts of charity are encumbered. If not in coin you must pay in humiliation of spirit for every benefit received at the heads of philanthropy. As Cæsar had his Brutus, every bed of charity must have its toll of a bath, every loaf of bread its compensation of a private and personal inquisition. Wherefore it is better to be a guest of the law, which, though conducted by rules, does not meddle unduly with a gentleman's private affairs.

Soapy, having decided to go to the Island, at once set about accomplishing his desire. There were many easy ways of doing this. The pleasantest was to dine luxuriously at some expensive restaurant; and then, after declaring insolvency, be handed over quietly and without uproar to a policeman. An accommodating magistrate would do the rest.

Soapy left his bench and strolled out of the square and across the level sea of asphalt, where Broadway and Fifth Avenue flow together. Up Broadway he turned, and halted at a glittering café, where are gathered together nightly the choicest products of the grape, the silkworm, and the protoplasm.

Soapy had confidence in himself from the lowest button of his vest upward. He was shaven, and his coat was decent and his neat black, ready-tied four-in-hand had been presented to him by a lady missionary on Thanksgiving Day. If he could reach a table in the restaurant unsuspected success would be his. The portion of him that would show above the table would raise no doubt in the waiter's mind. A roasted mallard duck, thought Soapy, would be about the thing—with a bottle of Chablis, and then Camembert, a demi-tasse and a cigar. One dollar for the cigar would be enough. The total would not be so high as to call forth any supreme manifestation of revenge from the café management; and yet the meat would leave him filled and happy for the journey to his winter refuge.

But as Soapy set foot inside the restaurant door the head waiter's eye fell upon his frayed trousers and decadent shoes. Strong and ready hands turned him about and conveyed him in silence and haste to the sidewalk and averted the ignoble fate of the menaced mallard.

Soapy turned off Broadway. It seemed that his route of the coveted Island was not to be an epicurean one. Some other way of entering limbo must be thought of.

At a corner of Sixth Avenue electric lights and cunningly displayed wares behind plate-glass made a shop window conspicuous. Soapy took a cobblestone and dashed it through the glass. People came running around the corner, a policeman in the lead. Soapy stood still, with his hands in his pockets, and smiled at the sight of brass buttons.

"Where's the man that done that?" inquired the officer, excitedly.

" Don't you figure out that I might have had something to do with it ? " said Soapy, not without sarcasm, but friendly, as one greets good fortune.

The policeman's mind refused to accept Soapy even as a clue. Men who smash windows do not remain to parley with the law's minions. They take to their heels. The policeman saw a man halfway down the block running to catch a car. With drawn club he joined in the pursuit. Soapy, with disgust in his heart, loafed along, twice unsuccessful.

On the opposite side of the street was a restaurant of no great pretensions. It catered to large appetites and modest purses. Its crockery and atmosphere were thick; its soup and napery thin. Into this place Soapy took his accusive shoes and telltale trousers without challenge. At a table he sat and consumed beefsteak, flapjacks, doughnuts and pie. And then to the waiter he betrayed the fact that the minutest coin and himself were strangers.

" Now, get busy and call a cop," said Soapy. "And don't keep a gentleman waiting."

" No cop for youse," said the waiter, with a voice like butter cakes and an eye like the cherry in a Manhattan cocktail. " Hey, Con ! "

Neatly upon his left ear on the callous pavement two waiters pitched Soapy. He arose joint by joint, as a carpenter's rule opens, and beat the dust from his clothes. Arrest seemed but a rosy dream. The Island seemed very far away. A policeman who stood before a drug store two doors away laughed and walked down the street.

Five blocks Soapy travelled before his courage permitted him to woo capture again. This time the opportunity presented what he fatuously termed to himself a " cinch." A young woman of a modest and pleasing guise was standing before a show window gazing with sprightly interest at its display of shaving mugs and inkstands, and two yards from the window a large policeman of severe demeanor leaned against a water plug.

It was Soapy's design to assume the rôle of the despicable and execrated " masher." The refined and elegant appearance of his victim and the contiguity of the conscientious cop encouraged him to believe that he would soon feel the pleasant official clutch upon his arm that would insure his winter quarters on the right little, tight little isle.

Soapy straightened the lady missionary's ready-made tie, dragged his shrinking cuffs into the open, set his hat at a killing cant and sidled toward the young woman. He made eyes at her, was taken with sudden coughs and " hems," smiled, smirked and went brazenly through the impudent and contemptible litany of the

" masher." With half an eye Soapy saw that the policeman was watching him fixedly. The young woman moved away a few steps, and again bestowed her absorbed attention upon the shaving mugs. Soapy followed, boldly stepping to her side, raised his hat and said :

" Ah there, Bedelia ! Don't you want to come and play in my yard ? "

The policeman was still looking. The persecuted young woman had but to beckon a finger and Soapy would be practically en route for his insular haven. Already he imagined he could feel the cozy warmth of the station-house. The young woman faced him and, stretching out a hand, caught Soapy's coat sleeve.

" Sure, Mike," she said joyfully, " if you'll blow me to a pail of suds. I'd have spoke to you sooner, but the cop was watching."

With the young woman playing the clinging ivy to his oak Soapy walked past the policeman overcome with gloom. He seemed doomed to liberty.

At the next corner he shook off his companion and ran. He halted in the district where by night are found the lightest streets, hearts, vows, and librettos. Women in furs and men in greatcoats moved gaily in the wintry air. A sudden fear seized Soapy that some dreadful enchantment had rendered him immune to arrest. The thought brought a little of panic upon it, and when he came upon another policeman lounging grandly in front of a transplendent theatre he caught at the immediate straw of " disorderly conduct."

On the sidewalk Soapy began to yell drunken gibberish at the top of his harsh voice. He danced, howled, raved, and otherwise disturbed the welkin.

The policeman twirled his club, turned his back to Soapy and remarked to a citizen.

" 'Tis one of them Yale lads celebratin' the goose egg they give to the Hartford College. Noisy; but no harm. We've instructions to lave them be."

Disconsolate, Soapy ceased his unavailing racket. Would never a policeman lay hands on him ? In his fancy the Island seemed an unattainable Arcadia. He buttoned his thin coat against the chilling wind.

In a cigar store he saw a well-dressed man lighting a cigar at a swinging light. His silk umbrella he had set by the door on entering. Soapy stepped inside, secured the umbrella and sauntered off with it slowly. The man at the cigar light followed hastily.

" My umbrella," he said, sternly.

" Oh, is it ? " sneered Soapy, adding insult to petty larceny. " Well, why don't you call a policeman ? I took it. Your umbrella ! Why don't you call a cop? There stands one on the corner."

The umbrella owner slowed his steps. Soapy did likewise, with a presentiment that luck would again run against him. The policeman looked at the two curiously.

" Of course," said the umbrella man—" that is—well, you know how these mistakes occur—I—if it's your umbrella I hope you'll excuse me—I picked it up this morning in a restaurant—If you recognize it as yours, why—I hope you'll ——"

" Of course it's mine," said Soapy, viciously.

The ex-umbrella man retreated. The policeman hurried to assist a tall blonde in an opera cloak across the street in front of a street car that was approaching two blocks away.

Soapy walked eastward through a street damaged by improvements. He hurled the umbrella wrathfully into an excavation. He muttered against the men who wear helmets and carry clubs. Because he wanted to fall into their clutches, they seemed to regard him as a king who could do no wrong.

At length Soapy reached one of the avenues to the east where the glitter and turmoil was but faint. He set his face down this toward Madison Square, for the homing instinct survives even when the home is a park bench.

But on an unusually quiet corner Soapy came to a standstill. Here was an old church, quaint and rambling and gabled. Through one violet-stained window a soft light glowed, where, no doubt, the organist loitered over the keys, making sure of his mastery of the coming Sabbath anthem. For there drifted out to Soapy's ears sweet music that caught and held him transfixed against the convolutions of the iron fence.

The moon was above, lustrous and serene; vehicles and pedestrians were few; sparrows twittered sleepily in the eaves—for a little while the scene might have been a country churchyard. And the anthem that the organist played cemented Soapy to the iron fence, for he had known it well in the days when his life contained such things as mothers and roses and ambitions and friends and immaculate thoughts and collars.

The conjunction of Soapy's receptive state of mind and the influences about the old church wrought a sudden and wonderful change in his soul. He viewed with swift horror the pit into which he had tumbled, the degraded days, unworthy desires, dead hopes, wrecked faculties and base motives that made up his existence.

And also in a moment his heart responded thrillingly to this novel mood. An instantaneous and strong impulse moved him to battle with his desperate fate. He would pull himself out of the mire; he would make a man of himself again; he would conquer the evil that had taken possession of him. There was time; he was comparatively young yet : he would resurrect his old eager ambitions and pursue them without faltering. Those solemn but sweet organ notes had set up a revolution in him. To-morrow he would go into the roaring down-town district and find work. A fur importer had once offered him a place as driver. He would find him to-morrow and ask for the position. He would be somebody in the world. He would——

Soapy felt a hand laid on his arm. He looked quickly around into the broad face of a policeman.

" What are you doin' here ? " asked the officer.

" Nothin'," said Soapy.

" Then come along," said the policeman.

" Three months on the Island," said the Magistrate in the Police Court the next morning.

AN ADJUSTMENT OF NATURE

IN an art exhibition the other day I saw a painting that had been sold for $5,000. The painter was a young scrub out of the West named Kraft, who had a favorite food and a pet theory. His pabulum was an unquenchable belief in the Unerring Artistic Adjustment of Nature. His theory was fixed around corned-beef hash with poached egg. There was a story behind the picture, so I went home and let it drip out of a fountain-pen. The idea of Kraft —but that is not the beginning of the story.

Three years ago Kraft, Bill Judkins (a poet), and I took our meals at Cypher's, on Eighth Avenue. I say " took." When we had money, Cypher got it " off of " us, as he expressed it. We had no credit; we went in, called for food and ate it. We paid or we did not pay. We had confidence in Cypher's sullenness and smouldering ferocity. Deep down in his sunless soul he was either a prince, a fool, or an artist. He sat at a worm-eaten desk, covered with files of waiter's checks so old that I was sure the bottomest one was for clams that Hendrik Hudson had eaten and paid for. Cypher had the power, in common with Napoleon III and the goggle-eyed perch, of throwing a film over his eyes, rendering opaque the windows of his soul. Once when we left him unpaid, with egregious excuses, I looked back and saw him shaking with inaudible laughter behind his film. Now and then we paid up back scores.

But the chief thing at Cypher's was Milly. Milly was a waitress. She was a grand example of Kraft's theory of the artistic adjustment of nature. She belonged, largely, to waiting, as Minerva did to the art of scrapping, or Venus to the science of serious flirtation. Pedestalled and in bronze she might have stood with the noblest of her heroic sisters as " Liver-and-Bacon Enlivening the World." She belonged to Cypher's. You expected to see her colossal figure loom through that reeking blue cloud of smoke from frying fat just as you expect the Palisades to appear through a drifting Hudson River fog. There amid the steam of vegetables and the vapors of acres of " ham and," the crash of crockery, the clatter of steel, the screaming of " short orders," the cries of the hungering and all the horrid tumult of feeding man, surrounded by swarms of the buzzing winged beasts bequeathed us by Pharaoh, Milly steered her magnificent way like some great liner cleaving among the canoes of howling savages.

Our Goddess of Grub was built on lines so majestic that they could be followed only with awe. Her sleeves were always rolled above her elbows. She could have taken us three musketeers in her two hands and dropped us out of the window. She had seen fewer years than any of us, but she was of such superb Evehood and simplicity that she mothered us from the beginning. Cypher's store of eatables she poured out upon us with royal indifference to price and quantity, as from a cornucopia that knew no exhaustion. Her voice rang like a great silver bell; her smile was many-toothed and frequent; she seemed like a yellow sunrise on mountain tops. I never saw her but I thought of the Yosemite. And yet, somehow, I could never think of her as existing outside of Cypher's. There nature had placed her and she had taken root and grown mightily. She seemed happy, and took her few poor dollars on Saturday nights with the flushed pleasure of a child that receives an unexpected donation.

It was Kraft who first voiced the fear that each of us must have held latently. It came up apropos, of course, of certain questions of art at which we were hammering. One of us compared the harmony existing between a Haydn symphony and pistache ice cream to the exquisite congruity between Milly and Cypher's.

" There is a certain fate hanging over Milly," said Kraft, " and if it overtakes her she is lost to Cypher's and to us."

" She will grow fat ? " asked Judkins, fearsomely.

" She will go to night school and become refined ? " I ventured, anxiously.

" It is this," said Kraft, punctuating in a puddle of spilled coffee with a stiff forefinger. " Cæsar had his Brutus—the cotton has its bollworm, the chorus girl has her Pittsburger, the summer boarder has his poison ivy, the hero has his Carnegie medal, art has its Morgan, the rose has its——"

" Speak," I interrupted, much perturbed. " You do not think that Milly will begin to lace ? "

" One day," concluded Kraft, solemnly, " there will come to Cypher's for a plate of beans a millionaire lumberman from Wisconsin, and he will marry Milly."

" Never ! " exclaimed Judkins and I, in horror.

" A lumberman," repeated Kraft, hoarsely.

" And a millionaire lumberman ! " I sighed despairingly.

" From Wisconsin ! " groaned Judkins.

We agreed that the awful fate seemed to menace her. Few things were less improbable. Milly, like some vast virgin stretch of pine woods, was made to catch the lumberman's eye. And well we knew the habits of the Badgers, once fortune smiled upon them. Straight to New York they hie, and lay their goods at the feet of the girl who serves them beans in a beanery. Why, the alphabet itself connives. The Sunday newspaper's headliner's work is cut for him.

" Winsome Waitress Wins Wealthy Wisconsin Woodsman."

For a while we felt that Milly was on the verge of being lost to us.

It was our love of the Unerring Artistic Adjustment of Nature that inspired us. We could not give her over to a lumberman, doubly accursed by wealth and provincialism. We shuddered to think of Milly, with her voice modulated and her elbows covered, pouring tea in the marble teepee of a tree murderer. No ! In Cypher's she belonged—in the bacon smoke, the cabbage perfume, the grand, Wagnerian chorus of hurled ironstone china and rattling casters.

Our fears must have been prophetic, for on that same evening the wildwood discharged upon us Milly's preordained confiscator —our fee to adjustment and order. But Alaska and not Wisconsin bore the burden of the visitation.

We were at our supper of beef stew and dried apples when he trotted in as if on the heels of a dog team, and made one of the mess at our table. With the freedom of the camps he assaulted our ears and claimed the fellowship of men lost in the wilds of a hash house. We embraced him as a specimen, and in three minutes we had all but died for one another as friends.

He was rugged and bearded and wind-dried. He had just come off the " trail," he said, at one of the North River ferries. I fancied I could see the snow dust of Chilcoot yet powdering his shoulders. And then he strewed the table with the nuggets, stuffed ptarmigans, bead work and seal pelts of the returned Klondiker, and began to prate to us of his millions.

" Bank drafts for two millions," was his summing up, " and a thousand a day piling up from my claims. And now I want some beef stew and canned peaches. I never got off the train since I mushed out of Seattle, and I'm hungry. The stuff the niggers feed you on pullmans don't count. You gentlemen order what you want."

And then Milly loomed up with a thousand dishes on her bare arm—loomed up big and white and pink and awful as Mount Saint Elias—with a smile like day breaking in a gulch. And the Klondiker threw down his pelts and nuggets as dross, and let his jaw fall halfway, and stared at her. You could almost see the diamond tiaras on Milly's brow and the hand-embroidered silk Paris gowns that he meant to buy for her.

At last the bollworm had attacked the cotton—the poison ivy was reaching out its tendrils to entwine the summer boarder—the millionaire lumberman, thinly disguised as the Alaskan miner, was about to engulf our Milly and upset Nature's adjustment.

Kraft was the first to act. He leaped up and pounded the Klondiker's back. " Come out and drink," he shouted. " Drink first and eat afterward." Judkins seized one arm and I the other. Gaily, roaringly, irresistibly, in jolly-good-fellow style, we dragged him from the restaurant to a café, stuffing his pockets with his embalmed birds and indigestible nuggets.

There he rumbled a roughly good-humored protest. " That's the girl for my money," he declared. " She can eat out of my skillet the rest of her life. Why, I never see such a fine girl. I'm going back there and ask her to marry me. I guess she won't want to sling hash any more when she sees the pile of dust I've got."

" You'll take another whiskey and milk now," Kraft persuaded, with Satan's smile. " I thought you up-country fellows were better sports."

Kraft spent his puny store of coin at the bar and then gave Judkins and me such an appealing look that we went down to the last dime we had in toasting our guest.

Then, when our ammunition was gone and the Klondiker, still somewhat sober, began to babble again of Milly, Kraft whispered into his ear such a polite, barked insult relating to people who were miserly with their funds, that the miner crashed down handful after handful of silver and notes, calling for all the fluids in the world to drown the imputation.

Thus the work was accomplished. With his own guns we drove him from the field. And then we had him carted to a distant small hotel and put to bed with his nuggets and baby seal-skins stuffed around him.

" He will never find Cypher's again," said Kraft. " He will propose to the first white apron he sees in a dairy restaurant to-morrow. And Milly—I mean the Natural Adjustment—is saved. !"

And back to Cypher's went we three, and finding customers scarce, we joined hands and did an Indian dance with Milly in the centre.

This, I say, happened three years ago. And about that time a little luck descended upon us three, and we were enabled to buy costlier and less wholesome food than Cypher's. Our paths separated, and I saw Kraft no more and Judkins seldom.

But, as I said, I saw a painting the other day that was sold for $5,000. The title was " Boadicea," and the figures seemed to fill all out-of-doors.   But of all the picture's admirers who stood before it, I believe I was the only one who longed for Boadicea to stalk from her frame bringing me corned-beef hash with poached egg.

I hurried away to see Kraft. His satanic eyes were the same, his hair was worse tangled, but his clothes had been made by a tailor.

" I didn't know," I said to him.

" We've bought a cottage in the Bronx with the money," said he. "Any evening at 7."

" Then," said I, " when you led us against the lumberman— the—Klondiker—it wasn't altogether on account of the Unerring Artisitc Adjustment of Nature ? "

" Well, not altogether," said Kraft, with a grin.

MEMOIRS OF A YELLOW DOG

I DON'T suppose it will knock any of you people off your perch to read a contribution from an animal. Mr. Kipling and a good many others have demonstrated the fact that animals can express themselves in remunerative English, and no magazine goes to press nowadays without an animal story in it, except the old-style monthlies that are still running pictures of Bryan and the Mont Pelée horror.

But you needn't look for any stuck-up literature in my piece, such as Bearoo, the bear, and Snakoo, the snake, and Tammanoo, the tiger, talk in the jungle books. A yellow dog that's spent most of his life in a cheap New York flat, sleeping in a corner on an old sateen underskirt (the one she spilled port wine on at the Lady 'Longshoremen's banquet), mustn't be expected to perform any tricks with the art of speech.

I was born a yellow pup; date, locality, pedigree and weight unknown. The first thing I can recollect, an old woman had me in a basket at Broadway and Twenty-third trying to sell me to a fat lady. Old Mother Hubbard was boosting me to beat the band as a genuine Pomeranian-Hambletonian-Red-Irish-Cochin-China-Stoke-Pogis fox terrier. The fat lady chased a V around among the samples of gros grain flannelette in her shopping bag till she cornered it, and gave up. From that moment I was a pet—a mamma's own wootsey squidlums. Say, gentle reader, did you ever have a 200-pound woman breathing a flavor of Camembert cheese and Peau d'Espagne pick you up and wallop her nose all over you, remarking all the time in an Emma Eames tone of voioe : " Oh, oo's um oodlum, doodlum, woodlum, toodlum, bitsy-witsy skoodlums ? "

From pedigreed yellow pup I grew up to be an anonymous yellow cur looking like a cross between an Angora cat and a box of lemons. But my mistress never tumbled. She thought that the two primeval pups that Noah chased into the ark were but a colateral branch of my ancestors. It took two policemen to keep her from entering me at the Madison Square Garden for the Siberian bloodhound prize.

I'll tell you about that flat. The house was the ordinary thing in New York, paved with Parian marble in the entrance hall and cobble-stones above the first floor. Our flat was three—well, not flights—climbs up. My mistress rented it unfurnished, and put in the regular things—1903 antique upholstered parlor set, oil chromo of geisha in a Harlem tea house, rubber plant and husbands.

By Sirius ! there was a biped I felt sorry for. He was a little man with sandy hair and whiskers a good deal like mine. Henpecked ? —well, toucans and flamingoes and pelicans all had their bills in him. He wiped the dishes and listened to my mistress tell about the cheap, ragged things the lady with the squirrel-skin coat on the second floor hung out on her line to dry. And every evening while she was getting supper she made him take me out on the end of a string for a walk.

If men knew how women pass the time when they are alone they'd never marry. Laura Lean Jibbey, peanut brittle, a little almond cream on the neck muscles, dishes unwashed, half an hour's talk with the iceman, reading a package of old letters, a couple of pickles and two bottles of malt extract, one hour peeking through a hole in the window shade into the flat across the airshaft—that's about all there is to it. Twenty minutes before time for him to come home from work she straightens up the house, fixes her rat so it won't show, and gets out a lot of sewing for a ten-minute bluff.

I led a dog's life in that flat. 'Most all day I lay there in my corner watching that fat woman kill time. I slept sometimes and had pipe dreams about being out chasing cats into basements and growling at old ladies with black mittens, as a dog was intended to do. Then she would pounce upon me with a lot of that drivelling poodle palaver and kiss me on the nose—but what could I do ? A dog can't chew cloves.

I began to feel sorry for Hubby, dog my cats if I didn't. We looked so much alike that people noticed it when we went out; so we shook the streets that Morgan's cab drives down, and took to climbing the piles of last December's snow on the streets where cheap people live.

One evening when we were thus promenading, and I was trying to look like a prize St. Bernard, and the old man was trying to look like he wouldn't have murdered the first organ-grinder he heard play Mendelssohn's wedding-march, I looked up at him and said, in my way :

" What are you looking so sour about, you oakum trimmed lobster ? She don't kiss you. You don't have to sit on her lap and listen to talk that would make the book of a musical comedy sound like the maxims of Epictetus. You ought to be thankful you're not a dog. Brace up, Benedick, and bid the blues begone."

The matrimonial mishap looked down at me with almost canine intelligence in his face.

" Why, doggie," says he, " good doggie. You almost look like you could speak. What it is, doggie—Cats."

Cats ! Could speak !

But, of course, he couldn't understand. Humans were denied the speech of animals. The only common ground of communication upon which dogs and men can get together is in fiction.

In the flat across the hall from us lived a lady with a black-and-tan terrier. Her husband strung it and took it out every evening, but he always came home cheerful and whistling. One day I touched noses with the black-and-tan in the hall, and I struck him for an elucidation.

" See here, Wiggle-and-Skip," I says, " you know that it ain't the nature of a real man to play dry nurse to a dog in public. I never saw one leashed to a bow-wow yet that didn't look like he'd like to lick every other man that looked at him. But your boss comes in every day as perky and set up as an amateur prestidigitator doing the egg trick. How does he do it ? Don't tell me he likes it."

" Him ? " says the black-and-tan. " Why, he uses Nature's Own Remedy. He gets spifflicated. At first when we go out he's as shy as the man on the steamer who would rather play pedro when they make 'em all jackpots. By the time we've been in eight saloons he don't care whether the thing on the end of his line is a dog or a catfish. I've lost two inches of my tail trying to sidestep those swinging doors."

The pointer I got from the terrier—vaudeville please copy—set me to thinking.

One evening about 6 o'clock my mistress ordered him to get busy and do the ozone act for Lovey. I have concealed it until now, but that is what she called me. The black-and-tan was called " Tweetness." I consider that I have the bulge on him as far as you could chase a rabbit. Still " Lovey " is something of a nomenclatural tin can on the tail of one's self-respect.

At a quiet place on a safe street I tightened the line of my custodian in front of an attractive, refined saloon. I made a dead-ahead scramble for the doors, whining like a dog in the press despatches that lets the family know that little Alice is bogged while gathering lilies in the brook.

" Why, darn my eyes," says the old man, with a grin; " darn my eyes if the saffron-colored son of a seltzer lemonade ain't asking me in to take a drink. Lemme see—how long's it been since I saved shoe leather by keeping one foot on the foot-rest ? I believe I'll——"

I knew I had him. Hot Scotches he took, sitting at a table. For an hour he kept the Campbells coming. I sat by his side rapping for the waiter with my tail, and eating free lunch such as mamma in her flat never equalled with her homemade truck bought at a delicatessen store eight minutes before papa comes home.

When the products of Scotland were all exhausted except the rye bread the old man unwound me from the table leg and played me outside like a fisherman plays a salmon. Out there he took off my collar and threw it into the street.

" Poor doggie," says he; " good doggie. She shan't kiss you any more. 'S a darned shame. Good doggie, go away and get run over by a street car and be happy.''

I refused to leave. I leaped and frisked around the old man's legs happy as a pug on a rug.

" You old flea-headed woodchuck-chaser," I said to him—" you moon-baying, rabbit-pointing, egg-stealing old beagle, can't you see that I don't want to leave you ? Can't you see that we're both Pups in the Wood and the missis is the cruel uncle after you with the dish towel and me with the flea liniment and a pink bow to tie on my tail. Why not cut that all out and be pards forever more ? "

Maybe you'll say he didn't understand—maybe he didn't. But he kind of got a grip on the Hot Scotches, and stood still for a minute, thinking.

" Doggie," says he, finally, " we don't live more than a dozen lives on this earth, and very few of us live to be more than 300. If I ever see that flat any more I'm a flat, and if you do you're flatter; and that's no flattery. I'm offering 60 to 1 that Westward Ho wins out by the length of a dachshund."

There was no string, but I frolicked along with my master to the Twenty-third Street ferry. And the cats on the route saw reason to give thanks that prehensile claws had been given to them.

On the Jersey side my master said to a stranger who stood eating a currant bun :

" Me and my doggie, we are bound for the Rocky Mountains."

But what pleased me most was when my old man pulled both of my ears until I howled, and said :

" You common, monkey-headed, rat-tailed, sulphur-colored son of a door mat, do you know what I'm going to call you ? "

I thought of " Lovey," and I whined dolefully.

" I'm going to call you ' Pete,' " says my master; and if I'd had five tails I couldn't have done enough wagging to do justice to the occasion.

THE LOVE-PHILTRE OF IKEY SCHOENSTEIN

THE Blue Light Drug Store is downtown, between the Bowery and First Avenue, where the distance between the two streets is the shortest. The Blue Light does not consider that pharmacy is a thing of bric-à-brac, scent and ice-cream soda. If you ask it for pain-killer it will not give you a bonbon.

The Blue Light scorns the labor-saving arts of modern pharmacy. It macerates its opium and percolates its own laudanum and paregoric. To this day pills are made behind its tall prescription desk— pills rolled out on its own pill-tile, divided with a spatula, rolled with the finger and thumb, dusted with calcined magnesia and delivered in little round pasteboard pill-boxes. The store is on a corner about which coveys of ragged-plumed, hilarious children play and become candidates for the cough drops and soothing syrups that wait for them inside.

Ikey Schoenstein was the night clerk of the Blue Light and the friend of his customers. Thus it is on the East Side, where the heart of pharmacy is not glacé. There, as it should be, the druggist is a counsellor, a confessor, an adviser, an able and willing missionary and mentor whose learning is respected, whose occult wisdom is venerated and whose medicine is often poured, untasted, into the gutter. Therefore Ikey's corniform, be-spectacled nose and narrow, knowledge-bowed figure was well known in the vicinity of the Blue Light, and his advice and notice was much desired.

Ikey roomed and breakfasted at Mrs. Riddle's two squares

away. Mrs. Riddle had a daughter named Rosy. The circum-locution has been in vain—you must have guessed it—Ikey adored Rosy. She tinctured all his thoughts; she was the compound extract of all that was chemically pure and officinal—the dispensatory contained nothing equal to her. But Ikey was timid, and his hopes remained insoluble in the menstruum of his backwardness and fears. Behind his counter he was a superior being, calmly conscious of special knowledge and worth; outside he was a weak-kneed, purblind, motorman-cursed rambler, with ill-fitting clothes stained with chemicals and smelling of socotrine aloes and valerianate of ammonia.

The fly in Ikey's ointment (thrice welcome, pat trope!) was Chunk McGowan.

Mr. McGowan was also striving to catch the bright smiles tossed about by Rosy. But he was no out-fielder as Ikey was; he picked them off the bat. At the same time he was Ikey's friend and customer, and often dropped in at the Blue Light Drug Store to have a bruise painted with iodine or get a cut rubber-plastered after a pleasant evening spent along the Bowery.

One afternoon McGowan drifted in in his silent, easy way, and sat, comely, smooth-faced, hard, indomitable, good-natured, upon a stool.

"Ikey," said he, when his friend had fetched his mortar and sat opposite, grinding gum benzoin to a powder, "get busy with your ear. It's drugs for me if you've got the line I need."

Ikey scanned the countenance of Mr. McGowan for the usual evidence of conflict, but found none.

"Take your coat off," he ordered. "I guess already that you have been stuck in the ribs with a knife. I have many times told you those Dagoes would do you up."

Mr. McGowan smiled. "Not them," he said. "Not any Dagoes. But you've located the diagnosis all right enough—it's under my coat, near the ribs. Say! Ikey—Rosy and me are goin' to run away and get married to-night."

Ikey's left forefinger was doubled over the edge of the mortar, holding it steady. He gave it a wild rap with the pestle, but felt it not. Meanwhile Mr. McGowan's smile faded to a look of perplexed gloom.

"That is," he continued, "if she keeps in the notion until the time comes. We've been layin' pipes for the getaway for two weeks. One day she says she will; the same evenin' she says nixy. We've agreed on to-night, and Rosy's stuck to the affirmative this time for two whole days. But it's five hours yet till the time, and I'm afraid she'll stand me up when it comes to the scratch."

"You said you wanted drugs," remarked Ikey.

Mr. McGowan looked ill at ease and harassed—a condition opposed to his usual line of demeanor. He made a patent-medicine almanac into a roll and fitted it with unprofitable carefulness about his finger.

" I wouldn't have this double handicap make a false start to-night for a million." he said. " I've got a little flat up in Harlem all ready, with chrysanthemums on the table and a kettle ready to boil. And I've engaged a pulpit pounder to be ready at his house for us at 9 : 30. It's got to come off. And if Rosy don't change her mind again ! "—Mr. McGowan ceased, a prey to his doubts.

" I don't see then yet," said Ikey, shortly, " what makes it that you talk of drugs, or what I can be doing about it."

" Old man Riddle don't like me a little bit," went on the uneasy suitor, bent upon marshalling his arguments. " For a week he hasn't let Rosy step outside the door with me. It it wasn't for losin' a boarder they'd have bounced me long ago. I'm makin' $20 a week and she'll never regret flyin' the coop with Chunk McGowan."

" You will excuse me, Chunk," said Ikey. " I must make a prescription that is to be called for soon."

" Say," said McGowan, looking up suddenly, " say, Ikey, ain't there a drug of some kind—some kind of powders that'll make a girl like you better if you give 'em to her ? "

Ikey's lip beneath his nose curled with the scorn of superior enlightenment; but before he could answer, McGowan continued:

" Tim Lacy told me he got some once from a croaker uptown and fed 'em to his girl in soda water. From the very first dose he was ace-high and everybody else looked like thirty cents to her. They was married in less than two weeks."

Strong and simple was Chunk McGowan. A better reader of men than Ikey was could have seen that his tough frame was strung upon fine wires. Like a good general who was about to invade the enemy's territory he was seeking to guard every point against possible failure.

" I thought," went on Chunk, hopefully, " that if I had one of them powders to give Rosy when I see her at supper to-night it might brace her up and keep her from reneging on the proposition to skip. I guess she don't need a mule team to drag her away, but women are better at coaching than they are at running bases. If the stuff'll work just for a couple of hours it'll do the trick."

" When is this foolishness of running away to be happening ? ' asked Ikey.

" Nine o'clock," said Mr. McGowan. " Supper's at seven. At eight Rosy goes to bed with a headache, at nine old Parvenzano lets me through to his backyard, where there's a board off Riddle's fence, next door. I go under her window and help her down the fire-escape. We've got to make it early on the preacher's account. It's all dead easy if Rosy don't balk when the flag drops. Can you fix me one of them powders, Ikey ? "

Ikey Schoenstein rubbed his nose slowly.

" Chunk," said he, " it is of drugs of that nature that pharmaceutists must have much carefulness. To you alone of my acquaintance would I intrust a powder like that. But for you I shall make it, and you shall see how it makes Rosy to think of you."

Ikey went behind the prescription desk. There he crushed to a powder two soluble tablets, each containing a quarter of a grain of morphia. To them he added a little sugar of milk to increase the bulk, and folded the mixture neatly in a white paper. Taken by an adult this powder would insure several hours of heavy slumber without danger to the sleeper. This he handed to Chunk McGowan, telling him to administer it in a liquid if possible, and received the hearty thanks of the backyard Lochinvar.

The subtlety of Ikey's action becomes apparent upon recital of his subsequent move. He sent a messenger for Mr. Riddle and disclosed the plans of Mr. McGowan for eloping with Rosy. Mr. Riddle was a stout man, brick-dusty of complexion and sudden in action.

" Much obliged," he said, briefly, to Ikey. " The lazy Irish loafer ! My own room's just above Rosy's. I'll just go up there myself after supper and load the shot-gun and wait. If he comes in my backyard he'll go away in a ambulance instead of a bridal chaise."

With Rosy held in the clutches of Morpheus and for a many-hours deep slumber, and the blood-thirsty parent waiting, armed and forewarned, Ikey felt that his rival was close, indeed, upon discomfiture.

All night in the Blue Light Drug Store he waited at his duties for chance news of the tragedy, but none came.

At eight o'clock in the morning the day clerk arrived and Ikey started hurriedly for Mrs. Riddle's to learn the outcome. And, lo ! as he stepped out of the store who but Chunk McGowan sprang from a passing street car and grasped his hand—Chunk McGowan with a victor's smile and flushed with joy.

" Pulled it off," said Chunk with Elysium in his grin. " Rosy hit the fire-escape on time to a second, and we was under the wire at the Reverend's at 9.30$\frac{1}{4}$. She's up at the flat—she cooked eggs this mornin' in a blue kimono—Lord ! how lucky I am ! You must pace up some day, Ikey, and feed with us. I've got a job down near the bridge, and that's where I'm heading for now."

" The—the—powder ? " stammered Ikey.

" Oh, that stuff you gave me ! " said Chunk, broadening his grin; " well, it was this way. I sat down at the supper table last night at Riddle's, and I looked at Rosy, and I says to myself, ' Chunk, if you get the girl get her on the square—don't try any hocus-pocus with a thoroughbred like her.' And I keeps the paper you give me in my pocket. And then my lamps fall on another party present, who, I says to myself, is failin' in a proper affection toward his comin' son-in-law, so I watches my chance and dumps that powder in old man Riddle's coffee—see ? "

MAMMON AND THE ARCHER

OLD Anthony Rockwall, retired manufacturer and proprietor of Rockwall's Eureka Soap, looked out the library window of his Fifth Avenue mansion and grinned. His neighbour to the right —the aristocratic clubman, G. Van Schuylight Suffolk-Jones— came out to his waiting motor-car, wrinkling a contumelious nostril, as usual, at the Italian renaissance sculpture of the soap palace's elevation.

" Stuck-up old statuette of nothing doing ! " commented the ex-Soap King. " The Eden Musée'll get that old frozen Nesselrode yet if he don't watch out. I'll have this house painted red, white, and blue next summer and see if that'll make his Dutch nose turn up any higher."

And then Anthony Rockwall, who never cared for bells, went to the door of his library and shouted " Mike ! " in the same voice that had once chipped off pieces of the welkin on the Kansas prairies.

" Tell my son," said Anthony to the answering menial, " to come in here before he leaves the house."

When young Rockwall entered the library the old man laid aside his newspaper, looked at him with a kindly grimness on his big, smooth, ruddy countenance, rumpled his mop of white hair with one hand and rattled the keys in his pocket with the other.

" Richard," said Anthony Rockwall. " what do you pay for the soap that you use ? "

Richard, only six months home from college, was startled a little. He had not yet taken the measure of this sire of his, who was as full of unexpectednesses as a girl at her first party.

" Six dollars a dozen, I think, dad."

" And your clothes ? "

" I suppose about sixty dollars, as a rule."

" You're a gentleman," said Anthony, decidedly. " I've heard of these young bloods spending $24 a dozen for soap, and going over the hundred mark for clothes. You've got as much money to waste as any of 'em, and yet you stick to what's decent and moderate. Now I use the old Eureka—not only for sentiment, but it's the purest soap made. Whenever you pay more than 10 cents a cake for soap you buy bad perfumes and labels. But 50 cents is doing very well for a young man in your generation, position and condition. As I said, you're a gentleman. They say it takes three generations to make one. They're off. Money'll do it as slick as soap grease. It's made you one. By hokey! it's almost made one of me. I'm nearly as impolite and disagreeable and ill-mannered as these two old knickerbocker gents on each side of me that can't sleep of nights because I bought in between 'em."

"There are some things that money can't accomplish," remarked young Rockwall, rather gloomily.

"Now, don't say that," said old Anthony, shocked. "I bet my money on money every time. I've been through the encyclopædia down to Y looking for something you can't buy with it; and I expect to have to take up the appendix next week. I'm for money against the field. Tell me something money won't buy."

"For one thing," answered Richard, rankling a little, "it won't buy one into the exclusive circles of society."

"Oho! won't it?" thundered the champion of the root of evil. "You tell me where your exclusive circles would be if the first Astor hadn't had the money to pay for his steerage passage over?"

Richard sighed.

"And that's what I was coming to," said the old man, less boisterously. "That's why I asked you to come in. There's something going wrong with you, boy. I've been noticing it for two weeks. Out with it. I guess I could lay my hands on eleven millions within twenty-four hours, besides the real estate. If it's your liver, there's the *Rambler* down in the bay, coaled, and ready to steam down to the Bahamas in two days."

"Not a bad guess, dad; you haven't missed it far."

"Ah," said Anthony, keenly; "what's her name?"

Richard began to walk up and down the library floor. There was enough comradeship and sympathy in this crude old father of his to draw his confidence.

"Why don't you ask her?" demanded old Anthony. "She'll jump at you. You've got the money and the looks, and you're a decent boy. Your hands are clean. You've got no Eureka soap on 'em. You've been to college, but she'll overlook that."

"I haven't had a chance," said Richard.

"Make one," said Anthony. "Take her for a walk in the park,

or a straw ride, or walk home with her from church. Chance !
Pshaw ! "

" You don't know the social mill, dad. She's part of the stream
that turns it. Every hour and minute of her time is arranged for
days in advance. I must have that girl, dad, or this town is a black-
jack swamp forevermore. And I can't write it—I can't do that."

" Tut ! " said the old man. " Do you mean to tell me that with
all the money I've got you can't get an hour or two of a girl's time
for yourself ? "

" I've put it off too late. She's going to sail for Europe at noon
day after to-morrow for a two years' stay. I'm to see her alone to-
morrow evening for a few minutes. She's at Larchmont now at
her aunt's. I can't go there. But I'm allowed to meet her with a
cab at the Grand Central Station to-morrow evening at the 8.30
train. We drive down Broadway to Wallack's at a gallop, where
her mother and a box party will be waiting for us in the lobby.
Do you think she would listen to a declaration from me during that
six or eight minutes under those circumstances ? No. And what
chance would I have in the theatre or afterward ? None. No, dad,
this is one tangle that your money can't unravel. We can't buy
one minute of time with cash; if we could, rich people would live
longer. There's no hope of getting a talk with Miss Lantry before
she sails."

"All right, Richard, my boy," said Old Anthony, cheerfully.
" You may run along down to your club now. I'm glad it ain't
your liver. But don't forget to burn a few punk sticks in the joss
house to the great god Mazuma from time to time. You say money
won't buy time ? Well, of course, you can't order eternity wrapped
up and delivered at your residence for a price, but I've seen Father
Time get pretty bad stone bruises on his heels when he walked
through the gold diggings."

That night came Aunt Ellen, gentle, sentimental, wrinkled,
sighing, oppressed by wealth, in to Brother Anthony at his evening
paper, and began discourse on the subject of lovers' woes.

" He told me all about it," said Brother Anthony, yawning. " I
told him my bank account was at his service. And then he
began to knock money. Said money couldn't help. Said the
rules of society couldn't be bucked for a yard by a team of ten-
millionaires."

" Oh, Anthony," sighed Aunt Ellen, " I wish you would not
think so much of money. Wealth is nothing where a true affection
is concerned. Love is all-powerful. If he only had spoken earlier !
She could not have refused our Richard. But now I fear it is too
late. He will have no opportunity to address her. All your gold
cannot bring happiness to your son."

At eight o'clock the next evening Aunt Ellen took a quaint old gold ring from a moth-eaten case and gave it to Richard.

" Wear it to-night, nephew," she begged. " Your mother gave it to me. Good luck in love she said it brought. She asked me to give it to you when you had found the one you loved."

Young Rockwall took the ring reverently and tried it on his smallest finger. It slipped as far as the second joint and stopped. He took it off and stuffed it into his vest pocket, after the manner of man. And then he 'phoned for his cab.

At the station he captured Miss Lantry out of the gabbing mob at eight thirty-two."

" We mustn't keep mamma and the others waiting." said she.

" To Wallack's Theatre as fast as you can drive ! " said Richard, loyally.

They whirled up Forty-second to Broadway, and then down the white-starred lane that leads from the soft meadows of sunset to the rocky hills of morning.

At Thirty-fourth Street young Richard quickly thrust up the trap and ordered the cabman to stop.

" I've dropped a ring," he apologized, as he climbed out. " It was my mother's, and I'd hate to lose it. I won't detain you a minute—I saw where it fell."

In less than a minute he was back in the cab with the ring.

But within that minute a crosstown car had stopped directly in front of the cab. The cab-man tried to pass to the left, but a heavy express wagon cut him off. He tried the right and had to back away from a furniture van that had no business to be there. He tried to back out, but dropped his reins and swore dutifully. He was blockaded in a tangled mess of vehicles and horses. He

One of those street blockades had occurred that sometimes tie up commerce and movement quite suddenly in the big city.

" Why don't you drive on ? " said Miss Lantry, impatiently. " We'll be late."

Richard stood up in the cab and looked around. He saw a congested flood of wagons, trucks, cabs, vans and street cars filling the vast space where Broadway, Sixth Avenue, and Thirty-fourth Street cross one another as a twenty-six inch maiden fills her twenty-two inch girdle. And still from all the cross streets they were hurrying and rattling toward the converging point at full speed, and hurling themselves into the straggling mass, locking wheels and adding their drivers' imprecations to the clamor. The entire traffic of Manhattan seemed to have jammed itself around them. The oldest New Yorker among the thousands of spectators that lined the sidewalks had not witnessed a street blockade of the proportions of this one.

" I'm very sorry," said Richard, as he resumed his seat, " but it looks as if we are stuck. They won't get this jumble loosened up in an hour. It was my fault. If I hadn't dropped the ring we——"

" Let me see the ring," said Miss Lantry. " Now that it can't be helped, I don't care. I think theatres are stupid anyway."

At 11 o'clock that night somebody tapped lightly on Anthony Rockwall's door.

" Come in." shouted Anthony, who was in a red dressing-gown, reading a book of piratical adventures.

Somebody was Aunt Ellen, looking like a gray-haired angel that had been left on earth by mistake.

" They're engaged, Anthony," she said, softly. " She has promised to marry our Richard. On their way to the theatre there was a street blockade, and it was two hours before their cab could get out of it.

" And oh, Brother Anthony, don't ever boast of the power of money again. A little emblem of true love—a little ring that symbolized unending and unmercenary affection—was the cause of our Richard finding his happiness. He dropped it in the street, and got out to recover it. And before they could continue the blockade occurred. He spoke to his love and won her there while the cab was hemmed in. Money is dross compared with true love, Anthony."

" All right," said old Anthony. " I'm glad the boy has got what he wanted. I told him I wouldn't spare any expense in the matter if——"

" But Brother Anthony, what good could your money have done ? "

" Sister," said Anthony Rockwall. " I've got my pirate in a devil of a scrape. His ship has just been scuttled, and he's too good a judge of the value of money to let drown. I wish you would let me go on with this chapter."

The story should end here. I wish it would as heartily as you who read it wish it did. But we must go to the bottom of the well for truth.

The next day a person with red hands and a blue polka-dot necktie, who called himself Kelly, called at Anthony Rockwall's house, and was at once received in the library.

" Well," said Anthony, reaching for his check-book, " it was a good bilin' of soap. Let's see—you had $5,000 in cash."

" I paid out $300 more of my own," said Kelly. " I had to go a little above the estimate. I got the express wagons and cabs mostly for $5; but the trucks and two-horse teams mostly raised me to $10. The motormen wanted $10, and some of the loaded teams $20. The cops struck me hardest—$50 I paid two, and the rest $20 and $25. But didn't it work beautiful, Mr. Rockwall? I'm glad William A. Brady wasn't onto that little outdoor vehicle mob scene. I wouldn't want William to break his heart with jealousy. And never a rehearsal, either! The boys was on time to the fraction of a second. It was two hours before a snake could get below Greeley's statue."

"Thirteen hundred—there you are, Kelly," said Anthony, tearing off a check. "Your thousand, and the $300 you were out. You don't despise money, do you, Kelly?"

"Me?" said Kelly. "I can lick the man that invented poverty."

Anthony called Kelly when he was at the door.

"You didn't notice," said he, "anywhere in the tie-up, a kind of a fat boy without any clothes on shooting arrows around with a bow did you?"

"Why, no," said Kelly, mystified. "I didn't. If he was like you say, maybe the cops pinched him before I got there."

"I thought the little rascal wouldn't be on hand." chuckled Anthony. "Goodby, Kelly."

SPRINGTIME À LA CARTE

IT was a day in March.

Never, never begin a story this way when you write one. No opening could possibly be worse. It is unimaginative, flat, dry, and likely to consist of mere wind. But in this instance it is allowable. For the following paragraph, which should have inaugurated the narrative, is too wildly extravagant and preposterous to be flaunted in the face of the reader without preparation.

Sarah was crying over her bill of fare.

Think of a New York girl shedding tears on the menu card!

To account for this you will be allowed to guess that the lobsters were all out, or that she had sworn ice-cream off during Lent, or that she had ordered onions, or that she had just come from a Hackett matinée. And then, all these theories being wrong, you will please let the story proceed.

The gentleman who announced that the world was an oyster which he with his sword would open made a larger hit than he deserved. It is not difficult to open an oyster with a sword. But did you ever notice any one try to open the terrestrial bivalve with a typewriter? Like to wait for a dozen raw opened that way?

Sarah had managed to pry apart the shells with her unhandy weapon far enough to nibble a wee bit at the cold and clammy world within. She knew no more shorthand than if she had been a graduate in stenography just let slip upon the world by a business college. So, not being able to stenog, she could not enter that bright galaxy of office talent. She was a free-lance typewriter and canvassed for odd jobs of copying.

The most brilliant and crowning feat of Sarah's battle with the world was the deal she made with Schulenberg's Home Restaurant. The restaurant was next door to the old red brick in which she hall-roomed. One evening after dining at Schulenberg's 40-cent, five-course *table d'hôte* (served as fast as you throw the five baseballs at the colored gentleman's head) Sarah took away with her the bill of fare. It was written in an almost unreadable script neither English nor German, and so arranged that if you were not careful you began with a tooth-pick and rice pudding and ended with soup and the day of the week.

The next day Sarah showed Schulenberg a neat card on which the menu was beautifully typewritten with the viands temptingly marshalled under their right and proper heads from " hors d'œuvre " to " not responsible for over-coats and umbrellas."

Schulenberg became a naturalized citizen on the spot. Before Sarah left him she had him willingly committed to an agreement. She was to furnish typewritten bills of fare for the twenty-one tables in the restaurant—a new bill for each day's dinner, and new ones for breakfast and lunch as often as changes occurred in the food or as neatness required.

In return for this Schulenberg was to send three meals per diem to Sarah's hall room by a waiter—an obsequious one if possible—and furnish her each afternoon with a pencil draft of what Fate had in store for Schulenberg's customers on the morrow.

Mutual satisfaction resulted from the agreement. Schulenberg's patrons now knew what the food they ate was called even if its nature sometimes puzzled them. And Sarah had food during a cold, dull winter, which was the main thing with her.

And then the almanac lied, and said that spring had come. Spring comes when it comes. The frozen snows of January still lay like adamant in the cross-town streets. The hand-organs still played " In the Good Old Summertime," with their December vivacity and expression. Men began to make thirty-day notes to buy Easter dresses. Janitors shut off steam. And when these things happen one may know that the city is still in the clutches of winter.

One afternoon Sarah shivered in her elegant hall bedroom; " house heated; scrupulously clean; conveniences; seen to be appreciated." She had no work to do except Schulenberg's menu cards. Sarah sat in her squeaky willow rocker, and looked out the window. The calendar on the wall kept crying to her : " Springtime is here, Sarah—springtime is here, I tell you. Look at me, Sarah, my figures show it. You've got a neat figure yourself, Sarah—a—nice springtime figure—why do you look out the window so sadly ? "

Sarah's room was at the back of the house. Looking out the window she could see the windowless rear brick wall of the box factory on the next street. But the wall was clearest crystal; and Sarah was looking down a grassy lane shaded with cherry trees and elms and bordered with raspberry bushes and Cherokee roses.

Spring's real harbingers are too subtle for the eye and ear. Some must have the flowering crocus, the wood-starring dogwood, the voice of bluebird—even so gross a reminder as the farewell handshake of the retiring buckwheat and oyster before they can welcome the Lady in Green to their dull bosoms. But to old earth's choicest kind there come straight, sweet messages from his newest bride, telling them they shall be no stepchildren unless they choose to be.

On the previous summer Sarah had gone into the country and loved a farmer.

(In writing your story never hark back thus. It is bad art, and cripples interest. Let it march, march.)

Sarah stayed two weeks at Sunnybrook Farm. There she learned to love old Farmer Franklin's son Walter. Farmers have been loved and wedded and turned out to grass in less time. But young Walter Franklin was a modern agriculturist. He had a telephone in his cow house, and he could figure up exactly what effect next year's Canada wheat crop would have on potatoes planted in the dark of the moon.

It was in this shaded and raspberried lane that Walter had wooed and won her. And together they had sat and woven a crown of dandelions for her hair. He had immoderately praised the effect of the yellow blossoms against her brown tresses; and she had left the chaplet there, and walked back to the house swinging her straw sailor in her hands.

They were to marry in the spring—at the very first signs of spring, Walter said. And Sarah came back to the city to pound her typewriter.

A knock at the door dispelled Sarah's visions of that happy day. A waiter had brought the rough pencil draft of the Home Restaurant's next day fare in old Schulenberg's angular hand.

Sarah sat down to her typewriter and slipped a card between the rollers. She was a nimble worker. Generally in an hour and a half the twenty-one menu cards were written and ready.

To-day there were more changes on the bill of fare than usual. The soups were lighter; pork was eliminated from the entrées, figuring only with Russian turnips among the roasts. The gracious spirit of spring pervaded the entire menu. Lamb, that lately capered on the greening hillsides, was becoming exploited with the sauce that commemorated its gambols. The song of the oyster, though not silenced, was *dimuendo con amore*. The frying-pan seemed to be held, inactive, behind the beneficent bars of the broiler. The pie list swelled; the richer puddings had vanished; the sausage, with his drapery wrapped about him, barely lingered in a pleasant thanatopsis with the buckwheats and the sweet but doomed maple.

Sarah's fingers danced like midgets above a summer stream. Down through the courses she worked, giving each item its position according to its length with an accurate eye.

Just above the desserts came the list of vegetables. Carrots and peas, asparagus on toast, the perennial tomatoes and corn and succotash, lima beans, cabbage—and then——

Sarah was crying over her bill of fare. Tears from the depths of some divine despair rose in her heart and gathered to her eyes. Down went her head on the little typewriter stand; and the keyboard rattled a dry accompaniment to her moist sobs.

For she had received no letter from Walter in two weeks, and the next item on the bill of fare was dandelions—dandelions with some kind of egg—but bother the egg !—dandelions, with whose golden blooms Walter had crowned her his queen of love and future bride—dandelions, the harbingers of spring, her sorrow's crown of sorrow—reminder of her happiest days.

Madam, I dare you to smile until you suffer this test : Let the Marechal Niel roses that Percy brought you on the night you gave him your heart be served as a salad with French dressing before your eyes at a Schulenberg *table d'hôte*. Had Juliet so seen her love tokens dishonored the sooner would she have sought the lethean herbs of the good apothecary.

But what witch is Spring ! Into the great cold city of stone and iron a message had to be sent. There was none to convey it but the little hardy courier of the fields with his rough green coat and modest air. He is a true soldier of fortune, this *dent-de-lion*—this lion's tooth, as the French chefs call him. Flowered, he will assist at love-making, wreathed in my lady's nut-brown hair; young and callow and unblossomed, he goes into the boiling pot and delivers the word of his sovereign mistress.

By and by Sarah forced back her tears. The cards must be written. But, still in a faint, golden glow from her dandelion dream, she fingered the typewriter keys absently for a little while, with her mind and heart in the meadow lane with her young farmer. But soon she came swiftly back to the rock-bound lanes of Manhattan, and the typewriter began to rattle and jump like a strike-breaker's motor car.

At 6 o'clock the waiter brought her dinner and carried away the typewritten bill of fare. When Sarah ate she set aside, with a sigh, the dish of dandelions with its crowning ovarious accompaniment. As this dark mass had been transformed from a bright and love-indorsed flower to be an ignominious vegetable, so had her summer hopes wilted and perished. Love may, as Shakespeare said, feed on itself : but Sarah could not bring herself to eat the dandelions that had graced, as ornaments, the first spiritual banquet of her heart's true affection.

At 7.30 the couple in the next room began to quarrel : the man in the room above sought for A on his flute; the gas went a little lower; three coal wagons started to unload—the only sound of which the phonograph is jealous; the cats on back fences slowly retreated toward Mukden. By these signs Sarah knew that it was time for her to read.

She got out "The Cloister and the Hearth,"the best non-selling book of the month, settled her feet on her trunk, and began to wander with Gerard.

The front door bell rang. The landlady answered it. Sarah left Gerard and Denys treed by a bear and listened. Oh, yes; you would, just as she did !

And then a strong voice was heard in the hall below, and Sarah jumped for her door, leaving the book on the floor and the first round easily the bear's.

You have guessed it. She reached the top of the stairs just as her farmer came up, three at a jump, and reaped and garnered her, with nothing left for the gleaners.

"Why haven't you written—oh, why ? " cried Sarah.

"New York is a pretty large town," said Walter Franklin. " I came in a week ago to your old address. I found that you went away on a Thursday. That consoled some; it eliminated the possible Friday bad luck. But it didn't prevent my hunting for you with police and otherwise ever since ! "

" I wrote ! " said Sarah, vehemently.

" Never got it ! "

" Then how did you find me ? "

The young farmer smiled a springtime smile.

" I dropped into that Home Restaurant next door this evening," said he. " I don't care who knows it; I like a dish of some kind of greens at this time of the year. I ran my eye down that nice typewritten bill of fare looking for something in that line. When I got below cabbage I turned my chair over and hollered for the proprietor. He told me where you lived."

" I remember," sighed Sarah, happily. " That was dandelions below cabbage."

" I'd know that cranky capital W 'way above the line that your typewriter makes anywhere in the world," said Franklin.

" Why, there's no W in dandelions," said Sarah in surprise.

The young man drew the bill of fare from his pocket and pointed to a line.

Sarah recognized the first card she had typewritten that afternoon. There was still the rayed splotch in the upper right-hand corner where a tear had fallen. But over the spot where one should have read the name of the meadow plant, the clinging memory of their golden blossoms had allowed her fingers to strike strange keys.

Between the red cabbage and the stuffed green peppers was the item :

`''Dearest Walter, with hard-boiled egg.''`

THE GREEN DOOR

SUPPOSE you should be walking down Broadway after dinner, with ten minutes allotted to the consummation of your cigar while you are choosing between a diverting tragedy and something serious in the way of vaudeville. Suddenly a hand is laid upon your arm. You turn to look into the thrilling eyes of a beautiful woman, wonderful in diamonds and Russian sables. She thrusts hurriedly into your hand an extremely hot buttered roll, flashes out a tiny pair of scissors, snips off the second button of your overcoat, meaningly ejaculates the one word, " parallelogram ! " and swiftly flies down a cross street, looking back fearfully over her shoulder.

That would be pure adventure. Would you accept it ? Not you. You would flush with embarrassment; you would sheepishly drop the roll and continue down Broadway, fumbling feebly for the missing button. This you would do unless you are one of the blessed few in whom the pure spirit of adventure is not dead.

True adventurers have never been plentiful. They who are set down in print as such have been mostly business men with newly invented methods. They have been out after the things they wanted —golden fleeces, holy grails, lady loves, treasure, crowns and fame. The true adventurer goes forth aimless and uncalculating to meet and greet unknown fate. A fine example was the Prodigal Son—when he started back home.

Half-adventurers — brave and splendid figures — have been numerous. From the Crusades to the Palisades they have enriched the arts of history and fiction and the trade of historical fiction. But each of them had a prize to win, a goal to kick, an axe to grind, a race to run, a new thrust in tierce to deliver, a name to carve, a crow to pick—so they were not followers of true adventure.

In the big city the twin spirits Romance and Adventure are always abroad seeking worthy wooers. As we roam the streets they slyly peep at us and challenge us in twenty different guises. Without knowing why, we look up suddenly to see in a window a face that seems to belong to our gallery of intimate portraits; in a sleeping thoroughfare we hear a cry of agony and fear coming from an empty and shuttered house; instead of at our familiar curb a cab-driver deposits us before a strange door, which one, with a smile, opens for us and bids us enter; a slip of paper, written upon, flutters down to our feet from the high lattices of Chance; we exchange glances of instantaneous hate, affection, and fear with hurrying strangers in the passing crowds; a sudden souse of rain—and our umbrella may be sheltering the daughter of the Full Moon and first cousin of the Sidereal System; at every corner handkerchiefs drop, fingers beckon, eyes besiege, and the lost, the lonely, the rapturous, the mysterious, the perilous changing clues of adventure are slipped into our fingers. But few of us are willing to hold and follow them. We are grown stiff with the ramrod of convention down our backs. We pass on; and some day we come, at the end of a very dull life, to reflect that our romance has been a pallid thing of a marriage or two, a satin rosette kept in a safe-deposit drawer, and a lifelong feud with a steam radiator.

Rudolf Steiner was a true adventurer. Few were the evenings on which he did not go forth from his hall bedchamber in search of the unexpected and the egregious. The most interesting thing in life seemed to him to be what might lie just around the next corner. Sometimes his willingness to tempt fate led him into strange paths. Twice he had spent the night in a station-house; again and again he had found himself the dupe of ingenious and mercenary tricksters; his watch and money had been the price of one flattering allurement. But with undiminished ardor he picked up every glove cast before him into the merry lists of adventure.

One evening Rudolf was strolling along a cross-town street in the older central part of the city. Two streams of people filled the side-walks—the home-hurrying, and that restless contingent that abandons home for the specious welcome of the thousand-candle-power *table d'hôte*.

The young adventurer was of pleasing presence, and moved

serenely and watchfully. By daylight he was a salesman in a piano store. He wore his tie drawn through a topaz ring instead of fastened with a stick pin; and once he had written to the editor of a magazine that "Junie's Love Test," by Miss Libbey, had been the book that had most influenced his life.

During his walk a violent chattering of teeth in a glass case on the sidewalk seemed at first to draw his attention (with a qualm) to a restaurant before which it was set; but a second glance revealed the electric letters of a dentist's sign high above the next door. A giant negro, fantastically dressed in a red embroidered coat, yellow trousers and a military cap, discreetly distributed cards to those of the passing crowd who consented to take them.

This mode of dentistic advertising was a common sight to Rudolf. Usually he passed the dispenser of the dentist's cards without reducing his store; but to-night the African slipped one into his hand so deftly that he retained it there smiling a little at the successful feat.

When he had travelled a few yards further he glanced at the card indifferently. Surprised, he turned it over and looked again with interest. One side of the card was blank; on the other was written in ink three words, "The Green Door." And then Rudolf saw, three steps in front of him, a man throw down the card the negro had given him as he passed. Rudolf picked it up. It was printed with the dentist's name and address and the usual schedule of "plate work" and "bridge work" and "crowns," and specious promises of "painless" operations.

The adventurous piano salesman halted at the corner and considered. Then he crossed the street walked down a block, recrossed and joined the upward current of people again. Without seeming to notice the negro as he passed the second time, he carelessly took the card that was handed him. Ten steps away he inspected it. In the same handwriting that appeared on the first card "The Green Door" was inscribed upon it. Three or four cards were tossed to the pavement by pedestrians both following and leading him. These fell blank side up. Rudolf turned them over. Every one bore the printed legend of the dental "parlors."

Rarely did the arch sprite Adventure need to beckon twice to Rudolf Steiner, his true follower. But twice it had been done, and the quest was on.

Rudolf walked slowly back to where the giant negro stood by the case of rattling teeth. This time as he passed he received no card. In spite of his gaudy and ridiculous garb, the Ethiopian displayed a natural barbaric dignity as he stood, offering the cards suavely to some, allowing others to pass unmolested. Every half minute he chanted a harsh, unintelligible phrase akin to the jabber of car conductors and grand opera. And not only did he withhold a card this time but it seemed to Rudolf that he received from the shining and massive black countenance a look of cold, almost contemptuous disdain.

The look stung the adventurer. He read in it a silent accusation that he had been found wanting. Whatever the mysterious written words on the cards might mean, the black had selected him twice from the throng for their recipient ; and now seemed to have condemned him as deficient in the wit and spirit to engage the enigma.

Standing aside from the rush, the young man made a rapid estimate of the building in which he conceived that his adventure must lie. Five stories high it rose. A small restaurant occupied the basement.

The first floor, now closed, seemed to house millinery or furs. The second floor, by the winking electric letters, was the dentist's. Above this a polyglot babel of signs struggled to indicate the abodes of palmists, dressmakers, musicians, and doctors. Still higher up draped curtains and milk bottles white on the window sills proclaimed the regions of domesticity.

After concluding his survey Rudolf walked briskly up the high flight of stone steps into the house. Up two flights of the carpeted stairway he continued; and at its top paused. The hallway there was dimly lighted by two pale jets of gas—one far to his right, the other nearer, to his left. He looked toward the nearer light and saw, within its wan halo, a green door. For one moment he hesitated : then he seemed to see the contumelious sneer of the African juggler of cards; and then he walked straight to the green door and knocked against it.

Moments like those that passed before his knock was answered measure the quick breath of true adventure. What might not be behind those green panels ! Gamesters at play; cunning rogues baiting their traps with subtle skill; beauty in love with courage, and thus planning to be sought by it; danger, death, love disappointment, ridicule—any of these might respond to that temerarious rap.

A faint rustle was heard inside, and the door slowly opened. A girl not yet twenty stood there white-faced and tottering. She loosed the knob and swayed weakly, groping with one hand. Rudolf caught her and laid her on a faded couch that stood against the wall. He closed the door and took a swift glance around the room by the light of a flickering gas jet. Neat, but extreme poverty was the story that he read.

The girl lay still, as if in a faint. Rudolf looked around the room excitedly for a barrel. People must be rolled upon a barrel who

—no, no; that was for drowned persons. He began to fan her with his hat. That was successful, for he struck her nose with the brim of his derby and she opened her eyes. And then the young man saw that hers, indeed, was the one missing face from his heart's gallery of intimate portraits. The frank, gray eyes, the little nose, turning pertly outward; the chestnut hair, curling like the tendrils of a pea vine, seemed the right end and reward of all his wonderful adventures. But the face was woefully thin and pale.

The girl looked at him calmly, and then smiled.

" Fainted, didn't I ? " she asked, weakly. " Well, who wouldn't? You try going without anything to eat for three days and see ! "

" Himmel ! " exclaimed Rudolf, jumping up. " Wait till I come back."

He dashed out the green door and down the stairs. In twenty minutes he was back again kicking at the door with his toe for her to open it. With both arms he hugged an array of wares from the grocery and the restaurant. On the table he laid them—bread and butter, cold meats, cakes, pies, pickles, oysters, a roasted chicken, a bottle of milk and one of red-hot tea.

" This is ridiculous," said Rudolf, blustering, " to go without eating. You must quit making election bets of this kind. Supper is ready." He helped her to a chair at the table and asked : " Is there a cup for the tea ? " " On the shelf by the window," she answered. When he turned again with the cup he saw her, with eyes shining rapturously, beginning upon a huge Dill pickle that she had rooted out from the paper bags with a woman's unerring instinct. He took it from her, laughingly, and poured the cup full of milk. " Drink that first," he ordered, " and then you shall have some tea, and then a chicken wing. If you are very good you shall have a pickle to-morrow. And now, if you'll allow me to be your guest we'll have supper."

He drew up the other chair. The tea brightened the girl's eyes and brought back some of her color. She began to eat with a sort of dainty ferocity like some starved wild animal. She seemed to regard the young man's presence and the aid he had rendered her as a natural thing—not as though she undervalued the conventions; but as one whose great stress gave her the right to put aside the artificial for the human. But gradually, with the return of strength and comfort, came also a sense of the little conventions that belong; and she began to tell him her little story. It was one of a thousand such as the city yawns at every day—the shop girl's story of insufficient wages, further reduced by " fines," that go to swell the store's profits; of time lost through illness; and then of lost positions, lost hope, and—the knock of the adventurer upon the green door.

But to Rudolf the history sounded as big as the Iliad or the crisis in " Junie's Love Test."

" To think of you going through all that," he exclaimed.

" It was something fierce," said the girl, solemnly.

" And you have no relatives or friends in the city ? "

" None whatever."

" I am all alone in the world, too," said Rudolf, after a pause.

" I am glad of that," said the girl, promptly; and somehow it pleased the young man to hear that she approved of his bereft condition.

Very suddenly her eyelids dropped and she sighed deeply.

" I'm awfully sleepy," she said, " and I feel so good."

Rudolf rose and took his hat.

" Then I'll say good-night. A long night's sleep will be fine for you."

He held out his hand, and she took it and said " good-night." But her eyes asked a question so eloquently, so frankly and pathetically that he answered it with words.

" Oh, I'm coming back to-morrow to see how you are getting along. You can't get rid of me so easily."

Then, at the door, as though the way of his coming had been so much less important than the fact that he had come, she asked : " How did you come to knock at my door ? "

He looked at her for a moment, remembering the cards, and felt a sudden jealous pain. What if they had fallen into other hands as adventurous as his ? Quickly he decided that she must never know the truth. He would never let her know that he was aware of the strange expedient to which she had been driven by her great distress.

" One of our piano tuners lives in this house," he said. " I knocked at your door by mistake."

The last thing he saw in the room before the green door closed was her smile.

At the head of the stairway he paused and looked curiously about him. And then he went along the hallway to its other end; and, coming back, ascended to the floor above and continued his puzzled explorations. Every door that he found in the house was painted green.

Wondering, he descended to the sidewalk. The fantastic African was still there. Rudolf confronted him with his two cards in his hand.

" Will you tell me why you gave me these cards and what they mean ? " he asked.

In a broad, good-natured grin the negro exhibited a splendid advertisement of his master's profession.

"Dar it is, boss," he said, pointing down the street. "But I 'spect you is a little late for de fust act."

Looking the way he pointed Rudolf saw above the entrance to a theatre the blazing electric sign of its new play, "The Green Door."

"I'm informed dat it's a fust-rate show, sah," said the negro. "De agent what represents it pussented me with a dollar, sah, to distribute a few of his cards along with de doctah's. May I offer you one of de doctah's cards, suh?"

At the corner of the block in which he lived Rudolf stopped for a glass of beer and a cigar. When he had come out with his lighted weed he buttoned his coat, pushed back his hat and said, stoutly to the lamp post on the corner:

"All the same, I believe it was the hand of Fate that doped out the way for me to find her."

Which conclusion, under the circumstances, certainly admits Rudolf Steiner to the ranks of the true followers of Romance and Adventure.

FROM THE CABBY'S SEAT

THE cabby has his point of view. It is more single-minded, perhaps, than that of a follower of any other calling. From the high, swaying seat of his hansom he looks upon his fellow-men as nomadic particles, of no account except when possessed of migratory desires. He is Jehu, and you are goods in transit. Be you President, or vagabond, to cabby you are only a Fare. He takes you up, cracks his whip, joggles your vertebrae and sets you down.

When time for payment arrives, if you exhibit a familiarity with legal rates you come to know what contempt is; if you find that you have left your pocket-book behind you are made to realize the mildness of Dante's imagination.

It is not an extravagant theory that the cabby's singleness of purpose and concentrated view of life are the results of the hansom's peculiar construction. The cock-of-the-roost sits aloft like Jupiter on an unsharable seat, holding your fate between two thongs of inconstant leather. Helpless, ridiculous, confined, bobbing like a toy mandarin, you sit like a rat in a trap—you, before whom butlers cringe on solid land—and must squeak upward through a slit in your peripatetic sarcophagus to make your feeble wishes known.

Then, in a cab, you are not even an occupant; you are contents. You are a cargo at sea, and the "cherub that sits up aloft" has Davy Jones's street and number by heart.

One night there were sounds of revelry in the big brick tenement house next door but one to McGary's Family Café. The sounds seemed to emanate from the apartments of the Walsh family. The sidewalk was obstructed by a assortment of interested neighbors, who opened a lane from time to time for a hurrying messenger bearing from McGary's goods pertinent to festivity and diversion. The sidewalk contingent was engaged in comment and discussion from which it made no effort to eliminate the news that Norah Walsh was being married.

In the fulness of time there was an eruption of the merry-makers to the sidewalk. The uninvited guests enveloped and permeated them, and upon the night air rose joyous cries, congratulations, laughter, and unclassified noises born of McGary's oblations to the hymeneal scene.

Close to the curb stood Jerry O'Donovan's cab. Night-hawk was Jerry called; but no more lustrous or cleaner hansom than his ever closed its doors upon point lace and November violets. And Jerry's horse! I am within bounds when I tell you that he was stuffed with oats until one of those old ladies who leave their dishes unwashed at home and go about having expressmen arrested, would have smiled—yes, smiled—to have seen him.

Among the shifting, sonorous, pulsing crowd glimpses could be had of Jerry's high hat, battered by the winds and rains of many years; of his nose like a carrot, battered by the frolicsome, athletic progeny of millionaires and by contumacious fares; of his brass-buttoned green coat, admired in the vicinity of McGary's. It was plain that Jerry had usurped the functions of his cab, and was carrying a " load." Indeed, the figure may be extended and he be likened to a bread-wagon if we admit the testimony of a youthful spectator, who was heard to remark " Jerry has got a bun."

From somewhere among the throng in the street or else out of the thin stream of pedestrians a young woman tripped and stood by the cab. The professional hawk's eye of Jerry caught the movement. He made a lurch for the cab, overturning three or four onlookers and himself—no! he caught the cap of a water-plug and kept his feet. Like a sailor shinning up the ratlins during a squall Jerry mounted to his professional seat. Once he was there McGary's liquids were baffled. He seesawed on the mizzenmast of his craft as safe as a Steeple Jack rigged to the flagpole of a skyscraper.

" Step in, lady," said Jerry, gathering his lines.

The young woman stepped into the cab; the doors shut with a bang; Jerry's whip cracked in the air; the crowd in the gutter scattered, and the fine hansom dashed away 'crosstown.

When the oat-spry horse had hedged a little his first spurt of speed

Jerry broke the lid of his cab and called down through the aperture in the voice of a cracked megaphone, trying to please.

" Where, now, will ye be drivin' to ? "

" Anywhere you please," came up the answer, musical and contented.

" 'Tis drivin' for pleasure she is," thought Jerry. And then he suggested as a matter of course :

" Take a thrip around in the park, lady. 'Twill be ilegant cool and fine."

" Just as you like," answered the fare, pleasantly.

The cab headed for Fifth Avenue and sped up that perfect street. Jerry bounced and swayed in his seat. The potent fluids of McGary were disquieted and they sent new fumes to his head. He sang an ancient song of Killisnook and brandished his whip like a baton.

Inside the cab the fare sat up straight on the cushions, looking to right and left at the lights and houses. Even in the shadowed hansom her eyes shone like stars at twilight.

When they reached Fifty-ninth Street Jerry's head was bobbing and his reins were slack. But his horse turned in through the park gate and began the old familiar nocturnal round. And then the fare leaned back, entranced, and breathed deep the clean, whole-some odors of grass and leaf and bloom. And the wise beast in the shafts, knowing his ground, struck into his by-the-hour gait and kept to the right of the road.

Habit also struggled successfully against Jerry's increasing torpor. He raised the hatch of his storm-tossed vessel and made the inquiry that cabbies do make in the park.

" Like shtop at the Cas-sino, lady ? Gezzer r'freshm's, 'n lish'n the music. Ev'body shtops."

" I think that would be nice," said the fare.

They reigned up with a plunge at the Casino entrance. The cab doors flew open. The fare stepped directly upon the floor. At once she was caught in a web of ravishing music and dazzled by a pano-rama of lights and colors. Some one slipped a little square card into her hand on which was printed a number—34. She looked around and saw her cab twenty yards away already lining up in its place among the waiting mass of carriages, cabs, and motor cars. And then a man who seemed to be all shirt-front danced backward before her; and next she was seated at a little table by a railing over which climbed a jessamine vine.

There seemed to be a wordless invitation to purchase; she con-sulted a collection of small coins in a thin purse, and received from them license to order a glass of beer. There she sat, inhaling and absorbing it all—the new-colored, new-shaped life in a fairy palace in an enchanted wood.

At fifty tables sat princes and queens clad in all the silks and gems of the world. And now and then one of them would look curiously at Jerry's fare. They saw a plain figure dressed in a pink silk of the kind that is tempered by the word "foulard," and a plain face that wore a look of love of life that the queens envied.

Twice the long hands of the clocks went round. Royalties thinned from their *al fresco* thrones, and buzzed or clattered away in their vehicles of state. The music retired into cases of wood and bags of leather and baize. Waiters removed cloths pointedly near the plain figure sitting almost alone.

Jerry's fare rose, and held out her numbered card simply :

" Is there anything coming on the ticket ? " she asked.

A waiter told her it was her cab check, and that she should give it to the man at the entrance. This man took it, and called the number. Only three hansoms stood in line. The driver of one of them went and routed out Jerry asleep in his cab. He swore deeply, climbed to the captain's bridge and steered his craft to the pier. His fare entered, and the cab whirled into the cool fastnesses of the park along the shortest homeward cuts.

At the gate a glimmer of reason in the form of sudden suspicion seized upon Jerry's beclouded mind. One or two things occurred to him. He stopped his horse, raised the trap and dropped his phonographic voice, like a lead plummet, through the aperture.

" I want to see four dollars before goin' any further on th' thrip. Have ye got th' dough ? "

" Four dollars ! " laughed the fare, softly, " dear me, no. I've only got a few pennies and a dime or two."

Jerry shut down the trap and slashed his oat-fed horse. The clatter of hoofs strangled but could not drown the sound of his profanity. He shouted choking and gurgling curses at the starry heavens; he cut viciously with his whip at passing vehicles; he scattered fierce and everchanging oaths and imprecations along the streets, so that a late truck driver, crawling homeward, heard and was abashed. But he knew his recourse, and made for it at a gallop.

At the house with the green lights beside the steps he pulled up. He flung wide the cab doors and tumbled heavily to the ground.

" Come on, you," he said, roughly.

His fare came forth with the Casino dreamy smile still on her plain face. Jerry took her by the arm and led her into the police station. A gray-moustached sergeant looked keenly across the desk. He and the cabby were no strangers.

" Sargeant," began Jerry in his old raucous, martyred, thunderous tones of complaint. " I've got a fare here that——"

Jerry paused. He drew a knotted, red hand across his brow. The fog set up by McGary was beginning to clear away.

"A fare, sargeant," he continued, with a grin, " that I want to introduce to ye. It's me wife that I married at ould man Walsh's this evening. And a divil of a time we had, tis thrue. Shake hands with th' sargeant, Norah, and we'll be off to home."

Before stepping into the cab Norah sighed profoundly.

" I've had such a nice time, Jerry," said she.

AN UNFINISHED STORY

WE no longer groan and heap ashes upon our heads when the flames of Tophet are mentioned. For, even the preachers have begun to tell us that God is radium, or ether or some scientific compound, and that the worst we wicked ones may expect is a chemical reaction. This is a pleasing hypothesis; but there lingers yet some of the old, goodly terror of orthodoxy.

There are but two subjects upon which one may discourse with a free imagination, and without the possibility of being controverted. You may talk of your dreams; and you may tell what you heard a parrot say. Both Morpheus and the bird are incompetent witnesses; and your listener dare not attack your recital. The baseless fabric of a vision, then, shall furnish my theme—chosen with apologies and regrets instead of the more limited field of pretty Polly's small talk.

I had a dream that was so far removed from the higher criticism that it had to do with the ancient, respectable, and lamented bar-of-judgment theory.

Gabriel had played his trump; and those of us who could not follow suit were arraigned for examination. I noticed at one side a gathering of professional bondsmen in solemn black and collars that buttoned behind; but it seemed there was some trouble about their real estate titles; and they did not appear to be getting any of us out.

A fly cop—an angel policeman—flew over to me and took me by the left wing. Near at hand was a group of very prosperous-looking spirits arraigned for judgment.

" Do you belong with that bunch ? " the policeman asked.

" Who are they ? " was my answer.

" Why," said he, " they are——"

But this irrelevant stuff is taking up space that the story should occupy.

Dulcie worked in a department store. She sold Hamburg edging, or stuffed peppers, or automobiles, or other little trinkets such as they keep in department stores. Of what she earned, Dulcie received six dollars per week. The remainder was credited to her and debited to somebody else's account in the ledger kept by G—— Oh, primal energy, you say, Reverend Doctor—— Well, then, in the Ledger of Primal Energy.

During her first year in the store, Dulcie was paid five dollars per week. It would be instructive to know how she lived on that amount. Don't care ? Very well; probably you are interested in larger amounts. Six dollars is a larger amount. I will tell you how she lived on six dollars per week.

One afternoon at six, when Dulcie was sticking her hat pin within an eighth of an inch of her *medulla oblongata*, she said to her chum, Sadie—the girl that waits on you with her left side :

" Say, Sade, I made a date for dinner this evening with Piggy."

" You never did ! " exclaimed Sadie, admiringly. " Well, ain't you the lucky one ? Piggy's an awful swell; and he always takes a girl to swell places. He took Blanche up to the Hoffman House one evening, where they have swell music, and you see a lot of swells. You'll have a swell time, Dulce."

Dulcie hurried homeward. Her eyes were shining, and her cheeks showed the delicate pink of life's—real life's—approaching dawn. It was Friday; and she had fifty cents left of her last week's wages.

The streets were filled with the rush-hour floods of people. The electric lights of Broadway were glowing—calling moths from miles, from leagues, from hundreds of leagues out of darkness around to come in and attend the singeing school. Men in accurate clothes, with faces like those carved on cherry stones by the old salts in sailors' homes, turned and stared at Dulcie as she sped, unheeding, past them. Manhattan, the night-blooming cereus, was beginning to unfold its dead-white, heavy-odored petals.

Dulcie stopped in a store where goods were cheap and bought an imitation lace collar with her fifty cents. That money was to have been spent otherwise—fifteen cents for supper, ten cents for breakfast, ten cents for lunch. Another dime was to be added to her small store of savings; and five cents was to be squandered for licorice drops—the kind that made your cheek look like the toothache, and last as long. The licorice was an extravagance— almost a carouse—but what is life without pleasures ?

Dulcie lived in a furnished room. There is this difference between a furnished room and a boarding-house. In a furnished room, other people do not know it when you go hungry.

Dulcie went up to her room—the third-floor-back in a West Side brownstone-front. She lit the gas. Scientists tell us that the

diamond is the hardest substance known. Their mistake. Land-
ladies know of a compound beside which the diamond is as putty.
They pack it in the tips of gas-burners; and one may stand on a
chair and dig at it in vain until one's fingers are pink and bruised.
A hairpin will not remove it; therefore let us call it immovable.

So Dulcie lit the gas. In its one-fourth-candle-power glow we
will observe the room.

Couch-bed, dresser, table, washstand, chair—of this much the
landlady was guilty. The rest was Dulcie's. On the dresser were
her treasures—a gilt china vase presented to her by Sadie, a calendar issued by a pickle works, a book on the divination of dreams,
some rice powder in a glass dish, and a cluster of artificial cherries
tied with a pink ribbon.

Against the wrinkly mirror stood pictures of General Kitchener,
William Muldoon, the Duchess of Marlborough, and Benvenuto
Cellini. Against one wall was a plaster of Paris plaque of an
O'Callahan in a Roman helmet. Near it was a violent oleograph
of a lemon-colored child assaulting an inflammatory butterfly.
This was Dulcie's final judgment in art; but it had never been
upset. Her rest had never been disturbed by whispers of stolen
copes; no critic had elevated his eyebrows at her infantile
entomologist.

Piggy was to call for her at seven. While she swiftly makes ready,
let us discreetly face the other way and gossip.

For the room, Dulcie paid two dollars per week. On week-days
her breakfast cost ten cents; she made coffee and cooked an egg
over the gaslight while she was dressing. On Sunday mornings
she feasted royally on veal chops and pineapple fritters at " Billy's "
restaurant, at a cost of twenty-five cents—and tipped the waitress
ten cents. New York presents so many temptations for one to run
into extravagance. She had her lunches in the department-store
restaurant at a cost of sixty cents for the week; dinners were $1.05.
The evening papers—show me a New Yorker going without his
daily paper !—came to six cents; and two Sunday papers—one
for the personal column and the other to read—were ten cents.
The total amounts to $4.76. Now, one has to buy clothes, and——

I give it up. I hear of wonderful bargains in fabrics, and of
miracles performed with needle and thread; but I am in doubt.
I hold my pen poised in vain when I would add to Dulcie's life
some of those joys that belong to women by virtue of all the unwritten, sacred, natural, inactive ordinances of the equity of heaven.
Twice she had been to Coney Island and had ridden the hobby-
horses. 'Tis a weary thing to count your pleasures by summers
instead of by hours.

Piggy needs but a word. When the girls named him, an undeserving stigma was cast upon the noble family of swine. The words-of-three-letters lesson in the old blue spelling book begins with Piggy's biography. He was fat; he had the soul of a rat, the habits of a bat, and the magnanimity of a cat. . . . He wore expensive clothes; and was a connoisseur in starvation. He could look at a shop-girl and tell you to an hour how long it had been since she had eaten anything more nourishing than marshmallows and tea. He hung about the shopping districts, and prowled around in department stores with his invitations to dinner. Men who escort dogs upon the streets at the end of a string look down upon him. He is a type; I can dwell upon him no longer; my pen is not the kind intended for him; I am no carpenter.

At ten minutes to seven Dulcie was ready. She looked at herself in the wrinkly mirror. The reflection was satisfactory. The dark blue dress, fitting without a wrinkle, the hat with its jaunty black feather, the but-slightly-soiled gloves—all representing self-denial, even of food itself—were vastly becoming.

Dulcie forgot everything else for a moment except that she was beautiful, and that life was about to lift a corner of its mysterious veil for her to observe its wonders. No gentleman had ever asked her out before. Now she was going for a brief moment into the glitter and exalted show.

The girls said that Piggy was a " spender." There would be a grand dinner, and music, and splendidly dressed ladies to look at and things to eat that strangely twisted the girls' jaws when they tried to tell about them. No doubt she would be asked out again.

There was a blue pongee suit in a window that she knew—by saving twenty cents a week instead of ten in—let's see——Oh, it would run into years ! But there was a second-hand store in Seventh Avenue where——

Somebody knocked at the door. Dulcie opened it. The landlady stood there with a spurious smile, sniffing for cooking by stolen gas.

" A gentleman's downstairs to see you," she said. " Name is Mr. Wiggins." By such epithet was Piggy known to unfortunate ones who had to take him seriously.

Dulcie turned to the dresser to get her handkerchief; and then she stopped still, and bit her underlip hard. While looking in her mirror she had seen fairyland and herself, a princess, just awakening from a long slumber. She had forgotten one that was watching her with sad beautiful, stern eyes—the only one there was to approve or condemn what she did. Straight and slender and tall, with a look of sorrowful reproach on his handsome, melancholy face, General Kitchener fixed his wonderful eyes on her out of his gilt photograph frame on the dresser.

Dulcie turned like an automatic doll to the landlady.

" Tell him I can't go," she said, dully. " Tell him I'm sick, or something. Tell him I'm not going out. "

After the door was closed and locked, Dulcie fell upon her bed, crushing her black tip, and cried for ten minutes. General Kitchener was her only friend. He was Dulcie's ideal of a gallant knight. He looked as if he might have a secret sorrow, and his wonderful moustache was a dream, and she was a little afraid of that stern yet tender look in his eyes. She used to have little fancies that he would call at the house sometime, and ask for her, with his sword clanking against his high boots. Once, when a boy was rattling a piece of chain against a lamp post she had opened the window and looked out. But there was no use. She knew that General Kitchener was away over in Japan, leading his army against the savage Turks; and he would never step out of his gilt frame for her. Yet one look from him had vanquished Piggy that night. Yes, for that night.

When her cry was over Dulcie got up and took off her best dress, and put on her old blue kimono. She wanted no dinner. She sang two verses of " Sammy." Then she became intensely interested in a little red speck on the side of her nose. And after that was attended to, she drew up a chair to the rickety table, and told her fortune with an old deck of cards.

" The horrid, impudent thing ! " she said aloud. "And I never gave him a word or a look to make him think it ! "

At nine o'clock Dulcie took a tin box of crackers and a little pot of raspberry jam out of her trunk and had a feast. She offered General Kitchener some jam on a cracker; but he only looked at her as the sphinx would have looked at a butterfly—if there are butterflies in the desert.

" Don't eat if you don't want to," said Dulcie. "And don't put on so many airs and scold so with your eyes. I wonder if you'd be so superior and snippy if you had to live on six dollars a week."

It was not a good sign for Dulcie to be rude to General Kitchener. And then she turned Benvenuto Cellini face downward with a severe gesture. But that was not inexcusable; for she had always thought he was Henry VIII, and she did not approve of him.

At half-past nine Dulcie took a last look at the pictures on the dresser, turned out the light and skipped into bed. It was an awful thing to go to bed with a goodnight look at General Kitchener, William Muldoon, the Duchess of Marlborough, and Benvenuto Cellini.

This story doesn't really get anywhere at all. The rest of it comes later—sometime when Piggy asks Dulcie again to dine with him, and she is feeling lonelier than usual, and General Kitchener happens to be looking the other way; and then——

As I said before, I dreamed that I was standing near a crowd of prosperous-looking angels, and a policeman took me by the wing and asked if I belonged with them.

" Who are they ? " I asked.

" Why," said he, " they are the men who hired working-girls, and paid 'em five or six dollars a week to live on. Are you one of the bunch ? "

" Not on your immortality," said I. " I'm only a fellow that set fire to an orphan asylum, and murdered a blind man for his pennies."

THE CALIPH, CUPID AND THE CLOCK

PRINCE MICHAEL, of the Electorate of Valleluna, sat on his favorite bench in the park. The coolness of the September night quickened the life in him like a rare, tonic wine. The benches were not filled; for park loungers, with their stagnant blood, are prompt to detect and fly home from the crispness of early autumn. The moon was just clearing the roofs of the range of dwellings that bounded the quadrangle on the east. Children laughed and played about the fine-sprayed fountain. In the shadowed spots fauns and hamadryads wooed, unconscious of the gaze of mortal eyes. A hand-organ—Philomel by the grace of our stage carpenter, Fancy —fluted and droned in a side street. Around the enchanted boundaries of the little park street cars spat and mewed and the stilted trains roared like tigers and lions prowling for a place to enter. And above the trees shone the great, round, shining face of an illuminated clock in the tower of an antique public building.

Prince Michael's shoes were wrecked far beyond the skill of the carefullest cobbler. The ragman would have declined any negotiations concerning his clothes. The two weeks' stubble on his face was gray and brown and red and greenish yellow—as if it had been made up from individual contributions from the chorus of a musical comedy. No man existed who had money enough to wear so bad a hat as his.

Prince Michael sat on his favorite bench and smiled. It was a diverting thought to him that he was wealthy enough to buy every one of those close-ranged, bulky, window-lit mansions that faced him, if he chose. He could have matched gold, equipages, jewels, art treasures, estates and acres with any Crœsus in this proud city of Manhattan, and scarcely have entered upon the bulk of his holdings. He could have sat at table with reigning sovereigns. The social world, the world of art, the fellowship of the elect, adulation, imitation, the homage of the fairest, honors from the highest, praise from the wisest, flattery, esteem, credit, pleasure, fame—all the honey of life was waiting in the comb in the hive of the world for Prince Michael, of the Electorate of Valleluna, whenever he might choose to take it. But his choice was to sit in rags and dinginess on a bench in a park. For he had tasted of the fruit of the tree of life, and, finding it bitter in his mouth, had stepped out of Eden for a time to seek distraction close to the un-armored, beating heart of the world.

These thoughts strayed dreamily through the mind of Prince Michael, as he smiled under the stubble of his polychromatic beard. Lounging thus, clad as the poorest of mendicants in the parks, he loved to study humanity. He found in altruism more pleasure than his riches, his station and all the grosser sweets of life had given him. It was his chief solace and satisfaction to alleviate individual distress, to confer favors upon worthy ones who had need of succor, to dazzle unfortunates by unexpected and bewildering gifts of truly royal magnificence, bestowed, however, with wisdom and judiciousness.

And as Prince Michael's eye rested upon the glowing face of the great clock in the tower, his smile, altruistic as it was, became slightly tinged with contempt. Big thoughts were the Prince's; and it was always with a shake of his head that he considered the subjugation of the world to the arbitrary measures of Time. The comings and goings of people in hurry and dread, controlled by the little metal moving hands of a clock, always made him sad.

By and by came a young man in evening clothes and sat upon the third bench from the Prince. For half an hour he smoked cigars with nervous haste, and then he fell to watching the face of the illuminated clock above the trees. His perturbation was evident, and the Prince noted, in sorrow, that its cause was connected, in some manner, with the slowly moving hands of the time-piece.

His Highness arose and went to the young man's bench.

" I beg your pardon for addressing you," he said, " but I perceive that you are disturbed in mind. If it may serve to mitigate the liberty I have taken I will add that I am Prince Michael, heir to the throne of the Electorate of Valleluna. I appear incognito, of course, as you may gather from my appearance. It is a fancy of mine to render aid to others whom I think worthy of it. Perhaps the matter that seems to distress you is one that would more readily yield to our mutual efforts."

The young man looked up brightly at the Prince. Brightly, but the perpendicular line of perplexity between his brows was not smoothed away. He laughed, and even then it did not. But he accepted the momentary diversion.

" Glad to meet you, Prince," he said, good humoredly. " Yes, I'd say you were incog. all right. Thanks for your offer of assistance —but I don't see where your butting-in would help things any. It's a kind of private affair, you know—but thanks all the same."

Prince Michael sat at the young man's side. He was often rebuffed but never offensively. His courteous manner and words forbade that.

" Clocks," said the Prince, " are shackles on the feet of mankind. I have obesrved you looking persistently at that clock. Its face is that of a tyrant, its numbers are false as those on a lottery ticket; its hands are those of a bunco steerer, who makes an appointment with you to your ruin. Let me entreat you to throw off its humiliating bonds and cease to order your affairs by that insensate monitor of brass and steel."

" I don't usually," said the young man. " I carry a watch except when I've got my radiant rags on."

" I know human nature as I do the trees and grass," said the Prince, with earnest dignity. " I am a master of philosophy, a graduate in art, and I hold the purse of a Fortunatus. There are few mortal misfortunes that I cannot alleviate or overcome. I have read your countenance, and found in it honesty and nobility as well as distress. I beg of you to accept my advice or aid. Do not belie the intelligence I see in your face by judging from my appearance of my ability to defeat your troubles."

The young man glanced at the clock again and frowned darkly. When his gaze strayed from the glowing horologue of time it rested intently upon a four-story red brick house in the row of dwellings opposite to where he sat. The shades were drawn, and the lights in many rooms shone dimly through them.

" Ten minutes to nine ! " exclaimed the young man, with an impatient gesture of despair. He turned his back upon the house and took a rapid step or two in a contrary direction.

" Remain ! " commanded Prince Michael, in so potent a voice that the disturbed one wheeled around with a somewhat chagrined laugh.

" I'll give her the ten minutes and then I'm off," he muttered, and then aloud to the Prince : " I'll join you in confounding all clocks, my friend, and throw in women, too."

" Sit down," said the Prince, calmly. " I do not accept your addition. Women are the natural enemies of clocks, and, therefore, the allies of those who would seek liberation from these monsters that measure our follies and limit our pleasures. If you will so far confide in me I would ask you to relate to me your story."

The young man threw himself upon the bench with a reckless laugh.

"Your Royal Highness, I will," he said, in tones of mock deference. "Do you see yonder house—the one with the three upper windows lighted? Well, at 6 o'clock I stood in that house with the young lady I am—that is, I was—engaged to. I had been doing wrong, my dear Prince—I had been a naughty boy, and she had heard of it. I wanted to be forgiven, of course—we are always wanting women to forgive us, aren't we, Prince?

"'I want time to think it over,' said she. 'There is one thing certain; I will either fully forgive you, or I will never see your face again. There will be no half-way business. At half-past eight,' she said, 'at exactly half-past eight you may be watching the middle upper window of the top floor. If I decide to forgive I will hang out of that window a white silk scarf. You will know by that that all is as was before, and you may come to me. If you see no scarf you may consider that everything between us is ended forever.' That," concluded the young man, bitterly, "is why I have been watching that clock. The time for the signal to appear has passed twenty-three minutes ago. Do you wonder that I am a little disturbed, my Prince of Rags and Whiskers?"

"Let me repeat to you," said Prince Michael, in his even, well-modulated tones, "that women are the natural enemies of clocks. Clocks are an evil, women a blessing. The signal may yet appear."

"Never, on your principality!" exclaimed the young man, hopelessly. "You don't know Marian—of course. She's always on time, to the minute. That was the first thing about her that attracted me. I've got the mitten instead of the scarf. I ought to have known at 8.31 that my goose was cooked. I'll go West on the 11.45 to-night with Jack Milburn. The jig's up. I'll try Jack's ranch awhile and top off with the Klondike and whiskey. Good-night—er—er—Prince."

Prince Michael smiled his enigmatic, gentle, comprehending smile and caught the coat sleeve of the other. The brilliant light in the Prince's eyes was softening to a dreamier, cloudy translucence.

"Wait," he said solemnly, "till the clock strikes. I have wealth and power and knowledge above most men, but when the clock strikes I am afraid. Stay by me until then. This woman shall be yours. You have the word of the hereditary Prince of Valleluna. On the day of your marriage I will give you $100,000 and a palace on the Hudson. But there must be no clocks in that palace—they measure our follies and limit our pleasures. Do you agree to that?"

"Of course," said the young man, cheerfully, "they're a nuisance, anyway—always ticking and striking and getting you late for dinner."

He glanced again at the clock in the tower. The hands stood at three minutes to nine.

"I think," said Prince Michael, "that I will sleep a little. The day has been fatiguing."

He stretched himself upon a bench with the manner of one who had slept thus before.

"You will find me in this park on any evening when the weather is suitable," said the Prince, sleepily. "Come to me when your marriage day is set and I will give you a check for the money."

"Thanks, Your Highness," said the young man, seriously. "It doesn't look as if I would need that palace on the Hudson, but I appreciate your offer, just the same."

Prince Michael sank into deep slumber. His battered hat rolled from the bench to the ground. The young man lifted it, placed it over the frowsy face and moved one of the grotesquely relaxed limbs into a more comfortable position. "Poor devil!" he said, as he drew the tattered clothes closer about the Prince's breast.

Sonorous and startling came the stroke of 9 from the clock tower. The young man sighed again, turned his face for one last look at the house of his relinquished hopes—and cried aloud profane words of holy rapture.

From the middle upper window blossomed in the dusk a waving, snowy, fluttering, wonderful, divine emblem of forgiveness and promised joy.

By came a citizen, rotund, comfortable, home-hurrying, unknowing of the delights of waving silken scarfs on the borders of dimly-lit parks.

"Will you oblige me with the time, sir?" asked the young man; and the citizen, shrewdly conjecturing his watch to be safe, dragged it out and announced:

"Twenty-nine and half minutes past eight, sir."

And then, from habit, he glanced at the clock in the tower, and made further oration.

"By George! that clock's half an hour fast! First time in ten years I've known it to be off. This watch of mine never varies a——"

But the citizen was talking to vacancy. He turned and saw his hearer, a fast receding black shadow flying in the direction of a house with three lighted upper windows.

And in the morning came along two policeman on their way to the beats they owned. The park was deserted save for one dilapidated figure that sprawled, asleep, on a bench. They stopped and gazed upon it.

"It's Dopy Mike," said one. "He hits the pipe every night. Park bum for twenty years. On his last legs, I guess."

The other policeman stooped and looked at something crumpled and crisp in the hand of the sleeper.

" Gee ! " he remarked. " He's doped out a fifty-dollar bill, anyway. Wish I knew the brand of hop that he smokes."

And then " Rap, rap, rap ! " went the club of realism against the shoe soles of Prince Michael, of the Electorate of Valleluna.

SISTERS OF THE GOLDEN CIRCLE

THE Rubberneck Auto was about ready to start. The merry top-riders had been assigned to their seats by the gentlemanly conductor. The sidewalk was blockaded with sightseers who had gathered to stare at sightseers, justifying the natural law that every creature on earth is preyed upon by some other creature.

The megaphone man raised his instrument of torture; the inside of the great automobile began to thump and throb like the heart of a coffee drinker. The top-riders nervously clung to the seats; the old lady from Valparaiso, Indiana, shrieked to be put ashore. But, before a wheel turns, listen to a brief preamble through the cardiaphone, which shall point out to you an object of interest on life's sightseeing tour.

Swift and comprehensive is the recognition of white man for white man in African wilds; instant and sure is the spiritual greeting between mother and babe; unhesitatingly do master and dog commune across the slight gulf between animal and man; immeasurably quick and sapient are the brief messages between one and one's beloved. But all these instances set forth only slow and groping interchange of sympathy and thought beside one other instance which the Rubberneck coach shall disclose. You shall learn (if you have not learned already) what two beings of all earth's living inhabitants most quickly look into each other's hearts and souls when they meet face to face.

The gong whirred, and the Glaring-at-Gotham car moved majestically upon its instructive tour.

On the highest, rear seat was James William, of Cloverdale, Missouri, and his Bride.

Capitalize it, friend typo—that last word—word of words in the epiphany of life and love. The scent of the flowers, the booty of the bee, the primal drip of spring waters, the overture of the lark, the twist of lemon peel on the cocktail of creation—such is the bride. Holy is the wife; revered the mother; galliptious is the summer girl —but the bride is the certified check among the wedding presents that the gods send in when man is married to mortality.

The car glided up the Golden Way. On the bridge of the great cruiser the captain stood, trumpeting the sights of the big city to his passengers. Wide-mouthed and open-eared they heard the sights of the metropolis thundered forth to their eyes. Confused, delirious with excitement and provincial longings, they tried to make ocular responses to the megaphonic ritual. In the solemn spires of spreading cathedrals they saw the home of the Vanderbilts; in the busy bulk of the Grand Central depot they viewed, wonderingly, the frugal cot of Russel Sage. Bidden to observe the highlands of the Hudson, they gaped, unsuspecting, at the up-turned mountains of a new-laid sewer.

To many the elevated railroad was the Rialto, on the stations of which uniformed men sat and made chop suey of your tickets. And to this day in the outlying districts many have it that Chuck Connors, with his hand on his heart, leads reform; and that but for the noble municipal efforts of one Parkhurst, a district attorney, the notorious " Bishop " Potter gang would have destroyed law and order from the Bowery to the Harlem River.

But I beg you to observe Mrs. James Williams—Hattie Chalmers that was—once the belle of Cloverdale. Pale-blue is the bride's, if she will; and this color she had honored. Willingly had the moss rosebud loaned to her cheeks of its pink—and as for the violet !—her eyes will do very well as they are, thank you. A useless strip of white chaf—oh, no, he was guiding the auto car—of white chiffon—or perhaps it was grenadine or tulle—was tied beneath her chin, pretending to hold her bonnet in place. But you know as well as I do that the hat pins did the work.

And on Mrs. James Williams's face was recorded a little library of the world's best thoughts in three volumes. Volume No. 1 contained the belief that James Williams was about the right sort of thing. Volume No. 2 was an essay on the world, declaring it to be a very excellent place. Volume No. 3 disclosed the belief that in occupying the highest seat in a Rubberneck auto they were travelling the pace that passes all understanding.

James Williams, you would have guessed, was about twenty-four. It will gratify you to know that your estimate was so accurate. He was exactly twenty-three years, eleven months and twenty-nine days old. He was well built, active, strong-jawed, good-natured, and rising. He was on his wedding trip.

Dear kind fairy, please cut out those orders for money and 40 H. P. touring cars and fame and a new growth of hair and the presidency of the boat club. Instead of any of them turn backward —oh, turn backward and give us just a teeny-weeny bit of our wedding trip over again. Just an hour, dear fairy, so we can remember how the grass and poplar trees looked, and the bow of those bonnet strings tied beneath her chin—even if it was the hat pins that did the work. Can't do it? Very well; hurry up with that touring car and the oil stock, then.

Just in front of Mrs. James Williams sat a girl in a loose tan jacket and a straw hat adorned with grapes and roses. Only in dreams and milliners' shops do we, alas! gather grapes and roses at one swipe. This girl gazed with large blue eyes, credulous, when the megaphone man roared his doctrine that millionaires were things about which we should be concerned. Between blasts she resorted to Epictetian philosophy in the form of pepsin chewing gum.

At this girl's right hand sat a young man about twenty-four. He was well built, active, strong-jawed, and good-natured. But if his description seems to follow that of James Williams, divest it of anything Cloverdalian. This man belonged to hard streets and sharp corners. He looked keenly about him, seeming to begrudge the asphalt under the feet of those upon whom he looked down from his perch.

While the megaphone barks at a famous hostelry, let me whisper you through the low-tuned cardiaphone to sit tight; for now things are about to happen, and the great city will close over them again as over a scrap of ticker tape floating down from the den of a Broad Street bear.

The girl in the tan jacket twisted around to view the pilgrims on the last seat. The other passengers she had absorbed; the seat behind her was her Bluebeard's chamber.

Her eyes met those of Mrs. James Williams. Between two ticks of a watch they exchanged their life's experiences, histories, hopes and fancies. And all, mind you, with the eye, before two men could have decided whether to draw steel or borrow a match.

The bride leaned forward low. She and the girl spoke rapidly together, their tongues moving quickly like those of two serpents— a comparison that is not meant to go further. Two smiles and a dozen nods closed the conference.

And now in the broad, quiet avenue in front of the Rubberneck car a man in dark clothes stood with uplifted hand. From the sidewalk another hurried to join him.

The girl in the fruitful hat quickly seized her companion by the arm and whispered in his ear. That young man exhibited proof of ability to act promptly. Crouching low, he slid over the edge of the car, hung lightly for an instant, and then disappeared. Half a dozen of the top-riders observed his feat wonderingly, but made no comment, deeming it prudent not to express surprise at what might be the conventional manner of alighting in this bewildering city. The truant passenger dodged a hansom and then floated past,

like a leaf on a stream between a furniture van and a florist's
delivery wagon.

The girl in the tan jacket turned again, and looked into the eyes
of Mrs. James Williams. Then she faced about and sat still while
the Rubberneck auto stopped at the flash of the badge under the
coat of the plainclothes man.

"What's eating you?" demanded the megaphonist, abandon-
ing his professional discourse for pure English.

"Keep her at anchor for a minute," ordered the officer.
"There's a man on board we want—a Philadelphia burglar called
'Pinky' McGuire. There he is on the back seat. Look out for the
side, Donovan."

Donovan went to the hind wheel and looked up at James
Williams.

"Come down, old sport," he said pleasantly. "We've got you.
Back to Sleepytown for yours. It ain't a bad idea, hidin' on a
Rubberneck, though. I'll remember that."

Softly through the megaphone came the advice of the conductor:

"Better step off, sir, and explain. The car must proceed on its
tour."

James Williams belonged among the level heads. With necessary
slowness he picked his way through the passengers down to the
steps at the front of the car. His wife followed, but she first turned
her eyes and saw the escaped tourist glide from behind the furniture van and slip behind a tree on the edge of the little park, not
fifty feet away.

Descended to the ground, James Williams faced his captors with
a smile. He was thinking what a good story he would have to tell
in Cloverdale about having been mistaken for a burglar. The
Rubberneck coach lingered, out of respect for its patrons. What
could be a more interesting sight than this?

"My name is James Williams, of Cloverdale, Missouri," he
said, kindly, so that they would not be too greatly mortified. "I
have letters here that will show——"

"You'll come with us, please," announced the plainclothes man.
"'Pinky' McGuire's description fits you like flannel washed in hot
suds. A detective saw you on the Rubberneck up at Central Park
and 'phoned down to take you in. Do your explaining at the
station-house."

James Williams's wife—his bride of two weeks—looked him in
the face with a strange, soft radiance in her eyes and a flush on her
cheeks, looked him in the face and said:

"Go with 'em quietly, 'Pinky,' and maybe it'll be in your
favor."

And then as the Glaring-at-Gotham car rolled away she turned and threw a kiss—his wife threw a kiss—at some one high up on the seats of the Rubberneck.

"Your girl gives you good advice, McGuire," said Donovan. "Come on now."

And then madness descended upon and occupied James Williams. He pushed his hat far upon the back of his head.

"My wife seems to think I am a burglar," he said, recklessly. "I never heard of her being crazy; therefore I must be. And if I'm crazy, they can't do anything to me for killing you two fools in my madness."

Whereupon he resisted arrest so cheerfully and industriously that cops had to be whistled for, and afterwards the reserves, to disperse a few thousand delighted spectators.

At the station-house the desk sergeant asked for his name.

"McDoodle, the Pink, or Pinky the Brute, I forgot which," was James Williams's answer. "But you can bet I'm a burglar; don't leave that out. And you might add that it took five of 'em to pluck the Pink. I'd especially like to have that in the records."

In an hour came Mrs. James Williams, with Uncle Thomas, of Madison Avenue, in a respect-compelling motor car and proofs of the hero's innocence—for all the world like the third act of a drama backed by an automobile mfg. co.

After the police had sternly reprimanded James Williams for imitating a copyrighted burglar and given him as honorable a discharge as the department was capable of, Mrs. Williams rearrested him and swept him into an angle of the station-house. James Williams regarded her with one eye. He always said that Donovan closed the other while somebody was holding his good right hand. Never before had he given her a word of reproach or of reproof.

"If you can explain," he began rather stiffly, "why you——"

"Dear," she interrupted, "listen. It was an hour's pain and trial to you. I did it for her—I mean the girl who spoke to me on the coach. I was so happy, Jim—so happy with you that I didn't dare to refuse that happiness to another. Jim, they were married only this morning—those two; and I wanted him to get away. While they were struggling with you I saw him slip from behind his tree and hurry across the park. That's all of it, dear—I had to do it."

Thus does one sister of the plain gold band know another who stands in the enchanted light that shines but once and briefly for each one. By rice and satin bows does mere man become aware of weddings. But bride knoweth bride at the glance of an eye. And between them swiftly passes comfort and meaning in a language that man and widows wot not of.

THE ROMANCE OF A BUSY BROKER

PITCHER, confidential clerk in the office, of Harvey Maxwell broker, allowed a look of mild interest and surprise to visit his usually expressionless countenance when his employer briskly entered at half-past nine in company with his young lady stenographer. With a snappy " Good-morning, Pitcher," Maxwell dashed at his desk as though he were intending to leap over it, and then plunged into the great heap of letters and telegrams waiting there for him.

The young lady had been Maxwell's stenographer for a year. She was beautiful in a way that was decidedly unstenographic. She forewent the pomp of the alluring pompadour. She wore no chains, bracelets, or lockets. She had not the air of being about to accept an invitation to luncheon. Her dress was gray and plain, but it fitted her figure with fidelity and discretion. In her neat black turban hat was the gold-green wing of a macaw. On this morning she was softly and shyly radiant. Her eyes were dreamily bright, her cheeks genuine peach-blow, her expression a happy one, tinged with reminiscence.

Pitcher, still mildly curious, noticed a difference in her ways this morning. Instead of going straight into the adjoining room, where her desk was, she lingered, slightly irresolute, in the outer office. Once she moved over by Maxwell's desk, near enough for him to be aware of her presence.

The machine sitting at that desk was no longer a man; it was a busy New York broker, moved by buzzing wheels and uncoiling springs.

" Well—what is it ? Anything ? " asked Maxwell, sharply. His opened mail lay like a bank of stage snow on his crowded desk. His keen gray eye, impersonal and brusque, flashed upon her half impatiently.

" Nothing," answered the stenographer, moving away with a little smile.

" Mr. Pitcher," she said to the confidential clerk, " did Mr. Maxwell say anything yesterday about engaging another stenographer ? "

" He did," answered Pitcher. " He told me to get another one. I notified the agency yesterday afternoon to send over a few samples this morning. It's 9.45 o'clock, and not a single picture hat or piece of pineapple chewing gum has showed up yet."

" I will do the work as usual, then," said the young lady, " until some one comes to fill the place." And she went to her desk at once and hung the black turban hat with the gold-green macaw wing in its accustomed place.

He who has been denied the spectacle of a busy Manhattan broker during a rush of business is handicapped for the profession of anthropology. The poet sings of the " crowded hour of glorious life." The broker's hour is not only crowded, but the minutes and seconds are hanging to all the straps and packing both front and rear platforms.

And this day was Harvey Maxwell's busy day. The ticker began to reel out jerkily its fitful coils of tape, the desk telephone had a chronic attack of buzzing. Men began to throng into the office and call at him over the railing, jovially, sharply, viciously, excitedly. Messenger boys ran in and out with messages and telegrams. The clerks in the office jumped about like sailors during a storm. Even Pitcher's face relaxed into something resembling animation.

On the Exchange there were hurricanes and landslides and snow-storms and glaciers and volcanoes, and those elemental distur-bances were reproduced in miniature in the broker's offices. Maxwell shoved his chair against the wall and transacted business after the manner of a toe dancer. He jumped from ticker to 'phone, from desk to door with the trained agility of a harlequin.

In the midst of this growing and important stress the broker became suddenly aware of a high-rolled fringe of golden hair under a nodding canopy of velvet and ostrich tips, an imitation sealskin sacque and a string of beads as large as hickory nuts, ending near the floor with a silver heart. There was a self-possessed young lady connected with these accessories; and Pitcher was there to con-strue her.

" Lady from the Stenographer's Agency to see about the position," said Pitcher.

Maxwell turned half around, with his hands full of papers and ticker tape.

" What position ? " he asked, with a frown.

" Position of stenographer," said Pitcher. " You told me yester-day to call them up and have one sent over this morning."

" You are losing your mind, Pitcher," said Maxwell. " Why should I have given you any such instructions ? Miss Leslie has given perfect satisfaction during the year she has been here. The place is hers as long as she chooses to retain it. There's no place open here, madam. Countermand that order with the agency, Pitcher, and don't bring any more of 'em in here."

The silver heart left the office, swinging and banging itself independently against the office furniture as it indignantly departed. Pitcher seized a moment to remark to the bookkeeper that the " old man " seemed to get more absent-minded and forgetful every day of the world.

The rush and pace of business grew fiercer and faster. On the floor they were pounding half a dozen stocks in which Maxwell's customers were heavy investors. Orders to buy and sell were coming and going as swift as the flight of swallows. Some of his own holdings were imperilled, and the man was working like some high-geared, delicate, strong machine—strung to full tension, going at full speed, accurate, never hesitating, with the proper word and decision and act ready and prompt as clockwork. Stocks and bonds, loans and mortgages, margins and securities—here was a world of finance, and there was no room in it for the human world or the world of nature.

When the luncheon hour drew near there came a slight lull in the uproar.

Maxwell stood by his desk with his hands full of telegrams and memoranda, with a fountain pen over his right ear and his hair hanging in disorderly strings over his forehead. His window was open, for the beloved janitress Spring had turned on a little warmth through the waking registers of the earth.

And through the window came a wandering—perhaps a lost—odor—a delicate, sweet odor of lilac that fixed the broker for a moment immovable. For this odor belonged to Miss Leslie; it was her own, and hers only.

The odor brought her vividly, almost tangibly before him. The world of finance dwindled suddenly to a speck. And she was in the next room—twenty steps away.

" By George, I'll do it now," said Maxwell, half aloud. " I'll ask her now. I wonder I didn't do it long ago."

He dashed into the inner office with the haste of a short trying to cover. He charged upon the desk of the stenographer.

She looked up at him with a smile. A soft pink crept over her cheek, and her eyes were kind and frank. Maxwell leaned one elbow on her desk. He still clutched fluttering papers with both hands and the pen was above his ear.

" Miss Leslie," he began, hurriedly. " I have but a moment to spare. I want to say something in that moment. Will you be my wife ? I haven't had time to make love to you in the ordinary way, but I really do love you. Talk quick, please—those fellows are clubbing the stuffing out of Union Pacific."

" Oh, what are you talking about ? " exclaimed the young lady. She rose to her feet and gazed upon him, round-eyed.

" Don't you understand ? " said Maxwell, restively. " I want you to marry me. I love you, Miss Leslie. I wanted to tell you, and I snatched a minute when things had slackened up a bit. They're calling me for the 'phone now. Tell 'em to wait a minute, Pitcher. Won't you, Miss Leslie?"

The stenographer acted very queerly. At first she seemed overcome with amazement; then tears flowed from her wondering eyes; and then she smiled sunnily through them, and one of her arms slid tenderly about the broker's neck.

"I know now," she said, softly. "It's this old business that has driven everything else out of your head for the time. I was frightened at first. Don't you remember, Harvey? We were married last evening at 8 o'clock in the Little Church around the Corner."

AFTER TWENTY YEARS

THE policeman on the beat moved up the avenue impressively. The impressiveness was habitual and not for show, for spectators were few. The time was barely 10 o'clock at night, but chilly gusts of wind with a taste of rain in them had well nigh depeopled the streets.

Trying doors as he went, twirling his club with many intricate and artful movements, turning now and then to cast his watchful eye adown the pacific thoroughfare, the officer, with his stalwart form and slight swagger, made a fine picture of a guardian of the peace. The vicinity was one that kept early hours. Now and then you might see the lights of a cigar store or of an all-night lunch counter; but the majority of the doors belonged to business places that had long since been closed.

When about midway of a certain block the policeman suddenly slowed his walk. In the doorway of a darkened hardware store a man leaned, with an unlighted cigar in his mouth. As the policeman walked up to him the man spoke up quickly.

"It's all right, officer," he said, reassuringly. "I'm just waiting for a friend. It's an appointment made twenty years ago. Sounds a little funny to you, doesn't it? Well, I'll explain if you'd like to make certain it's all straight. About that long ago there used to be a restaurant where this store stands—'Big Joe Brady's restaurant'".

"Until five years ago," said the policeman. "It was torn down then."

The man in the doorway struck a match and lit his cigar. The light showed a pale, square-jawed face with keen eyes, and a little white scar near his right eyebrow. His scarfpin was a large diamond, oddly set.

"Twenty years ago to-night," said the man, "I dined here at
'Big Joe' Brady's with Jimmy Wells, my best chum, and the finest
chap in the world. He and I were raised here in New York, just
like two brothers, together. I was eighteen and Jimmy was twenty.
The next morning I was to start for the West to make my fortune.
You couldn't have dragged Jimmy out of New York; he thought
it was the only place on earth. Well, we agreed that night that
we would meet here again exactly twenty years from that date and
time, no matter what our conditions might be or from what distance
we might have to come. We figured that in twenty years each of
us ought to have our destiny worked out and our fortunes made,
whatever they were going to be."

"It sounds pretty interesting," said the policeman. "Rather
a long time between meets, though, it seems to me. Haven't you
heard from your friend since you left?"

"Well, yes, for a time we corresponded," said the other. "But
after a year or two we lost track of each other. You see, the West
is a pretty big proposition, and I kept hustling around over it
pretty lively. But I know Jimmy will meet me here if he's alive,
for he always was the truest, stanchest old chap in the world. He'll
never forget. I came a thousand miles to stand in this door to-night,
and it's worth it if my old partner turns up."

The waiting man pulled out a handsome watch, the lids of it
set with small diamonds.

"Three minutes to ten," he announced. "It was exactly ten
o'clock when we parted here at the restaurant door."

"Did pretty well out West, didn't you?" asked the policeman.

"You bet! I hope Jimmy has done half as well. He was a kind
of plodder, though, good fellow as he was. I've had to compete
with some of the sharpest wits going to get my pile. A man gets
in a groove in New York. It takes the West to put a razor-edge
on him."

The policeman twirled his club and took a step or two.

"I'll be on my way. Hope your friend comes around all right.
Going to call time on him sharp?"

"I should say not!" said the other. "I'll give him half an
hour at least. If Jimmy is alive on earth he'll be here by that time.
So long, officer."

"Good-night, sir," said the policeman, passing on along his
beat, trying doors as he went.

There was now a fine, cold drizzle falling, and the wind had
risen from its uncertain puffs into a steady blow. The few foot
passengers astir in that quarter hurried dismally and silently along
with coat collars turned high and pocketed hands. And in the door
of the hardware store the man who had come a thousand miles to

fill an appointment, uncertain almost to absurdity, with the friend of his youth, smoked his cigar and waited.

About twenty minutes he waited, and then a tall man in a long overcoat, with collar turned up to his ears, hurried across from the opposite side of the street. He went directly to the waiting man.

" Is that you, Bob ? " he asked, doubtfully.

" Is that you, Jimmy Wells ? " cried the man in the door.

" Bless my heart ! " exclaimed the new arrival, grasping both the other's hands with his own. " It's Bob, sure as fate. I was certain I'd find you here if you were still in existence. Well, well, well !—twenty years is a long time. The old restaurant's gone, Bob ; I wish it had lasted, so we could have had another dinner there. How has the West treated you, old man ? "

" Bully ; it has given me everything I asked it for. You've changed lots, Jimmy. I never thought you were so tall by two or three inches."

" Oh, I grew a bit after I was twenty."

" Doing well in New York, Jimmy ? "

" Moderately. I have a position in one of the city departments. Come on, Bob ; we'll go around to a place I know of, and have a good long talk about old times."

The two men started up the street, arm in arm. The man from the West, his egotism enlarged by success, was beginning to outline the history of his career. The other, submerged in his overcoat, listened with interest.

At the corner stood a drug store, brilliant with electric lights. When they came into this glare each of them turned simultaneously to gaze upon the other's face.

The man from the West stopped suddenly and released his arm.

" You're not Jimmy Wells," he snapped. " Twenty years is a long time, but not long enough to change a man's nose from a Roman to a pug."

" It sometimes changes a good man into a bad one," said the tall man. " You've been under arrest for ten minutes, ' Silky ' Bob. Chicago thinks you may have dropped over our way and wires us she wants to have a chat with you. Going quietly, are you ? That's sensible. Now, before we go to the station here's a note I was asked to hand you. You may read it here at the window. It's from Patrolman Wells."

The man from the West unfolded the little piece of paper handed him. His hand was steady when he began to read, but it trembled a little by the time he had finished. The note was rather short.

Bob : I was at the appointed place on time. When you struck the match to light your cigar I saw it was the face of the man wanted in Chicago. Somehow I couldn't do it myself, so I went around and got a plain clothes man to do the job.

JIMMY.

LOST ON DRESS PARADE

Mr. TOWERS CHANDLER was pressing his evening suit in his hall bedroom. One iron was heating on a small gas stove; the other was being pushed vigorously back and forth to make the desirable crease that would be seen later on extending in straight lines from Mr. Chandler's patent leather shoes to the edge of his low-cut vest. So much of the hero's toilet may be intrusted to our confidence. The remainder may be guessed by those whom genteel poverty has driven to ignoble expedient. Our next view of him shall be as he descends the steps of his lodging-house immaculately and correctly clothed; calm, assured, handsome—in appearance the typical New York young clubman setting out, slightly bored, to inaugurate the pleasures of the evening.

Chandler's honorarium was $18 per week. He was employed in the office of an architect. He was twenty-two years old; he considered architecture to be truly an art; and he honestly believed —though he would not have dared to admit it in New York— that the Flatiron Building was inferior in design to the great cathedral in Milan.

Out of each week's earnings Chandler set aside $1. At the end of each ten weeks with the extra capital thus accumulated, he purchased one gentleman's evening from the bargain counter of stingy old Father Time. He arrayed himself in the regalia of millionaires and presidents; he took himself to the quarter where life is brightest and showiest, and there dined with taste and luxury. With ten dollars a man may, for a few hours, play the wealthy idler to perfection. The sum is ample for a well-considered meal, a bottle bearing a respectable label, commensurate tips, a smoke, cab fare, and the ordinary etceteras.

This one delectable evening culled from each dull seventy was to Chandler a source of renascent bliss. To the society bud comes but one début; it stands alone sweet in her memory when her hair was whitened; but to Chandler each ten weeks brought a joy as keen, as thrilling, as new as the first had been. To sit among *bon vivants* under palms in the swirl of concealed music, to look upon the *habitués* of such a paradise and to be looked upon by them— what is a girl's first dance and short-sleeved tulle compared with this?

Up Broadway Chandler moved with the vespertine dress parade. For this evening he was an exhibit as well as a gazer. For the next sixty-nine evenings he would be dining in cheviot and worsted at dubious *table d'hôtes*, at whirlwind lunch counters, on sandwiches and beer in his hall bedroom. He was willing to do that, for he was a true son of the great city of razzle-dazzle, and to him one evening in the limelight made up for many dark ones.

Chandler protracted his walk until the Forties began to intersect the great and glittering primrose way, for the evening was yet young, and when one is of the *beau monde* only one day in seventy, one loves to protract the pleasure. Eyes bright, sinister, curious, admiring, provocative, alluring were bent upon him, for his garb and air proclaimed him a devotee to the hour of solace and pleasure.

At a certain corner he came to a standstill, proposing to himself the question of turning back toward the showy and fashionable restaurant in which he usually dined on the evenings of his especial luxury. Just then a girl scuddled lightly around the corner, slipped on a patch of icy snow and fell plump upon the sidewalk.

Chandler assisted her to her feet with instant and solicitous courtesy. The girl hobbled to the wall of the building, leaned against it, and thanked him demurely.

" I think my ankle is strained," she said. " It twisted when I fell."

" Does it pain you much ? " inquired Chandler.

" Only when I rest my weight upon it. I think I will be able to walk in a minute or two."

" If I can be of any further service," suggested the young man, " I will call a cab, or——"

" Thank you," said the girl, softly but heartily. " I am sure you need not trouble yourself any further. It was so awkward of me. And my shoe heels are horridly commonsense; I can't blame them at all."

Chandler looked at the girl and found her swiftly drawing his interest. She was pretty in a refined way; and her eye was both merry and kind. She was inexpensively clothed in a plain black dress that suggested a sort of uniform such as shop-girls wear. Her glossy dark-brown hair showed its coils beneath a cheap hat of black straw whose only ornament was a velvet ribbon and bow. She could have posed as a model for the self-respecting working girl of the best type.

A sudden idea came into the head of the young architect. He would ask this girl to dine with him. Here was the element that his splendid but solitary periodic feats had lacked. His brief season of elegant luxury would be doubly enjoyable if he could add to it a lady's society. This girl was a lady, he was sure—her manner and speech settled that. And in spite of her extremely plain attire he felt that he would be pleased to sit at table with her.

These thoughts passed swiftly through his mind, and he decided to ask her. It was a breach of etiquette, of course, but oftentimes wage-earning girls waived formalities in matters of this kind. They were generally shrewd judges of men; and thought better of their own judgment than they did of useless conventions. His ten dollars, discreetly expended, would enable the two to dine very well indeed. The dinner would no doubt be a wonderful experience thrown into the dull routine of the girl's life; and her lively appreciation of it would add to his own triumph and pleasure.

" I think," he said to her, with frank gravity, " that your foot needs a longer rest than you suppose. Now, I am going to suggest a way in which you can give it that and at the same time do me a favor. I was on my way to dine all by my lonely self when you came tumbling around the corner. You come with me and we'll have a cozy dinner and a pleasant talk together, and by that time your game ankle will carry you home very nicely, I am sure."

The girl looked quickly up into Chandler's clear, pleasant countenance. Her eyes twinkled once very brightly, and then she smiled ingenuously.

" But we don't know each other—it wouldn't be right, would it ? " she said, doubtfully.

" There is nothing wrong about it," said the young man, candidly. " I'll introduce myself—permit me—Mr. Towers Chandler. After our dinner, which I will try to make as pleasant as possible, I will bid you good-evening, or attend you safely to your door, whichever you prefer."

" But, dear me ! " said the girl, with a glance at Chandler's faultless attire. " In this old dress and hat ! "

" Never mind that," said Chandler, cheerfully. " I'm sure you look more charming in them than any one we shall see in the most elaborate dinner toilette."

" My ankle does hurt yet." admitted the girl, attempting a limping step. " I think I will accept your invitation, Mr. Chandler. You may call me—Miss Marian."

" Come then, Miss Marian," said the young architect, gaily, but with perfect courtesy; " you will not have far to walk. There is a very respectable and good restaurant in the next block. You will have to lean on my arm—so—and walk slowly. It is lonely dining all by one's self. I'm just a little bit glad that you slipped on the ice. "

When the two were established at a well-appointed table, with a promising waiter hovering in attendance, Chandler began to experience the real joy that his regular outing always brought to him.

The restaurant was not so showy or pretentious as the one further down Broadway, which he always preferred, but it was nearly so. The tables were well filled with prosperous-looking diners, there was a good orchestra, playing softly enough to make conversation a possible pleasure, and the cuisine and service were beyond criticism. His companion, even in her cheap hat and dress, held herself with an air that added distinction to the natural beauty of her face and figure. And it is certain that she looked at Chandler, with his animated but self-possessed manner and his kindling and frank blue eyes, with something not far from admiration in her own charming face.

Then it was that the Madness of Manhattan, the Frenzy of Fuss and Feathers, the Bacillus of Brag, the Provincial Plague of Pose seized upon Towers Chandler. He was on Broadway, surrounded by pomp and style, and there were eyes to look at him. On the stage of that comedy he had assumed to play the one-night part of a butterfly of fashion and an idler of means and taste. He was dressed for the part, and all his good angels had not the power to prevent him from acting it.

So he began to prate to Miss Marian of clubs, of teas, of golf and riding and kennels and cotillions and tours abroad and threw out hints of a yacht lying at Larchmont. He could see that she was vastly impressed by this vague talk, so he endorsed his pose by random insinuations concerning great wealth, and mentioned familiarly a few names that are handled reverently by the proletariat. It was Chandler's short little day, and he was wringing from it the best that could be had, as he saw it. And yet once or twice he saw the pure gold of this girl shine through the mist that his egotism had raised between him and all objects.

" This way of living that you speak of," she said, " sounds so futile and purposeless. Haven't you any work to do in the world that might interest you more ? "

" My dear Miss Marian," he exclaimed—" work ! Think of dressing every day for dinner, of making half a dozen calls in an afternoon—with a policeman at every corner ready to jump into your auto and take you to the station, if you get up any greater speed than a donkey cart's gait. We do-nothings are the hardest workers in the land."

The dinner was concluded, the waiter generously tipped, and the two walked out to the corner where they met. Miss Marian walked very well now; her limp was scarcely noticeable.

"Thank you for a nice time," she said, frankly. "I must run home now. I liked the dinner very much, Mr. Chandler."

He shook hands with her, smiling cordially, and said something about a game of bridge at his club. He watched her for a moment, walking rather rapidly eastward, and then he found a cab to drive him slowly homeward.

In his chilly bedroom Chandler laid away his evening clothes for a sixty-nine days' rest. He went about it thoughtfully.

"That was a stunning girl," he said to himself. "She's all right, too, I'd be sworn, even if she does have to work. Perhaps if I'd told her the truth instead of all that razzle-dazzle we might—but, confound it! I had to play up to my clothes."

Thus spoke the brave who was born and reared in the wigwams of the tribe of the Manhattans.

The girl, after leaving her entertainer, sped swiftly cross-town until she arrived at a handsome and sedate mansion two squares to the east, facing on that avenue which is the highway of Mammon and the auxiliary gods. Here she entered hurriedly and ascended to a room where a handsome young lady in an elaborate house dress was looking anxiously out of the window.

"Oh, you madcap!" exclaimed the elder girl, when the other entered. "When will you quit frightening us this way? It's two hours since you ran out in that rag of an old dress and Marie's hat. Mamma had been so alarmed. She sent Louis in the auto to try to find you. You are a bad, thoughtless Puss."

The elder girl touched a button, and a maid came in a moment.

"Marie, tell mamma that Miss Marian has returned."

"Don't scold, Sister. I only ran down to Mme. Theo's to tell her to use mauve insertion instead of pink. My costume and Marie's hat were just what I needed. Every one thought I was a shop-girl, I am sure."

"Dinner is over, dear; you stayed so late."

"I know. I slipped on the sidewalk and turned my ankle. I could not walk, so I hobbled into a restaurant and sat there until I was better. That is why I was so long."

The two girls sat in the window seat, looking out at the lights and the stream of hurrying vehicles in the avenue. The younger one cuddled down with her head in her sister's lap.

"We will have to marry some day," she said, dreamily—"both of us. We have so much money that we will not be allowed to disappoint the public. Do you want me to tell you the kind of a man I could love, Sis?"

"Go on, you scatterbrain," smiled the other.

"I could love a man with dark and kind blue eyes, who is gentle and respectful to poor girls, who is handsome and good and does not try to flirt. But I could love him only if he had an ambition, an object, some work to do in the world. I would not care how poor he was if I could help him build his way up. But, Sister dear, the kind of man we always meet—the man who lives an idle life between society and his clubs—I could not love a man like that, even if his eyes were blue and he were so kind to poor girls whom he met in the street."

BY COURIER

IT was neither the season nor the hour when the Park had frequenters; and it is likely that the young lady, who was seated on one of the benches at the side of the walk, had merely obeyed a sudden impulse to sit for a while and enjoy a foretaste of coming Spring.

She rested there, pensive and still. A certain melancholy that touched her countenance must have been of recent birth, for it had not yet altered the fine and youthful contours of her cheek, nor subdued the arch though resolute curve of her lips.

A tall young man came striding through the park along the path near which she sat. Behind him tagged a boy carrying a suit-case. At sight of the young lady, the man's face changed to red and back to pale again. He watched her countenance as he drew nearer, with hope and anxiety mingled on his own. He passed within a few yards of her, but he saw no evidence that she was aware of his presence or existence.

Some fifty yards further on he suddenly stopped and sat on a bench at one side. The boy dropped the suit-case and stared at him with wondering, shrewd eyes. The young man took out his handkerchief and wiped his brow. It was a good handkerchief, a good brow, and the young man was good to look at. He said to the boy :

" I want you to take a message to that young lady on that bench. Tell her I am on my way to the station, to leave for San Francisco, where I shall join that Alaska moose-hunting expedition. Tell her that, since she has commanded me neither to speak nor to write to her, I take this means of making one last appeal to her sense of justice, for the sake of what has been. Tell her that to condemn and discard one who has not deserved such treatment, without giving him her reasons or a chance to explain is contrary to her nature as I believe it to be. Tell her that I have thus, to a certain degree, disobeyed her injunctions, in the hope that she may yet be inclined to see justice done. Go, and tell her that."

The young man dropped a half-dollar into the boy's hand. The boy looked at him for a moment with bright, canny eyes out of a dirty, intelligent face, and then set off at a run. He approached the lady on the bench a little doubtfully, but unembarrassed. He touched the brim of an old plaid bicycle cap perched on the back of his head. The lady looked at him coolly, without prejudice or favor.

" Lady," he said, " dat gent on de oder bench sent yer a song and dance by me. If yer don't know de guy, and he's tryin' to do de Johnny act, say de word, and I'll call a cop in t'ree minutes. If yer does know him, and he's on de square, w'y I'll spiel yer de bunch of hot air he sent yer."

The young lady betrayed a faint interest.

"A song and dance!" she said, in a deliberate, sweet voice that seemed to clothe her words in a diaphanous garment of impalpable irony. "A new idea—in the troubadour line, I suppose. I—used to know the gentleman who sent you so I think it will hardly be necessary to call the police. You may execute your song and dance, but do not sing too loudly. It is a little early yet for open-air vaudeville, and we might attract attention."

"Awe," said the boy, with a shrug down the length of him, " yer know what I mean, lady. 'Tain't a turn, it's wind. He told me to tell yer he's got his collars and cuffs in dat grip for a scoot clean out to 'Frisco. Den he's goin' to shoot snow-birds in de Klondike. He says yer told him not to send 'round no more pink notes nor come hangin' over de garden gate, and he takes dis means of puttin' yer wise. He says yer refereed him out like a has-been, and never give him no chance to kick at de decision. He says yer swiped him, and never said why."

The slightly awakened interest in the young lady's eyes did not abate. Perhaps it was caused by either the originality or the audacity of the snow-bird hunter, in thus circumventing her express commands against the ordinary modes of communication. She fixed her eye on a statue standing disconsolate in the dishevelled park, and spoke into the transmitter.:

" Tell the gentleman that I need not repeat to him a description of my ideals. He knows what they have been and what they still are. So far as they touch on this case, absolute loyalty and truth are the ones paramount. Tell him that I have studied my own heart as well as one can, and I know its weakness as well as I do its needs. That is why I decline to hear his pleas, whatever they may be. I did not condemn him through hearsay or doubtful evidence, and that is why I made no charge. But, since he persists in hearing what he already well knows, you may convey the matter.

" Tell him that I entered the conservatory that evening from the rear, to cut a rose for my mother. Tell him I saw him and Miss Ashburton beneath the pink oleander. The tableau was pretty, but the pose and juxtaposition were too eloquent and evident to require explanation. I left the conservatory, and, at the same time, the rose and my ideal. You may carry that song and dance to your impresario."

" I'm shy on one word, lady. Jux—jux—put me wise on dat, will yer ? "

" Juxtaposition—or you may call it propinquity—or, if you like, being rather too near for one maintaining the position of an ideal."

The gravel spun from beneath the boy's feet. He stood by the other bench. The man's eyes interrogated him, hungrily. The boy's were shining with the impersonal zeal of the translator.

" De lady says dat she's on to de fact dat gals is dead easy when a feller come spielin' ghost stories and tryin' to make up, and dat's why she won't listen to no soft-soap. She says she caught yer dead to rights, huggin' a bunch o' calico in de hot-house. She side-stepped in to pull some posies and yer was squeezin' der oder gal to beat de band. She says it looked cute, all right all right, but it made her sick. She says yer better git busy, and make a sneak for de train."

The young man gave a low whistle and his eyes flashed with a sudden thought. His hand flew to the inside pocket of his coat, and drew out a handful of letters. Selecting one, he handed it to the boy, following it with a silver dollar from his vest-pocket.

" Give that letter to the lady," he said, " and ask her to read it. Tell her that it should explain the situation. Tell her that, if she had mingled a little trust with her conception of the ideal, much heartache might have been avoided. Tell her that loyalty she prizes so much has never wavered. Tell her I am waiting for an answer."

The messenger stood before the lady.

" De gent says he's had de ski-bunk put on him widout no cause. He says he's no bum guy; and, lady, yer read dat letter, and I'll bet yer he's a white sport, all right."

The young lady unfolded the letter, somewhat doubtfully, and read it.

DEAR DR. ARNOLD : I want to thank you for your most kind and opportune aid to my daughter last Friday evening, when she was overcome by an attack of her old heart-trouble in the conservatory at Mrs. Waldron's reception. Had you not been near to catch her as she fell and to render proper attention, we might have lost her. I would be glad if you would call and undertake the treatment of her case.

Gratefully yours,
ROBERT ASHBURTON.

The young lady refolded the letter, and handed it to the boy.

" De gent wants an answer," said the messenger. " What's de word? "

The lady's eyes suddenly flashed on him, bright, smiling, and wet.

" Tell that guy on the other bench," she said, with a happy, tremulous laugh, " that his girl wants him."

THE FURNISHED ROOM

RESTLESS, shifting, fugacious as time itself is a certain vast bulk of the population of the red brick district of the lower West Side. Homeless, they have a hundred homes. They flit from furnished room to furnished room, transients forever—transients in abode, transients in heart and mind. They sing " Home, Sweet Home " in ragtime; they carry their *lares et penates* in a bandbox; their vine is entwined about a picture hat; a rubber plant is their fig tree.

Hence the houses of this district, having had a thousand dwellers, should have a thousand tales to tell, mostly dull ones, no doubt; but it would be strange if there could not be found a ghost or two in the wake of all these vagrant guests.

One evening after dark a young man prowled among these crumbling red mansions, ringing their bells. At the twelfth he rested his lean hand-baggage upon the step and wiped the dust from his hatband and forehead. The bell sounded faint and far away in some remote, hollow depths.

To the door of this, the twelfth house whose bell he had rung, came a house-keeper who made him think of an unwholesome, surfeited worm that had eaten its nut to a hollow shell and now sought to fill the vacancy with edible lodgers.

He asked if there was a room to let.

" Come in," said the housekeeper. Her voice came from her throat; her throat seemed lined with fur. " I have the third-floor back, vacant since a week back. Should you wish to look at it ? "

The young man followed her up the stairs. A faint light from no particular source mitigated the shadows of the halls. They trod noiselessly upon a stair carpet that its own loom would have for-

sworn. It seemed to have become vegetable; to have degenerated
in that rank, sunless air to lush lichen or spreading moss that grew
in patches to the stair-case and was viscid under the foot like organic
matter. At each turn of the stairs were vacant niches in the wall.
Perhaps plants had once been set within them. If so they had died
in that foul and tainted air. It may be that statues of the saints
had stood there, but it was not difficult to conceive that imps and
devils had dragged them forth in the darkness and down to the
unholy depths of some furnished pit below.

" This is the room," said the housekeeper, from her furry throat.
" It's a nice room. It ain't often vacant. I had some most elegant
people in it last summer—no trouble at all, and paid in advance
to the minute. The water's at the end of the hall. Sprowls and
Mooney kept it three months. They done a vaudeville sketch.
Miss B'retta Sprowls—you may have heard of her—Oh, that was
just the stage names—right there over the dresser is where the
marriage certificate hung, framed. The gas is here, and you see
there is plenty of closet room. It's a room everybody likes. It
never stays idle long."

" Do you have many theatrical people rooming here ? " asked
the young man.

" They comes and goes. A good proportion of my lodgers is
connected with the theatres. Yes, sir, this is the theatrical district.
Actor people never stays long anywhere. I get my share. Yes, they
comes and they goes."

He engaged the room, paying for a week in advance. He was
tired, he said, and would take possession at once. He counted out
the money. The room had been made ready, she said, even to
towels and water. As the housekeeper moved away he put, for the
thousandth time, the question that he carried at the end of his
tongue.

"A young girl—Miss Vashner—Miss Eloise Vashner—do you
remember such a one among your lodgers ? She would be singing
on the stage, most likely. A fair girl, of medium height and slender,
with reddish, gold hair and dark mole near her left eyebrow."

" No, I don't remember the name. Them stage people has names
they change as often as their rooms. They comes and they goes.
No, I don't call that one to mind."

No. Always no. Five months of ceaseless interrogation and the
inevitable negative. So much time spent by days in questioning
managers, agents, schools and choruses; by night among the
audiences of theatres from all-star casts down to music halls so low
that he dreaded to find what he most hoped for. He who had loved
her best had tried to find her. He was sure that since her disappearance from home this great, water-girt city held her somewhere,

but it was like a monstrous quicksand, shifting its particles constantly, with no foundation, its upper granules of to-day buried to-morrow in ooze and slime.

The furnished room received its latest guest with a first glow of pseudo-hospitality, a hectic, haggard, perfunctory welcome like the specious smile of a demirep. The sophistical comfort came in reflected gleams from the decayed furniture, the ragged brocade upholstery of a couch and two chairs, a foot-wide cheap pier glass between the two windows, from one or two gilt picture frames and a brass bedstead in a corner.

The guest reclined, inert, upon a chair, while the room, confused in speech as though it were an apartment in Babel, tried to discourse to him of its divers tenantry.

A polychromatic rug like some brilliant-flowered rectangular, tropical islet lay surrounded by a billowy sea of soiled matting. Upon the gay-papered wall were those pictures that pursue the homeless one from house to house—The Huguenot Lovers, The First Quarrel, The Wedding Breakfast, Psyche at the Fountain. The mantel's chastely severe outline was ingloriously veiled behind some pert drapery drawn rakishly askew like the sashes of the Amazonian ballet. Upon it was some desolate flotsam cast aside by the room's marooned when a lucky sail had borne them to a fresh port—a trifling vase or two, pictures of actresses, a medicine bottle, some stray cards out of a deck.

One by one, as the characters of a cryptograph became explicit, the little signs left by the furnished room's procession of guests developed a significance. The threadbare space in the rug in front of the dresser told that lovely woman had marched in the throng. The tiny fingerprints on the wall spoke of little prisoners trying to feel their way to sun and air. A splattered stain, raying like the shadow of a bursting bomb, witnessed where a hurled glass or bottle had splintered with its contents against the wall. Across the pier glass had been scrawled with a diamond in staggering letters the name " Marie." It seemed that the succession of dwellers in the furnished room had turned in fury—perhaps tempted beyond forebearance by its garish coldness—and wreaked upon it their passions. The furniture was chipped and bruised; the couch, distorted by bursting springs, seemed a horrible monster that had been slain during the stress of some grotesque convulsion. Some more potent upheaval had cloven a great slice from the marble mantel. Each plank in the floor owned its particular cant and shriek as from a separate and individual agony. It seemed incredible that all this malice and injury had been wrought upon the room by those who had called it for a time their home; and yet it may have been the cheated home instinct surviving blindly, the resentful rage at false household gods that had kindled their wrath. A hut that is our own we can sweep and adorn and cherish.

The young tenant in the chair allowed these thoughts to file, soft-shod, through his mind, while there drifted into the room furnished sounds and furnished scents. He heard in one room a tittering and incontinent, slack laughter; in others the monologue of a scold, the rattling of dice, a lullaby, and one crying dully; above him a banjo tinkled with spirit. Doors banged somewhere; the elevated trains roared intermittently; a cat yowled miserably upon a back fence. And he breathed the breath of the house—a dank savor rather than a smell—a cold, musty effluvium as from underground vaults mingled with the reeking exhalations of linoleum and mildewed and rotten woodwork.

Then suddenly, as he rested there, the room was filled with the strong, sweet odor of mignonette. It came as upon a single buffet of wind with such sureness and fragrance and emphasis that it almost seemed a living visitant. And the man cried aloud : " What, dear ? " as if he had been called, and sprang up and faced about. The rich odor clung to him and wrapped him around. He reached out his arms for it, all his senses for the time confused and commingled. How could one be peremptorily called by an odor ? Surely it must have been a sound. But, was it not the sound that had touched, that had caressed him ?

" She has been in this room," he cried, and he sprang to wrest from it a token, for he knew he would recognize the smallest thing that had belonged to her or that she had touched. This enveloping scent of mignonette, the odor that she had loved and made her own—whence came it ?

The room had been but carelessly set in order. Scattered upon the flimsy dresser scarf were half a dozen hairpins—those discreet, indistinguishable friends of womankind, feminine of gender, infinite mood and uncommunicative of tense. These he ignored, conscious of their triumphant lack of identity. Ransacking the drawers of the dresser he came upon a discarded, tiny, ragged handkerchief. He pressed it to his face. It was racy and insolent with heliotrope; he hurled it to the floor. In another drawer he found odd buttons, a theatre programme, a pawnbroker's card, two lost marshmallows, a book on the divination of dreams. In the last was a woman's black satin hair bow, which halted him, poised between ice and fire. But the black satin hair bow also is femininity's demure, impersonal common ornament and tells no tales.

And then he traversed the room like a hound on the scent, skimming the walls, considering the corners of the bulging matting on his hands and knees, rummaging mantel and tables, the curtains and hangings, the drunken cabinet in the corner, for a visible sign, unable to perceive that she was there beside, around, against, within, above him, clinging to him, wooing him, calling him so poignantly through the finer senses that even his grosser ones became cognizant of the call. Once again he answered loudly : " Yes, dear ! " and turned, wild-eyed, to gaze on vacancy, for he could not yet discern form and color and love and outstretched arms in the odor of mignonette. Oh, God ! whence that odor, and since when have odors had a voice to call ? Thus he groped.

He burrowed in crevices and corners, and found corks and cigarettes. These he passed in passive contempt. But once he found in a fold of the matting a half-smoked cigar, and this he ground beneath his heel with a green and trenchant oath. He sifted the room from end to end. He found dreary and ignoble small records of many a peripatetic tenant; but of her whom he sought, and who may have lodged there, and whose spirit seemed to hover there, he found no trace.

And then he thought of the housekeeper.

He ran from the haunted room downstairs and to a door that showed a crack of light. She came out to his knock. He smothered his excitement as best he could.

" Will you tell me, madam," he besought her, " who occupied the room I have before I came ? "

" Yes, sir. I can tell you again. 'Twas Sprowls and Mooney, as I said. Miss B'retta Sprowls it was in the theatres, but Missis Mooney she was. My house is well known for respectability. The marriage certificate hung, framed, on a nail over——"

" What kind of a lady was Miss Sprowls—in looks, I mean ? "

" Why, black-haired, sir, short, and stout, with a comical face. They left a week ago Tuesday."

" And before they occupied it ? "

" Why, there was a single gentleman connected with the draying business. He left owing me a week. Before him was Missis Crowder and her two children, that stayed four months; and back of them was old Mr. Doyle, whose sons paid for him. He kept the room six months. That goes back a year, sir, and further I do not remember."

He thanked her and crept back to his room. The room was dead. The essence that had vivified it was gone. The perfume of mignonette had departed. In its place was the old, stale, odor of mouldy house furniture, of atmosphere in storage.

The ebbing of his hope drained his faith. He sat staring at the yellow, singing gaslight. Soon he walked to the bed and began to tear the sheets into strips. With the blade of his knife he drove them tightly into every crevice around windows and door. When all was snug and taut he turned out the light, turned the gas full on again and laid himself gratefully upon the bed.

*   *   *   *   *

It was Mrs. McCool's night to go with the can for beer. So she fetched it and sat with Mrs. Purdy in one of those subterranean retreats where housekeepers foregather and the worm dieth seldom.

"I rented out my third-floor-back this evening," said Mrs. Purdy, across a fine circle of foam. "A young man took it. He went up to bed two hours ago."

"Now, did ye, Mrs. Purdy, ma'am?" said Mrs. McCool, with intense admiration. "You do be a wonder for rentin' rooms of that kind. And did ye tell him, then?" she concluded in a husky whisper laden with mystery.

"Rooms," said Mrs. Purdy, in her furriest tones, "are furnished for to rent. I did not tell him, Mrs. McCool."

"'Tis right ye are, ma'am; 'tis by renting rooms we kape alive. Ye have the rale sense for business, ma'am. There be many people will rayjict the rentin' of a room if they be tould a suicide has been after dyin' in the bed of it."

"As you say, we has our living to be making," remarked Mrs. Purdy.

"Yis, ma'am; 'tis true. 'Tis just one wake ago this day I helped ye lay out the third-floor-back. A pretty slip of a colleen she was to be killin' herself wid the gas—a swate little face she had, Mrs. Purdy, ma'am."

"She'd a-been called handsome, as you say," said Mrs. Purdy, assenting but critical, "but for that mole she had a-growin' by her left eyebrow. Do fill up your glass again, Mrs. McCool."

THE BRIEF DÉBUT OF TILDY

IF you do not know Bogle's Chop House and Family Restaurant it is your loss. For if you are one of the fortunate ones who dine expensively you should be interested to know how the other half consumes provisions. And if you belong to the half to whom waiters' checks are things of moment, you should know Bogle's, for there you get your money's worth—in quantity, at least.

Bogle's is situated in that highway of *bourgeoisie,* that boulevard of Brown-Jones-and-Robinson, Eighth Avenue. There are two rows of tables in the room, six in each row. On each table is a caster-stand, containing cruets of condiments and seasons. From the pepper cruet you may shake a cloud of something tasteless and melancholy, like volcanic dust. From the salt cruet you may expect nothing. Though a man should extract a sanguinary stream from the pallid turnip, yet will his prowess be balked when he comes to wrest salt from Bogle's cruets. Also upon each table stands the counterfeit of that benign sauce made " from the recipe of a nobleman in India."

At the cashier's desk sits Bogle, cold, sordid, slow, smouldering, and takes your money. Behind a mountain of toothpicks he makes your change, files your check, and ejects at you, like a toad, a word about the weather. Beyond a corroboration of his meteorological statement you would better not venture. You are not Bogle's friend; you are a fed, transient customer, and you and he may not meet until the blowing of Gabriel's dinner horn. So take your change and go—to the devil if you like. There you have Bogle's sentiments.

The needs of Bogle's customers were supplied by two waitresses and a Voice. One of the waitresses was named Aileen. She was tall, beautiful, lively, gracious and learned in persiflage. Her other name ? There was no more necessity for another name at Bogle's than there was for finger-bowls.

The name of the other waitress was Tildy. Why do you suggest Matilda ? Please listen this time—Tildy—Tildy. Tildy was dumpy, plain-faced, and too anxious to please. Repeat the last clause to yourself once or twice, and make the acquaintance of the duplicate infinite.

The Voice at Bogle's was invisible. It came from the kitchen, and did not shine in the way of originality. It was a heathen Voice, and contented itself with vain repetitions of exclamations emitted by the waitresses concerning food.

Will it tire you to be told again that Aileen was beautiful ? Had she donned a few hundred dollars' worth of clothes and joined the Easter parade, and had you seen her, you would have hastened to say so yourself.

The customers at Bogle's were her slaves. Six tables full she could wait upon at once. They who were in a hurry restrained their impatience for the joy of merely gazing upon her swiftly moving, graceful figure. They who had finished eating ate more that they might continue in the light of her smiles. Every man there—and they were mostly men—tried to make his impression upon her.

Aileen could successfully exchange repartee against a dozen at once. And every smile that she sent forth lodged, like pellets from a scatter-gun, in as many hearts. And all this while she would be performing astounding feats with orders of pork and beans, pot roasts, ham-and, sausage-and-the-wheats, and any quantity of things on the iron and in the pan and straight up and on the side. With all this feasting and flirting and merry exchange of wit

Bogle's came mighty near being a salon, with Aileen for its Madame Recamier.

If the transients were entranced by the fascinating Aileen, the regulars were her adorer. There was much rivalry among many of the steady customers. Aileen could have had an engagement every evening. At least twice a week some one took her to a theatre or to a dance. One stout gentleman whom she and Tildy had privately christened " The Hog " presented her with a turquoise ring. Another one known as " Freshy ," who rode on the Traction Company's repair wagon, was going to give her a poodle as soon as his brother got the hauling contract in the Ninth. And the man who always ate spareribs and spinach and said he was a stock broker asked her to go to " Parsifal " with him.

" I don't know where this place is," said Aileen while talking it over with Tildy, " but the wedding-ring's got to be on before I put a stitch into a travelling dress—ain't that right? Well, I guess! "

But, Tildy !

In steaming, chattering, cabbage-scented Bogle's there was almost a heart tragedy. Tildy with the blunt-nose, the hay-colored hair, the freckled skin, the bag-o'-meal figure, had never had an admirer. Not a man followed her with his eyes when she went to and fro in the restaurant save now and then when they glared with the beast-hunger for food. None of them bantered her gaily to coquettish interchanges of wit. None of them loudly " jollied " her of mornings as they did Aileen, accusing her, when the eggs were slow in coming, of late hours in the company of envied swains. No one had ever given her a turquoise ring or invited her upon a voyage to mysterious, distant " Parsifal."

Tildy was a good waitress, and the men tolerated her. They who sat at her tables spoke to her briefly with quotations from the bill of fare; and then raised their voices in honeyed and otherwise-flavored accents, eloquently addressed to the fair Aileen. They writhed in their chairs to gaze around and over the impending form of Tildy, that Aileen's pulchritude might season and make ambrosia of their bacon and eggs.

And Tildy was content to be the unwooed drudge if Aileen could receive the flattery and the homage. The blunt nose was loyal to the short Grecian. She was Aileen's friend; and she was glad to see her rule hearts and wean the attention of men from smoking pot-pie and lemon meringue. But deep below our freckles and hay-colored hair the unhandsomest of us dream of a prince or a princess, not vicarious, but coming to us alone.

There was a morning when Aileen tripped in to work with a slightly bruised eye; and Tildy's solicitude was almost enough to heal any optic.

"Fresh guy," explained Aileen, "last night as I was going home at Twenty-third and Sixth. Sashayed up, so he did, and made a break. I turned him down, cold, and he made a sneak; but followed me down to Eighteenth, and tried his hot air again. Gee! but I slapped him a good one, side of the face. Then he give me that eye. Does it look real awful, Til? I should hate that Mr. Nicholson should see it when he comes in for his tea and toast at ten."

Tildy listened to the adventure with breathless admiration. No man had ever tried to follow her. She was safe abroad at any hour of the twenty-four. What bliss it must have been to have had a man follow one and black one's eye for love!

Among the customers at Bogle's was a young man named Seeders, who worked in a laundry office. Mr. Seeders was thin and had light hair, and appeared to have been recently rough-dried and starched. He was too diffident to aspire to Aileen's notice; so he usually sat at one of Tildy's tables, where he devoted himself to silence and boiled weakfish.

One day when Mr. Seeders came in to dinner he had been drinking beer. There were only two or three customers in the restaurant. When Mr. Seeders had finished his weakfish he got up, put his arm around Tildy's waist, kissed her loudly and impudently, walked out upon the street, snapped his fingers in the direction of the laundry, and hied himself to play pennies in the slot machines at the Amusement Arcade.

For a few moments Tildy stood petrified. Then she was aware of Aileen shaking at her an arch forefinger, and saying:

"Why, Til, you naughty girl! Ain't you getting to be awful, Miss Slyboots! First thing I know you'll be stealing some of my fellows. I must keep an eye on you, my lady."

Another thing dawned upon Tildy's recovering wits. In a moment she had advanced from a hopeless, lowly admirer to be an Eve-sister of the potent Aileen. She herself was now a man-charmer, a mark for Cupid, a Sabine who must be coy when the Romans were at their banquet boards. Man had found her waist achievable and her lips desirable. The sudden and amatory Seeders had, as it were, performed for her a miraculous piece of one-day laundry work. He had taken the sackcloth of her uncomeliness, had washed, dried, starched and ironed it, and returned it to her sheer embroidered lawn—the robe of Venus herself.

The freckles on Tildy's cheeks merged into a rosy flush. Now both Circe and Psyche peeped from her brightened eyes. Not even Aileen herself had been publicly embraced and kissed in the restaurant.

Tildy could not keep the delightful secret. When trade was slack she went and stood at Bogle's desk. Her eyes were shining; she tried not to let her words sound proud and boastful.

" A gentleman insulted me to-day," she said. " He hugged me around the waist and kissed me."

" That so ? " said Bogle, cracking open his business armor. "After this week you get a dollar a week more."

At the next regular meal when Tildy set food before customers with whom she had acquaintance she said to each of them modestly, as one whose merit needed no bolstering :

" A gentleman insulted me to-day in the restaurant. He put his arms around my waist and kissed me."

The diners accepted the revelation in various ways—some incredulously, some with congratulations : others turned upon her the stream of badinage that had hitherto been directed at Aileen alone. And Tildy's heart swelled in her bosom, for she saw at last the towers of Romance rise above the horizon of the gray plain in which she had for so long travelled.

For two days Mr. Seeders came not again. During that time, Tildy established herself firmly as a woman to be wooed. She bought ribbons, and arranged her hair like Aileen's, and tightened her waist two inches. She had a thrilling but delightful fear that Mr. Seeders would rush in suddenly and shoot her with a pistol. He must have loved her desperately; and impulsive lovers are always blindly jealous.

Even Aileen had not been shot at with a pistol. And then Tildy rather hoped that he would not shoot at her, for she was always loyal to Aileen; and she did not want to over-shadow her friend.

At 4 o'clock on the afternoon of the third day Mr. Seeders came in. There were no customers at the tables. At the back end of the restaurant Tildy was refilling the mustard pots and Aileen was quartering pies. Mr. Seeders walked back to where they stood.

Tildy looked up and saw him, gasped, and pressed the mustard spoon against her heart. A red hair-bow was in her hair; she wore Venus's Eighth Avenue badge, the blue bead necklace with the swinging silver symbolic heart.

Mr. Seeders was flushed and embarrassed. He plunged one hand into his hip pocket and the other into a fresh pumpkin pie.

" Miss Tildy," said he, " I want to apologize for what I done the other evenin'. Tell you the truth, I was pretty well tanked up or I wouldn't of done it. I wouldn't do no lady that a-way when I was sober. So I hope, Miss Tildy, you'll accept my 'pology, and believe that I wouldn't 't of done it if I'd known what I was doin' and hadn't of been drunk."

With this handsome plea Mr. Seeders backed away, and departed, feeling that reparation had been made.

But behind the convenient screen Tildy had thrown herself flat upon a table among the butter chips and the coffee cups, and was sobbing her heart out—out and back again to the gray plain wherein travel they with blunt noses and hay-colored hair. From her knot she had torn the red hair-bow and cast it upon the floor. Seeders she despised utterly; she had but taken his kiss as that of a pioneer and prophetic prince who might have set the clocks going and the pages to running in fairyland. But the kiss had been maudlin and unmeant; the court had not stirred at the false alarm; she must forevermore remain the Sleeping Beauty.

Yet not all was lost. Aileen's arm was around her; and Tildy's red hand groped among the butter chips till it found the warm clasp of her friend's.

"Don't you fret, Til," said Aileen, who did not understand entirely. "That turnip-faced little clothespin of a Seeders ain't worth it. He ain't anything of a gentleman or he wouldn't ever of apologized."

THE TRIMMED LAMP

CONTENTS

THE TRIMMED LAMP

O F course there are two sides to the question. Let us look at the other. We often hear " shop-girls " spoken of. No such persons exist. There are girls who work in shops. They make their living that way. But why turn their occupation into an adjective ? Let us be fair. We do not refer to the girls who live on Fifth Avenue as " marriage-girls."

Lou and Nancy were chums. They came to the big city to find work because there was not enough to eat at their homes to go around. Nancy was nineteen; Lou was twenty. Both were pretty, active country girls who had no ambition to go on the stage.

The little cherub that sits up aloft guided them to a cheap and respectable boarding-house. Both found positions and became wage-earners. They remained chums. It is at the end of six months that I would beg you to step forward and be introduced to them. Meddlesome Reader : My Lady Friends, Miss Nancy and Miss Lou. While you are shaking hands please take notice—cautiously —of their attire. Yes, cautiously; for they are as quick to resent a stare as a lady in a fox at the horse show is.

Lou is a piece-work ironer in a hand laundry. She is clothed in a badly fitting purple dress, and her hat plume is four inches too long; but her ermine muff and scarf cost $25, and its fellow beasts will be ticketed in the windows at $7.98 before the season is over. Her cheeks are pink, and her light blue eyes bright. Contentment radiates from her.

Nancy you would call a shop-girl—because you have the habit. There is no type; but a perverse generation is always seeking a type; so this is what the type should be. She has the high-ratted pompadour and the exaggerated straight-front. Her skirt is shoddy, but has the correct flare. No furs protect her against the bitter spring air, but she wears her short broadcloth jacket as jauntily as though it were Persian lamb ! On her face and in her eyes, re- morseless type-seeker, is the typical shop-girl expression. It is a look of silent but contemptuous revolt against cheated womanhood ; of sad prophecy of the vengeance to come. When she laughs her loudest the look is still there. The same look can be seen in the eyes of Russian peasants; and those of us left will see it some day on Gabriel's face when he comes to blow us up. It is a look that should wither and abash man; but he has been known to smirk at it and offer flowers—with a string tied to them.

Now lift your hat and come away, while you receive Lou's cheery " See you again," and the sardonic, sweet smile of Nancy that seems, somehow, to miss you and go fluttering like a white moth up over the housetops to the stars.

The two waited on the corner for Dan. Dan was Lou's steady company. Faithful ? Well, he was on hand when Mary would have had to hire a dozen subpœna servers to find her lamb.

" Ain't you cold, Nancy ? " said Lou. " Say, whata chump you are for working in that old store for $8 a week ! I made $18.50 last week. Of course ironing ain't as swell work as selling lace behind a counter, but it pays. None of us ironers make less than $10. And I don't know that it's any less respectful work, either."

" You can have it," said Nancy, with uplifted nose. " I'll take my eight a week and hall bedroom. I like to be among nice things and swell people. And look what a chance I've got ! Why, one of our glove girls married a Pittsburg—steel maker, or blacksmith or something—the other day worth a million dollars. I'll catch a swell myself some time. I ain't bragging on my looks or anything; but I'll take my chances where there's big prizes offered. What show would a girl have in a laundry ? "

" Why, that's where I met Dan," said Lou, triumphantly. " He came in for his Sunday shirt and collars and saw me at the first board, ironing. We all try to get to work at the first board. Ella Maginnis was sick that day, and I had her place. He said he noticed my arms first, how round and white they was. I had my sleeves rolled up. Some nice fellows come into laundries. You can tell 'em by their bringing their clothes in suit cases, and turning in the door sharp and sudden."

" How can you wear a waist like that, Lou ? " said Nancy, gazing down at the offending article with sweet scorn in her heavy-lidded eyes. " It shows fierce taste."

" This waist ? " said Lou, with wide-eyed indignation. " Why, I paid $16 for this waist. It's worth twenty-five. A woman left it to be laundered, and never called for it. The boss sold it to me. It's got yards and yards of hand embroidery on it. Better talk about that ugly, plain thing you've got on."

" This ugly, plain thing," said Nancy, calmly, " was copied from one that Mrs. Van Alstyne Fisher was wearing. The girls say her bill in the store last year was $12,000. I made mine, myself. It cost me $1.50. Ten feet away you couldn't tell it from hers."

" Oh, well," said Lou, good-naturedly, " if you want to starve and put on airs, go ahead. But I'll take my job and good wages; and after hours give me something as fancy and attractive to wear as I am able to buy."

But just then Dan came—a serious young man with a ready-made necktie, who had escaped the city's brand of frivolity—an electrician earning $30 per week who looked upon Lou with the sad eyes of Romeo, and thought her embroidered waist a web in which any fly should delight to be caught.

" My friend, Mr. Owens—shake hands with Miss Danforth," said Lou.

" I'm mighty glad to know you, Miss Danforth," said Dan, with outstretched hand. " I've heard Lou speak of you so often."

" Thanks," said Nancy, touching his fingers with the tips of her cool ones, " I've heard her mention you—a few times."

Lou giggled.

" Did you get that handshake from Mrs. Van Alstyne Fisher, Nance ? " she asked.

" If I did, you can feel safe in copying it," said Nancy.

" Oh, I couldn't use it at all. It's too stylish for me. It's intended to set off diamond rings, that high shake is. Wait till I get a few and then I'll try it."

" Learn it first," said Nancy, wisely, " and you'll be more likely to get the rings."

" Now, to settle this argument," said Dan, with his ready, cheerful smile, " let me make a proposition. As I can't take both of you up to Tiffany's and do the right thing, what do you say to a little vaudeville ? I've got the tickets. How about looking at stage diamonds since we can't shake hands with the real sparklers ? "

The faithful squire took his place close to the curb; Lou next, a little peacocky in her bright and pretty clothes; Nancy on the inside, slender, and soberly clothed as the sparrow, but with the true Van Alstyne Fisher walk—thus they set out for their evening's moderate diversion.

I do not suppose that many look upon a great department store as an educational institution. But the one in which Nancy worked was something like that to her. She was surrounded by beautiful things that breathed of taste and refinement. If you live in an atmosphere of luxury, luxury is yours whether your money pays for it, or another's.

The people she served were mostly women whose dress, manners, and position in the social world were quoted as criterions. From them Nancy began to take toll—the best from each according to her view.

From one she would copy and practise a gesture, from another an eloquent lifting of an eyebrow, from others, a manner of walking, of carrying a purse, of smiling, of greeting a friend, of addressing " inferiors in station." From her best beloved model, Mrs. Van Alstyne Fisher, she made requisition for that excellent thing, a soft, low voice as clear as silver and as perfect in articulation as the notes of a thrush. Suffused in the aura of this high social refinement and good breeding, it was impossible for her to escape a deeper effect of it. As good habits are said to be better than good principles, so, perhaps, good manners are better than good habits. The teachings of your parents may not keep alive your New England conscience; but if you sit on a straight-back chair and repeat the words " prisms and pilgrims " forty times the devil will flee from you. And when Nancy spoke in the Van Alstyne Fisher tones she felt the thrill of *noblesse oblige* to her very bones.

There was another source of learning in the great departmental school. Whenever you see three or four shop-girls gather in a bunch and jingle their wire bracelets as an accompaniment to apparently frivolous conversation, do not think that they are there for the purpose of criticizing the way Ethel does her back hair. The meeting may lack the dignity of the deliberative bodies of man; but it has all the importance of the occasion on which Eve and her first daughter first put their heads together to make Adam understand his proper place in the household. It is Woman's Conference for Common Defense and Exchange of Strategical Theories of Attack and Repulse upon and against the World, which is a Stage, and Man, its Audience who Persists in Throwing Bouquets Thereupon. Woman, the most helpless of the young of any animal—with the fawn's grace but without its fleetness; with the bird's beauty but without its power of flight; with the honey-bee's burden of sweetness but without its—— Oh, let's drop that simile —some of us may have been stung.

During this council of war they pass weapons one to another, and exchange stratagems that each has devised and formulated out of the tactics of life.

" I says to 'im," says Sadie, " ain't you the fresh thing ! Who do you suppose I am, to be addressing such a remark to me ? And what do you think he says back to me ? "

The heads, brown, black, flaxen, red, and yellow bob together; the answer is given; and the parry to the thrust is decided upon, to be used by each thereafter in passages-at-arms with the common enemy, man.

Thus Nancy learned the art of defense; and to women successful defense means victory.

The curriculum of a department store is a wide one. Perhaps no other college could have fitted her as well for her life's ambition —the drawing of a matrimonial prize.

Her station in the store was a favored one. The music room was near enough for her to hear and become familiar with the works of the best composers—at least to acquire the familiarity that passed for appreciation in the social world in which she was vaguely trying to set a tentative and aspiring foot. She absorbed the educating influence of art wares, of costly and dainty fabrics, of adornments that are almost culture to women.

The other girls soon became aware of Nancy's ambition. " Here comes your millionaire, Nancy," they would call to her whenever any man who looked the rôle approached her counter. It got to be a habit of men, who were hanging about while their women folk were shopping, to stroll over to the handkerchief counter and dawdle over the cambric squares. Nancy's imitation high-bred air and genuine dainty beauty was what attracted. Many men thus came to display their graces before her. Some of them may have been millionaires; others were certainly no more than their sedulous apes. Nancy learned to discriminate. There was a window at the end of the handkerchief counter; and she could see the rows of vehicles waiting for the shoppers in the street below. She looked and perceived that automobiles differ as well as do their owners.

Once a fascinating gentleman bought four dozen handkerchiefs, and wooed her across the counter with a King Cophetua air. When he had gone one of the girls said :

" What's wrong, Nance, that you didn't warm up to that fellow? He looks the swell article, all right, to me."

" Him ? " said Nancy, with her coolest, sweetest, most impersonal, Van Alstyne Fisher smile; " not for mine. I saw him drive up outside. A 12 H. P. machine and an Irish chauffeur ! And you saw what kind of handkerchiefs he bought—silk ! And he's got dactylis on him. Give me the real thing or nothing, if you please."

Two of the most " refined " women in the store—a forelady and a cashier—had a few " swell gentlemen friends " with whom they now and then dined. Once they included Nancy in an invitation. The dinner took place in a spectacular café whose tables are engaged for New Year's Eve a year in advance. There were two " gentlemen friends "—one without any hair on his head—high living ungrew it; and we can prove it—the other a young man whose worth and sophistication he impressed upon you in two convincing ways— he swore that all the wine was corked; and he wore diamond cuff buttons. This young man perceived irresistible excellencies in Nancy. His taste ran to shop-girls; and here was one that added the voice and manners of his high social world to the franker charms of her own caste. So, on the following day, he appeared in the store and made her a serious proposal of marriage over a box of hemstitched, grass-bleached Irish linens. Nancy declined. A brown pompadour ten feet away had been using her eyes and ears. When the rejected suitor had gone she heaped carboys of upbraidings and horror upon Nancy's head.

" What a terrible little fool you are ! That fellow's a millionaire—he's a nephew of old Van Skittles himself. And he was talking on the level, too. Have you gone crazy, Nance ? "

" Have I ? " said Nancy. " I didn't take him, did I ? He isn't a millionaire so hard that you could notice it, anyhow. His family only allows him $20,000 a year to spend. The bald-headed fellow was guying him about it the other night at supper."

The brown pompadour came nearer and narrowed her eyes.

" Say, what do you want ? " she inquired, in a voice hoarse for lack of chewing-gum. "Ain't that enough for you ? Do you want to be a Mormon, and marry Rockefeller and Gladstone Dowie and the King of Spain and the whole bunch ? Ain't $20,000 a year enough for you ? "

Nancy flushed a little under the level gaze of the black, shallow eyes.

" It wasn't altogether the money, Carrie," she explained. " His friend caught him in a rank lie the other night at dinner. It was about some girl he said he hadn't been to the theater with. Well, I can't stand a liar. Put everything together—I don't like him; and that settles it. When I sell out it's not going to be on any bargain day. I've got to have something that sits up in a chair like a man, anyhow. Yes, I'm looking out for a catch; but it's got to be able to do something more than make a noise like a toy bank."

" The physiopathic ward for yours ! " said the brown pompadour, walking away.

These high ideas, if not ideals—Nancy continued to cultivate on $8 per week. She bivouacked on the trail of the great unknown " catch " eating her dry bread and tightening her belt day by day. On her face was the faint, soldierly, sweet, grim smile of the pre-ordained man-hunter. The store was her forest; and many times she raised her rifle at game that seemed broad-antlered and big; but always some deep unerring instinct—perhaps of the huntress, perhaps of the woman—made her hold her fire and take up the trail again.

Lou flourished in the laundry. Out of her $18.50 per week she paid $6 for her room and board. The rest went mainly for clothes. Her opportunities for bettering her taste and manners were few compared with Nancys'. In the steaming laundry there was nothing but work, work and her thoughts of the evening pleasures to come. Many costly and showy fabrics passed under her iron; and it may be that her growing fondness for dress was thus transmitted to her through the conducting metal.

When the day's work was over Dan awaited outside, her faithful shadow in whatever light she stood.

Sometimes he cast an honest and troubled glance at Lou's

clothes that increased in conspicuity rather than in style; but this was no disloyalty; he deprecated the attention they called to her in the streets.

And Lou was no less faithful to her chum. There was a law that Nancy should go with them on whatsoever outings they might take. Dan bore the extra burden heartily and in good cheer. It might be said that Lou furnished the color, Nancy the tone, and Dan the weight of the distraction-seeking trio. The escort, in his neat but obviously ready-made suit, his ready-made tie and unfailing, genial, ready-made wit never startled or clashed. He was of that good kind that you are likely to forget while they are present, but remember distinctly after they are gone.

To Nancy's superior taste the flavor of these ready-made pleasures was sometimes a little bitter : but she was young; and youth is a gourmand, when it cannot be a gourmet.

" Dan is always wanting me to marry him right away," Lou told her once. " But why should I ? I'm independent. I can do as I please with the money I earn; and he never would agree for me to keep on working afterward. And say, Nance, what do you want to stick to that old store for, and half starve and half dress yourself ? I could get you a place in the laundry right now if you'd come. It seems to me that you could afford to be a little less stuck-up if you could make a good deal more money."

" I don't think I'm stuck-up, Lou," said Nancy, " but I'd rather live on half rations and stay where I am. I suppose I've got the habit. It's the chance that I want. I don't expect to be always behind a counter. I'm learning something new every day. I'm right up against refined and rich people all the time—even if I do only wait on them; and I'm not missing any pointers that I see passing around."

" Caught your millionaire yet ? " asked Lou with her teasing laugh.

" I haven't selected one yet," answered Nancy. " I've been looking them over."

" Goodness ! the idea of picking over 'em ! Don't you ever let one get by you, Nance—even if he's a few dollars shy. But of course you're joking—millionaires don't think about working girls like us."

" It might be better for them if they did," said Nancy, with cool wisdom. " Some of us could teach them how to take care of their money."

" If one was to speak to me," laughed Lou, " I know I'd have a duck-fit."

" That's because you don't know any. The only difference between swells and other people is you have to watch 'em closer.

Don't you think that red silk lining is just a little bit too bright for that coat, Lou ? "

Lou looked at the plain, dull olive jacket of her friend.

" Well, no I don't—but it may seem so beside that faded-looking thing you've got on."

" This jacket," said Nancy, complacently, " has exactly the cut and fit of one that Mrs. Van Alstyne Fisher was wearing the other day. The material cost me $3.98. I suppose hers cost about $200 more."

" Oh, well," said Lou, lightly, " it don't strike me as millionaire bait. Shouldn't wonder if I catch one before you do, anyway."

Truly it would have taken a philosopher to decide upon the values of the theories held by the two friends. Lou, lacking that certain pride and fastidiousness that keeps stores and desks filled with girls working for the barest living, thumped away gaily with her iron in the noisy and stifling laundry. Her wages supported her even beyond the point of comfort : so that her dress profited until sometimes she cast a sidelong glance of impatience at the neat but inelegant apparel of Dan—Dan the constant, the immutable, the undeviating.

As for Nancy, her case was one of tens of thousands. Silk and jewels and laces and ornaments and the perfume and music of the fine world of good-breeding and taste—these were made for woman; they are her equitable portion. Let her keep near them if they are a part of life to her, and if she will. She is no traitor to herself, as Esau was; for she keeps her birthright and the pottage she earns is often very scant.

In this atmosphere Nancy belonged; and she throve in it and ate her frugal meals and schemed over her cheap dresses with a determined and contented mind. She already knew woman; and she was studying man, the animal, both as to his habits and eligibility. Some day she would bring down the game that she wanted; but she promised herself it would be what seemed to her the biggest and the best, and nothing smaller.

Thus she kept her lamp trimmed and burning to receive the bridegroom when he should come.

But, another lesson she learned, perhaps unconsciously. Her standard of values began to shift and change. Sometimes the dollar-mark grew blurred in her mind's eye, and shaped itself into letters that spelled such words as " truth " and " honor " and now and then just " kindness." Let us make a likeness of one who hunts the moose or elk in some mighty wood. He sees a little dell, mossy and embowered, where a rill trickles, babbling to him of rest and comfort. At these times the spear of Nimrod himself grows blunt.

So, Nancy wondered sometimes if Persian lamb was always quoted at its market value by the hearts that it covered.

One Thursday evening Nancy left the store and turned across Sixth Avenue westward to the laundry. She was expected to go with Lou and Dan to a musical comedy.

Dan was just coming out of the laundry when she arrived. There was a queer, strained look on his face.

" I thought I would drop around to see if they had heard from her," he said.

" Heard from who ? " asked Nancy. " Isn't Lou there ? "

" I thought you knew," said Dan. " She hasn't been here or at the house where she lived since Monday. She moved all her things from here. She told one of the girls in the laundry she might be going to Europe."

" Hasn't anybody seen her anywhere ? " asked Nancy.

Dan looked at her with his jaws set grimly, and a steely gleam in his steady gray eyes.

" They told me in the laundry," he said, harshly, " that they saw her pass yesterday—in an automobile. With one of the millionaires, I suppose, that you and Lou were forever busying your brains about."

For the first time Nancy quailed before a man. She laid her hand that trembled slightly on Dan's sleeve.

" You've no right to say such a thing to me, Dan—as if I had anything to do with it ! "

" I didn't mean it that way," said Dan, softening. He fumbled in his vest pocket.

" I've got the tickets for the show to-night," he said, with a gallant show of lightness. " If you——"

Nancy admired pluck whenever she saw it.

" I'll go with you, Dan," she said.

Three months went by before Nancy saw Lou again.

At twilight one evening the shop-girl was hurrying home along the border of a little quiet park. She heard her name called, and wheeled about in time to catch Lou rushing into her arms.

After the first embrace they drew their heads back as serpents do, ready to attack or to charm, with a thousand questions trembling on their swift tongues. And then Nancy noticed that prosperity had descended upon Lou, manifesting itself in costly furs, flashing gems, and creations of the tailor's art.

" You little fool ! " cried Lou, loudly and affectionately. " I see you are still working in that store, and as shabby as ever. And how about that big catch you were going to make—nothing doing yet, I suppose ? "

And then Lou looked, and saw that something better than

prosperity had descended upon Nancy—something that shone brighter than gems in her eyes and redder than a rose in her cheeks, and that danced like electricity anxious to be loosed from the tip of her tongue.

"Yes, I'm still in the store," said Nancy, "but I'm going to leave it next week. I've made my catch—the biggest catch in the world. You won't mind now Lou, will you?—I'm going to be married to Dan—to Dan !—he's my Dan now—why, Lou ! "

Around the corner of the park strolled one of those new-crop, smooth-faced young policemen that are making the force more endurable—at least to the eye. He saw a woman with an expensive fur coat and diamond-ringed hands crouching down against the iron fence of the park sobbing turbulently, while a slender, plainly dressed working girl leaned close, trying to console her. But the Gibsonian cop, being of the new order, passed on, pretending not to notice, for he was wise enough to know that these matters are beyond help so far as the power he represents is concerned, though he rap the pavement with his nightstick till the sound goes up to the furthermost stars.

A MADISON SQUARE ARABIAN NIGHT

To Carson Chalmers, in his apartment near the square, Phillips brought the evening mail. Besides the routine correspondence there were two items bearing the same foreign postmark.

One of the incoming parcels contained a photograph of a woman. The other contained an interminable letter, over which Chalmers hung, absorbed, for a long time. The letter was from another woman; and it contained poisoned barbs, sweetly dipped in honey, and feathered with innuendoes concerning the photographed woman.

Chalmers tore this letter into a thousand bits and began to wear out his expensive rug by striding back and forth upon it. Thus an animal from the jungle acts when it is caged, and thus a caged man acts when he is housed in a jungle of doubt.

By and by the restless mood was overcome. The rug was not an enchanted one. For sixteen feet he could travel along it; three thousand miles was beyond its powers to aid.

Phillips appeared. He never entered; he invariably appeared, like a well-oiled genie.

"Will you dine here, sir, or out ? " he asked.

"Here," said Chalmers, " and in half an hour." He listened

glumly to the January blasts making an Æolian trombone of the empty street.

"Wait," he said to the disappearing genie. "As I came home across the end of the square I saw many men standing there in rows. There was one mounted upon something, talking. Why do those men stand in rows, and why are they there?"

"They are homeless men, sir," said Phillips. "The man standing on the box tries to get lodging for them for the night. People come around to listen and give him money. Then he sends as many as the money will pay for to some lodging-house. That is why they stand in rows; they get sent to bed in order as they come."

"By the time dinner is served," said Chalmers, "have one of those men here. He will dine with me."

"W-w-which——" began Phillips, stammering for the first time during his service.

"Choose one at random," said Chalmers. "You might see that he is reasonably sober—and a certain amount of cleanliness will not be held against him. That is all."

It was an unusual thing for Carson Chalmers to play the Caliph. But on that night he felt the inefficacy of conventional antidotes to melancholy. Something wanton and egregious, something high-flavored and Arabian, he must have to lighten his mood.

On the half hour Phillips had finished his duties as slave of the lamp. The waiters from the restaurant below had whisked aloft the delectable dinner. The dining table, laid for two, glowed cheerily in the glow of the pink-shaded candles.

And now Phillips, as though he ushered a cardinal—or held in charge a burglar—wafted in the shivering guest who had been haled from the line of mendicant lodgers.

It is a common thing to call such men wrecks; if the comparison be used here it is the specific one of a derelict come to grief through fire. Even yet some flickering combustion illuminated the drifting hulk. His face and hands had been recently washed—a rite insisted upon by Phillips as a memorial to the slaughtered conventions. In the candle-light he stood, a flaw in the decorous fittings of the apartment. His face was a sickly white, covered almost to the eyes with a stubble the shade of a red Irish setter's coat. Phillips's comb had failed to control the pale brown hair, long matted and con-formed to the contour of a constantly worn hat. His eyes were full of hopeless, tricky defiance like that seen in a cur's that is cornered by his tormentors. His shabby coat was buttoned high, but a quarter inch of redeeming collar showed above it. His manner was singularly free from embarrassment when Chalmers rose from his chair across the round dining table.

" If you will oblige me," said the host, " I will be glad to have your company at dinner."

" My name is Plumer," said the highway guest, in harsh and aggressive tones. " If you're like me, you like to know the name of the party you're dining with."

" I was going on to say," continued Chalmers somewhat hastily, " that mine is Chalmers. Will you sit opposite ? "

Plumer, of the ruffled plumes, bent his knee for Phillips to slide the chair beneath him. He had an air of having sat at attended boards before. Phillips set out the anchovies and olives.

" Good ! " barked Plumer; " going to be in courses, is it ? All right, my jovial ruler of Bagdad. I'm your Scheherezade all the way to the toothpicks. You're the first Caliph with a genuine Oriental flavor I've struck since frost. What luck ! And I was forty-third in line. I finished counting, just as your welcome emissary arrived to bid me to the feast. I had about as much chance of getting a bed to-night as I have of being the next President. How will you have the sad story of my life, Mr. Al Raschid—a chapter with each course or the whole edition with the cigars and coffee ? "

" The situation does not seem a novel one to you," said Chalmers with a smile.

" By the chin whiskers of the prophet—no ! " answered the guest. " New York's as full of cheap Haroun al Raschids as Bagdad is of fleas. I've been held up for my story with a loaded meal pointed at my head twenty times. Catch anybody in New York giving you something for nothing ! They spell curiosity and charity with the same set of building blocks. Lots of 'em will stake you to a dime and chop-suey; and a few of 'em will play Caliph to the tune of a top sirloin; but every one of 'em will stand over you till they screw your autobiography out of you with foot notes, appendix and un-published fragments. Oh, I know what to do when I see victuals coming toward me in little old Bagdad-on-the-Subway. I strike the asphalt three times with my forehead and get ready to spiel yarns for my supper. I claim descent from the late Tommy Tucker, who was forced to hand out vocal harmony for his pre-digested wheaterina and spoopju."

" I do not ask your story," said Chalmers. " I tell you frankly that it was a sudden whim that prompted me to send for some stranger to dine with me. I assure you you will not suffer through any curiosity of mine."

" Oh, fudge ! " exclaimed the guest, enthusiastically tackling his soup; " I don't mind it a bit. I'm a regular Oriental magazine with a red cover and the leaves cut when the Caliph walks abroad. In fact, we fellows in the bed line have a sort of union rate for things of this sort. Somebody's always stopping and wanting to know what brought us down so low in the world. For a sandwich and a glass of beer I tell 'em that drink did it. For corned beef and cabbage and a cup of coffee I give 'em the hard-hearted-landlord —six-months-in-the-hospital-lost-job story. A sirloin steak and a quarter for a bed gets the Wall Street tragedy of the swept-away fortune and the gradual descent. This is the first spread of this kind I've stumbled against. I haven't got a story to fit it. I'll tell you what, Mr. Chalmers, I'm going to tell you the truth for this, if you'll listen to it. It'll be harder for you to believe than the made-up ones."

An hour later the Arabian guest lay back with a sigh of satisfaction while Phillips brought the coffee and cigars and cleared the table.

" Did you ever hear of Sherrard Plumer ? " he asked, with a strange smile.

" I remember the name," said Chalmers. " He was a painter, I think, of a good deal of prominence a few years ago."

" Five years," said the guest. " Then I went down like a chunk of lead. I'm Sherrard Plumer ! I sold the last portrait I painted for $2,000. After that I couldn't have found a sitter for a gratis picture."

" What was the trouble ? " Chalmers could not resist asking.

" Funny thing," answered Plumer, grimly. " Never quite understood it myself. For a while I swam like a cork. I broke into the swell crowd and got commissions right and left. The newspapers called me a fashionable painter. Then the funny things began to happen. Whenever I finished a picture people would come to see it, and whisper and look queerly at one another.

" I soon found out what the trouble was. I had a knack of bringing out in the face of a portrait the hidden character of the original. I don't know how I did it—I painted what I saw—but I know it did me. Some of my sitters were fearfully enraged and refused their pictures. I painted the portrait of a very beautiful and popular society dame. When it was finished her husband looked at it with a peculiar expression on his face, and the next week he sued for divorce.

" I remember one case of a prominent banker who sat to me. While I had his portrait on exhibition in my studio an acquaintance of his came in to look at it, ' Bless me,' says he, ' does he really look like that ? ' I told him it was considered a faithful likeness. ' I never noticed that expression about his eyes before,' said he; ' I think I'll drop downtown and change my bank account.' He did drop down, but the bank account was gone and so was Mr. Banker.

" It wasn't long till they put me out of business. People don't want their secret meannesses shown up in a picture. They can smile and twist their own faces and deceive you, but the picture can't. I couldn't get an order for another picture, and I had to give up. I worked as a newspaper artist for a while, and then for a lithographer, but my work with them got me into the same trouble. If I drew from a photograph my drawing showed up characteristics and expressions that you couldn't find in the photo, but I guess they were in the original, all right. The customers raised lively rows, especially the women, and I never could hold a job long. So I began to rest my weary head upon the breast of Old Booze for comfort. And pretty soon I was in the free-bed line and doing oral fiction for hand-outs among the food bazaars. Does the truthful statement weary thee, O Caliph ? I can turn on the Wall Street disaster stop if you prefer, but that requires a tear, and I'm afraid I can't hustle one up after that good dinner."

" No, no," said Chalmers, earnestly, " you interest me very much. Did all of your portraits reveal some unpleasant trait, or were there some that did not suffer from the ordeal of your peculiar brush ? "

" Some ? Yes," said Plumer. " Children generally, a good many women and a sufficient number of men. All people aren't bad, you know. When they were all right the pictures were all right. As I said, I don't explain it, but I'm telling you facts."

On Chalmer's writing-table lay the photograph that he had received that day in the foreign mail. Ten minutes later he had Plumer at work making a sketch from it in pastels. At the end of an hour the artist rose and stretched wearily. " It's done," he yawned. " You'll excuse me for being so long. I got interested in the job. Lordy ! but I'm tired. No bed last night, you know. Guess it'll have to be good-night now, O Commander of the Faithful ! "

Chalmers went as far as the door with him and slipped some bills into his hand.

" Oh ! I'll take 'em," said Plumer. "All that's included in the fall. Thanks. And for the very good dinner. I shall sleep on feathers to-night and dream of Bagdad. I hope it won't turn out to be a dream in the morning. Farewell, most excellent Caliph ! "

Again Chalmers paced restlessly upon his rug. But his beat lay as far from the table whereon lay the pastel sketch as the room would permit. Twice, thrice, he tried to approach it, but failed. He could see the dun and gold and brown of the colors, but there was a wall about it built by his fears that kept him at a distance. He sat down and tried to calm himself. He sprang up and rang for Phillips.

"There is a young artist in this building," he said—"a Mr. Reineman—do you know which is his apartment?"

"Top floor, front, sir," said Phillips.

"Go up and ask him to favor me with his presence here for a few minutes."

Reineman came at once. Chalmers introduced himself.

"Mr. Reineman," said he, "there is a little pastel sketch on yonder table. I would be glad if you will give me your opinion of it as to its artistic merits and as a picture."

The young artist advanced to the table and took up the sketch. Chalmers half turned away, leaning upon the back of a chair.

"How—do—you find it?" he asked, slowly.

"As a drawing," said the artist, "I can't praise it enough. It's the work of a master—bold and fine and true. It puzzles me a little; I haven't seen any pastel work near as good in years."

"The face, man—the subject—the original—what would you say of that?"

"The face," said Reineman, "is the face of one of God's own angels. May I ask who—"

"My wife!" shouted Chalmers, wheeling and pouncing upon the astonished artist, gripping his hand and pounding his back. "She is traveling in Europe. Take that sketch, boy, and paint the picture of your life from it and leave the price to me."

THE RUBÁIYÁT OF A SCOTCH HIGHBALL

THIS document is intended to strike somewhere between a temperance lecture and the "Bartender's Guide." Relative to the latter, drink shall swell the theme and be set forth in abundance. Agreeably to the former, not an elbow shall be crooked.

Bob Babbitt was "off the stuff." Which means—as you will discover by referring to the unabridged dictionary of Bohemia—that he had "cut out the booze," that he was "on the water wagon." The reason for Bob's sudden attitude of hostility toward the "demon rum"—as the white ribboners miscall whiskey (see the "Bartender's Guide"), should be of interest to reformers and saloon-keepers.

There is always hope for a man who, when sober, will not concede or acknowledge that he was ever drunk. But when a man will say (in the apt words of the phrase-distiller), "I had a beautiful skate on last night," you will have to put stuff in his coffee as well as pray for him.

One evening on his way home Babbitt dropped in at the Broadway bar that he liked best. Always there were three or four fellows there from the downtown offices whom he knew. And then there would be highballs and stories, and he would hurry home to dinner a little late but feeling good, and a little sorry for the poor Standard Oil Company. On this evening as he entered he heard some one say : " Babbitt was in last night as full as a boiled owl."

Babbitt walked to the bar, and saw in the mirror that his face was as white as chalk. For the first time he had looked Truth in the eyes. Others had lied to him; he had dissembled with himself. He was a drunkard, and had not known it. What he had fondly imagined was a pleasant exhilaration had been maudlin intoxication. His fancied wit had been drivel, his gay humors nothing but the noisy vagaries of a sot. But, never again !

" A glass of seltzer," he said to the bartender.

A little silence fell upon the group of his cronies, who had been expecting him to join them.

" Going off the stuff, Bob ? " one of them asked politely and with more formality than the highballs ever called forth.

" Yes," said Babbitt.

Some one of the group took up the unwashed thread of a story he had been telling; the bartender shoved over a dime and a nickel change from the quarter, ungarnished with his customary smile; and Babbitt walked out.

Now, Babbitt had a home and a wife—but that is another story. And I will tell you that story, which will show you a better habit and a worse story than you could find in the man who invented the phrase.

It began away up in Sullivan County, where so many rivers and so much trouble begins—or begin; how would say that ? It was July, and Jessie was a summer boarder at the Mountain Squint Hotel, and Bob, who was just out of college, saw her one day— and they were married in September. That's the tabloid novel— one swallow of water, and it's gone.

But those July days !

Let the exclamation point expound it, for I shall not. For particulars you might read up on " Romeo and Juliet," and Abraham Lincoln's thrilling sonnet about " You can fool some of the people," &c., and Darwin's works.

But one thing I must tell you about. Both of them were made over Omar's Rubaiyat. They knew every verse of the old bluffer by heart—not consecutively, but picking 'em out here and there as you fork the mushrooms in a fifty-cent steak à la Bordelaise. Sullivan County is full of rocks and trees; and Jessie used to sit on them, and—please be good—used to sit on the rocks; and Bob had a way of standing behind her with his hands over her shoulders holding her hands, and his face close to hers, and they would repeat over and over their favorite verses of the old tent-maker. They saw only the poetry and philosophy of the lines then—indeed, they agreed that the Wine was only an image, and that what was meant to be celebrated was some divinity, or maybe Love or Life. However, at that time neither of them had tasted the stuff that goes with a sixty-cent *table d'hôte*.

Where was I ? Oh, they married and came to New York. Bob showed his college diploma, and accepted a position filling ink-stands in a lawyer's office at $15 a week. At the end of two years he had worked up to $50, and gotten his first taste of Bohemia— the kind that won't stand the borax and formaldehyde tests.

They had two furnished rooms and a little kitchen. To Jess, accustomed to the mild but beautiful savor of a country town, the dreggy Bohemia was sugar and spice. She hung fish seines on the walls of her rooms, and bought a rakish-looking sideboard, and learned to play the banjo. Twice or thrice a week they dined at French or Italian *tables d'hôte* in a cloud of smoke, and brag and unshorn hair. Jess learned to drink a cocktail in order to get the cherry. At home she smoked a cigarette after dinner. She learned to pronounce Chianti, and leave her olive stones for the waiter to pick up. Once she essayed to say la, la la ! in a crowd but got only as far as the second one. They met one or two couples while dining out and became friendly with them. The sideboard was stocked with Scotch and rye and a liqueur. They had their new friends in to dinner and all were laughing at nothing by 1 A. M. Some plastering fell in the room below them, for which Bob had to pay $4.50. Thus they footed it merrily on the ragged frontiers of the country that has no boundary lines or government.

And soon Bob fell in with his cronies and learned to keep his foot on the little rail six inches above the floor for an hour or so every afternoon before he went home. Drink always rubbed him the right way, and he would reach his rooms as jolly as a sandboy. Jessie would meet him at the door, and generally they would dance some insane kind of a rigadoon about the floor by way of greeting. Once when Bob's feet became confused and he tumbled headlong over a foot-stool Jessie laughed so heartily and long that he had to throw all the couch pillows at her to make her hush.

In such wise life was speeding for them on the day when Bob Babbitt first felt the power that the giftie gi'ed him.

But let us get back to our lamb and mint sauce.

When Bob got home that evening he found Jessie in a long apron cutting up a lobster for the Newburg. Usually when Bob came in mellow from his hour at the bar his welcome was hilarious, though somewhat tinctured with Scotch smoke.

By screams and snatches of song and certain audible testimonials of domestic felicity was his advent proclaimed. When she heard his foot on the stairs the old maid in the hall room always stuffed cotton into her ears. At first Jessie had shrunk from the rudeness and flavor of these spiritual greetings, but as the fog of the false Bohemia gradually encompassed her she came to accept them as love's true and proper greeting.

Bob came in without a word, smiled, kissed her neatly but noiselessly, took up a paper and sat down. In the hall room the old maid held her two plugs of cotton poised, filled with anxiety.

Jessie dropped lobster and knife and ran to him with frightened eyes.

" What's the matter, Bob, are you ill ? "

" Not at all, dear."

" Then what's the matter with you ? "

" Nothing."

Hearken, brethren. When She-who-has-a-right-to-ask interrogates you concerning a change she finds in your mood answer her thus : Tell her that you, in a sudden rage, have murdered your grandmother; tell her that you have robbed orphans and that remorse has stricken you; tell her your fortune is swept away; that you are beset by enemies, by bunions, by any kind of malevolent fate; but do not, if peace and happiness are worth as much as a grain of mustard seed to you—do not answer her " Nothing."

Jessie went back to the lobster in silence. She cast looks of darkest suspicion at Bob. He had never acted that way before.

When the dinner was on the table she set out the bottle of Scotch and the glasses. Bob declined. " Tell you the truth, Jess," he said. " I've cut out the drink. Help yourself, of course. If you don't mind I'll try some of the seltzer straight."

" You've stopped drinking ? " she said, looking at him steadily and unsmilingly. " What for ? "

" It wasn't doing me any good," said Bob. " Don't you approve of the idea ? "

Jessie raised her eyebrows and one shoulder slightly.

" Entirely," she said with a sculptured smile. " I could not conscientiously advise any one to drink or smoke, or whistle on Sunday."

The meal was finished almost in silence. Bob tried to make talk, but his efforts lacked the stimulus of previous evenings. He felt miserable, and once or twice his eye wandered toward the bottle, but each time the scathing words of his bibulous friend sounded in his ear, and his mouth set with determination.

Jessie felt the change deeply. The essence of their lives seemed to have departed suddenly. The restless fever, the false gayety, the

unnatural excitement of the shoddy Bohemia in which they lived
had dropped away in the space of the popping of a cork. She stole
curious and forlorn glances at the dejected Bob, who bore the
guilty look of at least a wife-beater or a family tyrant.

After dinner the colored maid who came in daily to perform such
chores cleared away the things. Jessie, with an unreadable countenance, brought back the bottle of Scotch and the glasses and a
bowl of cracked ice and set them on the table.

"May I ask," she said, with some of the ice in her tones,
"whether I am to be included in your sudden spasm of goodness?
If not, I'll make one for myself. It's rather chilly this evening, for
some reason."

"Oh, come now, Jess," said Bob, good-naturedly, "don't be
too rough on me. Help yourself, by all means. There's no danger
of your overdoing it. But I thought there was with me; and that's
why I quit. Have yours, and then let's get out the banjo and try
over that new quickstep."

"I've heard," said Jessie in the tones of the oracle, "that
drinking alone is a pernicious habit. No, I don't think I feel like
playing this evening. If we are going to reform we may as well
abandon the evil habit of banjo-playing, too."

She took up a book and sat in her little willow rocker on the
other side of the table. Neither of them spoke for half an hour.

And then Bob laid down his paper and got up with a strange,
absent look on his face and went behind her chair and reached
over her shoulders, taking her hands in his, and laid his face close
to hers.

In a moment to Jessie the walls of the seine-hung room vanished,
and she saw the Sullivan County hills and rills. Bob felt her hands
quiver in his as he began the verse from Old Omar:

> "Come, fill the Cup, and in the Fire of Spring
>   The Winter Garment of Repentance fling:
> The Bird of Time has but a little way
>   To fly—and Lo! the Bird is on the Wing!"

And then he walked to the table and poured a stiff drink of
Scotch into a glass.

But in that moment a mountain breeze had somehow found its
way in and blown away the mist of the false Bohemia.

Jessie leaped and with one fierce sweep of her hand sent the
bottle and glasses crashing to the floor. The same motion of her
arm carried it around Bob's neck, where it met its mate and fastened
tight.

"Oh, my God, Bobbie—not that verse—I see now. I wasn't
always such a fool, was I? The other one, boy—the one that says:

' Remould it to the Heart's Desire.' Say that one—' to the Heart's Desire.' "

" I know that one," said Bob. " It goes :

> " Ah ! Love, could you and I with Him conspire
> To grasp this sorry Scheme of Things entire
> Would not we——"

" Let me finish it," said Jessie.

> " Would not we shatter it to bits—and then
> Remould it nearer to the Heart's Desire ! "

" It's shattered all right," said Bob, crunching some glass under his heel.

In some dungeon below the accurate ear of Mrs. Pickens, the landlady, located the smash.

" It's that wild Mr. Babbitt coming home soused again," she said. "And he's got such a nice little wife, too ! "

THE PENDULUM

" EIGHTY-FIRST STREET—let 'em out, please," yelled the shepherd in blue.

A flock of citizen sheep scrambled out and another flock scrambled aboard. Ding-ding ! The cattle cars of the Manhattan Elevated rattled away, and John Perkins drifted down the stairway of the station with the released flock.

John walked slowly toward his flat. Slowly, because in the lexicon of his daily life there was no such word as " perhaps." There are no surprises awaiting a man who has been married two years and lives in a flat. As he walked John Perkins prophesied to himself with gloomy and downtrodden cynicism the foregone conclusions of the monotonous day.

Katy would meet him at the door with a kiss flavored with cold cream and butter-scotch. He would remove his coat, sit upon a macadamized lounge and read, in the evening paper, of Russians and Japs slaughtered by the deadly linotype. For dinner there would be pot roast, a salad flavored with a dressing warranted not to crack or injure the leather, stewed rhubarb and the bottle of strawberry marmalade blushing at the certificate of chemical purity on its lable. After dinner Katy would show him the new patch in her crazy quilt that the iceman had cut for her off the end of his four-in-hand. At half-past seven they would spread newspapers over the furniture to catch the pieces of plastering that fell when the fat man in the flat overhead began to take his physical culture exercises. Exactly at eight Hickey & Mooney, of the vaudeville team (unbooked) in the flat across the hall, would yield to the gentle influence of delirium tremens and begin to overturn chairs under the delusion that Hammerstein was pursuing them with a five-hundred-dollar-a-week contract. Then the gent at the window across the air-shaft would get out his flute; the nightly gas leak would steal forth to frolic in the highways; the dumb-waiter would slip off its trolley; the janitor would drive Mrs. Zanowitski's five children once more across the Yalu; the lady with the champagne shoes and the Skye terrier would trip down-stairs and paste her Thursday name over her bell and letter-box —and the evening routine of the Frogmore flats would be under way.

John Perkins knew these things would happen. And he knew that at a quarter past eight he would summon his nerve and reach for his hat, and that his wife would deliver this speech in a querulous tone :

" Now, where are you going, I'd like to know, John Perkins ? "

" Thought I'd drop up to McCloskey's," he would answer, " and play a game or two of pool with the fellows."

Of late such had been John Perkins's habit. At ten or eleven he would return. Sometimes Katy would be asleep; sometimes waiting up, ready to melt in the crucible of her ire a little more gold plating from the wrought steel chains of matrimony. For these things Cupid will have to answer when he stands at the bar of justice with his victims from the Frogmore flats.

To-night John Perkins encountered a tremendous upheaval of the commonplace when he reached his door. No Katy was there with her affectionate, confectionate kiss. The three rooms seemed in portentous disorder. All about lay her things in confusion. Shoes in the middle of the floor, curling tongs, hair bows, kimonos, powder box, jumbled together on dresser and chairs—this was not Katy's way. With a sinking heart John saw the comb with a curling cloud of her brown hair among its teeth. Some unusual hurry and perturbation must have possessed her, for she always carefully placed these combings in the little blue vase on the mantel to be some day formed into the coveted feminine " rat."

Hanging conspicuously to the gas jet by a string was a folded paper. John seized it. It was a note from his wife running thus :

DEAR JOHN :

I just had a telegram saying mother is very sick. I am going to take the 4 : 30 train. Brother Sam is going to meet me at the depot there. There is cold mutton in the icebox. I hope it isn't her quinzy

again. Pay the milkman 50 cents. She had it bad last spring.
Don't forget to write to the company about the gas meter, and
your good socks are in the top drawer. I will write to-morrow.

Hastily,

KATY.

Never during their two years of matrimony had he and Katy
been separated for a night. John read the note over and over in
a dumbfounded way. Here was a break in a routine that had never
varied, and it left him dazed.

There on the back of a chair hung, pathetically empty and
formless, the red wrapper with black dots that she always wore
while getting the meals. Her week-day clothes had been tossed
here and there in her haste. A little paper bag of her favorite
butter-scotch lay with its string yet unwound. A daily paper
sprawled on the floor, gaping rectangularly where a railroad time-
table had been clipped from it. Everything in the room spoke of
a loss, of an essence gone, of its soul and life departed. John
Perkins stood among the dead remains with a queer feeling of
desolation in his heart.

He began to set the rooms tidy as well as he could. When he
touched her clothes a thrill of something like terror went through
him. He had never thought what existence would be without Katy.
She had become so thoroughly annealed into his life that she was
like the air he breathed—necessary but scarcely noticed. Now,
without warning, she was gone, vanished, as completely absent as
if she had never existed. Of course it would be only for a few days,
or at most a week or two, but it seemed to him as if the very hand
of death had pointed a finger at his secure and uneventful home.

John dragged the cold mutton from the ice-box, made coffee,
and sat down to a lonely meal face to face with the strawberry
marmalade's shameless certificate of purity. Bright among withdrawn blessings now appeared to him the ghosts of pot roasts and
the salad with tan polish dressing. His home was dismantled. A
quinzied mother-in-law had knocked his lares and penates sky-
high. After his solitary meal John sat at a front window.

He did not care to smoke. Outside the city roared to him to
come join in its dance of folly and pleasure. The night was his.
He might go forth unquestioned and thrum the strings of jollity
as free as any gay bachelor there. He might carouse and wander
and have his fling until dawn if he liked; and there would be no
wrathful Katy waiting for him, bearing the chalice that held the
dregs of his joy. He might play pool at McCloskey's with his
roistering friends until Aurora dimmed the electric bulbs if he
chose. The hymeneal strings that had curbed him always when the

Frogmore flats had palled upon him were loosened. Katy was gone.

John Perkins was not accustomed to analyzing his emotions. But as he sat in his Katy-bereft 10 x 12 parlor he hit unerringly upon the keynote of his discomfort. He knew now that Katy was necessary to his happiness. His feeling for her, lulled into unconsciousness by the dull round of domesticity, had been sharply stirred by the loss of her presence. Has it not been dinned into us by proverb and sermon and fable that we never prize the music till the sweet-voiced bird has flown—or in other no less florid and true utterances?

"I'm a double-dyed dub," mused John Perkins, "the way I've been treating Katy. Off every night playing pool and bumming with the boys instead of staying home with her. The poor girl here all alone with nothing to amuse her, and me acting that way! John Perkins, you're the worst kind of a shine. I'm going to make it up for the little girl. I'll take her out and let her see some amusement. And I'll cut out the McCloskey gang right from this minute."

Yes, there was the city roaring outside for John Perkins to come dance in the train of Momus. And at McCloskey's the boys were knocking the balls idly into the pockets against the hour for the nightly game. But no primrose way nor clicking cue could woo the remorseful soul of Perkins the bereft. The thing that was his, lightly held and half scorned, had been taken away from him, and he wanted it. Backward to a certain man named Adam, whom the cherubim bounced from the orchard, could Perkins, the remorseful, trace his descent.

Near the right hand of John Perkins stood a chair. On the back of it stood Katy's blue shirtwaist. It still retained something of her contour. Midway of the sleeves were fine, individual wrinkles made by the movements of her arms in working for his comfort and pleasure. A delicate but impelling odor of bluebells came from it. John took it and looked long and soberly at the unresponsive grenadine. Katy had never been unresponsive. Tears:—yes, tears—came into John Perkins's eyes. When she came back things would be different. He would make up for all his neglect. What was life without her?

The door opened. Katy walked in carrying a little hand satchel. John stared at her stupidly.

"My! I'm glad to get back," said Katy. "Ma wasn't sick to amount to anything. Sam was at the depot, and said she just had a little spell, and got all right soon after they telegraphed. So I took the next train back. I'm just dying for a cup of coffee."

Nobody heard the click and rattle of the cogwheels as the third-floor-front of the Frogmore flats buzzed its machinery back into the Order of Things. A band slipped, a spring was touched, the gear was adjusted and the wheels revolve in their old orbit.

John Perkins looked at the clock. It was 8.15. He reached for his hat and walked to the door.

"Now, where are you going, I'd like to know, John Perkins?" asked Katy, in a querulous tone.

"Thought I'd drop up to McCloskey's," said John, "and play a game or two of pool with the fellows."

TWO THANKSGIVING DAY GENTLEMEN

THERE is one day that is ours. There is one day when all we Americans who are not self-made go back to the old home to eat saleratus biscuits and marvel how much nearer to the porch the old pump looks than it used to. Bless the day. President Roosevelt gives it to us. We hear some talk of the Puritans, but don't just remember who they were. Bet we can lick 'em, anyhow, if they try to land again. Plymouth Rocks? Well, that sounds more familiar. Lots of us have had to come down to hens since the Turkey Trust got its work in. But somebody in Washington is leaking out advance information to 'em about these Thanksgiving proclamations.

The big city east of the cranberry bogs has made Thanksgiving Day an institution. The last Thursday in November is the only day in the year on which it recognizes the part of America lying across the ferries. It is the one day that is purely American. Yes, a day of celebration, exclusively American.

And now for the story which is to prove to you that we have traditions on this side of the ocean that are becoming older at a much rapider rate than those of England are—thanks to our git-up and enterprise.

Stuffy Pete took his seat on the third bench to the right as you enter Union Square from the east, at the walk opposite the fountain. Every Thanksgiving Day for nine years he had taken his seat there promptly at 1 o'clock. For every time he had done so things had happened to him—Charles Dickensy things that swelled his waist-coat above his heart, and equally on the other side.

But to-day Stuffy Pete's appearance at the annual trysting place seemed to have been rather the result of habit than of the yearly hunger which, as the philanthropists seem to think, afflicts the poor at such extended intervals.

Certainly Pete was not hungry. He had just come from a feast that had left him of his powers barely those of respiration and locomotion. His eyes were like two pale gooseberries firmly imbedded in a swollen and gravy-smeared mask of putty. His breath came in short wheezes; a senatorial roll of adipose tissue denied a fashionable set to his upturned coat collar. Buttons that had been sewed upon his clothes by kind Salvation fingers a week before flew like popcorn, strewing the earth around him. Ragged he was, with a split shirt front open to the wishbone; but the November breeze, carrying fine snowflakes, brought him only a grateful coolness. For Stuffy Pete was overcharged with the caloric produced by a super-bountiful dinner. beginning with oysters and ending with plum pudding, and including (it seemed to him) all the roast turkey and baked potatoes and chicken salad and squash pie and ice cream in the world. Wherefore he sat, gorged, and gazed upon the world with after-dinner contempt.

The meal had been an unexpected one. He was passing a red brick mansion near the beginning of Fifth Avenue, in which lived two old ladies of ancient family and a reverence for traditions. They even denied the existence of New York, and believed that Thanksgiving Day was declared solely for Washington Square. One of their traditional habits was to station a servant at the postern gate with orders to admit the first hungry wayfarer that came along after the hour of noon had struck, and banquet him to a finish. Stuffy Pete happened to pass by on his way to the park, and the seneschals gathered him in and upheld the custom of the castle.

After Stuffy Pete had gazed straight before him for ten minutes he was conscious of a desire for a more varied field of vision. With a tremendous effort he moved his head slowly to the left. And then his eyes bulged out fearfully, and his breath ceased, and the rough-shod ends of his short legs wriggled and rustled on the gravel.

For the Old Gentleman was coming across Fourth Avenue toward his bench.

Every Thanksgiving Day for nine years the Old Gentleman had come there and found Stuffy Pete on his bench. That was a thing that the Old Gentleman was trying to make a tradition of. Every Thanksgiving Day for nine years he had found Stuffy there, and had led him to a restaurant and watched him eat a big dinner. They do those things in England unconsciously. But this is a young country, and nine years is not so bad. The Old Gentleman was a stanch American patriot, and considered himself a pioneer in American tradition. In order to become picturesque we must keep on doing one thing for a long time without ever letting it get away from us. Something like collecting the weekly dimes in industrial insurance. Or cleaning the streets.

The Old Gentleman moved, straight and stately, toward the

Institution that he was rearing. Truly, the annual feeling of Stuffy Pete was nothing national in its character, such as the Magna Charta or jam for breakfast was in England. But it was a step. It was almost feudal. It showed, at least, that a Custom was not impossible to New Y—ahem !—America.

The Old Gentleman was thin and tall and sixty. He was dressed all in black, and wore the old-fashioned kind of glasses that won't stay on your nose. His hair was whiter and thinner than it had been last year, and he seemed to make more use of his big, knobby cane with the crooked handle.

As his established benefactor came up Stuffy wheezed and shuddered like some woman's over-fat pug when a street dog bristles up at him. He would have flown, but all the skill of Santos-Dumont could not have separated him from his bench. Well had the myrmidons of the two old ladies done their work.

" Good morning," said the Old Gentleman. " I am glad to perceive that the vicissitudes of another year have spared you to move in health about the beautiful world. For that blessing alone this day of thanksgiving is well proclaimed to each of us. If you will come with me, my man, I will provide you with a dinner that should make your physical being accord with the mental."

That is what the Old Gentleman said every time. Every Thanksgiving Day for nine years. The words themselves almost formed an Institution. Nothing could be compared with them except the Declaration of Independence. Always before they had been music in Stuffy's ears. But now he looked up at the Old Gentleman's face with tearful agony in his own. The fine snow almost sizzled when it fell upon his perspiring brow. But the Old Gentleman shivered a little and turned his back to the wind.

Stuffy had always wondered why the Old Gentleman spoke his speech rather sadly. He did not know that it was because he was wishing every time that he had a son to succeed him. A son who would come there after he was gone—a son who would stand proud and strong before some subsequent Stuffy, and say : " In memory of my father." Then it would be an Institution.

But the Old Gentleman had no relatives. He lived in rented rooms in one of the decayed old family brownstone mansions in one of the quiet streets east of the park. In the winter he raised fuchsias in a little conservatory the size of a steamer trunk. In the spring he walked in the Easter parade. In the summer he lived at a farm-house in the New Jersey hills, and sat in a wicker armchair, speaking of a butterfly, the ornithoptera amphrisius, that he hoped to find some day. In the autumn he fed Stuffy a dinner. These were the Old Gentleman's occupations.

Stuffy Pete looked up at him for a half minute, stewing and

helpless in his own self-pity. The Old Gentleman's eyes were bright with the giving-pleasure. His face was getting more lined each year, but his little black necktie was in as jaunty a bow as ever, and his linen was beautiful and white, and his gray mustache was curled gracefully at the ends. And then Stuffy made a noise that sounded like peas bubbling in a pot. Speech was intended; and as the Old Gentleman had heard the sounds nine times before, he rightly construed them into Stuffy's old formula of acceptance.

"Thankee, sir. I'll go with ye, and much obliged. I'm very hungry, sir."

The coma of repletion had not prevented from entering Stuffy's mind the conviction that he was the basis of an Institution. His Thanksgiving appetite was not his own; it belonged by all the sacred rights of established custom, if not by the actual Statute of Limitations, to this kind old gentleman who had pre-empted it. True, America is free; but in order to establish tradition some one must be a repetend—a repeating decimal. The heroes are not all heroes of steel and gold. See one here that wielded only weapons of iron, bady silvered, and tin.

The Old Gentleman led his annual protégé southward to the restaurant, and to the table where the feast had always occurred. They were recognized.

"Here comes de old guy," said a waiter, "dat blows dat same bum to a meal every Thanksgiving."

The Old Gentleman sat across the table glowing like a smoked pearl at his corner-stone of future ancient Tradition. The waiters heaped the table with holiday food—and Stuffy, with a sigh that was mistaken for hunger's expression, raised knife and fork and carved for himself a crown of imperishable bay.

No more valiant hero ever fought his way through the ranks of of an enemy. Turkey, chops, soups, vegetables, pies, disappeared before him as fast as they could be served. Gorged nearly to the uttermost when he entered the restaurant, the smell of food had almost caused him to lose his honor as a gentleman, but he rallied like a true knight. He saw the look of beneficent happiness on the Old Gentleman's face—a happier look than even the fuchsias and the ornithoptera amphrisius had ever brought to it—and he had not the heart to see it wane.

In an hour Stuffy leaned back with a battle won.

"Thankee kindly, sir," he puffed like a leaky steam pipe; "thankee kindly for a hearty meal."

Then he arose heavily with glazed eyes and started toward the kitchen. A waiter turned him about like a top, and pointed him toward the door. The Old Gentleman carefully counted out $1.30 in silver change, leaving three nickels for the waiter.

They parted as they did each year at the door, the Old Gentleman going south, Stuffy north.

Around the first corner Stuffy turned, and stood for one minute. Then he seemed to puff out his rags as an owl puffs out his feathers, and fell to the sidewalk like a sunstricken horse.

When the ambulance came the young surgeon and the driver cursed softly at his weight. There was no smell of whiskey to justify a transfer to the patrol wagon, so Stuffy and his two dinners went to the hospital. There they stretched him on a bed and began to test him for strange diseases, with the hope of getting a chance at some problem with the bare steel.

And lo! an hour later another ambulance brought the Old Gentleman. And they laid him on another bed and spoke of appendicitis, for he looked good for the bill.

But pretty soon one of the young doctors met one of the young nurses whose eyes he liked, and stopped to chat with her about the cases.

"That nice old gentleman over there, now," he said, "you wouldn't think that was a case of almost starvation. Proud old family, I guess. He told me he hadn't eaten a thing for three days."

THE ASSESSOR OF SUCCESS

HASTINGS BEAUCHAMP MORLEY sauntered across Union Square with a pitying look at the hundreds that lolled upon the park benches. They were a motley lot, he thought; the men with stolid, animal, unshaven faces; the women wriggling and self-conscious, twining and untwining their feet that hung four inches above the gravelled walks.

Were I Mr. Carnegie or Mr. Rockefeller I would put a few millions in my inside pocket and make an appointment with all the Park Commissioners (around the corner, if necessary) and arrange for benches in all the parks of the world low enough for women to sit upon, and rest their feet upon the ground. After that I might furnish libraries to towns that would pay for 'em, or build sanitariums for crank professors, and call 'em colleges, if I wanted to.

Women's rights societies have been laboring for many years after equality with man. With what result? When they sit on a bench they must twist their ankles together and uncomfortably swing their highest French heels clear of earthly support. Begin at the bottom, ladies. Get your feet on the ground, and then rise to theories of mental quality.

Hastings Beauchamp Morley was carefully and neatly dressed. That was the result of an instinct due to his birth and breeding. It is denied us to look further into a man's bosom than the starch on his shirt front; so it is left to us only to recount his walks and conversation.

Morley had not a cent in his pockets; but he smiled pityingly at a hundred grimy, unfortunate ones who had no more, and who would have no more when the sun's first rays yellowed the tall paper-cutter building on the west side of the square. But Morley would have enough by them. Sundown had seen his pockets empty before; but sunrise had always seen them lined.

First he went to the house of a clergyman off Madison Avenue and presented a forged letter of introduction that holily purported to issue from a pastorate in Indiana. This netted him $5 when backed up by a realistic romance of a delayed remittance.

On the sidewalk, twenty steps from the clergyman's door, a pale-faced, fat man huskily enveloped him with a raised red fist and the voice of a bell buoy, demanding payment of an old score.

" Why, Bergman, man," sang Morley, dulcetly, " is this you ? I was just on my way up to your place to settle up. That remittance from my aunt arrived only this morning. Wrong address was the trouble. Come up to the corner and I'll square up. Glad to see you. Saves me a walk."

Four drinks placated the emotional Bergman. There was an air about Morley when he was backed by money in hand that would have stayed off a call loan at Rothschilds'. When he was penniless his bluff was pitched half a tone lower, but few were competent to detect the difference in the notes.

" You gum to mine blace and bay me tomorrow, Mr. Morley," said Bergman. " Oxcuse me dat I dun you on der street. But I haf not seen you in dree mont'. Pros't ! "

Morley walked away with a crooked smile on his pale, smooth face. The credulous, drink-softened German amused him. He would have to avoid Twenty-ninth Street in the future. He had not been aware that Bergman ever went home by that route.

At the door of a darkened house two squares to the north Morley knocked with a peculiar sequence of raps. The door opened to the length of a six-inch chain, and the pompous, important black face of an African guardian imposed itself in the opening. Morley was admitted.

In a third-story room, in an atmosphere opaque with smoke, he hung for ten minutes above a roulette wheel. Then downstairs he crept, and was out-sped by the important Negro, jingling in his pocket the 40 cents in silver that remained to him of his five-dollar capital. At the corner he lingered, undecided.

Across the street was a drug store, well lighted, sending forth gleams from the German silver and crystal of its soda fountain and glasses. Along came a youngster of five, headed for the dispensary, stepping high with the consequence of a big errand, possibly one to which his advancing age had earned him promotion. In his hand he clutched something tightly, publicly, proudly, conspicuously.

Morley stopped him with his winning smile and soft speech.

" Me ? " said the youngster. " I'm doin' to the drug 'tore for Mamma. She gave me a dollar to buy a bottle of med'cin."

" Now, now, now ! " said Morley. " Such a big man you are to be doing errands for Mamma. I must go along with my little man to see that the cars don't run over him. And on the way we'll have some chocolates. Or would he rather have lemon drops ? "

Morley entered the drug store leading the child by the hand. He presented the prescription that had been wrapped around the money.

On his face was a smile, predatory, parental, polite, profound.

"Aqua pura, one pint," said he to the druggist. " Sodium chloride, ten grains. Fiat solution. And don't try to skin me, because I know all about the number of gallons of H_2O in the Croton reservoir, and I always use the other ingredient on my potatoes."

" Fifteen cents," said the druggist, with a wink, after he had compounded the order. " I see you understand pharmacy. A dollar is the regular price."

" To gulls," said Morley, smilingly.

He settled the wrapped bottle carefully in the child's arms and escorted him to the corner. In his own pocket he dropped the 85 cents accruing to him by virtue of his chemical knowledge.

" Look out for the cars, sonny," he said, cheerfully, to his small victim.

Two street cars suddenly swooped in opposite directions upon the youngster. Morley dashed between them and pinned the infantile messenger by the neck, holding him in safety. Then from the corner of his street he sent him on his way, swindled, happy, and sticky with vile, cheap candy from the Italian's fruit stand.

Morley went to a restaurant and ordered a sirloin and a pint of inexpensive Château Breuille. He laughed noiselessly, but so genuinely that the waiter ventured to premise that good news had come his way.

" Why, no," said Morley, who seldom held conversation with any one. " It is not that. It is something else that amuses me. Do you know what three diversions of people are easiest to overreach in transactions of all kinds ? "

" Sure," said the waiter, calculating the size of the tip promised by the careful knot of Morley's tie; " there's the buyers from the dry goods stores in the South during August, and honeymooners from Staten Island, and——"

" Wrong ! " said Morley, chuckling happily. " The answer is just—men, women, and children. The world—well, say New York and as far as summer boarders can swim out from Long Island— is full of greenhorns. Two minutes longer on the broiler would have made this steak fit to be eaten by a gentleman, François."

" If yez t'inks it's on de bum," said the waiter, " Oi'll——"

Morley lifted his hand in protest—slightly martyred protest.

" It will do," he said, magnanimously. "And now, green Chartreuse, frappé and a demitasse."

Morley went out leisurely and stood on a corner where two tradeful arteries of the city cross. With a solitary dime in his pocket, he stood on the curb watching with confident, cynical, smiling eyes the tides of people that flowed past him. Into that stream he must cast his net and draw fish for his further sustenance and need. Good Izaak Walton had not the half of his self-reliance and bait-lore.

A joyful party of four—two women and two men—fell upon him with cries of delight. There was a dinner party on—where had he been for a fortnight past ?—what luck to thus run upon him ! They surrounded and engulfed him—he must join them—tra la la—and the rest.

One with a white hat plume curving to the shoulder touched his sleeve, and cast at the others a triumphant look that said : " See what I can do with him ? " and added her queen's command to the invitations.

" I leave you to imagine," said Morley, pathetically, " how it desolates me to forego the pleasure. But my friend Carruthers, of the New York Yacht Club, is to pick me up here in his motor car at 8."

The white plume tossed, and the quartet danced like midges around an arc light down the frolicsome way.

Morley stood, turning over and over the dime in his pocket and laughing gleefully to himself.

" 'Front,' " he chanted under his breath; " 'front' does it. It is trumps in the game. How they take it in ! Men, women, and children—forgeries, water-and-salt lies—how they all take it in ! "

An old man with an ill-fitting suit, a straggling gray beard, and a corpulent umbrella hopped from the conglomeration of cabs and street cars to the side-walk at Morley's side.

" Stranger," said he, " excuse me for troubling you, but do you know anybody in this here town named Solomon Smothers ? He's my son, and I've come down from Ellenville to visit him. Be darned if I know what I done with his street and number."

" I do not, sir," said Morley, half closing his eyes to veil the joy in them. " You had better apply to the police."

" The police ! " said the old man. " I ain't done nothin' to call in the police about. I just come down to see Ben. He lives in a five-story house, he writes me. If you know anybody by that name and could——"

" I told you I did not," said Morely, coldly. " I know no one by the name of Smithers, and I advise you to——"

" Smothers not Smithers," interrupted the old man, hopefully. "A heavy-set man, sandy complected, about twenty-nine, two front teeth out, about five foot——"

" Oh, ' Smothers !' " exclaimed Morley. " Sol Smothers ? Why, he lives in the next house to me. I thought you said ' Smithers.' "

Morley looked at his watch. You must have a watch. You can do it for a dollar. Better go hungry than forego a gunmetal or the ninety-eight-cent one that the railroads—according to these watch-makers—are run by.

" The Bishop of Long Island," said Morley, " was to meet me here at 8 to dine with me at the Kingfishers' Club. But I can't leave the father of my friend Sol Smothers alone on the street. By St. Swithin, Mr. Smothers, we Wall Street men have to work ! Tired is no name for it ! I was about to step across to the other corner and have a glass of ginger ale with a dash of sherry when you approached me. You must let me take you to Sol's house, Mr. Smothers. But before we take the car I hope you will join me in——"

An hour later Morley seated himself on the end of a quiet bench in Madison Square, with a twenty-five-cent cigar between his lips and $140 in deeply creased bills in his inside pocket. Content, light-hearted, ironical, keenly philosophic, he watched the moon drifting in and out amidst a maze of flying clouds. An old, ragged man with a low-bowed head sat at the other end of the bench.

Presently the old man stirred and looked at his bench companion. In Morley's appearance he seemed to recognize something superior to the usual nightly occupants of the benches.

" Kind sir," he whined, " if you could spare a dime or even a few pennies to one who——"

Morley cut short his stereotyped appeal by throwing him a dollar.

" God bless you ! " said the old man. " I've been trying to find work for——"

" Work ! " echoed Morley with his ringing laugh. " You are a fool, my friend. The world is a rock to you, no doubt; but you must be an Aaron and smite it with your rod. Then things better than water will gush out of it for you. That is what the world is for. It gives to me whatever I want from it."

" God has blessed you," said the old man. " It is only work that I have known. And now I can get no more."

" I must go home," said Morley, rising and buttoning his coat. " I stopped here only for a smoke. I hope you may find work."

" May your kindness be rewarded this night," said the old man.

" Oh," said Morley, " you have your wish already. I am satisfied. I think good luck follows me like a dog. I am for yonder bright hotel across the square for the night. And what a moon that is lighting up the city to-night. I think no one enjoys the moonlight and such little things as I do. Well, a good-night to you."

Morley walked to the corner where he would cross to his hotel He blew slow streams of smoke from his cigar heavenward. A policeman passing saluted to his benign nod. What a fine moon it was.

The clock struck nine as a girl just entering womanhood stopped on the corner waiting for the approaching car. She was hurrying as if homeward from employment or delay. Her eyes were clear and pure, she was dressed in simple white, she looked eagerly for the car and neither to the right nor the left.

Morley knew her. Eight years before he had sat on the same bench with her at school. There had been no sentiment between them—nothing but the friendship of innocent days.

But he turned down the side street to a quiet spot and laid his suddenly burning face against the cool iron of a lamp-post, and said dully :

" God ! I wish I could die."

THE BUYER FROM CACTUS CITY

IT is well that hay fever and colds do not obtain in the healthful vicinity of Cactus City, Texas, for the dry goods emporium of Navarro & Platt, situated there, is not to be sneezed at.

Twenty thousand people in Cactus City scatter their silver coin with liberal hands for the things that their hearts desire. The bulk of this semi-precious metal goes to Navarro & Platt. Their huge brick building covers enough ground to graze a dozen head of sheep. You can buy of them a rattlesnake-skin necktie, an automobile, or an eighty-five dollar, latest style, lady's tan coat in twenty different shades. Navarro & Platt first introduced pennies west of the Colorado River. They had been ranchmen with business heads, who saw that the world did not necessarily have to cease its revolutions after free grass went out.

Every Spring, Navarro, senior partner, fifty-five, half-Spanish, cosmopolitan, able, polished, had " gone on " to New York to buy goods. This year he shied at taking up the long trail. He was undoubtedly growing older; and he looked at his watch several times a day before the hour came for his siesta.

" John," he said, to his junior partner, " you shall go on this year to buy the goods."

Platt looked tired.

" I'm told," said he, " that New York is a plumb dead town; but I'll go. I can take a whirl in San Antone for a few days on my way and have some fun."

Two weeks later a man in a Texas full dress suit—black frock coat, broad-brimmed soft white hat, and lay-down collar 3-4 inch high, with black, wrought-iron necktie—entered the wholesale cloak and suit establishment of Zizzbaum & Son, on lower Broadway.

Old Zizzbaum had the eye of an osprey, the memory of an elephant, and a mind that unfolded from him in three movements like the puzzle of the carpenter's rule. He rolled to the front like a brunette polar bear, and shook Platt's hand.

"And how is the good Mr. Navarro in Texas ? " he said. " The trip was too long for him this year, so ? We welcome Mr. Platt instead."

" A bull's eye," said Platt, " and I'd give forty acres of unirrigated Pecos County land to know how you did it."

" I knew," grinned Zizzbaum, " just as I know that the rainfall in El Paso for the year was 28.5 inches, or an increase of 15 inches, and that therefore Navarro & Platt will buy a $15,000 stock of suits this spring instead of $10,000, as in a dry year. But that will be to-morrow. There is first a cigar in my private office that will remove from your mouth the taste of the ones you smuggle across the Rio Grande and like—because they are smuggled."

It was late in the afternoon and businesss for the day had ended. Zizzbaum left Platt with a half-smoked cigar, and came out of the private office to Son, who was arranging his diamond scarfpin before a mirror, ready to leave.

" Abey," he said, " you will have to take Mr. Platt around to-night and show him things. They are customers for ten years. Mr. Navarro and I we played chess every moment of spare time when he came. That is good, but Mr. Platt is a young man and this is his first visit to New York. He should amuse easily."

" All right," said Abey, screwing the guard tightly on his pin. " I'll take him on. After he's seen the Flatiron and the head waiter at the Hotel Astor and heard the phonograph play ' Under the Old Apple Tree ' it'll be half-past ten, and Mr. Texas will be ready to roll up in his blanket. I've got a supper engagement at 11 : 30, but he'll be all to the Mrs. Winslow before then."

The next morning at 10 Platt walked into the store ready to do business. He had a bunch of hyacinths pinned on his lapel. Zizzbaum himself waited on him. Navarro & Platt were good customers, and never failed to take their discount for cash.

" And what did you think of our little town ? " asked Zizzbaum, with the fatuous smile of the Manhattanite.

" I shouldn't care to live in it," said the Texan. " Your son and I knocked around quite a little last night. You've got good water, but Cactus City is better lit up."

" We've got a few lights on Broadway, don't you think, Mr. Platt ? "

" And a good many shadows," said Platt. " I think I like your horses best. I haven't seen a crowbait since I've been in town."

Zizzbaum led him up stairs to show the samples of suits.

" Ask Miss Asher to come," he said to a clerk.

Miss Asher came, and Platt, of Navarro & Platt, felt for the first time the wonderful bright light of romance and glory descend upon him. He stood still as a granite cliff above the cañon of the Colorado, with his wide-open eyes fixed upon her. She noticed his look and flushed a little, which was contrary to her custom.

Miss Asher was the crack model of Zizzbaum & Son. She was of the blond type known as " medium," and her measurements even went the required 38-25-42 standard a little better. She had been at Zizzbaum's two years, and knew her business. Her eye was bright, but cool; and had she chosen to match her gaze against the optic of the famed basilisk, that fabulous monster's gaze would have wavered and softened first. Incidently, she knew buyers.

" Now, Mr. Platt," said Zizzbaum, " I want you to see these princess gowns in the light shades. They will be the thing in your climate. This first, if you please, Miss Asher."

Swiftly in and out of the dressing-room the prize model flew, each time wearing a new costume and looking more stunning with every change. She posed with absolute self-possession before the stricken buyer, who stood, tongue-tied and motionless, while Zizzbaum orated oilily of the styles. On the model's face was her faint, impersonal professional smile that seemed to cover something like weariness or contempt.

When the display was over Platt seemed to hesitate. Zizzbaum was a little anxious, thinking that his customer might be inclined to try elsewhere. But Platt was only looking over in his mind the best building sites in Cactus City, trying to select one on which to build a house for his wife-to-be—who was just then in the dressing-room taking off an evening gown of lavender and tulle.

" Take your time, Mr. Platt," said Zizzbaum. " Think it over to-night. You won't find anybody else meet our prices on goods like these. I'm afraid you're having a dull time in New York, Mr. Platt. A young man like you—of course, you miss the society of the ladies. Wouldn't you like a nice young lady to take out for dinner this evening? Miss Asher, now, is a very nice young lady; she will make it agreeable for you."

" Why, she doesn't know me," said Platt, wonderingly. " She doesn't know anything about me. Would she go? I'm not acquainted with her."

" Would she go? " repeated Zizzbaum, with uplifted eyebrows. " Sure, she would go. I will introduce you. Sure, she would go."

He called Miss Asher loudly.

She came, calm and slightly contemptuous, in her white shirt waist and plain black skirt.

" Mr. Platt would like the pleasure of your company to dinner this evening," said Zizzbaum, walking away.

" Sure," said Miss Asher, looking at the ceiling. " I'd be much pleased. Nine-eleven West Twentieth Street. What time? "

" Say seven o'clock."

"All right, but please don't come ahead of time. I room with a school teacher, and she doesn't allow any gentleman to call in the room. There isn't any parlor, so you'll have to wait in the hall. I'll be ready."

At half-past seven Platt and Miss Asher sat at a table in a Broadway restaurant. She was dressed in a plain, filmy black. Platt didn't know that it was all a part of her day's work.

With the unobtrusive aid of a good waiter he managed to order a respectable dinner, minus the usual Broadway preliminaries.

Miss Asher flashed upon him a dazzling smile.

" Mayn't I have something to drink? " she asked.

" Why, certainly," said Platt. " Anything you want."

" A dry Martini," she said to the waiter.

When it was brought and set before her Platt reached over and took it away.

" What is this? " he asked.

" A cocktail, of course."

" I thought it was some kind of tea you ordered. This is liquor. You can't drink this. What is your first name? "

" To my intimate friends," said Miss Asher, freezingly, " it is ' Helen.' "

' Listen, Helen," said Platt, leaning over the table. " For many years every time the spring flowers blossomed out on the prairies

I got to thinking of somebody that I'd never seen or heard of. I knew it was you the minute I saw you yesterday. I'm going back home to-morrow, and you're going with me. I know it, for I saw it in your eyes when you first looked at me. You needn't kick, for you've got to fall into line. Here's a little trick I picked out for you on my way over."

He flicked a two-carat diamond solitaire ring across the table. Miss Asher flipped it back to him with her fork.

" Don't get fresh," she said, severely.

" I'm worth a hundred thousand dollars," said Platt. " I'll build you the finest house in west Texas."

" You can't buy me, Mr. Buyer," said Miss Asher, " if you had a hundred million. I didn't think I'd have to call you down. You didn't look like the others to me at first, but I see you're all alike."

" All who ? " asked Platt.

" All you buyers. You think because we girls have to go out to dinner with you or lose our jobs that you're privileged to say what you please. Well, forget it. I thought you were different from the others, but I see I was mistaken."

Platt struck his fingers on the table with a gesture of sudden, illuminating satisfaction.

" I've got it ! " he exclaimed, almost hilariously—" the Nicholson place, over on the north side. There's a big grove of live oaks and a natural lake. The old house can be pulled down and the new one set further back."

" Put out your pipe," said Miss Asher. " I'm sorry to wake you up, but you fellows might as well get wise, once for all, to where you stand. I'm supposed to go to dinner with you and help jolly you along so you'll trade with old Zizzy, but don't expect to find me in any of the suits you buy."

" Do you mean to tell me," said Platt, " that you go out this way with customers, and they all—they all talk to you like I have?"

" They all make plays," said Miss Asher. " But I must say that you've got 'em beat in one respect. They generally talk diamonds, while you've actually dug one up."

" How long have you been working, Helen ? "

" Got my name pat, haven't you ? I've been supporting myself for eight years. I was a cash girl and a wrapper and then a shop girl until I was grown, and then I got to be a suit model. Mr. Texas Man, don't you think a little wine would make this dinner a little less dry ? "

" You're not going to drink wine any more, dear. It's awful to to think how——I'll come to the store to-morrow and get you. I want you to pick out an automobile before we leave. That's all we need to buy here."

" Oh, cut that out. If you knew how sick I am of hearing such talk."

After the dinner they walked down Broadway and came upon Diana's little wooded park. The trees caught Platt's eye at once, and he must turn along under the winding walk beneath them. The lights shone upon two bright tears in the model's eyes.

" I don't like that," said Platt. " What's the matter ? "

" Don't you mind," said Miss Asher. " Well, its because—well, I didn't think you were that kind when I first saw you. But you are all alike. And now will you take me home, or will I have to call a cop ? "

Platt took her to the door of her boarding-house. They stood for a minute in the vestibule. She looked at him with such scorn in her eyes that even his heart of oak began to waver. His arm was halfway around her waist, when she struck him a stinging blow on the face with her open hand.

As he stepped back a ring fell from somewhere and bounded on the tiled floor. Platt groped for it and found it.

" Now, take your useless diamond and go, Mr. Buyer," she said.

" This was the other one—the wedding ring," said the Texan, holding the smooth gold band on the palm of his hand.

Miss Asher's eyes blazed upon him in the half darkness.

" Was that what you meant ?—did you——"

Somebody opened the door from inside the house..

" Good-night," said Platt. " I'll see you at the store to-morrow."

Miss Asher ran up to her room and shook the school teacher until she sat up in bed ready to scream " Fire ! "

" Where is it ? " she cried.

" That's what I want to know," said the model. " You've studied geography, Emma, and you ought to know. Where is a town called Cac—Cac—Carac—Caracas City, I think they called it ? "

" How dare you wake me up for that ? " said the school teacher. " Caracas is in Venezuela, of course."

" What's it like ? "

" Why, it's principally earthquakes and Negroes and monkeys and malarial fever and volcanoes."

" I don't care," said Miss Asher, blithely; " I'm going there to-morrow."

THE BADGE OF POLICEMAN O'ROON

IT cannot be denied that men and women have looked upon one another for the first time and become instantly enamored. It is a risky process, this love at first sight, before she has seen him in Bradstreet or he has seen her in curl papers. But these things do happen; and one instance must form a theme for this story— though not, thank Heaven, to the overshadowing of more vital and important subjects, such as drink, policemen, horses, and earldoms.

During a certain war a troop calling itself the Gentle Riders rode into history and one or two ambuscades. The Gentle Riders were recruited from the aristocracy of the wild men of the West and the wild men of the aristocracy of the East. In khaki there is little telling them one from another, so they became good friends and comrades all around.

Ellsworth Remsen, whose old Knickerbocker descent atoned for his modest rating at only ten millions, ate his canned beef gayly by the campfires of the Gentle Riders. The war was a great lark to him, so that he scarcely regretted polo and planked shad.

One of the troopers was a well-set-up, affable, cool young man, who called himself O'Roon. To this young man Remsen took an especial liking. The two rode side by side during the famous mooted up-hill charge that was disputed so hotly at the time by the Spaniards and afterward by the Democrats.

After the war Remsen came back to his polo and shad. One day a well-set-up, affable, cool young man disturbed him at his club, and he and O'Roon were soon pounding each other and exchanging opprobrious epithets after the manner of long-lost friends. O'Roon looked seedy and out of luck and perfectly contented. But it seemed that his content was only apparent.

"Get me a job, Remsen," he said. "I've just handed a barber my last shilling."

"No trouble at all," said Remsen. "I know a lot of men who have banks and stores and things downtown. Any particular line you fancy?"

"Yes," said O'Roon, with a look of interest. "I took a walk in your Central Park this morning. I'd like to be one of those bobbies on horseback. That would be about the ticket. Besides, it's the only thing I could do. I can ride a little and the fresh air suits me. Think you could land that for me?"

Remsen was sure that he could. And in a very short time he did.

And they who were not above looking at mounted policemen
might have seen a well-set-up, affable, cool young man on a
prancing chestnut steed attending to his duties along the drive-
ways of the park.

And now at the extreme risk of wearying old gentlemen who
carry leather fob chains, and elderly ladies who—but no ! grandmother herself yet thrills at foolish, immortal Romeo—there must
be a hint of love at first sight.

It came just as Remsen was strolling into Fifth Avenue from his
club a few doors away.

A motor car was creeping along foot by foot, impeded by a
freshet of vehicles that filled the street. In the car was a chauffeur
and an old gentleman with snowy side whiskers and a Scotch plaid
cap which could not be worn while automobiling except by a
personage. Not even a wine agent would dare do it. But these
two were of no consequence—except, perhaps, for the guiding of
the machine and the paying for it. At the old gentleman's side sat
a young lady more beautiful than pomegranate blossoms, more
exquisite than the first quarter moon viewed at twilight through
the tops of oleanders. Remsen saw her and knew his fate. He could
have flung himself under the very wheels that conveyed her, but
he knew that would be the last means of attracting the attention
of those who ride in motor cars. Slowly the auto passed, and, if
we place the poets above the autoists, carried the heart of Remsen
with it. Here was a large city of millions, and many women who
at a certain distance appear to resemble pomegranate blossoms.
Yet he hoped to see her again; for each one fancies that his
romance has its own tutelary guardian and divinity.

Luckily for Remsen's peace of mind there came a diversion in
the guise of a reunion of the Gentle Riders of the city. There were
not many of them—perhaps a score—and there was wassail and
things to eat, and speeches and the Spaniard was bearded again in
recapitulation. And when daylight threatened them the survivors
prepared to depart. But some remained upon the battlefield. One
of these was Trooper O'Roon, who was not seasoned to potent
liquids. His legs declined to fulfil the obligations they had sworn
to the police department.

"I'm stewed, Remsen," said O'Roon to his friend. "Why do
they build hotels that go round and round like catherine wheels ?
They'll take away my shield and break me. I can think and talk
con-con-consec-sec-secutively, but I s-s-stammer with my feet.
I've got to go on duty in three hours. The jig is up, Remsen. The
jig is up, I tell you."

"Look at me," said Remsen, who was his smiling self, pointing
to his own face; "whom do you see here ? "

"Goo' fellow," said O'Roon, dizzily, "Goo' old Remsen."

"Not so," said Remsen. "You see Mounted Policeman O'Roon. Look at your face—no; you can't do that without a glass—but look at mine, and think of yours. How much alike are we? As two French *table d'hôte* dinners. With your badge, on your horse, in your uniform, will I charm nurse-maids and prevent the grass from growing under people's feet in the Park this day. I will have your badge and your honor, besides having the jolliest lark I've been blessed with since we licked Spain."

Promptly on time the counterfeit presentment of Mounted Policeman O'Roon single-footed into the Park on his chestnut steed. In a uniform two men who are unlike will look alike; two who somewhat resemble each other in feature and figure will appear as twin brothers. So Remsen trotted down the bridle paths, enjoying himself hugely, so few real pleasures do ten-millionaires have.

Along the driveway in the early morning spun a victoria drawn by a pair of fiery bays. There was something foreign about the affair, for the Park is rarely used in the morning, except by unimportant people who love to be healthy, poor, and wise. In the vehicle sat an old gentleman with snowy side-whiskers and a Scotch plaid cap which could not be worn while driving except by a personage. At his side sat the lady of Remsen's heart—the lady who looked like pomegranate blossoms and the gibbous moon.

Remsen met them coming. At the instant of their passing her eyes looked into his, and but for the ever coward's heart of a true lover he could have sworn that she flushed a faint pink. He trotted on for twenty yards, and then wheeled his horse at the sound of runaway hoofs. The bays had bolted.

Remsen sent his chestnut after the victoria like a shot. There was work cut out for the impersonator of Policeman O'Roon. The chestnut ranged alongside the off bay thirty seconds after the chase began, rolled his eye back at Remsen, and said in the only manner open to policeman's horses:

"Well, you duffer, are you going to do your share? You're not O'Roon, but it seems to me if you'd lean to the right you could reach the reins of that foolish slow-running bay—ah! you're all right; O'Roon couldn't have done it more neatly!"

The runaway team was tugged to an inglorious halt by Remsen's tough muscles. The driver released his hands from the wrapped reins, jumped from his seat and stood at the head of the team. The chestnut, approving his new rider, danced and pranced, reviling equinely the subdued bays. Remsen, lingering, was dimly conscious of a vague, impossible, unnecessary old gentleman in a Scotch cap who talked incessantly about something. And he was

acutely conscious of a pair of violet eyes that would have drawn
Saint Pyrites from his iron pillar—or whatever the allusion is—
and of the lady's smile and look—a little frightened, but a look
that, with the ever coward heart of a true lover, he could not yet
construe. They were asking his name and bestowing upon him
well-bred thanks for his heroic deed, and the Scotch cap was
especially babbling and insistent. But the eloquent appeal was
in the eyes of the lady.

A little thrill of satisfaction ran through Remsen, because he
had a name to give which, without undue pride, was worthy of
being spoken in high places, and a small fortune which, with due
pride, he could leave at his end without disgrace.

He opened his lips to speak and closed them again.

Who was he? Mounted Policeman O'Roon. The badge and the
honor of his comrade were in his hands. If Ellsworth Remsen,
ten-millionaire and Knickerbocker, had just rescued pomegranate
blossoms and Scotch cap from possible death, where was Policeman O'Roon? Off his beat, exposed, disgraced, discharged. Love
had come, but before that there had been something that demanded precedence—the fellowship of men on battlefields fighting
an alien foe.

Remsen touched his cap, looked between the chestnut's ears,
and took refuge in vernacularity.

" Don't mention it," he said, stolidly. " We policemen are paid
to do these things. It's our duty."

At the end of the day Remsen sent the chestnut to his stable
and went to O'Roon's room. The policeman was again a well-set-
up, affable, cool young man who sat by the window smoking
cigars.

" I wish you and the rest of the police force and all badges,
horses, brass buttons, and men who can't drink two glasses of *brut*
without getting upset were at the devil," said Remsen, feelingly.

O'Roon smiled with evident satisfaction.

" Good old Remsen," he said, affably, " I know all about it.
They trailed me down and cornered me here two hours ago. There
was a little row at home, you know, and I cut sticks just to show
them. I don't believe I told you that my Governor was the Earl
of Ardsley. Funny you should bob against them in the Park. If
you damaged that horse of mine I'll never forgive you. I'm going
to buy him and take him back with me. Oh, yes, and I think my
sister—Lady Angela, you know—wants particularly for you to
come up to the hotel with me this evening. Didn't lose my badge,
did you, Remsen? I've got to turn that in at Headquarters when
I resign."

BRICKDUST ROW

BLINKER was displeased. A man of less culture and poise and wealth would have sworn. But Blinker always remembered that he was a gentleman—a thing that no gentleman should do. So he merely looked bored and sardonic while he rode in a hansom to the centre of disturbance, which was the Broadway office of Lawyer Oldport, who was agent for the Blinker estate.

" I don't see," said Blinker, " why I should be always signing confounded papers. I am packed, and was to have left for the North Woods this morning. Now I must wait until to-morrow morning. I hate night trains. My best razors are, of course, at the bottom of some unidentifiable trunk. It is a plot to drive me to bay rum and a monologuing, thumb-handed barber. Give me a pen that doesn't scratch. I hate pens that scratch."

" Sit down," said double-chinned, gray Lawyer Oldport. " The worst has not been told you. Oh, the hardships of the rich ! The papers are not yet ready to sign. They will be laid before you to-morrow at eleven. You will miss another day. Twice shall the barber tweak the helpless nose of a Blinker. Be thankful that your sorrows do not embrace a haircut."

" If," said Blinker, rising, " the act did not involve more signing of papers I would take my business out of your hands at once. Give me a cigar, please."

" If," said Lawyer Oldport, " I had cared to see an old friend's son gulped down at one mouthful by sharks I would have ordered you to take it away long ago. Now, let's quit fooling, Alexander. Besides the grinding task of signing your name some thirty times to-morrow, I must impose upon you the consideration of a matter of business—of business, and I may say humanity or right. I spoke to you about this five years ago, but you would not listen—you were in a hurry for a coaching trip, I think. The subject has come up again. The property——"

" Oh, property ! " interrupted Blinker. " Dear Mr. Oldport, I think you mentioned to-morrow. Let's have it all at one dose to-morrow—signatures and property and snappy rubber bands and that smelly sealing-wax and all. Have luncheon with me ? Well, I'll try to remember to drop in at eleven to-morrow. Morning."

The Blinker wealth was in lands, tenements, and hereditaments, as the legal phrase goes. Lawyer Oldport had once taken Alexander in his little pulmonary gasoline runabout to see the many buildings and rows of buildings that he owned in the city. For

Alexander was sole heir. They had amused Blinker very much. The houses looked so incapable of producing the big sums of money that Lawyer Oldport kept piling up in banks for him to spend.

In the evening Blinker went to one of his clubs, intending to dine. Nobody was there except some old fogies playing whist who spoke to him with grave politeness and glared at him with savage contempt. Everybody was out of town. But here he was kept in like a schoolboy to write his name over and over on pieces of paper. His wounds were deep.

Blinker turned his back on the fogies, and said to the club steward who had come forward with some nonsense about cold fresh salmon roe :

" Symons, I'm going to Coney Island." He said it as one might say : "All's off, I'm going to jump into the river."

The joke pleased Symons. He laughed within a sixteenth of a note of the audibility permitted by the laws governing employees.

" Certainly, sir," he tittered. " Of course, sir, I think I can see you at Coney, Mr. Blinker."

Blinker got a paper and looked up the movements of Sunday steamboats. Then he found a cab at the first corner and drove to a North River pier. He stood in line, as democratic as you or I, and bought a ticket, and was trampled upon and shoved forward until, at last, he found himself on the upper deck of the boat staring brazenly at a girl who sat alone upon a camp stool. But Blinker did not intend to be brazen; the girl was so wonderfully good looking that he forgot for one minute that he was the prince incog, and behaved just as he did in society.

She was looking at him, too, and not severely. A puff of wind threatened Blinker's straw hat. He caught it warily and settled it again. The movement gave the effect of a bow. The girl nodded and smiled, and in another instant he was seated at her side. She was dressed all in white, she was paler than Blinker imagined milkmaids and girls of humble stations to be, but she was as tidy as a cherry blossom, and her steady, supremely frank gray eyes looked out from the intrepid depths of an unshadowed and untroubled soul.

" How dare you raise your hat to me ? " she asked, with a smile-redeemed severity.

" I didn't," Blinker said, but he quickly covered the mistake by extending it to " I didn't know how to keep from it after I saw you."

" I do not allow gentlemen to sit by me to whom I have not been introduced." she said with a sudden haughtiness that deceived him. He rose reluctantly, but her clear, teasing laugh brought him down to his chair again.

" I guess you weren't going far," she declared, with beauty's magnificent self-confidence.

" Are you going to Coney Island ? " asked Blinker.

" Me ? " She turned upon him wide-open eyes full of bantering surprise. " Why, what a question ! Can't you see that I'm riding a bicycle in the park ? " Her drollery took the form of impertinence.

" And I'm laying bricks on a tall factory chimney," said Blinker. " Mayn't we see Coney together ? I'm all alone and I've never been there before."

" It depends," said the girl, " on how nicely you behave. I'll consider your application until we get there."

Blinker took pains to provide against the rejection of his application. He strove to please. To adopt the metaphor of his non-sensical phrase, he laid brick upon brick on the tall chimney of his devoirs until, at length, the structure was stable and complete. The manners of the best society come around finally to simplicity; and as the girl's way was that naturally, they were on a mutual plane of communication from the beginning.

He learned that she was twenty, and her name was Florence; that she trimmed hats in a millinery shop; that she lived in a furnished room with her best chum Ella, who was cashier in a shoe store; and that a glass of milk from the bottle on the window-sill and an egg that boils itself while you twist up your hair makes a breakfast good enough for any one. Florence laughed when she heard " Blinker."

" Well," she said. " It certainly shows that you have imagination. It gives the ' Smiths' a chance for a little rest, anyhow."

They landed at Coney, and were dashed on the crest of a great human wave of mad pleasure-seekers into the walks and avenues of Fairyland gone into vaudeville.

With a curious eye, a critical mind, and a fairly witheld judgment Blinker considered the temples, pagodas and kiosks of popularized delights. Hoi polloi trampled, hustled, and crowded him. Basket parties bumped him; sticky children tumbled, howling, under his feet, candying his clothes. Insolent youths strolling among the booths with hard-won canes under one arm and easily won girls on the other, blew defiant smoke from cheap cigars into his face. The publicity gentlemen with megaphones, each before his own stupendous attraction, roared like Niagara in his ears. Music of all kinds that could be tortured from brass, reed, hide, or string, fought in the air to gain space for its vibrations against its competitors. But what held Blinker in awful fascination was the mob, the multitude, the proletariat shrieking, struggling, hurrying, panting, hurling itself in incontinent frenzy, with un-abashed abandon, into the ridiculous sham palaces of trumpery and tinsel pleasures. The vulgarity of it, its brutal overriding of all the tenets of repression and taste that were held by his caste, repelled him strongly.

In the midst of his disgust he turned and looked down at Florence by his side. She was ready with her quick smile and upturned, happy eyes, as bright and clear as the water in trout pools. The eyes were saying that they had the right to be shining and happy, for was their owner not with her (for the present) Man, her Gentleman Friend and holder of the keys to the enchanted city of fun.

Blinker did not read her look accurately, but by some miracle he suddenly saw Coney aright.

He no longer saw a mass of vulgarians seeking gross joys. He now looked clearly upon a hundred thousand true idealists. Their offenses were wiped out. Counterfeit and false though the garish joys of these spangled temples were, he perceived that deep under the gilt surface they offered saving and apposite balm and satisfaction to the restless human heart. Here, at least, was the husk of Romance, the empty but shining casque of Chivalry, the breath-catching though safe-guarded dip and flight of Adventure, the magic carpet that transports you to the realms of fairyland, though its journey be through but a few poor yards of space. He no longer saw a rabble, but his brothers seeking the ideal. There was no magic of poesy here or of art; but the glamour of their imagination turned yellow calico into cloth of gold and the megaphone into the silver trumpets of joy's heralds.

Almost humbled, Blinker rolled up the shirt sleeves of his mind and joined the idealists.

" You are the lady doctor," he said to Florence. " How shall we go about doing this jolly conglomeration of fairy tales, incorporated ? "

" We will begin there," said the Princess, pointing to a fun pagoda on the edge of the sea, " and we will take them all in, one by one."

They caught the eight o'clock returning boat and sat, filled with pleasant fatigue, against the rail in the bow, listening to the Italians' fiddle and harp. Blinker had thrown off all care. The North Woods seemed to him an uninhabitable wilderness. What a fuss he had made over signing his name—pooh ! he could sign it a hundred times. And her name was as pretty as she was— " Florence," he said it to himself a great many times.

As the boat was nearing its pier in the North River a two-funnelled, drab, foreign-looking sea-going steamer was dropping down toward the bay. The boat turned its nose in towards its slip. The steamer veered as if to seek mid-stream, and then yawed, seemed to increase its speed and struck the Coney boat on the side near the stern, cutting into it with a terrifying shock and crash.

While the six-hundred passengers on the boat were mostly tumbling about the decks in a shrieking panic the captain was shouting at the steamer that it should not back off and leave the rent exposed for the water to enter. But the steamer tore its way out like a savage sawfish and cleaved its heartless way, full speed ahead.

The boat began to sink at its stern, but moved slowly toward the slip. The passengers were a frantic mob, unpleasant to behold.

Blinker held Florence tightly until the boat had righted itself. She made no sound or sign of fear. He stood on a camp stool, ripped off the slats above his head and pulled down a number of the life preservers. He began to buckle one around Florence. The rotten canvas spilt and the fraudulent granulated cork came pouring out in a stream. Florence caught a handful of it and laughed gleefully.

" It looks like breakfast food," she said. " Take it off. They're no good."

She unbuckled it and threw it on the deck. She made Blinker sit down and sat by his side and put her hand in his. " What'll you bet we don't reach the pier all right ? " she said, and began to hum a song.

And now the captain moved among the passengers and compelled order. The boat would undoubtedly make her slip, he said, and ordered the women and children to the bow, where they could land first. The boat, very low in the water at the stern, tried gallantly to make his promise good.

" Florence," said Blinker, as she held him close by an arm and hand, " I love you."

" That's what they all say," she replied, lightly.

" I am not one of ' they all,' " he persisted. " I never knew any one I could love before. I could pass my life with you and be happy every day. I am rich. I can make things all right for you."

" That's what they all say," said the girl again, weaving the words into her little, reckless song.

" Don't say that again," said Blinker in a tone that made her look at him in frank surprise.

" Why shouldn't I say it ? " she asked, calmly. " They all do."

" Who are ' they ' ? " he asked, jealous for the first time in his existence.

" Why, the fellows I know."

" Do you know so many ? "

" Oh, well, I'm not a wall flower," she answered with modest complacency.

" Where do you see these—these men ? At your home ? "

" Of course not. I meet them just as I did you. Sometimes on the boat, sometimes in the park, sometimes on the street. I'm a pretty good judge of a man. I can tell in a minute if a fellow is one who is likely to get fresh."

" What do you mean by ' fresh ' ? "

" Who, try to kiss you—me, I mean."

" Do any of them try that ? " asked Blinker, clenching his teeth.

" Sure. All men do. You know that."

" Do you allow them ? "

" Some. Not many. They won't take you out anywhere unless you do."

She turned her head and looked searchingly at Blinker. Her eyes were as innocent as a child's. There was a puzzled look in them, as though she did not understand him.

" What's wrong about my meeting fellows ? " she asked, wonderingly.

" Everything," he answered, almost savagely. " Why don't you entertain your company in the house where you live ? Is it necessary to pick up Tom, Dick, and Harry on the streets ? "

She kept her absolutely ingenuous eyes upon his.

" If you could see the place where I live you wouldn't ask that. I live in Brickdust Row. They call it that because there's red dust from the bricks crumbling over everything. I've lived there for more than four years. There's no place to receive company. You can't have anybody come to your room. What else is there to do ? A girl has got to meet the men, hasn't she ? "

" Yes," he said, hoarsely. "A girl has got to meet a—has got to meet the men."

" The first time one spoke to me on the street," she continued, " I ran home and cried all night. But you get used to it. I meet a good many nice fellows at church. I go on rainy days and stand in the vestibule until one comes up with an umbrella. I wish there was a parlor, so I could ask you to call, Mr. Blinker—are you really sure it isn't ' Smith,' now ? "

The boat landed safely. Blinker had a confused impression of walking with the girl through quiet crosstown streets until she stopped at a corner and held out her hand.

" I live just one more block over," she said. " Thank you for a very pleasant afternoon."

Blinker muttered something and plunged northward till he found a cab. A big, gray church loomed slowly at his right. Blinker shook his fist at it through the window.

" I gave you a thousand dollars last week," he cried under his breath, " and she meets them in your very doors. There is something wrong; there is something wrong."

At eleven the next day Blinker signed his name thirty times with a new pen provided by Lawyer Oldport.

"Now let me get to the woods," he said, surlily.

"You are not looking well," said Lawyer Oldport. "The trip will do you good. But listen, if you will, to that little matter of business of which I spoke to you yesterday, and also five years ago. There are some buildings, fifteen in number, of which there are new five-year leases to be signed. Your father contemplated a change in the lease provisions, but never made it. He intended that the parlors of these houses should not be sub-let, but that the tenants should be allowed to use them for reception rooms. These houses are in the shopping districts, and are mainly tenanted by young working girls. As it is they are forced to seek companionship outside. This row of red brick——"

Blinker interrupted him with a loud, discordant laugh.

"Brickdust Row for an even hundred," he cried. "And I own it. Have I guessed right?"

"The tenants have some such name for it," said Lawyer Oldport.

Blinker arose and jammed his hat down on his eyes.

"Do what you please with it," he said, harshly. "Remodel it, burn it, raze it to the ground. But, man, it's too late, I tell you. It's too late. It's too late. It's too late."

THE MAKING OF A NEW YORKER

BESIDES many things, Raggles was a poet. He was called a tramp; but that was only an elliptical way of saying that he was a philosopher, an artist, a traveller, a naturalist, and a discoverer. But most of all he was a poet. In all his life he never wrote a line of verse; he lived his poetry. His Odyssey would have been a Limerick, had it been written. But, to linger with the primary proposition, Raggles was a poet.

Raggles's speciality, had he been driven to ink and paper, would have been sonnets to the cities. He studied cities as women study their reflections in mirrors; as children study the glue and sawdust of a dislocated doll; as the men who write about wild animals study the cages in the zoo. A city to Raggles was not merely a pile of bricks and mortar, peopled by a certain number of inhabitants; it was a thing with soul characteristic and distinct; an individual conglomeration of life, with its own peculiar essence, flavor, and feeling. Two thousand miles to the north and south, east and west, Raggles wandered in poetic fervor, taking the cities to his breast. He footed it on dusty roads, or sped magnificently in freight cars, counting time as of no account. And when he had found the heart of a city and listened to its secret confession, he strayed on, restless, to another. Fickle Raggles!—but perhaps he had not met the civic corporation that could engage and hold his critical fancy.

Through the ancient poets we have learned that the cities are feminine. So they were to poet Raggles; and his mind carried a concrete and clear conception of the figure that symbolized and typified each one that he had wooed.

Chicago seemed to swoop down upon him with a breezy suggestion of Mrs. Partington, plumes and patchouli, and to disturb his rest with a soaring and beautiful song of future promise. But Raggles would awake to a sense of shivering cold and a haunting impression of ideals lost in a depressing aura of potato salad and fish.

Thus Chicago affected him. Perhaps there is a vagueness and inaccuracy in the description; but that is Raggles's fault. He should have recorded his sensations in magazine poems.

Pittsburg impressed him as the play of " Othello " performed in the Russian language in a railroad station by Dockstader's minstrels. A royal and generous lady this Pittsburg, though— homely, hearty, with flushed face, washing the dishes in a silk dress and white kid slippers, and bidding Raggles sit before the roaring fireplace and drink champagne with his pigs' feet and fried potatoes.

New Orleans had simply gazed down upon him from a balcony. He could see her pensive, starry eyes and catch the flutter of her fan, and that was all. Only once he came face to face with her. It was at dawn, when she was flushing the red bricks of the banquette with a pail of water. She laughed and hummed a chansonette and filled Raggles's shoes with ice-cold water. Allons!

Boston construed herself to the poetic Raggles in an erratic and singular way. It seemed to him that he had drunk cold tea and that the city was a white, cold cloth that had been bound tightly around his brow to spur him to some unknown but tremendous mental effort. And, after all, he came to shovel snow for a livelihood; and the cloth, becoming wet, tightened its knots and could not be removed.

Indefinite and unintelligible ideas, you will say; but your disapprobation should be tempered with gratitudes, for these are poets' fancies—and suppose you had come upon them in verse!

One day Raggles came and laid siege to the heart of the great city of Manhattan. She was the greatest of all; and he wanted to learn her note in the scale; to taste and appraise and classify and solve and label her and arrange her with the other cities that had given him up the secret of their individuality. And here we cease to be Raggles's translator and become his chronicler.

Raggles landed from a ferry-boat one morning and walked into the core of the town with the blasé air of a cosmopolite. He was dressed with care to play the rôle of an " unidentified man." No country, race, class, clique, union, party clan, or bowling association could have claimed him. His clothing, which had been donated to him piece-meal by citizens of different height, but same number of inches around the heart, was not yet as uncomfortable to his figure as those specimens of raiment, self-measured, that are railroaded to you by trans-continental tailors with a suit case, suspenders, silk handkerchief and pearl studs as a bonus. Without money—as a poet should be—but with the ardor of an astronomer discovering a new star in the chorus of the milky way, or a man who has seen ink suddenly flow from his fountain pen, Raggles wandered into the great city.

Late in the afternoon he drew out of the roar and commotion with a look of dumb terror on his countenance. He was defeated, puzzled, discomfited, frightened. Other cities had been to him as long primer to read; as country maidens quickly to fathom; as send-price-of-subscription-with-answer rebuses to solve; as oyster cocktails to swallow; but here was one as cold, glittering, serene, impossible as a four-carat diamond in a window to a lover outside fingering damply in his pocket his ribbon-counter salary.

The greetings of the other cities he had known—their homespun kindliness, their human gamut of rough charity, friendly curses, garrulous curiosity, and easily estimated credulity or indifference. This city of Manhattan gave him no clue; it was walled against him. Like a river of adamant it flowed past him in the streets. Never an eye was turned upon him; no voice spoke to him. His heart yearned for the clap of Pittsburg's sooty hand on his shoulder; for Chicago's menacing but social yawp in his ear; for the pale and eleemosynary stare through the Bostonian eyeglass—even for the precipitate but unmalicious boot-toe of Louisville or St. Louis.

On Broadway Raggles, successful suitor of many cities, stood, bashful, like any country swain. For the first time he experienced the poignant humiliation of being ignored. And when he tried to reduce this brilliant, swiftly changing, ice-cold city to a formula he failed utterly. Poet though he was, it offered him no color similes, no points of comparison, no flaw in its polished facets, no handle by which he could hold it up and view its shape and structure, as he familiarly and often contemptuously had done with other towns. The houses were interminable ramparts loopholed for defense; the people were bright but bloodless spectres passing in sinister and selfish array.

The thing that weighed heaviest on Raggles's soul and clogged his poet's fancy was the spirit of absolute egotism that seemed to saturate the people as toys are saturated with paint. Each one that he considered appeared a monster of abominable and insolent conceit. Humanity was gone from them; they were toddling idols of stone and varnish, worshipping themselves and greedy for though oblivious of worship from their fellow graven images. Frozen, cruel, implacable, impervious, cut to an identical pattern, they hurried on their ways like statues brought by some miracle to motion, while soul and feeling lay unaroused in the reluctant marble.

Gradually Raggles became conscious of certain types. One was an elderly gentleman with a snow-white, short beard, pink, unwrinkled face, and stony, sharp blue eyes, attired in the fashion of a gilded youth, who seemed to personify the city's wealth, ripeness and frigid unconcern. Another type was a woman, tall, beautiful, clear as a steel engraving, goddess-like, calm, clothed like the princesses of old, with eyes as coldly blue as the reflection of sunlight on a glacier. And another was a by-product of this town of marionettes—a broad, swaggering, grim, threateningly sedate fellow, with a jowl as large as a harvested wheat field, the complexion of a baptized infant, and the knuckles of a prize-fighter. This type leaned against cigar signs and viewed the world with frappéd contumely.

A poet is a sensitive creature, and Raggles soon shriveled in the bleak embrace of the undecipherable. The chill, sphinx-like, ironical, illegible, unnatural, ruthless expression of the city left him downcast and bewildered. Had it no heart? Better the woodpile, the scolding of vinegar-faced housewives at back doors, the kindly spleen of bartenders behind provincial free-lunch counters, the amiable truculence of rural constables, the kicks, arrests, and happy-go-lucky chances of the other vulgar, loud, crude cities than this freezing heartlessness.

Raggles summoned his courage and sought alms from the populace. Unheeding, regardless, they passed on without the wink of an eyelash to testify that they were conscious of his existence. And then he said to himself that this fair but pitiless city of Manhattan was without a soul; that its inhabitants were mannikins moved by wires and springs, and that he was alone in a great wilderness.

Raggles started to cross the street. There was a blast, a roar, a hissing and a crash as something struck him and hurled him over and over six yards from where he had been. As he was coming down like the stick of a rocket the earth and all the cities thereof turned to a fractured dream.

Raggles opened his eyes. First an odor made itself known to him —an odor of the earliest spring flowers of Paradise. And then a hand soft as a falling petal touched his brow. Bending over him was the woman clothed like the princess of old, with blue eyes, now soft and humid with human sympathy. Under his head on the pavement were silks and furs. With Raggles's hat in his hand and with his face pinker than ever from a vehement outburst of oratory against reckless driving, stood the elderly gentleman who personified the city's wealth and ripeness. From a near-by café hurried the by-product with the vast jowl and baby complexion, bearing a glass full of crimson fluid that suggested delightful possibilities.

"Drink dis, sport," said the by-product, holding the glass to Raggles's lips.

Hundreds of people huddled around in a moment, their faces wearing the deepest concern. Two flattering and gorgeous policemen got into the circle and pressed back the overplus of Samaritans. An old lady in a black shawl spoke loudly of camphor; a newsboy slipped one of his papers beneath Raggles's elbow, where it lay on the muddy pavement. A brisk young man with a notebook was asking for names.

A bell clanged importantly, and the ambulance cleaned a lane through the crowd. A cool surgeon slipped into the midst of affairs.

"How do you feel, old man?" asked the surgeon, stooping easily to his task. The princess of silks and satins wiped a red drop or two from Raggles's brow with a fragrant cobweb.

"Me?" said Raggles, with a seraphic smile, "I feel fine."

He had found the heart of his new city.

In three days they let him leave his cot for the convalescent ward in the hospital. He had been in there an hour when the attendants heard sounds of conflict. Upon investigation they found that Raggles has assaulted and damaged a brother convalescent— a glowering transient whom a freight train collision had sent in to be patched up.

"What's all this about?" inquired the head nurse.

"He was runnin' down me town," said Raggles.

"What town?" asked the nurse.

"Noo York," said Raggles.

VANITY AND SOME SABLES

When "Kid" Brady was sent to the ropes by Molly Mc-Keever's blue-black eyes he withdrew from the Stovepipe Gang. So much for the power of a colleen's blanderin' tongue and stubborn true-heartedness. If you are a man who read this, may such an influence be sent you before 2 o'clock to-morrow; if you are a woman, may your Pomeranian greet you this morning with a cold nose—a sign of doghealth and your happiness.

The Stovepipe Gang borrowed its name from a sub-district of the city called the "Stovepipe," which is a narrow and natural extension of the familiar district known as "Hell's Kitchen." The "Stovepipe" strip of town runs along Eleventh and Twelfth avenues on the river, and bends a hard and sooty elbow around little, lost, homeless De Witt Clinton park. Consider that a stovepipe is an important factor in any kitchen and the situation is analyzed. The chefs in "Hell's Kitchen" are many, and the "Stovepipe" gang wears the cordon blue.

The members of this unchartered but widely known brotherhood appeared to pass their time on street corners arrayed like the lilies of the conservatory and busy with nail files and penknives. Thus displayed as a guarantee of good faith, they carried on an innocuous conversation in a 200-word vocabulary, to the causual observer as innocent and immaterial as that heard in the clubs seven blocks to the east.

But off exhibition the "Stovepipes" were not mere street corner ornaments addicted to posing and manicuring. Their serious occupation was the separating of citizens from their coin and valuables. Preferably this was done by weird and singular tricks without noise or bloodshed; but whenever the citizen honored by their attentions refused to impoverish himself gracefully, his objections came to be spread finally upon some police station blotter or hospital register.

The police held the "Stovepipe" gang in perpetual suspicion and respect. As the nightingale's liquid note is heard in the deepest shadows, so along the "Stovepipe's" dark and narrow confines the whistle for reserves punctures the dull ear of night. Whenever there was smoke in the "Stovepipe" the tasselled men in blue knew there was a fire in "Hell's Kitchen."

"Kid" Brady promised Molly to be good. "Kid" was the vainest, the strongest, the wariest, and the most successful plotter in the gang. Therefore, the boys were sorry to give him up.

But they witnessed his fall to a virtuous life without protest. For, in the Kitchen it is considered neither unmanly nor improper for a guy to do as his girl advises.

Black her eyes for love's sake, if you will; but it is all-to-the-good business to do a thing when she wants you to do it.

" Turn off the hydrant," said the Kid, one night when Molly, tearful, besought him to amend his ways. " I'm going to cut out the gang. You for mine, and the simple life on the side. I'll tell you, Moll—I'll get work; and in a year we'll get married. I'll do it for you. We'll get a flat and a flute, and a sewing machine and a rubber plant and live as honest as we can."

" Oh, Kid," sighed Molly, wiping the powder off his shoulder with her handkerchief, " I'd rather hear you say that than to own all of New York. And we can be happy on so little. ! "

The Kid looked down at his speckless cuffs and shining patent leathers with a suspicion of melancholy.

" It'll hurt hardest in the rags department," said he. " I've kind of always liked to rig out swell when I could. You know how I hate cheap things, Moll. This suit set me back sixty-five. Anything in the wearing apparel line has got to be just so, or it's to the misfit parlors for it, for mine. If I work I won't have so much coin to hand over to the little man with the big shears."

" Never mind, Kid. I'll like you just as much in a blue jumper as I would in a red automobile."

Before the Kid had grown large enough to knock out his father he had been compelled to learn the plumber's art. So now back to this honorable and useful profession he returned. But it was as an assistant that he engaged himself; and it is the master plumber and not the assistant, who wears diamonds as large as hailstones and looks contemptuously upon the marble colonnades of Senator Clark's mansion.

Eight months went by as smoothly and surely as though they had " elapsed " on a theatre program. The Kid worked away at his pipes and solder with no symptoms of backsliding. The Stovepipe gang continued its piracy on the high avenues, cracked policeman's heads, held up late travelers, invented new methods of peaceful plundering, copied Fifth Avenue's cut of clothes and neckwear fancies, and comported itself according to its lawless bylaws. But the Kid stood firm and faithful to his Molly, even though the polish was gone from his fingernails and it took him 15 minutes to tie his purple silk ascot so that the worn places would not show.

One evening he brought a mysterious bundle with him to Molly's house.

" Open that, Moll ! " he said in his large, quiet way. " It's for you."

Molly's eager fingers tore off the wrappings. She shrieked aloud, and in rushed a sprinkling of little McKeevers, and Ma McKeever, dishwashy, but an undeniable relative of the late Mrs. Eve.

Again Molly shrieked, and something dark and long and sinuous flew and enveloped her neck like an anaconda.

" Russian sables," said the Kid, pridefully, enjoying the sight of Molly's round cheek against the clinging fur. " The real thing. They don't grow anything in Russia too good for you, Moll."

Molly plunged her hands into the muff, over-turned a row of the family infants, and flew to the mirror. Hint for the beauty column. To make bright eyes, rosy cheeks, and a bewitching smile : Recipe—one set Russian sables. Apply.

When they were alone Molly became aware of a small cake of the ice of common sense floating down the full tide of her happiness.

" You're a bird, all right, Kid," she admitted, gratefully. " I never had any furs on before in my life. But ain't Russian sables awful expensive ? Seems to me I've heard they were."

" Have I ever chucked any bargain-sale stuff at you, Moll ? " asked the Kid, with calm dignity. " Did you ever notice me leaning on the remnant counter or peering in the window of the five-and-ten ? Call that scarf $250 and the muff $175 and you won't make any mistake about the price of Russian sables. The swell goods for me. Say, they look fine on you, Moll."

Molly hugged the sables to her bosom in rapture. And then her smile went away little by little, and she looked the Kid straight in the eye sadly and steadily.

He knew what every look of hers meant; and he laughed with a faint flush upon his face.

" Cut it out," he said, with affectionate roughness. " I told you I was done with that. I bought 'em and paid for 'em, all right, with my own money."

" Out of the money you worked for, Kid ? Out of $75 a month ? "

" Sure. I been saving up."

" Let's see—saved $425 in eight months, Kid ? "

" Ah, let up," said the Kid, with some heat. " I had some money when I went to work. Do you think I've been holding 'em up again ? I told you I'd quit. They're paid for on the square. Put 'em on and come out for a walk."

Molly calmed her doubts. Sables are soothing. Proud as a queen she went forth in the streets at the Kid's side. In all that region of low-lying streets Russian sables had never been seen before. The word sped, and the doors and windows blossomed with heads eager to see the swell furs Kid Brady had given his girl. All down the street there were " Oh's " and "Ah's" and the reported fabulous sum paid for the sables was passed from lip to lip, increasing as it went. At her right elbow sauntered the Kid with the air of a prince. Work had not diminished his love of pomp and show and his passion for the costly and genuine. On a corner they saw a group of the Stovepipe Gang loafing, immaculate. They raised their hats to the Kid's girl and went on with their calm, unaccented palaver.

Three blocks behind the admired couple strolled Detective Ransom, of the Central office. Ransom was the only detective on the force who could walk abroad with safety in the Stovepipe district. He was fair dealing and unafraid and went there with the hypothesis that the inhabitants were human. Many liked him, and now and then would tip off to him something that he was looking for.

"What's the excitement down the street?" asked Ransom of a pale youth in a red sweater.

"Dey're out rubberin' at a set of buffalo robes Kid Brady staked his girl to," answered the youth. "Some say he paid $900 for de skins. Dey're swell all right enough."

"I hear Brady has been working at his old trade for nearly a year," said the detective. "He doesn't travel with the gang any more, does he?"

"He's workin', all right," said the red sweater, "but—say, sport, are you trailin' anything in the fur line? A job in a plumbin' shop don't match wid dem skins de Kid's girl's got on."

Ransom overtook the strolling couple on an empty street near the river bank. He touched the Kid's arm from behind.

"Let me see you a moment, Brady," he said, quietly. His eye rested for a second on the long fur scarf thrown stylishly back over Molly's left shoulder. The Kid, with his old-time police-hating frown on his face, stepped a yard or two aside with the detective.

"Did you go to Mrs. Hethcote's on West 7—th Street yesterday to fix a leaky water pipe?" asked Ransom.

"I did," said the Kid. "What of it?"

"The lady's $1,000 set of Russian sables went out of the house about the same time you did. The description fits the ones this lady has on."

"To h—Harlem with you," cried the Kid, angrily. "You know I've cut out that sort of thing, Ransom. I bought them sables yesterday at——"

The Kid stopped short.

"I know you've been working straight lately," said Ransom. "I'll give you every chance. I'll go with you where you say you bought the furs and investigate. The lady can wear 'em along with us and nobody'll be on. That's fair, Brady."

"Come on," agreed the Kid, hotly. And then he stopped suddenly in his tracks and looked with an odd smile at Molly's distressed and anxious face.

"No use," he said, grimly. "They're the Hethcote sables, all right. You'll have to turn 'em over, Moll, but they ain't too good for you if they cost a million."

Molly, with anguish in her face, hung upon the Kid's arm.

"Oh, Kiddy, you've broken my heart," she said. "I was so proud of you—and now they'll do you—and where's our happiness gone?"

"Go home," said the Kid, wildly. "Come on, Ransom—take the furs. Let's get away from here. Wait a minute—I've a good mind to—— No, I'll be d— if I can do it—run along, Moll—I'm ready, Ransom"

Around the corner of a lumber-yard came Policeman Kohen on his way to his beat along the river. The detective signed to him for assistance. Kohen joined the group. Ransom explained.

"Sure," said Kohen. "I hear about those saples dat vas stole. You say you have dem here?"

Policeman Kohen took the end of Molly's late scarf in his hands and looked at it closely.

"Once," he said, "I sold furs in Sixth Avenue. Yes, dese are saples. Dey came from Alaska. Dis scarf is vort $12 and dis muff——"

"Biff!" came the palm of the Kid's powerful hand upon the policeman's mouth. Kohen staggered and rallied. Molly screamed. The detective threw himself upon Brady and with Kohen's aid got the nippers on his wrist.

"The scarf is vort $12 and the muff is vort $9," persisted the policeman. "Vot is dis talk about $1,000 saples?"

The Kid sat upon a pile of lumber and his face turned dark red.

"Correct, Solomonski!" he declared, viciously. "I paid $21.50 for the set. I'd rather have got six months and not have told it. Me, the swell guy that wouldn't look at anything cheap! I'm a plain bluffer. Moll—my salary couldn't spell sables in Russian."

Molly cast herself upon his neck.

"What do I care for all the sables and money in the world," she cried. "It's my Kiddy I want. Oh, you dear, stuck-up, crazy blockhead!"

"You can take dose nippers off," said Kohen to the detective. "Before I leaf de station de report come in dat de lady vind her saples—hanging in her wardrobe. Young man, I excuse you dat punch in my vace—dis von time."

Ransom handed Molly her furs. Her eyes were smiling upon

the Kid. She wound the scarf and threw the end over her left shoulder with a duchess's grace.

" A gouple of young vools," said Policemaṇ Kohen to Ransom; " come on away."

THE SOCIAL TRIANGLE

A T the stroke of six Ikey Snigglefritz laid down his goose. Ikey was a tailor's apprentice. Are there tailors' apprentices nowadays ?

At any rate, Ikey toiled and snipped and basted and pressed and patched and sponged all day in the steamy fetor of a tailor-shop. But when work was done Ikey hitched his wagon to such stars as his firmament let shine.

It was Saturday night, and the boss laid twelve begrimed and begrudged dollars in his hand. Ikey dabbled discreetly in water, donned coat, hat and collar with its frazzled tie, and chalcedony pin, and set forth in pursuit of his ideals.

For each of us, when our day's work is done, must seek our ideal, whether it be love or pinochle or lobster à la Newburg, or the sweet silence of the musty bookshelves.

Behold Ikey as he ambles up the street beneath the roaring " El " between the rows of reeking sweatshops. Pallid, stooping, insignificant, squalid, doomed to exist forever in penury of body and mind, yet, as he swings his cheap cane and projects the noisome inhalations from his cigarette you perceive that he nurtures in his narrow bosom the bacillus of society.

Ikey's legs carried him to and into that famous place of enter-tainment known as the Café Maginnis—famous because it was the rendezvous of Billy McMahan, the greatest man, the most wonder-ful man, Ikey thought, that the world had ever produced.

Billy McMahan was the district leader. Upon him the Tiger purred, and his hand held manna to scatter. Now, as Ikey entered, McMahan stood, flushed and triumphant and mighty, the centre of a huzzaing concourse of his lieutenants and constituents. It seems there had been an election; a signal victory had been won; the city had been swept back into line by a resistless besom of ballots.

Ikey slunk along the bar and gazed, breath-quickened, at his idol.

How magnificent was Billy McMahan, with his great, smooth, laughing face; his gray eye, shrewd as a chicken's hawk; his diamond ring, his voice like a bugle call, his prince's air, his plump

and active roll of money, his clarion call to friend and comrade—
oh, what a king of men he was! How he obscured his lieutenants,
though they themselves loomed large and serious, blue of chin and
important of mien, with hands buried deep in the pockets of their
short overcoats! But Billy—oh, what small avail are words to paint
for you his glory as seen by Ikey Snigglefritz!

The Café Maginnis rang to the note of victory. The white-coated
bartenders threw themselves featfully upon bottle, cork and glass.
From a score of clear Havanas the air received its paradox of
clouds. The leal and the hopeful shook Billy McMahan's hand.
And there was born suddenly in the worshipful soul of Ikey
Snigglefritz an audacious, thrilling impulse.

He stepped forward into the little cleared space in which
majesty moved, and held out his hand.

Billy McMahan grasped it unhesitatingly, shook it and smiled.

Made mad now by the gods who were about to destroy him,
Ikey threw away his scabbard and charged upon Olympus.

"Have a drink with me, Billy," he said familiarly, "you and
your friends?"

"Don't mind if I do, old man," said the great leader, "just to
keep the ball rolling."

The last spark of Ikey's reason fled.

"Wine," he called to the bartender, waving a trembling hand.

The corks of three bottles were drawn; the champagne bubbled
in the long row of glasses set upon the bar. Billy McMahan took
his and nodded, with his beaming smile, at Ikey. The lieutenants and satellites took theirs and growled "Here's to you."
Ikey took his nectar in delirium. All drank.

Ikey threw his week's wages in a crumpled roll upon the bar.

"C'rect," said the bartender, smoothing the twelve one-dollar
notes. The crowd surged around Billy McMahan again. Some one
was telling how Brannigan fixed 'em over in the Eleventh. Ikey
leaned against the bar a while, and then went out.

He went down Hester street and up Chrystie, and down Delancey
to where he lived. And there his women folk, a bibulous mother
and three dingy sisters, pounced upon him for his wages. And at
his confession they shrieked and objurgated him in the pithy
rhetoric of the locality.

But even as they plucked at him and struck him Ikey remained
in his ecstatic trance of joy. His head was in the clouds; the star
was drawing his wagon. Compared with what he had achieved
the loss of wages and the bray of women's tongues were slight
affairs. He had shaken the hand of Billy McMahan.

       ★   ★   ★   ★   ★

Billy McMahan had a wife, and upon her visiting cards was engraved the name " Mrs. William Darragh McMahan," And there was a certain vexation attendant upon these cards; for, small as they were, there were houses in which they could not be inserted. Billy McMahan was a dictator in politics, a four-walled tower in business, a mogul, dread, loved and obeyed among his own people. He was growing rich; the daily papers had a dozen men on his trail to chronicle his every word of wisdom ; he had been honored in caricature holding the Tiger cringing in leash.

But the heart of Billy was sometimes sore within him. There was a race of men from which he stood apart but that he viewed with the eyes of Moses looking over into the promised land. He, too, had ideals, even as had Ikey Snigglefritz; and sometimes, hopeless of attaining them, his own solid success was as dust and ashes in his mouth. And Mrs. William Darragh McMahan wore a look of discontent upon her plump but pretty face, and the very rustle of her silks seemed a sigh.

There was a brave and conspicuous assemblage in the dining saloon of a noted hostelry where Fashion loves to display her charms. At one table sat Billy McMahan and his wife. Mostly silent they were, but the accessories they enjoyed little needed the indorsement of speech. Mrs. McMahan's diamonds were outshone by few in the room. The waiter bore the costliest brands of wine to their table. In evening dress, with an expression of gloom upon his smooth and massive countenance, you would look in vain for a more striking figure than Billy's.

Four tables away sat alone a tall, slender man, about thirty, with thoughtful, melancholy eyes, a Van Dyke beard and peculiarly white, thin hands. He was dining on filet mignon, dry toast and apollinaris. That man was Cortlandt Van Duyckink, a man worth eighty millions, who inherited and held a sacred seat in the exclusive inner circle of society.

Billy McMahan spoke to no one around him, because he knew no one. Van Duyckink kept his eyes on his plate because he knew that every one present was hungry to catch his. He could bestow knighthood and prestige by a nod, and he was chary of creating a too extensive nobility.

And then Billy McMahan conceived and accomplished the most startling and audacious act of his life. He rose deliberately and walked over to Cortlandt Van Ducykink's table and held out his hand.

" Say, Mr. Van Duyckink," he said, " I've heard you was talking about starting some reforms among the poor people down in my district. I'm McMahan, you know. Say, now, if that's straight I'll do all I can to help you. And what I says goes in that neck of the woods, don't it? Oh, says, I rather guess it does."

Van Duyckink's rather somber eyes lighted up. He rose to his lank height and grasped Billy McMahan's hand.

" Thank you, Mr. McMahan," he said, in his deep, serious tones. " I have been thinking of doing some work of that sort. I shall be glad of your assistance. It pleases me to have become acquainted with you."

Billy walked back to his seat. His shoulder was tingling from the accolade bestowed by royalty. A hundred eyes were now turned upon him in envy and new admiration. Mrs. William Darragh McMahan trembled with ecstasy, so that her diamonds smote the eye almost with pain. And now it was apparent that at many tables there were those who suddenly remembered that they enjoyed Mr. McMahan's acquaintance. He saw smiles and bows about him. He became enveloped in the aura of dizzy greatness. His campaign coolness deserted him.

" Wine for that gang ! " he commanded the waiter, pointing with his finger. " Wine over there. Wine to those three gents by that green bush. Tell 'em it's on me. D——n it ! Wine for everybody ! "

The waiter ventured to whisper that it was perhaps inexpedient to carry out the order, in consideration of the dignity of the house and its custom.

" All right," said Billy, " if it's against the rules. I wonder if 'twould do to send my friend Van Duyckink a bottle ? No ? Well, it'll flow all right at the caffy to-night, just the same. It'll be rubber boots for anybody who comes in there any time up to 2 A. M."

Billy McMahan was happy.

He had shaken the hand of Cortlandt Van Duyckink.

*   *   *   *   *

The big pale-gray auto with its shining metal work looked out of place moving slowly among the push carts and trash-heaps on the lower east side. So did Cortlandt Van Duyckink, with his aristocratic face and white, thin hands, as he steered carefully between the groups of ragged, scurrying youngsters in the streets. And so did Miss Constance Schuyler, with her dim, ascetic beauty, seated at his side.

" Oh, Cortlandt," she breathed, " isn't it sad that human beings have to live in such wretchedness and poverty ? And you—how noble it is of you to think of them, to give your time and money to improve their condition ! "

Van Duyckink turned his solemn eyes upon her.

" It is little," he said, sadly, " that I can do. The question is a

large one, and belongs to society. But even individual effort is not
thrown away. Look, Constance! On this street I have arranged to
build soup kitchens, where no one who is hungry will be turned
away. And down this other street are the old buildings that I shall
cause to be torn down and there erect others in place of those death-
traps of fire and disease."

Down Delancey slowly crept the pale-gray auto. Away from it
toddled coveys of wondering, tangle-haired, barefooted, unwashed
children. It stopped before a crazy brick structure, foul and awry.

Van Duyckink alighted to examine at a better perspective one
of the leaning walls. Down the steps of the building came a young
man who seemed to epitomize its degradation, squalor and in-
felicity—a narrow-chested, pale unsavory young man, puffing at
a cigarette.

Obeying a sudden impulse, Van Duyckink stepped out and
warmly grasped the hand of what seemed to him a living rebuke.

"I want to know you people," he said, sincerely. "I am going
to help you as much as I can. We shall be friends."

As the auto crept carefully away Cortlandt Van Duyckink felt
an unaccustomed glow about his heart. He was near to being a
happy man.

He had shaken the hand of Ikey Snigglefritz.

THE PURPLE DRESS

WE are to consider the shade known as purple. It is a color
justly in repute among the sons and daughters of man.
Emperors claim it for their especial dye. Good fellows everywhere
seek to bring their noses to the genial hue that follows the com-
mingling of the red and blue. We say of princes that they are born
to the purple; and no doubt they are, for the colic tinges their faces
with the royal tint equally with the snub-nosed countenance of a
woodchopper's brat. All women love it—when it is the fashion.

And now purple is being worn. You notice it on the streets. Of
course other colors are quite stylish as well—in fact, I saw a lovely
thing the other day in olive-green albatross, with a triple-lapped
flounce skirt trimmed with insert squares of silk, and a draped
fichu of lace opening over a shirred vest and double puff sleeves
with a lace band holding two gathered frills—but you see lots of
purple too. Oh, yes, you do; just take a walk down Twenty-third
Street any afternoon.

Therefore Maida—the girl with the big brown eyes and cinna-
mon-colored hair in the Bee-Hive Store—said to Grace—the girl

with the rhinestone brooch and peppermint-pepsin flavor to her speech—" I'm going to have a purple dress—a tailor-made purple dress—for Thanksgiving."

" Oh, are you," said Grace, putting away some $7\frac{1}{2}$ gloves into the $6\frac{3}{4}$ box. "Well, it's me for red. You see more red on Fifth Avenue. And the men all seem to like it."

" I like purple best," said Maida. "And old Schlegel has promised to make it for $8. It's going to be lovely. I'm going to have a plaited skirt and a blouse coat trimmed with a band of galloon under a white cloth collar with two rows of——"

" Sly boots ! " said Grace with an educated wink.

"—soutache braid over a surpliced white vest; and a plaited basque and——"

" Sly boots—sly boots ! " repeated Grace.

"—plaited gigot sleeves with a drawn velvet ribbon over an inside cuff. What do you mean by saying that ? "

" You think Mr. Ramsay likes purple. I heard him say yesterday he thought some of the dark shades of red were stunning."

" I don't care," said Maida. " I prefer purple, and them that don't like it can just take the other side of the street."

Which suggests the thought that after all, the followers of purple may be subject to slight delusions. Danger is near when a maiden thinks she can wear purple regardless of complexions and opinions; and when emperors think their purple robes will wear forever.

Maida had saved $18 after eight months of economy; and this had bought the goods for the purple dress and paid Schlegel $4 on the making of it. On the day before Thanksgiving she would have just enough to pay the remaining $4. And then for a holiday in a new dress—can earth offer anything more enchanting ?

Old Bachman, the proprietor of the Bee-Hive Store, always gave a Thanksgiving dinner to his employees. On every one of the subsequent 364 days, excusing Sundays, he would remind them of the joys of the past banquet and the hopes of the coming ones, thus inciting them to increased enthusiasm in work. The dinner was given in the store on one of the long tables in the middle of the room. They tacked wrapping paper over the front windows; and the turkeys and other good things were brought in the back way from the restaurant on the corner. You will perceive that the Bee-Hive was not a fashionable department store, with escalators and pompadours. It was almost small enough to be called an emporium; and you could actually go in there and get waited on and walk out again. And always at the Thanksgiving dinners Mr. Ramsay——

Oh, bother ! I should have mentioned Mr. Ramsay first of all. He is more important than purple or green, or even the red cran-

berry sauce. Mr. Ramsay was the head clerk; and as far as I am
concerned I am for him. He never pinched the girls' arms when
he passed them in dark corners of the store; and when he told
them stories when business was dull and the girls giggled and said :
" Oh, pshaw ! " it wasn't G. Bernard they meant at all. Besides
being a gentleman, Mr. Ramsay was queer and original in other
ways. He was a health crank, and believed that people should
never eat anything that was good for them. He was violently
opposed to anybody being comfortable, and coming in out of snow
storms, or wearing overshoes, or taking medicine, or coddling
themselves in any way. Every one of the ten girls in the store had
little pork-chop-and-fried-onion dreams every night of becoming
Mrs. Ramsay. For, next year old Bachman was going to take him
in for a partner. And each one of them knew that if she should
catch him she would knock those cranky health notions of his sky
high before the wedding cake indigestion was over.

Mr. Ramsay was master of ceremonies at the dinners. Always
they had two Italians in to play a violin and harp and had a little
dance in the store.

And here were two dresses being conceived to charm Ramsay—
one purple and the other red. Of course, the other eight girls were
going to have dresses too, but they didn't count. Very likely they'd
wear some shirt-waist-and-black-skirt-affairs—nothing as resplen-
dent as purple or red.

Grace had saved her money, too. She was going to buy her dress
ready-made. Oh, what's the use of bothering with a tailor—when
you've got a figger it's easy to get a fit—the ready-made are intended for a perfect figger—except I have to have 'em all taken
in at the waist—the average figger is so large waisted.

The night before Thanksgiving came. Maida hurried home,
keen and bright with the thoughts of the blessed morrow. Her
thoughts were of purple, but they were white themselves—the
joyous enthusiasm of the young for the pleasures that youth must
have or wither. She knew purple would become her, and—for the
thousandth time she tried to assure herself that it was purple Mr.
Ramsay said he liked and not red. She was going home first to
get the $4 wrapped in a piece of tissue paper in the bottom drawer
of her dresser, and then she was going to pay Schlegel and take
the dress home herself.

Grace lived in the same house. She occupied the hall room
above Maida's.

At home Maida found clamor and confusion. The landlady's
tongue clattering sourly in the halls like a churn dasher dabbing
in buttermilk. And then Grace come down to her room crying with
eyes as red as any dress.

" She says I've got to get out," said Grace. " The old beast. Because I owe her $4. She's put my trunk in the hall and locked the door. I can't go anywhere else. I haven't got a cent of money."

" You had some yesterday," said Maida.

" I paid it on my dress," said Grace. " I thought she'd wait till next week for the rent."

Sniffle, sniffle, sob, sniffle.

Out came—out it had to come—Maida's $4.

" You blessed darling," cried Grace, now a rainbow instead of sunset. " I'll pay the mean old thing and then I'm going to try on my dress. I think it's heavenly. Come up and look at it. I'll pay the money back, a dollar a week—honest I will."

Thanksgiving.

The dinner was to be at noon. At a quarter to twelve Grace switched into Maida's room. Yes, she looked charming. Red was her color. Maida sat by the window in her old cheviot skirt and blue waist darning a st——. Oh, doing fancy work.

" Why, goodness me ! ain't you dressed yet ? " shrilled the red one. " How does it fit in the back ? Don't you think these velvet tabs look awful swell ? Why ain't you dressed, Maida ? "

" My dress didn't get finished in time," said Maida. " I'm not going to the dinner."

" That's too bad. Why, I'm awfully sorry, Maida. Why don't you put on anything and come along—it's just the store folks, you know, and they won't mind."

" I was set on my purple," said Maida. " If I can't have it I won't go at all. Don't bother about me. Run along or you'll be late. You look awful nice in red."

At her window Maida sat through the long morning and past the time of the dinner at the store. In her mind she could hear the girls shrieking over a pull-bone, could hear old Bachman's roar over his own deeply-concealed jokes, could see the diamonds of fat Mrs. Bachman, who came to the store only on Thanksgiving days, could see Mr. Ramsay moving about, alert, kindly, looking to the comfort of all.

At four in the afternoon, with an expressionless face and a lifeless air she slowly made her way to Schlegel's shop and told him she could not pay the $4 due on the dress.

" Gott ! " cried Schlegel, angrily. " For what do you look so glum ? Take him away. He is ready. Pay me some time. Haf I not seen you pass mine shop every day in two years ? If I make clothes is it that I do not know how to read beoples because ? You will pay me some time when you can. Take him away. He is made goot; and if you look bretty in him all right. So. Pay me when you can."

Maida breathed a millionth part of the thanks in her heart, and hurried away with her dress. As she left the shop a smart dash of rain struck upon her face. She smiled and did not feel it.

Ladies who shop in carriages, you do not understand. Girls whose wardrobes are charged to the old man's account, you cannot begin to comprehend—you could not understand why Maida did not feel the cold dash of the Thanksgiving rain.

At five o'clock she went out upon the street wearing her purple dress. The rain had increased, and it beat down upon her in a steady, wind-blown pour. People were scurrying home and to cars with close-held umbrellas and tight buttoned raincoats. Many of them turned their heads to marvel at this beautiful, serene, happy-eyed girl in the purple dress walking through the storm as though she were strolling in a garden under summer skies.

I say you do not understand it, ladies of the full purse and varied wardrobe. You do not know what it is to live with a perpetual longing for pretty things—to starve eight months in order to bring a purple dress and a holiday together. What difference if it rained, hailed, blew, snowed, cycloned?

Maida had no umbrella nor overshoes. She had her purple dress and she walked abroad. Let the elements do their worst. A starved heart must have one crumb during a year. The rain ran down and dripped from her fingers.

Some one turned a corner and blocked her way. She looked up into Mr. Ramsay's eyes, sparkling with admiration and interest.

" Why, Miss Maida," said he, " you look simply magnificent in your new dress. I was greatly disappointed not to see you at our dinner. And of all the girls I ever knew, you show the greatest sense and intelligence. There is nothing more healthful and invigorating than braving the weather as you are doing. May I walk with you ? "

And Maida blushed and sneezed.

THE FOREIGN POLICY OF COMPANY 99

JOHN BYRNES, hose-cart driver of Engine Company No. 99, was afflicted with what his comrades called Japanitis.

Byrnes had a war map spread permanently upon a table in the second story of the engine-house, and he could explain to you at any hour of the day or night the exact positions, conditions and intentions of both the Russian and Japanese armies. He had little clusters of pins stuck in the map which represented the opposing forces, and these he moved about from day to day in conformity with the war news in the daily papers.

Wherever the Japs won a victory John Byrnes would shift his pins, and then he would execute a war dance of delight, and the other firemen would hear him yell : " Go it, you blamed little, sawed-off, huckleberry-eyed, monkey-faced hot tamales ! Eat 'em up, you little sleight-o'-hand, bow-legged bull terriers—give 'em another of them Yalu looloos, and you'll eat rice in St. Petersburg. Talk about your Russians—say, wouldn't they give you painsky when it comes to a scrapovitch ? "

Not even on the fair island of Nippon was there a more enthusiastic champion of the Mikado's men. Supporters of the Russian cause did well to keep clear of Engine-House No. 99.

Sometimes all thoughts of the Japs left John Byrnes's head. That was when the alarm of fire had sounded and he was strapped in his driver's seat on the swaying cart, guiding Erebus and Joe, the finest team in the whole department—according to the crew of 99.

Of all the codes adopted by man for regulating his actions toward his fellow-mortals, the greatest are these—the code of King Arthur's Knights of the Round Table, the Constitution of the United States and the unwritten rules of the New York Fire Department. The Round Table methods are no longer practicable since the invention of street cars and breach-of-promise suits, and our Constitution is being found more and more unconstitutional every day, so the code of our firemen must be considered in the lead, with the Golden Rule and Jeffries's new punch trying for place and show.

The Constitution says that one man is as good as another; but the Fire Department says he is better. This is a too generous theory, but the law will not allow itself to be construed otherwise. All of which comes perilously near to being a paradox, and commends itself to the attention of the S. P. C. A.

One of the transatlantic liners dumped out at Ellis Island a lump of protozoa which was expected to evolve into an American citizen. A steward kicked him down the gangway, a doctor pounced upon his eyes like a raven, seeking for trachoma or ophthalmia; he was hustled ashore and ejected into the city in the name of Liberty— perhaps, theoretically, thus inoculating against kingocracy with a drop of its own virus. This hypodermic injection of Europeanism wandered happily into the veins of the city with the broad grin of a pleased child. It was not burdened with baggage, cares or ambitions. Its body was lithely built and clothed in a sort of foreign fustian; its face was brightly vacant, with a small, flat nose, and was mostly covered by a thick, ragged, curling beard like the coat of a spaniel. In the pocket of the imported Thing were a few coins

—denarii—scudi—kopecks—pfennigs—pilasters—whatever the financial nomenclature of his unknown country may have been.

Prattling to himself, always broadly grinning, pleased by the roar, and movement of the barbarous city into which the steamship cut-rates had shunted him, the alien strayed away from the sea, which he hated, as far as the district covered by Engine Company No. 99. Light as a cork, he was kept bobbing along by the human tide, the crudest atom in all the silt of the stream that emptied into the reservoir of Liberty.

While crossing Third Avenue he slowed his steps, enchanted by the thunder of the elevated trains above him and the soothing crash of the wheels on the cobbles. And then there was a new, delightful chord in the uproar—the musical clanging of a gong and a great shining juggernaut belching fire and smoke, that people were hurrying to see.

This beautiful thing, entrancing to the eye, dashed past, and the protoplasmic immigrant stepped into the wake of it with his broad, enraptured, uncomprehending grin. And so stepping, stepped into the path of No. 99's flying hose-cart, with John Byrnes gripping, with arms of steel, the reins over the plunging backs of Erebus and Joe.

The unwritten constitutional code of the fireman has no exceptions or amendments. It is a simple thing—as simple as the rule of three. There was the heedless unit in the right of way; there was the hose-cart, and the iron pillar of the elevated railroad.

John Byrnes swung all his weight and muscle on the left rein. The team and cart swerved that way and crashed like a torpedo into the pillar. The men on the cart went flying like skittles. The driver's strap burst, the pillar rang with the shock, and John Byrnes fell on the car track with a broken shoulder twenty feet away, while Erebus—beautiful, raven-black, best-loved Erebus— lay whickering in his harness with a broken leg.

In consideration for the feelings of the Engine Company No. 99 the details will be lightly touched. The company does not like to be reminded of that day. There was a great crowd, and hurry calls were sent in; and while the ambulance gong was clearing the way the men of No. 99 heard the crack of the S. P. C. A. agent's pistol, and turned their heads away, not daring to look toward Erebus again.

When the fireman got back to the engine-house they found that one of them was dragging by the collar the cause of their desolation and grief. They set it in the middle of the floor and gathered grimly about it. Through its whiskers the calamitous object chattered effervescently and waved its hands.

" Sounds like a seidlitz powder," said Mike Dowling, disgustedly,

" and it makes me sicker than one. Call that a man !—that hoss was worth a steamer full of such two-legged animals. It's a immigrant—that's what it is."

" Look at the doctor's chalk mark on its coat," said Reilly, the desk man. " It's just landed. It must be a kind of a Dago or a Hun or one of them Finns, I guess. That's the kind of truck that Europe unloads onto us."

" Think of a thing like that getting in the way and laying John up in hospital and spoiling the best fire team in the city," groaned another fireman. " It ought to be taken down to the dock and drowned."

" Somebody go around and get Sloviski," suggested the engine driver, " and let's see what nation is responsible for this conglomeration of hair and head noises."

Sloviski kept a delicatessen store around the corner on Third Avenue, and was reputed to be a linguist.

One of the men fetched him—a fat, cringing man, with a discursive eye and the odors of many kinds of meats upon him.

" Take a whirl at this importation with your jaw-breakers, Sloviski," requested Mike Dowling. " We can't quite figure out whether he's from the Hackensack bottoms or Hongkong-on-the-Ganges."

Sloviski addressed the stranger in several dialects, that ranged in rhythm and cadence from the sounds produced by a tonsillitis gargle to the opening of a can of tomatoes with a pair of scissors. The immigrant replied in accents resembling the uncorking of a bottle of ginger ale.

" I have you his name," reported Sloviski. " You shall not pronounce it. Writing of it in paper is better." They gave him paper, and he wrote, " Demetre Svangvsk."

" Looks like short hand," said the desk man.

" He speaks some language," continued the interpreter, wiping his forehead, " of Austria and mixed with a little Turkish. And, den, he have some Magyar words and a Polish or two, and many like the Roumanian, but not without talk of one tribe in Bessarabia. I do not quite understand."

" Would you call him a Dago or a Polocker, or what ? " asked Mike, frowning at the polyglot description.

" He is a "—answered Sloviski—" he is a—I dink he come from —I dink he is a fool," he concluded, impatient at his linguistic failure, " and if you pleases I will go back at mine delicatessen."

" Whatever he is, he's a bird," said Mike Dowling; " and you want to watch him fly."

Taking by the wing the alien fowl that had fluttered into the nest of Liberty, Mike led him to the door of the engine-house and bestowed upon him a kick hearty enough to convey the entire animus of Company 99. Demetre Svangvsk hustled away down the sidewalk, turning once to show his ineradicable grin to the aggrieved firemen.

In three weeks John Byrnes was back at his post from the hospital. With great gusto he proceeded to bring his war map up to date. " My money on the Japs every time," he declared. " Why, look at them Russians—they're nothing but wolves. Wipe 'em out, I say—and the little old jiu-jitsu gang are just the cherry blossoms to do the trick, and don't you forget it ! "

The second day after Byrnes's reappearance came Demetre Svangvsk, the unidentified, to the engine-house, with a broader grin than ever. He managed to convey the idea that he wished to congratulate the hose-cart driver on his recovery and to apologize for having caused the accident. This he accomplished by so many extravagant gestures and explosive noises that the company was diverted for half an hour. Then they kicked him out again, and on the next day he came back grinning. How or where he lived no one knew. And then John Byrnes's nine-year-old son, Chris, who brought him convalescent delicacies from home to eat, took a fancy to Svangvsk, and they allowed him to loaf about the door of the engine-house occasionally.

One afternoon the big drab automobile of the Deputy Fire Commissioner buzzed up to the door of No. 99 and the Deputy stepped inside for an informal inspection. Then men kicked Svangvsk out a little harder than usual and proudly escorted the Deputy around 99, in which everything shone like my lady's mirror.

The Deputy respected the sorrow of the company concerning the loss of Erebus, and he had come to promise it another mate for Joe that would do him credit. So they let Joe out of his stall and showed the Deputy how deserving he was of the finest mate that could be in horsedom.

While they were circling around Joe confabbing, Chris climbed into the Deputy's auto and threw the power full on. The men heard a monster puffing and a shriek from the lad, and sprang out too late. The big auto shot away, luckily taking a straight course down the street. The boy knew nothing of its machinery; he sat clutching the cushions and howling. With the power on nothing could have stopped that auto except a brick house, and there was nothing for Chris to gain by such a stoppage.

Demetre Svangvsk was just coming in again with a grin for another kick when Chris played his merry little prank. While the others sprang for the door Demetre sprang for Joe. He glided upon the horse's bare back like a snake and shouted something at

him like the crack of a dozen whips. One of the firemen afterward
swore that Joe answered him back in the same language. Ten
seconds after the auto started the big horse was eating up the asphalt
behind it like a strip of macaroni.

Some people two blocks and a half away saw the rescue. They
said that the auto was nothing but a drab noise with a black speck
in the middle of it for Chris, when a big bay horse with a lizard
lying on its back cantered up alongside of it, and the lizard reached
over and picked the black speck out of the noise.

Only fifteen minutes after Svangvsk's last kicking at the hands
—or rather the feet—of Engine Company No. 99 he rode Joe back
through the door with the boy safe, but acutely conscious of the
licking he was going to receive.

Svangvsk slipped to the floor, leaned his head against Joe's and
made a noise like a clucking hen. Joe nodded and whistled loudly
through his notrils, putting to shame the knowledge of Sloviski,
of the delicatessen.

John Byrnes walked up to Svangvsk, who grinned, expecting to
be kicked. Byrnes gripped the outlander so strongly by the hand
that Demetre grinned anyhow, conceiving it to be a new form of
punishment.

" The heathen rides like a Cossack," remarked a fireman who
had seen a Wild West show—" they're the greatest riders in the
world."

The word seemed to electrify Svangvsk. He grinned wider than
ever.

" Yas—yas—me Cossack," he spluttered, striking his chest.

" Cossack ! " repeated John Byrnes, thoughtfully, " ain't that
a kind of a Russian ? "

" They're one of the Russian tribes, sure," said the desk man,
who read books between fire alarms.

Just then Alderman Foley, who was on his way home and did
not know of the runaway, stopped at the door of the engine-house
and called to Byrnes.

" Hello there, Jimmy, me boy—how's the war coming along ?
Japs still got the bear on the trot, have they ? "

" Oh, I don't know," said John Byrnes, argumentatively, " them
Japs haven't got any walkover. You wait till Kuropatkin gets a
good whack at 'em and they won't be knee-high to a puddle-
ducksky."

THE LOST BLEND

Since the bar has been blessed by the clergy, and cocktails open the dinners of the elect, one may speak of the saloon. Teetotalers need not listen, if they choose; there is always the slot restaurant, where a dime dropped into the cold bouillon aperture will bring forth a dry Martini.

Con Lantry worked on the sober side of the bar in Kenealy's café. You and I stood, one-legged like geese, on the other side and went into voluntary liquidation with our week's wages. Opposite danced Con, clean, temperate, clear-headed, polite, white-jacketed, punctual, trustworthy, young, responsible, and took our money.

The saloon (whether blessed or cursed) stood in one of those little " places " which are parallelograms instead of streets, and inhabited by laundries, decayed Knickerbocker families and Bohemians who have nothing to do with either.

Over the café lived Kenealy and his family. His daughter Katherine had eyes of dark Irish—but why should you be told? Be content with your Geraldine or your Eliza Ann. For Con dreamed of her; and when she called softly at the foot of the back stairs for the pitcher of beer for dinner, his heart went up and down like a milk punch in the shaker. Orderly and fit are the rules of Romance; and if you hurl the last shilling of your fortune upon the bar for whiskey, the bartender shall take it, and marry his boss's daughter, and good will grow out of it.

But not so Con. For in the presence of woman he was tongue-tied and scarlet. He who would quell with his eye the sonorous youth whom the claret punch made loquacious, or smash with lemon squeezer the obstreperous, or hurl gutterward the cantankerous without a wrinkle coming to his white lawn tie, when he stood before a woman he was voiceless, incoherent, stuttering, buried beneath a hot avalanche of bashfulness and misery. What then was he before Katherine? A trembler, with no word to say for himself, a stone without blarney, the dumbest lover that ever babbled of the weather in the presence of his divinity.

There came to Kenealy's two sunburned men, Riley and Mc-Quirk. They had conference with Kenealy; and then they took possession of a back room which they filled with bottles and siphons and jugs and druggist's measuring glasses. All the appurtenances and liquids of a saloon were there, but they dispensed no drinks. All day long the two sweltered in there, pouring and mixing unknown brews and decoctions from the liquors in their store. Riley had the education, and he figured on reams of paper, reducing gallons to ounces and quarts to fluid drams. McQuirk, a morose man with a red eye, dashed each unsuccessful completed mixture into the waste pipe with curses gentle, husky and deep. They labored heavily and untiringly to achieve some mysterious solution like two alchemists striving to resolve gold from the elements.

Into this back room one evening when his watch was done sauntered Con. His professional curiosity had been stirred by these occult bartenders at whose bar none drank, and who daily drew upon Kenealy's store of liquors to follow their consuming and fruitless experiments.

Down the back stairs came Katherine with her smile like sunrise on Gweebarra Bay.

" Good evening, Mr. Lantry," says she. "And what is the news to-day, if you please ? "

" It looks like r-rain," stammered the shy one, backing to the wall.

" It couldn't do better," said Katherine. " I'm thinking there's nothing the worse off for a little water." In the back room Riley and McQuirk toiled like bearded witches over their strange compounds. From fifty bottles they drew liquids carefully measured after Riley's figures, and shook the whole together in a great glass vessel. Then McQuirk would dash it out, with gloomy profanity, and they would begin again.

" Sit down," said Riley to Con, " and I'll tell you."

" Last summer me and Tim concludes that an American bar in this nation of Nicaragua would pay. There was a town on the coast where there's nothing to eat but quinine and nothing to drink but rum. The natives and foreigners lay down with chills and get up with fevers; and a good mixed drink is nature's remedy for all such tropical inconveniences.

" So we lays in a fine stock of wet goods in New York, and bar fixtures and glassware, and we sails for that Santa Palma town on a lime steamer. On the way me and Tim sees flying fish and play seven-up with the captain and steward, and already begins to feel like the high-ball kings of the tropics of Capricorn.

" When we gets in five hours of the country that we was going to introduce to long drinks and short change the captain calls us over to the starboard binnacle and recollects a few things.

" 'I forgot to tell you, boys,' says he, ' that Nicaragua slapped an import duty of 48 per cent. ad valorem on all bottled goods last month. The President took a bottle of Cincinnati hair tonic by mistake for tabasco sauce, and he's getting even. Barrelled goods is free.'

" 'Sorry you didn't mention it sooner,' says we. And we bought two forty-two gallon casks from the captain, and opened every bottle we had and dumped the stuff altogether in the casks. That 48 per cent. would have ruined us; so we took the chances on making that $1,200 cocktail rather than throw the stuff away.

" Well, when we landed we tapped one of the barrels. The mixture was something heartrending. It was the color of a plate of Bowery pea soup, and it tasted like one of those coffee substitutes your aunt makes you take for the heart trouble you get by picking losers. We gave a nigger four fingers of it to try it, and he lay under a cocoanut tree three days beating the sand with his heels and refused to sign a testimonial.

" But the other barrel ! Say, bartender, did you ever put on a straw hat with a yellow band around it and go up in a balloon with a pretty girl with $8,000,000 in your pocket all at the same time ? That's what the thirty drops of it would make you feel like. With two fingers of it inside you you would bury your face in your hands and cry because there wasn't anything more worth while around for you to lick than little Jim Jeffries. Yes, sir, that stuff in that second barrel was distilled elixir of battle, money and high life. It was the color of gold and as clear as glass, and it shone after dark like the sunshine was still in it. A thousand years from now you'll get a drink like that across the bar.

" Well, we started up business with that one line of drinks, and it was enough. The piebald gentry of that country stuck to it like a hive of bees. If that barrel had lasted that country would have become the greatest on earth. When we opened up of mornings we had a line of generals and colonels and ex-presidents and revolutionists a block long waiting to be served. We started in at 50 cents silver a drink. The last ten gallons went easy at $5 a gulp. It was wonderful stuff. It gave a man courage and ambition and nerve to do anything; at the same time he didn't care whether his money was tainted or fresh from the Ice Trust. When that barrel was half gone Nicaragua had repudiated the National debt, removed the duty on cigarettes and was about to declare war on the United States and England.

" 'Twas by accident we discovered this king of drinks, and 'twill be by good luck if we strike it again. For ten months we've been trying. Small lots at a time, we've mixed barrels of all the harmful ingredients known to the profession of drinking. Ye could have stocked ten bars with the whiskies, brandies, cordials, bitters, gins and wines me and Tim have wasted. A glorious drink like that to be denied the world ! 'Tis a sorrow and a loss of money. The United States as a nation would welcome a drink of that sort, and pay for it."

All the while McQuirk had been carefully measuring and pouring together small quantities of various spirits, as Riley called them, from his latest pencilled prescription. The completed mixture was of a vile, mottled chocolate color. McQuirk tasted it, and hurled it, with appropriate epithets, into the waste sink.

" 'Tis a strange story, even if true," said Con. " I'll be going now along to my supper."

" Take a drink," said Riley. " We've all kinds except the lost blend."

" I never drink," said Con, " anything stronger than water. I am just after meeting Miss Katherine by the stairs. She said a true word, ' There's not anything,' says she, ' but is better off for a little water.' "

When Con had left them Riley almost felled McQuirk by a blow on the back.

" Did ye hear that ? " he shouted. " Two fools are we. The six dozen bottles of 'pollinaris we had on the ship—ye opened them yourself—which barrel did ye pour them in—which barrel, ye mudhead ? "

" I mind," said McQuirk, slowly, " 'twas in the second barrel we opened. I mind the blue piece of paper pasted on the side of it."

" We've got it now," cried Riley. " 'Twas that we lacked. 'Tis the water that does the trick. Everything else we had right. Hurry, man, and get two bottles of 'pollinaris from the bar, while I figure out the proportionments with me pencil."

An hour later Con strolled down the sidewalk toward Kenealy's café. Thus faithful employees haunt, during their recreation hours, the vicinity where they labor, drawn by some mysterious attraction.

A police patrol wagon stood at the side door. Three able cops were half carrying, half hustling Riley and McQuirk up its rear steps. The eyes and faces of each bore the bruises and cuts of sanguinary and assiduous conflict. Yet they whooped with strange joy, and directed upon the police the feeble remnants of their pugnacious madness.

" Began fighting each other in the back room," explained Kenealy to Con. "And singing ! That was worse. Smashed everything pretty much up. But they're good men. They'll pay for everything. Trying to invent some new kind of cocktail, they was. I'll see they come out all right in the morning."

Con sauntered into the back room to view the battlefield. As he went through the hall Katherine was just coming down the stairs.

" Good evening again, Mr. Lantry," said she. "And is there no news from the weather yet ? "

" Still threatens r-rain," said Con. slipping past with red in his smooth, pale cheek.

Riley and McQuirk had indeed waged a great and friendly battle. Broken bottles and glasses were everywhere. The room was full of alcohol fumes; the floor was variegated with spirituous puddles.

On the table stood a 32-ounce glass graduated measure. In the bottom of it were two tablespoonfuls of liquid—a bright golden liquid that seemed to hold the sunshine a prisoner in its auriferous depths.

Con smelled it. He tasted it. He drank it.

As he returned through the hall Katherine was just going up the stairs.

" No news yet, Mr. Lantry ? " she asked with her teasing laugh.

Con lifted her clear from the floor and held her there.

" The news is," he said, " that we're to be married."

" Put me down, sir ! " she cried indignantly, " or I will—— Oh, Con, oh, wherever did you get the nerve to say it ? "

A HARLEM TRAGEDY

HARLEM.

Mrs. Fink had dropped into Mrs. Cassidy's flat one flight below.

"Ain't it a beaut ? " said Mrs. Cassidy.

She turned her face proudly for her friend Mrs. Fink to see. One eye was nearly closed, with a great, greenish-purple bruise around it. Her lip was cut and bleeding a little and there were red finger-marks on each side of her neck.

" My husband wouldn't ever think of doing that to me," said Mrs. Fink, concealing her envy.

" I wouldn't have a man," declared Mrs. Cassidy, " that didn't beat me up at least once a week. Shows he thinks something of you. Say ! but that last dose Jack gave me wasn't no homeopathic one. I can see no stars yet. But he'll be the sweetest man in town for the rest of the week to make up for it. This eye is good for theater tickets and a silk shirt waist at the very least."

" I should hope," said Mrs. Fink, assuming complacency, " that Mr. Fink is too much of a gentleman ever to raise his hand against me."

" Oh, go on, Maggie ! " said Mrs. Cassidy, laughing and applying witch hazel, " you're only jealous. Your old man is too frappéd and slow to ever give you a punch. He just sits down and practises physical culture with a newspaper when he comes home—now ain't that the truth?"

"Mr. Fink certainly peruses of the papers when he comes home," acknowledged Mrs. Fink, with a toss of her head; "but he certainly don't ever make no Steve O'Donnell out of me just to amuse himself—that's a sure thing."

Mrs. Cassidy laughed the contented laugh of the guarded and happy matron. With the air of Cornelia exhibiting her jewels, she drew down the collar of her kimono and revealed another treasured bruise, maroon-colored, edged with olive and orange —a bruise now nearly well, but still to memory dear.

Mrs. Fink capitulated. The formal light in her eye softened to envious admiration. She and Mrs. Cassidy had been chums in the downtown paper-box factory before they had married, one year before. Now she and her man occupied the flat above Mame and her man. Therefore she could not put on airs with Mame.

"Don't it hurt when he soaks you?" asked Mrs. Fink, curiously.

"Hurt!"—Mrs. Cassidy gave a soprano scream of delight. "Well, say—did you ever have a brick house fall on you?—well, that's just the way it feels—just like when they're digging you out of the ruins. Jack's got a left that spells two matinées and a new pair of Oxfords—and his right!—well, it takes a trip to Coney and six pairs of openwork silk lisle threads to make that good."

"But what does he beat you for?" inquired Mrs. Fink, with wide-open eyes.

"Silly!" said Mrs. Cassidy, indulgently. "Why, because he's full. It's generally on Saturday nights."

"But what cause do you give him?" persisted the seeker after knowledge.

"Why, didn't I marry him? Jack comes in tanked up; and I'm here, ain't I? Who else has he got a right to beat? I'd just like to catch him once beating anybody else! Sometimes it's because supper ain't ready; and sometimes it's because it is. Jack ain't particular about causes. He just lushes till he remembers he's married, and then he makes for home and does me up. Saturday nights I just move the furniture with sharp corners out of the way, so I won't cut my head when he gets his work in. He's got a left swing that jars you! Sometimes I take the count in the first round; but when I feel like having a good time during the week or want some new rags I come up again for more punishment. That's what I done last night. Jack knows I've been wanting a black silk waist for a month, and I didn't think just one black eye would bring it. Tell you what, Mag, I'll bet you the ice cream he brings it to-night."

Mrs. Fink was thinking deeply.

" My Mart," she said, " never hit me a lick in his life. It's just like you said, Mame; he comes in grouchy and ain't got a word to say. He never takes me out anywhere. He's a chair-warmer at home for fair. He buys me things, but he looks so glum about it that I never appreciate 'em."

Mrs. Cassidy slipped an arm around her chum.

" You poor thing ! " she said. " But everybody can't have a husband like Jack. Marriage wouldn't be no failure if they was all like him. These discontented wives you hear about—what they need is a man to come home and kick their slats in once a week, and then make it up in kisses, and chocolate creams. That'd give 'em some interest in life. What I want is a masterful man that slugs you when he's jagged and hugs you when he ain't jagged. Preserve me from the man that ain't got the sand to do neither ! "

Mrs. Fink sighed.

The hallways were suddenly filled with sound. The door flew open at the kick of Mr. Cassidy. His arms were occupied with bundles. Mame flew and hung about his neck. Her sound eye sparkled with the love light that shines in the eye of the Maori maid when she recovers consciousness in the hut of the wooer who has stunned and dragged her there.

" Hello, old girl ! " shouted Mr. Cassidy. He shed his bundles and lifted her off her feet in a mighty hug. " I got tickets for Barnum & Bailey's, and if you'll bust the string of one of them bundles I guess you'll find that silk waist—why, good evening, Mrs. Fink—I didn't see you at first. How's old Mart coming along ? "

" He's very well, Mr. Cassidy—thanks," said Mrs. Fink. " I must be going along up now. Mart'll be home for supper soon. I'll bring you down the pattern you wanted to-morrow, Mame,"

Mrs. Fink went up to her flat and had a little cry. It was a meaningless cry, the kind of cry that only a woman knows about, a cry from no particular cause, altogether an absurd cry; the most transient and the most hopeless cry in the repertory of grief. Why had Martin never thrashed her ? He was as big and strong as Jack Cassidy. Did he not care for her at all ? He never quarrelled; he came home and lounged about silent, glum, idle. He was a fairly good provider, but he ignored the spices of life.

Mrs. Fink's ship of dreams was becalmed. Her captain ranged between plum duff and his hammock. If only he would shiver his timbers or stamp his foot on the quarter-deck now and then ! And she had thought to sail so merrily, touching at ports in the Delectable Isles ! But now, to vary the figure, she was ready to throw up the sponge, tired out, without a scratch to show for all those tame rounds with her sparring partner. For one moment she almost hated Mame—Mame, with her cuts and bruises, her salve of presents and kisses; her stormy voyage with her fighting, brutal, loving mate.

Mr. Fink came home at 7. He was permeated with the curse of domesticity. Beyond the portals of his cozy home he cared not to roam, to roam. He was the man who had caught the street car, the anaconda that had swallowed its prey, the tree that lay as it had fallen.

" Like the supper, Mart ? " asked Mrs. Fink, who had striven over it.

" M-m-m-yep," grunted Mr. Fink.

After supper he gathered his newspapers to read. He sat in his stocking feet.

Arise, some new Dante, and sing me the· befitting corner of perdition for the man who sitteth in the house in his stockinged feet. Sisters in Patience who by reason of ties or duty have endured it in silk, yarn, cotton, lisle thread or woollen—does not the new canto belong ?

The next day was Labor Day. The occupations of Mr. Cassidy and Mr. Fink ceased for one passage of the sun. Labor, triumphant, would parade and otherwise disport itself.

Mrs. Fink took Mrs. Cassidy's pattern down early. Mame had on her new silk waist. Even her damaged eye managed to emit a holiday gleam. Jack was fruitfully penitent, and there was a hilarious scheme for the day afoot, with parks and picnics and Pilsener in it.

A rising, indignant jealousy seized Mrs. Fink as she returned to her flat above. Oh, happy Mame, with her bruises and her quick-following balm ! But was Mame to have a monopoly of happiness ? Surely Martin Fink was as good a man as Jack Cassidy. Was his wife to go always unbelabored and uncaressed ? A sudden, brilliant breathless idea came to Mrs. Fink. She would show Mame that there were husbands as able to use their fists and perhaps to be as tender afterward as any Jack.

The holiday promised to be a nominal one with the Finks. Mrs. Fink had the stationary washtubs in the kitchen filled with a two-weeks' wash that had been soaking overnight. Mr. Fink sat in his stockinged feet reading a newspaper. Thus Labor Day presaged to speed.

Jealousy surged high in Mrs. Fink's heart and higher still surged an audacious resolve. If her man would not strike her—if he would not so far prove his manhood, his prerogative and his interst in conjugal affairs, he must be prompted to do his duty.

Mr. Fink lit his pipe and peacefully rubbed an ankle with a stockinged toe. He reposed in the state of matrimony like a lump of unblended suet in a pudding. This was his level Elysium—to sit at ease vicariously girdling the world in print amid the wifely splashing of suds and the agreeable smells of breakfast dishes departed and dinner ones to come. Many ideas were far from his mind; but the furthest one was the thought of beating his wife.

Mrs. Fink turned on the hot water and set the washboards in the suds. Up from the flat below came the gay laugh of Mrs. Cassidy. It sounded like a taunt, a flaunting of her own happiness in the face of the unslugged bride above. Now was Mrs. Fink's time.

Suddenly she turned like a fury upon the man reading.

" You lazy loafer ! " she cried, " must I work my arms off washing and toiling for the ugly likes of you ? Are you a man or are you a kitchen hound ? "

Mr. Fink dropped his paper, motionless from surprise. She feared that he would not strike—that the provocation had been insufficient. She leaped at him and struck him fiercely in the face with her clenched hand. In that instant she felt a thrill of love for him such as she had not felt for many a day. Rise up, Martin Fink, and come into your kingdom ! Oh, she must feel the weight of his hand now—just to show that he cared—just to show that he cared !

Mr. Fink sprang to his feet—Maggie caught him again on the jaw with a wide swing of her other hand. She closed her eyes in that fearful, blissful moment before his blow should come—she whispered his name to herself—she leaned to the expected shock, hungry for it.

In the flat below Mr. Cassidy, with a shamed and contrite face was powdering Mame's eye in preparation for their junket. From the flat above came the sound of a woman's voice, high-raised, a bumping, a stumbling and a shuffling, a chair overturned—unmistakable sounds of domestic conflict.

" Mart and Mag scrapping ? " postulated Mr. Cassidy. " Didn't know they ever indulged. Shall I trot up and see if they need a sponge holder ? "

One of Mrs. Cassidy's eyes sparkled like a diamond. The other twinkled at least like paste.

" Oh, oh," she said, softly and without apparent meaning, in the feminine ejaculatory manner. "I wonder if—wonder if ! Wait, Jack, till I go up and see."

Up the stairs she sped. As her foot struck the hallway above out from the kitchen door of her flat wildly flounced Mrs. Fink.

" Oh, Maggie," cried Mrs. Cassidy, in a delighted whisper; " did he ? Oh, did he ? "

Mrs. Fink ran and laid her face upon her chum's shoulder and sobbed hopelessly.

Mrs. Cassidy took Maggie's face between her hands and lifted it gently. Tear-stained it was, flushing and paling, but its velvety, pink-and-white, becomingly freckled surface was unscratched, unbruised, unmarred by the recreant fist of Mr. Fink.

" Tell me, Maggie," pleaded Mame, " or I'll go in there and find out. What was it ? Did he hurt you—what did he do ? "

Mrs. Fink's face went down again despairingly on the bosom of her friend.

" For God's sake don't open that door, Mame," she sobbed. "And don't ever tell nobody—keep it under your hat. He—he never touched me, and—he's—oh, Gawd—he's washin' the clothes —he's washin' the clothes ! "

"THE GUILTY PARTY"

A RED-HAIRED, unshaven, untidy man sat in a rocking chair by a window. He had just lighted a pipe, and was puffing blue clouds with great satisfaction. He had removed his shoes and donned a pair of blue, faded carpet-slippers. With the morbid thirst of the confirmed daily news drinker, he awkwardly folded back the pages of an evening paper, eagerly gulping down the strong, black headlines, to be followed as a chaser by the milder details of the smaller type.

In an adjoining room a woman was cooking supper. Odors from strong bacon and boiling coffee contended against the cut-plug fumes from the vespertine pipe.

Outside was one of those crowded streets of the east side, in which, as twilight falls, Satan sets up his recruiting office. A mighty host of children danced and ran and played in the street. Some in rags, some in clean white and beribboned, some wild and restless as young hawks, some gentle-faced and shrinking, some shrieking rude and sinful words, some listening, awed, but soon, grown familiar, to embrace—here were the children playing in the corridors of the House of Sin. Above the playground forever hovered a great bird. The bird was known to humorists as the stork. But the people of Chrystie Street were better ornithologists. They called it a vulture.

A little girl of twelve came up timidly to the man reading and resting by the window, and said :

" Papa, won't you play a game of checkers with me if you aren't too tired ? "

The red-haired, unshaven, untidy man sitting shoeless by the window answered, with a frown.

"Checkers. No, I won't. Can't a man who works hard all day have a little rest when he comes home ? Why don't you go out and play with the other kids on the sidewalk ? "

The woman who was cooking came to the door.

"John," she said. " I don't like for Lizzie to play in the street. They learn too much there that ain't good for 'em. She's been in the house all day long. It seems that you might give up a little of your time to amuse her when you come home."

"Let her go out and play like the rest of 'em if she wants to be amused," said the red-haired, unshaven, untidy man, " and don't bother me."

★   ★   ★   ★   ★

"You're on," said Kid Mullaly. " Fifty dollars to $25 I take Annie to the dance. Put up."

The Kid's black eyes were snapping with the fire of the baited and challenged. He drew out his " roll " and slapped five tens upon the bar. The three or four young fellows who were thus " taken " more slowly produced their stake. The bartender, ex-officio stakeholder, took the money, laboriously wrapped it, recorded the bet with an inch-long pencil and stuffed the whole into a corner of the cash register.

"And, oh, what'll be done to you'll be a plenty," said a bettor, with anticipatory glee.

"That's my lookout," said the " Kid," sternly. " Fill 'em up all around, Mike."

After the round Burke, the Kid's sponge, sponge-holder, pal, mentor and Grand Vizier, drew him out to the bootblack stand at the saloon corner where all the official and important matters of the Small Hours Social Club were settled. As Tony polished the light tan shoes of the club's President and Secretary for the fifth time that day, Burke spake words of wisdom to his chief.

"Cut that blonde out, Kid," was his advice, " or there'll be trouble. What do you want to throw down that girl of yours for ? You'll never find one that'll freeze to you like Liz has. She's worth a hallful of Annies."

"I'm no Annie admirer ! " said the Kid, dropping a cigarette ash on his polished toe, and wiping it off on Tony's shoulder. "But I want to teach Liz a lesson. She thinks I belong to her. She's been bragging that I daren't speak to another girl. Liz is all right—in some ways. She's drinking a little too much lately. And she uses language that a lady oughtn't."

"You're engaged, ain't you ? " asked Burke.

" Sure. We'll get married next year, maybe."

" I saw you make her drink her first glass of beer," said Burke. " That was two years ago, when she used to come down to the corner of Chrystie bareheaded to meet you after supper. She was a quiet sort of a kid then, and couldn't speak without blushing."

" She's a little spitfire, sometimes, now," said the Kid. " I hate jealousy. That's why I'm going to the dance with Annie. It'll teach her some sense."

" Well, you better look a little out," were Burke's last words. " If Liz was my girl and I was to sneak out to a dance coupled up with an Annie, I'd want a suit of chain armor on under my gladsome rags, all right."

Through the land of the stork-vulture wandered Liz. Her black eyes searched the passing crowds fierily but vaguely. Now and then she hummed bars of foolish little songs. Between times she set her small, white teeth together, and spake crisp words that the east side has added to language.

Liz's skirt was green silk. Her waist was a large brown-and-pink plaid, well-fitting and not without style. She wore a cluster ring of huge imitation rubies, and a locket that banged her knees at the bottom of a silver chain. Her shoes were run down over twisted high heels, and were strangers to polish. Her hat would scarcely have passed into a flour barrel.

The " Family Entrance " of the Blue Jay Café received her. At a table she sat, and punched the button with the air of milady ringing for her carriage. The waiter came with his large-chinned, low-voiced manner of respectful familiarity. Liz smoothed her silken skirt with a satisfied wriggle. She made the most of it. Here she could order and be waited upon. It was all that her world offered her of the prerogative of woman.

" Whiskey, Tommy," she said as her sisters further uptown murmer, " Champagne, James."

" Sure, Miss Lizzie. What,ll the chaser be ? "

" Seltzer. And say, Tommy, has the Kid been around to-day ? "

" Why, no, Miss Lizzie, I haven't saw him to-day."

Fluently came the " Miss Lizzie," for the Kid was known to be one who required rigid upholdment of the dignity of his fiancée.

" I'm lookin' for 'm," said Liz, after the chaser had spluttered under her nose. " It's got to me that he says he'll take Annie Karlson to the dance. Let him. The pink-eyed white rat ! I'm lookin' for 'm. You know me, Tommy. Two years me and the Kid's been engaged. Look at that ring. Five hundred, he said it cost. Let him take her to the dance. What'll I do ? I'll cut his heart out. Another whiskey, Tommy."

" I wouldn't listen to no such reports, Miss Lizzie," said the waiter smoothly, from the narrow opening above his chin. " Kid Mullaly's not the guy to throw a lady like you down. Seltzer on the side ? "

" Two years," repeated Liz, softening a little to sentiment under the magic of the distiller's art. " I always used to play out on the street of evenin's 'cause there was nothin' doin' for me at home. For a long time I just sat on doorsteps and looked at the lights and the people goin' by. And then the Kid came along one evenin' and sized me up, and I was mashed on the spot for fair. The first drink he made me take, I cried all night at home, and got a lickin' for makin' a noise. And now—say, Tommy, you ever see this Annie Karlson ? If it wasn't for peroxide the chloroform limit would have put her out long ago. Oh, I'm lookin' for 'm. You tell the Kid if he comes in. Me ? I'll cut his heart out. Leave it to me. Another whiskey, Tommy."

A little unsteadily, but with watchful and brilliant eyes, Liz walked up the avenue. On the doorstep of a brick tenement a curly-haired child sat, puzzling over the convolutions of a tangled string. Liz flopped down beside her, with a crooked, shifting smile on her flushed face. But her eyes had grown clear and artless of a sudden.

" Let me show you how to make a cat's-cradle, kid," she said, tucking her green silk skirt under her rusty shoes.

And while they sat there the lights were being turned on for the dance in the hall of the Small Hours Social Club. It was a bi-monthly dance, a dress affair in which the members took great pride and bestirred themselves huskily to further and adorn.

At 9 o'clock the President, Kid Mullaly, paced upon the floor with a lady on his arm. As the Lorelei's was her hair golden. Her " yes " was softened to a " yah," but its quality of assent was patent to the most Milesian ears. She stepped upon her own train and blushed, and—she smiled into the eyes of Kid Mullaly.

And then, as the two stood in the middle of the waxed floor, the thing happened to prevent which many lamps are burning nightly in many studies and libraries.

Out from the circle of spectators in the hall leaped Fate in a green silk skirt, under the *nom de guerre* of " Liz." Her eyes were hard and blacker than jet. She did not scream or waver. Most unwomanly, she cried out one oath—the Kid's own favorite oath —and in his own deep voice; and then while the Small Hours Social Club went frantically to pieces, she made good her boast to Tommy, the waiter—made good as far as the length of her knife blade and the stength of her arm permitted.

And next came the primal instinct of self-preservation—or was it self-annihilation, the instinct that society has grafted on the natural branch?

Liz ran out and down the street swift and true as a woodcock flying through a grove of saplings at dusk.

And then followed the big city's biggest shame, its most ancient and rotten surviving canker, its pollution and disgrace, its blight and perversion, its forever infamy and guilt, fostered, unreproved and cherished, handed down from a long-ago century of the basest barbarity—the Hue and Cry. Nowhere but in the big cities does it survive, and here most of all, where the ultimate perfection of culture, citizenship and alleged superiority joins, bawling, in the chase.

They pursued—a shrieking mob of fathers, mothers, lovers and maidens—howling, yelling, calling, whistling, crying for blood. Well may the wolf in the big city stand outside the door. Well may his heart, the gentler, falter at the siege. Knowing her way, and hungry for her surcease, she darted down the familiar ways until at last her feet struck the dull solidity of the rotting pier. And then it was but a few more panting steps—and good mother East River took Liz to her bosom, smoothed her muddily but quickly, and settled in five minutes the problem that keeps lights burning o' nights in thousands of pastorates and colleges.

* * * * *

It's mighty funny what kind of dreams one has sometimes. Poets call them visions, but a vision is only a dream in blank verse. I dreamed the rest of this story.

I thought I was in the next world. I don't know how I got there; I suppose I had been riding on the Ninth Avenue elevated or taking patent medicine or trying to pull Jim Jeffries's nose, or doing some such little injudicious stunt. But, anyhow, there I was, and there was a great crowd of us outside the court-room where the judgments were going on. And every now and then a very beautiful and imposing court-officer angel would come outside the door and call another case.

While I was considering my own worldly sins and wondering whether there would be any use of my trying to prove an alibi by claiming that I lived in New Jersey, the bailiff angel came to the door and sang out:

" Case No. 99,852,743."

Up stepped a plain-clothes man—there were lots of 'em there, dressed exactly like preachers and hustling us spirits around just like cops do on earth—and by the arm he dragged—whom, do you think? Why, Liz!

The court officer took her inside and closed the door. I went up to Mr. Fly-Cop and inquired about the case.

" A very sad one," says he, laying the points of his manicured fingers together. "An utterly incorrigible girl. I am Special Terrestrial Officer the Reverend Jones. The case was assigned to me. The girl murdered her fiancé and committed suicide. She had no defense. My report to the court relates the facts in detail, all of which are substantiated by reliable witnesses. The wages of sin is death. Praise the Lord."

The court officer opened the door and stepped out.

" Poor girl," said Special Terrestrial Officer the Reverend Jones, with a tear in his eye. " It was one of the saddest cases that I ever met with. Of course she was——"

" Discharged," said the court officer. " Come here, Jonesy. First thing you know you'll be switched to the pot-pie squad. How would you like to be on the missionary force in the South Sea Islands—hey ? Now, you quit making these false arrests, or you'll be transferred—see ? The guilty party you've got to look for in this case is a red-haired, unshaven, untidy man, sitting by the window reading, in his stocking feet, while his children play in the streets. Get a move on you."

Now, wasn't that a silly dream ?

ACCORDING TO THEIR LIGHTS

SOMEWHERE in the depths of the big city, where the unquiet dregs are forever being shaken together, young Murray and the Captain had met and become friends. Both were at the lowest ebb possible to their fortunes; both had fallen from at least an intermediate Heaven of respectability and importance, and both were typical products of the monstrous and peculiar social curriculum of their over-weening and bumptious civic alma mater.

The Captain was no longer a captain. One of those sudden moral cataclysms that sometimes sweep the city had hurled him from a high and profitable position in the Police Department, ripping off his badge and buttons and washing into the hands of his lawyers the solid pieces of real estate that his frugality had enabled him to accumulate. The passing of the flood left him low and dry. One month after his dishabilitation a saloon-keeper plucked him by the neck from his free-lunch counter as a tabby plucks a strange kitten from her nest, and cast him asphaltward. This seems low enough. But after that he acquired a pair of cloth-top, button Congress gaiters and wrote complaining letters to the newspapers. And then he fought the attendant at the Municipal Lodging House who tried to give him a bath. When Murray first saw him he was holding the hand of an Italian woman who sold apples and garlic on Essex Street, and quoting the words of a song book ballad.

Murray's fall had been more Luciferian, if less spectacular. All the pretty, tiny little kickshaws of Gotham had once been his. The megaphone man roars out at you to observe the house of his uncle on a grand and revered avenue. But there had been an awful row about something, and the prince had been escorted to the door by the butler, which, in said avenue, is equivalent to the impact of the avuncular shoe. A weak Prince Hal, without inheritance or sword, he drifted downward to meet his humorless Falstaff, and to pick the crusts of the streets with him.

One evening they sat on a bench in a little downtown park. The great bulk of the Captain, which starvation seemed to increase —drawing irony instead of pity to his petitions for aid—was heaped against the arm of the bench in a shapeless mass. His red face, spotted by tufts of vermilion, week-old whiskers and topped by a sagging white straw hat, looked, in the gloom, like one of those structures that you may observe in a dark Third Avenue window, challenging your imagination to say whether it be something recent in the way of ladies' hats or a strawberry shortcake. A tight-drawn belt—last relic of his official spruceness—made a deep furrow in his circumference. The Captain's shoes were buttonless. In a smothered bass he cursed his star of ill-luck.

Murray, at his side, was shrunk into his dingy and ragged suit of blue serge. His hat was pulled low; he sat quiet and a little indistinct, like some ghost that had been dispossessed.

" I'm hungry," growled the Captain—" by the top sirloin of the Bull of Bashan, I'm starving to death. Right now I could eat a Bowery restaurant clear through to the stovepipe in the alley. Can't you think of nothing, Murray ? You sit there with your shoulders scrunched up, giving an imitation of Reginald Vanderbilt driving his coach—what good are them airs doing you now ? Think of some place we can get something to chew."

" You forget, my dear Captain," said Murray, without moving, " that our last attempt at dining was at my suggestion."

" You bet it was," groaned the Captain, " you bet your life it was. Have you got any more like that to make—hey ? "

" I admit we failed," sighed Murray. " I was sure Malone would be good for one more free lunch after the way he talked baseball with me the last time I spent a nickel in his establishment."

" I had this hand," said the Captain, extending the unfortunate member—" I had this hand on the drumstick of a turkey and two sardine sandwiches when them waiters grabbed us."

" I was within two inches of the olives," said Murray. " Stuffed olives. I haven't tasted one in a year."

" What'll we do ? " grumbled the Captain. " We can't starve."

" Can't we ? " said Murray, quietly. " I'm glad to hear that. I was afraid we could."

" You wait here," said the Captain, rising heavily and puffily to his feet. " I'm going to try to make one more turn. You stay here till I come back, Murray. I won't be over half an hour. If I turn the trick I'll come back flush."

He made some elephantine attempts at smartening his appearance. He gave his fiery mustache a heavenward twist; he dragged into sight a pair of black-edged cuffs, deepened the crease in his middle by tightening his belt another hole, and set off, jaunty as a zoo rhinoceros, across the south end of the park.

When he was out of sight Murray also left the park, hurrying swiftly eastward. He stopped at a building whose steps were flanked by two green lights.

" A police captain named Maroney," he said to the desk sergeant, " was dismissed from the force after being tried under charges three years ago. I believe sentence was suspended. Is this man wanted now by the police ? "

" Why are ye asking ? " inquired the sergeant, with a frown.

" I thought there might be a reward standing," explained Murray, easily. " I know the man well. He seems to be keeping himself pretty shady at present. I could lay my hands on him at any time. If there should be a reward——"

" There's no reward," interrupted the sergeant, shortly. " The man's not wanted. And neither are ye. So, get out. Ye are frindly with um' and ye would be selling um. Out with ye quick, or I'll give ye a start."

Murray gazed at the officer with serene and virtuous dignity.

" I would be simply doing my duty as a citizen and gentleman," he said, severely, " if I could assist the law in laying hold of one of its offenders."

Murray hurried back to the bench in the park. He folded his arms and shrank within his clothes to his ghost-like presentment.

Ten minutes afterward the Captain arrived at the rendezvous, windy and thunderous as a dog-day in Kansas. His collar had been torn away; his straw hat had been twisted and battered; his shirt with ox-blood stripes split to the waist. And from head to knee he was drenched with some vile and ignoble greasy fluid that loudly proclaimed to the nose its component leaven of garlic and kitchen stuff.

" For Heaven's sake, Captain," sniffed Murray, " I doubt that I would have waited for you if I had suspected you were so desperate as to resort to swill barrels. I——"

" Cheese it," said the Captain, harshly. " I'm not hogging it yet. It's all on the outside. I went around on Essex and proposed marriage to that Catrina that's got the fruit shop there. Now, that business could be built up. She's a peach as far as a Dago could be. I thought I had that senoreena mashed sure last week. But look what she done to me ! I guess I got too fresh. Well there's another scheme queered."

" You don't mean to say," said Murray, with infinite contempt, " that you would have married that woman to help yourself out of your disgraceful troubles ! "

" Me ? " said the Captain. " I'd marry the Empress of China for one bowl of chop suey. I'd commit murder for a plate of beef stew. I'd steal a wafer from a waif. I'd be a Mormon for a bowl of chowder."

" I think," said Murray, resting his head on his hands, " that I would play Judas for the price of one drink of whiskey. For thirty pieces of silver I would——"

" Oh, come now ! " exclaimed the Captain in dismay. " You wouldn't do that, Murray ? I always thought that Kike's squeal on his boss was about the lowest-down play that ever happened. A man that gives his friend away is worse than a pirate."

Through the park stepped a large man scanning the benches where the electric light fell.

" Is that you, Mac ? " he said, halting before the derelicts. His diamond stickpin dazzled. His diamond-studded fob chain assisted. He was big and smooth and well fed. " Yes, I see it's you," he continued. " They told me at Mike's that I might find you over here. Let me see you a few minutes, Mac."

The Captain lifted himself with a grunt of alacrity. If Charlie Finnegan had come down in the bottomless pit to seek him there must be something doing. Charlie guided him by an arm into a patch of shadow.

" You know, Mac," he said, " they're trying Inspector Pickering on graft charges."

" He was my inspector," said the Captain.

" O'Shea wants the job," went on Finnegan. " He must have it. It's for the good of the organization. Pickering must go under. Your testimony will do it. He was your ' man higher up ' when you were on the force. His share of the boodle passed through your hands. You must go on the stand and testify against him."

" He was "—began the Captain.

" Wait a minute," said Finnegan. A bundle of yellowish stuff came out of his inside pocket. " Five hundred dollars in it for you. Two-fifty on the spot, and the rest——"

" He was my friend, I say," finished the Captain. " I'll see you and the gang, and the city, and the party in the flames of Hades before I'll take the stand against Dan Pickering. I'm down and out; but I'm no traitor to a man that's been my friend." The Captain's voice rose and boomed like a split trombone. " Get out of this park, Charlie Finnegan, where us thieves and tramps and boozers are your betters; and take your dirty money with you."

Finnegan drifted out by another walk. The Captain returned to his seat.

" I couldn't avoid hearing," said Murray, drearily. " I think you are the biggest fool I ever saw."

" What would you have done ? " asked the Captain.

" Nailed Pickering to the cross," said Murray.

" Sonny," said the Captain, huskily and without heat. " You and me are different. New York is divided into two parts—above Forty-second Street, and below Fourteenth. You come from the other part. We both act according to our lights."

An illuminated clock above the trees retailed the information that it lacked the half hour of twelve. Both men rose from the bench and moved away together as if seized by the same idea. They left the park, struck through a narrow cross street, and came into Broadway, at this hour as dark, echoing and de-peopled as a by-way in Pompeii.

Northward they turned; and a policeman who glanced at their unkempt and slinking figures withheld the attention and suspicion that he would have granted them at any other hour and place. For on every street in that part of the city other unkempt and slinking figures were shuffling and hurrying toward a converging point—a point that is marked by no monument save that groove on the pavement worn by tens of thousands of waiting feet.

At Ninth Street a tall man wearing an opera hat alighted from a Broadway car and turned his face westward. But he saw Murray, pounced upon him and dragged him under a street light. The Captain lumbered slowly to the corner, like a wounded bear, and waited, growling.

" Jerry ! " cried the hatted one. " How fortunate ! I was to begin a search for you to-morrow. The old gentleman has capitulated. You're to be restored to favor. Congratulate you. Come to the office in the morning and get all the money you want. I've liberal instructions in that respect."

" And the little matrimonial arrangement ? " said Murray, with his head turned sidewise.

" Why—er—well, of course, your uncle understands—expects

that the engagement between you and Miss Vanderhurst shall be——"

" Good night," said Murray, moving away.

" You madman ! " cried the other, catching his arm. " Would you give up two millions on account of——"

" Did you ever see her nose, old man ? " asked Murray, solemnly.

" But, listen to reason, Jerry. Miss Vanderhurst is an heiress, and——"

" Did you ever see it ? "

" Yes, I admit that her nose, isn't——"

" Good night ! " said Murray. " My friend is waiting for me. I am quoting him when I authorize you to report that there is ' nothing doing.' Good night."

A wriggling line of waiting men extended from a door in Tenth Street far up Broadway, on the outer edge of the pavement. The Captain and Murray fell in at the tail of the quivering millipede.

" Twenty feet longer than it was last night," said Murray, looking up at his measuring angle of Grace Church.

" Half an hour," growled the Captain, " before we get our punk."

The city clocks began to strike 12; the Bread Line moved forward slowly, its leathern feet sliding on the stones with the sound of a hissing serpent, as they who had lived according to their lights closed up in the rear.

A MIDSUMMER KNIGHT'S DREAM

> " *The knights are dead ;*
> *Their swords are rust.*
> *Except a few who have to hust-*
> *Le all the time*
> *To raise the dust.*"

DEAR READER : It was summertime. The sun glared down upon the city with pitiless ferocity. It is difficult for the sun to be ferocious and exhibit compunction simultaneously. The heat was—oh, bother thermometers!—who cares for standard measures, anyhow ? It was so hot that——

The roof gardens put on so many extra waiters that you could hope to get your gin fizz now—as soon as all the other people got theirs. The hospitals were putting in extra cots for bystanders. For when little woolly dogs loll their tongues out and say " woof, woof ! " at the fleas that bite 'em, and nervous old black bombazine

ladies screech " Mad dog ! " and policemen begin to shoot, somebody is going to get hurt. The man from Pompton, N. J., who always wears an overcoat in July, had turned up in a Broadway
hotel drinking hot Scotches and enjoying his annual ray from the
calcium. Philanthropists were petitioning the Legislature to pass
a bill requiring builders to make tenement fire-escapes more com-
modious, so that families might die all together of the heat instead
of one or two at a time. So many men were telling you about the
number of baths they took each day that you wondered how they
got along after the real lessee of the apartment came back to town
and thanked 'em for taking such good care of it. The young man
who called loudly for cold beef and beer in the restaurant, pro-
testing that roast pullet and Burgundy was really too heavy for such
weather, blushed when he met your eye, for you had heard him
all winter calling, in modest tones, for the same ascetic viands.
Soup, pocketbooks, shirt waists, actors and baseball excuses grew
thinner. Yes, it was summertime.

A man stood at Thirty-fourth Street waiting for a downtown
car. A man of forty, gray-haired, pink-faced, keen, nervous, plainly
dressed, with a harassed look around the eyes. He wiped his forehead and laughed loudly when a fat man with an outing look
stopped and spoke with him.

" No, siree," he shouted with defiance and scorn. " None of
your old mosquito-haunted swamps and skyscraper mountains
without elevators for me. When I want to get away from hot
weather I know how to do it. New York, sir, is the finest summer
resort in the country. Keep in the shade and watch your diet,
and don't get too far away from an electric fan. Talk about your
Adirondacks and your Catskills ! There's more solid comfort in
the borough of Manhattan than in all the rest of the country
together. No, siree ! No tramping up perpendicular cliffs and
being waked up at 4 in the morning by a million flies, and eating
canned goods straight from the city for me. Little old New York
will take a few select summer boarders; comforts and conveniences
of home—that's the ad. that I answer every time."

" You need a vacation," said the fat man, looking closely at the
other. " You haven't been away from town in years. Better come
with me for two weeks, anyhow. The trout in the Beaverkill are
jumping at anything now that looks like a fly. Harding writes me
that he landed a three-pound brown last week."

" Nonsense ! " cried the other man. " Go ahead, if you like,
and boggle around in rubber boots wearing yourself out trying to
catch fish. When I want one I go to a cool restaurant and order it.
I laugh at you fellows whenever I think of you hustling around in
the heat in the country thinking you are having a good time. For

me Father Knickerbocker's little improved farm with the big shady lane running through the middle of it."

The fat man sighed over his friend and went his way. The man who thought New York was the greatest summer resort in the country boarded a car and went buzzing down to his office. On the way he threw away his newspaper and looked up at a ragged patch of sky above the housetops.

"Three pounds !" he muttered, absently. "And Harding isn't a liar. I believe, if I could—but it's impossible—they've got to have another month—another month at least."

In his office the upholder of urban midsummer joys dived, head foremost, into the swimming pool of business. Adkins, his clerk, came and added a spray of letters, memoranda and telegrams.

At 5 o'clock in the afternoon the busy man leaned back in his office chair, put his feet on the desk and mused aloud :

"I wonder what kind of bait Harding used."

*   *   *   *   *

She was all in white that day; and thereby Compton lost a bet to Gaines. Compton had wagered she would wear light blue, for she knew that was his favorite color, and Compton was a millionaire's son, and that almost laid him open to the charge of betting on a sure thing. But white was her choice, and Gaines held up his head with twenty-five's lordly air.

The little summer hotel in the mountains had a lively crowd that year. There were two or three young college men and a couple of artists and a young naval officer on one side. On the other there were enough beauties among the young ladies for the correspondent of a society paper to refer to them as a " bevy." But the moon among the stars was Mary Sewell. Each one of the young men greatly desired to arrange matters so that he could pay her millinery bills, and fix the furnace, and have her do away with the " Sewell " part of her name forever. Those who could stay only a week or two went away hinting at pistols and blighted hearts. But Compton stayed like the mountains themselves, for he could afford it. And Gaines stayed because he was a fighter and wasn't afraid of millionaires' sons, and—well, he adored the country.

" What do you think, Miss Mary ? " he said once. " I knew a duffer in New York who claimed to like it in the summer time. Said you could keep cooler there than you could in the woods. Wasn't he an awful silly ? I don't think I could breathe on Broadway after the 1st of June."

" Mamma was thinking of going back week after next," said Miss Mary with a lovely frown.

" But when you think of it," said Gaines, " there are lots of jolly places in town in the summer. The roof gardens, you know, and the—er—the roof gardens."

Deepest blue was the lake that day—the day when they had the mock tournament, and the men rode clumsy farm horses around in a glade in the woods and caught curtain rings on the end of a lance. Such fun !

Cool and dry as the finest wine came the breath of the shadowed forest. The valley below was a vision seen through an opal haze. A white mist from hidden falls blurred the green of a hand's breadth of tree tops halfway down the gorge. Youth made merry hand-in-hand with young summer. Nothing on Broadway like that.

The villagers gathered to see the city folks pursue their mad drollery. The woods rang with the laughter of pixies and naiads and sprites. Gaines caught most of the rings. His was the privilege to crown the queen of the tournament. He was the conquering knight—as far as the rings went. On his arm he wore a white scarf. Compton wore light blue. She had declared her preference for blue, but she wore white that day.

Gaines looked about for the queen to crown her. He heard her merry laugh, as if from the clouds. She had slipped away and climbed Chimney Rock, a little granite bluff, and stood there, a white fairy among the laurels, fifty feet above their heads.

Instantly he and Compton accepted the implied challenge. The bluff was easily mounted at the rear, but the front offered small hold to hand or foot. Each man quickly selected his route and began to climb. A crevice, a bush, a slight projection, a vine or tree branch—all of these were aids that counted in the race. It was all foolery—there was no stake; but there was youth in it, cross reader, and light hearts, and something else that Miss Clay writes so charmingly about.

Gaines gave a great tug at the root of a laurel and pulled himself to Miss Mary's feet. On his arm he carried the wreath of roses; and while the villagers and summer boarders screamed and applauded below he placed it on the queen's brow.

" You are a gallant knight," said Miss Mary.

" If I could be your true knight always," began Gaines, but Miss Mary laughed him dumb, for Compton scrambled over the edge of the rock one minute behind time.

What a twilight that was when they drove back to the hotel ! The opal of the valley turned slowly to purple, the dark woods framed the lake as a mirror, the tonic air stirred the very soul in one. The first pale stars came out over the mountain tops where yet a faint glow of——

    *   *   *   *   *

" I beg your pardon, Mr. Gaines," said Adkins.

The man who believed New York to be the finest summer resort in the world opened his eyes and kicked over the mucilage bottle on his desk.

" I—I believe I was asleep," he said.

" It's the heat," said Adkins. " It's something awful in the city these——"

" Nonsense ! " said the other. " The city beats the country ten to one in summer. Fools go out tramping in muddy brooks and wear themselves out trying to catch little fish as long as your finger. Stay in town and keep comfortable—that's my idea."

" Some letters just came," said Adkins. " I thought you might like to glance at them before you go."

Let us look over his shoulder and read just a few lines one of them :

MY DEAR, DEAR HUSBAND : Just received your letter ordering us to stay another month. . . . Rita's cough is almost gone. . . . Johnny has simply gone wild like a little Indian. . . . Will be the making of both children . . . work so hard, and I know that your business can hardly afford to keep us here so long . . . best man that ever . . . you always pretend that you like the city in summer . . . trout fishing that you used to be so fond of . . . and all to keep us well and happy . . . come to you if it were not doing the babies so much good. . . . I stood last evening on Chimney Rock in exactly the same spot where I was when you put the wreath of roses on my head . . . through all the world . . . when you said you would be my true knight . . . fifteen years ago, dear, just think ! . . . have always been that to me . . . ever and ever.

MARY.

The man who said he thought New York the finest summer resort in the country dropped into a café on his way home and had a glass of beer under an electric fan.

" Wonder what kind of a fly old Harding used," he said to himself.

THE LAST LEAF

IN a little district west of Washington Square the streets have run crazy and broken themselves into small strips called "places." These "places" make strange angles and curves. One street crosses itself a time or two. An artist once discovered a valuable possibility in this street. Suppose a collector with a bill for paints, paper and canvas should, in traversing this route, suddenly meet himself coming back, without a cent having been paid on account!

So, to quaint old Greenwich Village the art people soon came prowling, hunting for north windows and eighteenth-century gables and Dutch attics and low rents. Then they imported some pewter mugs and a chafing dish or two from Sixth Avenue, and became a "colony."

At the top of a squatty, three-story brick Sue and Johnsy had their studio. "Johnsy" was familiar for Joanna. One was from Maine; the other from California. They had met at the *table d'hôte* of an Eighth Street "Delmonico's," and found their tastes in art, chicory salad and bishop sleeves so congenial that the joint studio resulted.

That was in May. In November a cold, unseen stranger, whom the doctors called Pneumonia, stalked about the colony, touching one here and there with his icy fingers. Over on the east side this ravager strode boldly, smiting his victims by scores, but his feet trod slowly through the maze of the narrow and moss-grown "places."

Mr. Pneumonia was not what you would call a chivalric old gentleman. A mite of a little woman with blood thinned by California zephyrs was hardly fair game for the red-fisted, short-breathed old duffer. But Johnsy he smote; and she lay, scarcely moving, on her painted iron bedstead, looking through the small Dutch window-panes at the blank side of the next brick house.

One morning the busy doctor invited Sue into the hallway with a shaggy, gray eyebrow.

"She has one chance in—let us say, ten," he said, as he shook down the mercury in his clinical thermometer. "And that chance is for her to want to live. This way people have of lining-up on the side of the undertaker makes the entire pharmacopœia look silly. Your little lady has made up her mind that she's not going to get well. Has she anything on her mind?"

"She—she wanted to paint the Bay of Naples some day," said Sue.

THE TRIMMED LAMP

" Paint ?—bosh ! Has she anything on her mind worth thinking about twice—a man, for instance ? "

" A man ? " said Sue, with a jew's-harp twang in her voice. " Is a man worth—but, no, doctor; there is nothing of the kind."

" Well, it is the weakness, then," said the doctor. " I will do all that science, so far as it may filter through my efforts, can accomplish. But whenever my patient begins to count the carriages in her funeral procession I subtract 50 per cent. from the curative power of medicines. If you will get her to ask one question about the new winter styles in cloak sleeves I will promise you a one-in-five chance for her, instead of one in ten."

After the doctor had gone Sue went into the workroom and cried a Japanese napkin to a pulp. Then she swaggered into Johnsy's room with her drawing board, whistling ragtime.

Johnsy, lay, scarcely making a ripple under the bedclothes, with her face toward the window. She stopped whistling, thinking she was asleep.

She arranged her board and began a pen-and-ink drawing to illustrate a magazine story. Young artists must pave their way to Art by drawing pictures for magazine stories that young authors write to pave their way to Literature.

As Sue was sketching a pair of elegant horseshow riding trousers and a monocle on the figure of the hero, an Idaho cowboy, she heard a low sound, several times repeated. She went quickly to the bedside.

Johnsy's eyes were open wide. She was looking out the window and counting—counting backward.

" Twelve," she said, and a little later " eleven "; and then " ten," and " nine "; and then " eight " and " seven ", almost together.

Sue looked solicitously out of the window. What was there to count? There was only a bare, dreary yard to be seen, and the blank side of the brick house twenty feet away. An old, old ivy vine, gnarled and decayed at the roots, climbed half way up the brick wall. The cold breath of autumn had stricken its leaves from the vine until its skeleton branches clung, almost bare, to the crumbling bricks.

" What is it, dear ? " asked Sue.

" Six," said Johnsy, in almost a whisper. " They're falling faster now. Three days ago there were almost a hundred. It made my head ache to count them. But now its easy. There goes another one. There are only five left now."

" Five what, dear. Tell your Sudie."

" Leaves. On the ivy vine. When the last one falls I must go, too. I've known that for three days. Didn't the doctor tell you ? "

" Oh, I never heard of such nonsense," complained Sue, with magnificent scorn. " What have old ivy leaves to do with your getting well ? And you used to love that vine, so, you naughty girl. Don't be a goosey. Why, the doctor told me this morning that your chances for getting well real soon were—let's see exactly what he said—he said the chances were ten to one ! Why, that's almost as good a chance as we have in New York when we ride on the street cars or walk past a new building. Try to take some broth now, and let Sudie go back to her drawing, so she can sell the editor man with it, and buy port wine for her sick child, and pork chops for her greedy self."

" You needn't get any more wine," said Johnsy, keeping her eyes fixed out the window. " There goes another. No, I don't want any broth. That leaves just four. I want to see the last one fall before it gets dark. Then I'll go, too."

" Johnsy, dear," said Sue, bending over her, " will you promise me to keep your eyes closed, and not look out the window until I am done working ? I must hand those drawings in by to-morrow. I need the light, or I would draw the shade down."

" Couldn't you draw in the other room ? " asked Johnsy, coldly.

" I'd rather be here by you," said Sue. " Besides, I don't want you to keep looking at those silly ivy leaves."

" Tell me as soon as you have finished," said Johnsy, closing her eyes, and lying white and still as a fallen statue, " because I want to see the last one fall. I'm tired of waiting. I'm tired of thinking. I want to turn loose my hold on everything, and go sailing down, down, just like one of those poor, tired leaves."

" Try to sleep," said Sue. " I must call Behrman up to be my model for the old hermit miner. I'll not be gone a minute. Don't try to move 'til I come back."

Old Behrman was a painter who lived on the ground floor beneath them. He was past sixty and had a Michael Angelo's Moses beard curling down from the head of a satyr along the body of an imp. Behrman was a failure in art. Forty years he had wielded the brush without getting near enough to touch the hem of his Mistress's robe. He had been always about to paint a master-piece, but had never yet begun it. For several years he had painted nothing except now and then a daub in the line of commerce or advertising. He earned a little by serving as a model to those young artists in the colony who could not pay the price of a professional. He drank gin to excess, and still talked of his coming master-piece. For the rest he was a fierce little old man, who scoffed terribly at softness in any one, and who regarded himself as especial mastiff-in-waiting to protect the two young artists in the studio above.

Sue found Behrman smelling strongly of juniper berries in his dimly lighted den below. In one corner was a blank canvas on an easel that had been waiting there for twenty-five years to receive the first line of the masterpiece. She told him of Johnsy's fancy, and how she feared she would, indeed, light and fragile as a leaf herself, float away, when her slight hold upon the world grew weaker.

Old Behrman, with his red eyes plainly streaming, shouted his contempt and derision for such idiotic imaginings.

"Vass!" he cried. "Is dere people in de world mit der foolishness to die because leafs dey drop off from a confounded vine? I haf not heard of such a thing. No, I will not bose as a model for your fool hermit-dunderhead. Vy do you allow dot silly pusiness to come in der prain of her? Ach, dot poor leetle Miss Yohnsy."

"She is very ill and weak," said Sue, "and the fever has left her mind morbid and full of strange fancies. Very well, Mr. Behrman, if you do not care to pose for me, you needn't. But I think you are a horrid old—old flibbertigibbet."

"You are just like a woman!" yelled Behrman. "Who said I will not bose? Go on. I come mit you. For half an hour I haf peen trying to say dot I am ready to bose. Gott! dis is not any blace in which one so goot as Miss Yohnsy shall lie sick. Some day I vill baint a masterpiece, and ve shall all go away. Gott! yes."

Johnsy was sleeping when they went upstairs. Sue pulled the shade down to the window-sill, and motioned Behrman into the other room. In there they peered out the window fearfully at the ivy vine. Then they looked at each other for a moment without speaking. A persistent, cold rain was falling, mingled with snow. Behrman, in his old blue shirt, took his seat as the hermit-miner on an upturned kettle for a rock.

When Sue awoke from an hour's sleep the next morning she found Johnsy with dull, wide-open eyes staring at the drawn green shade.

"Pull it up; I want to see," she ordered, in a whisper.

Wearily Sue obeyed.

But, lo! after the beating rain and fierce gusts of wind that had endured through the livelong night, there yet stood out against the brick wall one ivy leaf. It was the last on the vine. Still dark green near its stem, but with its serrated edges tinted with the yellow of dissolution and decay, it hung bravely from a branch some twenty feet above the ground.

"It is the last one," said Johnsy. "I thought it would surely fall during the night. I heard the wind. It will fall to-day, and I shall die at the same time."

" Dear, dear ! " said Sue, leaning her worn face down to the pillow, " think of me, if you won't think of yourself. What would I do ? "

But Johnsy did not answer. The lonesomest thing in all the world is a soul when it is making ready to go on its mysterious, far journey. The fancy seemed to possess her more strongly as one by one the ties that bound her to friendship and to earth were loosed.

The day wore away, and even through the twilight they could see the lone ivy leaf clinging to its stem against the wall. And then, with the coming of the night the north wind was again loosed, while the rain still beat against the windows and pattered down from the low Dutch eaves.

When it was light enough Johnsy, the merciless, commanded that the shade be raised.

The ivy leaf was still there.

Johnsy lay for a long time looking at it. And then she called to Sue, who was stirring her chicken broth over the gas stove.

" I've been a bad girl, Sudie," said Johnsy. " Something has made that last leaf stay there to show me how wicked I was. It is a sin to want to die. You may bring me a little broth now, and some milk with a little port in it, and—no; bring me a hand-mirror first, and then pack some pillows about me, and I will sit up and watch you cook."

An hour later she said.

" Sudie, some day I hope to paint the Bay of Naples."

The doctor came in the afternoon, and Sue had an excuse to go into the hallway as he left.

" Even chances," said the doctor, taking Sue's thin, shaking hand in his. " With good nursing you'll win. And now I must see another case I have downstairs. Behrman, his name is—some kind of an artist, I believe. Pneumonia, too. He is an old, weak man, and the attack is acute. There is no hope for him; but he goes to the hospital to-day to be made more comfortable."

The next day the doctor said to Sue : " She's out of danger. You've won. Nutrition and care now—that's all."

And that afternoon Sue came to the bed where Johnsy lay, contentedly knitting a very blue and very useless woollen shoulder scarf, and put one arm around her, pillows and all.

" I have something to tell you, white mouse," she said. " Mr. Behrman died of pneumonia to-day in the hospital. He was ill only two days. The janitor found him on the morning of the first day in his room downstairs helpless with pain. His shoes and cloth-ing were wet through and icy cold. They couldn't imagine where he had been on such a dreadful night. And then they found a lantern, still lighted, and a ladder that had been dragged from its place, and some scattered brushes, and a palette with green and yellow colors mixed on it, and—look out the window, dear, at the last ivy leaf on the wall. Didn't you wonder why it never fluttered or moved when the wind blew? Ah, darling, it's Behrman's master-piece—he painted it there the night that the last leaf fell."

THE COUNT AND THE WEDDING GUEST

ONE evening when Andy Donovan went to dinner at his Second Avenue boarding-house, Mrs. Scott introduced him to a new boarder, a young lady, Miss Conway. Miss Conway was small and unobtrusive. She wore a plain, snuffy-brown dress, and bestowed her interest, which seemed languid, upon her plate. She lifted her diffident eyelids and shot one perspicuous, judicial glance at Mr. Donovan, politely murmured his name, and returned to her mutton. Mr. Donovan bowed with the grace and beaming smile that were rapidly winning for him social, business and political advancement, and erased the snuffy-brown one from the tablets of his consideration.

Two weeks later Andy was sitting on the front steps enjoying his cigar. There was a soft rustle behind and above him and Andy turned his head—and had his head turned.

Just coming out of the door was Miss Conway. She wore a night-black dress of *crêpe de—crêpe de*—oh, this thin black goods. Her hat was black, and from it drooped and fluttered an ebon veil, filmy as a spider's web. She stood on the top step and drew on black silk gloves. Not a speck of white or a spot of color about her dress anywhere. Her rich golden hair was drawn, with scarcely a ripple, into a shining, smooth knot low on her neck. Her face was plain rather than pretty, but it was now illuminated and made almost beautiful by her large gray eyes that gazed above the houses across the street into the sky with an expression of the most appealing sadness and melancholy.

Gather the idea, girls—all black, you know, with the preference for *crêpe de*—oh, *crêpe de Chine*—that's it. All black, and that sad, faraway look, and the hair shining under the black veil (you have to be a blonde, of course), and try to look as if, although your young life had been blighted just as it was about to give a hop-skip-and-a-jump over the threshold of life, a walk in the park might do you good, and be sure to happen out the door at the right moment, and—oh, it'll fetch 'em every time. But it's fierce, now, how cynical I am, ain't it?—to talk about mourning costumes this way.

Mr. Donovan suddenly reinscribed Miss Conway upon the tablets of his consideration. He threw away the remaining inch and a quarter of his cigar, that would have been good for eight minutes yet, and quickly shifted his center of gravity to his low-cut patent leathers.

"It's a fine, clear evening, Miss Conway," he said; and if the Weather Bureau could have heard the confident emphasis of his tones it would have hoisted the square white signal, and nailed it to the mast.

"To them that has the heart to enjoy it, it is, Mr. Donovan," said Miss Conway, with a sigh.

Mr. Donovan, in his heart, cursed fair weather. Heartless weather! It should hail and blow and snow to be consonant with the mood of Miss Conway.

"I hope none of your relatives—I hope you haven't sustained a loss?" ventured Mr. Donovan.

"Death has claimed," said Miss Conway, hesitating—"not a relative, but one who—but I will not intrude my grief upon you, Mr. Donovan."

"Intrude?" protested Mr. Donovan. "Why, say, Miss Conway, I'd be delighted, that is, I'd be sorry—I mean I'm sure nobody could sympathize with you truer than I would."

Miss Conway smiled a little smile. And oh, it was sadder than her expression in repose.

"'Laugh, and the world laughs with you; weep, and they give you the laugh,'" she quoted. "I have learned that, Mr. Donovan. I have no friends or acquaintances in this city. But you have been kind to me. I appreciate it highly."

He had passed her the pepper twice at the table.

"It's tough to be alone in New York—that's a cinch," said Mr. Donovan. "But, say—whenever this little old town does loosen up and get friendly it goes the limit. Say you took a little stroll in the park, Miss Conway—don't you think it might chase away some of your mullygrubs? And if you'd allow me——"

"Thanks, Mr. Donovan. I'd be pleased to accept of your escort if you think the company of one whose heart is filled with gloom could be anyways agreeable to you."

Through the open gates of the iron-railed, old, downtown park, where the elect once took the air, they strolled, and found a quiet bench.

There is this difference between the grief of youth and that of old age; youth's burden is lightened by as much of it as another shares; old age may give and give, but the sorrow remains the same.

"He was my fiancé," confided Miss Conway, at the end of an

hour. " We were going to be married next spring. I don't want
you to think that I am stringing you, Mr. Donovan, but he was
a real Count. He had an estate and a castle in Italy. Count
Fernando Mazzini was his name. I never saw the beat of him for
elegance. Papa objected, of course, and once we eloped, but Papa
overtook us, and took us back. I thought sure Papa and Fernando
would fight a duel. Papa has a livery business—in P'kipsee, you
know.

" Finally, Papa came 'round, all right, and said we might be
married next spring. Fernando showed him proofs of his title and
wealth, and then went over to Italy to get the castle fixed up for us.
Papa's very proud and, when Fernando wanted to give me several
thousand dollars for my trousseau he called him down something
awful. He wouldn't even let me take a ring or any presents from
him. And when Fernando sailed I came to the city and got a
position as cashier in a candy store.

" Three days ago I got a letter from Italy, forwarded from
P'kipsee, saying that Fernando had been killed in a gondola
accident.

" That is why I am in mourning. My heart, Mr. Donovan, will
remain forever in his grave. I guess I am poor company, Mr.
Donovan, but I cannot take any interest in no one. I should not
care to keep you from gayety and your friends who can smile and
entertain you. Perhaps you would prefer to walk back to the
house ? "

Now, girls, if you want to observe a young man hustle out after
a pick and shovel, just tell him that your heart is in some other
fellow's grave. Young men are grave-robbers by nature. Ask any
widow. Something must be done to restore that missing organ to
weeping angels in *crêpe de Chine*. Dead men certainly get the worst
of it from all sides.

" I'm awfully sorry," said Mr. Donovan, gently. " No, we
won't walk back to the house just yet. And don't say you haven't
no friends in this city, Miss Conway. I'm awfully sorry, and I want
you to believe I'm your friend, and that I'm awful sorry."

" I've got his picture here in my locket," said Miss Conway,
after wiping her eyes with her handkerchief. " I never showed it
to anybody; but I will to you, Mr. Donovan, because I believe you
to be a true friend."

Mr. Donovan gazed long and with much interest at the photograph in the locket that Miss Conway opened for him. The face
of Count Mazzini was one to command interest. It was a smooth,
intelligent, bright, almost a handsome face—the face of a strong,
cheerful man who might well be a leader among his fellows.

" I have a larger one, framed, in my room," said Miss Conway.

" When we return I will show you that. They are all I have to remind me of Fernando. But he ever will be present in my heart, that's a sure thing."

A subtle task confronted Mr. Donovan—that of supplanting the unfortunate Count in the heart of Miss Conway. This his admiration for her determined him to do. But the magnitude of the undertaking did not seem to weigh upon his spirits. The sympathetic but cheerful friend was the rôle he essayed; and he played it so successfully that the next half-hour found them conversing pensively across two plates of ice-cream, though yet there was no diminution of the sadness in Miss Conway's large gray eyes.

Before they parted in the hall that evening she ran upstairs and brought down the framed photograph wrapped lovingly in a white silk scarf. Mr. Donovan surveyed it with inscrutable eyes.

"He gave me this the night he left for Italy," said Miss Conway. "I had the one for the locket made from this."

"A fine-looking man," said Mr. Donovan, heartily. "How would it suit you, Miss Conway, to give me the pleasure of your company to Coney next Sunday afternoon?"

A month later they announced their engagement to Mrs. Scott and the other boarders. Miss Conway continued to wear black.

A week after the announcement the two sat on the same bench in the downtown park, while the fluttering leaves of the trees made a dim kinetoscopic picture of them in the moonlight. But Donovan had worn a look of abstracted gloom all day. He was so silent to-night that love's lips could not keep back any longer the questions that love's heart propounded.

"What's the matter, Andy, you are so solemn and grouchy to-night?"

"Nothing, Maggie."

"I know better. Can't I tell? You never acted this way before. What is it?"

"It's nothing much, Maggie."

"Yes it is; and I want to know. I'll bet it's some other girl you are thinking about. All right. Why don't you go get her if you want her? Take your arm away, if you please."

"I'll tell you then," said Andy, wisely, "but I guess you won't understand it exactly. You've heard of Mike Sullivan, haven't you? 'Big Mike' Sullivan, everybody calls him."

"No, I haven't," said Maggie. "And I don't want to, if he makes you act like this. Who is he?"

"He's the biggest man in New York," said Andy, almost reverently. "He can about do anything he wants to with Tammany or any other old thing in the political line. He's a mile high and as broad as East River. You say anything against Big

Mike, and you'll have a million men on your collarbone in about two seconds. Why, he made a visit over to the old country awhile back, and the kings took to their holes like rabbits.

"Well, Big Mike's a friend of mine. I ain't more than deuce-high in the district as far as influence goes, but Mike's as good a friend to a little man, or a poor man as he is to a big one. I met him to-day on the Bowery, and what do you think he does? Comes up and shakes hands. 'Andy,' says he, ' I've been keeping cases on you. You've been putting in some good licks over on your side of the street, and I'm proud of you. What'll you take to drink?' He takes a cigar and I take a highball. I told him I was going to get married in two weeks. 'Andy,' says he, ' send me an invitation, so I'll keep in mind of it, and I'll come to the wedding.' That's what Big Mike says to me; and he always does what he says.

"You don't understand it, Maggie, but I'd have one of my hands cut off to have Big Mike Sullivan at our wedding. It would be the proudest day of my life. When he goes to a man's wedding, there's a guy being married that's made for life. Now, that's why I'm maybe looking sore to-night."

"Why don't you invite him, then, if he's so much to the mustard?" said Maggie, lightly.

"There's a reason why I can't," said Andy, sadly. "There's a reason why he mustn't be there. Don't ask me what it is, for I can't tell you."

"Oh, I don't care," said Maggie. "It's something about politics, of course. But it's no reason why you can't smile at me."

"Maggie," said Andy, presently, "do you think as much of me as you did of your—as you did of the Count Mazzini?"

He waited a long time, but Maggie did not reply. And then, suddenly she leaned against his shoulder and began to cry—to cry and shake with sobs, holding his arm tightly, and wetting the *crêpe de Chine* with tears.

"There, there, there!" soothed Andy, putting aside his own trouble. "And what is it, now?"

"Andy," sobbed Maggie. "I've lied to you, and you'll never marry me, or love me any more. But I feel that I've got to tell. Andy, there never was so much as the little finger of a Count. I never had a beau in my life. But all the other girls had; and they talked about 'em; and that seemed to make the fellows like 'em more. And, Andy, I look swell in black—you know I do. So I went out to a photograph store and bought that picture, and had a little one made for my locket, and made up all that story about the Count and about his being killed, so I could wear black. And nobody can love a liar, and you'll shake me, Andy, and I'll die for shame. Oh, there never was anybody I liked but you—and that's all."

But instead of being pushed away, she found Andy's arm folding her closer. She looked up and saw his face cleared and smiling.

" Could you—could you forgive me, Andy ? "

" Sure," said Andy. " It's all right about that. Back to the cemetery for the Count. You've straightened everything out, Maggie. I was in hopes you would before the wedding-day. Bully girl ! "

" Andy," said Maggie, with a somewhat shy smile, after she had been thoroughly assured of forgiveness, " did you believe all that story about the Count ? "

" Well, not to any large extent," said Andy, reaching for his cigar case; " because it's Big Mike Sullivan's picture you've got in that locket of yours."

THE COUNTRY OF ELUSION

THE cunning writer will choose an indefinable subject; for he can then set down his theory of what it is; and next, at length, his conception of what it is not—and lo ! his paper is covered. Therefore let us follow the prolix and unmapable trail into that mooted country, Bohemia.

Grainger, sub-editor of *Doc's Magazine,* closed his roll-top desk, put on his hat, walked into the hall, punched the " down " button, and waited for the elevator.

Grainger's day had been trying. The chief had tried to ruin the magazine a dozen times by going against Grainger's ideas for running it. A lady whose grandfather had fought with McClellan had brought a portfolio of poems in person.

Grainger was curator of the Lion's House of the magazine. That day he had " lunched " an Arctic explorer, a short-story writer, and the famous conductor of a slaughter-house exposé. Consequently his mind was in a whirl of icebergs, Maupassant, and trichinosis.

But there was a surcease and a recourse; there was Bohemia. He would seek distraction there; and, let's see—he would call by for Mary Adrian.

Half an hour later he threaded his way like a Brazilian orchid-hunter through the palm forest in the tiled entrance hall of the " Idealia " apartment-house. One day the christeners of apartment-houses and the cognominators of sleeping-cars will meet, and there will be some jealous and sanguinary knifing.

The clerk breathed Grainger's name so languidly into the house telephone that it seemed it must surely drop, from sheer inertia, down to the janitor's regions. But, at length, it soared dilatorily up to Miss Adrian's ear. Certainly, Mr. Grainger was to come up immediately.

A colored maid with an Eliza-crossing-the-ice expression opened the door of the apartment for him. Grainger walked sideways down the narrow hall. A bunch of burnt-umber hair and a sea-green eye appeared in the crack of a door. A long, white, undraped arm came out, barring the way.

" So glad you came, Ricky, instead of any of the others," said the eye. " Light a cigarette and give it to me. Going to take me to dinner ? Fine. Go into the front room till I finish dressing. But don't sit in your usual chair. There's pie in it—Meringue. Kappelman threw it at Reeves last evening while he was reciting. Sophy has just come to straighten up. Is it lit ? Thanks. There's Scotch on the mantel—oh, no, it isn't—that's chartreuse. Ask Sophy to find you some. I won't be long."

Grainger escaped the meringue. As he waited his spirits sank still lower. The atmosphere of the room was as vapid as a zephyr wandering over a Vesuvian lava-bed. Relics of some feast lay about the room, scattered in places where even a prowling cat would have been surprised to find them. A straggling cluster of deep red roses in a marmalade jar bowed their heads over tobacco ashes and unwashed goblets. A chafing-dish stood on the piano; a leaf of sheet music supported a stack of sandwiches in a chair.

Mary came in, dressed and radiant. Her gown was of that thin, black fabric whose name through the change of a single vowel seems to summon visions ranging between the extremes of man's experience. Spelled with an " è " it belongs to Gallic witchery and diaphanous dreams; with an " a " it drapes lamentation and woe.

That evening they went to the Café André. And, as people would confide to you in a whisper that André's was the only truly Bohemian restaurant in town, it may be well to follow them.

André began his professional career as a waiter in a Bowery ten-cent eating-house. Had you seen him there you would have called him tough—to yourself. Not aloud, for he would have " soaked " you as quickly as he would have soaked his thumb in your coffee. He saved money and started a basement *table d'hôte* in Eight (or Ninth) Street. One afternoon André drank too much absinthe. He announced to his startled family that he was the Grand Llama of Thibet, therefore requiring an empty audience hall in which to be worshipped. He moved all the tables and chairs from the restaurant into the back yard, wrapped a red table-cloth around himself, and sat on a step-ladder for a throne. When the diners began to arrive, Madame in a flurry of despair, laid cloths and ushered them, trembling, outside. Between the tables clothes-lines were stretched, bearing the family wash. A party of Bohemia hunters greeted the artistic innovation with shrieks and acclamations of delight. That week's washing was not taken in for two years. When André came to his senses he had the menu printed on stiffly starched cuffs, and served the ices in little wooden tubs. Next he took down his sign and darkened the front of the house. When you went there to dine you fumbled for an electric button and pressed it. A lookout slid open a panel in the door, looked at you suspiciously, and asked if you were acquainted with Senator Herodotus Q. McMilligan, of the Chickasaw Nation. If you were, you were admitted and allowed to dine. If you were not, you were admitted and allowed to dine. There you have one of the abiding principles of Bohemia. When André had accumulated $20,000 he moved uptown, near Broadway, in the fierce light that beats upon the thrown-down. There we find him and leave him, with customers in pearls and automobile veils, striving to catch his excellently graduated nod of recognition.

There is a large round table in the northeast corner of André's at which six can sit. To this table Grainger and Mary Adrian made their way. Kappelman and Reeves were already there. And Miss Tooker, who designed the May cover for the *Ladies' Notathome Magazine*. And Mrs. Pothunter, who never drank anything but black-and-white highballs, being in mourning for her husband, who—oh, I've forgotten what he did—died, like as not.

Spaghetti-weary reader, wouldst take one penny in-the-slot peep into the fair land of Bohemia ? Then look; and when you think you have seen it you have not. And it is neither thimbleriggery nor astigmatism.

The walls of the Café André were covered with original sketches by the artists who furnished much of the color and sound of the place. Fair woman furnished the theme of the bulk of the drawings. When you say " sirens and siphons " you come near to estimating the alliterative atmosphere of André's.

First, I want you to meet my friend, Miss Adrian. Miss Tooker and Mrs. Pothunter you already know. While she tucks in the fingers of her elbow gloves you shall have her daguerreotype. So faint and uncertain shall the portrait be :

Age, somewhere between twenty-seven and high-neck evening dresses. Camaraderie in large bunches—whatever the fearful word may mean. Habitat—anywhere from Seattle to Tierra del Fuego. Temperament uncharted—she let Reeves squeeze her hand after he recited one of his poems; but she counted the change after sending him out with a dollar to buy some pickled pig's feet. Deportment 75 out of a possible 100. Morals 100.

Mary was one of the princesses of Bohemia. In the first place, it was a royal and a daring thing to have been named Mary. There are twenty Fifines and Héloïses to one Mary in the Country of Elusion.

Now her gloves are tucked in. Miss Tooker has assumed a June poster pose; Mrs. Pothunter has bitten her lips to make the red show; Reeves has several times felt his coat to make sure that his latest poem is in the pocket. (It had been neatly typewritten; but he has copied it on the backs of letters with a pencil.) Kappelman is underhandedly watching the clock. It is ten minutes to nine. When the hour comes it is to remind him of a story. Synopsis : A French girl says to her suitor : " Did you ask my father for my hand at nine o'clock this morning, as you said you would ? " " I did not," he replies. "At nine o'clock I was fighting a duel with swords in the Bois de Boulogne." " Coward ! " she hisses.

The dinner was ordered. You know how long the Bohemian feast of reason keeps up with the courses. Humor with the oysters; wit with the soup; repartee with the entrée; brag with the roast; knocks for Whistler and Kipling with the salad; songs with the coffee, the slapsticks with the cordials.

Between Miss Adrian's eyebrows was the pucker that shows the intense strain it requires to be at ease in Bohemia. Pat must come each sally, *mot,* and epigram. Every second of deliberation upon a reply costs you a bay leaf. Fine as a hair, a line began to curve from her nostrils to her mouth. To hold her own not a chance must be missed. A sentence addressed to her must be as a piccolo, each word of it a stop, which she must be prepared to seize upon and play. And she must always be quicker than a Micmac Indian to paddle the light canoe of conversation away from the rocks in the rapids that flow from the Pierian spring. For, plodding reader, the handwriting on the wall in the banquet hall of Bohemia is " *Laisser faire.*" The gray ghost that sometimes peeps through the rings of smoke is that of slain old King Convention. Freedom is the tyrant that holds them in slavery.

As the dinner waned, hands reached for the pepper cruet rather than for the shaker of Attic salt. Miss Tooker, with an elbow to business, leaned across the table toward Grainger, upsetting her glass of wine.

" Now, while you are fed and in good humor," she said, " I want to make a suggestion to you about a new cover."

" A good idea," said Grainger, mopping the tablecloth with his napkin. " I'll speak to the waiter about it."

Kappelman, the painter, was the cut-up. As a piece of delicate

Athenian wit he got up from his chair and waltzed down the room with a waiter. That dependent, no doubt an honest, pachydermatous, worthy, tax-paying, art-despising biped, released himself from the unequal encounter, carried his professional smile back to the dumb-waiter and dropped it down the shaft to eternal oblivion. Reeves began to make Keats turn in his grave. Mrs. Pothunter told the story of the man who met the widow on the train. Miss Adrian hummed what is still called a *chanson* in the cafés of Bridgeport. Grainger edited each individual effort with his assistant editor's smile, which meant : " Great ! but you'll have to send them in through the regular channels. If I were the chief now—but you know how it is."

And soon the head waiter bowed before them, desolated to relate that the closing hour had already become chronologically historical; so out all trooped into the starry midnight, filling the street with gay laughter, to be barked at by hopeful cabmen and enviously eyed by the dull inhabitants of an uninspired world.

Grainger left Mary at the elevator in the trackless palm forest of the Idealia. After he had gone she came down again carrying a small hand-bag, 'phoned for a cab, drove to the Grand Central Station, boarded a 12.55 commuter's train, rode four hours with her burnt-umber head bobbing against the red-plush back of the seat, and landed during a fresh, stinging, glorious sunrise at a deserted station, the size of a peach crate, called Crocusville.

She walked a mile and clicked the latch of a gate. A bare, brown cottage stood twenty yards back; an old man with a pearl-white, Calvinistic face and clothes dyed blacker than a raven in a coal-mine was washing his hands in a tin basin on the front porch.

" How are you Father ? " said Mary timidly.

" I am as well as Providence permits, Mary Ann. You will find your mother in the kitchen."

In the kitchen a cryptic, gray woman kissed her glacially on the forehead, and pointed out the potatoes which were not yet peeled for breakfast. Mary sat in a wooden chair and decorticated spuds, with a thrill in her heart.

For breakfast there were grace, cold bread, potatoes, bacon, and tea.

" You are pursuing the same avocation in the city concerning which you have advised us from time to time by letter, I trust," said her father.

" Yes," said Mary. " I am still reviewing books for the same publication."

After breakfast she helped wash the dishes, and then all three sat in straight-back chairs in the barefloored parlor.

" It is my custom," said the old man, " on the Sabbath day to

read aloud from the great work entitled the 'Apology for Autho-
rized and Set Forms of Liturgy, by the ecclesiastical philospher
and revered theologian, Jeremy Taylor."

" I know it," said Mary blissfully, folding her hands.

For two hours the numbers of the great Jeremy rolled forth like
the notes of an oratio played on the violoncello. Mary sat gloating
in the new sensation of racking physical discomfort that the wooden
chair brought her. Perhaps there is no happiness in life so perfect
as the martyr's. Jeremy's minor chords soothed her like the music
of tom-tom. " Why, oh why," she said to herself, " does some one
not write words to it ? "

At eleven they went to church in Crocusville. The back of the
pine bench on which she sat had a penitential forward tilt that
would have brought St. Simeon down, in jealousy, from his pillar.
The preacher singled her out, and thundered upon her vicarious
head the damnation of the world. At each side of her an adamant
parent held her rigidly to the bar of judgment. An ant crawled
upon her neck, but she dared not move. She lowered her eyes
before the congregation—a hundred-eyed Cerberus that watched
the gates through which her sins were fast thrusting her. Her soul
was filled with a delirious, almost a fanatic joy. For she was out
of the clutch of the tyrant, Freedom. Dogma and creed pinioned
her with beneficent cruelty, as steel braces bind the feet of a
crippled child. She was hedged, adjured, shackled, shored up,
strait-jacketed, silenced, ordered. When they came out the minister
stopped to greet them. Mary could only hang her head and answer
" Yes, sir," and " No, sir," to his questions. When she saw that
the other women carried their hymn-books at their waists with
their left hands, she blushed and moved hers there, too, from her
right.

She took the three-o'clock train back to the city. At nine she
sat at the round table for dinner in the Café André. Nearly the
same crowd was there.

" Where have you been to-day ? " asked Mrs. Pothunter. " I
'phoned to you at twelve."

" I have been away in Bohemia," answered Mary, with a
mystic smile.

There ! Mary has given it away. She has spoiled my climax.
For I was to have told you that Bohemia is nothing more than the
little country in which you do not live. If you try to obtain citizenship in it, at once the court and retinue pack the royal archives
and treasure and move away beyond the hills. It is a hillside that
you turn your head to peer at from the windows of the Through
Express.

At exactly half past eleven Kappelman, deceived by a new

softness and slowness of *riposte* and parry in Mary Adrian, tried to kiss her. Instantly she slapped his face with such strength and cold fury that he shrank down, sobered, with the flaming red print of a hand across his leering features. And all sounds ceased, as when the shadows of great wings came upon a flock of chattering sparrows. One had broken the paramount law of sham-Bohemia —the law of " *Laisser faire.*" The shock came not from the blow delivered, but from the blow received. With the effect of a school-master entering the play-room of his pupils was that blow administered. Women pulled down their sleeves and laid prim hands against their ruffled side locks. Men looked at their watches. There was nothing of the effect of a brawl about it; it was purely the still panic produced by the sound of the ax of the fly cop, Conscience, hammering at the gambling-house doors of the Heart.

With their punctilious putting on of cloaks, with their exaggerated pretense of not having seen or heard, with their stammering exchange of unaccustomed formalities, with their false show of a light-hearted exit I must take leave of my Bohemian party. Mary has robbed me of my climax; and she may go.

But I am not defeated. Somewhere there exists a great vault miles broad and miles long—more capacious than the champagne caves of France. In that vault are stored the anti-climaxes that should have been tagged to all the stories that have been told in the world. I shall cheat that vault of one deposit.

Minnie Brown, with her aunt, came from Crocusville down to the city to see the sights. And because she had escorted me to fishless trout streams and exhibited to me open-plumbed waterfalls and broken my camera while I Julyed in her village, I must escort her to the hives containing the synthetic clover honey of town.

Especially did the custom-made Bohemia charm her. The spaghetti wound its tendrils about her heart; the free red wine drowned her belief in the existence of commercialism in the world; she was dazed and enchanted by the rugose wit that can be churned out of California claret.

But one evening I got her away from the smell of halibut and linoleum long enough to read to her the manuscript of this story, which then ended before her entrance into it. I read it to her because I knew that all the printing-presses in the world were running to try to please her and some others. And I asked her about it. " I didn't quite catch the trains," said she. " How long was Mary in Crocusville.? "

" Ten hours and five minutes." I replied.

" Well, then the story may do," said Minnie. " But if she had stayed there a week Kappelman would have got his kiss."

THE FERRY OF UNFULFILMENT

At the street corner, as solid as granite in the " rush-hour " tide of humanity, stood the Man from Nome. The Arctic winds and sun had stained him berry-brown. His eye still held the azure glint of the glaciers.

He was as alert as a fox, as tough as a caribou cutlet and as broad-gauged as the aurora borealis. He stood sprayed by a Niagara of sound—the crash of the elevated trains, clanging cars, pounding of rubberless tires and the antiphony of the cab and truck-drivers indulging in scarifying repartee. And so, with his gold dust cashed in to the merry air of a hundred thousand, and with the cakes and ale of one week in Gotham turning bitter on his tongue, the Man from Nome sighed to set foot again in Chilkoot, the exit from the land of street noises and Dead Sea apple pies.

Up Sixth Avenue, with the tripping, scurrying, chattering, bright-eyed, homing tide came the Girl from Sieber-Mason's. The Man from Nome looked and saw, first, that she was supremely beautiful after his own conception of beauty; and next, that she moved with exactly the steady grace of a dog sled on a level crust of snow. His third sensation was an instantaneous conviction that he desired her greatly for his own. Thus quickly do men from Nome make up their minds. Besides, he was going back to the North in a short time and to act quickly was no less necessary.

A thousand girls from the great department store of Sieber-Mason flowed along the side-walk, making navigation dangerous to men whose feminine field of vision for three years has been chiefly limited to Siwash and Chilkat squaws. But the Man from Nome, loyal to her who had resurrected his long-cached heart, plunged into the stream of pulchritude and followed her.

Down Twenty-third Street she glided swiftly, looking to neither side; no more flirtatious than the bronze Diana above the Garden. Her fine brown hair was neatly braided; her neat waist and unwrinkled black skirt were eloquent of the double virtues—taste and economy. Ten yards behind followed the smitten Man from Nome.

Miss Claribel Colby, the Girl from Sieber-Mason's, belonged to that sad company of mariners known as Jersey commuters. She walked into the waiting-room of the ferry, and up the stairs, and by a marvellous swift, little run, caught the ferry-boat that was just going out. The Man from Nome closed up his ten yards in three jumps and gained the deck beside her.

Miss Colby chose a rather lonely seat on the outside of the upper cabin. The night was not cold, and she desired to be away from the curious eyes and tedious voices of the passengers. Besides, she was extremely weary and drooping from lack of sleep. On the previous night she had graced the annual ball and oyster fry of the West Side Wholesale Fish Dealers' Assistants' Social Club No. 2, thus reducing her usual time of sleep to only three hours.

And the day had been uncommonly troublous. Customers had been inordinately trying; the buyer in her department had scolded her roundly for letting her stock run down; her best friend, Mamie Tuthill, had snubbed her by going to lunch with that Dockery girl.

The Girl from Sieber-Mason's was in that relaxed, softened mood that often comes to the independent feminine wage-earner. It is a mood most propitious for the man who would woo her. Then she has yearnings to be set in some home and heart; to be comforted, and to hide behind some strong arm and rest, rest. But Miss Claribel Colby was also very sleepy.

There came to her side a strong man, browned and dressed carelessly in the best of clothes with his hat in his hand.

" Lady," said the Man from Nome, respectfully, " excuse me for speaking to you, but I—I—saw you on the street, and—and ____"

" Oh, gee ! " remarked the Girl from Sieber-Mason's, glancing up with the most capable coolness. "Ain't there any way to ever get rid of you mashers ? I've tried everything from eating onions to using hatpins. Be on your way, Freddie."

" I'm not one of that kind, lady," said the Man from Nome— " honest, I'm not. As I say, I saw you on the street, and I wanted to know you so bad I couldn't help followin' after you. I was afraid I wouldn't ever see you again in this big town unless I spoke; and that's why I done so."

Miss Colby looked once shrewdly at him in the dim light on the ferry-boat. No; he did not have the perfidious smirk or the brazen swagger of the lady-killer. Sincerity and modesty shone through his boreal tan. It seemed to her that it might be good to hear a little of what he had to say.

" You may sit down," she said, laying her hand over a yawn with ostentatious politeness; " and—mind—don't get fresh or I'll call the steward."

The Man from Nome sat by her side. He admired her greatly. He more than admired her. She had exactly the looks he had tried so long in vain to find in a woman. Could she ever come to like him? Well, that was to be seen. He must do all in his power to stake his claim, anyhow.

" My name's Blayden," said he—" Henry Blayden."

"Are you real sure it ain't Jones?" asked the girl, leaning toward him, with delicious, knowing raillery.

"I'm down from Nome," he went on with anxious seriousness. "I scraped together a pretty good lot of dust up there, and brought it down with me."

"Oh, say!" she rippled, pursuing persiflage with engaging lightness, "then you must be on the White Wings force. I thought I'd seen you somewhere."

"You didn't see me on the street to-day when I saw you."

"I never look at fellows on the street."

"Well, I looked at you; and I never looked at anything before that I thought was half as pretty."

"Shall I keep the change?"

"Yes, I reckon so. I reckon you could keep anything I've got. I reckon I'm what you would call a rough man, but I could be awful good to anybody I liked. I've had a rough time of it up yonder, but I beat the game. Nearly 5,000 ounces of dust was what I cleaned up while I was there."

"Goodness!" exclaimed Miss Colby, obligingly sympathetic. "It must be an awful dirty place, wherever it is."

And then her eyes closed. The voice of the Man from Nome had a monotony in its very earnestness. Besides, what dull talk was this of brooms and sweeping and dust? She leaned her head back against the wall.

"Miss," said the Man from Nome, with deeper earnestness and monotony, "I never saw anybody I liked as well as I do you. I know you can't think that way of me right yet; but can't you give me a chance? Won't you let me know you, and see if I can't make you like me?"

The head of the Girl from Sieber-Mason's slid over gently and rested upon his shoulder. Sweet sleep had won her, and she was dreaming rapturously of the Wholesale Fish Dealer's Assistants' ball.

The gentleman from Nome kept his arms to himself. He did not suspect sleep, and yet he was too wise to attribute the movement to surrender. He was greatly and blissfully thrilled, but he ended by regarding the head upon his shoulder as an encouraging preliminary, merely advanced as a harbinger of his success, and not to be taken advantage of.

One small speck of alloy discounted the gold of his satisfaction. Had he spoken too freely of his wealth? He wanted to be liked for himself.

"I want to say, Miss," he said, "that you can count on me. They know me in the Klondike from Juneau to Circle City and down the whole length of the Yukon. Many a night I've laid in the snow up there where I worked like a slave for three years, and wondered if I'd ever have anybody to like me. I didn't want all that dust just myself. I thought I'd meet just the right one some time, and I done it to-day. Money's a mighty good thing to have, but to have the love of the one you like best is better still. If you was ever to marry a man, Miss, which would you rather he'd have ? "

" Cash ! "

The word came sharply and loudly from Miss Colby's lips, giving evidence that in her dreams she was now behind her counter in the great department store of Sieber-Mason.

Her head suddenly bobbed over sideways. She awoke, sat straight, and rubbed her eyes. The man from Nome was gone.

" Gee ! I believe I've been asleep," said Miss Colby. " Wonder what became of the White Wings ! "

THE TALE OF A TAINTED TENNER

MONEY talks. But you may think that the conversation of a little old ten-dollar bill in New York would be nothing more than a whisper. Oh, very well ! Pass up this *sotto voce* auto-biography of an X if you like. If you are one of the kind that prefers to listen to John D's checkbook roar at you through a megaphone as it passes by, all right. But don't forget that small change can say a word to the point now and then. The next time you tip your grocer's clerk a silver quarter to give you extra weight of his boss's goods read the four words above the lady's head. How are they for repartee ?

I am a ten-dollar Treasury note, series of 1901. You may have seen one in a friend's hand. On my face, in the centre, is a picture of the bison Americanus, miscalled a buffalo by fifty or sixty millions of Americans. The heads of Capt. Lewis and Capt. Clark adorn the ends. On my back is the graceful figure of Liberty or Ceres or Maxine Elliot standing in the centre of the stage on a conservatory plant. My references is—or are—Section 3,588, Revised Statutes. Ten cold, hard dollars—I don't say whether silver, gold, lead or iron—Uncle Sam will hand you over his counter if you want to cash me in.

I beg you will excuse any conversational breaks that I make— thanks, I knew you would—got that sneaking little respect and agreeable feeling toward even an X, haven't you ? You see, a tainted bill doesn't have much chance to acquire a correct form of expression. I never knew a really cultured and educated person that could afford to hold a ten-spot any longer than it would take to do an Arthur Duffy to the nearest That's All ! sign or delicatessen store.

For a six-year-old, I've had a lively and gorgeous circulation. I guess I've paid as many debts as the man who dies. I've been owned by a good many kinds of people. But a little old ragged, damp, dingy five-dollar silver certificate gave me a jar one day. I was next to it in the fat and bad-smelling purse of a butcher.

" Hey, you Sitting Bull," says I, " don't scrouge so. Anyhow, don't you think it's about time you went in on a customs payment and got reissued ? For a series of 1899 you're a sight."

" Oh, don't get crackly just because you're a Buffalo bill," says the fiver. " You'd be limp, too, if you'd been stuffed down in a thick cotton-and-lisle-thread under an elastic all day, and the thermometer not a degree under 85 in the store."

" I never heard of a pocketbook like that," says I. " Who carried you ? "

" A shopgirl," says the five-spot.

" What's that ? " I had to ask.

" You'll never know till their millennium comes," says the fiver.

Just then a two-dollar bill behind me with a George Washington head, spoke up to the fiver :

" Aw, cut out yer kicks. Ain't lisle thread good enough for yer ? If you was under all cotton like I've been to-day, and choked up with factory dust till the lady with the cornucopia on me sneezed half a dozen times, you'd have some reason to complain."

That was the next day after I arrived in New York. I came in a $500 package of tens to a Brooklyn bank from one of its Pennsylvania correspondents—and I haven't made the acquaintance of any of the five and two spot's friends' pocket-books yet. Silk for mine, every time.

I was lucky money. I kept on the move. Sometimes I changed hands twenty times a day. I saw the inside of every business; I fought for my owner's every pleasure. It seemed that on Saturday nights I never missed being slapped down on a bar. Tens were always slapped down, while ones and twos were slid over to the bartenders folded. I got in the habit of looking for mine, and I managed to soak in a little straight or some spilled Martini or Manhattan whenever I could. Once I got tied up in a great greasy roll of bills in a pushcart peddler's jeans. I thought I never would get in circulation again, for the future department store owner lived on eight cents' worth of dog meat and onions a day. But this peddler got into trouble one day on account of having his cart too near a crossing, and I was rescued. I always will feel grateful to the cop that got me. He changed me at a cigar store near the

Bowery that was running a crap game in the back room. So it was the Captain of the precinct, after all, that did me the best turn, when he got his. He blew me for wine the next evening in a Broadway restaurant; and I really felt as glad to get back again as an Astor does when he sees the lights of Charing Cross.

A tainted ten certainly does get action on Broadway. I was alimony once, and got folded in a little dogskin purse among a lot of dimes. They were bragging about the busy times there were in Ossining whenever three girls got hold of one of them during the ice cream season. But it's Slow Moving Vehicles Keep to the Right for the little Bok tips when you think of the way we bison plasters refuse to stick to anything during the rush lobster hour.

The first I ever heard of tainted money was one night when a good thing with a Van to his name threw me over with some other bills to buy a stack of blues.

About midnight a big, easy-going man with a fat face like a monk's and the eye of a janitor with his wages raised took me and a lot of other notes and rolled us into what is termed a " wad " among the money tainters.

" Ticket me for five hundred," said he to the banker, " and look out for everything, Charlie. I'm going out for stroll in the glen before the moonlight fades from the brow of the cliff. If anybody finds the roof in their way there's $60,000 wrapped in a comic supplement in the upper left-hand corner of the safe. Be bold; everywhere be bold, but be not bowled over. 'Night."

I found myself between two $20 gold certificates. One of 'em says to me :

" Well, old shorthorn, you're in luck to-night. You'll see something of life. Old Jack's going to make the Tenderloin look like a hamburg steak."

" Explain," says I. " I'm used to joints, but I don't care for filet mignon with the kind of sauce you serve."

" 'Xcuse me," said the twenty. " Old Jack is the proprietor of this gambling house. He's going on a whiz to-night because he offered $50,000 to a church and it refused to accept it because they said his money was tainted."

" What is a church ? " I asked.

" Oh, I forgot," says the twenty, " that I was talking to a tenner. Of course you don't know. You're too much to put into the contribution basket, and not enough to buy anything at a bazaar. A church is—a large building in which penwipers and tidies are sold at $20 each."

I don't care much about chinning with gold certificates. There's a streak of yellow in 'em. All is not gold that quitters.

Old Jack certainly was a gild-edged sport. When it came his time to loosen up he never referred the waiter to an actuary.

By and by it got around that he was smiting the rock in the wilderness; and all along Broadway things with cold noses and hot gullets fell in on our trail. The third Jungle Book was there waiting for somebody to put covers on it. Old Jack's money may have had a taint to it, but all the same he had orders for his Camembert piling up on him every minute. First his friends rallied round him; and then the fellows that his friends knew by sight; and then a few of his enemies buried the hatchet; and finally he was buying souvenirs for so many Neapolitan fisher maidens and butterfly octettes that the head waiters were 'phoning all over town for Julian Mitchell to please come around and get them into some kind of order.

At last we floated into an uptown café that I knew by heart. When the hod-carriers' union in jackets and aprons saw us coming the chief goal kicker called out : " Six—eleven—forty-two— nineteen—twelve " to his men, and they put on nose guards till it was clear whether we meant Port Arthur or Portsmouth. But old Jack wasn't working for the furniture and glass factories that night. He sat down quiet and sang " Ramble " in a half-hearted way. His feelings had been hurt, so the twenty told me, because his offer to the church had been refused.

But the wassail went on; and Brady himself couldn't have hammered the thirst mob into a better imitation of the real penchant for the stuff that you screw out of a bottle with a napkin.

Old Jack paid the twenty above me for a round, leaving me on the outside of his roll. He laid the roll on the table and sent for the proprietor.

" Mike," says he, " here's money that the good people have refused. Will it buy of your wares in the name of the devil ? They say it's tainted."

" It will," says Mike, " and I'll put it in the drawer next to the bills that was paid to the parson's daughter for kisses at the church fair to build a new parsonage for the parson's daughter to live in."

At 1 o'clock when the hod-carriers were making ready to close up the front and keep the inside open, a woman slips in the door of the restaurant and comes up to Old Jack's table. You've seen the kind—black shawl, creepy hair, ragged skirt, white face, eyes a cross between Gabriel's and a sick kitten's—the kind of woman that's always on the lookout for an automobile or the mendicancy squad—and she stands there without a word and looks at the money.

Old Jack gets up, peels me off the roll and hands me to her with a bow.

" Madam," says he, just like actors I've heard, " here is a tainted bill. I am a gambler. This bill came to me to-night from a gentleman's son. Where he got it I do not know. If you will do me the favor to accept it, it is yours."

The woman took me with a trembling hand.

" Sir," said she, " I counted thousands of this issue of bills into packages when they were virgin from the presses. I was a clerk in the Treasury Department. There was an official to whom I owed my position. You say they are tainted now. If you only knew—but I won't say any more. Thank you with all my heart, sir—thank you—thank you."

Where do you suppose that woman carried me almost at a run ? To a bakery. Away from Old Jack and a sizzling good time to a bakery. And I got changed, and she does a Sheridan-twenty-miles-away with a dozen rolls and a section of jelly cake as big as a turbine water-wheel. Of course I lost sight of her then, for I was snowed up in the bakery, wondering whether I'd get changed at the drug store the next day in an alum deal or paid over to the cement works.

A week afterward I butted up against one of the one-dollar bills the baker had given the woman for change.

" Hallo, E35039669," says I, " weren't you in the change for me in a bakery last Saturday night ? "

" Yep," says the solitaire in his free and easy style.

" How did the deal turn out ? " I asked.

" She blew E17051431 for milk and round steak," says the one-spot. " She kept me till the rent man came. It was a bum room with a sick kid in it. But you ought to have seen him go for the bread and tincture of formaldehyde. Half-starved, I guess. Then she prayed some. Don't get stuck up, tenner, We one-spots hear ten prayers, where you hear one. She said something about ' who giveth to the poor.' Oh, let's cut out the slum talk. I'm certainly tired of the company that keeps me. I wish I was big enough to move in society with you tainted bills."

" Shut up," says I, " there's no such thing. I know the rest of it. There's a ' lendeth to the Lord ' somewhere in it. Now look on my back and read what you see there."

" This note is a legal tender at its face value for all debts public and private."

" This talk about tainted money makes me tired," says I.

ELSIE IN NEW YORK

No, bumptious reader, this story is not a continuation of the Elsie series. But if your Elsie had lived over here in our big city there might have been a chapter in her books not very different from this.

Especially for the vagrant feet of youth are the roads of Manhattan beset " with pitfall and with gin." But the civic guardians of the young have made themselves acquainted with the snares of the wicked and most of the dangerous paths are patrolled by their agents, who seek to turn straying ones away from the peril that menaces them. And this will tell you how they guided my Elsie safely through all peril to the goal that she was seeking.

Elsie's father had been a cutter for Fox & Otter, cloaks and furs, on lower Broadway. He was an old man, with a slow and limping gait, so a pot-hunter of a newly licensed chauffeur ran him down one day when livelier game was scarce. They took the old man home, where he lay on his bed for a year and then died, leaving $2.50 in cash and a letter from Mr. Otter offering to do anything he could to help his faithful old employee. The old cutter regarded this letter as a valuable legacy to his daughter, and he put it into her hands with pride as the shears of the dread Cleaner and Repairer snipped off his thread of life.

That was the landlord's cue; and forth he came and did his part in the great eviction scene. There was no snowstorm ready for Elsie to steal out into, drawing her little red woollen shawl about her shoulders, but she went out, regardless of the unities. And as for the red shawl—back to Blaney with it ! Elsie's fall tan coat was cheap, but it had the style and fit of the best at Fox & Otter's. And her lucky stars had given her good looks, and eyes as blue and innocent as the new shade of note paper, and she had $1 left of the $2.50. And the letter from Mr. Otter. Keep your eye on the letter from Mr. Otter. That is the clue. I desire that everything be made plain as we go. Detective stories are so plentiful now that they do not sell.

And so we find Elsie, thus equipped, starting out in the world to seek her fortune. One trouble about the letter from Mr. Otter was that it did not bear the new address of the firm, which had moved about a month before. But Elsie thought she could find it. She had heard that policemen, when politely addressed, or thumbscrewed by an investigation committee, will give up information and addresses. So she boarded a downtown car at One Hundred and Seventy-seventh Street and rode south to Forty-second, which she thought must surely be the end of the island. There she stood against the wall undecided, for the city's roar and dash was new to her. Up where she lived was rural New York, so far out that the milkmen awaken you in the morning by the squeaking of pumps instead of the rattling of cans.

A kind-faced, sunburned, young man in a soft-brimmed hat went past Elsie into the Grand Central Depot. That was Hank Ross, of the Sunflower Ranch, in Idaho, on his way home from a visit to the East. Hank's heart was heavy, for the Sunflower Ranch was a lonesome place, lacking the presence of a woman. He had hoped to find one during his visit who would congenially share his prosperity and home, but the girls of Gotham had not pleased his fancy. But, as he passed in, he noted, with a jumping of his pulses, the sweet, ingenous face of Elsie and her pose of doubt and loneliness. With true and honest Western impulse he said to himself that here was his mate. He could love her, he knew; and he would surround her with so much comfort, and cherish her so carefully that she would be happy, and make two sunflowers grow on the ranch where there grew but one before.

Hank turned and went back to her. Backed by his never-before-questioned honesty of purpose, he approached the girl and removed his soft-brimmed hat. Elsie had but time to sum up his handsome frank face with one shy look of modest admiration when a burly cop hurled himself upon the ranchman, seized him by the collar and backed him against the wall. Two blocks away a burglar was coming out of an apartment-house with a bag of silverware on his shoulder; but that is neither here nor there.

" Carry on yez mashin' tricks right before me eyes, will yez ? " shouted the cop. " I'll teach yez to speak to ladies on me beat that ye're not acquainted with. Come along."

Elsie turned away with a sigh as the ranchman was dragged away. She had liked the effect of his light blue eyes against his tanned complexion. She walked southward, thinking herself already in the district where her father used to work, and hoping to find some one who could direct her to the firm of Fox & Otter.

But did she want to find Mr. Otter ? She had inherited much of the old cutter's independence. How much better it would be if she could find work and support herself without calling on him for aid !

Elsie saw a sign " Employment Agency " and went in. Many girls were sitting against the wall in chairs. Several well-dressed ladies were looking them over. One white-haired, kind-faced old lady in rustling black silk hurried up to Elsie.

" My dear," she said in a sweet, gentle voice, " are you looking for a position ? I like your face and appearance so much. I want a young woman who will be half maid and half companion to me. You will have a good home and I will pay you $30 a month."

Before Elsie could stammer forth her gratified acceptance, a young woman with gold glasses on her bony nose and her hands in her jacket pockets seized her arm and drew her aside.

" I am Miss Ticklebaum," said she, " of the Association for the Prevention of Jobs Being Put Up on Working Girls Looking for Jobs. We prevented forty-seven girls from securing positions last week. I am here to protect you. Beware of any one who offers you a job. How do you know that this woman does not want to make you work as a breaker-boy in a coal mine or murder you to get your teeth ? If you accept work of any kind without permission of our association you will be arrested by one of our agents."

" But what am I to do ? " asked Elsie. " I have no home or money. I must do something. Why am I not allowed to accept this kind lady's offer ? "

" I do not know," said Miss Ticklebaum. " That is the affair of our Committee on the Abolishment of Employers. It is my duty simply to see that you do not get work. You will give me your name and address and report to our secretary every Thursday. We have 600 girls on the waiting list who will in time be allowed to accept positions as vacancies occur on our roll of Qualified Employers, which now comprise twenty-seven names. There is prayer, music and lemonade in our chapel the third Sunday of every month."

Elsie hurried away after thanking Miss Ticklebaum for her timely warning and advice. After all, it seemed that she must try to find Mr. Otter.

But after walking a few blocks she saw a sign, " Cashier wanted," in the window of a confectionery store. In she went and applied for the place, after casting a quick glance over her shoulder to assure herself that the job-preventer was not on her trail.

The proprietor of the confectionery was a benevolent old man with a peppermint flavor, who decided, after questioning Elsie pretty closely, that she was the very girl he wanted. Her services were needed at once, so Elsie, with a thankful heart, drew off her tan coat and prepared to mount the cashier's stool.

But before she could do so a gaunt lady wearing steel spectacles and black mittens stood before her, with a long finger pointing, and exclaimed : " Young woman, hesitate ! "

Elsie hesitated.

" Do you know," said the black-and-steel lady, " that in accepting this position you may this day cause the loss of a hundred lives in agonizing physical torture and the sending as many souls to perdition ? "

"Why, no," said Elsie, in frightened tones. "How could I do that ?"

" Rum," said the lady—" the demon rum. Do you know why so many lives are lost when a theatre catches fire ? Brandy balls. The demon rum lurking in brandy balls. Our society women while in theatres sit grossly intoxicated from eating these candies filled with brandy. When the fire fiend sweeps down upon them they are unable to escape. The candy stores are the devil's distilleries. If you assist in the distribution of these insidious confections you assist in the destruction of the bodies and souls of your fellow-beings, and in the filling of our jails, asylums and almshouses. Think, girl, ere you touch the money for which brandy balls are sold."

" Dear me," said Elsie, bewildered. " I didn't know there was rum in brandy balls. But I must live by some means. What shall I do ? "

" Decline the position," said the lady, " and come with me. I will tell you what to do."

After Elsie had told the confectioner that she had changed her mind about the cashiership she put on her coat and followed the lady to the sidewalk, where awaited an elegant victoria.

" Seek some other work," said the black-and-steel lady, " and assist in crushing the hydra-headed demon rum." And she got into the victoria and drove away.

" I guess that puts it up to Mr. Otter again." said Elsie, ruefully, turning down the street. "And I'm sorry, too, for I'd much rather make my way without help."

Near Fourteenth Street Elsie saw a placard tacked on the side of a doorway that read : " Fifty girls, neat sewers, wanted immediately on theatrical costumes. Good pay."

She was about to enter, when a solemn man, dressed all in black, laid his hand on her arm.

" My dear girl," he said, " I entreat you not to enter that dressing-room of the devil."

" Goodness me ! " exclaimed Elsie, with some impatience. " The devil seems to have a cinch on all the business in New York. What's wrong about the place ? "

" It is here," said the solemn man, " that the regalia of Satan —in other words, the costumes worn on the stage—are manufactured. The stage is the road to ruin and destruction. Would you imperil your soul by lending the work of your hands to its support? Do you know, my dear girl, what the theatre leads to ? Do you know where actors and actresses go after the curtain of the play-house has fallen upon them for the last time ? "

"Sure," said Elsie. "Into vaudeville. But do you think it would be wicked for me to make a little money to live on by sewing? I must get something to do pretty soon."

"The flesh-pots of Egypt," exclaimed the reverend gentleman, uplifting his hands. "I beseech you, my child, to turn away from this place of sin and iniquity."

"But what will I do for a living?" asked Elsie. "I don't care to sew for this musical comedy, if it's as rank as you say it is; but I've got to have a job."

"The Lord will provide," said the solemn man. "There is a free Bible class every Sunday afternoon in the basement of the cigar store next to the church. Peace be with you. Amen. Farewell."

Elsie went on her way. She was soon in the downtown district where factories abound. On a large brick building was a gilt sign, "Posey & Trimmer, Artificial Flowers." Below it was hung a newly stretched canvas bearing the words, "Five hundred girls wanted to learn trade. Good wages from the start. Apply one flight up."

Elsie started toward the door, near which were gathered in groups some twenty or thirty girls. One big girl with a black straw hat tipped down over her eyes stepped in front of her.

"Say, you'se," said the girl, "are you'se goin' in there after a job?"

"Yes," said Elsie; "I must have work."

"Now don't do it," said the girl. "I'm chairman of our Scab Committee. There's 400 of us girls locked out just because we demanded 50 cents a week raise in wages, and ice water, and for the foreman to shave off his mustache. You're too nice a looking girl to be a scab. Wouldn't you please help us along by trying to find a job somewhere else, or would you'se rather have your face pushed in?"

"I'll try somewhere else," said Elsie.

She walked aimlessly eastward on Broadway, and there her heart leaped to see the sign, "Fox & Otter," stretching entirely across the front of a tall building. It was as though an unseen guide had led her to it through the byways of her fruitless search for work.

She hurried into the store and sent in to Mr. Otter by a clerk her name and the letter he had written her father. She was shown directly into his private office.

Mr. Otter arose from his desk as Elsie entered and took both hands with a hearty smile of welcome. He was a slightly corpulent man of nearly middle age, a little bald, gold spectacled, polite, well dressed, radiating.

" Well, well, and so this is Beatty's little daughter ! Your father was one of our most efficient and valued employees. He left nothing ? Well, well. I hope we have not forgotten his faithful services. I am sure there is a vacancy now among our models. Oh, it is easy work—nothing easier."

Mr. Otter struck a bell. A long-nose clerk thrust a portion of himself inside the door.

" Send Miss Hawkins in," said Mr. Otter. Miss Hawkins came.

" Miss Hawkins," said Mr. Otter, " bring for Miss Beatty to try on one of those Russian sable coats and—let's see—one of those latest model black tulle hats with white tips."

Elsie stood before the full-length mirror with pink cheeks and quick breath. Her eyes shone like faint stars. She was beautiful. Alas ! she was beautiful.

I wish I could stop this story here. Confound it ! I will. No; it's got to run it out. I didn't make it up. I'm just repeating it.

I'd like to throw bouquets at the wise cop and the lady who rescues Girls from Jobs, and the prohibitionist who is trying to crush brandy balls, and the sky pilot who objects to costumes for stage people (there are others), and all the thousands of good people who are at work protecting young people from the pitfalls of a great city; and then wind up by pointing out how they were the means of Elsie reaching her father's benefactor and her kind friend and rescuer from poverty. This would make a fine Elsie story of the old sort. I'd like to do this; but there's just a word or two to follow.

While Elsie was admiring herself in the mirror, Mr. Otter went to the telephone booth and called up some number. Don't ask me what it was.

" Oscar," said he, " I want you to reserve the same table for me this evening. . . . What ? Why, the one in the Moorish room to the left of the shrubbery. . . . Yes; two. . . . Yes, the usual brand; and the '85 Johannisburger with the roast. If it isn't the right temperature I'll break your neck. . . . No; not her . . . No, indeed . . . A new one—a peacherino, Oscar, a peacherino ! "

Tired and tiresome reader, I will conclude, if you please, with a paraphrase of a few words that you will remember were written by him—by him of Gad's Hill, before whom, if you doff not your hat, you shall stand with a covered pumpkin—aye, sir, a pumpkin.

Lost, Your Excellency. Lost, Associations, and Societies. Lost, Right Reverends and Wrong Reverends of every order. Lost, Reformers and Lawmakers, born with heavenly compassion in your hearts, but with the reverence of money in your souls. And lost thus around us every day.

INDEX TO SHORT STORIES